Accelerated Reader

Freeglader

Reading Level: 6.4

Point Value: 13

Accelerated Reader

vox

Reading Level: 6.3

Point Value: 13

Accelerated Reader

Last of...

Reading Level: 5.7

Point Value: 12

D1271968

THE TWILIGHT WOODS

THE EDGELANDS

AUG 15 2011

THE ROOK TRILOGY

THE ROOK TRILOGY
A DOUBLEDAY BOOK 978 0 385 61569 3

Published in Great Britain by Doubleday,
an imprint of Random House Children's Books
A Random House Group Company

This collected edition published 2008
Text and illustrations copyright ©Paul Stewart and Chris Riddell, 2008

The Last of the Sky Pirates
First published by Doubleday in 2002
Text and illustrations copyright © Paul Stewart and Chris Riddell, 2002

Vox
First published by Doubleday in 2003
Text and illustrations copyright © Paul Stewart and Chris Riddell, 2003

Freeglader
First published by Doubleday in 2004
Text and illustrations copyright © Paul Stewart and Chris Riddell, 2004

1 3 5 7 9 10 8 6 4 2

The Random House Group Limited makes every effort to ensure that the papers used in its books
are made from trees that have been legally sourced from well-managed and credibly certified
forests. Our paper procurement policy can be found at: www.randomhouse.co.uk/paper.htm

RANDOM HOUSE CHILDREN'S BOOKS
61–63 Uxbridge Road, London W5 5SA

www.**kidsatrandomhouse**.co.uk
www.**rbooks**.co.uk

Addresses for companies within The Random House Group Limited can be found at:
www.randomhouse.co.uk/offices.htm

THE RANDOM HOUSE GROUP Limited Reg. No. 954009

A CIP catalogue record for this book is available from the British Library.

Printed in the UK by Clays Ltd, St Ives plc.

THE EDGE CHRONICLES

THE ROOK TRILOGY

PAUL STEWART & CHRIS RIDDELL

DOUBLEDAY

THE EDGE CHRONICLES

The Quint Trilogy
The Curse of the Gloamglozer
The Winter Knights
Clash of the Sky Galleons

The Twig Trilogy
Beyond the Deepwoods
Stormchaser
Midnight Over Sanctaphrax

The Rook Trilogy
The Last of the Sky Pirates
Vox
Freeglader

The Lost Barkscrolls
The Edge Chronicles Maps

COMING SOON:

EDGE 10: THE IMMORTALS

JOIN THE FREE ONLINE EDGE FAN CLUB AT

www.edgechronicles.co.uk

BARNABY GRIMES

CURSE OF THE NIGHT WOLF
RETURN OF THE EMERALD SKULL
LEGION OF THE DEAD

www.barnabygrimes.co.uk

For younger readers:

FAR-FLUNG ADVENTURES

Fergus Crane
Corby Flood
Hugo Pepper

www.farflungadventures.co.uk

For Joseph, William, Anna, Katy and Jack

INTRODUCTION

Far far away, jutting out into the emptiness beyond, like the figurehead of a mighty stone ship, is the Edge. A great river – the Edgewater – pours down endlessly from the overhanging rock. It was not always so. Fifty years earlier, almost to the day, the river ground to a halt.

This was no random occurrence, but rather a preordained event – for the stopping of the river heralded the arrival of the Mother Storm which, once every five or six millennia, would roar in from Open Sky to seed the Edge with new life.

With the Anchor Chain severed and the floating city of Sanctaphrax lost, the Mother Storm swept on to Riverrise. There, she discharged her vast reserves of energy, rejuvenating the river and sowing her precious seeds of new life.

The Edgewater flowed once more. Riverrise

blossomed. A new Sanctaphrax rock was born. Yet all was far from well on the Edge, for a terrible pestilence was already spreading out from the Stone Gardens.

Stone-sickness, it was called. It was a name that was all too soon on everyone's lips.

It halted new growth in the Stone Gardens where, for centuries, buoyant rocks had sprouted and grown; rocks that had become the flight-rocks of league ships and sky pirate vessels, enabling them to fly. It passed from sky ship to sky ship, caus- ing the flight-rocks of the leaguesmen and sky pirates alike to decay, lose buoyancy and plummet from the sky. It even attacked the great floating rock upon which New Sanctaphrax was being built, causing it to crumble and sink.

Some claimed that the Mother Storm had brought the terrible sickness with her from Open Sky. Some main- tained that Cloud Wolf – the valiant sky pirate captain who had perished inside the Mother Storm – had some- how infected her. Others insisted, with just as much conviction, that there was no connection between the arrival of the Mother Storm and the outbreak, but that stone-sickness was a punishment on those Edge- dwellers who had refused to give up their evil ways.

In short, no-one knew for sure. Only one thing was certain. Stone-sickness meant that life on the Edge would never be the same again.

The league ships were grounded. Sky-trade was at an end. With Undertown and New Sanctaphrax now cut off, the usurper Vox Verlix – the erstwhile cloudwatcher who had ousted the new Most High Academe of New Sanctaphrax – commissioned the building of the Great Mire Road to connect the twin cities to the Deepwoods. In order to complete the project he enlisted the help of both the fearsome shrykes and the Librarian Academics – a union of earth-scholars and disillusioned sky-scholars who had joined their ranks. The consequences were far-reaching.

In the Deepwoods permanent settlements began to spring up for the first time: the Eastern Roost of the shrykes, the Foundry Glade and the Goblin Nations, and far, far to the north-west, between the Silver Pastures and the Hundred Lakes, the Free Glades. In the Mire, a new settlement sprang up overnight, when the sky pirates scuttled all their sky ships together.

Meanwhile, back in Undertown and New Sanctaphrax, despite an uneasy temporary truce, the rift between the sky-scholar Guardians of Night and the Librarian Academics became greater than ever.

The Guardians of Night maintained that the answer to stone-sickness lay in the healing power of storms, believing that Midnight's Spike – at the top of the Sanctaphrax Tower of Night – would attract the electrical energy of passing storms and destroy the terrible pestilence. The Librarian Academics, on the other hand, believed not only that the cure must lie somewhere far out in the Deepwoods, but that, if struck, Midnight's

Spike would cause more harm than good.

As the years passed, the Guardians got the upper hand. Led by the notoriously brutal Most High Guardian, Orbix Xaxis, they imposed their will, manipulating the leagues, enslaving the Undertowners and driving the Librarian Academics, literally, underground – for the sewers of Undertown became their new refuge.

It is down here, in the dark, dank, dripping underground chambers, that an unassuming, yet adventurous, young under-librarian lives. He is thirteen. He is an orphan. When no-one is around, he likes nothing better than to sit at one of the many floating sumpwood desks and bury his head in a treatise-scroll – even though this is strictly forbidden to someone of his lowly status.

He assumes, wrongly, that no-one has ever seen him. However, his disobedience has been both noticed and noted. What is more, it is to have repercussions that no-one could ever have predicted.

The Deepwoods, the Stone Gardens, the Edgewater River. Undertown and Sanctaphrax. Names on a map.

Yet behind each name lie a thousand tales – tales that have been recorded in ancient scrolls, tales that have been passed down the generations by word of mouth – tales which even now are being told.

What follows is but one of those tales.

THE LAST OF THE SKY PIRATES

THE DEEP WOODS SETTLEMENTS

THE GOBLIN NATIONS

THE FOUNDRY GLADE

THE EASTERN ROOST

THE SILVER PASTURES

CHAPTER ONE

THE GREAT
STORM CHAMBER
LIBRARY

The young under-librarian awoke drenched in sweat. From all around, echoing down the tunnels of the Undertown sewers, came the sound of the piebald rats' shrill dawn chorus. How they knew the sun was rising over Undertown, high above them, was a mystery to Rook Barkwater. But they did know, and Rook was grateful to be awake. The other nineteen under-librarians in the small sleeping chamber twitched and stirred in their hammocks, but slept on. It would be another couple of hours before the tilderhorns sounded. Until then Rook had the sewers to himself.

He slipped out of the hammock, dressed quickly and stole across the cold floor. The oil lamp fixed to the damp, mossy wall flickered as he passed by. In the furthest hammock Millwist muttered in his sleep. Rook froze. It wouldn't do to be caught.

'For Sky's sake, don't wake up,' Rook whispered as Millwist scratched his nose. Then, with a small cry of anger or alarm, the youth rolled onto his side – and fell still.

Rook crept out of the chamber and into the gloom of the narrow corridor outside. The air was cold and clammy. His boots splashed in the puddles on the floor and water dripped down his neck.

When it rained in Undertown, the underground tunnels and pipes filled with water, and the librarian-scholars fought to keep it out of the network of sewers they called home. But still it seeped through the walls and dripped from every ceiling. It hissed on the wall lamps, sometimes extinguishing a flame completely. It fell on mattresses, on blankets, on weapons, clothes – and on the librarian-scholars themselves.

Rook shivered. The dream still echoed in his head. First came the wolves – always the wolves. White-collared. Bristling and baying. Their terrible yellow eyes flashing in the dark forest …

His father was shouting for him to hide; his mother was screaming. He didn't know what to do. He was running this way, that way. Everywhere were flashing yellow eyes and the sharp, barked commands of the slave-takers.

Rook swallowed hard. It was a nightmare, but what came next was worse; far worse.

He was alone now in the dark woods. The howling of the slavers' wolf pack was receding into the distance. The slave-takers had gone – and taken his mother and father with them. Rook would never see them again. He was four years old, alone in the vastness of the Deepwoods – and something was coming towards him. Something huge . . .

And then . . .

Then he'd woken up, drenched in sweat, with the shrill sounds of piebald rats in his ears. Just like the time before – and the time before that. The nightmare would return every few weeks, always the same and for as far back as he could remember.

Rook took the left fork at the end of the corridor and went immediately left again; then, fifty strides further on, he turned sharp right into the opening to a low, narrow pipe.

Newcomers to the sewers were forever getting lost in the perplexing labyrinth of pipes and tunnels. But not Rook Barkwater. He knew every cistern, every chamber, every channel. He knew that the pipe he was in was a short cut to the Great Storm Chamber Library – and that even though he had grown tall since he first discovered it, and now had to stoop and stumble his way along, it was still the quickest route.

Emerging at the far end, Rook looked round furtively. To his right, the broad Main Tunnel disappeared back into shadows. It was, he was pleased to see, deserted. To his left, it ended with a great, ornate arch, on the other side of which lay the chamber itself.

Rook took a step forwards and, as the cavernous library chamber opened up before him, his heart fluttered. No matter that he had seen it almost every day for the best part of a decade, the place never failed to amaze him.

The air was warm from the wood-burners, and wafted round in a gentle breeze by hundreds of softly fluttering wind-turners. The buoyant lecterns – which housed the vast library of precious barkscrolls and bound treatises – gently bobbed in their 'flocks', straining at the chains which secured them to the magnificent Blackwood Bridge below. The ornately carved bridge spanned the great, vaulted chamber, linking the two sides of the Grand Central Tunnel. Beside it was the older Lufwood Bridge and numerous gantries; below, the flowing waters of this, the largest of Undertown's sewers.

Rook stood for a moment at the entrance to the chamber, feeling the warmth seep into his bones. No dripping water or leaks of any kind were permitted here; nothing that could harm the precious library that so many earth-scholars had died to establish and protect.

The words of the ageing librarian, Alquix Venvax, came back to Rook. 'Remember, my lad,' he would say,

THE GREAT STORM CHAMBER LIBRARY

'this great library of ours represents just a fraction of the knowledge that lies out there in the Deepwoods. But it is precious. Never forget, Rook, that there are those who hate librarian academics and mistrust earth-scholarship; those who betrayed us and persecuted us, who blame us for stone-sickness and have forced us to seek refuge down here, far from the light of the sun. For every treatise produced, one librarian has suffered to write it, while another has died defending it. But we shall not give up. Librarian Knights elect will continue to travel to the Deepwoods, to gather invaluable information and increase our knowledge of the Edge. One day, my lad, it will be your turn.'

Rook crept out of the tunnel and onto the Blackwood Bridge, keeping his head down behind the balustrade. There was someone on the adjacent bridge, which was unusual for so early in the morning – and though it was probably just a lugtroll there to clean, Rook didn't want to take any chances.

Unconsciously, yet unavoidably, he counted off the mooring winch-rings as he passed. It was something every under-librarian did automatically, for those who made an error about which buoyant lectern was at the end of which chain did not last long in the Great Storm Chamber.

Rook's experience led him unerringly to the seventeenth lectern, where he knew he'd find one treatise in particular. *A Study of Banderbears' Behaviour in Their Natural Habitat*, it was called. Of all the countless leatherbound works in the library, this one was special; special for a very simple reason.

Rook Barkwater owed his life to the treatise, and he could never forget it.

Having checked that the lugtroll was definitely not spying on him, Rook gripped the winch-wheel and began turning it slowly round. Link by link, the chain wound its way round the central axle and the buoyant sumpwood lectern came lower. When it was at the same level as the mounting platform, Rook ratcheted the brake-lever across, and climbed aboard.

'Careful!' he whispered nervously, as the lectern dipped and swayed. He sat himself down on the bench and gripped the desk firmly. The last thing he wanted to do was keel over backwards and fall into the sluggish water of the underground river. At this time of day, there were no raft-hands to drag him out – and he was a hope- less swimmer.

The honey-coloured wood felt warm and silky to the touch. In the warm, dry conditions of the library cham- ber a well-seasoned piece of sumpwood timber was twice as light as air. However, as with all timbers of the first order of buoyant wood, the minutest shift in temperature or humidity could destabilize the timber – and so the sumpwood lecterns bobbed and jittered constantly, making sitting at one for any length of time an art in itself.

'Stop wobbling about, you stupid thing,' Rook told the lectern sternly. He shifted his position on the bench. The violent lurching eased. 'That's better,' he said. 'Now, just hold still while I . . .'

Squinting into the bright spherical light above the

lectern, Rook reached up and pulled a large, bound volume from the uppermost shelf of the floating lectern. It was the one about banderbears. As he laid the treatise out on the desk before him, he felt a familiar surge of excitement, tinged with just a hint of fear. He opened it up at random.

His head bowed forwards. His eyes narrowed in concentration. No longer was he sitting at a floating lectern, in a vaulted chamber, deep down underground . . .

Instead, Rook was *up there* – in the open, in the vast, mysterious Deepwoods, with no walls, no tunnels and no ceiling but the sky itself. The air was cool and filled with the sound of bird-cry and rodent-screech . . .

He turned his attention to the treatise. *The yodelled communication cry,* he read, *is meant for one specific banderbear alone. None, not even those who may be nearer, will answer a call intended for another. In this respect it is as if a name had been used. However, because, throughout my treatise-voyage, I never managed to get close enough to one to fully decipher the language, it is impossible to know for sure.*

Rook looked up. He could hear in his head the banderbear yodel, almost as if he had once heard one for himself . . .

22

One matter appears certain. It seems to be impossible for any banderbear to deceive any other about his/her identity. It is perhaps this fact that makes banderbears such solitary animals. Since their individuality cannot come from anonymity in a crowd, it must come from isolation from that crowd.

The further my travels take me . . .

Rook looked up from the neat script for a second time and stared into mid air. '*The further my travels take me . . .*' The words thrilled him. How he would love to explore the endless Deepwoods for himself, to spend time with banderbears, to hear their plaintive yodelling by the light of the full moon . . .

And then it struck him.

Of course! he thought, and smiled bitterly. Today wasn't just any old day. It was the day of the Announcement Ceremony, when three apprentice librarians would be selected to complete their education far off in the Deepwoods, at Lake Landing.

Rook wanted so, so much to be selected himself – but he knew that, despite Alquix Venvax's encouraging words, this would never happen. He was a foundling, a nobody. He'd been discovered, lost and alone, wandering through the Deepwoods, by the great Varis Lodd – or so he'd been told. Varis, daughter of the High Librarian, Fenbrus Lodd, was the author of the treatise Rook now held in his hands.

If she hadn't been out in the Deepwoods studying banderbears, she would never have stumbled across the abandoned child with no real memories – apart from his name, and a recurring nightmare of slave-takers and wolves and . . .

Yes, Rook Barkwater did indeed owe his life to this particular bound treatise.

Varis Lodd had brought him back to the sewers of Undertown along with her treatise on banderbears, and left him here to be raised by the librarian-scholars. The old librarian professor, Alquix Venvax, had befriended the sad, lonely little boy and done what he could, but Rook was well aware that an orphan with no family connections would never be more than an under-librarian. His lot was to remain down in the great library chamber, tending the buoyant lecterns and serving the professors and their apprentices.

Unlike Felix. Rook smiled to himself. If *he* couldn't go to Lake Landing, then at least Felix could.

Felix Lodd was Varis Lodd's baby brother – though he wasn't much of a baby any more. He was tall for his age, powerfully-built and athletic. Quick to smile and slow to anger, what he lacked in brains, he made up for in the size of his heart.

Felix was an apprentice and had made up his mind to look after the small orphan his sister had found. Rook sometimes thought Felix felt guilty that his beloved sister, whom he idolized, had simply left Rook with the librarian-scholars to fend for himself. It didn't matter. They were friends, best friends. Felix fought the apprentices who tried to bully Rook, and Rook helped Felix with those studies the older boy found difficult. Together they made a strong team. And now all the hard work was about to pay off, for Felix was one of the favourites to be picked to go to Lake Landing and complete his education. Rook felt so proud. One day, he might even be sitting at this lectern with Felix's treatise in his hand.

He picked up the volume and was just reaching up to return it to the high shelf when a bellowing voice echoed angrily round the great chamber.

'You, there!'

Rook froze. Surely he couldn't have been spotted. Not today. Whoever it was must be shouting at that lugtroll on the Lufwood Bridge.

'*Rook Barkwater!*'

Rook groaned. Steadying himself, he slid the treatise back into place and turned slowly round. That was when he first realized how high up he was. With all the violent dipping and swaying of the lectern when he'd first boarded, the brake-lever must have shifted, for the chain securing the lectern had completely unwound. Now he was trapped, far up in the air on the buoyant lectern, which was floating higher from the Blackwood Bridge than any of the others. It was no wonder he'd been spotted. Rook peered down and swallowed unhappily. Why did it have to be Ledmus Squinx who had done the spotting?

25

A fastidious, flabby individual with small pink eyes and bushy side-whiskers, Squinx was one of the library's various under-professors. He was unpopular, and with good reason – for Ledmus Squinx was both overbearing and vain. He liked order, and he liked comfort and – as he'd grown older – he'd also discovered a distinct aptitude for throwing his (increasing) weight around.

'Will you get down here, now!' he bellowed. Rook stared down at the portly, red-faced individual. His hands were on his hips; his lips were sneering. They both knew that Rook couldn't get down without the under-professor's help.

'I – I can't, sir.'

'Then you shouldn't be up there in the first place, should you?' said Squinx triumphantly. Rook hung his head. 'Should you?' he rasped.

'N-no, sir,' said Rook.

'No, sir!' Squinx barked back. 'You should not. Do you know how many rules and regulations you have broken, Rook?' He raised his left hand and began counting off the fingers. 'One, the buoyant lecterns are not to be used in the hours between lights-out and the tilderhorn call. Two, the buoyant lecterns are not to be used unless another is present to operate the winch. *Three, under no circumstances whatsoever,*' he hissed, speaking each word slowly and clearly, '*is an under-librarian ever to board a buoyant lectern.*' He smiled unpleasantly. 'Do I need to go on?'

'No, sir,' said Rook. 'Sorry, sir, but—'

'Be still,' Squinx snapped. He turned his attention

to the winch-wheel, which he turned round and round – puffing noisily as he did so – until the buoyant lectern was once again level with the mounting platform. 'Now, get out,' he ordered.

Rook stepped onto the Blackwood Bridge. Squinx seized him by both arms and pushed his face so close that their noses were almost touching.

'I will not tolerate such disobedience,' he thundered. 'Such insubordination. Such a flagrant disregard for the rules.' He took a deep breath. 'Your behaviour, Rook, has been totally unacceptable. How dare you even *think* of reading the library treatises! They are not for the likes of you.' He spat out the words with contempt. 'You! A mere under-librarian!'

'But . . . but, sir—'

'Silence!' Squinx shrieked. 'First I catch you flouting the library's most serious rules, and now you have the bare-faced cheek to answer back! Is there no end to your audacity? I'll have you sent to a punishment cell. I'll have you clapped in irons and flogged. I'll—'

'Is there some problem, Squinx?' a frail yet imperious voice interjected.

The under-professor turned. Rook looked up. It was Alquix Venvax, the ageing librarian professor. He pushed his glasses up his nose with a bony finger and peered at the under-professor.

'Problem, Squinx?' he repeated.

'Nothing I can't handle,' said Squinx, puffing out his chest.

Alquix nodded. 'I'm glad to hear it, Squinx. Very

glad.' He paused. 'Though something troubles me.'

'Sir?' said Squinx.

'Yes, something I thought I overheard,' said Alquix. 'Something about imprisonment cells and being clapped in irons. And . . . what was it? Ah, yes, being flogged!'

Squinx's flabby face turned from red to purple and beads of sweat began oozing from every pore. 'I . . . I . . . I . . .' he blustered.

The professor smiled. 'I'm sure I don't have to remind you, Squinx that, as an *under*-professor, you are in no position to hand out punishments.' He scratched at his right ear thoughtfully. 'Indeed, I believe that attempting to do so is itself a punishable offence . . .'

'I . . . I . . . that is, I didn't intend . . .' Squinx mumbled feverishly, and Rook had to bite into his lower lip to prevent himself from smiling. It was wonderful to see the bullying under-professor squirm.

'But, sir,' Squinx protested indignantly as he gathered his thoughts. 'He has broken rule after rule after rule.' His voice grew more confident. 'I caught him up on a buoyant lectern, reading, no less. He was reading an academic treatise. He—'

Alquix turned on Rook. 'You were doing *what*?' he said. 'Well, this puts a totally different complexion on the matter, doesn't it? Reading indeed!' He turned back to the now smugly beaming under-professor. 'I'll deal with this, Squinx. You may go.'

As the portly Ledmus Squinx waddled off, Rook waited nervously for Alquix to return his attention to him. The professor had seemed genuinely angry. This was unusual and Rook wondered whether, this time, he had gone too far. When the professor did finally turn to face him, however, his eyes were twinkling.

'Rook! Rook!' he said. 'Reading treatises again, eh? What are we going to do with you?'

'I'm sorry, sir,' said Rook. 'It's just that—'

'I know, Rook, I know,' the professor interrupted. 'The thirst for knowledge is a powerful force. But in future . . .' He paused and shook his head earnestly. Rook held his breath. 'In future,' he repeated, 'just don't get caught!'

He chuckled. Rook laughed too. The next moment the professor's face grew serious once more.

'You shouldn't be here anyway,' he said. 'The buoyant lecterns are closed. Had you forgotten that the Announcement Ceremony is to take place today?'

Just then the tilderhorns echoed round the cavernous chamber. It was seven hours.

'Oh, no,' Rook groaned. 'It's Felix's big day, and I promised to help him get ready. I mustn't let him down.'

'Calm down, Rook,' the professor said. 'If I know Felix Lodd, he'll still be fast asleep in his hammock.'

'Precisely!' said Rook. 'I said I'd wake him!'

'Did you now?' said the professor, smiling kindly. 'Go, then,' he said. 'If you hurry, you should both make it back here in time.'

'Thank you, Professor,' said Rook as he scurried back across the bridge.

'Oh, and Rook!' the professor called after him. 'While you're about it, smarten your*self* up a bit, lad.'

'Yes, sir,' Rook called back. 'And thank you, sir.'

He left the Storm Chamber, ducked down and darted back into the narrow pipe. As the darkness wrapped itself around him once again, his mood also darkened.

The memory of his nightmare came back to him: the snarls of woodwolves and the cries of slave-takers. And the terrible, terrible feeling of being alone . . .

And with Felix gone, he'd be alone again. A small, guilty thought crept into his mind. *What if Felix isn't picked? What if he oversleeps and . . .*

'No!' Rook slapped a fist to his temple. 'No! Felix is my friend!'

·CHAPTER TWO·

THE SEWERS

Pushing past the thick hammelhornskin door-hang-ing, Rook entered the sleeping chamber. Unlike the damp, spartan under-librarians' dormitory, the room was warm and cosy, for Felix Lodd enjoyed all the comforts of a senior apprentice. There was a wood-burning stove in the corner, woven hangings on the wall and straw matting on the floor. The tilderhorns trumpeted the last wake-up call as Rook approached the quilted hammock with its plump pillows and warm fleece blankets.

Rook stared down at his friend. He looked so contented, so carefree and, judging by the smile tug-ging at the corners of his mouth, as if he were having a pleasant dream. It seemed almost a shame to wake him.

'Felix,' said Rook urgently. He shook him by the shoulders. 'Felix, get up.'

Felix's eyes snapped open. 'What? What?' He peered up. 'Rook, is that you?' He smiled and stretched lazily. 'What time is it?'

'It's late, Felix—' Rook began.

'I was having the most amazing dream,' Felix interrupted him. 'I was flying, Rook. Flying above the Deepwoods! Just imagine! Flying up there in the clean, clear air! It was such an incredible feeling – swooping this way and that, skimming the tops of the trees . . . Until I hit turbulence and went into a tailspin.' His eyes narrowed. 'That must have been when you woke me up.'

Rook shook his head. 'You've forgotten, haven't you?' he said.

Felix yawned. 'Forgotten what?' he said.

'What day it is today! It's the Announcement Ceremony.'

Felix sprang out of the hammock, scattering pillows and cushions, and upending a small ornate lamp. 'The Announcement Ceremony!' he exclaimed. 'I thought it was tomorrow.' He looked round the sleeping chamber. 'Curse this stupid place!' he thundered, pulling his robes from the heavy leadwood chest beneath the hammock. 'There's no dawn, no dusk. How can anyone keep track of the time down here?'

'Don't worry,' Rook assured him. 'The last tilderhorn has only just sounded. If we hurry we can still make it to the Lufwood Bridge before the Professor of Darkness begins the oath – although all the best places will be taken.'

'I don't care if they are,' said Felix, fumbling to unknot his formal sash. 'The Announcement Ceremony can't come too soon for me. I'm dying to get out of this rain-soaked sewer and feel the wind on my face, to breathe in clean, fresh air . . .'

'Let me,' said Rook, taking the sash from his friend and deftly unknotting it. He handed it back to Felix, who was now struggling into the heavy robes of a senior apprentice.

Rook smiled sadly. This was the last time he would be able to help his friend out of some scrape or other – for today, the Professor of Darkness was bound to announce that Felix Lodd would be sent off to Lake Landing to complete his studies. There, Felix would have to look after himself; making sure that his work was submitted on time, that his robes were clean and mended, and that he didn't oversleep on important occasions. He wouldn't have Rook to look after him.

Then again, he'd soon make friends out there in the Free Glades because, wherever he went and whatever he did, Felix couldn't help being popular and the centre of attention. Just like his sister before him, Felix was about to set off on a great adventure and make a name for himself up there in the world of fresh air and sunlight. And he, Rook, would be left alone.

Felix tied the sash around his waist and stood back. Rook looked him up and down. It never failed to amaze him! Just a few minutes earlier, Felix had been snoring his head off. Now he stood before him

looking magnificent in
his ceremonial robes,
as if he had taken
hours, not minutes,
preparing.

'How do I look?'
he said.

Rook smiled.
'You'll do,' he said.

'Earth and Sky
be praised!' said
Felix. He picked
up two lanterns,
handing one
to Rook. 'Right,
then. Let's get
to the Lufwood
Bridge. They'll
be expecting
me.'

'Quiet, Felix! I'm
trying to listen.' Rook
stepped closer to the tunnel entrance he'd stopped
beside and motioned Felix to be still with a flap of his
hand. 'I thought I heard something,' he whispered. He
raised his lantern and pointed down the narrow, dripping pipe to his right. 'In there.'

Felix came closer. His eyes narrowed. 'Do you think
it's a—' he mouthed the word – 'muglump?'

'It sounded like one to me,' Rook replied softly.

Felix nodded. That was good enough for him. Rook was second to none when it came to identifying the numerous parasites and predators that lurked in the network of sewers. He drew his sword and, pushing Rook firmly to one side, advanced into the pipe.

'But, Felix . . .' said Rook as, head down, he trotted after him. 'What about the ceremony?'

'It'll just have to wait,' Felix told him. 'This is more important.' He continued along the pipe, pausing at the first fork he came to and listening, before storming on.

Rook struggled to keep up. 'Wait a moment,' he panted, as Felix took a third turning. 'Felix—'

'Shut up, Rook!' Felix hissed. 'If a muglump *has* broken into our sewers from Screetown, then none of us are safe.'

'Couldn't we just report it and leave it to the sewer patrols?' said Rook.

'Sewer patrols?' said Felix, and snorted. 'That useless bunch can't even keep the rats at bay, let alone a fully grown muglump on a blood-hunt.'

'But—'

'*Ssh!*' He stopped at a junction where five tunnels intersected, and crouched down. It was cold, dank. All around, the air echoed with the sound of dripping water. 'There it is,' Felix whispered the next moment.

Rook cocked his head to one side. Yes, he could hear it, too – the soft, whistling hiss of the creature's breathing and the *squelch-squelch-squelch* of its paw-pads. It sounded like a large one.

Lantern raised, Felix followed the noises into the tunnel opposite and continued. Rook followed him. He was trembling nervously. What if Felix was right? What if it *was* on a blood-hunt?

Although they could be vicious when cornered, the muglumps which infested the Undertown sewers were generally less aggressive than their Mire cousins. Perhaps it was due to the lack of direct sunlight. Or perhaps, the change in their diet – the piebald rats they now feasted on were both plumper and more plentiful than the bony oozefish of the Mire. Whatever. As a rule, the sewer-muglumps kept themselves to themselves. But every once in a while, one of their number would develop an insatiable appetite for blood that would draw it into the main sewers in search of larger prey. A blood-hunt. Stories of the havoc such muglumps could wreak were legion amongst the scholars.

'This way,' said Felix grimly as he turned abruptly right. 'I can *smell* it.'

'But Felix,' Rook protested. 'This tunnel, it's . . .'

Felix ignored him. The muglump was near, he was sure. It was time to close in. At a trot now, with his sword out in front of him like a bayonet, he charged down the tunnel. He was going to rid the sewers of this foul creature that had developed a taste for librarian blood once and for all.

Rook did his best to keep up. Raising his head, he saw that Felix had almost reached the end of the tunnel.

'Felix, be careful!' he shouted. 'It's a dead— *Aargh!*' he

cried as his foot slipped, his ankle turned and he came crashing down to the floor of the tunnel. '—end,' he muttered.

He pulled himself up. 'Felix?' he called. Then a second time, louder, 'Felix!' Still nothing. 'Felix, what's—'

'It must be here *some*where!' came Felix's voice, frustration turning to anger in his voice.

'Felix?' Rook shouted. 'Hang on! I'm coming . . .' Limping slightly, he hurried on as fast as he could. His breath came in puffy clouds. Water dripped down his neck. He pulled his dagger from its sheath. 'Felix, are you all right?' he asked anxiously.

'Dead end,' said Felix. His voice was flat. 'Where did it go?'

Rook reached the end of the tunnel and looked into the cistern it had led to. Felix was standing at the far side, his back turned away.

'FELIX! WATCH OUT!' Rook bellowed. 'ABOVE YOU!'

Felix spun round. He looked up into the shadows above his head and found himself staring into the yellow eyes and slavering crimson mouth of the muglump.

It was huge – with a swollen belly, a long, whiplash
tail and six thick-set limbs. It was standing on the ceiling,
its body tensed, its rapier claws glinting.

'Come on, then, you hideous monstrosity,' Felix
challenged it through clenched teeth.

The creature's nasal-flaps fluttered as it sniffed at the
air and a long glistening tongue licked round its lips. Its
eyes narrowed. It drew back, ready to pounce.

Felix brandished his sword menacingly. 'Guard the
exit, Rook,' he said. 'This one isn't going to escape.'

Rook took up a position at the end of the pipe. He

gripped his dagger tenaciously – although he couldn't help wondering how much use it would be against the muglump's thirty terrible blades if the creature *did* turn on him.

Eyeing Felix's sword warily, the muglump retreated. Walking slowly backwards, it crossed the ceiling – *squelch, squelch, squelch.* Rook swallowed nervously. It was heading for the exit pipe; it was heading for *him.*

'It's all right, Rook,' Felix reassured him. 'I'll get it. Just keep your nerve, and—'

Just then the muglump flipped down from the ceiling, twisted in mid air and landed on the ground directly in front of Rook. It glared at him, nasal-flaps rasping loudly, and snorted with fury.

Felix bounded across the cistern, his sword slicing through the air. Rook raised his dagger and held his ground – only to be batted aside the next instant by a mighty blow from the creature's whiplash tail. He fell heavily to the ground. The muglump bowled past him and into the tunnel.

'Don't let it get away!' Felix yelled.

Rook pulled himself up and sent the dagger flying through the air after the retreating muglump. With a rasping *crunch*, the gleaming blade severed the long, prehensile tail in one curving slash and embedded itself at the top of the creature's right hind-leg.

The muglump froze, and howled with agonizing pain. Then it turned, and Rook felt the creature's furious gaze burning into him.

'Well done, Rook,' came Felix's voice from behind him. 'Now move out of the way, and let me finish the job off.'

Wounded it may have been, but the muglump seemed no slower on five legs than on six. Before Felix had gone a dozen strides, the muglump had reached the end of the tunnel and disappeared.

'This time you've got away!' Felix roared after it. 'Next time you will not be so lucky! That, my evil friend, I guarantee!'

Rook poked at the severed tail with his boot. The question was, when would that 'next time' be? After all, Felix was about to be sent off to Lake Landing, where blood-crazed muglumps would be the last thing on his mind.

At that moment, from far away in the depths of the underground sewers, there came the roar of a cheering crowd. It throbbed along the tunnels, drowning out the noise of the dripping water. Felix turned to Rook. 'The Announcement Ceremony,' he said. 'It's started. Quickly, Rook, we must hurry. I'll never live it down if I miss my own name being announced!'

They had by now reached the end of the narrow pipe. Felix looked up and down the adjoining tunnel. 'Left, I think.'

'No,' said Rook. 'We'll go right. I know a quicker way.'

And he dashed off down the tunnel. 'Follow me,' he called back.

Rook skidded round into an abandoned, unlit pipe to his left. Felix followed, close on his heels. The pipe was old and cracked, with pools of water and jagged debris lying all along the floor. Nightspider webs – thick and soggy – wrapped themselves round the two youths' faces as they splashed and stumbled on.

'Are you sure this is – *ppttt, ppttt* – the right way?' said Felix, spitting out the cobwebs as he spoke. 'I can't hear the crowds any more.'

'That's because they've stopped cheering,' said Rook. 'Your father'll already be doing his stuff. Trust me, Felix. Have I ever let you down before?'

'No,' said Felix. He shook his head slowly. 'No, Rook, you haven't. I'm going to miss you, you know.'

Rook made no reply. He couldn't. The lump in his throat wouldn't let him.

'You're right!' Felix exclaimed a moment later as the deep, resonant voice of the High Librarian filtered down into the pipe. 'I'd know that voice anywhere.'

'Welcome!' cried Fenbrus Lodd. 'Welcome to the Great Storm Chamber Library, librarian academics of every echelon, on this, the occasion of the Announcement . . .'

'We sound near,' said Felix.

'We *are* near,' said Rook. 'A little bit further and ...
yes, here we are.' He darted off into a broader pipe
which, fifty strides on, abruptly emerged into the Grand
Central Tunnel. Rook sighed with relief. They'd made it.
The arched entrance to the Great Storm Chamber stood
before them.

'Come on,' said Felix grimly. 'There's probably only
standing room left.'

Rook looked ahead at the vast crowds who had
gathered to witness the Announcement Ceremony. They
were spilling out of the Storm Chamber and jostling for
position. 'We'll be lucky to get beyond the door,' he said.

'No problem,' said Felix. 'Mind your backs!' he
shouted good-naturedly. 'Make way for an apprentice
with an appointment at Lake Landing!'

·CHAPTER THREE·

THE ANNOUNCEMENT CEREMONY

With so many crammed together in the great chamber – packing the Blackwood Bridge, clinging to the jutting gantries and perched on the skittish buoyant lecterns – the place was warmer than ever. Both Felix and Rook were soon dripping with sweat, and when their wet clothes began to dry they also began to steam.

Having forged their way right to the front of the crowd on the Blackwood Bridge, Rook and Felix stood on the lower rail of the carved balustrade and looked across to the smaller Lufwood Bridge. Below them, the channel of water – sluggish after so long without a decent downpour outside – was covered with rafts, each one weighed down with still more spectators and held in place by the raft-hands' hooked poles.

'They're all there,' Felix noted, jerking his chin towards the stage on the Lufwood Bridge.

Rook nodded. Seated on high-backed chairs on either side of the High Librarian's speaking-balcony, from which Fenbrus Lodd was addressing the crowd, were the Professors of Light and Darkness, Ulbus Vespius and Tallus Penitax. Both were former sky-scholars who, appalled by the behaviour of the Guardians of Night, had decided to throw in their lot with the Librarian Academics. Flanking them, six on either side, were the elders of the library.

Fenbrus Lodd's voice echoed round the hushed chamber. 'Never has the Council of Three had such a hard task selecting those who are to journey to Lake Landing. Not, I should add, because there was a lack of suitable candidates, but rather the opposite. Each of your library elders put up an excellent contender, and argued well in his or her favour . . .'

Rook looked at the dozen venerable individuals, one after the other. Their backgrounds were wildly varied. Some were brilliant earth-scholars who had returned from exile to help with the new underground library; others had been eminent sky-scholars who, like the Professors of Darkness and Light themselves, had changed sides when the evil Guardians of Night took over Sanctaphrax – and then there were those whose histories were an absolute secret. His gaze fell on Alquix Venvax. The kindly professor who had taken him under his wing was a case in point. His past was a mystery.

'As always,' the High Librarian continued, 'the short-list has been whittled down to the three individuals who we, the Council of Three, consider best suited to the task ahead . . .'

Rook glanced round at Felix. His face was glowing with keen expectation. The pair of them had talked often about what being selected would involve. First the journey, through Undertown, over the Great Mire Road and on into the Deepwoods, aided by those loyal to the librarian-scholars. Then, after a period of intense study (which Felix usually chose to gloss over) the building of his own sky-craft. Finally Felix's dreams of flying were to come true.

'. . . sacred, but also arduous,' the High Librarian was saying. His voice dropped. 'And deeply perilous. Those of you who are selected must fight against over-confidence, for that is your worst enemy. You must remain on your guard. The world outside is a dangerous place.'

Just then Rook's and Alquix Venvax's eyes met. The professor acknowledged the young under-librarian with a slight nod. Rook nodded back, and hoped Alquix hadn't noticed how red his cheeks had become. The professor, he'd heard, was intending to take him on as his permanent personal assistant when he came of age. Rook knew he should be grateful – it was, after all, what most under-librarians dreamed of. But for Rook, the thought of spending the rest of his life down in the airless, sunless underground system of tunnels and chambers was, instead, an absolute nightmare.

'And so, Edge scholars, one and all,' Fenbrus Lodd proclaimed, his voice laden with occasion, 'the time has come for the Announcement.'

The chamber fell still. All that could be heard was a soft, distant dripping which echoed round the vaulted ceiling and, like great wings beating, the flutter of the wind-turners. All eyes fell on the scroll which the High Librarian, Fenbrus Lodd, now unfurled before them.

'The first Librarian Knight elect shall be Stob Lummus,' he announced.

The news was greeted with clapping and cheering, and the traditional *whoop-whoop-whooping* of the apprentices, while the professors nodded approvingly. As Stob Lummus was a brilliant scholar, his selection came as no surprise to them – although a couple of the older, wiser academics present noted that he would soon learn that barkscroll-learning alone was not enough to ensure success. Rook and Felix looked down to see a stocky youth with a broad back and a shock of thick, dark hair being hoisted up onto his neighbours' shoulders.

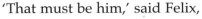

'That must be him,' said Felix, peering down more closely. He was feeling a little uneasy not to have been announced first. 'Stob Lummus,' he said finally, and shrugged. 'I don't think I know him.'

Rook frowned. '*I* might,' he said thoughtfully. 'From down in the Eastern Reaches. I think he's the son of that big guard in the sewer patrol – you know, the one with the scar . . .'

'The son of a guard, eh?' said Felix. He stared across at his own father. There was a time when the other apprentices had accused him of being at an unfair advantage with so eminent an academic as his father. Felix didn't see it that way. If anything, being the son of the High Librarian and brother to the famous Varis Lodd meant that everyone seemed to expect great things of him. He had to be twice as good at everything as anyone else. Sometimes he just didn't think he was up to it. He often saw disappointment in the eyes of his tutors. Only Rook continued to have absolute faith in his friend.

'Your turn next,' he whispered.

Felix nodded, but made no reply. As Stob Lummus reached the side of the stage, Fenbrus Lodd raised the scroll for a second time. Once again, the chamber fell

47

into a silence that seemed to quiver with expectation.

'The second Librarian Knight elect shall be . . .' Felix swallowed hard. Rook bit into his lower lip. 'Magda Burlix.'

There was a sharp intake of breath from, it seemed, every onlooker present. The shocked gasp echoed round the chamber walls. The next moment, as the person in question revealed herself, the crowd split itself into two. Half of them raised their hands and clapped; the other half kept their hands in their pockets and turned to their neighbours to express their surprise.

Magda Burlix, tall with piercing green eyes and three thick plaits, emerged from one of the rafts. She was hauled up onto the Lufwood Bridge, where she took her place beside Stob Lummus.

From the back of the chamber came the sound of booing. But the clapping grew louder to drown it out, and a lone voice from near the Central Tunnel cried out, 'Another Varis Lodd!'

Those in favour of the announcement cheered gleefully. Those against fell silent, for how could they reject Magda Burlix's selection without also dismissing the finest, bravest, cleverest Librarian Knight ever to have been ennobled?

Felix stared directly ahead, fighting back the tears. With such a father and such a sister, how could he fail? Yet if he did, how could he ever show his face again? He turned to Rook and seized him by the sleeve. 'I'm not going to make it, am I?' he said. 'Am I, Rook? They're not going to announce my name.'

'Of course they are,' said Rook. 'There's no-one here who is better than you, Felix. At one-to-one combat, you're unbeaten. At swordplay, you're the best. At pummelball and parajousting . . .'

Felix shook his head. 'It's the studying,' he said. 'It's always let me down. The learning. The memorizing. Without your help I wouldn't even have got this far.'

'Nonsense,' said Rook reassuringly. 'Besides, who needs books when they fight as well as you do?'

Felix nodded. 'I suppose you're right,' he said. He paused and looked at Rook properly. 'Do you think I'm being foolish?'

'No, not foolish,' said Rook. 'But you're worrying needlessly. There's one perfectly good reason your name hasn't been announced yet.'

'There is?' said Felix.

'Yes,' said Rook and smiled. 'They're saving the best till last.'

For the third time, an expectant hush fell over the great chamber. The High Librarian scratched at his thick, bushy beard and returned his attention to the scroll.

'The third Librarian Knight elect . . .' Fenbrus paused and looked round. For a fleeting moment his gaze rested on the spot on the Blackwood Bridge where the two friends were standing.

Rook sighed sadly. This was it, then. Felix's selection would be announced and the two of them, who had once been like brothers, would be separated, probably for

ever. Felix would leave for Lake Landing that evening –
while he, Rook, would remain underground. 'I'll miss
you,' he whispered.

'Same here,' Felix whispered back.

Fenbrus Lodd returned his attention to the scroll
before him. '... will be ...'

As one, the entire assembled gathering held its breath.
The High Librarian cleared his throat. He looked up
again. 'Rook Barkwater.'

For a moment there was complete silence in the chamber. No-one, but no-one, could believe what he or she
had just heard.

Rook Barkwater?

The youth wasn't even an apprentice! A mere under-
librarian, that's all *he* was; a lectern-tender, a
chain-turner ... How could such a lowly individual
have been accorded so high an honour? It was incredible. It was unheard of.

Low muttering grew in volume until the whole
chamber was in uproar. The gantries and bridges
trembled and, as the atmosphere grew more heated and

steamy, so the buoyant lecterns dipped and swayed wildly. Several senior apprentices fell into the water, and had to be retrieved by the raft-hands.

Dazed, Rook looked along the line of academics on the Lufwood Bridge. He saw Tallus Penitax, the Professor of Darkness, looking at him levelly, his brows knitted and his heavy arms folded. He saw Alquix Venvax nodding enthusiastically – and he remembered his professor telling him to smarten himself up. Now he knew why. The fact was, however, that the chase for the muglump had left him looking even scruffier than usual. Still, there was nothing to be done.

Rook climbed down from the balustrade, head in a whirl and knees knocking, and turned to go back along the Blackwood Bridge. The rowdy crowd parted before him. Their faces, shocked and questioning, were a blur to Rook. As he stumbled on, murmurs and whispers filled the air.

'An under-librarian!' said one. 'What next? A sewer cleaner?'

'I, for one, have never heard of him,' said another.

'Apparently he's Varis Lodd's foundling,' said a third scornfully.

'And a friend of that fool son of the High Librarian!' added someone else.

On the Lufwood Bridge at last, Rook advanced slowly towards the stage, where Ulbus Vespius, Tallus Penitax and Fenbrus Lodd stood waiting in a triangle. Following Stob and Magda's lead, Rook went from one to the other. Each of the venerable academics congratulated each of the librarian knights elect and presented objects to help them with the task ahead.

Ulbus Vespius was handing out pairs of pale yellow stones. 'Sky-crystals,' he told Rook. 'Keep them in separate pockets, for they glow when close to each other. And if you rub them together, they spark.'

'Thank you, sir,' said Rook. 'Thank you.' He moved on.

The Professor of Darkness was next. Having congratulated Magda, he turned to the bashful youth.

'Well done,' he said gruffly, and leaned forward to tie a folded square of glistening black material around Rook's neck like a scarf. 'The Cover of Darkness is woven from the finest silk that nightspiders can produce,' he explained. 'Open it up and wrap it round you when you need either to hide away or travel unseen.'

Once again, Rook gave thanks and moved on. Fenbrus Lodd, High Librarian of the Great Storm Chamber, stood before him.

'Congratulations, lad,' he said, and reached down to

place a talisman over Rook's head. 'It is a bloodoak tooth – engraved with your name,' he added. 'It will offer you some protection from the dangers of the Deepwoods.'

Rook looked down at the pointed claw-like object which gleamed in the lamplight. 'Thank you,' he said uncertainly. 'But . . .'

'But?' said Fenbrus.

'Please, sir,' Rook mumbled. 'It's just . . . It should be Felix going, not me,' he said. 'Surely there's been a mistake.'

Fenbrus took a step forwards and gripped Rook by the arms. 'There has been no mistake,' he said. 'Even though he is my own son, I cannot pretend that Felix is cut out for the task ahead. Certainly, he has the boldness, the courage and the strength required, but he has no natural aptitude for study – and without that, his other qualities count for nought.'

'But—' Rook said for a second time.

'Enough,' Fenbrus interrupted him. 'The decision was unanimous.' He smiled. 'Though given the powerful arguments put forward by your proposer, that was hardly a surprise.'

Rook nodded. 'Professor Venvax has always been good to me,' he said.

The High Librarian frowned. 'I'm sure he has – yet it was not he who offered you up for selection.'

Rook was confused. 'It wasn't?' he said.

'No, it was not,' came a voice from behind him. Rook turned to see Alquix Venvax himself standing there. 'Indeed, if it had been down to me alone, you would have become my personal assistant—'

'It was *I* who put your name forward for selection.'
The Professor of Darkness stepped forwards. He looked
quite different in the formal ceremonial robes of his
office, rather than the usual harness and jerkin of a sky-
flyer. His dark, attentive eyes darted this way and that,
seemingly missing nothing.

'You?' said Rook, surprised – and blushed at how
insolent he must have sounded. 'I mean . . . thank you,
sir,' he added.

The Professor of Darkness nodded. 'I've had my eye
on you for some while now, Rook,' he said. 'Your
perseverance and rigour have impressed me greatly –
even though your willingness to bend the rules can, at
times, be a little alarming.'

Rook's eyes widened. The professor clearly knew all
about his reading the treatises.

'Remember, Rook. While such behaviour was under-
standable in an under-librarian, it is completely
unacceptable in a librarian knight elect. I shall continue
to keep an eye on you.' His eyebrows came together
sternly. 'Do not disappoint me, Rook.'

'I won't,' Rook assured him.

The professor nodded approvingly. 'You have a long
and difficult journey ahead of you. The treatise you will
produce is precious, for it is only by librarian-academics
constantly adding to our knowledge of the Edge that we
will keep the dark ignorance of the Guardians of Night
at bay – and in due course, Earth and Sky willing,
discover the cure to stone-sickness. If you are to return

safely and successfully, Rook, you must travel in secret and trust no-one. A single careless word, and you could all perish!'

Just then a dozen tilderhorns trumpeted loudly, announcing that it was time for the three young hopefuls to take the Scholarship Oath. Rook took his place between the others.

The High Librarian raised his head. 'Do you, Stob Lummus, Magda Burlix and Rook Barkwater, swear to serve Edge Scholarship, both Earth and Sky, for the good of all?'

Three voices rang out in response. With his eyes fixed on the High Librarian's face, however, Rook was aware of no-one but himself. He heard the words come out of his mouth – words he'd always longed to say, but never dared to imagine that he ever would.

'With my heart and my head, I do.'

The Most High Guardian of Night, Orbix Xaxis, was standing on one of the uppermost gantries of the Tower of Night. A tall, imposing figure, he was wearing the heavy black robes of public office – and the dark glasses and metal mask of his own private fears. The glasses, he hoped, would repel any who would try to curse him with the evil eye, while the mask – which had a filter of phraxdust behind the muzzle – purified the germ-laden air he breathed.

From below him there came the clanking and clunking of the mounted swivel telescopes turning this way and that as the Guardians scanned the early morning sky for any sign of illicit skycraft in flight. Sky flight, both in Sanctaphrax and Undertown, was strictly forbidden.

Xaxis stared out into open sky. The high winds and driving rain which had been forecast only the day before had, once again, failed to materialize. 'Surely a storm must come soon,' he muttered to himself. He looked up at Midnight's Spike, the tall, elegant lightning conductor which pointed up to the sky from the top of the tower, and shook his head. 'Fifty years, and nothing. But soon. Soon a storm is bound to come,' he hissed, 'and when it does, the great Sanctaphrax rock will be healed, cured, restored . . .' His eyes glinted unpleasantly behind the dark glasses. 'And when *that* happens—'

Just then there was a knock at the door. Xaxis turned and, with a flourish of his cape, stepped back through the open window and into his reception chamber.

'Enter,' he called, his imperious voice muffled somewhat by the mask.

MIDNIGHT'S SPIKE

The door opened, and a youth dressed in the black robes of the Guardians of Night walked in. He was pallid, angular, with shadowy rings beneath his violet eyes and his hair shorn to a dark stubble.

'Ah, Xanth,' said Orbix, recognizing the youth at once. 'What brings you here? Has the execution taken place already?'

'It has, sir – but that is not the reason for my visit.' He paused. There was something deeply disturbing about never being able to see the Most High Guardian's eyes. It was only his rasping voice that gave any clue as to what he was thinking.

'Well?' Orbix demanded.

'I have information,' said Xanth simply.

Orbix nodded. Xanth Filatine was, without doubt, the most promising apprentice to have come his way in many years. Now that Orbix had prised him away from that obese fop, Vox Verlix, the youth was shaping up well. 'Information?' he said. 'What information?'

'It concerns the librarian knights,' he said, and spat on the floor. 'A recently captured prisoner has just revealed some interesting facts about them under interrogation.'

'Go on,' said Orbix, rubbing his gloved hands together.

'They are about to send three more apprentice treatise scholars off to the Deepwoods. Tomorrow morning, when—'

'Then we must seize them.' Orbix smiled behind the metal mask. 'Three more traitors to add to the hanging gantries.'

'If you please, sir,' said Xanth, his nasal voice little more than a whisper, 'I think I may have a better idea.'

Orbix glowered at the youth. He didn't like his plans being questioned. 'A *better* idea?' he growled.

'Well, not better, as such,' said Xanth, back-tracking. 'But an alternative that you might like to consider.'

'Go on,' said Orbix.

'Sir, if the renegades were followed, in secret, this could be the chance we have been waiting for to uncover the entire network of traitors. We could expose each and every enemy of the Tower of Night operating between Undertown and the so-called *Free* Glades.'

'But—' Orbix began.

'As I see it, the choice is this,' Xanth went on hurriedly. 'The three apprentices now. Or the whole treacherous set-up tomorrow.'

Orbix raised an eyebrow. 'And who might be the spy to carry out such a task?' he asked.

Xanth lowered his head modestly.

'I see,' said Orbix. He tapped thoughtfully on the muzzle of the mask with the tips of his bony fingers.

The proposal was interesting, very interesting. For so long now, he had dreamed of capturing those two turn-coats, Ulbus Vespius and Tallus Penitax, the treacherous Professors of Light and Darkness – and torturing them until they repented for going over to the other side and begged for his forgiveness. He *would* forgive them, of course. He would forgive all those who fell into his clutches – even Fenbrus Lodd.

And then he would have them executed.

'Very well, Xanth,' he said at last. 'I give you my permission to go.'

'Thank you, sir. Thank you,' said Xanth, emotion sounding in his voice for the first time since their meeting had begun. 'You won't regret your decision, sir. I give my word.'

'I hope not, Xanth,' came the icy response. 'Indeed, I make you this promise. If you should let me down, then it is *you* who will live to regret my decision.'

With Orbix Xaxis's
doomladen words
echoing round his
head, Xanth left the
chamber and headed
back down the
flights of stairs.
Hood raised and
gown wrapped
close about him, he
kept to the shadows
and out of sight. Past
the look-out gantries
he went; past the
guards' quarters and
great halls, the laborato-
ries and kitchens, and on
down into the dark, dismal dungeons in the lower reaches of the sinister Tower of Night.

All round him he heard the low, whimpering moan of the prisoners. Hundreds of them, there were – earth-scholars, sky pirates, suspected spies and traitors, even Guardians who had fallen from favour. Each one had been locked up, pending a trial which would take years to come – and almost certainly end up with an execution. In the meantime, they had to remain in their cells – if cell was the right word for the precarious ledges which jut-ted out into the vast atrium at the centre of the tower.

Xanth stopped on a half-landing, where one of the descending flights of stairs became two, and turned to the door facing him. He slid the round spy-hole cover to one side and peered through. The prisoner was still sitting in exactly the same position as when Xanth had left him, nearly two hours earlier.

'It's me,' he hissed. 'I'm back.'

The hunched figure did not move.

'You were right,' said Xanth, louder now. 'It worked.' Still the prisoner did not stir. Xanth frowned. 'I thought you might be interested in my good news,' he said peevishly.

The figure turned and stared back at the spy-hole. He was old. His eyes were sunken; his cheeks hollow. His thick, grey beard and thinning hair were dark with years of filth. He raised one shaggy eyebrow. 'Interested?' he said. 'Aye, Xanth, I suppose I am.' He looked round his cell and shook his head wearily. The small ledge, sticking out into the cavernous, echoing atrium, had no walls, yet escape was impossible. Apart from the door, which was kept securely bolted from the outside, the only way out was down – down to cer-tain death on the ground, far below. He turned back to the spy-hole. 'But I am also envious beyond words.'

Xanth swallowed with embarrassment. Here, deep
down in the stinking bowels of the atrium, the cell was
about as bad as it could be. There was a table where,
being an academic, the prisoner was forced to do work
for the Guardians, and a filthy straw mattress. And that
was it. For as long as Xanth had been alive, and many,
many long years before that, the cell had been the
prisoner's entire world.

'I . . . I'm so sorry,' said Xanth. 'I didn't think.'

'You didn't think,' he murmured. 'How ironic that is,
Xanth, for I do little else *but* think. I think of everything
that has happened – of what I have lost, of what has been
taken from me . . .' He paused, and when he looked up
again he was smiling. 'You will enjoy the Deepwoods,
Xanth. I know you will. It is dangerous there, of course,
with more perils than you could imagine. Yet it is a
wondrous place – exciting, beautiful . . .'

Xanth nodded enthusiastically. It was, after all, their
long conversations about the endless forest which had
triggered his interest in the Deepwoods in the first place.
They'd talked about woodtroll paths and reed-eel beds,
about waif country and (Xanth's favourite) about sacred
Riverrise, high up in the distant mountains. Yet it was a
place the prisoner would only ever visit again in his
memory, for Xanth knew that the Most High Guardian of
Night considered him too important ever to be released
– and no-one had ever escaped from the dungeons of the
Tower of Night.

Just then a pair of soiled ratbirds landed on the corner

of the prisoner's sleeping ledge. He flapped his thin, grimy hands at them, sending them screeching back into the air. 'And stay gone!' he shouted after them. 'I'm not dead yet.' He snorted. 'There'll be time enough to pick my bones clean when I am. Eh, Xanth?'

The young apprentice Guardian winced uneasily. 'Please don't talk like that,' he said. 'Something'll turn up. I know it will . . .'

'Hush now, Xanth,' the prisoner cautioned. 'Such words are treason. If you do not wish to end up on your own dungeon ledge, you'd better be careful.' He returned his attention to the barkscroll. 'I will be thinking of you,' he said.

The following morning Rook Barkwater stood in the cold, damp dormitory, stuffing all his belongings – which were few – into a backpack. He untied and reknotted the black scarf around his neck. He inspected the talisman. He rubbed the two sky-crystals together and watched the sparks tumble down to the floor, where they fizzed and disappeared.

'Where is Felix?' he wondered. He hadn't laid eyes on him since the moment his own name had been announced from the Lufwood Bridge. He had found his sleeping chamber empty, the hammock unslept in – and none of the other senior apprentices seemed to have seen him. Rook was confused. Surely, desperately disappointed as he was, Felix wouldn't let him leave without saying goodbye.

Would he?

As he pushed the last of his meagre belongings into the backpack and tightened the drawstring, Rook sighed unhappily. Just then there came a noise from the end of the long thin room, and the door burst open. Rook spun round.

'Felix,' he said as a figure appeared. 'At last! I was beginning to think . . .' He fell still. It was not Felix at all.

'Come on, Rook,' said Stob Lummus impatiently. 'Aren't you ready yet?'

'We've been waiting for simply ages,' added Magda Burlix, and pursed her lips primly. 'There's still a lot to be done before we can depart.'

Rook pulled the backpack shut and swung it up onto his shoulder. As he did so, he noticed something shiny which had been lying on the hammock beneath his backpack. Rook gasped. It was Felix's ceremonial sword.

'Thank you, Felix,' he whispered, as he belted it round his waist and trotted after the others. 'And fare you well, wherever you may be.'

CHAPTER FOUR

THE GREAT
MIRE ROAD

It was late afternoon before the three young librarian knights elect were ready. First, they had to be fitted with their respective outfits. A long, flowing cape for Magda Burlix, with little bundles of bright materials hanging in bunches amidst clusters of shiny pins and thimbles of all sizes.

'Finest silks from the workshops of Undertown,' she smiled, turning to look at herself in the mirror. 'Something to suit every shryke-matron. How about you, madam? Can I interest you in twenty rolls of this very fine spider-silk?'

Rook smiled, but Stob Lummus, the other librarian, turned away. 'It won't be so funny when you're on the Mire road surrounded by shryke guards, Magda,' he said sharply. Stob adjusted the tall, conical hat of a timber trader, and pulled the rather moth-eaten tilder coat on over the heavy sample-laden waistcoat he wore.

'As for you!' He turned to Rook, contempt plain in his dark brown eyes and curling upper lip. 'Don't encourage her, *under*-librarian!'

Rook turned away, his face burning, and fumbled with the straps of his tool harness.

'What a natural knife-sharpener you make,' sneered Stob. 'Must run in the family.'

Rook didn't rise to the bait. As Felix had so often told him, 'You're equal to any and better than most.' Good old Felix!

Rook sighed as he thought of his old friend. He wouldn't like to guess how many times Felix had come to his aid over the years, defending him against overbearing professors and aggressive apprentices – for bullies came in all shapes and sizes.

'Ready?' It was the Professor of Darkness. He looked strained and tired. 'Here are your papers. Stob, you are a timber merchant from the Foundry Glade. Magda, you are a silk trader carrying samples to the Eastern Roost. And you, my boy,' said the professor, laying a hand on Rook's shoulder, 'you are a lowly knife-sharpener and tool-mender. Slip away quietly now – and look out for the bloodoak pendants. Those who wear them are friends to the librarian knights and will protect and guide you. The first of your contacts will make themselves known to you at the tollgate to the Great Mire Road. Sky speed, and may Earth protect you.'

Stob stepped forwards.

'No,' said the professor. 'Rook, you lead the way. You know the tunnels better than anyone.'

Stob shot Rook a black look.

'It's this way,' Rook told the others some time later as he led them through the labyrinth of underground sewage tunnels. He was heading for an overflow pipe in the boom-docks which, in times of heavy rain, emptied directly into the Edgewater River. It was not the closest to the Great Mire Road tollgate but, being so well concealed by the overhead jetties, it was considered by the Professor of Darkness to be the safest.

One after the other, the three of them emerged into the eerie half-light of shadows and setting sun. The air was cold, and took Rook by surprise. He swallowed it in great greedy lungfuls. Compared with the stale, tepid atmosphere of the sewers they had left behind, it tasted wonderfully fresh – even here, on the muddy shoreline of the sluggish river.

To their right stood a tall pillar. A single piece of cloth, nailed to its side, fluttered in the rising breeze.

'Look at that,' Rook murmured.

Stob frowned. 'I believe it's a posting-pole,' he said. 'I've read about them somewhere. Before the Edge was blighted with stone-sickness, sky ship captains with berths to spare would advertise—'

'Not that,' Rook interrupted. He nodded past the pillar at the huge sun, deep crimson and pulsating. '*That*,' he murmured in awe. 'It's been so long . . .'

Magda, who had herself been standing with her mouth open, shook her head. 'It's incredible, isn't it?' she said. 'I mean, I knew the sun was up there above us the whole time, but actually to see it – to feel it—'

'But you mustn't look at it directly,' Stob interrupted stiffly. 'Ever. I read that it can blind you if you stare for too long, even when it's this low in the sky . . .'

'The colour of the clouds,' Rook whispered reverently. 'And the way they glow! They're so beautiful.'

'They make my spider-silk samples look dull in comparison,' said Magda, nodding.

'What nonsense,' said Stob. 'Sunsets are just dust particles in upper sky . . .'

'Read that somewhere, did you?' said Magda, lightly.

Stob nodded. 'If you must know, it was in an old sky-scholar scroll I uncovered in—' He heard Magda's sigh of irritation and stopped himself. 'We should be making tracks,' he said. He strode off, not looking back.

Magda followed. 'Come on, Rook,' she called back gently. 'We mustn't get separated.'

'Coming,' said Rook. Reluctantly, he dragged himself away from the dazzling evening sky.

Rook's senses were on fire and, as he followed the other two up a rotting wooden flight of stairs to the quayside promenade, along a winding alleyway and onto the main thoroughfare which led to the beginning of the Great Mire Road, he was bombarded with sights, sounds, smells – and distant memories which tugged at his feelings. The cool caress of night air coming in from open sky. The smudge and twinkle of the first emerging stars. The smells of roast meats and strange spices from the ramshackle stalls they passed. Goblins shouting down to passing cloddertrogs, timber wagons creaking along narrow alleys and boots clattering on the cobbled streets. By the time the massive lamplit towers of the Great Mire Road gateway came into view, Stob, Magda and Rook were walking in the midst of a large and growing crowd, streaming both to and from the road's great entrance.

'Busy 'ere this evening, innit, Maz?' said a voice behind them.

'You can say that again,' came the reply.

'I said, it's busy here this evening . . .'

'Oh, Sisal, you are a one!'

Rook glanced round to see two grinning mobgnomes with a bundle of costumes, robes and frock coats on hangers draped over their left arms, hurrying past them. To their left was a gnokgoblin sitting astride a prowlgrin which was pulling a low cart, laden with boxes labelled FINEST PEWTER CUTLERY. Behind him an officious-looking lugtroll was shouting out orders at half a dozen cloddertrogs who were staggering along beneath the weight of a long, heavy roll of red and purple tapestry. And following them, a contingent of gyle goblins bearing pallets of gleaming flagons, goblets and urns above their heads . . .

Nobody paid any heed to the sullen timber merchant, the young silk-seller or the lowly knife-sharpener who followed close on their footsteps. Rook felt overwhelmed yet exhilarated to be a part of all this great activity. From every corner of Undertown, merchants and dealers were converging on the Great Mire Road. For though some of the more heavy industry had shifted to the Foundry Glade, where wood-fuel was cheap – and labour cheaper still – the majority of manufactured goods were still produced in the traditional workshops and factories of Undertown. On the other side they would barter and sell their wares in the Eastern Roost.

'Mind your backs!' roared a rough voice from near the gateway. 'Coming through.'

Ahead of him, Rook saw the crowds part as an approaching hammelhorn-drawn wagon rolled into view. It was long and flat – and followed by two others. On the bench at the front of each one were two seated leaguesmen and a swarthy flat-head goblin, who stood on the driving platform, holding a knot of reins with one hand and cracking a whip with the other. Rook craned his neck to see what load was being carried beneath the huge tarpaulins. Raw materials of some kind, that much was certain, for everything manufactured in Undertown – from bracelets to bricks – was made from materials brought in from outside.

'It's timber,' Rook heard Stob telling Magda in that bossy, rather haughty voice of his. 'Ironwood, by the look of it. No doubt bound for the Sanctaphrax forest,' he continued. 'Sheer madness, if you ask me, but then –' his voice dropped to a low whisper – 'that's the Guardians of Night for you.'

'*Ssh!*' Magda warned him under her breath 'There are spies everywhere,' she breathed.

Stob's eyes narrowed. Even though he knew she was right, he didn't like to be told. And as the third load of ironwood rumbled past, and the departing crowd surged forwards once again, Stob marched ahead, demanding that the others keep up.

Magda turned to Rook, rolled her eyes and smiled conspiratorially. Rook increased his pace to keep up with her.

'The Guardians,' he whispered. 'Do you think they know what we're doing?'

Magda shrugged. 'I wouldn't be surprised,' she said. 'But knowing and *finding* are two different things!' she added fiercely.

'What about the Most High Academe?' asked Rook. 'They say he has an army of goblin mercenaries on duty day and night, just to hunt down librarian knights . . .'

Magda tossed her head back contemptuously. 'The Most High Academe, Vox Verlix, that great sack of oak-wine – *hah*! He's finished.' She paused. 'Of course, you know it's him who's responsible for that.' She pointed to the tall towers of the Mire road looming up ahead of them.

Rook gasped. 'He built *that*!'

Magda nodded. 'Oh, yes,' she said. 'After stone-sickness put an end to sky-trade, he designed and supervised the building of the Great Mire Road so that we humble merchants of Undertown could trade with the Deepwoods. Clever person, old Vox. At least, he was once. Too clever! Mother Scab-beak and the Shryke Sisterhood seized control of it, and there was nothing he could do to stop them.'

'What about his goblin mercenaries?' asked Rook.

'Them? They're worse than the shrykes. Vox recruited them to guard the slaves he used to build the Great Mire Road, and they ended up holding him to ransom. He has to pay them off constantly. Otherwise they'd throw him out of that fancy palace of his – and he knows it. The goblins and the shrykes have made an alliance to control the trade between Undertown and the Deepwoods, and Vox Verlix, the so-called Most High Academe, is nothing more than their puppet. Anyway, it's not him we have to worry about,' Magda added darkly. 'It's the Guardians of Night who are really dangerous.'

Rook shivered and adjusted the tool-harness on his back. It suddenly felt very heavy.

Magda shook her head. 'It was also Vox Verlix who designed the Tower of Night for the Guardians,' she said. 'It was supposed to tap the power of a passing storm and thereby heal the great floating rock.' She stopped and looked over her shoulder. 'You can see it over there in the distance. Evil-looking monstrosity.'

Rook nodded, and glanced back. There, huge and threatening, was the great wooden structure, towering high above the rooftops of even the tallest Undertown buildings. Its narrow spire – Midnight's Spike – pointed up accusingly at the sky.

'And it was Vox,' she went on, turning back, 'who, when that same great floating rock began to crumble and sink, was forced by the Guardians to keep it shored up with timbers. Hundreds, thousands of ironwood timbers. The Sanctaphrax Forest.'

'Yes, I know about that,' said Rook, remembering his studies. It's that vast wooden scaffold of pillars and crossbeams that keeps the floating rock from sinking right down to the ground, isn't it?'

'Precisely,' said Magda. 'According to many scholars, that must never be allowed to happen. If the floating rock touches the ground, they say, it would mean that the power of the storm would pass straight through the stricken rock to the ground beneath, failing to heal it. Hence the so-called *forest* – which, unlike the Tower of Night and the Mire road, will go on being built for ever,' she added, 'for the lower the rock sinks, the more

timbers are needed to support it. Stob is right. It *is* madness – Careful, Rook!'

Too late. Rook walked slap-bang into an oncoming
tufted goblin. There was a *thud*, followed by a *crash*,
followed by the sound of round objects clattering over
the cobbles and loud, angry swearing. Rook, who had
been looking back at the angular Tower of Night
silhouetted against the darkening sky, spun round. The
goblin was lying on his back, dazed and cursing loudly,
with Magda crouching down next to him. The crate he
had dropped had upturned and its contents – a consignment of choicest woodapples – were rolling noisily over
the cobbled street in all directions. As for Stob, he was
nowhere to be seen.

Rook's heart began to pound. He was meant to be
travelling as inconspicuously as possible, yet here he
was drawing attention, not only to himself, but also to
Magda. A small crowd had collected round the ranting
goblin. If the guards were to get wind of what was going
on, he ran the risk of sabotaging the entire trip before
they even got properly started.

'I'm so sorry,' he said as he scurried about, retrieving
the woodapples. 'It was entirely my fault. I wasn't looking where I was going.'

'Yeah, well,' said the tufted goblin, making a great
show of dipping his finger into the soft red flesh of a
shattered woodapple. 'That's all very well, but what
about the fruit what's got smashed up? I'm just a poor
fruit vendor . . .' He left the words hanging in mid air.

'I . . . I'll make good the loss, of course,' said Rook

uneasily. He looked up at Magda. 'Won't we?'

Without a word, Magda reached into her cloak and pulled out a leather pouch. She loosened the drawstring. 'Here,' she said, placing a small gold piece into the goblin's palm. 'This is for the damaged fruit.' The goblin nodded, his eyes glinting craftily. 'And this,' she said, as she added a second coin, 'is for any bumps or bruises suffered.' She stood up, yanked the goblin to his feet and smiled fiercely. 'I trust the matter is settled, then,' she said.

'Y-yes, I suppose so,' the goblin stammered. 'Though—'

'Excellent,' Magda announced. She turned and, with Rook in tow, strode back off into the crowd.

'You handled that very . . . confidently,' said Rook.

Magda tossed her plaits back and laughed. 'I have three older brothers,' she explained. 'I've had to learn how to hold my own.'

Rook smiled. He was growing to like this travelling companion. Although at first she had seemed imposing, abrupt – abrasive even – now he was beginning to see her in a different light. She was practical, she was forthright, she spoke her mind and acted decisively. Rook realized, now, why she had been selected to go to the Free Glades. In comparison, Stob seemed cold, aloof, bookish . . . He frowned. 'Where *is* Stob?' he wondered out loud.

Magda shook her head. 'That's what I was just asking myself,' she said, and looked round. 'We must stick together.'

They were, by now, almost at the entrance to the Great Mire Road, with the gateway towers reaching far up above their heads. If everything went as planned, then someone would make themselves known to them – someone who would guide them safely through the toll-gate. Rook fingered his bloodoak tooth and searched the crowd for anyone wearing something similar.

Stob was nowhere to be seen, and the large square in front of the tollgate was thronging. The noise was colossal, and the smells! Everything from the sour stench of pickled tripweed barrels to the overpowering sweet-ness of vats of barkcat-musk perfume. Here, where the in-trade and out-trade converged, were merchants and pedlars, prowlgrin-riders and hammelhorn-drivers, carts, carriages and cargo of every description.

There were armed guards and tally-shrykes, smugglers and slavers, food vendors, bar-tenders, entre-preneurs and money-lenders. There were creatures and characters from every corner of the Edge – lugtrolls, gabtrolls, woodtrolls, cloddertrogs and termagants, nightwaifs and flitterwaifs, and goblins of every description. And there, standing in the shadows of a tall loading-derrick, his body half turned away, was Stob Lummus himself.

'He's talking to someone,' Rook hissed. His voice

dropped. 'It must be our contact.' And he went to step forwards, only to find Magda's firm grip on his arm holding him back.

'I'm not so sure,' she said. 'Listen.'

Rook cocked his head to one side and concentrated on the gruff voice coming from the depths of the shadows. 'What was that? Bloodoak *what*?' the voice complained tetchily. 'You must speak up!'

'I said,' he heard Stob replying in a sibilant stage-whisper, 'that is an interesting charm you're wearing.

Bloodoak tooth, if I'm not mistaken—'

'What?' demanded the voice, and Rook caught the flash of something metallic. 'What's it got to do with you?'

Magda shook her head. 'Surely that can't be our contact,' she said.

'Indeed it's not, missy,' came a sing-song voice behind her. '*I* am.' Both Magda and Rook turned to see a dumpy gnokgoblin wearing a long cape and head scarf, and carrying a covered basket on one of her stubby arms. Around her neck glinted an ornate pendant, the centre-piece of which was a glistening red tooth.

'My name is Tegan,' she said. 'Your friend has made an unfortunate, not to say foolish, mistake—'

'He's no friend of mine,' Magda cut in sharply.

'Friend, companion, fellow-traveller,' said Tegan, 'the precise nature of your relationship is unimportant. All that matters is that he is in danger.' She shook her head and tutted with concern. 'This could be serious,' she said. 'Very serious. You must go and get him before he gives all of us away. Quickly, now.'

Neither Magda nor Rook needed to be told twice. They darted across the square, dodging through the streaming crowds, and into the shadows at the bottom of the loading-derrick.

'There you are, Stob!' cried Rook, grabbing one of his arms. 'We've been looking everywhere for you,' said Magda, as she took hold of the other. 'Off we go!'

'No, no,' said Stob urgently, and tried to shake them off. His voice lowered to a conspiratorial whisper. 'I've found our first contact,' he said.

Rook and Magda glanced round at the old woodtroll who was standing beside them. He was plump and bandy-legged, and the plaits in his beard had turned white. He had a brass ear-trumpet raised to one ear, while round his neck were clustered trinkets and lucky charms of all shapes and sizes. A dullish brown tusk on a leather cord nestled in the white whiskers.

'No, you haven't,' said Magda.

'Trouble is,' Stob said, 'he's a bit deaf.'

'I heard that!' said the woodtroll indignantly.

'So are you, Stob!' Magda said in a clipped whisper. 'I'm telling you, he's *not* the contact. Now, *come on.*' With that, she and Rook tightened their grip and frogmarched Stob away.

'Here!' the woodtroll called after them. 'What's this all about?'

Magda turned to Stob questioningly. Stob shrugged. 'Didn't you see it?' he said. 'The pendant – a bloodoak tooth on a leather strip—'

'That was no bloodoak tooth,' said Magda. 'It was a whitecollar woodwolf fang.' She tutted. 'Call yourself a librarian scholar!'

Even as he heard her accusing words, Rook realized that he, too, might just as easily have been fooled. At a glance, in the jostling crowd, the wolf fang could easily be confused with a bloodoak tooth. Stob's big mistake had been to approach the old woodtroll rather than wait to be approached.

'You made it, then,' the gnokgoblin said to them when they arrived back by her side. 'Well done. I was beginning to worry.'

'Yes,' said Magda. 'Though no thanks to—'

'Who is this?' said Stob, butting in. He was feeling both foolish and resentful. 'Can we trust her?'

Tegan nodded sagely. 'You are wise to be sceptical,' she said. 'For "Trust no-one" is as good a motto as any for you to stick to on your long journey.'

'You still haven't given us a reason for trusting you,' said Stob rudely.

Without saying a word, the gnokgoblin reached forwards and fingered the carved bloodoak tooth round his neck, then nodded towards the two others. 'Rather a coincidence for three travellers to be wearing the same earth-studies talisman, don't you think?' she said. 'Unless Fenbrus Lodd is now handing them out to all and sundry.'

'No,' Stob conceded. 'So far as I know, they are given only to librarian knights elect, and their supporters.'

'Then nothing has changed,' said Tegan. She opened the front of her cape to reveal her own ornate talisman.

'You?' said Stob, surprised. 'You're our contact?'

'You seem surprised,' said the gnokgoblin. 'Over the years I have done my best to be useful to scholars and academics of every persuasion. Acting as a counsellor

here, a guide there...' Her voice took on an icy edge.
'Anything, rather than allow the Edge to slide into the
dark oblivion those cohorts of the Tower of Night would
foist upon us all.'

'Well said,' Magda agreed.

The gnokgoblin looked around anxiously. 'We have
already been standing here for too long. It's not safe.' She
turned back to them and her face broke into a smile. 'The
three of you have got a long and difficult journey ahead
of you, but with a little luck and a lot of perseverance, I
just know you're going to succeed.'

Rook suddenly felt buoyed up by the gnokgoblin's
confidence, and grinned from ear to ear. He could hardly
wait to get going.

'Right, then,' said Tegan. 'It's high time we saw about
your tally-discs. Keep close together – and let me do all
the talking.'

As they approached the Great Mire Road, Rook saw
that there was a row of tally-huts and barriers strung out
in a line between the huge towers. Individual queues led
to each one. The gnokgoblin led them straight to the
tally-hut closest to the left-hand tower.

Ahead, on an ornately carved throne, sat a large shryke
matron, bedecked in jewels and rich fabrics. On either
side of the throne sprouted enormous carved claws which
barred the way through. The shryke eyed each trader with
yellow, unblinking eyes, before scrutinizing the tattered,
much-thumbed papers handed to her.

'Pass!' Her voice rasped out as she flicked the lever at
her side with an evil-looking talon. The carved claws

clicked open and the trader walked through. 'Next!'

'Pass!' *Click*. 'Next! Pass!' *Click*. 'Next!'

Rook jumped. To his surprise, he realized that Stob and Magda were through. It was his turn. His heart leaped into his mouth.

'Remember,' Tegan whispered in his ear. 'Let me do the talking.'

'*Next!*' The shryke's voice was shrill with irritation. Tegan pushed Rook forward. Somehow, Rook made his legs work. With a trembling hand, he offered up his false documents, trying not to look at the yellow eyes that seemed to be boring into his skull. What if there was some mistake with his papers? What if the shryke asked him about his so-called line of business? What did Rook know about knife-sharpening? A cold panic began to build in the pit of his stomach.

'Knife-sharpener?' The shryke cocked her large head to one side. The feathers at her neck ruffled, the jewels clinked, her terrible curved beak came towards Rook's down-turned face. 'Don't look old enough to play with knives, do he?' the shryke cackled nastily. 'Well, sonny? Goblin stolen your tongue?'

Tegan stepped forward. 'It's his first time,' she smiled. 'Obviously he's overcome with the beauty of your plumage, Sister Sagsplit.'

The shryke laughed. 'Tegan, you old charmer. Is he with you?'

Tegan nodded.

'I might have known,' said the shryke. 'Through you go.'

The talon flicked the lever. Rook took his papers and
tally-disc, and stumbled through the opening claw-stile.
Magda and Stob were waiting on the other side.

'What kept you?' Magda sounded panicky.

'Stopped for a chat, no doubt,' said Stob smugly.

'Shut up, Stob,' said Magda. She clasped Rook's hand.
'Are you all right? You look very pale.'

'I'm fine,' said Rook shakily. 'It's just, I've never seen a
shryke before. They're so . . . so . . .'

'You'll see plenty more on the Mire road,' said Tegan,
motioning them forward.

'*You?* Don't you mean *we?*' said Magda.

'Yeah, I thought you were coming with us,' said Stob.

'My place is here,' Tegan explained. 'My role is to get
travellers safely through the tollgate tally-huts and onto
the Great Mire Road. Others will make themselves
known to you along the way.' She gave them each a
brief, but heartfelt hug. 'Take care, beware and well may
you fare, my dears,' she said. And with that, she was
gone.

The three young librarian knights elect suddenly felt
very alone. From behind them, there came the loud noise
of clattering and chattering as a contingent of rowdy
mobgnomes lugging a vast range of ironware products,
from buckets and bellows to wrought-iron railings, drew
closer and overtook them. Without saying a word to one
another – but instinctively aware that there was safety in
numbers – Stob and Magda attached themselves to the
back of the group, and Rook brought up the rear.

Ever since the young under-librarian's name had

THE GREAT MIRE ROAD

echoed round the high vaulted ceiling of the Great Storm Chamber, Rook Barkwater had felt he was in a dream, scarcely able to believe the events unfolding before him. Now, as he stared ahead at the magnificent raised road, with its ironwood pylons and huge floating lufwood barges; with its look-out posts, its toll-towers and its blazing beacons snaking away into the distance far ahead, his head reeled and his body tingled with excitement.

'This is it,' he whispered softly. 'There's no turning back now. The greatest adventure of my life has already begun.'

Back at the tally-hut, there was a soft *click* as the claw-stile opened once more. An angular figure in dark robes slipped through. As he lowered his hood, the moon glinted on high cheekbones and closely cropped hair.

CHAPTER FIVE

DEADBOLT VULPOON

They had been walking for hours over the slippery boarded walkway. All around them traders, merchants and itinerant labourers just like themselves trudged on, backs bent under heavy burdens, eyes staring fixedly down. Few spoke, and when they did, it was in whispers. It was dangerous to attract attention on the Great Mire Road.

Rook glanced up. Ahead, the timber walkway snaked off into the distance like some gigantic hover worm. To their left and right, the Mire mud glistened in the fading light.

'Keep your eyes down!' Stob's whisper was urgent and threatening.

'Remember,' said Magda softly, placing a hand on Rook's shoulder. 'To look directly into a shryke guard's eyes is punishable by death.'

Rook shuddered. Just then, ahead of them, he heard

the clicking sound of clawed feet on the wooden boards and the brittle crack of a bone-flail. Shryke guards were approaching.

Rook's heart missed a beat.

'Steady,' Stob hissed. 'We mustn't draw attention to ourselves. Just keep moving. And you—' he jabbed Rook nastily in the back – 'keep your eyes to yourself!'

'It's all right,' whispered Magda. 'Here, take my hand, Rook.'

Rook grasped Magda's hand gratefully, fighting the urge to turn tail and flee.

The clawed feet clicked nearer. Ahead, the slow-moving crowd seemed to melt away into the shadows cast by the blazing beacons that were strung out high above them at hundred-stride intervals along the way. Rook couldn't help himself. He glanced up.

There ahead of him, staring back with cruel, yellow unblinking eyes, was a tall mottled shryke guard, resplendent in burnished metal breast-plate and great curved beaked helmet. A razor-sharp talon moved to her side, where the vicious-looking bone-flail was strapped. With a rustle of feathers, the guard drew the flail. Rook was transfixed with fright. He looked down instantly and squeezed Magda's hand with all his might. He heard Magda gasp.

'How *dare* you!' The screech pierced the air like a dart.

Rook closed his eyes and hunched his shoulders, waiting for the blow he felt must surely come.

'Mercy, mercy,' a goblin's frightened voice cried out pitifully. 'I didn't mean to . . . I beg you. I—'

The bone-flail cracked to life in the evening air, followed by the sound of a skull shattering. Rook opened one eye. In front of him, in the harsh glare of an overhead beacon, a small goblin lay at the shryke's feet. A pool of blood spilled out across the surrounding boards.

'Goblin scum!' the shryke squawked, and behind her two other guards clacked their beaks with amusement.

The shryke swung the flail over her shoulder, and the three of them strode on. Magda pulled Rook to one side as they passed. He felt faint. Rook had witnessed, and experienced, violence before – the viciousness of an angry professor, the brutality of the fights that had occasionally broken out amongst the apprentices and under-librarians . . .

But this. This was different. It was a cold violence, callous and passionless – and all the more shocking for that.

'That was close,' said Stob quietly, behind them. 'Come on, now. Keep moving, or we'll never make it to the toll-tower. There's a rest platform there,' he added.

Rook glanced down at the body on the road and, with a jolt, recognized the pack on the hapless goblin's back.

The goblin had been a knife-grinder, just like himself. Hands were now grasping the body, dragging it into the shadows. Rook heard a distant muffled thud as something landed far below in the soft Mire mud. All that was left of the goblin was a small blood-red stain in the wood, which marked what had happened. It occurred to Rook that, along the length of the Great Mire Road, he had seen many such stains.

Rook turned to Magda. 'This is a terrible place,' he said weakly.

'Courage, Rook,' said Magda kindly. 'We can stop for the night at the rest platform. There'll be someone there to meet us, I'm sure.'

Rook stopped. 'Couldn't we just stay here? Night's closing in, the road seems to be getting more and more slippery – and I'm so hungry.'

'We keep on to the toll-tower,' said Stob firmly. '*Then* we stop for something to eat. Rook!' he snapped. 'Do keep up.'

Rook was motionless, rigid. His eyes and mouth were open wide, his face drained of all colour. He had seen something hanging from a great beacon-pole, just up ahead.

'What's the matter?' said Magda. 'Rook, what is it?'

Rook pointed. Magda looked round – and gasped. Her hand shot up to her mouth.

'Earth and Sky,' Stob groaned as he, too, saw what Rook had seen. 'That is . . . dis-*gus*-ting,' he murmured.

Rook shuddered. 'Why do they do it? What could possibly justify *that*?'

He stared up at the hang-
ing-cage. It was a mesh of
interlocking bars, shaped
like a sphere and suspended
from a gantry fixed to the
top of the tall, fluted ironwood beacon-pole. There
was a dead body inside it, its
limbs contorted, its head
bathed in shadows. A growing flock of white ravens
was flapping round, land-
ing on the bars and pecking
fiercely through the gaps.

All at once the corpse
slumped forwards. The
largest white raven of all gave a
loud *kraaak*, beat the other
birds away and stabbed at the
head, once, twice.

Rook screwed his eyes shut, but too late to avoid seeing the unfortunate creature's dead eyes being plucked
out of its skull. One. Two. The sudden jerkiness of the
movement . . . A strand of something glistened in the
yellow lamplight. Rook abruptly bent over double as if
he'd been struck a blow to the belly and retched emptily
as he staggered over the bloodstained boards.

'Come on, now,' Magda said gently. 'Pull yourself
together.' Then, supporting him with her arm, she handed
Rook her water-container. 'Drink some of this,' she said.

'That's it. Now, breathe deeply. In, out. In, out . . .'

Slowly, Rook's legs stopped shaking, his heart quietened, and the choking feelings of nausea began to subside. 'You were right, Rook,' he heard Magda saying in a quavering voice. 'This is indeed a terrible place.' They rejoined the slow-moving file of travellers on the Mire road, and continued in silence.

With the toll-tower no more than a hundred strides away now and the wind coming from the west, the acrid smoke from the tilder-fat beacon at its top blew back along the Mire road into their faces. It made Rook's eyes water. It made his heart pound. After all, if no-one appeared soon to help them through this stage of their journey, they would have to deal with the shryke toll-guards on their own – and having just seen what they were capable of . . .

'I am a knife-sharpener, if it pleases you,' he practised breathlessly. 'A knife-sharpener from the Goblin Glades – I mean, *Nations*. The Goblin *Nations*. That's it. I'm a knife-sharpener from the Goblin Nations.'

In the event, the imposing shryke at the desk took their money, stamped their papers and waved them on without even raising her crested head. Rook kept his eyes firmly on his feet, which were now aching from the hours of walking. Presenting their papers was clearly a mere formality, he realized, important only when it was *not* done – for if the shryke guards ever found a trader or merchant without the most up-to-date stamps during one of their random inspections, the punishment was both swift and severe.

Rook didn't want to think about it. He followed the other two out onto a wide landing of lufwood planks, crammed with numerous stalls. Run by mobgnomes and gabtrolls they were, slaughterers, woodtrolls and gnokgoblins – each one vying with his or her neighbour for the passing trade.

There were lucky charms for sale: talismans, amulets and birth-stones. There were crossbows and long-bows, daggers and clubs. There were purses, baskets and bags. There were potions and poultices, tinctures and salves. There were street plans for newcomers to Undertown and charts of the endless forest (often hopelessly in-accurate, though none who purchased them would ever find their way back to complain) for those who hoped to travel in the Deepwoods.

And there were food stalls. Lots of them, each one laden with delicacies from all parts of the Edge. There were gnokgoblin meatloaves on offer, woodtroll tilder sausages, and sweetbreads cooked to a traditional cloddertrog recipe. There were pies and pastries, puddings and tarts; honey-soaked milkcakes and slices of candied oaksap. In short, there was something for everyone, whatever their taste, and the air was filled with an intoxicating mixture of aromas – sweet, rich, juicy, creamy, tangy – all mingling together in the brazier-warmed air.

Yet Rook was no longer hungry. His appetite had been lost to the memory of that dead prisoner in the cage, with his torn flesh and his stolen eyes.

'You must try to eat,' said Magda.

Rook shook his head mutely.

'Then I'll get something for you,' she said. 'For later.'

'As you wish,' said Rook wearily. It was sleep he needed, not food.

'There are hammock shelters and sleeping pallets close by,' came a soft, yet penetrating voice by his side. 'If you require, I can take you there.'

Rook looked down to find a short, wiry waif standing by his side. With his pale, almost luminous skin and his huge bat-like ears, he looked like a greywaif, or possibly a night-waif . . .

'A *night*waif,' the character confirmed. 'Greywaifs are generally larger and—' he gestured towards his mouth – 'they have those rubbery barbels hanging down from round here . . .' He frowned. 'But you're right, Rook. And I apologize. My name is Partifule.'

Rook scowled. He'd always found the mind-reading ability of waifs – whatever their variety – deeply disturbing. It made him feel exposed, vulnerable – and how could you ever trust a creature that made you feel like that?

Partifule sighed. 'That is our curse,' he said. 'In waif country, reading the minds of others is essential for our survival; a gift to enable us to see through the darkness. Here, however, it is a curse – spoiling every friendship and turning so many of us into spies who sell their services to the highest bidder.'

And you? Rook wondered with a shudder. How much have you been paid to spy on us?

Partifule sighed a second time. 'I give my services for free,' he said. 'And I am no spy. Perhaps *this* will help you to trust me.' He pulled his cape apart and there, nestling in the folds of the shirt beneath, was a red bloodoak tooth hanging from a delicate silver chain. 'I have been assigned the task of guarding you all while you sleep this first night. You must be fully rested for what lies ahead.' And he added, in response to Rook's unspoken question, 'The Twilight Woods.'

Rook smiled. For the first time that day he felt himself relax. Stob and Magda returned from the stalls, food wrapped in small, neat bundles. Magda handed one to Rook, who put it in his pocket.

'Who's that?' Stob demanded, his voice cold and imperious.

'Partifule, at your service,' came the reply and, for a second time, he revealed the bloodoak tooth.

'He's going to show us where we can bed down for the night,' Rook explained, 'and keep watch while we sleep.'

'Is he now?' said Stob. 'And slit our throats while we're snoring, eh?'

'Stob,' said Magda, sounding angry and embarrassed. 'He's wearing the tooth.' She turned to the nightwaif. 'Greetings, Partifule,' she said as she shook the creature's damp, bony hand. 'And apologies for our companion's rudeness.'

'Better safe than sorry,' Stob muttered.

'Indeed,' Partifule agreed. 'And, of course, Stob, you must feel free to spend the night on watch with me,' he said. 'I'd welcome the company.'

Stob made no verbal reply, but from the amused expression that played around the nightwaif's face, Rook knew that he had *thought* something back.

'Come on, then,' said Partifule. 'Stick together. It's just over here.'

They picked their way through the crowds gathered round the stalls, and across the landing to its outer edge. There, Partifule showed them the long, covered stall, with hammocks strung from its beams. To the right were row upon row of pallets, each one padded with a thick mattress of straw.

'Hammock shelter or sleeping pallet?' Magda asked Rook.

'Oh, a sleeping pallet, definitely,' said Rook. He gazed up into the speckled inky blackness above him. 'I've wanted to sleep out under the starry canopy of the sky for so long—'

'Well, now's your chance,' Partifule broke in. 'In fact, you should all be settling down for the night. It's almost midnight and you've got a long day ahead of you.'

None of the three young librarian knights elect needed any persuasion. It had been a long, draining day. Before Partifule had even taken up his look-out position at the end of his pallet, Stob, Magda and Rook were settling down to sleep.

Rook was just dozing off when, above the coughs and snores of the sleepers all around him, he heard a voice.

'Wa-ter,' it rasped. '*Waooooh*-ter.'

Rook got up slowly and picked his way through the pallets to the very edge of the landing. There, in front of him, were two hanging-cages next to each other. His blood turned cold in his veins. The first contained a bleached skeleton, with one bony hand reaching out of the cage pleadingly and the skull resting against the bars, its jaws set in a permanent grimace. The second cage appeared to be empty.

'Wa-ter.'

There was the voice again, but weaker now. Rook cautiously approached the cages. The skeleton couldn't have spoken, which meant . . . He peered up into the shadows within the second cage, and gasped. It wasn't empty after all.

'Wa-ter,' the voice repeated.

Rook hurriedly unclipped the leather water-bottle from his belt and held it up – but although he stretched as high as possible, he couldn't reach the cage. 'Here,' he called. 'Here's some water.'

'Water?' said the voice.

'Yes, here below you,' said Rook. For a moment

nothing happened. Then a great ham of a hand shot out from the bottom of the cage and grabbed the water-bottle. 'You're welcome,' said Rook, as he watched the hand and the water-bottle disappear back inside the cage.

There came the sound of slurping and swallowing – followed by a loud burp. The empty water-container dropped out of the cage and fell at Rook's feet. He bent down to retrieve it.

'Forgive me,' came the voice from above his head, weak still, but less rasping. 'But my need was indeed great.' The hand descended for a second time. 'And if you had a little something to eat, too . . .'

Rook searched his pockets, and found the bundle Magda had given him. He'd forgotten even to open it. He passed the warm package up to the waiting hand. The sound of hungry chomping and chewing filled the air.

'Mmm . . . mmmfff . . . Delicious – though perhaps it could do with a little extra salt.' He peered down at Rook and winked. 'You saved my life, young fellow.' He nodded towards the skeleton in the next cage. 'I did not wish to end up like my neighbour.'

Rook noticed the harsh edge to the voice. This was someone who was used to giving orders. He peered more closely inside the shadowy cage. Behind the bars, bathed in dark shadows and flickering lamp-light, was a hulking great figure, so immense that he was forced to crouch in the cage. Dressed in a frock coat, breeches and a tattered tricorn hat, he had dark curly hair, bushy eyebrows and a thick, black beard with what looked – Rook realized with a gasp – like ratbird skulls plaited into it. Bulging eyes glared out from the tangled bird's-nest of hair like two snowbird eggs.

Rook felt a surge of excitement. 'Are . . . are you a sky pirate?' he asked hesitantly.

A throaty laugh went up. 'Aye, lad. Long ago. A sky pirate captain, no less.' He paused. 'Not that that means anything these days – not since the Edge was stricken with stonesickness.'

'A *sky pirate captain*,' Rook whispered in awe, and felt tingles of excitement running up and down his spine. What must it be like, he wondered, to have sailed in a sky pirate ship, with the sun in your face and the wind in your hair? He had often read, late into the night at the lecterns of the underground library, of the Great Voyages of Exploration into the darkest Deepwoods and the fearful dangers encountered there; of the series of Noble Flights out into Open Sky itself – and, of course, all about the fierce and terrible battles the sky pirates had fought with the wicked leaguesmen in their determination to keep the skies open for free trade.

Ships with names like *Galerider*, *Stormchaser*, *Windcutter*, *Edgedancer* and the *Great Sky Whale*, sailed by legendary sky pirate captains. Ice Fox, Wind Jackal, Cloud Wolf. And, perhaps the most famous of them all, the great Captain Twig himself.

Rook stared more closely at the caged captain. Could *this* be the fabled Twig? Had the popular young captain he'd read so much about become the huge hairy hulk before him?

'Are you Captain—' he began.

'Vulpoon,' the sky pirate captain answered, his voice low, hushed. 'Deadbolt Vulpoon. But keep it to yourself.'

Rook frowned. *Vulpoon.* There was something familiar about it.

A little smile played around the captain's eyes. 'I see you recognize my name,' he said, unable to keep the pride from his voice. His voice dropped to a whisper. 'Those flea-ridden featherballs that captured me had no idea the size of the fish they had landed. If they had, I wouldn't be talking to you now.' The sky pirate captain laughed. 'If they knew it was Deadbolt Vulpoon in this stinking cage, they'd cart me off to the Wig-Wig Arena in the Eastern Roost faster than a three-master in a skystorm.' He played with one of the skulls in his thick beard. 'Instead, they've left me to waste away like a common Mire raider.'

'Can I help?' asked Rook.

'Thank you, lad, for the thought,' said the pirate, 'but unless you have the cage key of a shryke-sister, I'm done for like an oozefish on a mudflat.' He stroked his beard. 'There is one thing . . .'

'Name it,' said Rook.

'You could stay and talk a while. Three days and three nights I've been here, and you're the first who hasn't been too frightened of shrykes to approach the cage.' He paused. 'Yours will probably be the last kind voice I'll ever hear.'

'Of course,' said Rook. 'It would be an honour.' He slipped back into the nearby shadows and crouched down. 'So, what was it like?' he asked. 'Skysailing.'

'Skysailing?' said Vulpoon, and sighed with deep longing. 'Only the most incredible experience in the world, lad,' he said. 'Nothing compares to the feel of soaring up into the air and speeding across the sky, with the full sails creaking, the hull-weights whistling and the flight-rock – sensitive to every change in temperature – now rising, now falling. Angle, speed and balance, that's what it was all about.' He paused. 'Until the flight-rocks began to fall to the stone-sickness, that is.'

Rook stared at the sky pirate captain's crestfallen face.

'A terrible time, it was,' he continued. 'Of course, we'd known what was happening to the new floating rock of Sanctaphrax for some time. The loss of buoyancy. The gradual disintegration . . . But we made no connection between the plight of the New Sanctaphrax rock and our own precious flight-rocks. That was soon to change. First off, news started coming in of large, heavy traders simply crashing out of the sky. The broad tug boats followed, with league ships and patrol boats soon also becoming useless. The leagues fell into decline and the skies above Undertown emptied. A terrible time it was, lad. Terrible.

'At first, we sky pirates did very well out of the situation. Night after night, we would carry out raids on the Great Mire Road, knowing that none would be able to follow us. What was more, we became the main means of transportation for fleeing Undertowners—' he rubbed his forefinger and thumb together – 'for a price.' He sighed noisily. 'And then it happened.'

Rook waited expectantly. Vulpoon scratched beneath his chin.

'We thought we were clever,' he said. 'We thought that by keeping our distance from New Sanctaphrax we would avoid the sickness. But we were wrong. Whether it travelled in on the wind, or had simply been incubating inside the stone, we'll never know . . . It was on the third day of the fourth quarter that the *Cloudbreaker* – one of the oldest and finest double-masters ever to have been built; a real beauty – just fell out of the sky like a speared ratbird and crash-landed in the Deepwoods below. Stone-sickness had finally caught up with us.

'Something had to be done if we were not all to go the same way, one by one. We had to convene to make plans. I dispatched a flock of ratbirds bearing word that an assembly was to be held at Wilderness Lair at the next full moon.' He sighed. 'And it was there, clinging to the underside of the jutting Edgelands rock like a collection of rock-limpets, that we decided to scuttle the entire fleet together—'

'The Armada of the Dead,' Rook gasped.

'You've heard of it, then?' said Vulpoon.

'Of course,' said Rook. 'Everyone has.' He didn't

mention *what* he'd heard – that it had become a renegade outpost attracting every dissident, runaway and more notorious denizen of the Mire.

Vulpoon was nodding sagely. 'What a night that was,' he murmured. 'We sailed together, that final time, across the sky from the misty Edgelands to the desolation of the Mire. And there, as one, we descended. All round us, a flock of white ravens flapped and screeched at the giants in their midst. We landed on the soft, sinking mud . . .' He looked up. 'That was nigh on thirty-five years since – and we're still there.'

Rook stared out across the mudflats of the Mire. 'It seems so very bleak,' he said.

'We get by,' said Vulpoon. 'A fleet of sky pirate ships was a pretty good basis for a settlement. And what we don't have, we go out and get.' A broad grin spread from ear to ear, revealing gums which bore more gaps than teeth. 'The occasional raid on the Great Mire Road. The odd skirmish with the shrykes . . .' He chuckled. 'There aren't many who haven't heard the name of Captain Deadbolt Vulpo—'

'*Thunderbolt!*' Rook blurted out. 'Thunderbolt Vulpoon. *That* was the name I was trying to remember.'

'He was my father,' the sky pirate captain said quietly. 'Executed in cold blood by the shrykes – those murderous, verminous, *pestilential* creatures. By Sky, how I'd like to wring every one of their scraggy necks.'

'The shrykes killed him,' Rook murmured.

'Aye, lad, in that evil Wig-Wig Arena of theirs,' he said. 'Yet it was a noble death, an honourable death – for he died that another might be saved.'

'He did?'

Deadbolt Vulpoon nodded, and wiped a tear from the corner of his eye. 'You may not have heard of him, but it was a certain Captain Twig they were actually after.'

'Oh, but I *have* heard of him,' said Rook. 'The young foundling, raised by Deepwoods woodtrolls, who was to become the most famous sky pirate captain of all time. Who has not heard of him?'

'Yes, well,' said Vulpoon, and puffed up his chest – as far as the confines of the cage would allow. 'Perhaps not *the* most famous.' He paused. 'Anyway, Twig'd been sentenced to death by the shrykes for some heinous crime, so he had. They were about to throw him to the bloodthirsty wig-wigs, when my father intervened – and sacrificed himself instead.'

'He must have been very brave,' said Rook.

Deadbolt Vulpoon sniffed, and wiped the corner of his other eye. 'Oh, he was,' he said. 'He certainly was.' He paused. 'If only there had been something left of him to bury, something to remember him by. But . . . well, I'm sure I don't need to tell you about wig-wigs. By the time they'd finished, there wasn't a scrap remaining.'

Rook nodded sympathetically and left a respectful pause before asking what he really wanted to know. 'And this Captain Twig?' he said. 'What happened to him? Is he with you at the Armada of the Dead? Or . . .'

'Or?' said Vulpoon.

'Or could those stories about him be true?' said Rook. 'That he alone refused to scuttle his ship. That he sailed off, back into the Deepwoods. That he lives there still, alone, unwashed and in total silence, wandering endlessly by day and sleeping in caterbird cocoons by night.'

'He did sail off into the Deepwoods,' Vulpoon concurred gruffly. 'As for the rest, I don't know. I've heard stories, of course. There have been sightings. *Soundings*, even – for some have returned with tales of him singing to the moon.' He shrugged. 'You have to take most of what you hear with a pinch of salt.' He looked up. His eyes narrowed. 'Shrykes,' he whispered urgently. 'You'd better make yourself scarce.'

'Shrykes!' Rook jumped. He turned and saw three of them, all bedecked in gaudy ornamentation, striding across the platform towards them. Rook shrank back into the shadows.

One of them cracked a flail ominously. Three pairs of

yellow eyes seemed to cut through the darkness and bore into Rook's. He held his breath.

'Not long now, Mire scum!' the lead shryke taunted. 'Where are your friends now?' She threw back her head and gave a cruel, screeching laugh.

Then, as one, the three of them turned and clicked back across the landing.

'*Phew*,' Rook murmured. 'I thought . . .'

'You were lucky just then,' said Deadbolt Vulpoon. 'But you must leave now. Thank you for the food and drink,' he whispered. 'And for listening.'

'It was nothing,' Rook replied. 'Good luck,' he murmured awkwardly.

Rook walked back to the sleeping pallets with a heavy heart, his parting words mocking him with their inadequacy. 'Good luck', indeed! What could he have been thinking? Magda rolled over and muttered something in her sleep, and next to her Stob snored noisily. Rook laid his head down on the soft mattress of straw and fell gratefully to sleep.

·CHAPTER SIX·

THE SKY PIRATE RAID

At first Rook's sleep was deep and dreamless. He was warm beneath the thick blankets and the straw was wonderfully soft. Later, however, a cold wind gathered. It plucked at his bedding and sent dark clouds scudding across the moon. The light seemed to be flashing – on, off, on, off – now bathing Rook's face in silver, now plunging it into darkness. His eyelids flickered.

He was on a sky ship; a huge vessel with two masts and a great brass harpoon at its prow. He was standing at the helm, with the wind in his hair and the sun in his eyes.

'More lift, Master Midshipman,' came a voice. It was the captain, a foppish creature with jewelled clothes and a great waxed moustache, and – Rook realized with a start – he was giving orders to *him*.

'Aye-aye, Captain,' he said and, with nimble fingers playing over the rows of bone-handled levers, he raised the hanging weights and adjusted the sails with the expertise of someone who had *the touch.*

'Thirty-five degrees to starboard!' the captain barked.

The sky ship soared and around him its crew cheered and called out to one another. Rook felt a surge of exhilaration. The shouts and cries of the sky pirates rose, getting louder and louder and—

'Wake up!' came an insistent voice.

Rook stirred. The dream began to fade. No, he thought muzzily, he didn't want to be dragged away. He was enjoying it all too much – the sensation of flight, his sudden expertise with the flight-levers . . .

'Wake up, *all* of you!' the voice insisted.

Rook's eyes snapped open. The sky ship disappeared – yet the sound of its crew seemed louder than ever. He turned to Partifule, who was shaking the snoring Stob roughly by the shoulders. 'Wh-what's happening,' he murmured.

'It's a raid,' the nightwaif whispered back. 'A sky-pirate raid.'

Rook was on his feet at once. 'It is?' he said. He peered into the darkness. Sure enough, figures with flaming torches were shinning up ropes attached to grappling-irons and swarming onto the landing near the cages. 'But this is fantastic!' Rook gasped. 'They've come to rescue Deadbolt Vulpoon.'

'Fantastic for your friend Vulpoon if he does manage to escape,' Partifule said. 'Not so great for the rest of us if the shrykes go into one of their rage-frenzies. Like creatures possessed, they are, screeching, screaming, spitting, slashing out at anything that moves . . . Rook!' he called out, as the youth hurried off. 'Come back!'

'I must help!' Rook called back.

'ROOK!' Magda shouted, as he disappeared into the shadowy and chaotic scene unfolding over by the hanging-cages.

Stob sat bolt upright, and looked round, bleary-eyed, startled. 'What? What?' he said.

'Oh, nothing,' said Magda. 'Nothing at all. Except we're in the middle of a sky-pirate raid. And the shrykes are about to go crazy. Oh, and Rook's decided he wants a better view.'

Stob jumped up from his pallet. 'Why didn't anyone wake me before?' he demanded.

Magda rolled her eyes impatiently.

'Never mind all that now,' said Partifule. 'We must get as far away from here as possible. *All* of us.' He stared back towards the cages, ears fluttering. 'I . . . I can hear Rook,' he said.

'Let's just go on without him,' said Stob. 'I can't think why an under-librarian was selected in the first place. Insolent, sloppy, disobedient—'

'Stob, be quiet,' Magda snapped. 'I'll go and get him.' And before anyone could stop her, she dashed off.

Unaware of the discord he was generating amongst his fellow-travellers, Rook darted ahead from shadow to shadow. All round him, the roaring sky pirates were homing in on the cage where Deadbolt Vulpoon was imprisoned. One had already shinned up the fluted column and had used a long pikestaff to jam the chain

and stop it from swinging. A second, at the very top, acted as look-out. Meanwhile, two more sky pirates – one, a brawny giant with thick, matted hair and an eye-patch; the other (on his shoulders) an angular individual with steel-framed, half-moon glasses – were standing directly beneath the cage. All round them, a dozen or more pirates formed a protective circle, their weapons glinting in the intermittent moonlight like the horns of a phalanx of hammelhorns. The raid must have been well-planned.

Rook listened, spellbound, to the flood of muttered expletives as the bespectacled sky pirate picked at the lock of the cage door with the long, thin blade of his knife. All at once there was a click.

'At last!' he exclaimed, but his triumph was drowned out by the wail of a loud klaxon splitting the air, and the look-out's bellowed warning.

'*Shrykes!*'

The effect that single word had on the scene was both immediate and absolute. Bystanders and spectators on the landing turned away from the spectacle of the sky-pirate breakout, some taking cover, others dashing this way, that way, desperate to escape, yet terrified of running slap-bang into the oncoming shrykes – while those who had been trying to sleep through the raid, now picked up their bedding and fled for their lives.

Back on the road, the merchants and traders who had decided to journey through the night were suddenly thrown into turmoil. Those on foot scurried into the shadows and concealed themselves and their wares; those on wagons and carts shouted at their hammel-horns and prowlgrins, and the sound of cracking whips rose up above the klaxon wail and panicked screaming. There were crashes and collisions, cries of anger and groans of dismay as the carts keeled over and spilt their loads. And underneath it all, the rhythmic screeching of the shrykes advancing down the Great Mire Road towards the landing.

'Fifty strides and counting!' the look-out cried, then added, 'I'm getting out of here.'

Rook stood rooted to the spot. He watched, mouth open and eyes unblinking, as the cage door flew back and Deadbolt Vulpoon himself squeezed his body through the narrow opening and dropped heavily to the boards below. He was free, Rook realized, his heart fluttering. The old sky pirate was free!

All at once an anguished cry rang out. Louder than the

klaxon, louder than the crowd, louder even than the shrieking shrykes. 'Spatch!' roared the voice.

It was the huge sky pirate with the eye-patch. He crouched down beside the companion who, only a moment before, had been on his shoulders. Now he was dead. A single crossbow bolt had shattered one of the half-moons of his glasses and lodged itself behind his eye.

'Oh, Spatch, my friend,' he wailed. '*Spatch!*'

'Come, Logg.' It was the captain himself. He laid a hand on the sky pirate's shoulder. 'There is nothing more we can do for him. We must leave before the rest of us taste the shrykes' weapons.'

'I'm not leaving Spatch here,' came the belligerent reply as he hoisted the limp body up onto his massive shoulders. 'He deserves a proper burial, so he does.'

'As you wish,' said Vulpoon. He raised his head and looked round at the expectant sky pirates, all waiting for his command. 'What are you waiting for, you mangy mire-rats? Let's get out of here!'

As one, the sky pirates turned on their heels – only to find their escape route cut off. The shryke guards had surrounded the landing on all sides and were closing in. The sky pirates had no choice but to fight.

'Forget what I said!' Vulpoon roared. 'ATTACK!'

The air abruptly shook with an explosion of noise as the sky pirates and the shrykes fell on one another. The shrykes swung their bone-flails, and fought with beak and claw, crossbow and evil spiked scythes. The pirates battled back with cutlass and pike and baked mire-mud slingshots that hissed like angry hover worms as they cut through the air.

The fight was short and vicious.

A crossbow bolt whistled past Rook's ear. He came to his senses, wild excitement turning to cold, stomach-churning fear. He flung himself behind an upturned cart, its cargo of heavy stone jars strewn around it.

In front of him two sky pirates – one tall and thin, one short and portly – stood back to back, battling with two shrykes. The pirates' swords glinted and clanged. The shrykes' claws flashed, their beaks gnashed. It looked as if the sky pirates were tiring when – as if to some unspoken command – both of them lunged forwards. Their attackers were skewered simultaneously. The sky pirates withdrew their swords and turned to face a fresh onslaught.

There were dead shrykes everywhere, but those who fell were instantly replaced by more of the frenzied bird-creatures, answering the klaxon-call and streaming down the Great Mire Road.

'Take the balustrades!' Rook heard Vulpoon bellow, and looked round to see the sky pirate captain fighting off two shrykes at the same time. 'And *keep* them,' he grunted as first one, then the other shryke fell lifeless to the ground. 'We all leave together,' Vulpoon cried. 'When *I* give the word.'

Just then Rook saw the flash of crimson and yellow feathers as a tall, muscular shryke guard emerged from the shadows behind Vulpoon. She was wearing a gleam-ing breast-plate and a plumed helmet. A spiked scythe was raised above her head.

'Captain!' screamed Rook, leaping to his feet.

Just in time, the sky pirate captain dodged sharply to his left. The scythe struck the wooden boards and stuck fast. Vulpoon swung his heavy cutlass. With an ear-piercing screech, the shryke hawked and spat. A glistening boll of saliva flew through the air and splattered into his face. Crying out in disgust, Vulpoon staggered backwards in the direction of the cart.

Rook gasped with surprise. This was no ordinary shryke guard, he realized. With her bright plumage and her stature, she must be one of the elite Shryke Sisterhood.

'Deadbolt Vulpoon!' the shryke-sister screeched, as she advanced towards him in a hissing whirr of bared talons. 'The great Deadbolt Vulpoon! Let's see how great you are now!'

Vulpoon was dazed and half-blinded. The shryke-sister contemptuously knocked his sword away. Then, balancing on one clawed foot, she slashed at his arm with the other.

'I'll rip out your heart!' she shrieked. 'And devour it!'

There was blood seeping through the sleeve of Vulpoon's jacket and dripping down the hand which clasped his sword. The sky pirate slumped to his knees in front of the upturned cart.

It was all but over.

Vulpoon had no sword. The shryke – eyes blazing, unblinking – approached with her razor-sharp talons outstretched.

'Fool,' she shrieked. 'Did you truly believe we were

unaware of who you are? Did you? You, great captain, were the bait to lure them here.' She nodded back to the battle for the balustrade continuing behind them. 'With you dead, they'll give up, and I will have rid the Edge of you and your sky pirate scum once and for all.'

Vulpoon made no reply. He was utterly defenceless. The shryke-sister seemed to enjoy toying with him.

'No longer shall I be a mere shryke-sister,' she screamed. 'I shall return to the Eastern Roost victorious and claim my reward.' She paused. 'Mother Hinnytalon of the Eastern Roost. It has a nice ring to it, don't you think,' she said, and shrieked with raucous laughter. 'There is only one thing standing between me and my goal,' she added. Her gaze hardened and fixed itself on Vulpoon. She raised her claws, ready to strike. 'You.'

'Wrong!' Rook cried out as he sprang to his feet, a heavy pot clutched tightly in his shaking hands raised high above his head.

Looking up at the cart, the shryke was stunned into inaction for a split second – and that was all it took. With a grunt of effort, Rook brought the heavy pot crashing down onto the shryke's head. It smashed into the helmet and shattered, sending pieces flying through the air, and the shryke staggering backwards.

Vulpoon made a lunge for his sword. In one graceful movement he straightened up and swung it round in a low, rising sweep, beheading the creature with a single blow. The plumed helmet clattered to the ground, while the head it had once protected bounced across the landing, beak agape and eyes bulging with surprise.

Vulpoon turned. His jaw dropped. 'You,' he said. 'Again.'

Just then a second voice called out. 'Rook. Quickly!' It was Magda. 'Come on,' she said through clenched teeth. 'We must leave now.'

'That is the second time you have saved me,' Vulpoon said. 'What did you say your name was?'

'Rook Barkwater, if it pleases you,' said Rook.

'It pleases me well, lad,' the sky pirate captain said. 'Rook Barkwater. I will never forget what you have done for me this night.' He nodded towards Magda. 'But your friend is right,' he said. 'You must leave now.'

'Captain,' roared a voice from behind him, and a swarthy individual grabbed at his arm. 'The balustrade is clear. Come quickly before more shryke reinforcements arrive.'

With the sky pirate pulling Vulpoon in one direction, and Magda dragging Rook away in the other, their gaze met for one last time.

'Fare you well, Rook Barkwater,' the captain called out.

'Goodbye, Captain,' Rook called back.

He and Magda hurried back to the sleeping stall to find Stob and Partifule sitting up on the driving seat of a sturdy hammelhorn-drawn cart.

'Where did you get that?' asked Magda.

'We found it abandoned,' said Stob. 'Lying on its side—'

'Just jump up,' Partifule shouted out urgently.

Magda and Rook leaped onto the back of the cart. Stob cracked the whip and the hammelhorn plodded off along the road as fast as it could, leaving the sky pirates and the shryke guards far behind them. The shuffling walkers on the road jostled and jumped out of their way, but the shrykes – hurrying to the landing where the battle still seemed to rage – paid them no heed.

As they rumbled on over the boards, the shouting grew distant and the klaxon-wail faded to nothing. Still they continued, driving on through darkness, mile after mile. Their pace slowed as they became snagged at the back of a convoy of heavy wagons. The darkest hour came and went. Soft strands of light threaded their way up from the horizon as the sun prepared to rise.

Rook's head spun. More had happened to him during that last day than would normally occur in an entire year. Yet they had made it. He turned to Magda and smiled. 'Do you think the worst is behind us?' he asked.

Stob glanced round. 'That shows how much you know, under-librarian,' he snarled unkindly. He turned back and nodded up ahead. 'Look.'

Rook climbed to his feet to get a better view. Although the sky was, for the most part, still swathed in impenetrable darkness, directly in front of them was a curious golden half-light, like the glow from a giant tilder-oil lamp.

'What is it?' asked Rook.

'Need you ask?' said Stob.

'We are approaching the Twilight Woods,' said Partifule, his voice hushed and reverent. 'Which, my young friends,' he continued, 'is the most treacherous and perilous place in all the Edge.'

CHAPTER SEVEN

THE TWILIGHT WOODS

The waif pulled gently at the reins, and the great lumbering hammelhorn snorted and came to a halt. It shook its shaggy head, with its immense curling horns, and waited patiently. Partifule got down from the wagon.

Rook sat up, suddenly wide awake, and looked around. The unfamiliar, eerie light bathed everything in a golden glow. A straggle of gnokgoblins pulling hand-carts clattered past, their heads down, their faces grim.

'Why have we stopped?' said Rook.

'Search me,' said Stob beside him, stifling a yawn.

'I must leave you now,' said Partifule.

Magda gasped. The waif turned to her, took her hand and gazed deeply into her eyes, listening to her thoughts. 'You will reach Lake Landing,' he said. 'Of that I am convinced. From the little time I have spent with you all, I have been impressed with your determination, your bravery –' he turned to Rook – 'your compassion.'

'And we with yours,' said Magda softly.

Partifule nodded and lowered his head. 'I have already come closer to the Twilight Woods than I like.' He looked up ahead at the line of trees, bathed in their alluring half-light, which signified the end of the Mire and the beginning of the treacherous woods. 'Even at this distance, the twilight glow fills my head with the strangest visions . . . and voices . . .' He shook his head. 'And for a waif, that is dangerous indeed.'

'Go, then,' said Magda. 'And thank you.'

'Yes, thank you, Partifule,' said Rook.

The pair of them turned to Stob. 'Thanks,' he muttered. Partifule nodded to each of them in turn. 'Ahead of you lies great danger. But you will not be alone. There is a guide waiting for you in the Eastern Roost. He is one of the greatest and bravest of us all. You will be in good hands, believe me.'

He turned away, tears welling in his dark eyes. His ears fluttered. 'Earth and Sky be with you,' he said softly. 'Farewell.'

As they approached the tally-hut, Rook could see the road ahead disappearing into the Twilight Woods. It shimmered and swayed, as if under water, before losing itself in the miasmic gloom beyond. Where it did so, Rook noticed that the very construction of the road seemed to alter.

It became narrow beyond the tally-hut, and the balustrades seemed to be closer together. They curved up like the bars of a cage. Above, there were two long cables – one on each side of the road – slung through great hanging hoops and snaking off into the distance.

The gnokgoblins emerged from the tally-hut with lengths of rope, which they threw over the cable-hooks above their heads. Then they attached both ends to their belts.

'Knot them firmly!' screeched a shryke guard, looking on. 'And keep moving, if you know what's good for you.'

Alone amongst the creatures of the Edge, shrykes were impervious to the effects of the treacherous forest. Their double eyelids ensured that its seductive visions had no power over them. It was this immunity which had enabled them to build the Great Mire Road, and now meant that any who crossed the Twilight Woods were dependent on the callous and unpredictable bird-creatures for safe passage.

'Next!' came the rasping voice of a tally-hen from the hut.

Rook, Stob and Magda got down from the cart and entered the hut. A large speckled tally-hen sat in the dimly lit interior behind an ornately carved lectern. She looked up.

'Three is it?' she squawked. 'That'll be nine gold pieces for the rope and three more for the cart. Hurry up, hurry up! Haven't got all day . . .'

Magda paid and the shryke handed them each a length of rope from a sack hanging from the side of the lectern, and a scrap of barkpaper with a symbol scrawled on it in brown ink.

'For the cart!' she snapped as Rook took it gingerly from her talons. 'Next!'

Outside, a shryke guard met them and snatched the barkpaper from Rook. She examined it with unblinking yellow eyes, handed it back and clicked her bone-flail. A second shryke appeared and climbed up into the driver's seat. With a vicious snap of the reins, she drove the hammelhorn on. The wagon clattered off along the timbered road and into the Twilight Woods in a cloud of glittering dust.

'Central Market, Holding Pens,' squawked the guard. 'It'll be waiting for you there.' She jerked her head to one side. 'Well, what are you waiting for?'

Magda stepped forward. She flung her rope up into the air and over the cable-hook. Stob and Rook followed suit. Rook flushed crimson as he fumbled with his leash-rope, making the knots round his belt as tight as possible.

'Tie them firmly!' commanded the guard. 'And keep moving.'

With a deep breath Rook plunged into the rippling twilight after the others. He felt the rope go taut and tug on him. Straining with exertion, he pushed on; the hook, rasping on the cable above, like a leadwood anchor-weight, pulling him back. Every movement was an effort. Every step, an achievement.

He struggled after the other two. Up ahead, the gnokgoblins laboured with their handcarts, their ropes swaying as they pulled at them. Behind him, Rook could see a small group of cloddertrogs milling round the tally-hut.

'Keep moving!' screeched the guard behind him. 'If one stops, you all stop! Any hold-ups and you'll be cut loose! Remember!'

Rook pressed resolutely on. Soon his lungs were on fire, his legs ached and he found himself gulping in the thick, humid air as fast as he could. His head was swimming, and everything swayed and swirled in front of his eyes. I can't keep going! he thought, fear churning in the pit of his stomach.

Behind him, the cloddertrogs panted and groaned. In front, Stob's back shimmered, sometimes close, sometimes impossibly far away. Then, just as Rook thought he was going to faint with exhaustion and be trampled on by the following cloddertrogs, the panic and fatigue suddenly seemed to disappear. He felt strength returning to his limbs. The rope seemed less like an anchor and more like a string holding a balloon. A sense of elation began to course through his body.

It was, Rook thought, like being immersed in a pool of warm, golden water which swirled round his body and made him feel oddly buoyant. It poured into his ears, his eyes, his nose, drowning out the grunts and groans of the cloddertrogs and turning the toasted-almond scented air to shimmering liquid. And when he went to speak, it filled his mouth with forgotten tastes of his earliest childhood, before the slave-takers had stolen his parents away – oak-flake rusks, smoky woodbee honey, delberry linctus . . .

There were voices too, calling from the shadowy depths. 'Come,' they called, their honeyed tones matching the thick, dappled light. 'Rook. *Rook!*'

Rook trembled. That voice, so familiar . . . He felt his throat aching with loss, with longing. 'Mother?' he said tremulously. 'Is that you?'

The woods swallowed up his words. Ahead of him, he was dimly aware of Stob waving his arms and laughing hysterically, and of Magda's great, gulping sobs. 'Keep moving,' he told himself. 'Keep moving.'

Rook tried to clear his mind, to ignore the voices and just look ahead – but the Twilight Woods seemed to have a hypnotic hold over him that he could not shake free.

He found himself looking into the endless expanse of golden forest. The trees, sparkling with a strange sepia dust, creaked and groaned with age as the soft, warm breeze stirred their branches. The air twisted and sighed. Something – or someone – flitted between the shadowy tree-trunks.

All at once a strange, spectral figure was emerging from the gloom. Rook stared with fascinated horror as it approached the road. Mounted on a prowlgrin, the apparition wore the tarnished antique armour of an ancient Knight Academic. It was as if an illustration in one of the library scrolls had come to life. The gauges and pipes, bolts and levers covering the rusting armour were all there; even in the twilight Rook could make

them out quite clearly. He reached out and tapped Stob on the shoulder.

'Do you see it?' Rook called. Stob kept on walking and made no reply. Rook hurried after him. 'A Knight Academic! Stob! Out there in the woods! He's getting closer!'

'Shut up and keep moving!' Stob growled back. 'Or a shryke guard will cut you loose. You heard what they said.'

'He's right, Rook,' Magda called back. Her voice was thick from crying. 'It'll soon be over if we just keep moving and don't lose our heads.'

Rook glanced back; the knight had vanished. He could hear muffled sighs and taunting whispers and, whichever way he looked, he caught sight of movement out of the corner of his eye – though when he tried to focus in on it, the movement ceased and he saw nothing.

Was anything real in the Twilight Woods? he wondered. Or was it inhabited solely by phantasms and ghosts – the spirits of those who had fallen victim to the seductive charms of the dimly lit forest?

Just then there was a loud *crash*. One of the gnok-goblins' handcarts had overturned, sending its cargo of metal pots clattering and clanging across the narrow road. The group came to a halt, twisting round on their leash-ropes as they attempted to right the cart and rescue its spilt contents. Soon they were all hopelessly tangled, and shouting at each other.

'Turn *this* way, Morkbuff!' wheezed their elderly leader. 'You, Pegg! Help him out . . . No, not like that!'

Magda, Stob and Rook came to a halt a few strides away. Behind them, the cloddertrogs approached.

'Keep moving!' they bellowed.

'We can't!' Rook called back. 'Or we'll get caught up with that lot.' He pointed at the tangle of goblins.

Another handcart crashed over.

'Somebody *do* something!' shouted Stob above the din.

'That's really helpful!' said Magda. 'What do you suggest?'

Around them, the Twilight Woods seemed to be listening. From the shadows, Rook was aware of movement. The Knight Academic reappeared.

'Look,' he whispered excitedly to the other two. 'He's back.'

They followed Rook's gaze.

'He's not the only one,' said Stob.

Sure enough, other figures were emerging from the shadowy gloom, as if drawn by the gnokgoblins' commotion. Rook shuddered. There were ragged, half-dead trogs, skeletal leaguesmen, several desperate-looking goblins, some with missing limbs and many bearing terrible wounds. They stood all round them; hollow-eyed, staring, silent.

The gnokgoblins saw the ghostly crowd they had attracted and fell still. The two groups watched each other in absolute silence; the living and the undead.

Despite the clammy heat, Rook felt icy sweat run over his face, into his eyes, down his back. 'This is a dreadful place,' he whispered.

Suddenly, there came the sound of furious screeching and squawking, and a squadron of shryke guards appeared through the gloom, glittering dust flying in their wake. Just as suddenly, the ghostly apparitions melted back into the woods.

'What's going on?' squawked the shrykes' leader, an imposing female with bright yellow plumage and a purple crest. 'Why is no-one moving?'

Everybody started talking at once.

'Silence!' roared the shryke, the feathers round her neck ruffling ominously. 'Twilight-crazy, the lot of you!' She turned to her second-in-command. 'Clear this featherless vermin off my road, Magclaw, and get the rest moving!'

'You heard what Sister Featherslash said!' rasped Magclaw, with a click of her bone-flail. 'Cut them loose! Now!'

The gnokgoblins began wailing, and Rook flinched as the shrykes began slashing at the snarled ropes with their razor-sharp scythes. The ropes fell to the ground.

The shrykes chased the weeping goblins into the woods.

'Get moving, the rest of you!' ordered Sister Featherslash. 'I'm sure you've all got important business in the beautiful Eastern Roost!' She cackled unpleasantly. 'If you ever get there.'

Magda, Stob and Rook set off quickly.

'I don't care what the Eastern Roost is like, it can't be worse than this,' said Magda. 'Can it?'

'Just keep moving,' said Stob. 'And try not to think about it.'

Rook looked back over his shoulder. In the eerie, dappled light, the elderly gnokgoblin was sitting on a tree-root, waving his arms and protesting loudly to thin air.

·CHAPTER EIGHT·

THE EASTERN ROOST

Out of the swirling twilight loomed a lufwood tree, so enormous that a gateway had been tunnelled through the middle of its vast trunk. It straddled the road, separating the Twilight Woods from the Eastern Roost beyond. High up, above the arched entrance, the cable to which the leash-ropes were attached came to an end.

Two shryke guards stood sentry, one on either side of the gateway. 'Untie your ropes!' one of them commanded harshly as Magda, Stob and Rook approached.

They quickly did as they were told. Already, the cloddertrogs were arriving behind them.

'Proceed by the Lower Levels to the Central Market!' barked the other guard. 'The upper roosts are for shrykes only.' Her yellow eyes glinted menacingly. 'You have been warned!'

Rook's head was beginning to clear as the strange,

penetrating atmosphere of the Twilight Woods released its grip. He squinted into the gloom beyond the Lufwood Gate.

The first thing that struck him was the smell. Beneath the roasting pinecoffee and sizzling tilder sausages, beneath the odours and scents, of leatherware, incense and the greasy smell of oil lamps, there was another smell. A rank and rancid smell. A smell that, as the wind stirred, grew more pungent, then less – but never faded completely.

Rook shivered.

'We're going to be fine,' Magda whispered, and squeezed his hand reassuringly. 'If we all stick together. We must head for the Central Market.'

Rook nodded. It wasn't only his sense of smell which had become so acute. After the sensory deprivation and confusion of the Twilight Woods, his senses were blazing. The air felt greasy, dirty. He could taste it in his mouth. His ears heard every screech, every squeal; every barked order and crack of the whip – every heartrending cry of despair. And as for his eyes . . .

'I've never seen anything like it,' Rook muttered, as they started along one of a series of walkways strung out between the trees, which led deeper and deeper into the thronging city.

Lights. Colour. Faces. Movement . . . Everywhere he looked, Rook was bombarded by a confusing mass of strange and disturbing sights. It was like a great patchwork quilt which, as he passed through it, threw up image after individual image.

A caged banderbear. A chained vulpoon. Tethered rotsuckers. Betting posts and gambling tables. Itinerants hawking lucky charms. A pair of shrykes, their flails clacking. Two more – one armed with a great studded club. An animated argument between a gnokgoblin and a cloddertrog. A lost woodtroll, screaming for its mother. Leather dealers, paper merchants, chandlers and coopers. Refreshment stalls selling snacks and beverages that Rook didn't even know existed. What was a wood-toad shake? Or a hot-bod? And what in Sky's name might gloamglozer tea taste of?

'It's this way,' he heard Stob saying, pointing up at a painted sign above their heads.

They descended three flights of rickety steps, zig-zagging downwards until they arrived at a bustling walkway in the trees. Burdened with its heavy load of merchants and marketeers, goblins, trogs and trolls streaming in both directions, the walkway dipped and bounced, creaking ominously as it swayed. Rook gripped the safety-rail anxiously.

'Don't look down,' Magda whispered, sensing Rook's nervousness.

But Rook couldn't help himself. He peered down into the depths below. Three levels beneath him, in the dark, acrid gloom, was the forest floor. It shimmered and writhed as if the earth itself were somehow alive. With a jolt, Rook realized that that was precisely what it was – for the forest floor was a living mass of tiny orange creatures.

'Wig-wigs,' he muttered uneasily.

Although he'd never seen one before, Rook had read about them in Varis Lodd's treatise on banderbears. They hunted in huge packs and could devour a creature as big as a banderbear in an instant – flesh, hair, bones, tusks; everything. Rook shuddered as it occurred to him that this vast city in the trees – the Eastern Roost – must provide an abundance of food for so many bloodthirsty scavengers to have congregated underneath. Giddy with foreboding, he
gripped
the rail
tightly.

'Come on, knife-grinder,' said Stob nastily. 'We don't have time for sightseeing.'

He pushed Rook roughly in the back and strode off along the walkway. Magda and a trembling Rook followed.

As the Central Market drew closer, the walkway grew broader – though no less congested. It became louder than ever and, with all the constant coming and going and general milling about, the three librarian apprentices were hard pushed to fight their way through.

'Stick together,' Stob called back as he reached the narrow entrance to the market.

'Easier said than done,' Magda grumbled, as the surging crowd threatened to separate them.' Hold my hand, Stob,' she said. 'And you, too, Rook.'

With Stob in front, the three of them forged onwards. The gateway came closer. They were shuffling now, with bodies all round them, pressing in tightly. Through the archway and . . . inside.

Rook took a deep breath as the crowd released its grip. He looked round at the others and smiled. They had made it to the Central Market.

Built on a platform which was supported by a scaffolding of trees, sawn off where they stood, the Central Market was open to the elements. The starry canopy looked almost close enough to touch as the stars shimmered in the heat thrown off by the braziers and spits.

THE CENTRAL MARKET OF THE EASTERN ROOST

Rook took out the scrap of barkpaper the shryke had given them and examined it.

'Now what?' said Stob, looking around.

'We find the cart,' said Magda, and then . . .'

'Yes?' said Stob meanly.

'One thing at a time,' said Magda, frowning and looking around. 'Over there, I think.'

They made their way across the bustling Central Market. There was everything there, and more – stuffed, pickled, roasted and tanned; woven, gilded and carved. They passed slaughterers with their hammelhorn enclosures and overflowing displays of leatherwear; woodtrolls at their timber stalls and goblin tinkers and ironmongers, all bargaining, bartering and hawking their wares. And as they got close to the Holding Pens, they became aware also of the constant flow of shryke-driven carts and heavy wagons arriving from the Twilight Woods. The drivers waved flaming torches to ward off the wig-wigs before climbing the swaying ramp that snaked up to the Central Market platform where the wagon owners waited anxiously by the stalls.

Rook stared in amazement at the sprawling Holding Pens before him. The atmosphere was urgent – and smelly. A vast sea of carts and wagons, and pack-animals tugging on their leashes, guarded by burly, sullen shrykes, was waiting to be reclaimed. The air resounded with discordant cries and voices raised in protest.

'But half my cargo has been stolen!' shouted a gnokgoblin.

'I've lost two hammelhorns!' a cloddertrog complained.

'Shryke tax!' laughed one of the guards. 'Perhaps you'd like to take your wagon through the Twilight Woods yourself next time? No? Didn't think so!' She cackled unpleasantly.

'Typical shryke robbery,' moaned a goblin as he barged past Rook. 'Just 'cause they're not affected by the Twilight Woods, they think they can rob us blind!'

Magda matched a sign above one of the pens with the scrawl on the barkpaper. 'Here!' she shouted excitedly to the other two. 'Over here!'

Stob and Rook joined her as she presented the paper to a scruffy, bored-looking shryke leaning against a fencepost.

'Over there,' said the shryke, waving a talon.

In the corner of the pen was a small, broken-down cart with a thin, ill-looking prowlgrin in harness.

'But that's not our cart,' Magda protested. 'Ours was a four-seater, pulled by a hammelhorn . . .'

'Take it or leave it,' sneered the shryke. She yawned and inspected her talons.

'They'll take it, mistress. A thousand thank-yous,' came a squeaky voice. A small, tatty shryke-mate stepped forward and took Magda by the arm.

'But—' said Magda.

'No *buts*, my child,' squeaked the shryke-mate. 'We have urgent business, and we mustn't take up any more of the generous mistress's valuable time.'

He bowed low to the shryke guard and ushered

Magda away. The other two followed.

'What's the big idea?' said Stob, grabbing the shryke-mate's puny wing and pulling the grasping talons from Magda's arm.

The shryke-mate cringed. 'A thousand apologies,' he whispered. 'But we can't speak here. It's too dangerous. Follow me.'

He reached inside his filthy tunic and flashed a bloodoak-tooth pendant at Stob, before turning and hurrying into the crowd.

'Wait for us!' said Stob. 'Come on, you two. Stop dithering! You heard what the shryke said.'

Magda and Rook exchanged quizzical glances before following Stob as he pushed through the crowd after the small, scruffy figure of the shryke-mate.

They caught up with him by a stall in the slaughterers area. Everything – from tooled amulets, breast-plates and leather gauntlets, to great hanging carcasses of hammelhorn, woodhog and tilder – was on offer. Stob stood at the middle of it all, scratching his head and looking round.

'He was here one second and gone the next,' he muttered angrily. 'Hey, you there!' he said, turning to a short, flame-haired slaughterer who was laying out smoked tilder hams on a nearby table. 'Did you see him? A mangy little shryke-mate . . .'

The slaughterer turned his back on Stob and looked right and left furtively.

'I said—' Stob's voice was raised in anger.

'I heard what you said,' the slaughterer replied softly,

without turning. 'You'll find Hekkle round the back, behind the curtain. And don't let appearances deceive you.'

Stob pushed rudely past the slaughterer and pulled aside the leather curtain at the back of the stall to reveal a small concealed chamber behind. Magda and Rook went with him.

'Thank you,' whispered Rook as they passed the slaughterer.

'Good luck,' came the gruff reply.

Sitting by a small lufwood stove on a tilderskin rug, was the shryke-mate. As the curtain fell back into place, the flames of the burning lufwood bathed everything in a soft purple glow.

'Please, my brave and intrepid friends,' said the shryke, 'be seated. We must hurry, for every moment you spend here in the Eastern Roost your lives are in danger.'

'Well, this place of yours looks nice and cosy,' said Stob, casually reaching out to stroke a hammelhornskin wall-hanging. As his fingers touched the fur, it instantly bristled, becoming as sharp as needles to the touch. 'Ouch!' he cried out in alarm.

'Don't be fooled,' said the shryke. 'There are shryke guards all around us, and they raid the lower roosts constantly, on the look-out for contraband or...' He hesitated. 'Spies.'

Rook gulped. Was that what they were to these terrifying feathered creatures? He remembered the terrible cages on the Mire road and suddenly felt very weak.

'Are you the guide we were told would meet us?' asked Magda.

Stob, sucking his finger, looked at the shryke-mate with open contempt.

'Indeed I am, most merciful mistress, indeed I am,' trilled the shryke-mate. 'My name is Hekkle, and you do me a thousand honours to allow me to serve you.'

'Yes, yes,' said Stob. 'But if we're in danger, why are we standing around here?'

'Patience, brave master,' said Hekkle, rummaging in a large trunk in the corner, 'and I will explain everything.'

Rook dropped to his knees. His head felt strangely light, and the lufwood glow was making him sleepy.

'The Eastern Roost is a closed city, my brave friends,' said Hekkle, pulling a bundle of dark robes from the trunk and laying them out. 'For visitors, there is only one way in and one way out and that, as you have seen, is by the eastern Lufwood Gate. The Undertown merchants – such as you pretend to be – arrive, sell their wares and return on the Great Mire Road back to Undertown, bearing the goods from the Deepwoods they have bought in the Central Market.'

'So, how do we get out of this accursed city and into the Deepwoods?' asked Stob impatiently.

'Only shrykes may leave or enter the Eastern Roost on the Deepwoods side of the city,' Hekkle continued. 'That way, merciful master, the Shryke Sisterhood controls all the trade between Undertown and the Deepwoods settlements. It's beautifully simple. The shrykes buy goods from the Deepwoods and bring them into the Roost, where they trade them for Undertown goods, which they use to buy more Deepwoods goods – thus making a profit from Undertowners and Deepwooders alike. That is why there is no way through the Eastern Roost for anyone who isn't a shryke.'

'So, you're saying we're trapped here?' said Magda, a hint of panic in her voice. 'That the only way out is back to Undertown the way we came?'

'No, not quite, merciful mistress,' said Hekkle, returning to the trunk.

'Then how *do* we get out of the Roost and into the Deepwoods?' Stob persisted.

'Simple,' said Hekkle, turning round. 'If only shrykes are permitted to leave by the western Deepwoods Gate, then you shall become shrykes!'

He held up three crude feathered masks, each with a curved, serrated beak and black staring eye-sockets.

'You can't be serious,' scoffed Stob. 'It'll never work!'

'Oh, but it has before,' said Hekkle, his voice suddenly serious and with a brittle, harsh edge to it. 'And it will again.' Looking at the three earnest faces in front of him, he suddenly laughed. 'You, my fine brave friends, will

be sooth-sisters – the venerated priestesses of the Golden
Nest. Here are your robes.' He held up the heavy black
garments, plain and drab compared to the gaudy
costumes most shrykes loved. 'And here are your
masks.' He handed them each a feathered head-dress.
'Hurry now. Time is short.'

They put Hekkle's costumes on over their merchants'
clothes, fastening up the robes at the front and securing
the masks on their heads. Hekkle slipped out of the
room, returning a moment later with a burnished milk-
wood mirror.

Rook turned and looked at himself. In the heavy robes
and ornate mask he looked the part – but for one thing.
'But, Hekkle,' he began, his voice muffled beneath the
beaked mask. 'The eyes. Surely our eyes will give us
away. I mean, look. They're not yellow, or fierce-looking,
or—'

'Silly me, oh merciful master,' laughed Hekkle. 'I was
forgetting. Here, take these. No self-respecting sooth-
sister would dream of appearing in public without them.'

He handed Rook a pair of spectacles with thick, black
lenses. Rook put them on over his mask with difficulty,
and clipped the nose-piece onto the false beak.

'But I can't see a thing!' he protested.

'Of course not,' chuckled Hekkle
indulgently. 'Sooth-sisters only per-
mit themselves to look upon the
clutch of eggs in the Golden
Nest, laid by the Roost Mother
herself. The rest of the time, they

wear spectacles of coal-glass to blot out impure sights.'

'But if we can't see—' began Rook.

'That's what I'm here for,' said Hekkle, bowing low. 'I shall be your guide. All sooth-sisters have them – at the end of a golden chain. But I must warn you.' Hekkle was suddenly solemn again, the harsh edge back in his voice. 'On no account are you to remove the spectacles. Just keep silent, and trust me. For if we are caught, the penalty for impersonating a shryke – and a sooth-sister at that – is terrible indeed, brave friends.'

'What is it?' Stob asked, trying to hide the nervousness in his voice.

'Roasting,' said Hekkle simply. 'Roasting alive, on a spit in the Central Market. Now, let's go.'

When Rook thought back to the ensuing journey to the Deepwoods Gate of the Eastern Roost, he could scarcely believe he had survived the terrifying experience. The sound of his own breathing inside the mask, the inky blackness of the coal-glass spectacles and the noises of the upper roosts – unfamiliar, and all the more sinister for that – haunted him in dreams for months afterwards.

They were climbing, climbing, constantly climbing. Even inside the mask, Rook sensed the air becoming fresher the higher they went. The cacophony of the lower roosts receded, to be replaced with the strange disturbing calls of the shrykes promenading along the upper walkways. There were coos, shrieks, and odd staccato throat-throbbings which built up to a sudden hooting scream.

'Steady,' whispered Hekkle, leading them on the end of his golden chain, like a tame lemkin. 'The sisters are just singing to one another. Nothing to worry about.'

But the sounds made Rook's blood run cold. How long had they been walking? In his growing panic it seemed like hours – although it could only have been minutes; half an hour at the most. He wanted to ask Hekkle, but he knew that it would be madness to utter so much as a single word. Behind him, Stob trod on the backs of his heels, and Rook bit his lip hard.

'Steady, your gracious holinesses,' cooed Hekkle, then, in a louder voice, 'Make way for the sooth-sisters! Make way!'

Rook was aware of the clattering of claws on the wooden walkway as respectful shryke-matrons moved aside.

'Give our blessings to the Golden Nest,' came a harsh shryke voice.

'May the egg-clutch prosper, sisters,' came another.

'Fruitful hatching!'

The calls sounded all round them. Rook's heart was thumping like a hammer. He battled to control his churning stomach and the panic rising in his throat.

'The sooth-sisters bless you,' called Hekkle in his sing-song voice. 'The sooth-sisters bless you.' He whispered urgently out of the side of his beak, 'We're nearly there. Keep together. One more walkway and we'll be at the prowlgrin corral beside the Deepwoods Gate.'

Stob stepped on the back of Rook's heel again. Rook stumbled heavily, the jolt almost dislodging his heavy coal-black spectacles. He screwed up his left eye as daylight flooded through a gap that had opened up between the mask and the lens. He felt the spectacles wobble on the beak.

'Careful, sister!' came a piercing voice.

Out of the corner of his eye Rook glimpsed a tall, imposing shryke-matron bedecked in finery, sitting on a raised bench and flanked on either side by smaller, but no less gaudy, companions. He was suddenly aware of a familiar overpowering stench. The shryke-matron's plumage ruffled and she let out a contented squawk as an acrid white shryke-dropping fell through the hole beneath her and down onto the lower roosts below.

'That's better,' she said, turning to her companion. 'Now, you were saying, Talonclaw . . .'

'Oh, yes,' said the shryke next to her, also letting a

sour-smelling spurt of droppings go. 'The sky pirate cut off her head with one blow. Leastways, that's what I heard.'

'Come now, sisters.' Hekkle's voice had that hard edge back in it. He pulled at Rook's robes. 'We must get to the prowlgrin corrals. We have nesting materials to gather in the Deepwoods, remember.'

Rook forced himself to put one foot in front of the other. He hunched his shoulders, convinced that the piercing yellow eyes of the shryke-matron seated on the ornate latrine would unmask him at any moment.

'Wait!' The matron's raucous cry rang out.

Rook froze. The spectacles rattled on the bridge of his beak. The matron rose from her seat and adjusted her skirts. Rook scarcely dared breathe. Behind him, the other two were rooted to the spot. The matron approached and Rook shut his eyes tight.

'May blessings attend your nest-building,' said the shryke-matron and bowed. Rook inclined his head gingerly in response, praying the spectacles would stay in place. The matron turned and her talons clicked on the wooden boards as she and her companions walked away.

'Quickly now.' Hekkle's voice sounded urgently in his ear. 'Before they return!'

They hurried on in a nightmare of tension and un-certainty, Rook catching glimpses of evil shryke faces as they made their way to the Deepwoods Gate, all the time in terror of his spectacles falling from his mask. The acrid smell of shryke droppings gave way to the warm, musty smell of prowlgrins. Rook could hear their soft, throaty purrs as they neared the corrals. It sounded strangely reassuring.

Hekkle guided them down a gangplank, and Rook could feel the heat given off by the roosting prowlgrins. He peered out of the side of his spectacles. The creatures were all round them, perching on broad branches and looking down on the newcomers with their sad, doleful eyes. Hekkle reached up and untied one of them. He passed the tether to Magda.

'Climb up,' he said. 'And take the reins. She won't move until you kick her.'

With Hekkle's help, Magda tentatively pulled herself up onto the prowlgrin's back, taking care not to let the shryke-mask slip. She reached round the harness for the reins and gripped them tightly. On either side, Rook and Stob did the same. Finally, Hekkle jumped up onto his own prowlgrin and pulled the great beast round.

'Kick!' he cried.

All four of them jabbed their heels into the prowlgrins' sides. The prowlgrins moved off, thrusting away from the broad perch with their hind-legs and clinging onto the one ahead with their fore-claws. Following the lead of Hekkle's prowlgrin, they clambered down onto a walkway. Rook glimpsed a large gateway up ahead.

'We're approaching the guard tower,' said Hekkle, reining in his prowlgrin. The others did the same. All four prowlgrins slowed to a sedate lope, placing their fore-paws down and swinging their hind-legs forward.

At the end of the long walkway, the guard tower came closer.

'What are we going to do?' said Magda.

'Nothing,' said Hekkle. 'Remember, you are sooth-sisters. You do not need to talk to mere guards. I shall speak for you.'

As they reached the guard tower, a tawny shryke with a rusty lance stepped forwards. Hekkle approached her. Rook, Magda and Stob stood apart and aloof, their heads raised imperiously, blind behind their spectacles.

'You heard me,' Rook heard Hekkle saying sternly a moment later. 'We seek nesting materials for the Golden Nest.' His voice dropped. 'Do you *dare* to stand in the sooth-sisters' way?'

'No, no,' the shryke guard said. 'Pass through.' She put her lance to her side, clicked her heels and bowed her head. Hekkle led his prowlgrin past. The others – keeping as rigid as possible as their prowlgrins lurched – followed close behind. Rook held his breath. He could only pray that the guard would neither see behind the spectacles nor hear the noisy hammering of his heart.

Step by faltering step, they left the Eastern Roost and entered the Deepwoods. The moment the last of them had crossed the boundary separating the two, Hekkle kicked his prowlgrin into action. The others followed suit, and all four of them hurtled off into the great forest, leaping from branch to branch.

'*Wahoo!*' Rook screeched, with a mixture of elation and relief. '*Waahoooo!*'

Hekkle laughed. 'Well done, brave friends,' he said. 'You have done well.'

'You are a brave guide,' said Rook. He glanced back over his shoulder. The guard tower had disappeared from view. 'We made it!' he gasped, and he tore off his shryke-mask, glasses and heavy robes and tossed them to the air.

Magda did the same. 'At last,' she sighed, tears of relief welling up in her eyes.

Stob pulled off his own mask and held it before him. 'I think I made a pretty convincing sooth-sister,' he said. 'Even if I do say so myself— *Whoooah!*' he cried out as his prowlgrin stumbled, and he almost lost his grip.

He gripped the reins tightly with both hands. The shryke-mask slipped from his fingers and bounced through the branches, down to the forest floor below. He noticed the others staring at him. 'What?' he said. '*What?*'

Back at the guard tower the shryke guard was receiving a second visitor, a callow youth with a dark stubble covering his scalp sitting astride a prowlgrin.

He had pulled back his hood and thrust a pass under the guard's beak.

'See here,' he said quietly. 'The gloamglozer seal of the Most High Guardian of Night. And here. The thumbprint of Vox Verlix. And here, the crossed-feather stamp of the Shryke Sisterhood. I trust that is authority enough for you. Well, is it?'

'Yes, sir. Sorry, sir,' the guard said, scraping her feet furiously. It was not proving to be her day. 'What was it you wanted to know?'

Xanth ran his fingertips lightly over his shaven skull. 'I asked whether any had recently passed this way?'

'Three sooth-sisters, sir,' said the guard, 'and an accompanying shryke-mate.'

'*Mm-hmm*,' said the youth. 'And did they say where they were bound?'

'On a nesting expedition,' said the guard promptly.

Xanth snorted. 'An expedition to the Free Glades more like,' he said.

The guard cocked her head in puzzlement. 'But shrykes don't go to the Free Glades,' she said.

'Precisely,' said Xanth. He turned away and tugged at the reins. The prowlgrin grunted, sniffed the air and was off, leaping from branch to branch.

Xanth held on tightly. He didn't look back.

·CHAPTER NINE·

THE DEEPWOODS

The four riders rode on hard into the Deepwoods, leaving the Eastern Roost far behind them. With the wind in their hair and their stomachs in their mouths, Stob, Magda and Rook clung desperately onto the reins as their prowlgrins – sure-footed, yet breathtakingly swift – hurtled on from branch to branch through the trees. For more than an hour they continued like this, neither pausing for breath nor descending to the forest floor. It was late afternoon by the time Hekkle finally signalled that he considered it safe to leave the trees.

'Are you sure?' Stob called back uneasily. 'What about the wig-wigs?'

'They seldom stray this far from the roosts,' Hekkle reassured him. 'Besides, you must be getting tired. It's much easier riding on the ground.'

Neither Magda nor Rook needed telling twice. The lurching, jolting ride had left the pair of them exhausted.

With a sharp kick and a downward tug on the reins, they began the long descent to the forest floor below. Hekkle followed them. Seeing that no harm had befallen his companions, and not wishing to be left behind, Stob came down close behind him.

Rook soon got into the rhythm of moving with his prowlgrin as it loped steadily forwards. 'I can hardly believe it,' he called across to Magda. 'All those long years spent down under the ground. You know, I must have dreamed about the Deepwoods almost every single night. And now, here I am.' He sighed. 'It's even more wonderful than I imagined.'

Massive, ancient trees rose up out of the forest floor like great pillars. Some were ridged, some were fluted, some were covered in great bulbous lumps and nodules – all of them were tall, reaching up through the green, shadowy air to find light above the dense canopy of leaves. Occasionally, the trees would thin out, allowing dazzling shafts of sunlight to slice down through the air and encouraging shrubs and bushes to grow below. There were combbushes humming in the soft breeze, clamshrubs snapping their shell-like flowers, and hairy-ivy, spiralling up round the thick tree-trunks and glittering like tinsel. And, as they pounded on, Rook saw the alluring turquoise glow of a lullabee glade far to his left.

'It's all so beautiful!' he cried out.

'. . . so beautiful!' his echo cried back.

There was a feverish rustling in a nearby bush and Rook caught a glimpse of something moving out of the

corner of his eye. He looked round to
see a small furry creature with deep
blue fur and wide, startled eyes
bounding across the leafy forest floor
to a tall lufwood tree, and scurrying
up into its branches.

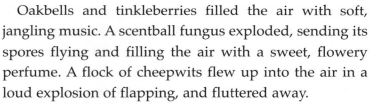

'A wild lemkin!' said Magda. 'Oh,
how sweet.'

Oakbells and tinkleberries filled the air with soft,
jangling music. A scentball fungus exploded, sending its
spores flying and filling the air with a sweet, flowery
perfume. A flock of cheepwits flew up into the air in a
loud explosion of flapping, and fluttered away.

'Wonderful!' bellowed Rook. 'It's all *wonderful*!'

'. . . *wonderful . . . derful . . . ful . . .*'

'Yes, wonderful, brave master,' came Hekkle's voice
by his side. 'But the Deepwoods is also treacherous.
More treacherous than you could believe. It is unwise to
draw attention to ourselves. We must travel discreetly,
silently, and remain vigilant at all times . . .'

Rook nodded absent-mindedly. They were passing
through a dappled glade of smaller trees – dewdrop
trees, their pearl-like leaves glistening in the yellowing
sunlight; weeping-willoaks and brackenpines. And
there, scurrying across the ground before him, a comical
family of weezits in a long line, largest at the front down
to smallest at the back, each one clutching the tail of the
one in front in its mouth.

'. . . And never become separated from the others,' he
heard Hekkle saying. Rook looked round. 'On no

account are you ever to wander off on your own, do you understand?'

'Yes,' said Rook. 'Yes, I do.'

Hekkle shook his head. 'I hope for your sake, brave master, that you truly do.' He reined in his prowlgrin and stopped beside an aged and ailing tree with sparse foliage, crumbling bark and the scars of many storms and lightning bolts. 'Hold my prowlgrin steady,' he told Rook.

Rook did so. Magda and Stob caught up, and the three of them watched Hekkle remove his backpack, climb onto the prowlgrin's back and reach up towards a rotten knot-hole high up on the trunk. He dangled a single talon down inside.

No-one spoke. No-one moved. Throughout their journey through the Deepwoods, Hekkle had stopped innumerable times just like this, and they had learned not to disturb him.

Sometimes he had stopped by fallen logs and broken branches and, having listened intently – head cocked and feathers quivering – had torn into the bark to reveal plump, pale grubs wriggling beneath. Once he had paused and scraped at the leaves beneath his feet – and discovered a nestful of squirming red worms. Another time he had thrust his beak into the soft, powdery wood of a rotting lullabee tree, and emerged with a fat caterpillar skewered on the end. Each new addition had ended up with the others in Hekkle's forage sack.

Stob leaned forwards. 'What's he doing now?' he whispered into Magda's ear.

Magda shrugged.

Since taking up his position on the prowlgrin's back, Hekkle had remained completely still – apart from the one talon. *Scritch scritch scritch.* The needle-sharp point of the claw scraped lightly at the swollen bark around the edge of the hole. *Scritch scritch scritch.*

Stob shook his head impatiently. Rook craned his neck to see better.

Scritch scritch . . .

All at once there was a loud scrabbling sound from inside the tree, a flash of pale orange from the entrance to the hole and Rook gasped as a set of vicious, glinting mandibles snapped shut around the curving talon. Hekkle did not flinch. Rook held the prowlgrin harness tight and watched intently as the shryke-mate slowly and smoothly drew his hooked talon away from the hole.

The creature came with it. It was sleek, with varnished armour, and multi-segmented like a string of mire-pearls. A pair of delicate white legs waved from each segment. Suddenly, perhaps sensing that it was exposed and wishing to return to the darkness, the creature squirmed and released its hold. But Hekkle was too quick for it. Stabbing into the hole with its beak it dragged the entire creature out – all stride and a half of it – and shook it until it fell still. Then, jumping down and loosening the drawstring to his forage sack, he dropped it in on top of the rest.

'A skewbald thousandfoot,' said Hekkle. 'Delicious . . .'

'Delicious?' said Stob. 'You mean you *eat* them?'

'Of course, brave master,' said Hekkle. 'The forest is full of food. It's just a matter of knowing where to look.'

Rook blanched. He'd assumed that Hekkle was simply collecting interesting specimens, perhaps to sell to the scholars in the Free Glades. 'Are you intending to *eat* all the stuff you've collected in that sack?' he asked.

'Of course, brave master,' said Hekkle and chuckled throatily. He swung the backpack over his shoulders and mounted his prowlgrin. 'The sun's getting low,' he said. 'We must make camp before darkness falls. Stay close, and keep your eyes peeled. We need to find a specially sturdy tree to rest up for the night. Then we can see about that meal.'

'I can't wait,' muttered Rook weakly.

'You first,' said Stob meanly, thrusting the skewer with the gimpelgrub on it into Rook's face.

Rook shuddered queasily. He was sure he'd just seen it wriggle.

'He doesn't have to if he doesn't want to,' said Magda. 'Oh, but I'm so hungry!'

'Eat!' chuckled Hekkle. 'Eat! I prefer them raw, but they're equally good cooked. Go on, it won't bite!'

'I'm not so sure,' said Rook, holding up the bright red fleshy grub. He closed his eyes, opened his mouth and bit down hard . . .

'I never thought I'd say it,' Rook said, 'but that was delicious.'

'Even the thousandfoot?' said Hekkle.

'*Especially* the thousandfoot,' said Rook, licking his fingers. 'In fact, is there any more?'

Hekkle poked about inside the hanging-stove. 'No,' he said at last. 'It's all gone. *Everything's* gone.'

'Pity,' said Rook and Stob together, and laughed.

They'd come across the tree just as the last rays of the sinking sun were being extinguished from the forest floor. It was a huge, spreading leadwood, with a gnarled grey trunk and broad, horizontal branches. As the prowlgrins had carried them up into the tree – leaping and grasping, leaping and grasping – so the sun had reappeared, treacly yellow and comfortingly warm.

High up in the tree, they had dismounted and Hekkle had tethered the prowlgrins to the stout branch they were perching on. Having travelled all day, the weary creatures were soon asleep. Hekkle had led the others up to the broad branches above the roosting prowlgrins and given the three young librarians the tasks which, as they journeyed further, were to become a daily routine.

Magda and Rook collected kindling and logs. Hekkle secured the hanging metal stove he had been carrying on his back to an overhanging branch. Stob tied up their three hammocks. Then, when they returned, Rook laid a fire inside the round stove, which Magda lit, using her sky-crystals. Meanwhile, Hekkle prepared the contents of his forage sack for cooking – washing, slicing, spicing and finally, when the fire was hot enough, placing them

on skewers which he slid into the glowing stove.

The flames had died down now, and the embers of the various pieces of wood that Rook and Magda had collected flickered with colour – now red, now purple, now turquoise – and gave off both sweet aromatic smells and the sound of soothing lullabies.

Magda yawned. 'I'm going to sleep well tonight,' she said.

'It's time you all got some sleep,' said Hekkle. 'Get into your hammocks, brave masters and mistress. I shall roost in the branches above your heads and sleep with one eye open. We shall be making an early start in the morning.'

Stob, Magda and Rook pulled themselves up and laid their weary bodies down in the swinging hammocks. The heat from the glowing stove warmed the chill air.

'Haven't you forgotten something?' Hekkle said, as he looked down from his perch. 'The Covers of Darkness will keep you safe from prying eyes.'

As one, the three librarian knights elect remembered the gift they had received from the Professor of Darkness. They sat up and untied the scarves from around their necks. Rook watched Stob and Magda unfold the flimsy material, wrap it around themselves and their hammocks – and disappear. With fumbling fingers, he opened up his own scarf. The nightspider-silk was as soft and fine as gossamer, and almost weightless. As he went to drape it over himself, the wind caught it, making it dance in the air like a shadow.

'Secure it to the rope by your head,' Hekkle instructed him. 'That's it.'

Rook lay back in the soft hammock, arms behind his head and looked upwards. Though concealing him totally, the cover was see-through, and Rook stared up into the canopy of angular leaves far above his head, silhouetted against the milky moonlit sky beyond. All round him, curious sounds filled the air. The screech of woodowls and razorflits. The coughing of fromps and squealing of quarms. And far, far away in the distance, the sound of a banderbear yodelling to another. Feeling warm, safe and secure, Rook smiled happily. 'I know that Hekkle said the forest can be treacherous,' he said quietly, 'but to me the Deepwoods still seems a wonderful, magical place . . .'

'Particularly after the horrors of the terrible Eastern Roost,' said Magda drowsily.

'Just think,' said Rook. 'One day, when we've completed our studies and set out on our treatise-voyages,
we'll fly over these woods.'

Magda stifled a tired yawn. 'I'm thinking of looking at
the life-cycle of the woodmoth,' she murmured.

'Woodmoths?' said Rook. 'I'm going to study banderbears.' The curious yodelling sound repeated, fainter
and farther away. 'I can't wait . . .'

'Go to sleep,' said Stob.

'Well said, Master Stob,' said Hekkle. 'We've got a
long day ahead of us.' He fluffed up his feathers against
the rising wind. 'Goodnight, brave masters, goodnight
brave mistress,' he said. 'And sleep well.'

'Night-night,' came Stob's sleepy voice.

'Goodnight, Hekkle,' said Rook.

Magda, already half-asleep, muttered softly and rolled
over.

Six days they travelled – six long, arduous days of hard
riding. After the initial thrill of being inside the dark,
mysterious forest, even Rook's enthusiasm was
beginning to wane. The going was tough and, when it
rained at night, they climbed out of their hammocks the
following morning feeling more tired and achy than
when they had turned in. But with their destination still
far off, they had no choice but to continue, no matter
how weary they felt.

Hekkle urged them on as best he could, encouraging
and reassuring them, producing delicious food night
after night and praising the contributions they were

beginning to make to the forage sack. But the un-remitting pressure of the long, difficult journey through the Deepwoods was taking its toll. Stob and Magda bickered constantly, while Rook's sleep was increasingly troubled.

On that sixth evening, as they tucked into their supper of grubs and fungus, the atmosphere was oppressive. Stob was in a foul mood, Magda was tearful, while Rook – who had drifted off to sleep and fallen from his prowl-grin earlier that day – was nursing a badly bruised knee.

'Any more for any more?' said Hekkle, offering round a tray of toasted ironwood bugs. The young librarians all declined. Hekkle looked at them fondly. 'You are doing so well,' he said.

Stob snorted.

'Believe me,' said Hekkle. 'I have never guided a more determined and courageous group through the Deepwoods than your good selves. Our progress has been phenomenal.' He clacked his beak. 'So much so that you'll be pleased to know our journey is coming to its end.'

'It is?' said Rook eagerly.

Hekkle nodded. 'We are getting close to the Silver Pastures,' he confirmed. His face grew serious and the familiar harsh tone to his voice returned. 'But I must tell you that this is the most perilous part of our expedition.'

Magda sniffed miserably.

'Naturally,' muttered Stob sullenly.

'This area attracts the most dangerous of creatures,' Hekkle went on. 'The pastures – and indeed the densely populated Free Glades beyond – offer rich pickings. From sun-up tomorrow, we must be extra vigilant. But fear not. We shall not fail – not having come so far.'

That night Rook slept worse than ever. Every squawk, every screech, every whispered breath of wind permeated his fitful sleep and turned his dreams to nightmares – to *the* nightmare.

'Mother! Father!' he cried out, but his voice was whisked away unheard as the slave-takers carried them both off. The whitecollar wolves snarled and howled. The slavers cackled. Rook turned away, trying to shut out the horrors of what had just taken place, when . . .

'No!' he screamed.

There it was again. Looming out of the darkness; something huge, something terrifying. Reaching towards him. Closer, closer . . .

'NO!' he screamed.

Rook's eyes snapped open. He sat bolt upright.

'It's all right, brave master,' came Hekkle's voice. The shryke was perched above the hammock, looking down at the youth sympathetically.

'H-Hekkle,' said Rook. 'Did I wake you?'

'No, brave master,' said Hekkle. 'Stob's snoring woke me hours ago.' He smiled kindly. 'Get up and get ready,' he said. 'The end is almost in sight.'

Despite Hekkle's words, the atmosphere that morning remained tense. They packed up quickly and in silence, and set off before the sun had risen high enough to strike the forest floor. On they travelled, through the morning and into the afternoon without once stopping.

'What about the forage sack?' asked Rook.

Hekkle smiled. 'Tonight you will feast on something grander,' he said. 'Hammelhorn, perhaps. Or if you're lucky, oakbuck.'

Rook peered ahead into the shadows and shook his head. 'It all still looks the same,' he said. 'How can you tell that the Silver Pastures are near?'

Hekkle's eyes narrowed and his head-feathers quivered. 'I can sense it, Master Rook,' he said quietly. He shuddered. 'Believe me, the pastures are not far now.'

As they journeyed further, the prowlgrins began to grow skittish. They snorted; they rolled their eyes. They pawed the ground and tossed their heads. Once, Rook's prowlgrin bolted, and it was only Hekkle's speedy reactions that prevented him from being whisked off into the endless forest alone.

'I thought I saw something out there,' said Magda a while later. 'Something watching us . . .'

Hekkle reined his prowlgrin in, and listened intently. 'Courage, Mistress Magda,' he said at last. 'It's probably just woodhogs scratching for oaktruffles. But we'd better move on quickly, just in case.'

Magda tried to smile bravely. So did the others. But as dark, purple-edged clouds moved in across the low sun, plunging the forest into shadow, their hearts beat fast.

In a loud hiss and a flash of yellow and green, a hover worm emerged from the undergrowth to their left and sped across their path, causing the prowlgrins to rear up in panic.

'Steady,' said Hekkle. 'Keep your nerve.'

Rook glanced round him constantly, his head jerking this way, that way, as he searched the shadows for whatever it was lurking just out of sight. His eyes focused in on a dark shape sliding off behind a tree. He shivered.

Crack.

'What was that?' gasped Stob.

'Stay calm, brave master,' said Hekkle. 'Fear amplifies the slightest of sounds.'

Crack.

'There it was again,' said Stob. He looked round nervously. 'From over there.'

Hekkle nodded. 'Stay close together,' he whispered. He kicked his prowlgrin's sides, urging it into a loping canter. The others did the same.

Crack.

The sound was behind them now, and fainter. 'I think we lost it,' said Hekkle, easing up. 'But just in case, no-one must make another sound until we get to the Silver Pastures—'

All at once something whistled over their heads. There was a thud and the sound of splintering wood. And there, inches from where Magda sat on her jittery prowlgrin, was a flint-tipped spear, embedded in the trunk of a great lufwood tree.

Magda screamed. Stob held on desperately as his prowlgrin reared up and squealed. A second spear flew past, hitting the forest floor and scattering the iron-wood cones which lay there.

'Take to the trees!' Hekkle cried. 'And try not to get separated!'

But it was no use. All round them the air suddenly pulsed with the sound of low, guttural voices grunting in unison, throwing the prowlgrins into a panic.

'*Urrgh. Aargh. Urrgh. Aargh. Urrgh. Aargh.*'

The prowlgrins leaped around in alarm – and there was nothing their riders could do to bring them back under control. A second flurry of spears flew through the air.

'*Urrgh. Aargh. Urrgh. Aargh. Urrgh. Aargh.*'

'Rook! Stob!' shouted Magda, as her prowlgrin thrashed about, trying its best to dislodge her. 'It won't climb! I can't make it—' She screamed as the prowlgrin suddenly bolted. 'Help!' she cried out. '*Help!*'

'Hold on!' Rook called to her.

He yanked the reins and tried to steer his own prowl-grin after her. But the creature had a mind of its own and, before he could do a thing about it, had tossed him off its back and leaped up into the low-slung branches of a huge ironwood tree.

'Stick together!' he heard Hekkle shouting.

Rook rolled over and looked round. Magda's faint voice floated back through from the shadows. Stob and Hekkle were nowhere to be seen.

'*Urrgh. Aargh. Urrgh. Aargh. Urrgh. Aargh.*'

Heart pounding, Rook looked up to see his prowlgrin perched on a branch of the ironwood tree above. He struggled to his feet, and cried out as searing pain shot through his injured knee. He fell to the ground again. 'Here, boy,' he whispered. 'Come here, boy.'

The prowlgrin watched him from the branch, with wide, terrified eyes. Rook gritted his teeth. There was nothing for it. If the prowlgrin wouldn't come to him, then he would have to go to the prowlgrin.

Head down, he began dragging himself across the forest floor to the foot of the ironwood tree. His knee felt as if there were a knife lodged beneath his knee-cap, jarring with every movement he made. Closer. Closer . . .

'*Urrgh. Aargh. Urrgh. Aargh. Urrgh. Aargh.*'

All at once another spear whistled through the air. It struck the prowlgrin in its side. With a low moan, the creature dropped like an ironwood cone, hit the ground with a thud – and fell still.

Rook froze. What now?

'*Urrgh. Aargh. Urrgh. Aargh. Urrgh. Aargh.*'

The chanting was louder than ever. It seemed to be coming from every direction. Rook was on his own – wounded and frightened. He couldn't run. He couldn't hide. And something huge was coming towards him . . . With a surge of panic mixed with nausea, Rook suddenly realized that it was as if his nightmare were actually coming true.

Then he saw it. Tall, brutal, half-formed – it looked like a larger, fiercer and much, much uglier version of a clod-dertrog. Its huge, blunt face was mottled and scarred. The flat nose sniffed the air, the heavy jutting brow frowned over deep-set, red eyes that scanned the gloom of the forest floor.

Rook shrank back down into the soft leaf-cover on the ground and held his breath. His only hope was that it did not see him.

'*Urrgh!*' it grunted over its shoulder, and was joined by another trog with jagged, yellow nails and long matted hair.

'*Aargh!*' its companion responded. It pulled a spear from the giant quiver slung across its shoulder and brandished it in the air. '*Aargh!*'

From all round came replies, and out of the shadows emerged more of the hulking great trogs. Rook trembled with terror. Each of the creatures had skulls – whole strings of them – tied on leather thongs around its neck. They rattled as the trogs walked, jaws grinning and empty eye-sockets staring out in all directions.

'*AARGH!*'

The first trog had spotted him. Their eyes met.

'No, no, no,' Rook muttered as he desperately tried to scuttle away on his backside, dragging himself along with his scrabbling hands.

The creature advanced unhurriedly. It drew back its heavy, muscular arm and threw the spear.

Rook ducked.

It whistled past him, and on into the tangled undergrowth behind. The creature drew another spear and lumbered forwards, the necklace of skulls rattling. Its mouth opened to reveal a set of long, wolf-like teeth.

'*AARGH!*' it roared.

A sharp pain shot up from Rook's injured knee. He collapsed. It was no good. There was nothing he could do. He could feel the pounding feet vibrating through the ground beneath him, he could smell rancid fat. The facets of the flint spear glinted in the dappled light as the trog raised it, ready to strike.

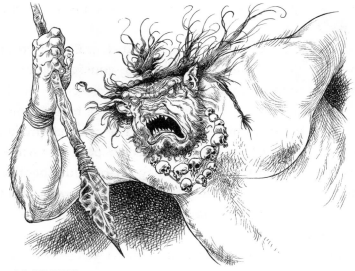

'*AARGH!*'

Rook closed his eyes. So this was how his nightmare ended, he thought bitterly.

Just then, from behind him, there came the sound of furious scratching, followed by a loud whirring noise. The trog cried out.

Rook looked round to see a dense swarm of small, silver-black angular creatures emerging from the undergrowth where the stray spear had landed. Despite the perilousness of his situation, the instincts of a true earthscholar were awakened in him. With their long, pointed

noses
and stubby
triangular
wings, they were
clearly related to the
ratbirds which had once
roosted in the bowels of the
great sky ships. Like the ratbirds,
they flew in flocks. Unlike their
harmless, scavenging cousins, however,
these small, vicious creatures seemed to be
hunters.

Wheeling through the air in a great cloud, the countless silvery creatures flapped in perfect synchronization. When one turned, they all turned. Together, they resembled nothing so much as a billowing sheet, tossing and turning in the wind.

'*AARGH!*' bellowed the trog.

The flock switched in mid air, and swooped down towards it. Roaring loudly, the trog swiped at them with its spear. Several of the tiny creatures plummeted to the ground – but with so many, the loss of half a dozen of their number meant nothing.

'*AARG—*'

As Rook stared, fascination replacing fear, the flock struck. It engulfed the trog in an instant. The sound of gnashing and slurping filled the air – but only for an instant.

The next, the creatures flapped back into the air, squealing loudly.

Rook felt the icy fear return. The flock had stripped the hapless trog to the bone. Where he had been standing a moment before, there now stood a white skeleton and empty, grinning skull which, as Rook watched, fell to the ground in a heap of bones. The gruesome necklace of skulls lay among them. The spear dropped down on top of them all.

At the sight of what had happened to their leader, the others let out a howl of alarm.

'*Aargh!*' they screamed. '*Urrgh!*' And they turned on their heels and hurtled back into the forest.

The flock of tiny, blood-crazed creatures wheeled round in the air – looking, for a moment, like a vast sky ship with billowing sails – before turning as one, and speeding off after the fleeing trogs.

For a moment Rook could not move. His breath came in short, jerky gasps. Beside him lay one of the small creatures, its neck broken. He picked it up. It was small – smaller than the palm of his hand and scaly. Four razor-sharp teeth protruded from its slack jaws.

Rook trembled. On their own, the creatures were nothing, yet when they swarmed they were transformed into a huge, fearsome predator.

Rook memorized every detail of the tiny creature, fascinated and repelled in equal measure. If he ever got back to the library, he would describe it and name it, and perhaps one day a young under-librarian would pick up his treatise and read about it, and wonder . . . He would call it a snicket.

Slowly and painfully, using one of the discarded spears which littered the forest floor for support, Rook climbed to his feet. He stared round into the gloomy shadows. Whichever way he turned, the forest looked the same. He sighed. He'd escaped the primitive skull-trogs, and the snickets – only to find himself lost and alone in the depths of the Deepwoods.

Back in the underground library, he had often wondered why so many of those who had written about the Deepwoods described it as *endless*. Of course it isn't endless, he would say. You can see that from the map. Look, here it becomes the Edgelands, and here it borders the Twilight Woods . . . After a week tramping through the forest, however, 'endless' seemed exactly the right word. It was so vast that anyone lost could wander for ever, and never find a way out.

Too frightened to call for his missing companions, Rook set off, orientating himself as best he could by the distant glow of the sun. His knee throbbed and, now that the dangers had passed, he was left feeling weak with hunger. He stumbled on, glancing round constantly, try-ing not to cry out as the forest sounds seemed to grow more and more sinister with every step he took. 'Stay calm,' he told himself.

But what was that? It sounded like footsteps – and they were coming towards him.

'It's all right,' he whispered, his voice breathless with rising fear. 'Don't panic.'

Yes. Yes. They were definitely footsteps. Heavy, sure-footed. Had one of the terrible skulltrogs come back to finish him off? He crouched down behind a vast trunk, festooned with hairy-ivy, and peered out tensely. The foliage parted and—

'Hekkle!' Rook cried.

'Master Rook!' the shryke exclaimed. 'Can it truly be you? Oh, brave master, praise be to Earth and Sky!' Rook climbed awkwardly to his feet. 'But you're hurt! What have you done?'

'It's my knee,' said Rook.

Hekkle dismounted and trotted towards him. Crouching down, he inspected it closely. 'It's swollen,' he said at last. 'But nothing too serious. Sit down for a moment, and I'll fix it up.'

Rook slumped back heavily to the ground. Hekkle removed a pot of green salve and a length of bandage from his backpack and began treating the knee.

'Did you see the flying creatures?' said Rook. 'Thousands of them, there were. They stripped that giant trog to the bone in a second.'

Hekkle nodded as he rubbed the salve into the joint. 'And not only him,' he said darkly.

Rook took a sharp intake of breath. 'You mean . . . ? Stob . . . Magda . . .'

Hekkle looked up. 'I meant the other trogs,' he said. 'The brave master and mistress are safe,' he said. 'They are waiting for us at the edge of the Silver Pastures.'

'Praise be to Earth and Sky, indeed,' Rook breathed.

'There,' said Hekkle, as he knotted the ends of the bandage securely. 'Now, let's get you up onto my prowlgrin.'

They set off at a brisk trot, with Hekkle at the front holding the reins, and Rook behind, gripping the saddle tightly. As they loped on, the trees around them began to thin out. A head wind, blowing into their faces, sent the dark clouds scudding away across the sky, and for the first time that day, as warm shafts of sunlight flooded the forest floor, Rook began to feel optimistic about what lay ahead.

'Not far now,' said Hekkle. He pointed to a line of tall lufwoods. 'Those trees mark the edge of the pastures.'

Rook grinned. They had made it. The next moment his happiness was complete. 'And look!' he cried out. 'Magda and Stob!'

'You're right, brave master,' said Hekkle. 'But . . . Oh, no!' His feathers ruffled and his eyes nearly popped out of his head. 'What is *that*?'

'What? What?' said Rook. He looked intently for any sign of danger, but could see none. Stob and Magda had dismounted next to a long log, tethered the prowlgrins to a nearby lufwood tree and were standing with their backs turned away, looking out across the pastures beyond. 'What is it?' said Rook. He was suddenly frightened.

Hekkle flicked the reins and kicked into the prowl-grin's side. 'Watch out, Master Stob!' he shrieked as they pounded across the ground, but the wind whipped his warning away. 'Mistress Magda!'

'What was that?' said Magda.

Stob shrugged. 'I didn't hear anything,' he said, sitting down on the log.

Magda turned. 'Look,' she said excitedly. 'It's Hekkle. And he's got Rook with him!'

Stob frowned. 'Why are they galloping like that? And waving their arms? You don't suppose any of those horrible trog things are . . . ?'

Magda jumped up onto the log for a better view. 'I don't think so,' she said. 'There's nothing chasing them.' She cupped her hands to her mouth. 'What's wrong?' she cried out. 'Are you all right?'

'Stop waving, brave mistress!' Hekkle screeched back. 'And get out of there! Both of you!'

Rook knew Hekkle well enough to understand that Magda and Stob must be in terrible danger. 'Run for your lives!' he screamed. 'NOW!'

All at once there was an ominous rumble and a loud hiss. The ground shook. The dead leaves flew up. A pair of fromps skittered across the ground and away.

Rook stared ahead in horror and disbelief as the log on which Stob sat and Magda stood quivered, swung round and abruptly reared up into the air. It writhed. It swayed. It opened at one end, revealing sharp fangs and a dark, cavernous throat – and howled and wheezed with a bloodthirsty rage.

'Stob,' Rook gasped.'Magda . . .'

CHAPTER TEN

THE SILVER PASTURES

Rook stared in horror as the enormous thrashing creature rose up on a cushion of air spurting from rows of knot-like ducts the length of its huge mossy body.

'A logworm!' Hekkle shouted. 'Save yourselves!' He kicked his prowlgrin hard with his heels.

Stob fell heavily just behind the hovering logworm, and remained motionless where he lay. Magda landed with a thud beside the tethered prowlgrins, which twisted and reared in panic as the logworm swung round in mid air.

'Stob!' Magda screamed as the creature's great gaping maw lurched towards her fallen companion. 'Watch out!'

The logworm instantly turned towards the sound of her voice. Magda screamed. The prowlgrins thrashed about, screeching and howling and rolling their eyes in terror. The logworm's ring of green eyes focused on the terrified creatures.

'For pity's sake, Magda!' shouted Rook from behind Hekkle. 'Get out of there . . .'

His voice was drowned out by a deafeningly loud hissing. The logworm's huge mouth was sucking in air with tremendous force. A flurry of leaves and cones disappeared inside the creature as it came down low, and advanced on Magda and the terrified prowlgrins. They squealed and screeched and fought against the tunnel of swirling air, while Magda gripped their straining tether-ropes desperately.

'Magda . . .' Rook gasped.

Hekkle brought their prowlgrin to a skidding halt, leaped from its back and raced towards her. 'Brave mistress!' he called and seized her tightly by the wrist. Her cloak billowed out in the twisting air as he dragged her away to safety, just in time.

There was loud *crack* as the first of the tethers snapped under the unrelenting pressure, and one of the squealing prowlgrins barrelled back towards the cavernous mouth of the logworm. It disappeared inside. With a hideous crunching sound, the log-worm's body arched and shivered as it squashed the life out of its still squealing prey.

Hekkle, dragging Magda with him, reached Stob and plucked at his shirt. 'Get up, brave master,' he said. 'Get up!'

The librarian apprentice groaned.

Just then there was another *crack*, and the second

screaming prowlgrin disappeared. The logworm belched thunderously.

Hekkle and Magda pulled Stob to his feet, and stumbled away from the writhing monster. Rook kicked into the sides of his panic-stricken mount.

'Come on, boy,' he said. 'They need our help—*Whoooah!*' he cried out.

The terrified prowlgrin let out an ear-splitting screech and reared up. At the sound, the logworm turned on them, and Rook found himself staring straight down the creature's blood-red throat. Its circle of green eyes fixed him with a malevolent intensity. With a sinister hiss, the logworm lurched towards them, sucking in everything in its way in huge, convulsive gulps.

Rook felt the prowlgrin being dragged backwards. It was like being caught inside a whirlwind. He tugged at the reins in a furious attempt to yank the creature out of the traction-like spiral of air which was drawing them closer and closer to the terrible gaping mouth. Suddenly, with a loud *crack*, the harness snapped. The reins came away in his hands.

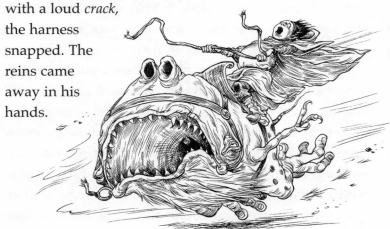

'No,' he groaned, tossing the useless bits of tilder-leather to the ground, and hanging on grimly round the creature's neck.

'Pick on someone your own size!' Hekkle's voice shrieked and, turning, Rook caught sight of the puny shryke-mate – feathers fluffed up and eyes glinting – beating the ground furiously with a lullabee branch. Distracted, the huge logworm roared with rage and twisted round to confront the shryke. Twigs, leaves, rocks and earth were thrown high up into the air.

Suddenly free, the prowlgrin tore off as fast as its powerful legs could take it. Rook held on desperately as they thundered through the suddenly thinning lufwood trees and on into the brilliant light and vast spaces of the Silver Pastures themselves.

Rook felt a great wave of relief wash over him. Vast and softly undulating, the pastures were spectacular. The silvery grey-green was broken only by the thick streaks of the black and brown herds of migrating hammelhorn and tilder, which stretched out as far as the eye could see.

The wide sky, cloudless now, was dotted with birds in flight – a flock of snowbirds, a cluster of cheepwits, songteals twittering loudly, a gladehawk hovering and waiting to dive and, far, far in the distance, a solitary caterbird flapping sedately. Below, the huge herds moved slowly through the pastures. The air was filled with the warm, musty smell of their thick fur mingling with the mouthwatering scent of crushed grass. Their deep lowing rumbled sonorously . . .

A loud hiss cut through the air directly behind him. The logworm! Rook kicked his heels into the galloping prowlgrin, not daring to look back. The huge beast had followed them out into this vast sea of grass. Ahead, a large herd of shaggy hammelhorns trumpeted loudly and, turning on their heels, stampeded off in a cloud of dust.

The logworm was almost on top of them. Rook could feel the twisting air tugging at his cape, his trousers, his hair, and making the prowlgrin pant with exertion.

'Faster! Faster!' Rook cried out in desperation. 'Don't give up now!' The prowlgrin snorted helplessly. It had done all it could; it could do no more. Clinging on tightly, Rook leaned forwards. 'You did your best,' he whispered.

The prowlgrin stumbled. Rook cried out. They crashed into the soft, herb-scented grass, Rook tumbling clear of his mount. The gaping maw of the logworm loomed over them, closer, closer . . .

'No!' he screamed. 'Not like this!'

All at once Rook caught sight of a blur of movement out of the corner of his eye. The next moment something struck him hard, knocking the air from his lungs, and – in a flurry of grasping hands, glinting wood and flapping sails – he was plucked from the ground.

Rook gasped. He was soaring up, up, up into the sky.

'Just in time, friend,' came a voice from behind him. Rook craned his neck round. He was on a skycraft! He was actually flying! There, astride a narrow seat behind him, was the pilot – a young, slightly built slaughterer, dressed in flight-suit and goggles. The skycraft lurched to the left. 'Stay still, friend,' he said firmly. 'She's not used to passengers.'

Rook turned back, scarcely able to believe what was happening. He wrapped his arms round the neck of the skycraft's roughly hewn figurehead and clung on tightly, his heart bubbling with joy.

Flying!

Far below, there came a long howl of despair. Rook looked down to see the brave yet hapless prowlgrin disappear inside the voracious log-like creature. A last plaintive squeal rose up through the air. Then nothing. Rook shuddered, and almost lost his grip on the figurehead.

'*Whooah*, steady there, friend!' the pilot shouted. 'First time in the air?'

Rook nodded and tried not to look down.

At that moment the fragile skycraft hit a pocket of turbulent air. It bucked and dipped, and went into a nose-dive. The slaughterer pilot's hands darted forwards and began tugging at a series of ropes, raising weights and shifting the sails round, while his feet balanced the craft with thin, curved stirrups. Rook gasped, stomach in his mouth, as the ground spiralled towards them.

'I know, I know,' the slaughterer muttered through clenched teeth, as he tugged on two of the ropes at the same time. 'You're not built for two, are you, old girl?'

The skycraft abruptly pulled out of the dive and soared back into the sky – only to be struck by a ferocious gust of wind slamming into its side. Rook's

stomach did a somersault as the buffeting crosswind threatened at any moment to send them into another terrifying spin. The patched sails billowed in and out; this side, that side . . .

'Help!' Rook shouted out despite himself, his cry whipped away on the battering wind. He glanced behind him.

With his jaw set grimly, the young slaughterer was gripping the steering-handles tightly. The skycraft juddered violently, threatening to shake itself to pieces at any moment.

'Easy, girl!' he coaxed as, balancing in the stirrups, he wrestled with the tangle of ropes.

Rook held his breath.

Slowly, slowly – his brow furrowed with concentration – the slaughterer brought the skycraft round. His feet were poised, ready for the moment when the wind struck them from the back. Rook gripped the carved wood with white-knuckled ferocity . . .

All at once the skycraft gave a violent shudder. The wind was directly behind them. The sails billowed, the ropes strained. With a terrible lurch – and an ominous crunch – the skycraft hurtled forwards like an arrow.

Nothing could have prepared Rook for the sudden burst of speed. It threw him back, snatched his breath away and plucked at the corners of his mouth. He screwed his eyes tightly shut.

'*Whup! Whup! Wahoo!*' he heard a moment later. He frowned in disbelief. Was the slaughterer seriously enjoying this – or had the young pilot gone mad with fear?

Rook risked another glance over his shoulder. Although they were travelling at breakneck speed, and at an alarmingly steep angle, the slaughterer did seem to be in control. Standing up in the stirrups, he was pulling in the sail-ropes one by one, reducing the bulge of the individual sails, while at the same time keeping the fragile craft expertly balanced. '*Whup! Whup! Wahoo!*' he cried out again. He *was* enjoying himself.

Ahead of him, Rook spotted a tall tower; a mass of roughly hewn timber that seemed to sprout from the pastures like a colossal wooden needle. Just below the point, Rook could make out a series of rough gantries and primitive walkways bedecked with lanterns that, even in the light of the pastures, seemed to be glowing.

'That's my beauty, I knew you could do it,' the slaughterer muttered under his breath. 'Nearly there . . . Nearly there . . .' He tugged on a thick, plaited black rope above his head, and the sail to Rook's left rose.

The effect was instantaneous. Instead of continuing forwards, the skycraft went into a slow, coiling turn, arcing through the air like a woodmaple-seed on the wind. Once round the tall needle of the tower it flew, then descended, inch perfect onto a rough plank gantry where the skycraft touched down.

Rook slumped forwards, exhilarated and exhausted in equal measure. The slaughterer tore off his goggles and leaped from the seat, his face bursting with pride. 'Yes,' he smiled, and stroked the skycraft's carved prow. 'I knew you wouldn't fail me.' He looked suddenly thoughtful. 'What does the Professor of Darkness know?' he said. 'More than a single pilot on a skycraft. Can't be done, eh? Well, we've shown him, haven't we, *Woodwasp*, old girl?' He patted the figure-head affectionately.

Rook tapped him on the shoulder. 'My name's Rook Barkwater, and I want to thank you from the bottom of my heart,' he began. He paused. 'Did you say *Professor of Darkness*? Are you also an apprentice?'

The slaughterer looked down and laughed. 'I, Knuckle, an apprentice?' he said. 'No. Just a simple herder, me. The professor is a . . . an acquaintance of mine.' He turned to face Rook, as if only now seeing him for the first time.

'But you fly so well,' said Rook. 'Who taught you, if not the masters of Lake Landing?'

'I taught myself,' said Knuckle. He patted the skycraft lovingly. 'Built her from scratch, I did. 'Course, I'd be the first to admit that she's not the most beautiful skycraft ever to fly, but the *Woodwasp* here is a remarkable creature. Obedient. Sensitive. Responsive . . .'

Rook was intrigued. 'You're talking about it as though it was alive,' he said.

'Aye, well, that's the secret of skycraft flight in a nutshell,' said Knuckle earnestly. 'You treat your sky-craft like a friend – with love, with tenderness, with respect – and she'll return the favour tenfold. When I saw you in trouble with that logworm, it was the *Woodwasp* herself who urged me to try to rescue you. "We can do it!" she told me. "The two of us together!" And she was right.'

'And thank Earth and Sky for that,' said Rook softly. 'Without you both, I would have perished.'

Suddenly, from all around, came the sound of voices. Rook looked out from the gantry to see half a dozen or so skycraft – each one piloted by a single pilot – looping down through the air towards them. Like Knuckle, they seemed to be slaughterers, flame-haired and clad in leather flight-suits. They waved down enthusiastically.

'That was amazing, Knuckle!' shouted one.

'The most incredible piece of flying I've ever seen!' shouted another.

'And with two people on board!' said a third, awestruck. 'If I hadn't seen it with my own eyes, I'd never have believed it possible!'

One by one, they landed their own skycraft on gantries below them, dismounted, and clambered up swaying ladders to join them. Knuckle bowed his head.

'It was nothing,' he said, modest, almost shy. 'It's all down to the *Woodwasp* here, the little beauty—'

'But you are an excellent pilot,' Rook butted in. He turned to the others. 'The way he swooped down and plucked me from the jaws of the logworm. The way he battled with the air-pockets and gale-force winds . . .' He shook his head with admiration. 'You should have seen it!' He glanced back towards the young slaughterer. 'Knuckle, here, was magnificent! He saved my life!'

'And who are *you*?' asked a short, sinewy slaughterer as he stepped forwards.

'Looks like a merchant to me,' came a voice.

'Probably one of those apprentices,' came another.

'He *is* an apprentice,' Knuckle answered for him. 'His name is Rook Barkwater.'

Rook nodded. 'I was travelling with two other apprentices,' he said. 'A shryke guide was taking us to the Free Glades. Have you seen them? Do you know if they're all right?'

'A shryke?' said Knuckle, and screwed up his nose.

The others muttered under their breath. Shrykes were clearly not popular among the group of slaughterers.

'This one's not like the others,' Rook assured them. 'He's kind, thoughtful—'

'Yeah, yeah, and I'm a tilder sausage,' came a loud voice, and they all laughed.

'You certainly fly like a tilder sausage,' said someone else. The laughter got louder.

Knuckle turned to Rook. 'Come,' he said, taking Rook by the arm. 'We'll get a better view from the west gantry. Perhaps we can spot your friends from there.'

*

187

Rook gasped as he peered down from the west gantry of the tower. On the ground, far below him, the herds of tilder and hammel-horn looked like woodants in the failing light. He clutched the balustrade nervously.

'It's so high,' he trembled.

'Wouldn't be much use for looking out of if it weren't,' said Knuckle.

'I know,' said Rook queasily. 'But does it have to sway like that?'

'The wind's getting up,' said Knuckle, and he scanned the sky thoughtfully. 'Looks like a sky-storm's brewing.'

Rook frowned. He turned to Knuckle. 'A sky-storm?' he said. 'With thunder and ball-lightning?'

Knuckle chuckled. 'Yeah, and hailstones the size of your fist if you're lucky.'

'The size of your fist,' Rook said softly.

The slaughterer looked at him quizzically. 'Are you telling me you've never seen a sky-storm before?'

Rook shook his head. 'Not that I remember,' he said

wistfully. 'I grew up in an underground world of pipes and chambers – dripping, enclosed, illuminated with artificial light . . .' He turned, tilted his head back and was bathed in the golden shafts of warm sunlight. 'Not like this. And as for the weather,' he said, turning back to Knuckle. 'Everything I know, I learned from barkscrolls and treatises.'

'So you've never smelt the whiff of toasted almonds in the air when lightning strikes? Nor heard the earth tremble as the thunder explodes? Nor felt the soft, icy kiss of a snowflake landing on your nose . . .?' He paused, suddenly noticing the blush spreading over Rook's cheeks. 'But I envy you, Rook Barkwater. It must be wonderful to have the chance to experience all these things for the first time – and be old enough to really appreciate them.'

Rook smiled. He hadn't thought of it like that.

'Now, let's see if we can spot these friends of yours,' Knuckle went on. 'They'll be making their way on foot if the logworm got your prowlgrins.'

'I hope so,' said Rook, following the slaughterer's gaze out across the silvery plains, over the heads of the grazing hammelhorns.

'That's where you came from,' he said. 'The Eastern Roost. If you look carefully, you can just see the top of the Roost Spike.'

Rook nodded. The sun was deep orange now and low in the sky, casting the trees in darkness. The spike stood out like a needle point and, as he watched, a light came on at its top. Knuckle's arm swung further round.

'Over there are the Goblin Nations,' he said. 'And there, due south, is the Foundry Glade. See how the sky is darker in that whole area? That's the filthy smoke constantly belching out from their factory chimneys.'

Rook could see the heavy black clouds, tinged with red, far in the distance. 'It looks like a terrible place,' he observed.

'Take my advice, friend,' said Knuckle earnestly. 'The Foundry Glade is no place for the likes of us. Ten times worse than Undertown, so they say – a place of fiery furnaces and slaves—'

'Slaves?' said Rook, shocked.

'And worse,' said Knuckle darkly. 'Not at all like the *Free* Glades.' The slaughterer smiled. 'Now the Free Glades are a sight to see, believe me!'

'Which way *are* the Free Glades?' said Rook.

Knuckle turned him round, till Rook was standing with his back to the sinking sun. 'Over there,' he said. 'Just beyond that ridge of ironwood trees; the most beautiful place in all the Edgelands.'

'So close?' said Rook, trembling with excitement. As he peered into the darkness, he was filled with a mixture of happiness and sadness. Overjoyed to discover that he had almost reached his destination, he had momentarily forgotten that his companions were not with him . . .

'Rook!' The voice echoed up on the swirling wind from the other side of the tower. '*Rook!*'

'Magda?' said Rook, hurrying to see. He clutched the rough wooden balustrade and looked down. A group of ant-like slaughterers were staring up. When Rook's head appeared they all started waving and pointing and shouting at once. 'Come down!' 'Come here!' 'Your friends . . .' And three individuals from the crowd were pushed forwards.

Rook cried out with joy. 'Magda!' he shouted. 'Stob! Hekkle!' And he turned on his heels, clambered down the ladders leading on to the walkways, and finally hurried down a creaking zigzag staircase.

'Rook!' Magda cried as he emerged at the bottom, and she rushed forwards to hug him, before bursting into tears. 'We . . . we thought we'd lost you for certain,' she sobbed. 'Then we saw that slaughterer swooping down . . .'

'And I thought I spotted you clinging on, brave master,' said Hekkle.

'You did,' Rook beamed and turned to Knuckle, who had followed him down. 'Knuckle, here, saved my life.'

Hekkle turned to him. 'You are a true friend of earth-and sky-studies,' he said.

Knuckle nodded uncertainly. Talking to a shryke clearly felt strange to him. 'Thanks,' he muttered. 'I just did what anyone else would have done.'

Magda broke away from Rook, and wrapped her arms tightly round the startled slaughterer. 'You're too modest, Knuckle!' she said. 'Thank you and thank you and thank you again,' she said, planting three kisses on his forehead.

The other slaughterers roared approvingly. Knuckle blushed, his normally red skin turning a deep shade of purple.

Hekkle's voice rose above the hub-
bub. 'It is time we left,' he said. Ignoring the protests and politely declining the offers of refresh- ment and a bed for the night, he raised his hands and appealed for quiet. 'Tonight,' he began. The slaughterers fell still. 'Tonight we will sup, dine and sleep in the Free Glades.'

A cheer went up. And as Hekkle led his small party away, the slaughterers waved and cried out. 'Good luck!' they shouted. And, 'Earth and Sky be with you!' And, 'Don't forget us!'

Rook turned. 'Never!' he shouted back. 'I'll never for- get you! Farewell, Knuckle! Farewell!'

The sun had set by now, and the colours on the horizon behind them had become muted and shrunk away to a thin, pale ribbon of light. Above their heads the stars were coming out and, as they climbed the steep ridge of ironwood trees, the first of the night creatures were already calling to one another in the darkness.

'The Free Glades,' Rook breathed. 'So close.'

'Not long now,' said Hekkle.

Though on a gentle incline, the ridge seemed to continue for ever. Each time they reached what they thought was the top, the slope continued upwards. The moon rose and shone down brightly. Rook wiped his glistening forehead. 'It's further than I thought,' he said. 'Knuckle made it sound so—'

'Sshhh!' Hekkle stopped and cocked his head to one side. 'Can you hear that?' he whispered.

Rook listened. 'Oh, no,' he groaned as, from his right, he heard the unmistakable – and terrifyingly familiar – sound of hissing. 'It can't be.'

'A logworm,' Magda gasped.

'I'm afraid so,' Hekkle whispered nervously. 'The woods all round the pastures are infested with the brutes. The pickings are just too good.'

'What shall we do, Hekkle?' whispered Stob.

Rook noticed that his apprentice companion's voice had lost its usual arrogant tone.

'Find a tree,' whispered Hekkle, 'and climb as swiftly and silently as you can. Go, now!'

They did as they were told. Quickly, noiselessly, they scaled an ironwood tree and crouched in its huge branches, like ratbirds, beneath their cloaks of nightspider-silk. The hissing grew louder as the logworm approached, and a flurry of leaves rose up in the air. The next moment its great slavering snout poked out from between the trees; its eyes and teeth glinted in the moonlight.

They held their breath and remained as still as their pounding hearts and trembling bodies would allow. Rook willed the creature to go.

Please, please, please . . .

All at once it grew darker as a cloud fell across the moon. Rook glanced down. Something was flapping past.

'Snickets!' he gasped.

'So that's what they're called,' he heard Stob mutter beside him.

The logworm hissed louder, and turned in their direction. Rook shrank back. Below them, the whirring swarm of snickets was spiralling up through the darkness like a great arrow-head. As it approached, the moon burst forth again and shone down brightly on the countless silver-black beating wings. The snickets were heading straight for them.

Rook groaned. If the logworm didn't get them, the snickets would. And when they were so close to their journey's end . . .

All at once and with no warning, the logworm swerved round to face the swarm. Rook gasped as the logworm   convulsed.

The snickets were being sucked  up into the vast, dark tunnel of the logworm.

It writhed and wriggled, sucking in more and more of the little creatures, its high-pitched hiss sounding like a great kettle letting off steam. As the last of the swarm disappeared inside the logworm, Rook turned to Hekkle.

'It's destroyed them all,' he said.

'On the contrary, brave master,' said Hekkle. 'Things in the Deepwoods are seldom what they seem.'

'But—' Rook began.

Just then the logworm let out a deafening cry of pain. The sound echoed round the trees, making the leaves tremble, and Rook felt the hairs on the back of his neck stand on end. As he watched, transfixed, the entire log-worm seemed to disappear before his eyes. The snickets were consuming it from within, each and every scrap! For a moment the vast swarm resembled the great hovering log it had just devoured. Then, as if at some unseen signal, the snickets twisted round in the air – no longer together, but singly and in pairs – and fluttered off in all directions.

Legs shaking, Rook climbed down from the ironwood tree. 'I . . . I don't understand,' he said. 'Why did the swarm disperse like that?'

Hekkle clambered down and stood beside Rook. 'Their feeding frenzy is over,' he said. 'They will only swarm again when their hunger once more drives them to it.' He laughed humourlessly. 'Now it is the turn of other creatures to feed,' he said. 'Many of their number will be picked off by predators.'

Rook shook his head in wonder. He'd read so much about the delicate balance of life in the Deepwoods, about the constant battle between predators and their prey. Now he was experiencing it first hand. It was fascinating how it all slotted together. How no single creature seemed ever to get the upper hand. How victor became victim and victim became victor, and the whole violent yet intricate process continued for ever and ever.

He thought of the treatise that lay ahead, and the banderbears he wanted to study. They, at least, were gentle creatures. Noble. Humble. Loyal. At least, that was what everyone believed – even Varis Lodd. Soon he wanted to find out for himself . . .

'Come, brave friends,' said Hekkle, setting off up the ridge once more. 'We're almost there.'

Stob and Magda followed. Rook brought up the rear, his heart thumping with expectation. As they approached the brow, he almost expected it to give way to yet another slope, and another one beyond that.

This time, however, they really had reached the top. The ground fell away before them, and in front – spread out in all their magnificence – were the Free Glades. To their right was a pool of honey-coloured lamplight. To their left, a flickering circle of burning torches, and beyond that, the low red glow of furnaces. Whilst far in the distance, shimmering like silver beneath the moon, were three lakes. In the centre of the largest one, twinkling brightly, was a tall, spired building, bedecked with coloured lights. It was there that, for the months of study which lay ahead, they were to stay.

'Lake Landing!' said Rook, pointing. 'Our new home.'

CHAPTER ELEVEN

STORMHORNET

Lake Landing

Spirits soaring, Rook, Magda and Stob raced down the steep incline, with Hekkle flapping behind them, clucking noisily. 'Careful, brave masters!' he called out breathlessly. 'Not so fast, brave mistress!'

They emerged from the trees onto a track – flattened and hardened by the passing of countless booted feet and wooden wheels – and there in front of them, like some magnificent jewel-encrusted tapestry, were the glades themselves.

Rook's pulse quickened as he looked round in wonder. In the moonlight, the diverse dwelling places of the numerous Free Glade denizens were picked out in luminous silver and long, sharp shadows. The three apprentices stopped and stared. The air was filled with smells and sounds. The tang of leather, the odour of stale beer, the aromatic scent of spices and herbs. And Rook could hear the buzz of distant voices – joyful voices, and singing and laughter. Hekkle bustled up behind them and tried to catch his breath. The feathers on his neck stood up in a ragged ruff and his thin pointed beak quivered. 'Over there, that's where the webfoot goblins live.' He nodded towards a group of huts floating on shimmering marshland to their left. 'Great eel-fishers,' he said, 'but not too particular in their personal habits. And those,' he said, pointing over his right shoulder to a tall, steep, pockmarked hill, 'are the cloddertrog caves. Now, they're really a sight to see. They say whole clans live in a single cave together; sometimes hundreds of them—'

All at once there was a clatter of hoofs behind them. They turned to see two gnokgoblins on prowlgrins approaching. Both the goblins and their mounts wore tooled-leather armour; the gnokgoblins carried long ironwood lances and large crescent-shaped shields. One stopped and, standing tall in his saddle, scanned the area. The other rode towards them.

'Advance and identify yourselves,' he barked.

Hekkle stepped forwards and produced the bloodoak-tooth medallion, which he held up. 'Friends of Earth and Sky,' he said.

Rook and the others revealed their medallions, too. The guard nodded. Up close, Rook noticed that the burnished leather of his armour was pitted and scratched with the scars of battle.

Just then a third guard appeared. 'Hey, Glock, Steg,' he shouted. 'Marauders have been sighted up in the Northern Fringes. We're needed there at once.'

The guard turned back to Hekkle and his three charges. 'Pass, friends,' he said, 'and fare you well.'

He tugged the reins, kicked hard, and galloped off after the others, his prowlgrin throwing up clods of earth with each bound.

'The Free Glades are beautiful and peaceful, brave friends,' said Hekkle. 'But many a brave soul has had to lay down his life to keep them that way. Come, let us continue to Lake Landing.'

They walked down a broad set of steps lit by huge, floating lanterns, and passed by a towering copse of dark trees, immense against the slate-grey sky.

'Who lives there?' said Rook.

'Waifs,' answered Hekkle. 'That is Waif Glen. Only the invited may go there, for the ways of waifs are secretive and mysterious, even here in the Free Glades.'

'And what's that?' said Rook excitedly, turning to his right.

In the distance, rows of lights illuminated narrow streets and the windows of clusters of ornate buildings – some broad and squat with spreading roofs; others tall, thin and topped with elegant towers.

Hekkle turned. 'That, brave master, is New Undertown. You'll find it very different from the old one. There is a welcome to be found for all in New Undertown – a hearty meal, and a free hammock in the hive-huts for those who want it.'

'Hive-huts?' said Rook excitedly. 'You mean those buildings over there – the ones that look like helmets?'

'That's right, brave master, they're—' Hekkle began.

'And what in Earth and Sky's name is *that* called?' said Rook, pointing at the tall, angular building with latticed walls and a high spire which dominated New Undertown.

'It's the Lufwood Tower, brave master,' said Hekkle. 'It's like Vox Verlix's palace in Old Undertown – except all are free to go there and speak their minds in its meeting chamber.'

'Can we visit the waifs? And the hive-huts?' said Rook eagerly. 'And the Lufwood Tower?'

'Oh, Master Rook!' Hekkle laughed and held up his hands in submission. 'Enough! Enough! There'll be time for all that, but first we *must* get to Lake Landing.'

Rook blushed. 'I'm sorry,' he said. 'It's just all so . . . so . . .' He swung his arms round in a wide arc. 'So . . .'

'Get a move on!' said Stob grumpily. 'I'm tired, and so is Magda.' Magda shrugged and smiled, but Rook noticed the dark rings under her eyes.

'Believe me,' said Hekkle, 'the best is still to come.' He took Rook by the hand. 'Come, brave master.'

They continued past Waif Glen, and the Leadwood Copse beyond. Behind them, the sounds of New Undertown receded and, as the moon rose higher in the indigo sky, the air grew strangely still.

Rook's eyes darted round – but he kept his questions to himself. There were flowers with huge white blooms, swaying in the silvery light. There were black and yellow birds in the branches, chirruping to the moon. The grass hissed. The path crunched. They came to an archway of sweet-scented woodjasmine, stepped through and . . .

'Oh, my!' gasped Rook.

Before them lay a lake. It was vast and still, and, like a giant mirror, reflected everything in it perfectly. Birds skimming its surface. The trees fringing its banks. And the huge moon, shining down out of the inky sky so brightly.

On a broad platform at the centre of the lake – wreathed in mist and twinkling with a thousand lanterns – was a tall, sprawling building, jagged against the sky. It had pointed turrets, jutting walkways, arch-windowed walls and long, sloping roofs.

Rook shook his head in amazement. 'I've never seen anywhere so beautiful,' he said softly. 'Even in my dreams.'

'The Lake Landing Academy,' said Hekkle. 'The jewel of the Free Glades, and beacon of hope to all who love and value freedom.'

LAKE LANDING

But no-one was listening to the shryke guide's words any more. One after the other, as if in a trance, the three young apprentices walked slowly down to the water's edge and climbed onto the long narrow jetty which crossed the lake to the landing of vast lufwood planks.

As Rook stepped onto the great central platform, something caught his eye and he looked up to see a small skycraft with a gleaming prow and snow-white billowing sails approaching. His heart skipped a beat. It was the most beautiful sight yet. The moonlight played on the ornately carved figurehead and sleek curves of the skycraft's body. The dark greens and browns of the young pilot's flight-suit contrasted with the warm gold of his wooden arm-plates and leg-guards. The skycraft's sails seemed to flow through the night air like liquid silver as it circled the landing. It was joined silently by another craft, and then another, and another.

One by one, they swooped down out of the sky in perfect formation, before touching down lightly on the landing-stage, side by side. Rook stared at the four young apprentices as they climbed down from their craft, and shook his head in awe.

'I'll never be able to fly that well,' he said.

'Yes, you will, brave master,' said Hekkle, coming up behind him. 'Trust me. You're not the first young apprentice who's stood awestruck on Lake Landing, full of self-doubt. Believe me, though, you'll learn.'

'But—' Rook began.

Hekkle clacked his beak softly. 'No "buts", brave master. From the first moment I clapped eyes on you, back in the Eastern Roost, I knew you were special. Sky-spirit and earth-sense, I call it.'

Rook blushed deep pink.

'They'll teach you well here at Lake Landing, but you've got something already – something that no amount of teaching can give you. Always remember that.'

Rook smiled awkwardly. 'Thank you, Hekkle,' he said. 'Thank you for everything. I'll miss you . . .'

'Welcome!' came a rather shrill voice from the far side of the landing. 'The new apprentices, is it? My, my, but you look fit to drop! Yes, yes, you certainly do, and no mistake!'

Rook turned to see a small, shabbily dressed gnok-goblin with a wrinkled face and stubby legs striding towards Stob and Magda, one hand clutching his robes, the other pressed against his heart in greeting. Rook went over to join them.

Stob had already taken control. 'Ah, my good fellow,' he said. 'See to our bags, would you, and then take us to the High Master of Lake Landing. I think he'll be interested to see us.'

'Indeed!' said the gnokgoblin, his face crumpling with amusement. He made no move towards the bags. 'Interested to see you, yes, indeed!'

Stob frowned. 'Well?' he said imperiously.

Hekkle turned to him. 'I don't think you quite understand, brave master,' he began.

'It's all right,' said Rook awkwardly, moving forwards. 'We can carry our own bags. After all, we've carried them this far.'

'Leave them, Rook,' said Stob sharply. 'A fine place this is! Upstart servants who refuse to do as they're told. Wait till the High Master hears of this!'

'I think,' said Hekkle quietly, 'he just has.'

'Stay out of this, Hekkle,' said Stob rudely, before rounding on the smiling gnokgoblin. 'Now, tell me your name this instant, you impudent wretch!'

Just then, as the gnokgoblin lowered his hands, Rook noticed the gold chain around his neck, glinting from beneath the simple robes. Each of the heavy links was in the shape of twisted leaves and feathers.

'Why, certainly, my fine, young and rather over-tired apprentice,' the gnokgoblin said. 'I am Parsimmon, High Master of Lake Landing.'

Stob turned a bright shade of crimson. 'I . . . I . . .' he stuttered.

But the High Master waved his apologies aside. 'You must be tired and hungry, all of you,' he said. 'Come inside and I'll show you your sleeping cabins. Then I'll take you to the upper refectory. There is food and drink waiting and . . .' He looked up. 'But what have we here? I was expecting only three, indeed I was. And yet, and yet . . .'

Stob, Magda and Rook turned to see a wiry figure with close-cropped hair crossing the walkway towards them. 'He's not with us, your Most Highness, sir,' said Stob, regaining the power of speech.

Parsimmon beckoned to the figure to approach. 'Welcome, welcome,' he said genially. 'And who might you be?'

'Xanth,' said the youth. He rubbed his hand over his scalp. 'Xanth Filatine. Sole survivor from the latest group of apprentices to set forth from the Great Storm Chamber Library.' He pulled a bloodoak-tooth pendant from his tattered gown and thrust it forward defiantly.

Rook noticed the youth's hands shaking. He frowned. There was something about this young apprentice that made him feel uneasy.

'They sent another group after us?' said Stob suspiciously. 'So soon?'

Xanth nodded. 'Word came back that you'd been lost in a shryke raid. The professors decided to despatch a second contingent of apprentices immediately.'

Stob humphed.

'I'm sure the professors know what they're doing,' said Hekkle.

'So, what happened to the others?' Stob demanded of the youth.

Xanth shook his head sadly. 'Dead,' he said quietly. 'All dead.' He swallowed noisily with choking emotion. 'I'm the only one who made it.'

Rook listened closely. Perhaps he had been too harsh.

'Bron Turnstone,' Xanth went on, his voice cracking with emotion. 'Ignis Gimlet. And our brave woodtroll guide, Rufus Snetterbark. A logworm got them all . . .'

'I don't know those names,' said Parsimmon, 'but it is always a terrible tragedy to lose any of our brave apprentices. And as you can see,' he said, nodding towards Rook and the others, 'this contingent did make it – which makes the losses all the more tragic.'

Xanth nodded silently and lowered his head. Tears welled up in his eyes.

'But *you* made it, Xanth Filatine,' said Parsimmon kindly. 'The journey to the Free Glades is never an easy one. Few are lucky enough to get through. And those who do . . .' He clapped the four new arrivals re-assuringly on the shoulder. 'You are very precious to us. We will teach you everything we know, and send you off on your treatise-voyage, so that you may add to our deepening knowledge of the Edge.' His eyes sparkled brightly. 'Yes, yes,' he said. 'Very precious, indeed.'

The Woodtroll Workshop

'Damn and blast!' Rook shouted, and sucked at his painfully throbbing thumb.

Stob chuckled. 'A fine way for a young scholar to talk,' he said.

'Another splinter?' came Magda's sympathetic voice. She was standing by her own workbench.

'Yes,' said Rook, wearily inspecting his hands. Apart from the jagged splinter – which he managed to pull from his thumb with his teeth – his hands were grazed, scarred and bruised black and blue. He looked bleakly at the huge sumpwood log clamped into the vice before him. Despite weeks of work, what should by now have been an elegant skycraft prow, was still no more than a shapeless lump. 'I'll never get the hang of this,' he muttered miserably.

Around them, the timber yards hummed with activity. Convoys of tall-sided log-carts swayed past the long, thatched woodsheds, the musky odour of the sweating hammelhorns pulling them mixing with the peppery scent of sawdust. Cloddertrog wagoneers shouted down to the woodtroll carpenters, while groups of woodtroll tree-fellers queued good-naturedly at the huge, ever-busy grindstones to sharpen their axes. Rook gazed out of the open-sided workshop at the cluster of woodtroll villages in the distance and let out a deep sigh.

'Don't give up,' said Magda.

Rook glanced over towards his friend. Her own prow was coming along beautifully. The wood was smooth and the figurehead was slowly taking on the appearance of a delicate woodmoth, with its bulging eyes and coiled feelers. Stob, too, had created something recognizable. A hammelhorn, stolid and lifelike. He was using a fine rasp to shape the long, curling horns. While Xanth – who was at his usual workbench apart from the others at the far end of the thatched workshop – was the farthest advanced of them all. With its long, crumpled snout and swept-back wings, the ratbird he had carved from the sumpwood was almost complete.

Oakley Gruffbark, the woodtroll master, his thick orange hair twisted into the traditional woodtroll tufts, stood beside him, running his leathery hands over the wood and inspecting the workmanship closely. 'Well, young'un, it's an unusual creature to carve, and that's the truth,' he was saying. 'Yet it seems to come from the heart . . .'

Stob snorted. 'A ratbird,' Rook heard him muttering scornfully. 'I wonder what *that* says about his heart?'

Rook said nothing. He'd distrusted Xanth at first, but the young apprentice kept himself to himself and, with his haunted-looking eyes and polite, quiet voice, Rook found it hard to dislike him. At least, Rook thought, Xanth had thought of *something* to carve. He picked up a plane from the workbench and attacked the lump of wood with a sudden fury. The air filled with muttered oaths, and a flurry of pale wood-shavings.

'Stupid! . . . Blasted! . . . Accursed!'

'No, no, no! That'll never do, Master Rook, indeed it won't!' came Gruffbark's urgent voice as he hurried over to his bench. He snatched the plane away. 'You must *feel* your wood, Master Rook,' he said. '*Know* it. Study it intimately, until you are familiar with every mark of its swirling grain, with the intricate pattern of knots, with the natural curve of its sweeping shape.' He paused. 'Only then will you find the creature hiding within . . .'

Rook looked up angrily, his eyes filling with tears. 'But I can't!' he said. 'There's nothing there!' Oakley shook his tufted head sympathetically. 'All those dreams of flying I've had, and I'm never even going to leave this workshop! It's hopeless! Useless! And so am I!'

The woodtroll's face creased into a warm smile. He fixed the youth with his deep, dark eyes and took his hands in his own. 'But there *is* something there, Rook,' he said patiently. 'Open your ears and your eyes, and let the wood speak to you.'

Rook shook his head mutely. The words meant nothing to him.

'It's getting late, and you're tired, young'un,' said Oakley. He clapped his hands together. 'Class dismissed.'

Rook turned and walked stiffly away. Outside, the parties of axe-carrying fellers and teams of carpenters were wandering out of the timber yards and off down the woodtroll paths towards their villages – and supper. Small groups passed him by, laughing and joking in the evening twilight glow. Magda caught him up and put her arm round his shoulders. 'You'll feel better after supper,' she said. 'I think it's your favourite tonight. Tilder stew.'

Magda was right on both counts. It *was* tilder stew, which *was* Rook's favourite. The upper refectory was busy tonight. Several visiting professors sat at the central table. A huge translucent spindlebug – the stew clearly visible digesting in his stomach – was in conversation with a tiny waif, her large ears flapping delicately as she ate. Parsimmon sat listening indulgently, his usual supper of barkbread and water untouched in front of him.

Rook, too, had little appetite. He stirred at the stew absent-mindedly, the spoon never leaving the bowl. He looked round at the others on the circular outer table, all tucking in hungrily. There were Magda and Stob, sharing a joke; and groups of other apprentices, loud and swaggering, at different stages in their learning; and Xanth, alone as usual, watching everything but saying nothing.

Rook sighed. If he couldn't even carve his prow, then how would he ever learn to fly?

A painful lump rose in his throat, which he could not swallow away. His eyes smarted and watered. He pushed the bowl back, climbed from the bench and quietly left the refectory. With the door closed behind him, he clambered down the circular staircase of the Academy Tower, passing the round doors of the sleeping cabins as he went, and on through the dark wooden colonnades where the skycraft lessons took place.

At the edge of the landing platform Rook stared out across the dark waters of the lake, his heart weary. The air was thick and heavy, smudging the stars and sliver of new moon, and muffling the night sounds coming from the Deepwoods beyond. Black, forbidding stormclouds rolled in from the north-west, making the air darker, denser – and charging it with a crackling force that made Rook's skin tingle.

The sky splintered and flashed as fine tendrils of lightning

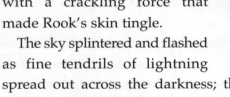

spread out across the darkness; the water shimmered with a pale green phosphorescence and, out of the corner of his eye, Rook caught sight of something darting across the lake. He couldn't quite make it out. The air seemed as heavy as a liquid and the lake blacker than it had ever looked before.

There it was again, a flash of yellow and red. And a perfect circular ripple spread out across the dark surface of the lake, growing in front of Rook's eyes, larger and larger, before fading away.

Suddenly, close by, there was the hum of swiftly beat-ing wings – and Rook saw it. A large, insect-like creature with an angular head and a long, slender body striped yellow and red. As he watched, it swooped and dived, sipping at the luminous water before looping back up into the air. Another perfect ripple spread out.

Rook was entranced. His heart soared and bubbled. The little creature was so graceful, so elegant – so perfect.

And as he stared, unblinking, it was as though he too were flying beside it, darting down to the surface of the water and soaring back up again. His stomach turned somersaults. His head spun. He opened his mouth, and laughed and laughed and laughed . . .

The following morning, after a deep dreamless sleep, Rook skipped breakfast and hurried to the timber yards before the others had even emerged from their sleeping cabins. He hugged the great slab of wood.

'Perfect,' he whispered, and his body tingled with the feelings of the previous evening.

With mallet and chisel, Rook began to shape the wood. Although it was still dark, he worked swiftly and confidently, and without a break. And each time when, for a moment, he was unsure what to do next, he would close his eyes and stroke the wood gently, for Oakley

Gruffbark was right. The wood *was* telling him what to do.

The rough form of the skycraft began to take shape: the narrow seat, the fixed keel and, at the front, the raised figurehead. Although lacking any fine detail, the angular head of the creature was already clearly recognizable. He was working on the curved neck when he heard footsteps approaching. The first woodtrolls must be arriving from the surrounding villages.

Rook felt a hand on his shoulder. 'Early start, young'un?' said Oakley, his rubbery face creasing with amusement. 'That's what I like to see. Now, what do we have here?' He raised his lantern and held it up to the wood. For the first time, Rook saw the carved prow clearly. A smile tugged at the corners of his mouth.

'I think I've found it,' he said.

'I think you have,' said Oakley. 'Do you know what it is?'

Rook shook his head.

'Why, young'un, it's a stormhornet,' Oakley told him. 'And you don't see many of them, I can tell you.'

Rook's heart fluttered. He lay his hands on the roughly hewn head of the creature. '*Stormhornet*,' he whispered.

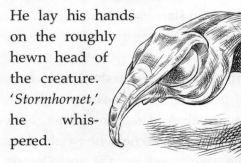

The Gardens of Light

Click click click click . . .

The rhythmical sound of claw on stone came closer.
Rook looked up from the bubbling pot in front of him, to
see their tutor – an ancient spindlebug, already in his
third century – tottering towards them. He was picking
his way along one of the narrow, raised walkways which
formed a winding network throughout the glowing
underground cavern. A laden tray was gripped tightly in
his claws.

Weeks after he had first set foot inside them, Rook still
couldn't get over the Gardens of Light. Hidden deep
below the huge Ironwood Glade, the vast illuminated
cavern was one of the most spectacular wonders in all

the Free Glades. It was here that the great glassy spindle-bugs grew the astonishing glowing fungus, the light from which shimmered on the cavern walls high above their heads and lent everything an eerie, yet ethereal beauty. Rook could have spent hours just gazing at the hypnotic shifting lights – if it wasn't for the varnishing.

'Nice glass of tea, Master Rook?' The ancient spindle-bug's voice, as thin and reedy as his long glass legs, snapped Rook out of his daydream. Tweezel towered above him.

'Thank you, sir,' said Rook, taking the glass of thin, amber liquid.

The spindlebug passed the tray to Magda, Stob and finally Xanth, who accepted the last glass with the faintest trace of a smile playing on his thin lips. Xanth really seemed to like Tweezel, Rook noticed. Although the young appren-tice was still quiet and reserved, the spindlebug seemed somehow able to get him to relax. Rook never could work out how.

Perhaps it was the old creature's quaint formality; the way he insisted they stop and drink his strange scented tea, bowing to each other after each sip, but saying nothing – not a single word – until the glass was empty. Or perhaps it was the long conversations the two of them had together about long-ago times, as the apprentices stirred the little pots of varnish over the small brass burners, adding a pinch of oak pepper here and a dash of wormdust there.

Rook would listen in as Tweezel told Xanth about places with strange names, like the Palace of Shadows and the Viaduct Steps, and tell stories of a young girl called Maris, whom the old creature had loved like a daughter. They spoke quietly, politely, never raising their voices. Rook couldn't always make out the details, and when he tried to join in, Xanth would smile and Tweezel would say, in that thin voice of his, 'Time for a nice glass of tea, I think, my dear scholars.'

They finished their glasses and bowed. The spindle-bug inspected their varnish pots.

'Not bad, Master Rook, but be careful not to overheat your varnish. It does so thin it, I find – and with quite tiresome results.'

Rook nodded. It was strange to think, looking at the clear, bubbling mixture in front of him, that without it there would be no sky-flight. The sumpwood of the sky-craft, once coated with the meticulously prepared and applied varnish, gained the enhanced buoyancy that made wood-flight possible. Some said that it was Tweezel himself who had invented the varnish, but whether this was true or not, all accepted that the spindlebug was the greatest authority on varnish and its preparation in all the Deepwoods.

'What shall we do with you, Mistress Magda? We can't have lumps, now, can we?'

Magda sighed. Varnish was proving far trickier than she'd ever expected.

'And as for you, Master Stob!' Tweezel tutted, peering into the apprentice's blackened, sticky varnish pot. 'I think you'd better start again. To the milking field with you!'

Stob groaned, and with a dark look at Rook and Xanth he picked up a tin pail and a pair of heavy gloves, and stomped off towards a field of glowing fungus, several walkways below.

'Now, Xanth, my dear young scholar.' The spindle-bug's antennae quivered as he peered down at the glistening brass pot. 'I do believe you're done! Quite remarkable! I have never seen a more perfect varnish, and at only the fiftieth attempt! You, Master Xanth, will be the first to varnish your skycraft. Congratulations! You've made an old spindlebug very happy!'

Xanth smiled and looked down modestly. Rook was pleased for his classmate – though he couldn't help also feeling a little jealous. He was still months away from making a perfect varnish for *his* skycraft.

Just then there was a high-pitched scream, followed by a string of loud curses.

'Not again!' said Tweezel, trilling with irritation. 'Follow me, everyone.'

Rook, Magda and Xanth clicked the lids over their burners and followed the spindlebug off the laboratory ledge and down the stone walkway towards the fungus fields. As they rounded a corner, they saw him.

Covered with glue and upside
down, Stob was stuck halfway
up the cavern wall. Ten feet
below him, snuffling amongst
the glowing toadstools, a huge
slime-mole swayed from side to
side, its translucent body
bulging and sloshing with
mole-glue. The sight of the
glistening creatures' jelly-like
bodies always made Rook's
stomach lurch queasily – and
milking them was one of his least
favourite tasks. But without mole-glue
there would be no varnish, and without varnish there
would be no wood-flight, and without wood-flight . . .

'Master Stob!' said Tweezel, his reedy voice sharp with
vexation. 'Don't tell me. You did it again, didn't you?
You milked it . . .'

'Yes,' said Stob weakly. 'From the wrong end.'

The Slaughterers Camp

'Behave yourselves, you stupid things!' came Magda's angry voice. 'Oh, no! Not again!'

Rook turned to see his friend hopelessly entangled in the gossamer light spider-silk sails. 'You've got to watch out for the crosswind, Magda,' he called over his shoulder, as he concentrated on controlling his own sails, which were billowing up into the warm air like two large, unruly kites.

He tugged on the silk cord in his right hand and the loft-sail gently folded in on itself. Then, having waited a split second, he swung his left arm round in a wide arc, playing out cord to the nether-sail. It, too, folded gracefully in on itself, and fell silently to the ground.

'How do you *do* that?' said Magda. She looked at the two neatly folded sails beside Rook, then at the tangled mess of cord and spider-silk wrapped round her own arms and trailing in the dust, and sighed deeply.

'You look like a bedraggled snowbird,' laughed Stob. He was sitting at a table eating tilder steaks with two flame-red slaughterers, who laughed good-naturedly with him.

In front of them the huge fire crackled in the vast iron brazier, throwing heat high into the clearing and warming the long family hammocks slung from the trees above.

Rook loved the slaughterers camp almost as much as the Gardens of Light. Especially at this time of day, when the evening shadows grew long, the camp fires were replenished and, one by one, the slaughterer families woke up and poked their flame-red heads from their hammocks to greet the new night. Soon, the communal breakfast would begin. Rook's stomach gurgled in anticipation of tilder steaks and honey-coated hammel-horn hams. But first, he must try to disentangle his poor friend.

He turned back to Magda, crouched down, and began gently tugging at the knotted ropes.

'Careful, now. Careful,' came a voice from behind him. It was Brisket, the slaughterer who had been assigned to teach the four apprentices all about sail-setting and ropecraft. 'Don't want to weaken the fibres now, do we?' he said. 'Let me have a look.'

Rook stood back. Brisket kneeled down and began teasing the ropes loose with one hand, while – taking care not to snag it – easing the sailcloth free with the other. Rook watched closely. Even though the slaughterer was little older than himself, his every move-ment revealed a lifetime of experience.

'My word, mistress!' he was saying. 'You really have got yourself in a tangle this time, haven't you?'

'I just don't understand it,' said Magda, her voice tear-ful and cross. 'I thought I was doing everything right.'

'Sail-setting is a difficult business,' said Brisket.

'But I did what you taught me,' said Magda. 'I threw out the loft-sail slowly, just as you said.'

'But you threw out into a crosswind,' Rook blurted out, stopping himself when he saw the hurt look on Magda's face.

'Rook's got a point,' said Brisket softly as he carefully folded Magda's sails. 'You must feel what the sail is telling you through the cord. You must watch how the wind shapes it, and let your movements flow. Never fight the sails, Mistress Magda.'

'But it's so hard,' said Magda disconsolately.

'I know, I know,' said Brisket understandingly. 'Get Master Rook here to help you. He's got the touch, and no mistake.' He paused, and tugged at a last knotted cord. The knot undid, the cord slid free. 'There, Mistress Magda,' said Brisket, handing her the sails. 'That's all for today. Now, who's for breakfast?'

Stob, Magda and Rook sat at a long table, which was weighed down by the sumptious spread of food laid out upon it. A little way off, Xanth stood practising his ropecraft. With one lazy movement, he lassoed the great curling horn of a hammelhorn which stood chewing the cud at the far side of its enclosure.

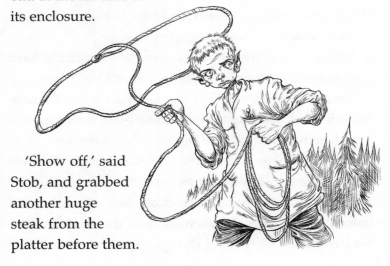

'Show off,' said Stob, and grabbed another huge steak from the platter before them.

'You'll turn into a hammelhorn if you eat any more,' said Magda.

Rook looked across at Xanth. Thanks to his success in varnishing, the young apprentice had gained a head start on the others. He'd already mastered sail-setting and was close to passing ropecraft. Despite this, Rook didn't feel jealous. Rather, he felt sorry for him. It was Xanth's haunted expression and quiet, lonely manner that touched him.

'Oh, he's all right,' he said to Stob, and turned back to his steaming tilder stew.

By now the communal tables were bursting with hungry, happy slaughterers, toasting the new night with mugs of woodale and bursting into song. Stob joined in, raising his mug high in the air.

Stob, Rook noticed, loved the slaughterers camp even more than he did. The arrogant, surly Stob he knew seemed to disappear in the company of slaughterers. He relaxed and become almost playful. For their part, the slaughterers had taken to Stob, treating the young apprentice like some sort of prize hammelhorn, to be fed and patted on the back.

Just then there was a loud cry from above their heads. Rook looked up. There, an arm waving in greeting, was Knuckle astride the *Woodwasp*, bearing down on them in a series of exquisitely executed loops. He had a lasso in his hand, which he was swinging round and round.

Lower he came, swooping down past the communal hammocks strung out between the ironwood trees, over the hammelhorn pens and tanning vats. When he was no more than a dozen strides away, he flicked his wrist forward. The rope coiled down like a striking woodcobra and circled Stob's raised hand. Knuckle jerked the lasso. The slip-knot tightened around the mug of woodale – which abruptly flew out of Stob's grasp and up into the air.

'Hey!' shouted Stob indignantly.

Knuckle smiled and took a gulp from the mug. 'Delicious!' he called down as he brought the little sky-craft in to land. 'Thanks, friend,' he said, handing the empty mug to Stob. 'I was feeling rather thirsty.'

Stob looked at the slaughterer for an instant – then a broad smile broke across his face and he threw back his head and roared with laughter. The slaughterers around them joined in.

'It's good to see you, Rook,' said Knuckle, sitting down next to him and helping himself to Rook's tilder stew. 'You look more grown-up each time I see you. You'll be off on your treatise-voyage in no time, I'll be bound.'

Rook smiled. 'If I can master ropecraft half as well as you, I hope to,' he said. 'The *Stormhornet*'s varnished, rigged and tethered at Lake Landing, just waiting to be flown – if the masters ever let me, that is.'

'Oh, they'll let you all right,' laughed Knuckle, his mouth full of stew. 'From what I hear, you're a natural, just like your friend Xanth over there.' He paused. A smile played on his lips. 'A stormhornet, eh? A rare creature, by all accounts. Swift and graceful, and with a sting in its tail; a harbinger of mighty storms brewing far off.' He clapped Rook on the shoulder. 'It's a fine name, Rook, my friend. A fine name!'

The Naming Rite

'We are assembled here, over Earth and under Sky, to welcome four apprentices to the Academy's long list of brave librarian knights, so we are,' announced Parsimmon, the High Master of the Lake Landing Academy. Behind him, the mighty Ironwood Glade cast its reflection in the glassy lake; above, the sky glowed a deep gold. The air was heavy and still.

Rook's heart give a little leap. He was standing in a line with Magda, Stob and Xanth. Before them, at the centre of a long, raised lufwood platform, stood Parsimmon, flanked on both sides by the tutors who had guided them through their long, arduous months of learning: Oakley Gruffbark, the wise and patient woodtroll, his tufted hair blazing a brilliant orange in the evening light; Tweezel, the ancient spindlebug, leaning on an ironwood staff and wheezing softly; and Brisket, the flame-red slaughterer, dressed in a heavy hammel-hornskin coat, with a length of rope coiled over one shoulder.

'You have done well, my young apprentices,' Parsimmon continued. 'Very well. For though many months more will pass before you are ready to depart on your treatise-voyages, this evening marks the completion of the first stage of your studies.' He turned to the row of skycraft, tethered to heavy rings at the back of the stage. 'You have carved your skycraft exquisitely, taking care to heed what the wood told you. You have prepared your varnish and applied it with care, to give them the gift of flight. You have rigged them with sails of finest woodspider-silk, tamed by your touch, and you have mastered ropecraft, to tether them and bring you safely back to earth. Well done, my fine young librarian knights!'

Rook lowered his head modestly. The tutors murmured their approval. Rook nudged Xanth and smiled. Xanth looked round and, for an instant, Rook thought he saw a flicker of sadness in his friend's eyes before he returned the smile.

'It is time,' Parsimmon continued, 'for you to name your skycraft which, tomorrow, you will fly for the first time.'

'At last,' Rook heard Stob mutter under his breath.

Magda felt for Rook's hand and squeezed it tightly. 'We did it,' she whispered.

Rook nodded, and looked up into the twilight sky, his eyes wide and heart singing. It was indeed a perfect evening, with the sun warm, the wind gentle, and small clouds rolling across the sky like orange and purple balls of fluff. The water of the lake ruffled like velvet.

'Step forward, Magda Burlix,' said Parsimmon.

Magda left the line. She climbed up onto the stage, shook the High Master's hand and crossed over to where her skycraft was tethered beside the others. She laid her hands upon the gently bobbing figurehead.

'By Earth and Sky, your name shall be *Woodmoth*,' she said, reciting the words she had been practising. 'Together, we shall set forth into the Deepwoods and return with a treatise entitled, *The Iridescence of Midnight Woodmoth Wings*.' She bowed her head and returned to her place in the line.

'Step forward, Stob Lummus,' said Parsimmon.

Stob came up and rested his hands on the ridged, curling horns of his figurehead. 'By Earth and Sky, your name shall be *Hammelhorn*,' he said in a loud, confident voice. 'Together, we shall set forth into the Deepwoods and return with a treatise entitled, *A Study of the Growth Rings of the Coppertree*.

As Xanth stepped forwards, he glanced round at Rook. He looked oddly troubled; sheepish, almost. Rook smiled at his friend encouragingly, but the expression in Xanth's eyes remained sad, haunted.

'By Earth and Sky, your name shall be *Ratbird*,' Xanth announced, his hands shaking as they clasped the creature's carved snout. 'Together, we shall set forth into the Deepwoods . . .' His head lowered and the thick hair which had grown unchecked since his arrival at Lake Landing flopped down over his eyes. His voice dropped. 'And return with a treatise entitled . . .' A faraway look came into his eyes as he raised his head. '*A Witnessing of the Hatching of a Caterbird from its Cocoon.*'

It was Rook's turn. He stepped up onto the stage, his heart bursting with pride and excitement, and walked slowly towards his skycraft. 'By Earth and Sky, your name shall be *Stormhornet,*' he said. 'Together we shall set forth into the Deepwoods and return with a treatise entitled, *An Eyewitness Account of the Mythical Great Convocation of Banderbears.*'

All four apprentices raised their right hands and touched their bloodoak pendants with their left. Then, heads raised and voices carrying across the dark waters of the lake, they announced in unison, 'This we pledge to do, or perish in the attempt.'

CHAPTER TWELVE

FLIGHT

Rook was awoken by shafts of light streaming through the grille of his sleeping-cabin door. He threw off his tilderwool blanket and flung the door open. 'Magda,' he called. 'Magda, are you up yet?'

'Down here, sleepy head,' came Magda's reply.

Screwing up his eyes against the light, Rook squinted down at the landing below. There, resplendent in their green flight-suits, goggles and golden wood-armour, stood Magda, Xanth and Stob.

'Why didn't you wake me?' Rook called angrily.

'We tried,' said Stob. 'But you were dead to the world, believe me.'

Rook scratched his head. He'd had the old familiar nightmare again the previous night, and had woken in the half-light of early dawn, exhausted. He must have nodded off again.

'Come and join us,' said Xanth. 'Your flight-suit's by your door.'

229

Sure enough, hanging from the iron hook outside his cabin was a green leather flight-suit with pockets and loops, as yet unfilled with equipment. Wooden leg-shields and arm-protectors dangled from their cord straps beside it. With trembling fingers Rook seized them and, fumbling clumsily, pulled the soft, burnished flight-suit on over his night clothes. His first flight! He was about to go on his first flight! Pausing only to adjust his new goggles, Rook dashed down the tower walkway to join his companions on the landing.

'Where are our skycraft?' he asked breathlessly.

'Over there,' said Magda, nodding towards the four skycraft, still tethered to the back of the lufwood stage.

There, gently bobbing in the breeze, was the *Ratbird*, the *Hammelhorn*, the *Woodmoth* – and the *Stormhornet*. Rook grinned. 'They look good, don't they?' he said.

'They'll look even better up in the sky,' said Stob. 'Where's our flight instructor? I thought he'd be here by now.'

'Patience,' said Magda. 'We've waited long enough. A few more minutes won't make any difference.'

As the early dawn mist began to lift over the lake, and the sounds of hammelhorn carts rumbling down the woodtroll paths towards the timber yards echoed through the air like distant thunder, the apprentices began to get impatient.

'Sunrise, the High Master said, didn't he?' said Stob. 'So where is our flight instructor?'

'Perhaps he overslept, whoever he is,' said Xanth.

'Forgotten all about us, more like,' said Stob irritably.

'Well, I'm not going to stand for it. How about you three?'

The others shrugged.

'Just once round the lake and back again,' Stob said. 'It can't do any harm. Who's up for it?'

'Me,' said Rook and Xanth together.

Magda nodded. 'All right,' she said quietly.

Rook ran to the *Stormhornet*. Now that it had been decided, he couldn't wait to be up in the sky. He released the tether, jumped up onto the saddle and, feet in the stirrups, grasped the two wooden rope-handles.

With nimble fingers, he raised the loft-sail and lowered the nether-sail – keeping a hold of the upper nether-sail rope as he did so. The two sails billowed out in front of him, just as they had so many times before, when he had been perched on top of the training block. This time, however, his craft was not secured to the ground.

With a tremble and a sigh, the elegant *Stormhornet* rose from the platform. For a second, it hovered there, its sails fluttering and flight-weights swaying.

Then, as the wind took it, Rook pulled on the pinner-rope, and the skycraft suddenly came to life and surged upwards into the crisp morning air.

Nothing could have prepared Rook for the thrill which raced through his body as the skycraft climbed ever higher. Not the buoyant lecterns, nor riding the prowlgrins as they leaped from tree to tree – nor even his brief flight with Knuckle. This time, he was in control. The *Stormhornet* responded to his every movement, dipping and swooping, rising and looping, utterly obedient to his command. It was exhilarating. It was awesome.

Once round the lake, Stob had said, yet now he was airborne, Rook had no intention of landing so soon. He looked round at the others. Stob was some way to his left, his flight steady and arrow-straight, the heavy hammelhorn prow seemingly butting its way through the currents of air. Magda, in contrast, seemed almost to be fluttering; this way and that she went, darting through the air, catching each gust and eddy for just a moment before changing course. Rook realigned the weights and sails, pulled the pinner-rope to his left and swooped down towards her. As their eyes met, they both burst out laughing.

'Isn't this the best thing ever?' said Rook, his voice snatched away on the wind.

'Incredible!' Magda shouted back.

Xanth, sleek and poised on the *Ratbird*, swooped down low over the lake, his trailing flight-weights skimming the still surface. Rook gasped at the elegance of his friend's flight. Xanth twitched the ropes and flew off, laughing.

Standing up in the stirrups, and tugging hard on the pinner-rope, Rook gave chase. Up to the top of the trees they flew, then, twisting round, they hurtled down, down like stones, before pulling out at the last moment, skimming the water again, and soaring back into the sky.

Xanth glanced round, his face glowing with excitement.

'Whup! Whup! Wahoo!' Rook cried.

'Wahoo!' Xanth bellowed and, turning away, darted back off towards the trees, looping the loop twice as he went.

This time Rook did not follow. Pulling the *Stormhornet* round, he flew back across the lake.

All at once he heard a cry of alarm, and spun round to see Stob and the *Hammelhorn* hurtling straight towards a great ironwood tree on the far edge of the lake. His hands were a blur of movement as they leaped around the ropes and levers, but the *Hammelhorn* was not responding. With a sickening crunch, the skycraft struck the tree's massive trunk, and fell.

Rook gasped and, distracted, let go of his own sail-ropes. The next moment he felt a heavy drag below him. Looking down, he saw, to his horror, that the nether-sail was half immersed in water. Desperately, he tried to raise it, while at the same time giving full head to the loft-sail. But it was no use. With a loud splash, the *Stormhornet* struck the lake.

The icy water snatched Rook's breath away and

chilled him instantly to the bone. He struggled desperately upwards, fighting against the weight of his wet
clothes, and emerged next to the *Stormhornet*, which was
bobbing about on the surface, pinned down by its
sodden sails. Gasping with relief, Rook grabbed hold of
the tether-rope, and clung on tightly.

Overhead, Magda seemed to stall. Her sails collapsed
and the *Woodmoth* lurched to one side. With a shrill
scream, she tumbled down towards the lake. There was
a resounding *splash*, followed, seconds later, by coughing
and spluttering as Magda sur-
faced beside Rook.

'It's all your fault, Rook!' she laughed. 'You put me
off!'

The *Woodmoth* dropped slowly down towards the
surface of the lake, landing close to the base of the ironwood tree where a disgruntled Stob sat rubbing his head
ruefully.

Xanth swooped in from overhead. 'Are you two all
right?' he called. 'It's a bit cold for a swim, if you ask
me.' He flew off with a laugh, circling the lake effortlessly on the soaring *Ratbird*, before turning back
towards Lake Landing.

'Just look at him,' said Magda. 'He makes it look so easy.' She shook her head. 'Who'd have thought it, eh? Quiet little Xanth, the best flyer of us all.'

'Beginner's luck,' said Rook, and smiled. 'I'll race you to the landing, come on!'

He and Magda splashed through the cold water, with Magda soon pulling in front. Ahead of them, Xanth was coming in to land, the *Ratbird* – sleek and swift – tilting into the wind.

'He's coming in too fast,' said Rook.

'Oh, he'll be all right,' Magda called back. 'Look at him, he's in control.'

The skycraft swooped low in an elegant arc and descended steeply. Just as it did so, a lone figure emerged from the Landing Tower and strode across the lufwood decking. At the sight of the figure, Xanth seemed to check his descent. The *Ratbird* reared up, its sails collapsed and the smooth arc turned into an ugly tumble. The next moment the skycraft crashed heavily into the landing, splintering its slender mast and throwing its rider clear.

Rook and Magda kicked out for the landing. The figure was crouching over the stricken body of their friend as they approached. At the same time Stob was running from the far edge of the lake, dragging the *Hammelhorn* behind him. Wet, breathless and shivering from the cold, Magda and Rook heaved themselves up onto the landing. Behind them, their skycraft bobbed on the water.

'Is he all right?' asked Magda.

'He'll live,' said the figure, without looking up. 'But

he's broken his leg badly. This is one apprentice who won't be flying again for a long time to come.'

Xanth groaned and opened his eyes. 'It hurts,' he said miserably.

'It's all my fault!' said Stob, running up, red-faced and with tears in his eyes. 'We were waiting for the flight instructor, but he didn't show up, so I thought it wouldn't do any harm just to take a short flight round the lake and back.' He shook his head. 'If I'd only known it would end like this . . .' He sank to his knees and grasped Xanth's hand. 'I'm sorry, Xanth. We should have waited for that stupid flight instructor. Now we'll have to postpone our first lesson.'

'I don't think so,' said the figure, standing up and turning to face them. '*I* am your "stupid" flight instructor.'

Stob groaned; he'd done it again.

'Perhaps you've heard of me,' she said. 'My name is Varis Lodd.'

Rook's jaw dropped. So this was the great Varis Lodd. Felix's sister. The librarian knight who had rescued him from the Deepwoods all those years ago. He wondered whether he should say something to her . . . Then again, he thought, she didn't even seem to recognize him – and why should she? He'd been a child of four when she'd rescued him, and she hadn't seen him since. He bit his tongue.

'And as for your first lesson . . .' Varis was saying. She paused and looked along the line of apprentices, one red-faced, one open-mouthed and one shivering; and at Xanth, prostrate on the landing, and moaning with pain. 'You have just learned it.'

As the moon peeked up above the horizon, broad and creamy yellow, Rook soared into the sky. Below him on Lake Landing, Varis Lodd and Parsimmon grew smaller and smaller.

Far to his left, a great caterbird, its black plumage and huge curved beak magnificent in the moonlight, flapped slowly across the sky. Xanth would have loved the sight. Rook remembered his friend's proposed treatise and wondered whether he would ever achieve his dreams. Poor Xanth. Even now, six long months after the terrible crash, he still walked with the aid of a stick, and had become even quieter and more haunted-looking, if that were possible.

Rook had always made a point of seeking Xanth out and including him in all the talk of sail-craft, flight-signing and wind-riding that accompanied their flight training. But there was no escaping the fact that, whenever he, Magda and Stob took to the air, Xanth was left behind, his pale face and dark eyes betraying his hurt and disappointment.

Tonight had been especially tough for Xanth because it was the night of their final flight. After this, Magda, Stob and Rook would be fully-fledged librarian knights,

ready to embark on their
treatise-voyages. The thrill
of it coursed through
Rook's body as
he realigned the
sails and pulled
hard on the
pinner-
rope. The
skycraft shifted round,
swooped down lower in the
sky and skirted the fringes of
the vast island of light and prosperity nestling in the
dark, mysterious Deepwoods.

'The Free Glades,' he whispered, as he steered the little
craft over each of the three glistening lakes in turn, past
the towering Ironwood Glade and back down towards
New Undertown.

He skimmed over the Lufwood Tower, the building
that had so impressed him when he first arrived in the
glades: how long ago that now seemed! Over the hive-
huts and the tufted goblins' long-houses he flew, and
round the gyle-goblin colony where small groups of the
bulbous-nosed goblins were wending their way home
from the surrounding fields – back to their Grossmother
and a supper of sweet gyle honey.

The moon rose higher. Tacking expertly against the gathering wind, Rook swooped down over the Tarry-vine Tavern, meeting-place for creatures from the farthest corners of the Deepwoods. How he'd loved sitting in its dark corners, listening to the tales of the old times, before stone-sickness, when the great sky ships had sailed the skies.

And now, here he was, in his own skycraft, with the moonlight in *his* eyes and the wind in *his* hair. He smiled, re-jigged the sails, stood up in the stirrups and flew up high over the tavern and beyond.

There were the timber yards, and the woodtroll villages beyond. 'Farewell, Oakley,' he whispered, remembering the kindly, tufty-haired old woodtroll. 'And thank you.'

There, beneath the huge Ironwood Glade, was the entrance to the Gardens of Light. How many times, labouring over his varnish stove, had he dreamed of this very night. But now the time had come, he knew he would miss the beautiful shimmering gardens – and his ancient spindlebug tutor. 'Farewell, Tweezel!' Rook whispered.

And there, shrouded in a fine red mist, the slaughterers camp. The huge fires were blazing beneath the sleeping hammocks, already swaying with waking slaughterers, making ready for a hard night's work. Rook could almost taste the spicy tilder sausages he'd eaten so many times. 'Farewell, Brisket!' he whispered. 'Enjoy your breakfast, kind master.'

He coaxed his craft into a long, slow turn, and headed back towards Lake Landing. In the distance, the Silver Pastures glistened in the moonlight. They'd never looked more beautiful, thought Rook. 'Farewell, Knuckle – my friend,' he said softly.

As he approached the Central Lake, Rook spotted Magda and Stob circling the landing, waiting for him to join them for their final descent. They, too, had been saying their last goodbyes. A lump came to Rook's throat.

There was heavy, arrogant Stob on his solid *Hammelhorn*. Quick to anger, slow to forgive – but now, Rook realized, for all his faults, like an older brother to him. And Magda, serious, sensitive Magda, on her *Woodmoth*, fluttering delicately on the wind. She was like a sister, sharing his triumphs and disasters alike, and always ready with a word of encouragement or a sympathetic look.

The three of them twisted down through the air in perfect harmony, furling their sails gracefully as they came lower, and landing in front of their flight instructor and the High Master soundlessly.

'Well done, all of you,' Varis Lodd said quietly. 'That was magnificent.'

Glowing with pleasure at her words of praise, Rook smiled. He remembered how haughty and aloof he had initially thought Varis Lodd to be. Yet how wrong he'd been. On that first morning, as she had turned and walked away, he'd run after her, keen to announce himself.

'I'm Rook Barkwater,' he had told her.

And she had turned, placed a hand on his shoulder and smiled warmly. 'I know,' she'd said. 'I'd know those deep blue eyes anywhere. But look at you! What a fine young apprentice you've turned into. Go and get your skycraft, Rook Barkwater, and then we shall have lunch together at my table.'

Ever since that moment Rook had felt close to her, as if the bond between them – established all those years ago when Varis had discovered him in the Deepwoods – had never been broken. Sometimes she reminded him of Felix, humorous and playful. At other times she could be as earnest and exacting as Alquix Venvax. Throughout it all, however, she had always been there for Rook; teaching him well and spurring him on to ever greater feats of achievement. And now here he was, standing before her, having completed the final flight of his studies.

'You are all now ready,' she said, bowing her head formally. 'It is time for you to embark on your treatise-voyages, friends of Earth and Sky.'

Parsimmon bowed his head in turn. 'Good luck in all your travels, and may you return safely to us in the Free Glades, my dear, precious librarian knights.'

Rook's heart was thumping fit to burst. He felt like

shouting out, with relief, with joy and anticipation, but instead he followed Stob and Magda's lead, bowing low and saying quietly, 'By Earth and Sky, we shall not fail you.'

Just then the heavy creaking sound of rough wheels on the lufwood decking interrupted the quiet ceremony, as a hammelhorn cart drew up, accompanied by two Free Glade guards on prowlgrins. Rook looked round.

A young apprentice lay groaning softly in the back of the cart, a dark stain spreading across the knife-grinder robes he wore. Parsimmon hurried over.

'We found him on the Northern Fringes,' the first guard, a gnokgoblin, reported, saluting the High Master. 'He says he was one of a group of apprentices from Undertown ambushed by shrykes. Says they knew they were coming.'

'Is this true?' said Parsimmon, kneeling down beside the stricken apprentice.

'Yes, master,' the apprentice whispered, his face pinched and white from the pain. 'They picked us out in the Eastern Roost, surrounded us on the upper gangways, and hacked us down, one by one . . .'

Parsimmon patted his hand. 'There, there, the journey is a terrible one indeed, but you have made it. That's the important thing. We will look after you now. You are very precious to us.' He motioned to the guards. 'Take him to the tower, and fetch Tweezel – we don't want to lose this brave young apprentice.'

The guards hurried off. Varis walked stiffly over to Parsimmon. 'I don't like it,' she said tersely. 'That is the third group that has been ambushed. We can't afford these losses, High Master. The Guardians of Night are growing stronger. I sense their hand in this.'

Parsimmon nodded sagely. 'You may be right, my dear Varis, but that is a matter for the Free Glades Council and our masters back in Old Undertown. Tonight, let us salute our brave young friends here, and talk no more about it.' He turned to Magda, Stob and Rook. 'Go now,' he said. 'Supper awaits you in the upper refectory.'

As he turned to follow the others, Rook caught sight of Xanth, half-hidden in shadow, his face ashen, his lips thin and bloodless. Their eyes met. 'Xanth,' Rook called out.

Xanth looked away shiftily.

'Xanth!' he called, louder. 'Come and join us.'

'Leave him,' said Magda. 'He knows where to find us if he wants to. He must be feeling pretty miserable at the moment – wishing his leg would mend, wishing he was us.'

Rook nodded. But though he knew Magda's words made sense, he didn't believe them. It wasn't sadness or regret, or even envy, that he had seen in Xanth's eyes.

It was guilt.

CHAPTER THIRTEEN

THE FOUNDRY GLADE

After a wild storm that raged through the night and late into the morning, the weather had finally cleared around noon. In its wake came fluffy white clouds which scudded across the gleaming sky, seemingly buffing it up as they passed, while down in the Deepwoods, it looked to Rook as if every leaf of every tree glinting in the shafts of silvery sunlight had been freshly waxed and polished.

He steered his skycraft expertly round a great lullabee tree and on low over the jagged thickets of razorthorn beyond, his heart racing with the excitement of it all. He could hardly believe it; so soon after his final flight as an apprentice, here he was with the great Varis Lodd and his best friend, Knuckle the slaughterer, flying through the Deepwoods on a raid!

Darting swiftly and silently through the dappled light of the forest, the three skycraft – the *Windhawk*,

Woodwasp and *Stormhornet* – kept low in amongst the towering trees. Rook's hands played with the rope-handles, coaxing the skycraft this way and that, up, down and from side to side. It was difficult flying, demanding his constant attention.

Every so often – more from nervousness than necessity – his hand would pat his flight-suit, checking that all the unfamiliar items of flight paraphernalia were still in place: his grappling-hook and a coil of rope; his water-flask and – Sky and Earth forbid he should ever need it – his lufwood box, courtesy of Tweezel the spindlebug, with its bandages, potions and salves. On his chest he wore his telescope, compass and scales; at his side, his knife, Felix's ornate sword and, slung through a leather loop on his belt, one of the small razor-sharp axes carried by all skycraft pilots. Now he felt like a real librarian knight, equipped for any eventuality. If only the uneasy fluttering in the pit of his stomach would go away.

Dense forest ahead, Varis Lodd signalled to her two companions and, as one, she, Knuckle and Rook soared up high into the air and burst through the forest canopy.

Rook gasped with wonder as the tops of the trees spread out all round him. He stood up in his carved stirrups and, with the warm wind in his face, gave the *Stormhornet* full sail. The skycraft trembled for a moment before throwing Rook back in his seat and leaping forwards.

Stay low, Varis signalled silently. It was important that they weren't spotted.

Rook pulled at the looped pinner-rope. The

Stormhornet swooped down obediently, and skimmed over the top of the watery forest, just like its yellow and red striped namesake that Rook had watched skimming the surface of the lake. How long ago that seemed now. Rook's thoughts began to wander.

He went back to the previous evening when, just as he had been about to turn in for the night, he had heard a light *tap-tap-tap* on the door of his sleeping cabin. It was Varis Lodd, her flight-suit fully equipped and a loaded crossbow at her side.

'Come with me,' she'd said. 'I have something to tell you.'

He had followed her down to Lake Landing, where Knuckle was waiting for them, twirling his lasso. Below them, the dark, turbulent waters of the lake surged and swelled; above, dark, boiling clouds tumbled in from the west. Varis had turned to address them both, her face sombre, her voice trembling with emotion. Rook had never seen her so upset.

'Your young friend, Xanth, approached me this evening,' she began. 'Since his injury, he's made himself useful by, shall we say, gathering information.'

'Spying?' said Rook, faintly shocked.

'You could call it that,' said Varis. 'In our war against the Guardians of Night and their allies, we need to be vigilant. Anyway, young Xanth had disturbing news.'

'Go on,' said Knuckle, letting the rope fall.

'Slavery has returned to the Foundry Glade.'

Knuckle shook his head bitterly. 'Will the Foundry Master never learn?'

Varis put a hand on the slaughterer's shoulder. 'Like you, Knuckle here lost his family to slave-takers,' she said to Rook. 'We thought we'd taught them and their goblin allies a lesson last time we raided, but it seems they're back to their old ways.'

'These slaves,' Rook remembered asking, 'are they slaughterers? Gnokgoblins?'

And Varis had shaken her head. 'They're ...' She had turned to Rook, her eyes filled with a mixture of anger and sorrow.

'What?'

'Banderbears, Rook,' she had said. 'Banderbears.'

The *Stormhornet* juddered as the memory of Varis's words made his fingers tremble. Banderbears! How could anyone enslave such mighty, noble creatures? The very thought of it made his blood boil. Yet that is exactly what Hemuel Spume, the Foundry Master, had done. What kind of an individual must he be to keep bander-bears in chains?

'You love banderbears as much as I do,' Varis had said. 'I knew you'd want to help rescue them.'

'And Stob and Magda?' Rook had asked.

Varis had shaken her head. 'The fewer the better on this sort of raid,' she'd said. 'And you two are the best flyers in the Free Glades.' She had paused. 'If you're with me, we'll need to fly into the Foundry Glade under the noses of Spume's goblin guards, release the bander-bears from their slave-hut and get away before we're discovered. It won't be easy.'

'We're with you,' Rook and Knuckle had both replied at the same time. It was then that Rook had first felt the fluttering in the pit of his stomach.

As the sun darkened and slid down towards the horizon, Rook felt the wind getting up once again. He trimmed his nether-sail and tightened his grip on the pinner-rope. Although the stiffening breeze would make their flight much quicker, it also made the skycraft skittish and wilful.

There it is, Knuckle signalled, signing the words quickly, thumb and forefinger coming together to form the unmistakable signal for *glade*.

Rook looked ahead. Far in the distance, he saw thick black smoke belching out of the tall foundry chimneys and staining the sky above with a dark smudge of filth. His heart missed a beat.

Tack down! Varis signalled urgently, the *Windhawk* darting back down into the forest.

Rook shifted the rope-handles, bringing in the nether-sail and letting out the loft-sail while, at the same time, shifting his balance in the stirrups and slowly raising the pinner-rope. He chewed his lower lip nervously. The *Stormhornet* dipped forwards and dived down through a break in the canopy of leaves. As it entered the protected shadowy half-light below, the wind immediately dropped and the delicate craft trembled and dropped. Rook's fingers darted round the ropes and levers. The skycraft righted itself and swooped on.

Varis flashed a quick signal – *Outstanding flying, Rook!* – and smiled.

Rook found himself grinning broadly, then flushed as blood rushed to his cheeks. He felt suddenly so proud that the great Varis Lodd should compliment him on his skill. He patted the *Stormhornet*'s prow. 'Well done,' he whispered.

The light began to fail as they journeyed on. Time and again, Rook had to swerve to avoid the trees and their great spreading branches which suddenly loomed up out of the gloom before him. Just ahead, he noticed an oily yellow light glowing between the trees.

Follow me, both of you, Varis signalled over her shoulder.

She flew steeply upwards and landed silently on the broad branch of a huge, ancient ironwood tree. Rook and Knuckle came down beside her. Varis signalled to the other two and pointed towards the source of the light ahead.

Rook unhooked his telescope and raised it to one eye. Peering through the overhanging branches, he studied the glade before him. Vast, sick, scarred, the clearing was like a great festering scab on the surface of the forest. It stank of sulphur, of pitch, of molten metal. It echoed to the percussive sounds of hammers clanking and wood being chopped; to the roar of the furnaces, to the whipcrack and barked commands of the goblin task-masters, and the synchronized crunch of spades and pickaxes digging deep down into the ore-pits.

Beneath it all, like a dark mournful choir, was the sonorous groaning of the labouring goblins. Rook trembled. What those poor, miserable creatures must be suffering to produce so terrible a sound . . .

Just then, cutting across the cacophony of heavy toil and deep despair, there came a long creak, followed by a dull thud. Rook swung his telescope round. A cloud of dust, billowing up at the edge of the great clearing, settled to reveal the latest felled tree lying on the ground where it had crashed down. Already, a team of goblins were scampering over its immense trunk, stripping it bare.

The beautiful forest! Rook signed.

Hemuel Spume, Varis signalled back, and drew a finger in a cutting motion across her throat.

Rook nodded.

Apart from the ash-heaps and earth-mounds which erupted from the bare earth like boils, there were also mountains of stripped logs, each one serving one of the foundries. Teams of stooped, bony goblins – their hooded robes tattered and their skin ingrained with years of grime – were removing the logs, one after the other, and dragging them with ropes and hooks towards

THE FOUNDRY GLADE

the foundries, and inside. Work-team after work-team, log after log – yet the tall, unsteady heaps never diminished in size, for no sooner was one tree-trunk removed, than it was replaced by another, newly felled, as the cancerous glade ate further and further into the surrounding forest.

Where are the banderbears? Rook signed, shoulders shrugging.

Knuckle tapped him on the shoulder and pointed.

A banderbear! Heart beating excitedly, Rook shifted his telescope round and homed in on the banderbear emerging from the bottom of the tall, bulbous foundry to his left. The sight shocked him to the marrow in his bones.

The poor creature, with its jutting ribs and sunken cheeks, looked half-starved. Its mossy fur was singed and lustre-less; all over its hunched, cringing body, bare patches of red-raw skin showed through. Shackled at its ankles and wrists, the bander-bear was being escorted by two goblins, each one armed with a long, heavy stick – which they used often and with obvious relish. The banderbear took the blows, nei-ther reacting nor resisting. And as Rook watched it slowly shuffling on towards the slave-hut, he realized that the creature's spirit had been crushed.

Five more banderbears appeared, one from each of the foundries. If anything, their condition was even worse than the first. None of them seemed able to move any faster, despite the vicious blows and angry oaths that rained down on them. One was limping badly. Another had an angry weeping burn on its shoulder. All of them were shivering violently, freezing cold now after their hours spent in the blistering heat.

Rook turned to Varis. Her eyes were blazing; her jaw clenched and unclenched. She gripped her crossbow in both hands. Rook – his pity turned to anger – felt for the dagger and sword at his belt, then looked back at the glade.

As he watched, the banderbears were led into the slave-hut and chained to the central pillars within. Despite the roof, the open-sided building offered no shelter from the biting wind, and the six shackled banderbears huddled together for warmth at the centre of the mattress of filthy straw, mute and trembling, their eyes lifeless and dull.

Rook scanned the glade through the telescope. It seemed almost empty. With the banderbears no longer stoking the furnaces, the foundries had fallen idle, and the last of the ore-workers, tree-fellers and log-pullers were disappearing inside their long-huts. The goblin guards followed them, laughing and joking.

Soon the only remaining individual to be seen was a lone guard, asleep at his post at the top of a look-out turret. An eerie silence descended over the Foundry Glade. Varis turned to Knuckle and Rook, her face suddenly serious.

Remember, she signalled. *We fly in, we fly out. No sound.*

Rook and Knuckle nodded.

Come, Varis motioned, raising her sails and flying up from the branch. *We're going in!*

As the *Stormhornet* rose up from the ironwood bough, the fluttering in Rook's stomach disappeared. Keeping close to Varis and Knuckle, he steered the skycraft through the last fringes of foliage, and into the desolation beyond. A calm, icy fury wrapped itself around him as he flew silently into the evil glade.

Varis and Rook swooped down over rows of long-huts and covered wagons, and hovered beside the banderbear slave-hut. At the same time Knuckle darted up towards the top of the look-out turret where the goblin guard was snoring noisily, winding the end of his lasso round his hand as he went. Rook watched as the slaughterer swooped in close and tossed the lasso. The spinning loop disappeared from view behind the parapet. Rook held his breath.

The next instant the lasso reappeared, a large bunch of keys held in its tightened knot.
The sleeping guard had not stirred.

Well done, Rook signalled, awestruck by the slaughterer's skill.

Rook, Varis motioned urgently. *Here*. She threw one end of her tether-rope to him.

Rook caught it and secured it round the neck of the stormhornet figurehead, binding the two skycraft together.

Varis swung her feet round and dropped down from the skycraft to the ground.

The *Windhawk* bucked and lurched, tugging on its tether-rope. The *Stormhornet* reared up in protest. Rook shifted in the stirrups and gripped the straining pinner-rope grimly as he struggled to keep both skycraft balanced and ready for their getaway.

'Steady,' he whispered softly. 'Easy does it.'

Knuckle swooped down close to the ground, tossing the bunch of keys to Varis as he flew past, before soaring back into the sky to keep a look-out for goblin guards. Inside the slave-hut, Varis set to work.

There was a *click*, followed by the clatter of falling chains. Then a second *click* . . .

Above Rook's head, Knuckle was slowly circling, keeping his eyes peeled.

With a final click and clatter, the last shackle tumbled to the ground.

'Go,' Rook heard Varis urge the banderbears. 'You're free!'

The poor creatures seemed dazed at first, but slowly – agonizingly slowly it seemed to Rook, who was battling to keep Varis's skycraft steady – first one, then another banderbear, climbed gingerly to its feet. Slowly, cautiously, they emerged into the glade, followed by Varis.

'Make for the tree-line,' Varis urged the shuffling giants desperately.

At the same moment a muffled sound came from the line of covered wagons. Rook spun round, his heart racing. Something was wrong.

All at once, the tilderskin tarpaulins flew back to reveal row after row of armed goblin guards.

'It's a trap!' Knuckle bellowed down. 'Get out of there!'

As one, the long-haired goblins drew their jagged-tooth rapiers and, with a bloodcurdling battle-cry, sprang forward.

The banderbears threw back their heads, bared their fangs and howled. Rearing up on their huge hind-quarters they lunged forwards, blind with rage, their great, sabre-like claws slashing through the air, desperate to get to the safety and freedom of the forest.

'Leave the banderbears!' shouted a voice. 'It's Lodd that we're after!'

Rook turned back to see a thin, wizened individual with long, coiling side-whiskers, a pinched face and darting eyes standing alone on one of the wagons. It was Hemuel Spume himself! He banged his heavy staff noisily on the boards. *'Get me Varis Lodd!'* he screeched.

Varis let fly a bolt from her crossbow. It thudded into the side of the wagon, inches from Spume's head. The Foundry Master squealed and leaped for cover. Varis raced over to where Rook held her skycraft ready. The goblins advanced, brandishing swords and a heavily weighted net. The tether-rope leaped from Rook's hand just as Varis clasped the *Windhawk*'s prow, and the sky-craft lurched to the side, throwing her to the ground.

Rook groaned. From behind him there came a loud howl of derision from the gleeful goblins.

'We've got her now!' one of them shouted.

'The great Varis Lodd!' taunted another.

'That'll teach her to— *Unnkh!*'

Rook looked round quickly. One of the goblin guards was lying on the ground, a bolt sticking out of his chest. Two more were crouched down beside him. Above them, crossbow raised, was Knuckle, coming in for another attack.

'Unnkh!' A second goblin crashed to the ground, blood pouring from the bolt in his back.

'Rook,' came Varis's voice, as she struggled awkwardly to her feet. 'Rook, help me.'

Rook reached forwards and grabbed the *Windhawk*'s

tether-rope, wrapping it back round his hand. The weight of the second skycraft almost pulled his arm out of its socket. Wincing with pain, he held on grimly. 'Get on board!' he shouted at Varis. 'Quick!'

The guards screeched with rage and surged forwards. *'Imbeciles!'* Hemuel Spume's furious voice echoed.

Knuckle swooped down a third time. The crossbow bolt hissed.

Rook let go of the tether-rope as Varis grabbed hold of the *Windhawk*. It juddered and listed dangerously to one side as she pulled herself up and swung her leg over the seat. The next moment she realigned the sails and the skycraft soared up into the air. Rook's heart sang as he flew up beside her, scattering goblins on every side. 'We made it!' he cried out.

'Thanks to you, Rook,' Varis called back. 'You saved my life.'

Knuckle swooped in towards them. 'Let's get out of here!' he shouted.

'But what about the banderbears?' Rook shouted back. 'Did they escape?'

'See for yourself!' Knuckle pointed down to his left.

There, at the edge of the clearing, the banderbears were disappearing into the forest. The goblin guards hung nervously back from the huge beasts, while Spume shouted curses and waved his stick furiously at the skycraft.

'Shoot them down!' he screamed.

'Scatter!' barked Varis, as a flurry of crossbow bolts hurtled past them.

Rook broke away. He curved down low over the huts and away from the goblins, following the retreating banderbears towards the cover of the tree-line.

The last banderbear turned. It was the one Rook had seen emerging first from the foundries – a massive female, with odd black markings circling one eye and crossing her snout.

Their eyes met.

'Watch out!' shouted Varis, somewhere above him.

Rook glanced back to see a goblin crouched down on one knee beside one of the empty wagons. He had a long-bow in his hands, trained on the motionless banderbear's heart.

With a twang and a hiss the arrow shot through the air. Rook swerved in front of the banderbear.

There was a soft thud as the arrow embedded itself in Rook's shoulder. The pain shot down his arm. He cried out.

'Hold on!' screamed Varis, swooping down towards him.

The goblin was reaching into his quiver for a second arrow when the bolt from Knuckle's crossbow struck him between the eyes. He slumped to the ground. Varis reached over and made a grab for Rook's dangling tether-rope. Shoulders braced, she dragged the wounded young apprentice towards the safety of the tree-line.

'Wuh-wuh!' the banderbear cried after them, and lumbered into the forest.

'It's going to be all right,' Varis called breathlessly

across to Rook. Grunting with effort, she fastened the end of the tether-rope to the *Windhawk* figurehead, then realigned the sails. As they dodged in and out of the tall trees, several crossbow bolts fell short behind them. 'Hold on, Rook!' she cried. 'Hold on!'

'Hold on,' Rook murmured. 'Hold on . . .' He leaned forwards and wrapped his arms around the *Stormhornet*'s elegant neck. All round him, the sea of silver-green treetops flashed past in a blur. His eyes closed.

Knuckle flew in close beside them. 'He looks in a bad way,' he shouted into the wind.

'The arrow,' Varis shouted back. 'It will have been poisoned, if I know long-haired goblins. We've got to get him to Lake Landing as quickly as possible. If we don't, he'll die.'

·CHAPTER FOURTEEN·

FEVER

A faint, milky light poured through the grille of the sleeping-cabin door, dimly illuminating the small room and falling across the carved, golden wood of the bed-shelf, where a bony figure with a bandaged shoulder lay sleeping fitfully. Tossing and turning beneath the tilderwool blanket, the hollow-cheeked young librarian knight was drenched in sweat. His legs kicked the blanket back. His eyelids flickered.

Wolves. There were woodwolves all round him, their yellow eyes flashing like bright coals. Howling. Growling. And voices – angry voices, frightened voices – shouting, raging . . .

'No, no,' he whimpered, his arms flailing wildly.

Now he was on his own in the silence of the vast, shadowy forest, overwhelmed with grief. A four-year-old once again, he began sobbing – loudly, uncontrollably, tears welling up in his eyes . . . He was lost and alone – and so, so terribly cold.

It was the old nightmare.

Suddenly, something loomed towards him out of the shadows. Something huge. Something menacing, with glinting teeth and blazing eyes . . .

'There, there,' came a voice.

Rook's eyes fluttered and opened. His shoulder throbbed.

Tweezel was standing above him, a lantern raised in one hand and a cold, damp mist-leaf in the other, which he pressed to Rook's glistening brow. The great spindlebug's glass body seemed to fill the entire cabin.

'Keep fighting, brave master,' he said, his reedy voice hushed with sympathy. 'The fever will soon break.'

He reached across, plumped up Rook's pillow and pulled the blanket back over him. Rook closed his eyes.

When he opened them again, the spindlebug had gone – though the lantern, low and sputtering now, still glimmered from the desk opposite. Rook looked round the small, shadowy cabin with its lufwood panelling and simple carved furniture. From the moment Parsimmon had first shown him to it on his arrival at Lake Landing– now already more than a year since – Rook had felt safe and secure inside the cocoon-like timber cabin.

He stared up at the ceiling, his gaze following the narrow planks of wood into the corners and down the walls. The soft amber light of the flickering lantern was mirrored in the varnished wood. Rook's eyelids grew heavy. The straight lines between the panels twisted and blurred. The dull ache in his shoulder throbbed, sapping his strength and spreading through his body like a slow-burning forest fire.

His eyes closed. His breathing became low and regular as Rook fell into a deep, dreamless sleep. When he woke again, the fever had returned.

One moment he was burning up, his bed-clothes drenched and his skin blistering hot. The next, as if plunged into icy water, he was bitterly cold, huddled up in a tight ball in the middle of the bed-shelf, teeth chattering and body violently shivering.

Noises from outside permeated his dreams. The night cries of the nocturnal Deepwoods creatures, the hushed yet excited chatter of the apprentices hurrying past his door; sometimes the wind howling or rain pounding on the roof, sometimes the turbulent lake slapping and sloshing beneath him – and just once, the distant yodelling cry of a solitary banderbear.

Rook lost all sense of time. Was it night? Was it morning? How long had he lain there, now moaning softly, now thrashing fretfully about, as he fought the goblin poison that coursed through his veins?

'It's all right,' he heard. 'Don't try to speak.'

He slowly opened his eyes. The room swam.

'We've come to say goodbye,' came a soothing voice.

'Goodbye,' Rook repeated, his own voice a low rasping growl.

Before him, two round faces emerged from the shimmering golden shadows. His neck lolled from side to side as he tried to hold their gaze. The effort was too great.

His eyes fluttered shut. A hand clasped his own. It was cool and soft. With one last effort he opened his eyes once again, and there, looking down at him, was Magda. Behind her, Stob.

Rook tried to speak. 'Magda . . .' he whispered, his cracked lips barely moving. His eyes closed.

'Rook,' she whispered back, her own eyes filling with tears, 'Stob and I depart on our treatise-voyages tomorrow . . .' She broke down. 'Oh, Stob!' she cried. 'Do you think he can even hear us?'

'He's a fighter,' came Stob's gruff voice. 'He won't give in – and Tweezel's doing all he can. Come, let's leave him to rest.'

The two apprentices rose to go. 'Fare you well, Rook,' they said softly.

Rook's eyelids flickered. He felt a light kiss brush his fevered brow, the lips cool and dry, and smelled the pine-like scent of Magda's thick hair. His body was impossibly heavy.

There was a click of the catch as the door closed. Rook was alone again.

Night followed day followed night. Time after time, as evening fell and the milky light from outside grew dim, the spindlebug came to light the oil lantern. He bathed Rook and tucked him in; he put droplets of potent medicine under his tongue and applied oily herbal unguents to the angry wound, and bandaged it up with fresh strips of gauzy cloth.

Sometimes Rook would wake to find Tweezel fussing about him attentively; mostly, he would sleep through the spindlebug's tender ministrations.

'Rook, can you hear me?' Rook opened his eyes. He knew that voice. 'It's me, Rook. Xanth.'

'Xanth?' he murmured, and winced as the searing pain in his shoulder shot down his arm.

Xanth winced with him. His face was pale and drawn, and his dark sunken eyes looked more haunted than ever. He pushed his hair off his forehead and took a step closer to the bed. The lantern in his hand swung to and fro. 'I came to say goodbye, Rook,' he told him.

'Goodbye,' said Rook dully. 'You as well? Magda and Stob . . .'

Xanth laughed bitterly. 'Magda and Stob! How I envy them,' he said. He put his head in his hands. 'There'll be no treatise-voyage for me, Rook. My path leads away from the Deepwoods and back to New Sanctaphrax.'

'New Sanctaphrax?' Rook struggled to clear his head. Was this really happening – or was it all just a fever-induced dream? 'But why, Xanth?' he murmured.

The apprentice turned away, and Rook could just make out his hunched-up shoulders in the shadows. When he spoke, his voice was low and thick with emotion. 'You have been a good friend to me, Rook Barkwater,' he said. 'When others ignored me or made fun of me, you were there, defending me, encouraging me . . .' He hesitated. 'And I have repaid your friendship with lies and treachery.'

'But . . . but how?' asked Rook. 'I don't understand.'

'I am a spy, Rook,' said Xanth. 'I serve Orbix Xaxis, the Most High Guardian of Night. The librarian knights are my enemies.' His eyes narrowed. 'Why do you suppose no groups of apprentices have reached Lake Landing since I arrived? Because I betrayed them, Rook. And how did the goblins at the Foundry Glade know that Varis Lodd was going to pay them a visit, eh? Because I set the trap, that's how. Oh, but Rook . . .' Xanth turned and kneeled beside the bed-shelf. He clasped Rook's hand, his own hands trembling with emotion. 'If I'd known that you – one of only two people I have ever called friend – were going to be on that raid, I would have warned you, Rook. You've got to believe me!'

Rook pulled his hand away. 'You? You betrayed us?' he said weakly. 'After all we've been through together . . . Oh, Xanth, how could you?'

'Because I belong to the Guardians of Night,' said Xanth bitterly. 'They own me, body and soul. Try as I might, there is nothing I can do to get away from them. Don't you think I'd rather stay out here in the beautiful Deepwoods if I could?' He shook his head. 'It's not

possible, Rook. I have gone too far. I have done too much damage. I cannot stay.' He sighed. 'I am as much a prisoner of the Tower of Night as my friend Cowlquape, to whom I must now return.'

Rook stared at Xanth through lowered lids. His temples pounded, his vision was blurred.

'It was Cowlquape who first filled my head with stories of the Deepwoods, and his adventures with Twig the sky pirate,' Xanth continued. 'Because of him, I had to come out here and see it all for myself – even if the only way I could do so was by becoming a spy.' He looked down miserably. 'I suppose I have betrayed you both.'

Rook turned away. The fever was returning with a savage intensity. Xanth? A traitor? He didn't want it to be true. Xanth was his friend. A deep sorrow mingled with the pain of his wound, and the shadows grew darker round his bed-shelf. Rook closed his eyes and let the fever wash over him.

Xanth looked down at the sleeping youth, and pulled the blanket up around his shoulders. 'Farewell, Rook,' he said. 'I doubt our paths will cross again.'

He stepped back, turned and crossed the floor to the circular doorway. He did not look back.

Fingers shaking with excitement, Rook dressed himself in the stiff, green leather flight-suit, secured the belt with its dagger and axe, and Felix's sword round his waist, swung the small backpack of provisions onto his shoulder and set off down the tower staircase. Although he was still a little weak, and his face was pale and drawn, with Tweezel's help he had managed to beat the goblin's poison. Now – two weeks after Stob and Magda had set forth – it was his turn to set off on his treatise-voyage.

Varis Lodd was at the foot of the tower to greet him. 'There were occasions,' she confessed, 'when I wondered if this day would ever come. But you made it, Rook. I'm so proud of you. And now, Librarian Knight,' she said, nodding towards the tethered *Stormhornet* which bobbed about at the back of the stage, 'your skycraft awaits.'

Rook stepped forward, wrapped his arms round the smooth wooden neck of the delicate creature and rubbed his cheek against its head. '*Stormhornet*,' he whispered. 'At last.'

Just then, from behind Rook, there came the sound of footsteps. He turned to see two figures approaching. One was Parsimmon, his tattered gown flapping. The other – tall, bearded and dressed in a black tunic – raised

his hand in greeting. Rook's gaze fell
upon the white crescent moon
emblazoned across his chest.

'The Professor of Darkness!'
he said, surprised.

'He arrived while you were
ill, Rook, bearing news of
Xanth's treachery,' said Varis.
'A bad business all round.'

Rook nodded sadly. The two
figures drew close. The professor took Rook's hand and
shook it firmly.

'Can this truly be the callow
youth who once tended the

buoyant lecterns on the Blackwood Bridge?' he said. His
eyes twinkled. 'I can scarce believe it. Here you are,
about to embark upon your treatise-voyage. We have
groomed and trained you. Now it is your chance to
contribute to the great canon of work already stored in
the Storm Chamber Library. You have done well, Rook.
Very well.' His expression clouded over. 'Though you
have hardly been helped by a certain friend, I believe.'

'Xanth?' Rook faltered. It all seemed like a dream to
him now, Xanth's confession and departure. He had
tried to put it out of his mind.

'Xanth Filatine,' the professor said, 'is a traitor!'

'A traitor,' Rook whispered softly. 'He . . . he came to
my cabin when I was ill, just before he . . . disappeared.'

'Fled back to his evil master, the Most High Guardian

of Night,' said the professor, shaking his head.

'Many good apprentices and their loyal guides have been lost because of that young wood-viper,' said Parsimmon sadly. 'But come, we are not here to talk of such things. Xanth Filatine will pay for his treachery soon enough. Now we shall celebrate the beginning of your great adventure, Master Rook.'

Rook nodded, but said nothing. He couldn't think of his former friend without a heavy ache of sadness forming in his chest. He tried to push the feelings away. Today was a day for celebration, not sadness, he told himself.

Varis stepped forwards. 'Rook, it is time for you to leave,' she said softly. As she spoke, the low sun rose up above the trees. She shielded her eyes with her hand. 'May your treatise-voyage be safe and fruitful.'

Rook looked up. He saw the professor, Parsimmon and Varis all smiling at him kindly. He smiled back. Beside him, the sails of the waiting *Stormhornet* fluttered in the light breeze.

Parsimmon nodded towards it. 'She's raring to go,' he said.

'And so am I!' said Rook, hardly daring to believe that the moment of his departure had finally arrived.

Checking his laden flight-suit and tightening the straps of his backpack, he turned away. He untethered the small craft and leaped into its saddle. The skittish *Stormhornet* bucked and lurched.

'Good luck, Rook!' said Varis.

Rook adjusted his goggles, took hold of the upper sail-rope and raised the loft-sail.

'Earth and Sky be with you, lad,' said the Professor of Darkness solemnly.

The nether-sail billowed out beneath him. The *Stormhornet* juddered upwards and hovered impatiently.

'And may you return successful from your treatise-voyage!' cried Parsimmon. 'Fare you well, Master Rook.'

'Fare you well!' shouted the others.

Rook pulled down sharply on the pinner-rope. The sails filled. The flight-weights swung. And Rook's heart soared as the skycraft flew steeply up into the cool, bright morning air.

'Farewell!' he shouted back.

Below him, Lake Landing quickly became smaller and smaller, and the three figures standing upon it – their arms waving and their faces turned up to the sky – grew so tiny, he could no longer see which was which.

'This is it,' Rook murmured happily, the fluttering back in the pit of his stomach as he skimmed the tops of the trees fringing the far side of the lake. Before him lay

the vast, mysterious Deepwoods, rippling in the wind like an endless ocean.

As the leaves rushed past him in a blur of greens and blues, he imagined his completed treatise nestling beside Varis Lodd's masterpiece, on the seventeenth buoyant lectern of the Blackwood Bridge, deep down in the Great Storm Chamber Library. He could see the bound leather volume with its gold lettering: *An Eyewitness Account of the Mythical Great Convocation of Banderbears* . . .

Far off in the distance a flock of snowbirds wheeled up from the trees below and soared into the air, their white wings flashing brightly in the rising sun. Farther still, a rotsucker flapped across the hazy sky. Beneath it, clutched in its claws, the egg-shaped silhouette of a great caterbird cocoon swung back and forth.

Rook frowned as the immensity of the Deepwoods – and his task – struck him. He pushed all thoughts of the completed treatise from his head; this was no time for daydreaming. He had come a long way since that morning when Fenbrus Lodd, the High Librarian, had announced that he, Rook Barkwater, had been selected as a librarian knight elect. He had journeyed to Lake Landing. He had built the *Stormhornet* with his very own hands and learned to fly. Now, finally, he was setting forth on his treatise-voyage.

'At last,' he whispered, as he swooped down low over the leafy canopy. 'Now it all begins.'

CHAPTER FIFTEEN

WUMERU

Rain was falling as Rook stirred from his sleep. He was high up on a colossal branch of an ironwood tree. The canopy he'd rigged up in the branches above his head, before turning in the night before, had kept the worst of it off him. But his hammock and sleeping bag were damp, and would have to be aired later if they were not to end up mildewy and rank.

Rubbing the sleep from his eyes, Rook got up. He yawned. He stretched. His breath came in wispy twists of mist. Shivering with cold, he lit the hanging copper stove, placed a small saucepan of water on its flickering, blue flame and went to check on the *Stormhornet*, tethered securely to one of the huge branch's offshoots.

'I trust you are well rested,' he whispered to the little skycraft. 'And not too wet to fly.'

He ran his fingers over its smooth, varnished prow, over each and every knotted rope and tethered sail. A shower of tiny raindrops glistened as they fell from the silky material. He tightened the flight-weights. He greased the levers . . . Everything seemed to be in order.

Behind him, the water started to bubble.

Rook hurriedly rolled up his hammock and sleeping bag, folded away the waterproof canopy, and secured all

three behind the *Stormhornet's* saddle. Then, back at the hanging-stove, he removed the saucepan from the heat, carefully capped the flame and poured the boiling water into a mug. He stirred in three spoonfuls of dried charlock leaves and wrapped his hands around the piping-hot mug.

He looked out from his vantage point on the ironwood branch. The rain had all but stopped and the forest was beginning to fill with birdsong as the sheltering cheepwits and songteals emerged from their shadowy perches and leafy hollows. He heard a rustle of leaves, and looked down to see a family of woodfowl foraging for food far below.

Rook sighed. He, too, should eat – yet all he had left from the previous evening was a thick slice of baked loafsap, wrapped up neatly in a broad, waxy leaf.

As he opened the small green package, the musty odour of the pappy fruit filled his nostrils and, although his stomach rumbled hungrily, his appetite completely disappeared. 'Stop being so fussy,' he told himself, biting off a large chunk and chewing gamely.

He knew from Varis Lodd's woodlore lessons that the edible loafsap was both nutritious and filling. He knew also that it was unwise to set out on an empty stomach ... But the fruit was so unpalatable! Rook took a sip of the charlock tea and swallowed the whole mouthful of claggy pulp in one go. He grimaced. 'That'll do,' he said, tossing the half-eaten slice away. It landed with a soft *thud*. The woodfowl darted off in all directions, squawking with alarm.

Rook climbed to his feet, packed up the precious stove and untethered the *Stormhornet*. The sunlight pierced the thinning clouds and, shining down through the gaps in the trees, gleamed on the burnished green leather of his flight-suit. In the weeks that had passed since he'd first set off from Lake Landing the stiffness of the leather had gone, and the flight-suit had moulded itself to the shape of his body, fitting him now like an extra layer of skin.

Rook glanced round one last time to make sure he hadn't left anything behind. Then, shifting the sails and weights, and tugging on the pinner-rope, he launched the *Stormhornet* into the dappled, forest air. 'Perhaps today,' he whispered, just as he whispered every morning. His breath came in soft, puffy clouds. 'Perhaps today will be the day.'

Three months Rook had been journeying; three long, tiring months. By day, when not foraging for food and water, he would scour the Deepwoods for any tell-tale signs of a banderbear – a woven sleeping nest, branches newly stripped of fruit, or heavy footprints in the soft, boggy places beside woodland springs. By night, he would rest up in the tall branches of the great trees, lying in his hammock and listening out for the curious yodelling of the creatures.

So far, he had heard them on three occasions. Each time, when he had risen the following morning, he had set off in the direction of their calls, his heart beating with anticipation. He still recalled the intense thrill he had felt in the Foundry Glade, when he saw those first banderbears. Now, he couldn't wait to see more – free, healthy banderbears in their own habitat – but as the sun had moved across the sky and the shadows had lengthened, Rook had, each time, been forced to concede defeat. The elusive creatures were proving far more difficult to locate than he could ever have imagined.

Yet his journey had not consisted only of disappointments. There had been triumphs, too, along the way; achievements, discoveries – each one faithfully recorded in his treatise-log in his small, neat handwriting, and illustrated with detailed pictures and diagrams.

Today I came across deep, tell-tale scratches in the bark of an ancient lufwood tree where a banderbear had sharpened its claws. Some scratches looked fresh, others were covered with green moss, suggesting that the tree is a regular scratching-post. I am greatly encouraged.

Four days he had camped high up at the top of a neighbouring lufwood, keeping constant watch. No

banderbear had appeared. On the morning of the fifth
day he had packed up and, with a heavy heart, set off
once more. That evening, having set up his hanging-
stove and hammock, the *Stormhornet* tethered safely to a
branch, he sharpened his stub of leadwood and recorded
a new entry.

After abandoning the scratching-post, I flew all day. Just
before midnight I spotted a small mound of oakgourd-peel
beneath one of the tall, bell-shaped trees – surely the sign of a
recently passing banderbear. My hopes were confirmed by the
presence of a banderbear footprint. I sat up most of the night
in a nearby ironwood tree, hoping the creature might return
for the few fruits remaining.

But again, the creature let him down. His journey continued bright and early the following morning.

The days began to blur into one another, with weeks
turning to months, and still no sight of the shy, retiring
creatures. Rook grew lean, yet strong; his senses razor-
sharp. He got to know the Deepwoods increasingly well.
Its changing moods. Its shifting character. The plants
and trees and creatures that dwelt in its dark, mysterious
shadows. What to eat and what to shun. Its sounds. Its
smells. And at night, he would record the fauna and
flora he encountered.

Today I discovered a woodbee hive. I was successful in
smoking the swarm out with a branch of smouldering lullabee
wood. The honey was delicious in the charlock tea, turning it
a surprising blue colour, like the sky before a storm . . .

I have just witnessed a halitoad stunning a fromp with a
blast of its noxious breath, seizing the creature in its long,

sticky tongue and swallowing it whole. The hideous beast then swelled to twice its size, before letting go a revolting belch. I stayed well hidden for an hour . . .

It has been a week of violent thunderstorms. Once, while I was taking shelter, an ironwood close by was struck by lightning and burst into flames. I heard an odd 'popping' sound, which turned out to be the tree's seedpods bursting open, and scattering their seeds far and wide. 'In death there is life,' as Tweezel would say. By Earth and Sky, the Deepwoods is a strange and wonderful place . . .

Today I witnessed something truly horrendous. Drawn towards it by the sound of desperate screeching and squealing, I came down in the air to see the unexpected spectacle of a hammelhorn, apparently in flight! Around its middle, gripping tightly, was a tarry-vine – the long, green, parasitic sidekick of the terrible bloodoak. The creature struggled, wriggled and writhed, but the tarry-vine was too strong for it. And when a second vine came to its aid, coiling round the hapless hammelhorn's neck, the struggle was over. The vines pulled the creature through the forest towards the gaping maw at the top of the bloodoak's thick, rubbery trunk. The ring of razor-sharp mandibles clattered loudly. With a sudden flick, the two vines released the hammelhorn, which dropped head-first down inside the great flesh-eating tree. The creature's muffled cries fell still. The vines turned red . . .

Rook lay the stubby twig of leadwood down. He was sitting cross-legged, high up in a spreading lullabee tree, his stove blazing, his hammock hanging absolutely motionless in the still, humid air. The moon shone down on his pinched, anxious-looking face. The hammelhorn had reminded him of his fellow apprentice.

'Are you safe, Stob?' he whispered. 'Have you found your coppertrees yet? Has your treatise work begun? Or . . .' He swallowed, and fought hard against the choking emotion which rose in his throat.

Just then, from above, Rook heard a soft scratching sound. He turned and looked up. Some way to his left, secured to the knobbly bark on the underside of a thick, horizontal branch, was what looked like a bunch of pine-grapes. Only the colour was different, parchment brown rather than purple – that, and the increasingly insistent scratching.

As Rook watched, one of the spherical pods split and opened. A small, bedraggled insect appeared at the papery entrance, crawled up onto the top of the branch and flapped its wings in the warm, moonlit air. The matted fur on its body dried and fluffed up. The wings thrummed softly as they stiffened.

'A woodmoth,' Rook whispered. 'First the hammel-horn. Now a woodmoth.' He smiled as memories of Magda flooded his thoughts.

Soon the first woodmoth was joined by others as the rest of the pods cracked open, one after the other, and the hatchlings emerged. Then, as the last of them climbed onto the branch and flapped its wings, the whole armada took to the air and fluttered through the shafts of moonlight.

Rook stared, unblinking, as the woodmoths performed their strange, exuberant dance – dipping and
diving like autumn leaves in a blustery wind, their
bright, iridescent wings sparkling like marsh-gems and
black diamonds in the silvery light.

How Magda would have loved the sight, he
thought, and smiled. Perhaps she already had.
Perhaps her treatise was already finished... His face
clouded over.

While his own was yet to begin.

Rook was thirsty. His canteen was empty and, apart
from a little sticky juice which he'd sucked from the
chewy flesh of a woodpear that morning, not a drop of
liquid had passed his lips for almost two days. His head
was throbbing. His vision was becoming blurred. His
concentration strayed . . .

'*Wooah*, there!' he cried out, as the nether-sail snagged
on a spike-bush branch and tipped the skycraft off-balance. Shocked by his own carelessness, Rook realigned
the sails and raised the flight-weights. The *Stormhornet*
lurched away from the danger unharmed and up above
the tops of the trees. But Rook knew he'd had a lucky
escape. He must find water before he blacked out
completely.

As the sun beat down ferociously, Rook slipped back
beneath the forest canopy and continued through the
dappled trees, keeping low and close to the forest floor.
He knew that sallowdrop trees, with their pale, pearly
fronds, grew near running water, and that clouds of

woodmidges often collected above underground pools – but he saw neither.

His mind was beginning to wander once more when, from his right, there came the unmistakable sound of babbling water. With a sudden burst of energy, Rook manoeuvred the *Stormhornet* skilfully about, swooped down through the air and round the cluster of tall lullabee trees before him.

And there, at the far side of a small, sandy clearing, bursting with lush vegetation, was a spring. It bubbled up from rocks on the side of a slope, trickled over a jutting lip of rock and splashed down into a deep green pool below.

'Thank Sky and Earth,' Rook whispered to the *Stormhornet*. 'At last.'

Yet he did not dare land. Not yet. Beautiful though this welcome oasis looked, he knew it would also be a perilous place, attracting some of the most dangerous Deepwoods creatures there were: rapier-toothed wood-cats, whitecollar wolves and, of course, wig-wigs which, though they themselves never needed to drink, frequented such places to prey on those that did.

Rook brought the skycraft down to land on a sturdy branch high up in one of the ancient lullabees. He put his telescope to his eye and, trying hard to ignore his dry mouth and burning brow, focused in on the spring below him.

As the time passed, several creatures appeared from the surrounding forest to drink at the babbling pool. A small herd of speckled tilder, a family of woodfowl, a solitary woodhog boar, with long curving tusks and small, suspicious eyes. A hover worm flitted over the surface of the water, bowing its head and sipping delicately, as the jets of air expelled from tiny ducts the length of its underbelly hissed softly.

Finally Rook could wait no longer. He tethered the *Stormhornet* securely, scurried down the great bulbous trunk of the lullabee to the ground and, looking all about him, crept towards the bubbling spring.

There, he quickly dropped to his knees, cupped his hands, and drank mouthful after mouthful of the cold, clear water. He felt it coursing down his throat and filling his stomach. Immediately his head stopped pounding and his eyes cleared. He hastily filled his canteen and was about to return to the *Stormhornet* to continue on his way, when something caught his eye.

A footprint.

Rook gasped and, scarcely able to believe his good fortune, crouched down for a better look at the broad marking in the soft, damp sand at the water's edge. Although smaller than the print he had seen beside the oakgourd tree, from the arrangement of pads and claws, there could be no doubt. It was a banderbear footprint. What was more, the impression was sharply defined. It had been made recently.

Bursting with excitement, Rook leaped to his feet and inspected the whole clearing. In amongst the footprints of all the other thirsty creatures were more of the small banderbear tracks. Some were faded and worn, some as fresh as the one at the water's edge – the banderbear must have returned several times to drink over the last few days.

Turning away, he scaled the lullabee tree. 'This is the place,' he confided to the *Stormhornet*. 'We shall wait here for a banderbear to appear, no matter how long it takes.'

Rook stayed awake that night. All round him, the sounds of the night creatures filled the air. Coughing fromps. Squealing quarms. Chattering razorflits . . . As the moon rose, blades of silver light cut through the surrounding trees, and speared the forest floor below. Rook's eyes were growing heavy when all at once, shortly before the dawn, he heard the sharp *crack* of a twig snapping in the shadows beneath him.

How could anything have got so close without me noticing? he wondered. He pointed his telescope down at the place where the noise had come from and adjusted the lens, until every leaf appeared in sharp focus. As he did so, the foliage trembled and abruptly parted, and out of the shadows stepped a tall, stocky creature.

It was a banderbear! Rook held his breath and tried not to tremble. He had finally found a wild banderbear!

The creature was truly magnificent, with bright eyes, sharp white tusks and long, gleaming claws. Though smaller than the banderbears he had seen at the Foundry Glade, it was nevertheless both tall and imposing and, given the half-starved appearance of those sorry

individuals, probably weighed more than them. As it lumbered towards the bubbling pool, its shiny coat gleamed – now dark brown, now pale green.

Rook watched it stoop down at the water's edge, lower its snout and begin lapping at the water. He was so excited, he could hardly breathe. His hands were trembling, his legs were shaking – he had difficulty keeping the telescope focused.

Just then there was a rustling in the leaves. The banderbear looked up, its delicate ears fluttering. It was probably just a fromp swinging through the trees, or a roosting woodfowl shifting position in its sleep. But the banderbear was taking no chances. As Rook watched, spellbound, the banderbear climbed to its feet and melted silently into the surrounding forest.

'Today,' Rook whispered, as he closed his telescope and clipped it back onto his flight-suit. 'Today *is* the day!'

The banderbear returned many times, and as the days passed, Rook observed it closely, keeping detailed notes of its behaviour and writing them up in his treatise-log. He recorded what time of day and night it appeared, and for how long. He documented each movement it made: every scratch, every gesture, every facial expression. And he drew pictures – dozens of them – trying to capture each individual characteristic of the creature: the curve of its tusks, the arch of its eyebrows, the grey mottled markings across its shoulders . . .

Several days into his vigil, Rook decided to track the

banderbear. As it lumbered off into the forest, he slipped the tether-rope of the *Stormhornet* and, keeping at a safe distance, flew after it. He was surprised how fast the creature travelled. Hovering silently up in the air, he watched it stop at a huge, spreading tree, and gorge itself on the dripping blue-black fruit which hung from its branches, before continuing on its way.

An idea formed in Rook's head. He swooped down and, keeping close to the tree, plucked an armful of the fruit. Then, having returned to the spring, he laid it out in small pile beside the bubbling water.

For the rest of the day – using a makeshift catapult to keep other visiting creatures away from the fruit – Rook made sure that the pile remained untouched, ready for the banderbear's return. When the banderbear did return – several hours later – it sniffed at the fruit suspiciously. Its ears fluttered wildly. It sniffed again.

'Go on,' Rook whispered urgently. The next moment he beamed broadly as the banderbear picked up the first piece of fruit in its sharp, yet delicate claws and bit into it. Gleaming red syrup dribbled down over its chin, and Rook noted the blissful expression – the drooping mouth and dreamy eyes – that passed across the creature's face.

When the first fruit was gone, it started on the second, then the third. It didn't stop until every last morsel had gone.

The following day Rook laid out more fruit. This time, however, when the banderbear came to eat it, he was crouched down on the ground behind the lullabee tree, watching it. Up so close, he realized just how enormous the creature was. Although clearly little more than an adolescent, it was already more than twice his own height and ten times as heavy, and from its shorter tusks and mane, Rook could tell it was a female.

It was four nights later when Rook plucked up the courage to take the next step. The banderbear returned at midnight to discover that no fruit had been left out for her. She sniffed round disappointedly and, with a low guttural groan, made do with a drink of spring water.

Heart in his mouth, Rook tentatively emerged from his hiding place. He held a piece of fruit in his trembling hands. The banderbear spun round, eyes wide and ears fluttering. For a terrible moment Rook thought she was about to turn on her heels and gallop back into the forest, never to return again now that her drinking place had been discovered.

'It's for you,' Rook whispered, holding his hands out.

The banderbear hesitated. She looked at the fruit, she looked at Rook, she looked back at the fruit – and something in her expression seemed to change, as if she had made the connection between the two.

Her right arm rose, and her great taloned paw fluttered by her chest. Rook held his breath. With her gaze fixed on Rook's eyes, the banderbear reached forwards and gingerly seized the fruit from his hand.

'Wuh-wuh,' she murmured.

Little by little as the weeks passed, Rook gained the confidence of the banderbear, until – by the time the ironwood's leaves were beginning to turn colour and fall – the two of them had become close. They foraged for food side by side. They watched out for one another. And at night Rook would help the banderbear build one of the great sleeping nests in the dense thickets of the forest floor. Intricately woven and expertly concealed, lined with moss and soft grasses and protected by branches of thornbush, the nests were spectacular constructions, and Rook could only marvel at the banderbear's skill.

He recorded everything in his treatise-log: the edible fruit and roots they ate, the building of the sleeping nests, the creature's finely tuned senses which enabled her to detect food, water, shelter, changes in the weather, danger ... And as the banderbear became more and more familiar to him, he began also to understand her language.

Rook had often read the part in Varis Lodd's seminal treatise – *A Study of Banderbears' Behaviour in Their Natural Habitat* – where she had outlined the possible meaning of some of the banderbears' more simple grunts and gestures. Varis had had to rely on observations taken from a distance. Now, closer to a banderbear in the wild than any librarian had come before, Rook was able to take the understanding of the subtle intricacies of their communication further.

As they journeyed together, he slowly began to master the banderbear's language and, though the creature appeared amused by his own attempts to communicate, they seemed to understand one another well enough. Rook loved the rough beauty of the language in which a tilt of the head or the shrug of the shoulders could convey so much.

'Wuh-wurreh-wum,' she told him, her head down and jaw jutting. *I am hungry, but step lightly for the air trembles.* (Beware, there is danger close by.)

'Weg-wuh-wurr,' she would growl, with one shoulder higher than the other and her ears flat against her head. *It is late, the new moon is a scythe, not a shield.* (I am anxious about proceeding further in the darkness.)

Even the creature's name was beautiful. Wumeru. *She with chipped tusk who walks in moonlight.*

Rook had never been so happy as he was now, spending every day and every night with the banderbear. He was becoming quite fluent now, and – he realized with a guilty jolt – so wrapped up in his life with Wumeru that he was neglecting his treatise-log. Still, there was always tomorrow. Or maybe the next day . . .

They were seated on the ground one late afternoon, sharing a supper of oaksaps and pinenuts. The dappled sunlight was golden orange. Wumeru turned towards him.

'Wuh-wurrah-wugh,' she grunted, and swept an arm round through the air. *The oaksap is sweet, the sun warms my body.*

'Wuh-wuh-wulloh,' Rook replied and cupped his hands together. *The pinenuts are good, my nose is fat.*

Wumeru's eyes crinkled with amusement. She leaned forwards, her face coming close to Rook's.

'What?' he said. 'Did I say something funny? I simply meant that their smell is . . .'

The banderbear covered her mouth with her paw. He should be quiet. She touched Rook's chest and her own in turn, then, concentrating hard, she uttered a single word; low, faltering, but unmistakeable – a word, Rook knew *he* had never given her.

'Fr-uh-nz.'

Rook trembled. *Friends?* Where could she possibly have heard the word before?

Some nights later Rook woke with a start and looked

up. The sky was clear and the moon was almost full. It shone down brightly on the forest, casting the treescape in silver and black. He climbed out of his hammock, high in the lufwood tree and looked down. Wumeru's sleeping nest was empty.

'Wumeru?' he called. 'Wuh-wurrah.' *Where are you?*

There was no reply. Rook walked along the branch to where the *Stormhornet* was tethered, and looked out across the dark forest.

And there she was, standing on a rocky incline not twenty strides away, motionless – apart from her fluttering ears – and staring intently at the distant horizon. Rook smiled and was about to call out his greetings, when he heard something that took his breath away.

Echoing across the night sky, came the yodelled cry of a distant banderbear. It was the first one Rook had heard since meeting his companion.

There it was again!

Wumeru! Rook recognized the name being called, and he felt a tingle run down his spine. The second banderbear was not merely calling out to any other; it was addressing his friend by name. *'Wumeru, Wumeru . . .'*

Over such a long distance, with the wind whipping half of the sounds away, it was difficult for Rook to make out exactly what the banderbear was saying. But he had no difficulty translating Wumeru's reply.

'Wuh-wuh. Wurruhma!' *I come, the full moon shines brightly; it is time at last.*

'Wumeru,' Rook called down, suddenly gripped by an incredible sense of expectation. 'What's happening?'

But Wumeru ignored him. She had ears only for the other banderbear. From the distance, the yodelling continued.

'What's that?' Rook murmured. *Make haste . . . The Valley of a Thousand Echoes awaits . . .*

Shaking with excitement, he fumbled for his treatise-log and leadwood stub, and began to write the words down in a trembling hand. 'Valley of a Thousand Echoes,' he whispered. 'Wumeru,' he called and looked down. *'Wumeru?'*

He fell still. The rock where the banderbear had been standing was empty. His friend had gone.

Wumeru had abandoned him.

·CHAPTER SIXTEEN·

THE GREAT CONVOCATION

Rook quickly gathered his belongings together and stowed them on the *Stormhornet*. He couldn't lose the banderbear. Not now. He was all fingers and thumbs unhooking the hanging-stove and, as he was folding it away, the flame-cap came loose and tumbled down into the darkness below.

'Blast,' Rook muttered breathlessly. It would take for ever to find the thing again, and meanwhile Wumeru was getting farther and farther away ... There was no choice. He would have to leave it.

Jumping astride the *Stormhornet*, he raised the sails, realigned the hanging weights and pulled on the pinner-rope, all in one smooth movement. The skycraft leaped from the branch, darted through the overhead canopy of leaves and soared off into the clear night sky beyond.

'Where are you?' Rook murmured, as he searched the forest floor ahead of him. The yodelling of the other banderbear had come from somewhere to the west – and that was where Rook set his course. Earth and Sky willing, Wumeru had headed off in the same direction. 'Where *are* you?' he whispered. 'You must be down there somewhere.'

Just then the trees began to thin beneath him, and Rook spotted his banderbear friend striding purposefully ahead. She was walking in an unwavering straight line, as if hypnotized. And as Rook caught up, he could hear her murmuring under her breath. The same sound, over and over – a word he didn't recognize.

'*Worrah, worrah . . .*'

'Not too close, now,' Rook whispered, patting the *Stormhornet*'s prow and raising the loft-sail. 'We don't want her to spot us. Not yet. Not until we know where she's heading.'

The *Stormhornet* slowed to little more than a hover, and Rook steered it gently to his right, where the forest was thicker and he could follow Wumeru without her seeing him. As he darted on from tree to tree – keeping to the shadows and taking care not to lose sight of her, even for a moment – Rook's hopes began to rise.

'The Valley of a Thousand Echoes,' he murmured. 'Is it too much to hope . . . ? Could it be . . . ? Could it actually be the place where the banderbears assemble? The Great Convocation?' He ran his fingers down the long, curved neck of the *Stormhornet*. 'Is that where Wumeru is heading?'

For several hours he flew on, keeping Wumeru constantly in sight. The other banderbear's yodel must certainly have been important; Rook had never seen his friend so determined. Usually she would amble slowly through the forest, leaving no trace of her passing. Tonight, as she blundered tirelessly on, she left a trail of trampled undergrowth and broken branches in her wake.

Suddenly the air was splintered with the sound of banderbears – seven or possibly eight of them, far ahead, yodelling in unison. '*Worrah, worrah, worrah, worrah . . . whoo!*'

It was the same sound that Wumeru herself had been chanting under her breath, and as the chorus of voices faded away, their calls were answered by others. Dozens of them. From every direction.

'*Worrah, worrah . . . whoo.*'

And from his right, louder than all the others, came Wumeru's answering cry. '*Worrah-whoo!*'

Rook's hopes soared. Surely it must be the convocation. What other reason could there be for so many of these solitary creatures to be gathering together in the forest?

'*Worrah-whoo!*' Wumeru called a second time, and Rook looked across to see that she had stopped some way up ahead on the crest of a rocky outcrop. Motionless save for her twitching ears, against the slate-grey sky the banderbear looked like a great boulder with a pair of cheepwits fluttering at its top.

Rook flew closer. 'Wumeru,' he called out. 'Wumeru, it's me.'

He landed the *Stormhornet* on the flat slab of rock just

behind her and jumped down. The banderbear turned to face him.

'Wuh-wuh,' said Rook, holding his open hand to his chest. *I woke alone. You abandoned me.* He sighed and touched his ear, then pointed down to the ground. 'Wurrah-wuh.' *Your parting words were silent, I followed you here.*

'Wuh!' grunted Wumeru, and sliced her claws down through the air like a great sword. Her eyes blazed. Her lips curled back, revealing her gleaming tusks and glinting fangs.

Nothing had prepared Rook for this. It was as if he were suddenly a stranger to her.

'But—' he began, his hands open in a gesture of supplication.

The banderbear let out a low, menacing growl that rose from the back of her throat. Could this strange, fearsome creature truly be gentle Wumeru, his friend? Never before had he heard her sound so full of rage. She lunged forwards and swiped at the air, her fangs bared.

'Wuh-wuh!' *No further! It is forbidden for you to follow my path!*

Rook took a step backwards, his hands still raised defensively. 'I'm sorry, Wumeru,' he said. 'I meant no harm.'

The banderbear grunted, turned and disappeared back into the trees. Rook watched her leave, a painful lump forming in his throat.

'What now?' he whispered, as he climbed back on to the *Stormhornet* and took to the air. As if in response, the yodelling voices echoed back.

'Worrah, worrah, worrah . . . whoo!'

Rook trembled. The banderbears were closer than ever. How could he resist their call? Yet dare he go on? If Wumeru discovered that he had followed her, there was no knowing what she would do. Then again, he could not leave. Not now. Not having come so far . . .

The yodelling grew louder. The ululating chanting rose and fell in waves.

Rook's mind was made up. Ever since he'd first picked up Varis Lodd's treatise in the library, he'd dreamed of this. He was a librarian knight, and this was the moment to prove it. He brought the *Stormhornet* down low, and landed on the sturdy branch of an iron-wood tree. He tied up the tether-rope tightly and scrambled down.

Keeping to the shadows, he passed the rocky out-crop where Wumeru had been standing and went on through the trees, following her trail of flattened undergrowth. Then, stepping cautiously ahead, he found himself on a high, jutting ledge which looked out over a bowl-shaped valley. At the very edge grew a tree – its roots clinging to the great fissured blocks of rock, its long, thick trunk curving out at an angle above the yawning chasm below.

Rook ran to the tree, climbed up and inched himself along its curved trunk out above the valley. All around him the low sound of chanting grew louder and louder . . .

'Sky above and Earth below!' he gasped as the scene abruptly opened up beneath him. 'There must be hundreds of them! *Thousands!*'

Rook shook his head in disbelief. Everywhere he looked there were banderbears gently swaying in the moonlit valley, each one calling out the same mesmeric chant: low, guttural, building at the back of the throat, only to soften into a long, tuneless moan. Some were alone, some in pairs, some in groups which grew bigger and smaller as the great lumbering creatures endlessly came together and drifted apart. Little by little, the chanting became synchronized, until the entire gathering was calling as one. The tree beneath him seemed to vibrate with the resonant booming.

'This is it,' Rook breathed. 'The Great Convocation of the Banderbears. I've *found* it.'

Gripping on tightly to the sloping tree-trunk with his legs, Rook rummaged in his backpack for the treatise-log and stub of leadwood. He had to capture every detail of the wondrous scene for his treatise.

Large groups constantly breaking up and reforming, he hurriedly scribbled down. *As if in some huge dance that every banderbear seems instinctively to understand . . . And the chanting – incredible, booming, resonant . . .*

From below him, the chanting grew in intensity. The tree trembled. And there was something else . . .

Hard to catch at first, but, yes, there it was again. Mingling with the overall chant, yet somehow distinct from it, single banderbear calls were rising and falling against the background throb. Rook could just make out snippets.

I, from the lone ridges of the twin peaks . . . I, from the high reaches of the mist-canyons . . . I from the sombre shadows of the ironwood groves . . . from the lullabee forests . . . from the deepest, darkest nightwoods . . .

Rook listened, transfixed, as the individual voices came and went.

The snow-passes of the lofty Edgelands . . . The fur-damp swampwood glades . . . The turbulent thornwoods . . .

It was as if he were listening to a map; a map of the Deepwoods in banderbear song. They were singing of their homes and, as their chants intermingled, they became one great shared description of all the places the banderbears knew. Below him was a living library, as rich as the concealed library of Old Undertown itself, kept alive in the memories of the banderbears and shared amongst them at this Great Convocation. Head swimming with the beauty of it all, Rook swooned . . .

The treatise-log slipped from his grasp. He lunged forwards desperately as it tumbled down, missed it, and lost his balance in the process. Suddenly, to his horror, he found himself falling from the tree – legs pedalling and arms flailing, as he hurtled towards the ground below.

The next instant he struck the hard, packed earth with a loud *thud*. Everything went black.

*

Rook's head spun. He felt a warm wind blowing across his body and sensed a bright light shining in his face.

Where am I? he wondered.

His head throbbed. Everything was blurred and shifting. His breath came in short, sharp gasps and, as his head began to clear, he let out a cry of surprise.

All around him was a towering circle of banderbears, glaring down at him furiously. Their huge tusks glinted, and there was fire in their eyes – yet not one of them made a sound. The Valley of a Thousand Echoes was in absolute silence.

Rook swallowed hard.

All at once a mountainous male banderbear with jet-black fur and thick, curling tusks, leaned down. Rook saw the great paws swoop down towards him and felt the cold, hard claws clutch his body. The creature's fur smelled musty, its breath sour.

'*Aaargh!*' he cried out, his stomach turning somersaults, as he was lifted into the air.

'Wuh!' the banderbear roared. *How dare you!* And Rook felt the great creature's indignation and rage trembling through its entire body as it gripped him tightly and cried out, 'Wuh-wurrah!'

He had never seen a banderbear so angry, so . . . so *vengeful*. Stiff with terror, Rook was rigid in the creature's grip, as the other banderbears took up the same, blood-chilling cry, until the whole valley echoed with their roaring.

'Wuh-wug-wurrugh?' the great black banderbear boomed out above the tumult. *Who dares to steal the echoes of our valley and trespass on our sacred convocation?*

'Wuh,' Rook replied, his voice low and trembling. 'Wuh-woor.' Wriggling to free

his hand from the banderbear's crushing hold, he touched his heart lightly. *I come as a friend. I mean no harm.*

The banderbear hesitated. His startled eyes inspected Rook's face as if to say, *Who is this creature that knows the secret language of banderbears?*

Rook sensed the creature's confusion. 'Wurrah-wegga-weeg,' he said, his voice thin and warbling. *I am a friend of banderbears. She with chipped tusk who walks in moonlight and I have walked the same path.*

The banderbear's dark brow knitted and he looked round at the crowd of banderbears, scouring the sea of angry faces for Wumeru. When he caught sight of her, his eyes narrowed. 'Wuh?' he growled menacingly. *Is this true?*

Wumeru stepped forwards, head bowed and fluttering ears drooping. 'Wuh-wurroo. Wuh,' she said, without looking up. *My friend of the forest trail has brought only shame upon our companionship.* She turned away.

'Wumeru!' cried Rook desperately. 'Wumeru, *please*! I—'

The black banderbear raised him up high in the air once more. His grip tightened, his eyes grew cold. With Rook held aloft, he bellowed out loudly.

You, who have listened to words meant only for banderbears' ears, have committed the greatest sacrilege of all. Thief of our songs. Stealer of our chant. You must die!

Just then a solitary cry abruptly rose up above the gathering frenzy. 'WUH!' *STOP!*

The great black banderbear instantly froze. He looked round. Rook – dizzy and befuddled – could just make out a banderbear pushing through the crowd towards them.

'Wuh?' *Who speaks?* the black banderbear demanded.

The female stopped before him. 'Wuh-wuh. Wurra-woogh-weerlah,' she grunted, touching first her shoulder, then her chest. *I, Wuralo, who suffered much in the Foundry Glade. I know this one. He saved my life.*

With a start, Rook looked at the banderbear. She was heavier now than when he'd last seen her, and her coat was thick and glossy. But from her markings – the curious black line which circled one eye and crossed her snout – Rook knew that this was indeed the banderbear he had saved from the goblin's arrow.

The black banderbear hesitated. The female turned to

303

him and pressed her large, furry face up close to his.

'Wura-wuh-wurl!' *My heart cries for mercy. Spare him.* 'Wuh-wuh. Weera-weeg.' *I thought he fell to the poison-sticks. But he lives.*

'Wurra-woor-wuh,' Rook explained quietly. *I was indeed struck, yet my heart beat on. I carry the scar.* He opened the front of his shirt and pulled it back.

The black banderbear traced a claw delicately over the knot of healed skin. 'Wuh-wuh. Wurrh!' he cried. *It is true. You bear the mark of the poison-sticks.* He placed Rook down on the ground. *You risked your life for one of us?*

'Wuh-wurrel-lurragoom,' Rook explained. *I have loved banderbears from my first breath and will defend them to my last. I gladly risked my life in the Foundry Glade!*

The gathering of banderbears grunted softly and muttered beneath their breath.

'Wuh-wulla,' said Rook. *Believe me, I am a true friend of the banderbears!*

All at once, rising up above the general babble, a voice rang out. 'Wuh-wuh!'

Out of the corner of his eye Rook noticed a third banderbear approaching. She was old and stooped, her fur, silvery grey.

'Wurra-looma-weera-wuh,' she said, her voice cracked and frail. *I sense he speaks the truth. He is a friend of banderbears.*

The crowd, intrigued, turned and watched her walk up to the young intruder. A low murmur spread out through the ranks of attendant banderbears. The old, grey female leaned forwards and wrapped her great arms around him.

Rook smelled the warm, mossy scent of her fur, and felt her heart beating close to his. The sensation was extraordinary. He felt safe, protected, and found himself wishing that this comforting hug would never end.

At last, she released him and stared into his face, her dark eyes crinkling with affection. 'Wuh-wulla, wegeeral,' she whispered. *Friends until the last shadow of that final night.*

The surrounding banderbears grunted their approval. The black banderbear raised his great head. 'Wura-galuh-weer!' he proclaimed. *Gala, oldest of the old and wisest of the wise, has spoken. This is good enough for me.* 'Wuh-wurra-lowagh.' *We welcome you. You shall be Uralowa – he who took the poison-stick.*

The crowd of banderbears roared all the louder. Rook quivered with happiness. 'Thank you,' he said. 'Wuh!'

The black banderbear nodded earnestly. 'Wurrah-woor. Wuh-wuh.' *You are special. No others have witnessed our Great Convocation – save for one . . .*

Just then Rook sensed a movement behind him. He glanced back over his shoulder to see the great crowd of banderbears parting. A long, narrow passageway opened up between them and, as Rook peered down it, he saw a figure emerge from the other end and walk slowly towards him.

'What the—?' Rook whispered.

He stared at the figure, with his stooped shoulders and long, white matted hair and beard. His jerkin, trousers and boots were made from wild-leather, and stitched together with strips of thong. His threadbare hammelhornskin waistcoat flapped in the rising breeze. As he approached, Rook looked into the newcomer's face.

The skin was leathery and lined, every crease and every scar hinting at an episode in the stranger's past. But the eyes! Rook had never seen such eyes before. Marsh-gem green and crystal clear, they twinkled brightly in the moonlight, like the eyes of someone much younger.

He stopped in front of Rook. 'I believe this is yours,' he said.

Rook looked down to see his treatise-log clutched in the stranger's calloused hands. He reached out and took it gratefully. 'Th-thank you,' he said. 'But . . . who am I thanking?'

'My name is Twig,' came the reply. 'I used to be a sky pirate captain, a defender of Old Sanctaphrax. Now, like you, I am a friend of banderbears . . .' He smiled warmly, his eyes twinkling brighter than ever. 'Perhaps you've heard of me?'

CHAPTER SEVENTEEN

THE CAPTAIN'S
TALE

It was a glorious morning, Rook. I'll never forget it. A morning which, after the ferocious storm which had raged throughout the previous night, many of us thought we'd never live to see.' Twig's eyes became dreamy; he shook his head slowly from side to side. 'I can scarcely believe that fifty years has gone by since then.'

Rook looked at Twig thoughtfully. Fifty years. That would make the sky pirate captain nearly seventy years old. So much had changed in the Edge in that time.

'The old days – oh, the stories I could tell you of the old days,' Twig was saying. 'But that is for another time. With the passing through of the great Mother Storm, the waters of the Edge were rejuvenated and the glistening air that morning pulsated with hope for a bright new future.'

Rook nodded. From the texts and scrolls in the Great

Storm Chamber Library he had learned about the birth of the new rock and the subsequent founding of New Sanctaphrax. And how Vox Verlix had taken over from the first High Academe – an obscure youth, not up to the task – and built the foundations of what was later to become the Tower of Night. Now, speaking to this strange, ragged old sky pirate captain, the dry accounts he'd read came vividly to life.

'My work there finally done,' Twig continued, 'I boarded the *Skyraider* and prepared to depart, for it was time for me to set a course for the Deepwoods, to collect those faithful members of my crew who were still at Riverrise, awaiting my return.'

'Riverrise,' Rook breathed.

'Aye, lad,' said Twig. 'That was where I'd left them. There was Maugin – the best stone pilot that ever tended a flight-rock. And Woodfish, a waterwaif with powers of hearing that were truly remarkable, even by waif standards. And Goom.' He smiled and looked round. 'Dear Goom, the bravest banderbear a captain could wish for. I promised them faithfully that I would return for them – and, on that fine morning so long ago, that was just what I intended to do.'

Rook and Twig were sitting side by side on the log of a fallen tree at the edge of the valley clearing. Before them, the Great Convocation was in full sway, with the vast crowd of banderbears mingling and chanting and sharing their knowledge of the Deepwoods, one with the other, as the first blush of dawn tinged the edges of the sky.

'I had a good crew to aid me in my quest,' Twig went on. 'I can see their faces almost as clearly as I can see yours now. There was Bogwitt, the flat-head goblin – just the type to have fighting by your side in a battle. And Tarp Hammelherd, the slaughterer I had rescued from the drinking dens of Undertown. And my quartermaster, Wingnut Sleet – his face hideously scarred by a lightning bolt.' He sighed. 'And the others. Teasel the mobgnome – good with ropes, I recall. Stile, the cook, with his twisted spine and awkward walk. Old Jervis, the gnok-goblin – not much use, but a cheery soul. And, of course, Grimlock. Who could forget Grimlock!'

'Grimlock?' said Rook.

'A giant of a brogtroll,' said Twig. 'Not the sharpest arrow in the quiver, perhaps, but strong as a team of hammelhorns.' He smiled to himself. 'Anyway . . . Where was I? Ah, yes. Pausing only to bid farewell to the Most High Academe and wish him luck, we set forth, with the wind in our sails and hope in our hearts.' He turned to Rook, his eyes twinkling brightly. 'I can still remember how warm upon my back the sun was, as we soared off over the Mire and on towards the Deepwoods.' He smiled broadly. 'And how high my spirits flew . . . Riverrise! I was returning to Riverrise!'

Rook smiled with him, caught up in the enthusiasm of the old sky pirate captain.

'Of course,' Twig continued, his expression becoming serious, 'I knew it wasn't going to be easy. The voyage would be long and difficult. But I also knew that I needed to trust both my instincts and my senses.

Woodfish would be calling to me. I had to keep my mind focused so that I could follow his call.'

Twig's eyes had a faraway look in them as he went on. 'We sailed for several months,' he said, 'soon leaving woodtroll villages and goblin settlements far behind. Each morning I scanned the horizon and cleared my mind. All about us, the great Deepwoods stretched as far as the eye could see; dark, forbidding and endless. But we kept going, ever onwards, into the deepest, darkest places where the forest was so dense that no light penetrated. The air above it boiled with black, turbulent clouds and festering storms which buffeted and battered the *Skyraider* until it was as ragged and frayed as our nerves.'

Twig fell still. He put his head in his hands.

'What happened?' asked Rook. 'Did you hear the waif's call? Did you find Riverrise?'

Twig looked up, his eyes glistening. 'Nothing,' he said. 'I heard nothing but the taunting howl of the storms as they ripped through our sails – and the mocking silence of the Deepwoods during the lulls between.' He shivered. 'And worse . . .'

'Worse?' said Rook.

'The scream of Wingnut Sleet as a storm swept him from the quarterdeck, the last gasps of poor old Jervis, crushed by a falling section of rigging, and the incoherent babble of Teasel as he lost his mind and jumped from the mast into the blackness below. Stile, the old cook, died soon afterwards – of a broken heart, or so my crew said. And yet still we continued, because I couldn't give up, Rook. I couldn't. None of us could. You must understand.'

Rook patted the old sky pirate's tattered sleeve. 'I understand,' he whispered.

'Do you?' said Twig. 'Do you? Sixteen years we sailed, Rook. Sixteen long, lonely, frightening years, growing ragged, weary . . . defeated. And it was all my fault. I couldn't find my way back to Riverrise.' He looked up, his eyes shot with pain. 'I failed them, Rook. My crew . . . My friends . . .'

'You did your best,' said Rook.

'But my best just wasn't good enough,' said Twig bitterly. He shook his head. 'At last there were just four of us left. Bogwitt, Tarp Hammelherd, Grimlock – and myself. Flying the sky ship without a stone pilot had been difficult enough before, but now, with so few hands on board, it was all but impossible. To continue our search for Riverrise I needed to take on extra crew. So I turned back and set a course for a place I'd heard talked of in the woodtroll villages and rundown goblin hamlets we had passed through on our travels – a place that was said to be a beacon of hope in the darkness of the Deepwoods, offering a welcome to the weary and a haven to the lost—'

'The Free Glades!' Rook exclaimed. 'You visited the Free Glades!'

'That we did,' said Twig. 'New Undertown was no more than a collection of lufwood cabins back then, and the woodtroll villages were only just being established. But we did indeed find a welcome, at the Lake Landing Academy, from a young librarian by the name of Parsimmon—'

'Parsimmon,' Rook broke in excitedly. 'He's still there. Except he's the High Master now. He taught *me*.'

'Then you had a wise teacher, young Rook,' said Twig. 'I remember that evening well. We limped into the Free Glades and moored up at the Landing Tower. Caused a bit of a commotion, we did.' He smiled at the memory. 'I suppose we must have looked quite a sight to those young librarians, Parsimmon amongst them, who greeted us. Our clothes were no better than rags, and the poor old *Skyraider*'s hull was pitted and scarred, its sails in tatters. But they gathered round us and gawped, open-mouthed, until Parsimmon stepped forward and introduced himself.

'He said we looked as if we could do with a good meal and rest, and that we must dine with them in their refectory; and that he wouldn't take no for an answer! It was over supper – tilder stew and oakapple cider, as I recall – that we heard the terrible news, and realized why they were so surprised to see us.'

'What news?' asked Rook.

'Why, news of stone-sickness, of course,' said Twig. 'Parsimmon told me all about it. Both league ships and sky pirate ships were dropping out of the sky like stones, he said. Not a single flight from Old Sanctaphrax had reached the Free Glades for more than a year.

'The sickness had, it seemed, spread out from the stricken New Sanctaphrax rock. It was highly contagious, travelling from sky ship to sky ship like wild-fire. As the flight-rock of one sky ship crumbled, so the crew had to find work on another – infecting the flight-rock of the new ship as they did so. "The First Age of Flight was at an end" – those were his very words, and as I heard them I realized the awful truth.

'Though we had come to the Free Glades in desperate need of more crew-members, I could not risk taking anyone on board who might be contaminated. We had only escaped until then because we'd been out in the furthest parts of the Deepwoods for so long. I leaped up from the table, hurried back to the *Skyraider*, and departed at once.

'I called the crew together as soon as we'd left the Free Glades safely behind, and explained our situation. Tarp clapped me on the back, Bogwitt shook my hand and Grimlock almost broke my ribs with a great banderbear-hug. They all agreed they would stay with me in my search, even though, with just the four of us, it would be backbreaking work. Dear brave fellows, they were,' he said wistfully. 'Long gone now, of course.'

Twig looked into the distance for a long time, saying nothing. At last Rook asked, 'What happened?'

Twig's face grew sad. 'It was a stupid thing really. But deadly. You see, we needed provisions. So, not daring to venture into villages or settlements for fear of contamination, we scavenged in the Deepwoods themselves – for tilder and woodhog meat, fruits and roots we could dry or pickle, and twenty barrels of water which Grimlock, being so strong, managed to collect in a single afternoon.'

He shook his head miserably. 'It was the water which was to seal our fate, for poor, stupid Grimlock – Sky rest him – ignored that most important Deepwoods law of all. *Never drink from a still pool.* Grimlock had filled every single barrel with the same tainted water . . . But it was *my* fault, not his!' he said, his eyes blazing. 'I was the captain. I should have checked; I should have known . . .

'Before long, all of us had gone down with blackwater fever. I staved it off a while longer than the rest, but soon I too was held in its terrible grip. I vomited till my stomach was empty. I lost consciousness. How many days and nights I lay there on the deck, while the *Skyraider* drifted on across the Deepwoods unchecked, I will never know. Tossing and turning as the fever raged on, burning up one moment, shivering with bitter cold the next.'

Rook nodded sympathetically. He knew only too well how terrible a raging fever could be.

'It was daybreak when I finally came round. I sat up, my head spinning groggily, my stomach grumbling. A

cold, damp mist swirled through the air. It clung to my clothes, my hair, my skin, and had covered every surface of the *Skyraider* with a fine coating of slippery wetness. I struggled to my feet, looked around.

'There were no trees beneath us now, only rock; a vast, greasy-grey expanse, broken up into broad, flat slabs with deep cracks between them. I knew at once where I was, and my heart filled with dread. The Edgelands; an eerie wasteland of mists and nightmares.

'It was in the Edgelands, many years before, that I had come face to face with a horror I can scarcely bring myself to share with you. For me, you see, Rook, the Edgelands hold a particular terror, for it was there that I met the gloamglozer – and lived to tell the tale.'

Rook gasped. 'The gloamglozer! But how? When . . . ?'

'One day I'll tell you the whole story,' said Twig. 'But suffice to say, I survived, and vowed never to return to that accursed place. Yet, as fate would have it, it was to the Edgelands that the poor, battered old *Skyraider* had carried me. I looked around.' Twig's eyes grew sad. 'The *Skyraider* seemed deserted. My crew! Where were they? I hadn't seen or heard any of them since wakening. I called out, but there was no reply. I left the helm and dashed to the fore-deck. And . . . and there they were. All three of them . . .

'Oh, Rook,' he groaned. 'They were dead. Bogwitt. Tarp Hammelherd. Even poor Grimlock, great, powerful brogtroll that he was, had proved no match for black-water fever . . .' His voice faltered. 'Th-their bodies were sprawled out on the cold, wet deck, rigid in their death throes – arms reaching out, faces twisted with fear and horror. Each one of them had died a terrible death . . .' He swallowed hard. 'I performed the funeral rituals as best I could. It was the least I could do for a fine, loyal crew who had served me and the *Skyraider* so well . . .'

He fell still, and Rook watched as the tall, rugged sky pirate captain wiped a tear from his eyes. A lump formed in his own throat.

'You see, Rook, I had finally failed. There was nothing for it . . .' Twig took a deep breath. 'Sailing back to the Deepwoods was not an option. I could never have sailed the *Skyraider* single-handed,' he said. 'And so I tethered her to a great rocky outcrop that jutted out from the cliff-face, like some crouching demon, black against the sunrise, and left.'

'You mean, the *Skyraider* is still there!' gasped Rook.

'Aye, lad,' said Twig. 'If she hasn't rotted away or succumbed to stone-sickness in the meantime, then she *is* still there. A fine drizzle was falling the morning I bade her farewell. Despite what she'd been through, she looked magnificent, floating above that barren waste-land, a cruel reminder of all that had been lost.' He paused. 'The last sky ship . . .' Again Twig fell silent until – with a small sigh – he continued. 'Three days it took me to cross the treacherous Edgelands, and another two weeks before I chanced across a band of itinerant cloddertrogs who gave me food, drink and shelter. And I have wandered the Deepwoods ever since.

'Although there is now only me, and I am old and weary, I have never truly given up hope. I look for Riverrise on the horizon every morning when I wake, and I think of the friends I left there every evening when I lay myself down to sleep.

'I see their faces, Rook. Goom. Maugin. Woodfish. They are not angry with me. Sometimes I wish they were. The look of hope and trust in their eyes as they gaze upon me is a thousand times worse. I let them down, Rook,' he said. His voice broke. 'They believed in me . . . My poor, lost friends . . .' He held his head in his hands. 'I'm haunted by memories of all those I have known. The living and the dead, clustered together. Faces I'll never see again. My father. Tuntum. The old Professors of Light and Darkness. Hubble. Spooler. Spiker . . .' He shook his head. 'And the Most High Academe of Sanctaphrax, the way he looked on that morning so long ago when my quest began, as he waved us goodbye . . .'

Rook nodded. The captain's tale had come full circle.

'The excitement, touched with apprehension, in his smile. The pride in his stature. The hope in his eyes. He had once been my apprentice, and now he was the new Most High Academe of Sanctaphrax! How proud I was of him . . .' He shook his head. 'Poor, dear Cowlquape—'

'Cowlquape?' said Rook, startled. 'But I know that name.'

'Yes, Cowlquape Pentephraxis,' said Twig bitterly. 'Murdered long ago by that tyrant, Vox Verlix. I learned the news at Lake Landing.'

With a shock, Xanth's words came back to Rook. *I am as much a prisoner of the Tower of Night as my friend Cowlquape, to whom I must now return.* Despite the fever raging at the time, he was sure that was what Xanth had said. *It was Cowlquape who first filled my head with stories of the Deepwoods, and his adventures with Twig the sky pirate . . .*

Rook leaped to his feet. Twig's friend and Xanth's prisoner were one and the same.

'So young,' Twig was saying, 'and I left him to rebuild Sanctaphrax on his own, to go on this failed quest. If only I had got to Riverrise, I could have returned to help him and perhaps he'd still be alive today.'

'But he is!' shouted Rook, unable to keep quiet a moment longer. A couple of banderbears glanced round curiously in mid yodel. Rook seized Twig by the arms. 'He's alive!' he exclaimed. 'Cowlquape is alive!'

The colour drained from Twig's face. His jaw dropped. 'Alive?' he gasped.

CHAPTER EIGHTEEN

SKYRAIDER

Twig stared at Rook in astonishment. 'But how do you know he's still alive?' he demanded. 'Parsimmon said . . . Let me see . . . Yes, even after all this time, I can remember what he told me. When I asked after Cowlquape the High Academe, he shook his head and said, "Vox Verlix is the Most High Academe now. Cowlquape's name has been stricken from the records. Murder, plain and simple, so it was – though you'll find few in New Sanctaphrax who dare say as much." Those were his very words—'

'But he *is* alive,' said Rook. 'A prisoner in the Tower of Night. A friend . . .' He paused, a sudden twinge of pain in his chest. 'At least, I thought he was my friend,' he murmured. 'He told me that he had seen Cowlquape in the Tower of Night – and that he was very much alive. He even said that Cowlquape spoke to him of you, Twig, and the adventures you'd shared.'

'He did?' said Twig. He was on his feet now, clutching both Rook's hands and staring hard into his eyes. Around them, the banderbears were falling silent in the light of the new dawn, as Twig's excited voice echoed round the valley. 'What is this Tower of Night you speak of?'

Rook shook his head. 'You've been out here for a long time, Captain Twig,' said Rook. 'Many things have changed since you left. Parsimmon told you of Vox Verlix becoming Most High Academe, but that was only the start.'

'Tell me,' said Twig. 'Tell me everything you know!'

Banderbears were crowding about them now, great mountains of fur topped by twitching ears.

'When Vox Verlix became Most High Academe, he ordered the construction of a tall tower on New Sanctaphrax, even as the rock began to crumble with sickness. From what I've heard, and read in the library, he claimed stone-sickness was a sign that the academics had grown soft and complacent and that he, Vox, would do something about it.'

'That Vox!' snarled Twig. 'He was a bad lot when I first knew him as a young apprentice in Old Sanctaphrax.'

'It gets worse,' said Rook. 'You see, Vox founded a sect of Knights Academic, whom he called the Guardians of Night. They enslaved Undertowners and forced them to work, not only on his accursed tower, but on his other great schemes as well. The Great Mire Road. And the Sanctaphrax Forest that props up the sick rock—'

Twig's eyes blazed. 'Slavery?' he said angrily. 'In Undertown?'

'Yes, I know,' said Rook. 'It was a terrible betrayal of the principles which Undertown was founded upon, and there were many who resisted. But the Guardians of Night were brutal. They ensured that the schemes were completed. Those Knights Academic who disagreed with Vox's plans split away and joined with the earth-scholars to found the Librarians Academic.' He paused. 'We live in hiding in the sewers of Undertown . . .'

'Librarians living in sewers.' Twig shook his head sadly. 'That it should have come to this. Vox Verlix the bully, master of New Sanctaphrax!'

'Not quite,' said Rook. 'There's a twist in the tale.'

'Go on,' said Twig.

'Well, Vox didn't realize what a monster he'd created when he established the Guardians of Night. Soon a leader emerged from their ranks, one Orbix Xaxis, who declared himself the  Most High Guardian and took over the Tower of Night. Fearing for his life, Vox fled to an old palace in Undertown. The shrykes seized the opportunity to take full control of the Great Mire Road, and Vox was forced to rely on goblin mercenaries to hold on to what little power he had left in Undertown. These days, if the rumours are true, he spends his entire time alone in his dilapidated palace, too obese to leave his bed-chamber, drinking himself into a stupor each night with bottle after bottle of Oblivion.'

'Well, I, for one, am not in the least sorry for him,' said Twig. 'But tell me, Rook, what more do you know of this Tower of Night in which Cowlquape is held captive?'

Rook sighed. 'I know this much: they say no-one ever escapes from the Tower of Night. It is a vast, impenetrable fortress, with spiked gates and barred windows, rock-slings and harpoons, and great swivel catapults mounted on every jutting gantry. I've only seen it once myself, and that was from a distance, but I've heard stories from librarian knights who have seen it close up. Once, the great Varis Lodd even attacked it with a fleet of skycraft – but they proved no match for the tower's weapons.'

'Skycraft?' Twig said. 'Those little wooden things? I saw them at Lake Landing. No wonder they failed. Why, it'd be like woodmoths attacking a hammelhorn!'

'Armed guards patrol every corner of the tower,' Rook continued without a breath, 'each one trained to kill first and ask questions afterwards. The Tower of Night is impregnable. To attack it from the ground, you'd have to go through Screetown.' He shuddered. 'They say it's inhabited by strange, glistening creatures that constantly change their shape – rubble ghouls, they're called. And rock demons . . . And if you survived all that, there's the Sanctaphrax Forest – a mass of timber scaffolding that holds the rock up. It's infested with rotsuckers and razorflits, terrible creatures by all accounts. No, the only way to attack the tower is by air and, as you say, a skycraft is just too small—'

'But a sky ship isn't,' said Twig.

'A sky ship,' Rook breathed. All around them, the banderbears listened closely.

'Oh, Rook, lad,' said Twig, 'it would be like the old days when I sailed with my father, Cloud Wolf, on raids against those great over-stuffed league ships. The trick was to go in hard and fast, I remember, and be off again with whatever loot they had stashed away before they knew what had hit them. And that's what we shall do, Rook – in the *Skyraider*!'

'The *Skyraider*?' said Rook. 'But Twig, we don't have a crew.'

Just then there was flurry of movement behind them, and Rook turned to see the great female from the Foundry Glade, Wuralo, stepping forward. 'Wuh-wurra Tw-uh-ug-wuh,' she said, and raised a great paw to her chest. *I shall go with you, Captain Twig, friend of banderbears.*

Twig leaned forwards and clapped the great beast on the shoulders. 'Wuh-wuh,' he said, and swept his hand round in a languid arc. *Welcome! Friend!*

A second banderbear – a huge male with a deep scar in his shoulder – stepped up beside her. 'Wuh. Weega. Wuh-wuh.' *I, Weeg, shall also go with you.* 'Wurra-wuh!' He pointed to the skies, touched his scar and raised his head. *I served upon a sky pirate ship long ago, in the old days of which you speak.*

'Wuh-weelaru-waag!' boomed the giant black banderbear. *I know nothing of flight, but I am strong! They call me Rummel: he who is stronger than ironwood.*

Rummel was immediately joined by three others:

Meeru and Loom – twin males who had once tended timber barges – and Molleen, a wiry old female who'd worked long ago as an assistant to a stone pilot. Her lopsided grin revealed several missing teeth and only one chipped tusk.

'Wuh-leela, wuh-rulawah,' she yodelled softly. *I can tend your flight-rock, Captain Twig, if you'll have an old bag of bones like me.*

'Wuh-wuh,' said Twig. *Welcome, Molleen. She, who is a friend of stone.* He took a step backwards, and raised his arms. 'Thank you, friends,' he said. 'From the bottom of my heart, I thank you all. But we have enough volunteers.' He turned to Rook. 'I think we've found our crew.'

'Wuh-wuh!' came an insistent voice, and Rook turned to see Wumeru forcing her way through the crowd of banderbears. *Take me! Take me!*

Twig smiled. 'And what experience of skysailing could you possibly have, my young friend?'

'Wuh,' said Wumeru, her great head hanging low. *None. But my youth is my strength. I am powerful and eager . . .*

'Thank you, young friend,' Twig began, 'but as I said before, we now have enough volunteers—'

'Wuh . . .' Wumeru faltered. She looked at Rook forlornly, imploringly. 'Wuh . . .'

Rook turned to Twig. 'We'll need a ship's cook,' he said. 'And Wumeru is an excellent forager, I can vouch for that.'

'Wumeru?' said Twig. 'You know each other?'

Rook nodded. 'We are friends,' he said.

Twig's face crinkled into a warm smile. 'Friendship with a banderbear is the greatest friendship there is,' he said, pulling a pendant – a discoloured banderbear tooth with a hole through its centre – from inside his hammelhornskin waistcoat, and looking at it thoughtfully for a moment. '*I* know.' He turned to Wumeru. 'Welcome aboard,' he said. 'But I give you due warning. If you should ever serve up pickled tripweed, I shall have you sky-fired!'

Just then the rising sun broke through the high ridge of trees surrounding the valley and shone down brightly on the small group of waiting banderbears. Twig raised his head. 'Come, then, my brave crew,' he announced. 'Let us delay no longer. The *Skyraider* awaits us in the Edgelands.'

A roar of approval resounded all round the Valley of a

Thousand Echoes, and the cheering assembly of banderbears stepped aside to let Twig, Rook and the seven
volunteers pass between them.

'Cowlquape, my young friend,' Twig muttered under
his breath, 'I have lived too long with failure. This is one
quest that will not fail!'

They made excellent progress through the Deepwoods.
Never resting up for longer than an hour at a time, they
travelled by both day and night, orientating themselves
by the sun and the East Star as they headed north –
always north – through the deep, dark forest and on
towards the treacherous Edgelands.

Back in the saddle of the *Stormhornet*, Rook flitted
through the trees above Twig and the banderbears as the
group pressed on. The great creatures were speeding
through the forest silently and swiftly. And unlike
Wumeru who, as if in a trance when she was answering
the call to the Great Convocation, had battered her way
through the undergrowth leaving a trail of destruction
behind her, the banderbears left not a single sign of their
passing. Rook could only marvel at their agility, their
deftness, their stealth.

It struck him as strange that banderbears were such
solitary creatures, for together they worked so

cohesively and well. They each took it in turn to lead, falling back to be replaced by another when they tired; each kept an ear open and an eye out for any potential danger. Intrigued, Rook approached Wumeru during one of the short breaks they took to forage and take their bearings.

'Why *do* you live apart from one another?' he asked. 'You should form tribes. Work together. You're good at it!'

Wumeru looked up, ears fluttering wildly. 'Wuh-wuh. Wurra-waloo.' She slashed her paw through the air and tossed her head. *You are wrong. Banderbears can never live together. Together, we invite the fiercest predators. Alone, we can live longer, for we attract less attention.* She looked about her and smiled, her tusks glinting. 'Weeru-wuh!' *Though to be in a band like this, I almost wouldn't mind dying sooner.*

'Wug-wulla-wuh,' said Twig, approaching, his arms spread wide. *Don't speak of death, young Wumeru – though I am honoured to be facing it with you at my side.*

There was a rustle in the undergrowth and the huge figure of Rummel emerged, his arms full of branches of hyleberries. 'Wuh-wuh!' he grunted. *Quick, eat, for we must keep moving.*

They continued through the forest, Rook scouting ahead on the *Stormhornet* until, with a tug of the pinner-rope, he would twist elegantly round in the air and fly back the way he'd come, checking every inch along the strung-out line of banderbears. Weeg was currently leading the group, the great scar on his shoulder glinting in the half light. Meeru and Loom, walking side by side, followed some way behind. Shortly after them came Wuralo, her mottled shoulders hunched, and after her, the massive Rummel, with his strange, loping gait. There was then a long gap before Rook came to Wumeru who, though young, seemed to have less stamina than the others. Finally, after another long gap, he came to the stragglers: Molleen, who was older and slower than the rest, and Twig himself.

As Rook swooped down, the old sky pirate captain waved to him. Rook waved back, proud of the great captain's acknowledgement. And as he soared back into the air, he heard Twig murmuring words of encouragement to Molleen.

Not long now, old-timer. The flight-rock awaits your expert touch.

Darkness fell, but the banderbears – with Rook still up in the air above them – kept resolutely on. Through the night they journeyed, never easing up on their relentless pace, never making the slightest sound. The moon rose, crossed the sky and set far to their left. The sun came up, heating the damp, spongy earth and sending wisps of mist coiling up into the bright, glittering air.

All at once there came a yodelled cry from up ahead. It was Wuralo, now at the front of the line. *The Edgelands! We have reached the Edgelands!*

Twig yodelled back. *Wait for us. We'll soon be with you.*

Impatient to see the notorious Edgelands for himself, Rook gave full head to the skycraft sails and darted forward. Beneath him, the trees grew fewer and the undergrowth thinned. Silhouetted against the pale yellow sky ahead was Wuralo, looking back. She spotted the approaching skycraft and waved.

Rook signalled back and, shifting the weight-levers and sail-ropes, swooped down towards her. As he flew lower in the sky, the rising mist swirled around him, chilling him instantly to the bone. He landed on a flat slab next to the waiting banderbear, jumped down and wrapped the tether-rope round his hand.

'Wuh-wuh,' Wuralo greeted him. 'Wulloo-weg.' She hugged her arms tightly round her great stomach. *This place fills me with dread.*

Rook nodded as he looked around the broad expanse of greasy, grey rock. He had never been anywhere that made him feel so uneasy. Even the endless tunnels of the Undertown sewers, with their muglumps and vicious piebald rats, were nothing compared with the barren Edgelands.

It howled and sighed as the chill wind swept in from beyond the Edge and whistled along the cracks and gullies in the sprawling granite pavement. It clicked and whispered. It hummed and whined, as though it was alive. A sour, sulphurous odour snatched his breath away. His skin turned to clammy woodturkey-flesh as the coils of fetid mist wrapped themselves around him. The wind plucked at the *Stormhornet*, bobbing weightlessly by his side.

He saw Wumeru emerging from the woods, followed closely by Rummel, with Weeg and the twins – Meeru and Loom – behind him. Like Wuralo, they seemed deeply troubled by the eerie atmosphere of the bleak Edgelands, and clustered together for warmth and safety.

Twig and Molleen reached the desolate rockland last. Twig clapped a hand on Rook's shoulder. Rook could see he was trembling.

'I never thought I'd return to this terrible place,' said Twig, looking around uneasily. 'But somewhere out there the *Skyraider* is waiting for us. Follow me,' he said. 'And search the horizon for the great black demon crag!'

Twig strode off into the mist, with Rook by his side – the skycraft bobbing behind him as he slipped and slid over the treacherous rocks. The group of banderbears, still huddled together, followed close behind.

The wind continued to whine and whisper in Rook's ears and, as he trudged on, trying hard not to listen, wispy fingers of mist seemed to caress his face and stroke his hair.

'*Ugh!*' he groaned. 'This is a terrible, terrible place.'

'Courage, Rook,' said Twig. 'And keep looking for the crag.'

Rook strained to see through the dense, coiling mists. Ahead of them, the flat pavement seemed to stretch on for ever.

'Wait for the mists to clear,' said Twig. 'They will, if only for an instant – but that's all we'll need to spot our goal.' He pressed on. The wind howled round his ears, and strange voices seemed to snigger and jeer.

As Rook stumbled after him, the little skycraft at his side twisting and turning in the oncoming breeze, he could only pray that Twig was right. The mist closed in, blurring his vision and muffling his ears.

'Is everyone still here?' Twig called back.

'Wuh!' the banderbears replied with one voice. *We are all together*.

Occasionally, sudden squalls of turbulent air blew in, slamming into Rook's face and pitching him off balance. He would drop to the ground, clutching on tightly to the tether-rope, and wait for the wind to subside. The last time it happened, the air had cleared and, for the briefest of moments, he thought he caught a glimpse of the Edge itself. But then the mist had closed in again, and he'd been plunged back into whiteout blindness. 'I can't see a thing!' he called out nervously.

'It's all right, Rook,' said Twig. 'Trust me.'

Just then the mist thinned again, and Rook glimpsed

the cliff-edge a second time. Far in the distance a dark shape loomed. The mist thickened, and Rook lost sight of it. 'Did you see it, Captain?' he said excitedly. 'The crag!'

'I saw it,' said Twig. There was an odd catch in his voice. 'But I didn't see the *Skyraider*.'

They forged ahead in the face of the gusting wind and swirling mists, struggling to see more than a few feet ahead.

'I don't think I can go much further,' gasped Rook as he battled with the *Stormhornet*. Twig looked stooped and exhausted; the banderbears around him, bedraggled and miserable.

'We'll stop for a few moments,' shouted Twig above the howling wind.

The banderbears formed a huddle round Rook and the old sky pirate, offering a shield from the gale. Rook shivered unhappily. If only those mocking voices would stop, he would at least be able to think.

'We're lost, aren't we, Captain?' he said.

Twig didn't seem to hear him. He was gazing straight ahead. The wind had died down momentarily and the mist was rolling away. 'Look,' he said simply.

And there, looming above their heads, was the largest sky vessel Rook had ever seen. Its great battered prow alone was the size of twenty *Stormhornets*, its pitted, scarred hull as big as an Undertown tavern, while its mast towered up into the sky like a great ironwood pine. A mighty anchor chain descended to the black crag ahead, its dark bulk shielding the vessel in its lee.

'She's magnificent!' gasped Rook, then shook his head sadly as a thought struck him. No matter how wonderful it was to have created a wooden skycraft, the *Stormhornet* was, he realized, nothing compared with the *Skyraider*. The so-called Second Age of Flight, of which the librarian knights were so proud, was the merest shadow of what had existed before. So, so much had been lost.

'Come on, lad,' Twig called him, 'we have no time to lose. We must leave this accursed place! Take your skycraft and board the *Skyraider*. Throw down the rope-ladders and we'll climb aboard. Quick, now. Before the winds pick up again.'

Hurriedly Rook climbed onto the *Stormhornet* and took to the air. In moments, he was level with the battered balustrade of the mighty ship's foredeck. He secured the *Stormhornet* to the mast and jumped down to the deck. With trembling fingers, he untied the coiled rope-ladders and let them down. Instantly, the banderbears began clambering aboard, followed at last by Twig himself. As he set foot on the sky ship, the old sky pirate captain fell to his knees and kissed the deck.

'Thank Sky!' he whispered. 'I thought for a moment that I'd lost you.' He sprang to his feet. Suddenly, he no longer looked stooped. The years seemed to fall away, and a youthful glint came into his eyes. 'Come!' he cried. 'Let's get the *Skyraider* airborne!'

As one, the banderbears dispersed. Twig went with them. Rook was left on his own. He scuttled round the *Skyraider*, snooping into cupboards and locker-rooms, peering down below deck and watching the banderbears as they hurried this way and that, busily making the great sky pirate ship skyworthy.

Wumeru headed for the galleys below deck. Rummel unfurled the mainsail, checking it and double-checking it for any sign of major rents in the material. Wuralo saw to the ropes. Meeru and Loom climbed over the balustrades – one on the port side, one on the starboard side – and clambered round the hull-rigging beneath, ensuring that the hull-weights and rudder-wheel were all secure and in alignment. Weeg scaled the mast, inspecting the great wooden shaft for any trace of wood-rot or the tell-tale hairline fracture of timber fatigue as he climbed right up to the caternest at the very top.

From behind him Rook heard a hiss and a soft roar. Curious, he followed the sound, and stumbled across Twig himself – his head between the bars of the central cage – staring intently at the surface of the flight-rock. Beside him, adjusting the flames of the now blazing torches, was Molleen.

'Is it all right?' Rook asked.

Twig pulled away from the flight-rock and looked round. 'It shows no sign of the sickness,' he said.

'But that's wonderful news!' said Rook. 'We can fly!'

'Indeed we can,' said Twig. 'But we must make haste. For I fear the unseen sickness may already have struck.'

Rook frowned. 'But how?' he said.

Twig swept his arm round in a wide arc. 'Through the crew,' he said. 'You heard what they said. Most of them have had experience of life on board a sky ship. The danger is that one – or all – might be carrying the terrible sickness.'

Rook trembled uneasily. 'But how can we tell?' he said.

'We can't,' said Twig. 'Maybe the flight-rock has already been contaminated. Maybe not. Certainly, the closer we fly to the crumbling Sanctaphrax rock, the greater the risk. Make no mistake, Rook, this is a one-way voyage. The *Skyraider* won't be coming back. We must just hope and pray that it holds out long enough for us to make it to the Tower of Night.'

'Earth and Sky willing,' said Rook, his face pale and drawn.

'But cheer up, lad,' said Twig, clapping him on the shoulder. 'This is the beginning of a great adventure. Come with me.'

He turned away and, leaving Molleen to tend to the flight-rock, hurried round the narrow skirting-deck and up a short flight of stairs to the helm. He seized the great wheel and released the locking-lever. Then he tested the individual bone-handled flight-levers, one after the other, making sure that the ropes moved smoothly; raising and lowering the sails and hull-weights in preparation for take-off.

As he did so, the yodelled cries of the banderbear crew filled the air as, one by one, they announced that the various sections of the great sky pirate ship were just about in working order. When the last – Weeg – called down from the caternest that the mast was skyworthy, Twig clapped his hands together with glee.

'Prepare to launch!' he bellowed. 'Make ready to drop the anchor chain!'

'Wuh-wuh!' the banderbears bellowed back. *Aye-aye*.

With a mighty shudder and an ominous creak, the *Skyraider* began to lift up into the air. Twig let the heavy anchor chain fall away with a resounding *clang*.

'We shan't need that where we're going,' he called to the others.

The tattered sails billowed. The sky ship listed to one side and pulled away from the black crag. Higher and higher the great sky vessel flew, calmly, sedately, until, all at once, the wind caught it from behind and sent it soaring up into the air so fast that Rook's head spun and his stomach did somersaults.

'This is *amazing*!' he cried out. '*Incredible!* I can't believe that I'm actually flying on board a sky pirate ship!'

Twig chuckled. 'Neither can I, lad,' he said. 'Neither can I. Sky above, but I've missed it! The thrust of the sails, the sway of the weights – the wind in my hair. It's almost like the old days,' he said. 'As if I were a sky pirate once again.'

Rook turned to him, his eyes bright with excitement. 'But you *are*!' he said.

Twig nodded slowly, as his fingers danced over the flight-levers. 'Aye, Rook, I suppose I am,' he said. His brow furrowed. 'The *last* of the sky pirates.'

CHAPTER NINETEEN

THE TOWER OF NIGHT

It was the darkest hour just before the dawn. A fine dew, glistening in the overhead lamplight, covered the surface of the crumbling Sanctaphrax rock. From a shadowy crevice came a soft, slurping noise. Something was stirring.

A long, glistening tentacle appeared, then another – and the two gripped the rock and pulled. A dripping, jelly-like creature emerged. Three small round bumps on the top of its head grew large, cracked open and eyed the surroundings suspiciously. The tentacles reached out again and dragged it forwards.

Where the creature passed, the rock behind was left bone-dry, and as it slipped and slid about, it began to swell. Larger it became, larger and larger until, with a hiss and a spurt, three rear-tentacles suddenly uncoiled and squirted a thick, oily substance over the rock behind it. It had drunk enough.

The rubble ghoul slithered back down between the cracks in the broken rock. Having sated its thirst, it was now hungry.

Far, far above, a hammerhead goblin was also hungry. Ravenous, in fact. And thirsty. And cold. He stamped his great booted feet and pulled his black robes up against the icy air which, so high up the towering building, was cold enough to cover the wood of the jutting gantry with a feathery coating of frost.

'Just you wait till I get my hands on you, Gobrat, you useless, squint-eyed little runt!' he growled, and his breath came in dense puffs of cloud which glowed and squirmed in the yellow light of the hanging oil lamps. He paced back and forwards, slapping his arms against each other in an attempt to get warm. 'Leaving me here to do your guard-duty!' he complained. He should have been relieved at nine hours the previous night; now, the first rays of early morning sun were already lining the distant clouds with silver. 'All through the night I've been standing here!' he muttered angrily. 'I'll stove in your skull! I'll break every bone in your body! I'll— *Waaargh!*'

The heel of his boot skidded on an untouched patch of frost, and sent the goblin crashing to the floor. His heavy horned helmet came loose as his head slammed viciously down on the cold, hard wood with a loud *crack!*

Dazed, the hammerhead sat up. He saw the helmet scudding towards the edge of the gantry. Heart hammering furiously, he lunged forwards and grasped one of the helmet's curving horns just as it was about to tumble down from the high gantry.

'That was a close one,' he told himself grimly. 'You take care, now, Slab.' He climbed to his feet and put the helmet back on his head. If he'd lost it, the guard master would have clapped him in irons and thrown him into solitary confinement for a week as punishment.

Slab checked the rest of his equipment – the curved knife at his belt, the powerful-looking crossbow on his back, the heavy hooked pikestaff . . . Everything, he was relieved to discover, seemed to be in order.

Just then, in the distance, far below, came the sound of the bell at the top of Vox Verlix's Undertown palace tolling the hour. It was six. He'd now been on duty for eighteen hours! He stared out across the chasm of open sky as the sun slowly wobbled up above the horizon, shielding his eyes as the light grew dazzling. He looked down.

There, below, were the Stone Gardens, their once mighty rock-stacks now a mess of broken rubble littering the dead rock. Screetown and Undertown were wreathed in mist and, in the middle distance, the Great Mire Road was already teeming with countless tiny individuals as it wound its way back into the murky gloom and disappeared. For despite the bright start to the day, there were dark clouds rolling in from the Deepwoods far to the north-west, threatening rain, maybe even a lightning storm . . .

'A storm, after all this time.' Slab hawked and spat. 'That'd show those accursed librarian knights,' he growled. 'Think they're so clever, so they do – with their books and learning and their pathetic little skycraft.' He stared up into the great banks of cloud, praying for a lightning bolt to strike the top of the tower. 'But they'll learn one day. When Midnight's Spike heals the rock and we return to the skies, *then* they'll see—'

'Strength in night!' came a gruff voice behind him, and Slab turned to see a brawny, heavily tattooed flat-head who bore the scars of many a battle standing in front of him, his clenched right fist pressed against his breastplate in ritual greeting.

'Ah, Bragknot, strength in night!' Slab replied, and saluted in response. 'Am I glad to see you. Gobrat never showed up, the little—'

'Gobrat's gone missing,' said Bragknot. 'No-one seems to know *where* he is.'

'Soused on woodgrog and slumped in some dark corner, if I know him,' Slab muttered bitterly. He yawned.

'Eighteen hours without a break I've been up here. *Eighteen* hours . . .'

Bragknot shrugged. 'It happens,' he mumbled unsympathetically and looked all around, scanning the townscape below and squinting into the distance. 'Quiet watch, was it?' he said. 'No problems?'

'None,' said Slab.

The flat-head nodded towards the great banks of cloud looming closer. 'Looks like rain,' he commented. 'Just my luck!'

'Yeah, well, I'll leave you to it,' said Slab. 'I'm off to get my head down.'

'You do that,' said Bragknot, turning towards him. 'I'll—' He gasped and looked back over Slab's shoulder. 'Sky above! What is *that*?'

Slab chuckled. 'I'm not falling for that one again,' he said.

'I mean it, Slab!' said Bragknot. 'It's . . . it's . . .' He grabbed the smirking hammerhead by the shoulders and twisted him round. 'Look!'

Slab's eyes widened. His jaw dropped. This time, Bragknot had not been playing one of his stupid games. There really was something there.

'It can't be,' he whispered, trembling with awe as a great ghostly vessel emerged from the cover of dark, swirling cloud.

Too young to have seen one before, Slab stood transfixed, staring in disbelief at the vast, solid sky ship as it swept gracefully down through the air towards them. With its huge billowing sails and massive hull, it was

more awesome than he could ever have imagined.

'B-but how?' he faltered. 'How is it possible?' He shook his head. 'A sky ship still flying . . . Where did it come from?'

'Never mind all that!' bellowed Bragknot. 'Sound the alarms! Raise the guard! Mount the harpoons! *Come on*, Slab! We must—'

Just then Slab heard a high-pitched whistle and a soft thud. He spun round. Bragknot stood there, swaying slowly back and forwards on the spot. He looked back at Slab, his eyes filled with fear and confusion as his fingers closed gingerly round the ironwood bolt lodged in the side of his neck. His throat gurgled. Blood gushed down over his black robe. The next moment he staggered backwards and toppled over the edge of the gantry, dropping down silently out of sight.

A second bolt whistled in over Slab's head and embedded itself in a broad crossbeam behind him. A third shattered the hanging-lamp. It was followed by a dozen or more arrows, hissing in through the air and quivering where they struck.

'To the gantries!' Slab roared. 'We're under attack!'

'What is it? . . . What's going on?' several voices cried out from above and below him.

'Over there!' shouted someone from an upper gantry, pointing into the cloud, now swirling round the tower.

'A sky ship!' bellowed another.

'It's turning this way!' shouted yet another, a telescope raised to his eye. 'And it's got heavy weaponry aboard!'

A loud rasping klaxon sounded, followed by another and another . . . Soon, the whole Tower of Night echoed to the clamour of the Guardians answering the call to arms.

Head down, Slab dashed back along the exposed gantry. Skidding awkwardly on the slippery wood, he tumbled in through the doorway. Behind him there was a flash and an almighty splintering *crash* as an incoming ball of flaming ironwood severed the jutting gantry and sent it hurtling down below. Had it landed a second earlier, he too would be hurtling down with it.

Slab climbed shakily to his feet. All round him the air was filled with bellowed orders and screeched commands. Doors banged and shutters slammed as section after section within the great tower was sealed off to prevent an invasion. Heavy boots pounded up and down stairs as well-armed, black-robed Guardians hastened to the west side of the tower to repel the great attacking sky ship.

In all the chaos and confusion no-one noticed a small skycraft as it swooped down through the dark, swirling mist on the far side of the tower.

With the cloud as cover, the sky ship spat out a flaming salvo at the Tower of Night. Gantries splintered and shattered; great holes appeared in the walls and, where the heavy balls of flaming ironwood penetrated, small fires broke out.

Inside the tower the Guardians of Night were in turmoil, with the guard masters barking out a stream of orders.

'Shove that broken beam back into place!'

'Douse that fire!'

'Load the harpoons!'

'Prime the catapults!'

While some effected makeshift repairs and others smothered the flames with water and sand, small groups ventured out onto the jutting weapon-platforms where the heavyweight weaponry stood on plinths, bolted to the floor. Working in threes, they took up their battle positions. At the harpoon-turrets, one jumped into the firing seat and primed the shooting mechanism, one loaded a harpoon into the long chamber, while the third grabbed the wheel at the side of the turret and began turning. Slowly, as the sequence of internal cogs moved, the whole mechanism swung round. Then, seizing a second wheel, he altered the angle of the long barrel until the huge harpoon was pointing directly at the attacking sky ship. At the swivel catapults a similar process was taking place. When the launch trajectory had been secured, the guards – two at a time – heaved enormous, heavy boulders into each of the ladle-shaped firing bowls.

'Fire!' roared a guard master. Then another, higher up, bellowed the same command. And another, and another.

'Fire! . . . Fire! . . . Fire!'

A volley of harpoons and rocks exploded from the Tower of Night and hurtled towards the sky ship. One of the harpoons struck the starboard bow; a second skittered across the lower deck. Further back, a boulder dealt a glancing blow to the stern. All would have shattered a small skycraft, but the mighty sky ship barely seemed to flinch.

The Guardians of Night reloaded. The *Skyraider* rose up higher in the sky. The harpoon-turrets and swivel catapults were realigned.

'*FIRE!*'

The second bombardment did even less harm than the first, with not a single harpoon or boulder meeting its target. Peering through their telescopes into the swirling cloud, the guard masters saw the bearded figure at the helm – resplendent in satin frock coat and tricorn hat – barking commands of his own. The main-sail billowed. The stern hull-weights dropped. Abruptly, the hovering sky ship soared upwards, returning fire as it did so.

'They're heading for Midnight's Spike,' someone cried.

'Defend the spike!'

'Defend her with your lives!'

'*FIRE!*'

A third salvo of rocks and harpoons soared into the sky, a single rock hitting amidships, where a lone banderbear feverishly tended the great flight-rock. The banderbears at the rear of the ship replied with a heavy bombardment of the flaming ironwood balls. The walls of the tower suffered more damage and one harpoon-turret was destroyed by a direct hit. Two Guardians – one up high on a look-out gantry and one on a weapon-platform some way below – were struck by arrows simultaneously. The pair of them keeled forwards and, one after the other, tumbled down through the air as in some strange and terrible dance.

'More fire-power!' roared a guard master.

'Reinforcements to the spike chamber at once!' bellowed another.

'Alert the Most High Guardian!'

'Call Orbix Xaxis!'

Slab crouched down on the boards and peered out through the shattered wall. He had neither harpoon-turrets nor swivel catapults up here at the look-out gantry, yet the death of his comrade-in-arms would be avenged. With trembling hands, he raised the sight of the crossbow to his eye, slid the ironwood bolt into place and ratcheted the string back.

'This is for Bragknot,' he muttered grimly.

The sky ship loomed up before him, thick clouds of mist swirling around it. Slab lowered his head. He took aim. For the briefest of moments, the sky ship drew level. He fired the crossbow.

There was a thump. A *twang*. The bolt shot into the air and disappeared into the thick misty cloud. Slab held his breath. The next instant, rising up above the cacophony of noise from the tower itself, there came an anguished yodelling cry and, as the cloud fleetingly thinned out, he saw a banderbear clutch at its heart and fall off the sky ship.

'Got you!' Slab snarled, as the great hairy beast tumbled down through the air. He raised the crossbow to his eye a second time. As he looked through the view-finder, he saw three great flaming balls hurtling straight towards him.

Before he had a chance even to cry out, the ironwood balls struck – tearing apart the whole upper section of the tower and snuffing out the life of the hammerhead guard. The building shook from top to bottom. The sky ship rose higher, almost level with the great spike that topped the tower.

'They're using grappling-hooks!' screeched a guard from the base of the spike as a heavy three-pronged hook abruptly flew out from the *Skyraider* and hurtled towards it. 'They're trying to destroy Midnight's Spike!'

'Sacrilege!' bellowed another.

'Destroy the invaders!' roared yet another.

The Guardians intensified their efforts to repel the attacking sky ship with volley after volley of boulders and harpoons, arrows and crossbow bolts – and any-thing else they could lay their hands on. The air trembled with the din of battle. The *Skyraider* responded with arrows and crossbow bolts of its own, and the great flaming balls of ironwood which tore chunk after chunk from the dark tower. Numerous goblins, trogs and trolls in the black robes of the Guardians of Night plummeted to their deaths. Another grappling-iron clanged against Midnight's Spike. A second banderbear was struck . . .

On the other side of the tower the skycraft approached. Lightly, stealthily – like a woodmoth on the wing – it flitted up and down the great east wall, its rider looking for a place to enter. Finally he swooped down onto a small, jutting gantry, two-thirds of the way up, which appeared to be deserted.

The rider dismounted. As he tethered the skycraft securely to eye-hooks screwed into the wall, the weak milky sunlight penetrated the thick cloud and shone into his face. The youth – jaw set and brow creased with concentration – turned towards the small, dark entrance and disappeared inside.

*

As Rook peered into the gloom, the dark, menacing atmosphere assaulted his senses like a battering-ram slamming into locked fortress doors. It was dark within the tower despite the hanging-lamps, and the stench of death and rancid decay was overpowering. Rook faltered – numb, dumbstruck, incredulous that anyone could have created so evil a place.

He could hear voices, countless voices. Their muffled moans and feeble cries echoed in the darkness, a soft and terrible accompaniment to the bass rumbles and furious percussion of the battle raging far above him. 'Poor wretches,' Rook murmured. 'If only I could save you all.'

As his eyes grew accustomed to the gloom, he wrapped the cloak of nightspider-silk round his shoulders and ventured further into the tower. He found himself in a confusing labyrinth of narrow walkways and rickety flights of stairs sandwiched between the outer wall of the tower and an inner wall. At wild irregular angles, the wooden stairways zigzagged off in all directions – above and below him, and away to both sides. The sound of the hopeless, groaning prisoners grew louder, the foul stench more intense.

Rook's eyes followed the path of the walkway he was standing on. It led to a small, square landing, before doubling back on itself and rising steeply further up. At the far side of the landing, set into the shadowy inner wall of the tower, was a door.

Is that one of the cells? he wondered. There was only one way to find out.

Rook dashed up the stairs. On the landing, as he approached the heavy, wooden door, he saw what looked like markings. He pulled the sky-crystals from his pockets and, holding them together, used the pale light they emitted to examine the door more closely. Several names had been scratched crudely into hard wood: RILK TILDERHORN, LEMBEL FLITCH, REB MARWOOD, LOQUBAR AMSEL . . . Each of them had a line gouged through them. Only the name at the bottom remained untouched.

'Finius Flabtrix,' Rook whispered. 'An academic, by the sound of him.'

There was a shuttered spy-hole in the door and heavy bolts at the top and bottom. Rook reached forwards, slid aside the spy-hole cover and quickly glanced inside. He couldn't make out anything in the blackness, but the stench intensified. Gingerly he reached up and drew the top bolt across; then the bottom bolt. Slowly he pushed the heavy door open and looked in.

With no walls, no chains, no bars, the cell was nothing like he had ever seen. A narrow set of steps led from the door down to a single ledge, which jutted out from the wall into a cavernous atrium beyond. Apart from the door which, when shut, formed a smooth, unbroken part of the inward-sloping wall, the only way out was to step off the ledge and tumble down through the fetid air to certain death below. Looking out into the atrium, Rook could make out countless other ledges, each connected by their own steps to individual cell doors.

Appalled, his gaze fell upon the individual at the corner of the ledge before him. Curled up in a foetal ball, he lay on a stinking mattress of straw, bony arms hugged round bonier legs; his robes in tatters, his breath uneven, rasping. Long, matted hair hung down over his face. In places it had fallen out in clumps, leaving angry scab-encrusted patches all over his scalp. His beard was thick and soiled; his skin was covered in grime and red, weeping sores – the result of scratching and scratching with his filthy, jagged nails to relieve the intolerable itching of the tick-lice which burrowed beneath the surface to lay their eggs.

'Finius? Finius Flabtrix,' said Rook softly, moving closer. '*Professor* Finius Flabtrix?'

The breathing quickened. The eyelids flickered and opened for an instant but, though the eyes stared in his direction, Rook knew that they had not seen him. They closed again.

'Not my fault,' the old professor murmured, his voice hoarse and faltering. 'Not my fault. Not my fault . . .'

'It's all right, I won't hurt you,' Rook whispered, tears welling up in his eyes.

The professor ignored him, lost in his own private torment. Rook turned and made his way carefully back up the stairs and out through the cell door. There was no time to lose; the *Skyraider* couldn't keep the Guardians occupied for ever. He *must* find Cowlquape and get out of this terrible place.

He hurried down another walkway, and saw a row of cell doors embedded in the inner wall. Quickly, by the

THE DUNGEONS OF THE TOWER OF NIGHT

glow from the sky-crystals, he checked the names scratched into each door: JUG-JUG ROMPERSTAMP, Rook read. ELDRICK SWILL. RAIN HAWK III. SILVIX ARMENIUS. GROLL ... If the names were anything to go by, then the prisoners came from every walk of Edge life. Merchants and academics. Slaughterers, goblins and trolls. A former sky pirate ...

At some, Rook simply read off the name and continued without stopping. At others, he paused to look through the spy-hole – though each time he did so, he wished that he had not. The abject creatures inside were too terrible to witness. Jabbering. Twitching. Deranged. Some rocked slowly back and forwards, some ranted and raved, some paced round and round mumbling beneath their breath, while others – the worst of them; those who had given up all hope – simply lay on the ledge, waiting for death to come and embrace them.

A fiery anger spread through Rook's body. Curse the Guardians of Night! he thought bitterly. 'The dungeons are an abomination! An affront to every living creature in the Edge – to life itself! Why, if I was ever uncertain whether the war between the librarian knights and the Guardians of Night was a just one, then here is the proof,' he told himself. 'This is truly a battle between good and evil!'

'Well said,' came a voice close by.

Rook jumped. 'Who's that?' he whispered.

'Over here,' said the voice.

Rook approached a cell door. He looked down. CODSAP was scratched into its heavy, dark wood.

'Open the door,' came the voice. 'Give it a good shove. A *really* good shove! Go on!'

Rook unbolted the door, and gave it a hard push. There was a thud, and a muffled cry. Rook's heart missed a beat. What had happened? What had he *done*? He thrust his head inside the doorway just in time to see a green, scaly creature tumbling back off the stairs and down into the yawning void of the great atrium.

'No!' Rook bellowed, his howl of anguish spinning round and round the rank air. 'I'm sorry! I . . .'

Suddenly, there was a voice, speaking to him inside his head. 'Thank you, thank you, friend, for releasing me when I lacked the courage to jump . . .' The voice fell still.

Rook flinched. How long had the poor creature waited on the stairs for someone to come and end his suffering? He slammed the door shut with a helpless fury, the clang echoing loudly through the tower.

'*Ouch*,' came a voice from the shadows, somewhere to his left. 'Oh, my poor head. I knew I shouldn't have had all that woodgrog. Is that you, Slab?'

Rook drew his knife and silently followed the direction of the voice. There, just ahead, slumped in the corner of a landing, head in hands, was a sleepy flat-head goblin in the black robes of a Guardian of Night, a crossbow and an empty jar by his side.

In an instant Rook grabbed the crossbow, kicked the jar away and thrust his knife at the goblin's throat.

'Y-y-you're not Slab,' he stammered. Rook could see the whites of his eyes as the goblin's frightened face looked up into his. Wh-who are you?'

'Never mind who I am,' Rook whispered, stepping back and levelling the crossbow at the white gloam-glozer emblem on the goblin's chest. 'Who are *you*?'

'I'm Gobrat. I'm just a poor guard. A warder. Please don't hurt me.' He paused, a frown crossing his broad features. 'You're one of them librarian knights, ain't you? Oh, please have mercy, sir. I've never hurt no-one, honest I haven't.'

'And yet you wear the black robes of the Guardians of Night,' said Rook, a cold anger in his quiet voice.

'They took me in, sir, when I was starving in Undertown. I had nothing. They fed me and clothed me – but I'm just a poor goblin from the Edgewater slums at heart. Please don't kill me, sir.'

'A warder, you say,' said Rook.

'Yes, sir. I'm not proud of it, sir – but I does what I can for the poor wretches locked up here . . .'

Rook raised the crossbow to silence the flat-head. 'Take me to the cell of Cowlquape Pentephraxis and I'll spare your miserable life,' he said.

The goblin groaned. 'It'll be more than my life's worth if the High Master finds out I've led you to Cowlquape.'

'It'll be more than your life's worth if you don't,' said Rook, pulling back on the crossbow trigger.

'All right! All right!' The goblin got to his feet shakily. 'Follow me, sir, and be careful where you're pointing that there crossbow.'

Rook followed the flat-head through the endless maze of walkways and staircases, down into the depths of the

Tower of Night. As they continued, there was a loud crashing sound from high up above the atrium, and the stairs rattled as the tower shook.

'I suppose that's your lot up there,' said Gobrat, 'causing all that commotion.

It won't do any good, you know. You never learn! Skycrafts is no match for tower weapons.'

'Just keep walking,' said Rook, jabbing the crossbow into his back. 'How much further?'

'Not far,' said Gobrat, with a mirthless laugh. 'We're almost at the lower depths now, young sir.'

With the flat-head in front, they made their way down a sloping flight of stairs. Gobrat stopped at a heavily bolted door.

'Cowlquape Pentephraxis,' said Rook, reading off the name. 'This is it!'

Gobrat scowled. 'There. Now take my advice and get out of here smartish. The guards will be swarming all round once they've dealt with your comrades, and now I've helped you, my life isn't worth an oakapple pip!' The goblin pulled off his robe and threw it to the ground. 'I suppose it's back to the Edgewater slums for old Gobrat – if the rubble ghouls don't get me.'

Rook waved the flat-head away. 'You've been of valuable service to the librarian knights,' he said. 'Fare you well, Gobrat.'

With the flat-head gone, Rook returned his attention to the cell door. Having checked that the stairs inside were clear, he slid the bolts across and pushed the door open.

'Is that you, Xanth?' came a cracked, frail voice.

'No, Professor,' said Rook. 'I'm a librarian knight. I've come to rescue you.'

He descended the stairs, down to the primitive, wooden ledge. Here in the depths of the tower, the stench was indescribable. The former Most High Academe of New Sanctaphrax looked up at him. His body was bent and painfully thin. His grey hair, long and unkempt, his robes thread- bare.Worst of all were his eyes. Filled with the memories of horrors too terrible to forget, they stared ahead, lifeless, dull, unblinking . . .

'Professor, we *must* leave now,' said Rook. 'Time is running out.'

'Leave . . .' Cowlquape murmured. 'Time . . .'

Rook leaned forwards and, taking the professor gently but firmly by the arm, hoisted him up onto his feet. Then, taking his weight – which wasn't much – he guided him up the stairs.

'Wait! Wait!' Cowlquape called urgently, and broke away. He returned to the ledge, grabbed a roll of papers and barkscrolls and thrust them under his arm. He looked at Rook, a little smile playing round his mouth. 'Now I am ready to leave,' he said.

Up at Midnight's Spike the battle raged on. The crew of the *Skyraider* was down to five now. Rummel, the huge, black banderbear, had fallen first, fatally wounded by Slab's crossbow bolt. Meeru was next to fall, skewered by one of the great harpoons and torn away from the sky ship. Mindless with grief, his brother Loom had thrown himself off the stern after his beloved twin.

But Twig hadn't time to mourn the loss of the three brave banderbear volunteers, for Molleen had yodelled to him to come at once to the flight-rock cage. Calling Wumeru over, and telling her to hold the helm steady, Twig hurried down to the old banderbear's side.

'Wuh-wuh!' *Look!* Molleen pointed at a livid scar in the glowing flight-rock. 'Wegga-lura-meeragul. Wuh!' *The rock is wounded. I thought the weapons of the Dark Ones had not hurt it – but look, Captain!*

Twig looked. Where the Guardians' rock had struck, a deep crater had formed. It was growing like an ulcer, eating away at the flight-rock.

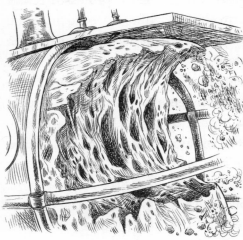

'Contamination!' Twig gasped. 'We haven't much time. Do what you can, Molleen, but be prepared to abandon ship.' He hurried back to the helm.

Despite her best attempts to keep it buoyant – dousing the flight-lamps, drenching the rock with chilled sand and, with Wumeru now by her side, desperately operating the cooling-fans – the rock continued to disintegrate. The crater in its surface became wider, deeper, and a growing trickle of dusty particles showered down through the air.

'Give me as much time as you can!' Twig shouted across to Molleen. 'We can't abandon Rook now,' he added, mopping the beads of sweat from his forehead. His hands darted over the bone-handled levers in a furious blur as he carried out ever-finer adjustments to the sails and weights in an effort to keep the leaning, lurching sky ship from rolling right over.

But he was fighting a losing battle. With every passing

minute the flight-rock became less and less buoyant. If the *Skyraider* was to remain airborne, it would have to be made lighter.

'Weeg!' Twig bellowed. 'To the hull-rigging with you! I want you to cut the weights.'

'Wuh-wuh,' he shouted back. *Cut the weights, Captain? But we'll become unstable.*

'It's a chance we'll have to take,' Twig shouted back. 'Start with the klute-hull-weights, then the peri-hull-weights. And if that's not enough, move on to the prow-and stern-weights . . . Sky willing, it'll give us the lift we need.' He frowned. '*Now*, Weeg!'

Grunting unhappily, the lanky banderbear hurried off to carry out the commands. Twig fingered the various bone and wood amulets around his neck. Far below him, on the platform beneath Midnight's Spike, stood a figure in black robes, fluttering in the mist, with a curious muzzle-like mask covering most of his face.

'Wuh! Wuh!' Molleen cried out. *The flight-rock! It's broken in two!*

'Hold it steady!' Twig told her. 'Just a little bit longer—'

At that moment a lufwood-flare soared up from the other side of the tower and blazed in the sky far above their heads, a brightly glowing streak of purple.

Twig gritted his teeth. 'Thank Sky!' he whispered. 'It's the signal! Rook is waiting for us!'

Just then Weeg must have severed the first hull-weight, for the sky ship gave a sudden jolt and rose up several strides into the air. A salvo of harpoons sailed harmlessly beneath its hull.

'Hold tight, Cowlquape, old friend,' said Twig grimly. 'We're coming to get you.'

Down on the platform at the base of Midnight's Spike, Orbix Xaxis stared up at the bright purple light suspiciously. 'It must be some sort of signal,' he said. He looked across at the *Skyraider*; his eyes narrowed. 'While you, up there, were keeping us busy . . .' he said slowly, thoughtfully, 'there was something else afoot. I smell a rat . . .' He paused. 'The dungeons!'

'I'll check them at once,' said the sallow, shaven-headed youth by his side, dashing off as fast as he could down the broken flight of stairs.

'You, Banjax,' the Most High Guardian shouted at one of the guard masters close by. 'Take two dozen Guardians and scour the dungeons for intruders. No-one must get in or out!'

'At once, High Guardian,' Banjax replied, and the air resounded with the tramp of the Guardians' heavy boots on the wooden stairs.

The Most High Guardian looked back up at the *Skyraider*. The sky ship had pulled away from Midnight's Spike at last, and seemed to be heading round in a great circle. 'So you think you've tricked the Most High Guardian of Night, do you?' he hissed.

Twig gripped the main-sail lever grimly. With the flight-rock irreparably weakened, he was dependent on the great, tattered sail for lift. Slowly, carefully, battling against treacherous draughts of misty air, he brought the *Skyraider* round to the east side of the tower and began the long, perilous descent.

Wumeru cried out. 'Wuh-wuh. Roo-wuh-ook!'

Peering down, Twig saw Rook standing on a jutting gantry, a third of the way down, together with . . . Twig gasped. Could that be him? Could that stooped, grey-haired figure truly be his apprentice, Cowlquape? He looked so frail, so fragile – so old.

'Prepare to board!' he bellowed down.

Rook looked up and waved wildly. The sky ship sank lower. The gantry came closer.

'Wumeru!' Twig shouted. 'Wuh-weela-wurr.' *Help Cowlquape aboard.*

'Professor,' said Rook urgently, 'you'll have to jump.'

'Jump?' the ancient professor croaked. 'I think my jumping days are over.'

'Try,' said Rook. 'You must try.'

He looked up. The *Skyraider* was just above them now. As it came down lower, he stepped behind Cowlquape and seized him by the shoulders.

The sky ship drew level, but did not slow down . . .

'No, no, I can't . . .' Cowlquape trembled, the years of being perched on the high prison ledge suddenly returning to him with full force as he looked down.

'Now!' shouted Twig.

Rook pushed Cowlquape off the gantry. At the same time Wumeru leaned forwards, arms outstretched. She caught the old professor in her great arms and lowered him gently onto the deck. 'Wuh-wuh,' she said softly. *You're safe now.*

Overjoyed, Twig locked the flight-levers and hurtled down to the foredeck to greet his old friend. He rushed up, arms open, and embraced him warmly.

'Cowlquape, Cowlquape,' he cried, his voice straining with emotion. 'I can't tell you what it means to see you again.'

'Nor I, you, Twig,' said Cowlquape. 'Nor I, you.'

At that moment the sky ship gave a sudden lurch. 'Hold on, old friend,' said Twig, pulling away. 'We're not quite safe yet. But fear not. I won't let you down.'

Back at the helm, Twig unlocked the levers and tried his best to right the stricken sky ship. 'Just a little bit longer,' he groaned, as it trembled and creaked.

'Wuh-wuh!' screamed Molleen. *The flight-rock's breaking up.*

Twig locked the helm and levers a second time, raced to the balustrade and bellowed down. 'The prow-weight, Weeg!' he roared. 'Then the stern-weight!'

'Wuh-wurra!' the banderbear shouted back. He'd already cut both of them free.

'The neben-hull-weights, then,' Twig shouted. 'Sever the neben-hull-weights – small, medium *and* large!'

Weeg made no reply, but the next moment the *Skyraider* leaped upwards abruptly, back past the gantry and – under Twig's expert guidance – soared round the tower and off into the cloudy sky.

As the sky ship sailed past, Orbix Xaxis – Most High Guardian of Night – raised his powerful, exquisitely tooled crossbow. He aimed it at the sky ship's helm, and fired.

Down on the gantry Rook untethered the *Stormhornet* and leaped into the saddle. Then, standing tall in the stirrups, he jerked the pinner-rope to his right, and rose up into the air – only to pull up sharply a moment later as the tether-rope went taut.

'*Ooof!*' he gasped as he was thrown forward in his seat.

Rather than soaring away from the gantry, the *Stormhornet* remained stuck, bobbing about in the air like a kite. Rook looked round. He had been careless. In his hurry, instead of reeling in the tether-rope and stowing it neatly, he had left it hanging loose. Now it was snagged on the gantry's jutting balustrade.

With trembling hands, Rook seized the rope. He tugged it and shook it for all he was worth – but the tether-rope was stuck fast. It would not budge. There was nothing for it but to land again, dismount and pull it free—

'Halt!'

The bellowed command cut through the air like a knife. Rook's heart missed a beat. He yanked desperately at the rope. It moved – but only a fraction, and wedged itself tighter than ever. A figure emerged from the doorway at the end of the gantry, crossbow in hand. He raised it to his eye. 'Halt, or I'll shoot!'

Rook stared at the wiry indi-vidual in the black uniform. Though his hair, shaved back to a shadowy stubble, was shorter than Rook had ever seen it before, the youth was unmistakable.

'Xanth,' he gasped.

Xanth lowered the crossbow. 'Rook? Rook Barkwater.' His dark eyes narrowed. 'Is that you?'

Rook raised his goggles. Their eyes met.

From behind Xanth came the sound of heavy boots pounding closer and closer. Rook's heart hammered furiously in his chest. Xanth stepped forwards.

'Please, Xanth,' said Rook quietly. 'For friendship's sake—'

The pounding of the boots grew louder. The unit of guards was almost upon them.

Xanth raised his crossbow and took aim. Rook closed his eyes.

There was a click, a *twang* and a whistle as the cross-bow loosed its bolt and sent it speeding towards the *Stormhornet*. Rook froze. The next instant – with a soft *thwpp* – the bolt sliced through the tether-rope and the *Stormhornet* catapulted forward into the air.

Seizing control of the skycraft, Rook darted up and off into the swirling mists. He flicked the pinner-rope to the left and felt the *Stormhornet* gather speed beneath him. As he flew on, he glanced over his shoulder and glimpsed Xanth – his shaven head gleaming in the bright rising sun – standing in the middle of a large group of Guardians.

Had Xanth shot the bolt through the tether-rope on purpose, deliberately setting him free? Rook desperately wanted to think so. 'Thank you,' he whispered.

As he left the Tower of Night behind, he saw the *Skyraider* in the sky up in front. But something was wrong. It wasn't waiting for him. Instead, listing heavily to one side, it was gathering speed. Past Undertown it went, with the boom-docks ahead . . .

If it didn't change course, it would sail over the great jutting Edge itself, and be lost in Open Sky.

·CHAPTER TWENTY·

RETURN

Realigning the nether-sail, Rook stood up in the stir-rups and sped forwards. As he battled to get closer to the *Skyraider*, he realized just how bad the situation had become. The flight-rock seemed to be crumbling, with ever larger chunks falling down from the cage. What was more, without its hull-weights, the sky ship looked out of control and at the mercy of the turbulent wind that held it in its grip.

As the *Skyraider* careered over the boom-docks, Rook could see the banderbears abandoning ship. With their parawings strapped to their backs, they leaped off the balustrades, tugged their rip-cords and sailed down to the ground below – Old Molleen, with no flight-rock left to tend; Wuralo, the female whose life he had saved at the Foundry Glade; and Wumeru, his friend. Last to jump was Weeg. As he launched himself off from the deck, Rook saw that he was carrying a ragged bundle in his paws. He gasped.

It was Cowlquape, wrapped up in the banderbear's protective embrace, like a babe in arms. The pair of them were swooping down through the sky towards the boom-docks. Pulling on the pinner-sail, Rook set the *Stormhornet* on a path to meet them. A cloud rolled in and he lost sight of the distant *Skyraider*.

'I just hope they've all made it,' Rook murmured, as he approached the muddy shores of the boom-docks and swooped in to land.

He brought the *Stormhornet* down next to one of the great overflow pipes that would lead them back into the labyrinth of sewer tunnels. The banderbears were huddled together.

'Where's the captain?' called Rook, tethering the *Stormhornet* and rushing over. Cowlquape pointed at the clearing horizon. Rook's eyes followed the direction of his bony finger.

High up in the sky and far out beyond the Edge, the *Skyraider* was still airborne – but only just. With no weights left to balance it, the sky pirate ship was on its side, juddering as it sailed on. The useless weight-ropes dangled; the sails flapped in the gathering wind. Rook raised his telescope to his eye and focused in on the helm.

'I can see him!' he said, his voice breaking with emotion. 'Why doesn't he abandon her?'

Wumeru was suddenly by Rook's side. 'Wuh-wug. Weela-lugg.' *He is mortally wounded, a crossbow bolt in his back.* She hung her head. *He chooses to die with his sky ship.*

They stood there, side by side, arms raised to shield

their eyes from the sun, watching the great sky ship sailing away.

'He was so brave,' Rook trembled. 'So selfless . . .' Suddenly, the *Skyraider* was flying no longer. The buoyant flight-rock had died, and the sky ship was dropping out of the sky like a stone. Down it came, gathering speed as it fell, before – in the blink of an eye – disappearing below the Edge. Rook gasped. Tears welled in his eyes. 'Oh, Captain Twig,' he murmured.

Wumeru clapped her arm around his shoulder and squeezed warmly. 'Wuh-wuh,' she said. *Wumeru is truly sorry.*

Rook sniffed, and wiped his eyes on his sleeve. Captain Twig was gone. For ever.

He turned back to where Cowlquape, Weeg and Molleen stood waiting. 'Come,' he said, 'the librarian scholars will welcome us in the sewers. I know the way.'

He looked back at the Edge one last time, standing silently for a moment, and was about to turn away when he caught sight of something out of the corner of his eye. Something huge. Something flapping . . . He squinted into the misty distance. It was a bird. A magnificent black and white bird with vast wings and a long, spreading tail.

'What's that?' Rook breathed.

'Why, it's a caterbird,' said Cowlquape. 'I do believe it's a caterbird!'

'It's magnificent,' said Rook. 'But wait . . . What's it got in its claws? Look!' He pointed at the small bundle clutched tightly in the enormous creature's great curved talons.

Cowlquape gasped. 'Of course – it has to be! I should have known at once!' He laughed joyfully and clapped his hands. 'It is *the* caterbird. The one whose hatching Twig was present at when he was a lad. The one who has watched over him ever since!'

Rook stared, wide-eyed. 'I wonder where it's taking him.'

Cowlquape shook his head. 'That I couldn't tell you, young librarian.'

The caterbird, with its precious load swinging below its great body, had wheeled round in the sky and was heading towards the Deepwoods. Suddenly Twig's words came back to Rook – about his quest; his endless, futile quest to return to his waiting crew.

'There's only one place it could be taking him,' he said, his heart soaring. 'To Riverrise.'

The old nightmare was back. The baying whitecollar woodwolves, their eyes flashing, their teeth bared and fur bristling. His father shouting, his mother screaming. Running . . . Running . . . Got to escape the wolves . . . Got to shake off the slave-takers . . .

Now he was alone, lost and wandering through the dark, menacing forest. Eyes glinted at him from the shadows. Growls, grunts and bloodthirsty cries echoed in the darkness. All at once he heard something else. Something close by – and coming closer, closer.

He looked up. A massive creature was looming towards him . . . But wait . . . Shouldn't he wake up now, just as he always did?

This time, however, was different. This time the creature continued inexorably towards him. He could hear its footfall, feel its hot, moist breath in his face. Sobbing loudly, knowing there was no escape, Rook reached out with his hand – into the darkness, into the unknown.

His fingers brushed against thick, warm fur. His heart pounded; his legs went weak. The sound of low, lulling grunts whispered into his ear as he was swept up off the ground and enfolded in the creature's huge, but gentle arms.

They smelt mossy. They cuddled him warmly, tenderly. Cradling him. Protecting him. Rook had never felt so safe or known so much comfort . . .

'Rook, are you awake?'

Rook's eyes opened. He knew that voice. He looked round the small, cosy room. The ornate oil lamp on the writing desk was still burning, casting a soft amber glow into every corner of the room and spilling out across his treatise-journal which lay open on the desk beneath it – and beside his bed sat Varis Lodd.

'I heard of your brave deeds from the Professor of Darkness the moment I arrived from the Free Glades,' she said. 'All Undertown is talking of it!' She paused. 'But what is it? You look as if you've seen a ghost.'

'Not a ghost,' said Rook. 'A dream. I had a dream. A dream I've had many times before, only this time . . . Varis, when you rescued me as a child, do you remember where exactly you found me?'

'Found you?' said Varis.

'In the Deepwoods,' he said. 'What happened? You've never really said—'

'You mean you don't know?' said Varis. 'I had no idea. I thought they would have told you. Your parents, they were taken by slavers. You escaped. Earth and Sky know how. And then . . . Oh, Rook, it was miraculous! I found you, all healthy and plump, tucked up asleep in a nest of woven grass—'

Rook stared at her. 'A nest?'

'That's right,' said Varis, nodding. 'An abandoned banderbear nest, though how you got there, I've no idea.'

Rook trembled as the memories came flooding back; the huge, enfolding arms, the warm breath, the thick fur, the steady thud of a heart beating next to his. Safe, protected, watched over, in the vast depths of the endless Deepwoods.

'I know how I got there,' said Rook, with a smile. 'I know.'

Vox

THE
EASTERN
BASKETS

THE
CEREMONIAL
CAGE

THE
ROCK
DEMONS
RAVINE

SCREETO

THE
SANCTAPHRAX
FOREST

THE
SUNKEN
PALACE

TO THE
STONE
GARDENS

THE SLAVE TRAIL

ROOK'S
CROSSING

THE
MISERY
HOLE

EASTERN
ENTRANCE
TO SEWERS

UNDER

TH

INTRODUCTION

Far far away, jutting out into the emptiness beyond, like the figurehead of a mighty stone ship, is the Edge. A river – the Edgewater – pours down from the overhanging rock. Though broad, the river is slow and sluggish. It has been many long decades since storms brought any significant rainfall in from Open Sky – though now, with the sky overcast and the air hot and heavy with moisture, it feels as though perhaps, at last, all that is about to change.

At the furthest point of the Edge, draped in the dark, swirling cloud, are the Stone Gardens. Once they were the source of the floating rocks which gave birth to sky-flight and formed the great Sanctaphrax rocks them-selves. Now the gardens are dead, for stone-sickness struck the Edge, grounding the sky ships, attacking the new Sanctaphrax rock and leaving the Stone Gardens a barren wasteland of broken stacks and rubble. Even the white ravens that once guarded them have gone.

Up in the Tower of Night, perched high on the crumbling Sanctaphrax rock, the Guardians – led by the merciless Orbix Xaxis – still believe that the lightning of a Great Storm will heal the ailing rock. They made preparations for its arrival and have waited impatiently for that day for many a long year.

Meanwhile, down in the library chambers of the underground sewers, their enemies – the librarian academics – disagree that lightning will heal the rock. Under the guidance of the High Librarian, Fenbrus Lodd, they study, learn, conjecture and experiment on pieces of the stricken rock, trying to find an alternative cure – while taking care to defend themselves against any who would seize the library and its secrets for themselves.

And there are many, quite apart from Orbix Xaxis, who would like to do just that. The brutal hammerhead goblin, General Tytugg, for instance, who so often dreams of having the same stranglehold over those who live beneath Undertown as those who live above, and who would fulfil these dreams were it not so perilous to attack. And Mother Muleclaw, shryke Mother of the Eastern Roost; she, too, would like to see an end to the library – to break, once and for all, the link between the librarians and the shrykes' sworn enemies in the Free Glades.

Ever vigilant, librarian knights patrol the skies at dusk and dawn – like young Rook Barkwater, fresh from the Free Glades, but already as seasoned a flier as any of his comrades who patrol in ones and twos each day. They keep to the shadows, skimming over the faded glory of Undertown in their sumpwood skycraft, darting round the jumble of debris and gaping crevices of Screetown, and flitting between the great wooden struts and pillars of the so-called Sanctaphrax Forest, that vast never-ending scaffold construction which keeps the stricken Sanctaphrax rock from ever touching the ground.

At the end of their forays, they return to the library with reports of the world above: strange disturbing reports of fireballs in the sky, and sightings of huge, mutant creatures in Screetown – whilst with every passing day, the weather seems to be getting more humid and oppressive.

Vox Verlix – nominal Leaguesmaster and Most High Academe of Sanctaphrax – knows all about the weather. Once he was the most promising cloudwatcher apprentice of his generation. Bully and genius, it was he who wrested power from Cowlquape Pentephraxis, the Most High Academe of New Sanctaphrax, taking the great chain of high office for himself; he who seized control of the mighty merchant leagues; he who oversaw the construction of the Tower of Night, the Great Mire Road, and the Sanctaphrax Forest.

These days, however, despite his grand titles and grander projects, Vox Verlix has little power. Time and again, he has been double-crossed. Orbix Xaxis seized the Tower of Night for himself, Mother Muleclaw took control of the Great Mire Road, while together with his army of goblins, General Tytugg – although content to keep a powerless puppet in place to hold the threat of a shryke attack at bay – rules Undertown with a rod of iron. Vox Verlix, it is generally believed, is little more than a prisoner in the crumbling Palace of Statues; drunken, powerless and obese.

He is, it is true, befuddled by his housekeeper's endless supply of oblivion for most of the time. Yet there are moments of lucidity; moments when – though Vox finds it hard to recall a single thing from the previous day – his memories of former glories are as fresh in his mind as they ever were.

And during those reveries of the past, he makes plans for the future. Intricate plans. *Vengeful* plans. For, alone and powerless as he is, Vox still cherishes dreams of vengeance on those he blames for his current plight. On the shrykes who strut and squawk on the Mire Road, on the goblins who march through the Undertown streets and on the sinister Guardians of Night, ever watchful from their great tower.

These are strange times. With the weather so hot, so humid, so charged with menace, it is like being trapped within a bubbling cauldron which is threatening at any moment to boil over. Slaves wilt in the suffocating heat. Guards squabble among themselves. In Screetown and the Sanctaphrax Forest, the creatures that live there are jittery and unpredictable.

Something is about to happen. Of that, there is no doubt. But what?

Rumours abound. Suspicions deepen. There are many questions but few answers. What are Orbix Xaxis and his Guardians of Night looking for as they gather each night and scan the skies? What is General Tytugg scheming in his Hive Towers fortress? Why has Mother Muleclaw gathered her shryke-sisters to her makeshift court at the end of the Great Mire Road? And what of the librarians, deep in their sewers, always mindful of those who live above them? What danger is it that they sense?

Only one individual is overlooked, forgotten and alone in his crumbling palace, seemingly oblivious to the world outside and lost in his own bitter dreams. Only one individual, who doesn't seem to care as Undertown simmers in the unbearable heat. Only one.

Vox Verlix.

The Deepwoods, the Stone Gardens, the Edgewater River. Undertown and Sanctaphrax. Names on a map.

Yet behind each name lie a thousand tales – tales that have been recorded in ancient scrolls, tales that have been passed down the generations by word of mouth – tales which even now are being told.

What follows is but one of those tales.

·CHAPTER ONE·

DAWN PATROL

It was cold in the great chamber; bitter cold. Above, through the frost-edged panes of the glass dome overhead, the stars glittered like phraxdust in the black sky. Below, at the large ring-shaped ironwood table, a hulking figure was hunched over a sheaf of sky charts, a carved tankard in front of him, and an upturned telescope by the foot of his chair. Loud snores echoed through the chamber as the figure's head slumped slowly forwards, a red gobbet of spittle bubbling on his lips.

The sky charts rustled like dead leaves as they were caught by an icy draught whistling through the chamber. The academic shivered in his sleep and the light *clink* of a phraxdust medallion tapping the heavy chain of office round his neck mingled with his snores.

He slumped further forward, cheeks wobbling and neck creasing into plump, grublike layers of fat. The dangling phraxdust medallion knocked against the rim of the all but empty tankard. The snores were deep and rumbling now and, as the sleeper's jowly face hovered over the table, the medallion hung down inside the tankard.

All at once, with a volcanic snore, the sagging figure fell completely forwards. He slammed his forehead on the edge of the table with a thud – and sat bolt upright. In front of him, there was a hiss, a crackle, a whiff of toasted wood-almonds – and the tankard abruptly exploded.

The academic was thrown back from his chair. He landed heavily on the other side of the chamber, twisting a leg and knocking his head sharply against the tiled floor.

From high above, like a faulty echo, there came an answering sound of breaking glass and an ear-splitting crash, as something hard and heavy burst through the dome and landed in the middle of the ironwood table, splitting it in two.

The academic coughed throatily as he heaved himself painfully to his feet. The air was thick with dust and smoke. His head throbbed, his ears were ringing, and wherever he looked, the after-image of the explosion flashed before him; now pink, now green. He coughed again and again, great convulsions racking his body.

At last the coughing subsided, and he fumbled for a spidersilk kerchief and wiped his streaming eyes. Above his head, he saw that several of the glass panels had shattered in the blast. At his feet, the jagged fragments glinted in the moonlight. He frowned as his gaze fell on the object nestling amongst the shards of glass and splinters of wood. It was a stone head dislodged from one of the statues on the roof, the thick frost coating its surface already melting and dripping down onto the floor.

Who is it this time? the academic wondered. Which venerable figure of rank has taken a tumble tonight?

He crouched down, seized the slippery head with both hands, rolled it over – and gasped with sudden foreboding. It was his own face staring back at him.

Although it was close to midnight, with the full moon dull and greasy yellow behind the thickening mist, the air – even high up at the top of the Tower of Night – was still clammy and warm. The Most High Guardian, Orbix Xaxis, emerged onto the main upper gantry, looked round uneasily, and began at once to fiddle urgently with the metal muzzle that covered his mouth and nose.

With the vents closed by spidersilk gauze, Orbix's face sweated beneath the mask and his voice took on a muffled and rasping tone – but at least it protected him from the vile contagion of the night. The High Guardian clicked the muzzle-guard securely into place. When the great purifying storm finally arrived, he thought with quiet satisfaction, the air would be fit to breathe again, but until that glorious day . . .

'The chosen ones await your bidding, master,' came a gruff voice behind him.

Orbix turned. The cage-master, Mollus Leddix, stood before him. Behind him, flanked by hulking flathead Guardians, were two young librarians, their faces white and drawn. One, a shock of ginger hair matted by a gash in his eyebrow, tried to stand up straight, but the muscles in his jaw betrayed his fear. His companion, smaller and slightly hunched, stared with pale blue eyes at his feet. Their arms were tied behind their backs.

Orbix thrust his muzzle into the smaller one's face, and took a long, deep sniff. A tear squeezed out from the librarian's eyelashes and slid down his cheek.

'Very good,' said Orbix at last. 'Sweet. Tender . . . Caught them in the sewers, did you?'

'One of them, master,' Leddix nodded. 'The other was shot down over Undertown.'

Orbix Xaxis tutted. 'You librarians,' he said softly. 'Will you never learn that it is we, the Guardians of Night, who are the masters?' He nodded to the flatheads. 'Put them in the cage,' he growled. 'And remove their gags. I want to hear them sing.'

The flatheads tore the knotted rope from the prisoners' mouths and bundled them to the end of the jutting gantry, where a heavy cage hung down from an overhead pulley. One of the Guardians opened the barred door. Another shoved the prisoners inside. The ginger-haired librarian stood stock-still, his head held high. Beside him, his companion followed his example.

Orbix snorted. They were all the same, these young librarians. Trying so hard to be brave, to hide their fear – he had yet to meet a single one prepared to plead for his life. A cold fury gripped him. They would be singing soon enough.

'Lower the cage,' he barked.

Leddix gave a signal, and a Guardian stepped forward, released the locking-bolt on the crank-wheel, and began turning. With a lurch, the cage began its long descent. Orbix Xaxis raised his arms and lifted his head. The moon-light glinted on his mask and tinted glasses.

'Thus perish all those who pollute the Great Sky with blasphemous flight!' his rasping voice rang out. 'For we, the Guardians, shall purify the Sky, ready for that Great Night. Hail, the Great Storm!'

The gantry filled with voices raised in salute. 'Hail, the Great Storm! Hail, the Great Storm!'

Far below them now, the cage continued down. Past the dark angular Tower of Night it went; past the surface of the crumbling Sanctaphrax rock and the vast network of scaffolding erected to support it, and on down into Screetown.

Inside the cage, the two librarians struggled to keep their balance as they stared out.

'Try not to look down,' said the ginger-haired one.

'I . . . I can't,' said his companion. 'I saw something down there in the darkness . . . Waiting . . .'

Created when massive chunks of stone had broken off from the crumbling Sanctaphrax rock, fallen and crushed the area of Undertown directly beneath, Screetown was a rubble-strewn wilderness. Every building had been demolished, every street destroyed, while the weight of the immense boulders crashing down was so great that the shock waves had opened up gaping canyons in the ground.

It was into the deepest of these canyons that the librarians were being lowered. All at once, the cage jerked to a standstill. The two young librarians fell against the bars of the cage as, far above their heads, the voice of the High Guardian rang out.

'Come, Demons of the Deep!' he cried. 'And rid the Sky of its polluters!' He turned to Leddix. 'Release them,' he hissed.

Leddix reached across and pulled on the stout wooden lever by his shoulder. There was a *hiss* as rope slid through the pulley-wheel, and a muffled *clank*. Far below, the bottom of the cage swung open and the librarians toppled down onto the steep, scree-covered slope beneath them with an anguished cry.

'Now, their song begins,' Orbix rasped from behind the mask. He stepped forward and peered down into the canyon.

Far beneath him, he could just make out the two young librarians, sliding and stumbling as they struggled to stop themselves slipping further down into the canyon. And there, emerging from the cracks and crevices all round them – in a shadowy flurry of flapping wings and scurrying claws – were the huge dark shapes of the creatures awaiting them.

The pale, young librarians let out loud, piercing screams. Like the contracting iris of a monstrous eye, the black shapes closed in around them – and blotted them out. From the canyon depths came a low chorus of howls and snarls, and the sound of tearing flesh. The screaming stopped.

Orbix turned away. 'Such a sweet song,' he mused. 'I never tire of it.'

'Master,' gasped Leddix, pointing up at the sky and falling to his knees. 'Look!'

Orbix spun round, to see a bright ball of flame hurtling from one side of the sky to the other in a blaze of blood-red light. Over his head it flew, wailing eerily; past the Stone Gardens and off into Open Sky beyond. Unblinking, Orbix watched it shrink to the size of a marsh-gem, a pinprick – and then disappear.

He held his breath.

The next instant, there was a distant explosion and a

flash of light. The misty clouds seemed to grow denser, dimming the yellow light of the moon. Orbix gripped the wooden lever to steady himself. The air grew heavier than ever.

'It is a sign,' he breathed. 'Look how the clouds grow thick, how the very air around us grows hotter. The sky is preparing for the arrival of that wondrous night.'

'Hail, the Great Storm!' barked Leddix, falling to his knees. The guards took up the cry once more. 'Hail, the Great Storm! Hail, the Great Storm!'

Several storeys below, in his study, Xanth Filatine – assistant to the High Guardian of Night – looked up from a barkscroll and shuddered. There must have been another Purification Ceremony – probably the two librarians he'd interrogated that afternoon. And after he'd specifically told Leddix he couldn't have them!

Xanth slammed a fist down on his desk. The evil skyslug had gone over his head to the High Guardian – and everybody knew how much Orbix Xaxis enjoyed his little rituals.

Xanth strode across to the window and looked out. 'Hail to the Great Storm,' he muttered bitterly.

*

As he looked down from the saddle of the *Stormhornet*, Rook Barkwater frowned. Something *was* going on at the Mire Gates. Usually at this time in the morning, there would be half a dozen shrykes at most on guard. Today there were hundreds of them.

Deftly lowering the loftsail and tugging the nether-sail rope hard to his right, he swooped in as close as he dared. He was counting on the thick stifling mist to help conceal him. Keeping low, he skirted the boom-docks. Then, taking both rope-handles in one hand, he raised his telescope to his eye with the other.

'Sky above!' he exclaimed.

Long columns of the bird-creatures were stretched back along the Great Mire Road as far as the eye could see. More ominously, from the way they were kitted out – with their shiny breastplates, plumed battle-helmets and multitude of terrible weapons – this was no mere gathering of the clans. The shrykes seemed to be mobilizing for war.

Rook knew he had to get back to the Great Library and make a report. Then it would be up to the High Librarian, Fenbrus Lodd, to decide what to do for the best. Tugging sharply on the loftsail rope, Rook brought the *Stormhornet* round and, staying low in the sky, headed back over Undertown.

These were, indeed, strange times. There were alleged goblin atrocities in Undertown, rumours of a thwarted slave uprising in the Sanctaphrax Forest and un-confirmed sightings of monstrous creatures emerging from the diseased rock itself. And then there was this strange weather. Like all librarian knights, Rook Barkwater had been briefed to take close note of the weather whilst on patrol.

But what was there to say? he wondered. That it was a little bit hotter than the morning before? A little bit more humid, more sultry, more oppressive? That the dense cover of cloud looked a little bit lower in the sky; the sun behind it, a little dimmer? Certainly he could confirm all these things. But that was all. As for *why* it was happening, that was anyone's guess. All Rook knew was that sunrise had become a drab affair, with the displays of dazzling colour and intricate cloud formations now seemingly things of the past.

Ploughing on through the hot, turgid air, Rook circled the tall, cracked towers of the Palace of Statues and swooped back down over the squalor and degradation of Undertown. He noted the dilapidated stores and run-down workshops opening up for business, the factories and foundries belching smoke, and on every street, the columns of chained slaves being driven by goblin guards from one part of town to the other as the night-shift was replaced by the day-shift.

'Poor creatures,' Rook whispered, his stomach churning.

The whole stinking place sickened him. And yet, as he swooped by unnoticed, Rook saw no sign that the goblins' behaviour was any more atrocious than normal. Nor, when he reached the jumbled framework of beams and pillars that formed the Sanctaphrax Forest, could he detect any hint of a recent uprising. It all looked like business as usual, with the slaves toiling and the goblins keeping them at their backbreaking work with random acts of casual brutality.

Away from the work gangs, the Sanctaphrax Forest was eerily quiet. Only the constant soft creaking of the wood broke the silence. Rook flitted in and out of the shadowy scaffolding uneasily. He'd never liked it here. Ever since the forest had first been erected it had become colonized by numerous unpleasant creatures: flocks of ratbirds, colonies of rabid fromps, weezits, razorflits . . .

Suddenly, from his right, he heard a sucking, slurping noise. He glanced round to see a dwarf-rotsucker on a broad horizontal beam crouched down next to a small egg-like cocoon. It had already drilled a hole in the side with its probing snout, and was now sucking out the putrid soup of a recent victim, now fully decomposed.

The rank stench of death filled the air. The rotsucker looked up from its meal, its glowing eyes boring into the shadows suspiciously. Rook glided on.

Swooping down lower in the sky, letting the light breeze do the work for him as he crossed the Edgewater

River, Rook found himself thinking about the under-ground library – and how glad he was not to be there now.

All those years he'd spent down in the dark, dripping sewers had left him with a fierce hunger for the world outside. He loved the freedom, and the space, and the wind in his hair and the sun in his face – and each time he soared up high on the *Stormhornet*, he was over-whelmed by the wonder of the endless expanse of sky all round him.

He looked down, and swallowed uneasily. Screetown.

Rook surveyed the scene of desolation below him. The debris, the destruction, the dark fissures that had opened up in the ground. He shuddered. Everywhere, there were shifting shadows sliding between the rocks, and curious glinting lights that were like eyes glaring back at him; widening greedily, sizing him up. Rook felt the evil of the place weighing him down. He tugged sharply on the sail ropes and the skycraft rose up in the sky.

Higher he flew, past the Sanctaphrax rock and on up above the Tower of Night. Far to his left, the Stone Gardens came into view. Pulling hard on the loftsail, Rook brought the *Stormhornet* about in the sky and prepared for the long swooping descent round the stacks of broken boulders at the furthest tip of the Edge.

His spirits lifted as he left Screetown behind him. It felt good to be high in the sky once more, the whole world spread out below him like a vast intricate map. *This* was where he belonged, up in wide open air. Not trapped below the ground like a piebald rat.

All at once, a sound broke into his thoughts: a great roaring, wailing sound that was coming up fast behind him. The next instant everything was a confusion of noise and heat and light. The *Stormhornet* reared beneath him and spun round. Rook couldn't see a thing. The wind was rushing all round him, tossing him about like a scrap of parchment. The acrid smell of burning spider-silk and toasted wood-almonds filled his nostrils.

'Sky save me,' he murmured, his words whipped away on the rushing air.

The fragile craft had gone into a plummeting tailspin, and together, the pair of them were tumbling out of the sky faster than a stricken flight-rock.

·C H A P T E R   T W O·

SCREETOWN

Clinging on grimly, Rook fought hard to control the *Stormhornet*'s steep dive. He leaned back in the stirrups and tried desperately to keep her nose up. But it was no good. The skycraft wasn't responding. The ground – a mosaic of rock stacks and ravines – hurtled up to meet them.

The last thing Rook remembered was making himself relax his muscles in preparation for the crash, just as he'd been taught to do in flight training. He released the carved wooden neck, pulled his feet out of the stirrups, and felt the *Stormhornet* slip away from beneath him.

For a moment, everything seemed to be sweeping past him in a smudged blur. There was a roaring of air and a flashing of light – then blackness.

Rook opened his eyes. His head was throbbing, there was something heavy pressing down on his chest, and his mouth was full of foul-tasting dust. But he was alive.

Above him, the chaotic silhouettes of rubble crags stood out against the muddy sky like brooding giants. Where was he? he wondered. Where was the *Stormhornet*? And what in Sky's name had happened? One moment he'd been swooping high in the sky beyond the great rock, the next he was . . .

Screetown!

An icy shiver ran through him. The treacherous winds had driven him back across the sky. Now he was inside that desolate wasteland of wrecked buildings and sprawling rockfalls, home to rubble ghouls and muglumps – and worse. From far above him came the raucous cawing of a lone white raven as it sliced across the dusty sky.

The important thing, he knew, was not to panic. He must stay calm. He must remember his training. After all, he was a librarian knight, he told himself; one of Varis Lodd's finest. He would survive. He had to survive. Varis would expect nothing less of him.

First of all, he must check for any injuries. Gingerly, he felt his head, his neck, and his chest . . . The pressure on his ribs, he discovered, came from a large piece of rubble that was making it hard to breathe. With a grunt, Rook gripped the boulder, slowly eased it off his chest and dropped it beside him. It disappeared into nothingness.

With a gasp, Rook turned to find himself staring down into a deep, dark chasm. He was lying on the very edge of a huge canyon. Far below, he could hear the boulder's clattering descent. Its muffled thuds echoed back – first loud, then softer, and then softer still – as it bounced

from rock to rock. And from the depths of the canyon, there came an answering call; a mewling cry which grew louder and louder, until the air echoed with sinister howls.

Anxiously, Rook rose to his feet and stepped back from the canyon's edge. Whatever lurked down there in those infernal depths, he had clearly awoken it. The cries grew louder, and he thought he heard the sound of shifting scree as something scrabbled closer.

He didn't wait to see what it was. Turning away, Rook began to pick his way through the piles of rubble as quickly as he dared. The treacherous rubble below his feet slipped and slid. The air was thick with choking dust.

'Find shelter,' a voice inside his head whispered. 'Somewhere to hide.'

Rook clambered over the angular rock-scape, grazing his fingers and scraping his shins. There were great mountains of rubble looming up everywhere he looked; a chaos of cracked arches, fallen walls and leaning pillars, with jutting roofbeams silhouetted against the sepia-stained sky like the ribs of giant creatures.

The wind, though little more than a hot, malodorous draught, whistled softly between the rocks like an ancient goblin matron sucking air between her gappy teeth. The sun was low behind the cloudcover, with the sky already growing darker, yet the air beneath was hotter than ever. Rook wiped the sweat from his forehead; he was still finding it difficult to breathe. His head ached, and every jarred bone in his body throbbed with pain – but Rook dared not stop, not even for a moment.

The howls were getting closer, and whatever was making them, it was clearly no longer alone. Others had joined it in a chorus of yelps and shrieks. He had to find a hiding-place, and quickly.

Some way ahead a ruined archway poked up from the scree. Beneath it, Rook could see a crevice that looked just large enough for him to crawl through. He only hoped it didn't already have an occupant. He checked his equipment – water-bottle, grappling-hook, notebook, hover tincture, knife . . .

The cries seemed just behind him now; keening, high-pitched, and accompanied by a strange leathery rustling. Rook swallowed anxiously.

He was being hunted.

Drawing his knife, Rook made for the crevice. He crouched down, thrust his head into the entrance and listened. There was nothing. He sniffed. If some creature was using the place as a sanctuary, he should be able to smell its musty bedding or pungent droppings. Again, there was nothing; only the dry, sour odour of the crumbled rock itself.

Behind him, the howls rose up in a swirling discord.

'Earth guard and Sky protect me,' he murmured as he disappeared into the small opening.

It was narrower than he'd first thought and grew narrower still the further he scrambled into the dark, dusty crevice. Soon he was down on his front and wriggling between the great slabs of fallen rock. The gaps between them closed in, pressing into him from both sides, squeezing him

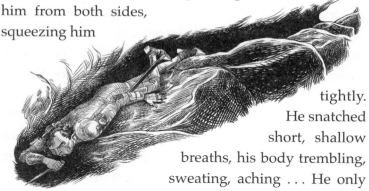

tightly. He snatched short, shallow breaths, his body trembling, sweating, aching . . . He only hoped he'd be able to get out again. Had he escaped the howling creatures, only to bury himself in his own grave? The thing was, he had to get far enough in to avoid a probing claw or tentacle.

'Just a few strides more,' he urged himself. 'Just . . .'

Rook could go no further. Ahead, the rubble was packed tight. He shifted himself awkwardly round, cracking his knee against a jutting rock. Ignoring the intense pain, he reached out and hurriedly grasped handful after handful of the sour dust, which he rubbed over his clothes, his face, and his hair. It stuck to the sweat, coating every inch of him and should, according to his training, obscure his own smell – at least, that was the theory.

All at once, there came a snuffling, sniffing sound from the opening to the crevice. Rook froze. The sniffing grew louder. Then there was a rough scratching noise, followed by the sound of falling debris. Something – a snout, a claw, a tentacle – was working its way into the crevice, searching for its elusive prey. Rook bit nervously into his lower lip.

The scratching stopped. The sniffing resumed – then it, too, stopped. Rook heard the leathery rustling as something big scuffled off heavily, howling with rage and frustration as it searched elsewhere. A dozen others answered its call. The leathery rustle grew more distant; the howls receded. The hunt seemed to be moving on.

When he was sure they'd gone, Rook began the arduous crawl back out of the crevice. At the end, he pushed aside the rocks that the creature had dislodged, and emerged, dust-covered and shaking. He wiped the sour particles from his lips and breathed in the evening air greedily. Then he peered about him, ready at the first sign of danger to disappear back into the hole.

The ground gave a little tremor – causing the rubble to shift and more dust to rise.

Must get my bearings, Rook thought grimly as he climbed to his feet. He had to get out of this place as soon as he could.

The Sanctaphrax rock loomed in the sky behind him and he could just make out the cracked towers of Undertown's northern heights far ahead. To his left and right, the skeletons of buildings rose up out of the debris like disfigured hands. Before him, a vast mound of stone blocks extended into the distance. Walking was impossible. He would have to clamber up the precariously balanced rocks on his hands and knees.

Rook knew the drill, of course. Test each foothold before committing your whole weight. And if you need to leap, then look carefully first.

By the time he reached the top of the first rubble mound, Rook was sweating heavily and panting like a shryke-sister's prowlgrin after a long patrol. He paused and straightened up. The towers of the northern heights were still in front of him – but by his reckoning it was already late afternoon. At this rate, he faced the very real prospect of having to survive a night in Screetown. He swallowed uneasily.

All at once, a colossal tremor knocked Rook off his feet. The rubble beneath him seemed to boil; great clouds of dust blacked out the evening sky, stinging his eyes and filling his mouth. Rook curled up into a ball and waited for the shaking to stop.

Slowly, the rubble settled and the rattle of shifting pebbles died away. The thick dust still hung in the hot, humid air but, as Rook wiped his eyes, it too began to clear. When he was sure it was over, he climbed shakily to his feet once more and looked around.

The rubble mounds just behind him had been flattened to reveal a line of splintered beams from some long-buried building. Beside them, only half-uncovered, the statue of a great Undertown artisan – long since forgotten – stood at a drunken angle, one arm, broken at the wrist, reaching up to the sky. And in the middle of it all – like a huge clenched fist – lay a massive chunk of rock. Rook looked up at the towering shape of the Sanctaphrax rock above him, propped up on its forest of wooden pillars, like some huge diseased oak-apple.

Despite the neverending work carried out on the Sanctaphrax Forest, crumbling pieces of the great rock were always falling. Most were small and insignificant, but every so often a great slab would break free and come crashing down onto Screetown.

Rook shuddered. 'That was close,' he murmured. 'Too close.'

He turned to go – then froze in his tracks. A hand of ice seemed to grip his heart.

'No,' he whispered. 'No, it can't be.'

But it was. Lying on the ground not half a dozen strides away was the *Stormhornet* – or what was left of it. The mast was blackened and in two pieces. A charred scrap of spidersilk and a twist of rope were all that remained of the sails. And as for the prow ... Rook picked his way over the uneven ground and, crouching down beside the skycraft, reached out tentatively.

His fingers confirmed what he hoped his eyes had only imagined. The neck of the *Stormhornet* was broken almost in two. Jagged splinters at the top of the stump glinted in the weak sunlight while the angular head – barely attached by a couple of thin, woody fibres – lolled forward.

A painful lump formed in Rook's throat. The sails and ropes could have been replaced; so could the mast. But with the neck of the craft broken, he knew that its spirit had been released. The *Stormhornet* would never fly again.

Rook fell to his knees. He raised the wooden head, held it gently in place, and hugged the prow tightly. Memories from the Free Glades came flooding back: Oakley Gruffbark, the woodtroll master-carver who had helped him find the stormhornet – *his* stormhornet – concealed within the slab of wood he had to carve; varnish-making in the Gardens of Light; sail-setting and ropecraft. Bit by bit, he'd worked on her, and learned to fly her . . .

'I . . . I carved you,' he whispered, his voice faltering. 'I named you. Together we rode the sky, you and I.' He sniffed. 'Farewell . . .' His chest felt tight, as though the boulder was back there, pressing down and making it difficult to breathe. '*Stormhornet* . . .'

Rook knew that his beloved skycraft was now just a piece of wood again. Her spirit had departed. With a heavy heart, he stood up and set off.

He did not look back.

Progress was slow as Rook struggled on. Navigating the jagged, uneven rubble became increasingly difficult and his throat was soon as parched as the rocky landscape he was crossing. Time and again he came to vast craters which took an age to cross. Down he would go, into the echoing bowl of boulders and up the other side, hoping and praying each time that when he emerged at the top, the towers of Undertown would look nearer.

'This time,' he whispered, the sound of his own voice oddly reassuring as he climbed the far side of a particularly large depression. 'This time, they'll look closer, they've got to . . .'

Once again, he was disappointed. The towers appeared as far away as ever. What was more, it was growing darker.

Must keep my head, he reminded himself. I can

survive a night in Screetown if I just follow my training and don't lose my nerve – Earth and Sky willing, he thought anxiously as a raucous shriek echoed round the desolation. The night-creatures were stirring.

He reached for his water-bottle and had it to his lips before remembering that it was empty.

'Stupid,' he muttered to himself, clipping the empty flask back into place. Varis would be disappointed in him for failing to conserve his meagre rations. He shook his head miserably. Perhaps he'd discover some more water and be able to refill it. But until then . . .

He picked up a smooth round pebble and popped it into his mouth. It was supposed to make his mouth water, to provide enough moisture to soothe his burning throat. But it didn't work. Rook spat the claggy stone out in disgust, and as he drove himself on, his thirst nagged at him constantly now that there was no means to slake it.

It was so hot. So humid. He wiped his hand gently across his brow and sucked the sweat from his finger-tips. The salty droplets only made him greedy for more.

Of course, there was water here in Screetown, dry and dusty though it appeared. Rook knew that it was just a matter of finding it. Ruptured pipes and broken fountains continued to flow; wells where, long ago, Undertowners had gathered to draw water and gossip, still tapped into the underground water-table. What he had to do was look out for moss, for grass, and scrubby bushes, whose roots, reaching down through the cracks in the rubble, were a sure sign of the presence of water –

that and the evidence of the Screetown creatures which drank it.

As he forged his way on, their shrieks and cries echoed through the sultry twilight air. Past a cracked tower he went, a great section of its once magnificent dome missing, like a bite from a giant woodsap. To his left, out of the corner of his eye, he caught sight of movement and turned to see something slither into the shadows. Rook moved quickly on.

He made his way over fallen pillars forming makeshift bridges; beneath a crumbling viaduct, its two rows of supports in various stages of collapse; through the lower window of a tall, unsteady facade, and on across a jagged carpet of slates – once a roof, now a treacherous floor. One slip and he would end up tumbling down into the cracks that gaped on either side of him. If he did, he knew that no-one would ever find him – until the scavengers came to pick his bones.

The towers of Undertown were still before him, but flat now against the sky in the fading light. Despite all his efforts, he was still making dismal progress. Every breath was an effort; every step a gamble. Panting noisily, he slipped and stumbled, grazing his knuckles and cracking his shins. And then, just when he thought things couldn't get any worse, something up ahead of him caught his eye; something that reminded him that in Screetown things could *always* get worse.

It was lying on a flat slab of rock: bright blue, furry, crushed. He approached cautiously, a numbing dread pounding in his temples. From its beaky snout and curved claws, Rook recognized the dead creature at once.

'A lemkin,' he gasped, and prodded at the desiccated body with his foot. A fine white dust trickled down from its mouth and empty eye-sockets. Rook looked away, but not before noticing that there was grey-green moss clinging to the rock. There must be water close by! Perhaps the lemkin had come searching for it – and perished in the process. Rook drew his sword and peered into the shadows.

From his left, he heard a soft, murmuring trickle. Water – running water. A broken pipe, maybe; or a little spring. Rook moved towards the sound, his senses on fire and his head spinning – the promise of the cool, refreshing water battling with the need to remain on his guard.

He climbed over a squat, rounded rock that looked like nothing so much as a grazing hammelhorn. The trickling sound grew louder. There, bubbling up from the ground in the shadow of two moss-covered slabs of rock, was a small spring. It overflowed and spread out, before disappearing back into the earth. The muddy ground around it was dappled with the footprints of numerous creatures – both predator and prey. Rook had just seen what had happened to the lemkin. He had no intention of suffering the same fate.

Keeping a close lookout, he crouched down – sword ready at his side – cupped his hands and plunged them into the small pool; and again, and again . . .

Water had never tasted as good!

His thirst quenched at last, Rook unclipped his water-bottle and dunked it into the clear water. Glugging bubbles hit the surface as it filled, and he glanced nervously round, terrified that some prowling Screetown creature might have heard.

Was that something glinting in the shadows? he wondered, his heart racing. And what was that *smell*? Steamy . . . Stagnant . . .

'Hurry up,' he muttered and shook the bottle under the water, trying to force it to fill more quickly. The air bubbles came out in a rush – then stopped completely as the water gushed in. Rook pushed the cork into place and was about to attach it back on his belt when he heard a noise behind him. Soft and slithering, it was – and the steamy, stagnant odour seemed to grow more intense.

Grasping his sword, Rook spun round. At first, he couldn't see anything untoward. Just rocks and shadows.

There's nothing there, he tried to reassure himself. It's just my mind playing tricks.

But even as he thought it, he realized that he was wrong. His gaze fell on a glint of light. It was a tentacle; a moist, translucent tentacle writhing out of a black crevice and probing the rock above. And as he watched – horrified, unable to tear him-self away – a second tentacle appeared. Together, the pair of them gripped the rock, quivered and tugged. The next instant, the glistening top of a jelly-like creature appeared from the narrow crack. It squeezed itself up out of the gap, like tilder-fat oozing from a split barrel.

'Earth and Sky!' Rook gasped, stepping back.

With a slimy *squelch*, the last of the great gelatinous creature eased itself out of the crevice. Trembling and wobbling, it resumed its more normal form. With a sickening jolt of recognition, Rook realized just what it was. The three flickering eye-bumps, the slimy transparent skin with the veins pulsing beneath it; the probing tentacles, the fluttering belly-frill, the vast body quivering with anticipation . . .

'A rubble ghoul,' he whispered.

The name was enough to make every hair on his body stand on end. He had pored over descriptions of them in the library treatises he'd read, descriptions that had

revolted him even then. But now, up close, he felt a wave of nausea wash over him.

Slurping loudly, the rubble ghoul slithered over the slab of rock, its three eyes glistening in the gloom. Rook took another step back. At the edge of the slab now, the creature flapped its belly-frill and rose up, seemingly weightless, into the air. It pulsated as it moved, like bellows – in, out, in, out – sucking in the humid air, and blowing it out again, as hot and dry as the blast from an oven.

Rook took yet another step back. The creature came closer. It was clearly thirsty – but then rubble ghouls, he knew, were *always* thirsty. Not for running water though. Even as he edged towards the babbling spring, Rook knew it wouldn't save him. No, the rubble ghoul took its sustenance from living bodies, sucking every drop of moisture from its victims. Lemkins or librarian knights, they weren't fussy what they drank.

At the next faltering step, Rook's back thudded against rock. He could go no further. He was trapped.

The rubble ghoul hovered before him, slurping and hissing. In, out, it went. In out. The air all round grew hotter, drier; the stagnant odour made him gag.

All at once, the great pulsing creature tilted back to reveal a huge iris-like opening at the centre of its quivering belly. Rook stared in horror as, slowly but surely, it began to open. A shower of bright pink suckered tentacles flipped out and danced in the scorching air.

The colour drained from Rook's face. What could he do?

*

421

Like a clump of noxious toadstools growing out of a grimy Undertown clearing, the Hive Towers – headquarters of General Tytugg and his elite hammerhead guard – gleamed in the fading light. Lamps had already been lit both inside and out. Dull, flickering yellow light glowed from the small windows in the towers and cone-

shaped roofs; torches fixed to the walls and the sides of the notorious Gates of Despair blazed. The rank odour of the burning fat mingled with the general filth – fungal, fetid, and foul.

Inside, the shadowy building was one vast, spartan open hall. At its centre was a great fire, the stinkwood logs the goblins preferred blazing fiercely. The flames were intensely hot; the smoke, pungent. Above the brazier hung a series of bubbling pots, each one tended by mobgnome slaves, their chains bolted to the floor. At the sides of the building, there were staircases leading up to platform after platform – all secured to the curving outer-walls but with no inner-walls to close them off into rooms. There were no secrets in the Hive Towers.

The whole place was seething. There were hammer-head goblins in every corner; rough and rowdy, their voices raised, and spoiling for a fight. Even those asleep on their hammocks strung out beneath the roof-beams were snoring, snorting, thrashing about and cursing loudly in their dreams.

Some were on duty, guarding the gates, the walls and the roofs. Some were at table in the slop-corners; others were seated on wooden benches tending to their equip-ment – patching rents in their jackets and re-soling their boots, cleaning blood from their swords and sharpening the vicious jags on their battle-scythes.

As a mobgnome slave scurried past a group of them, a jug clasped in her scrawny arms, one – a tattooed individual with a ring through his nose – stuck out a boot. The mobgnome went sprawling, her face thudding down into the rank, mouldering straw, her jug smashing and the hammelhorn-milk it had held slopping over the floor.

'Lick that up, clumsy slave-filth,' the hammerhead snarled.

Outside, a dozen or more – massive specimens, each of them, with heavy armour and bearing the scars of numerous hard battles – were locked in mock-combat, so fierce that it looked like the real thing.

Passing between the lot of them, a returning battalion of goblin guards was tramping up the stairs to the bulging armoury with a consignment of seized weapons.

Their victorious voices boomed round the hall.

'That'll teach them Undertown scumsacks not to mess with us,' one grunted. 'Whatever made them think they could get away with manufacturing weapons like that? And right under us noses!'

His neighbour chuckled. 'D'you hear that factory-master squeal when we strung him up?' he said. 'Like a stuck woodhog, he sounded.'

'Bled like one, too,' another chipped in.

'Still, the weapons'll come in useful,' the first hammer-head muttered, patting the great bundle of scythes, swords, maces and crossbows he and his neighbour were carrying between them. 'Rumour has it, there's a fresh contingent coming in from the Goblin Nations.'

Further down the stairs, a couple of goblins snorted dismissively.

'Goblin Nations,' one of them said, hawking and spitting down the stairwell.

'Milksops, the lot of them,' said the other. 'Settled down in villages just like that Free Glade scum, they have!'

Every self-respecting hammerhead goblin prided himself on his independence; with a weapon at his side and his birthing-bundle on his back, a hammerhead was always ready to pick up everything he owned and move on. Or should have been. Recently, though, several of their number had been tempted to settle down in permanent dwellings in the Goblin Nations; they'd become merchants, trappers – some, it was reported, were even taking up farming!

'General Tytugg will soon whip 'em into shape,' came a

voice from further up the stairs, and a cheer of derision and anticipation echoed round the building.

General Tytugg himself was unaware that his name had been mentioned. He didn't hear the raucous cheering, nor the spontaneous boot-pounding of approval that followed. Standing on the raised platform jutting out from the first storey, he only had eyes and ears for his prisoner.

'You *will* tell me, Huffknot,' he said, his voice gruff and menacing as he jerked the lugtroll's head sharply back. 'Of that, I give you my word.' He pulled a long rusty pin from the lapel of his leather battle-jacket and held it close to the lugtroll's terrified face.

'But ... but I don't ... I don't know anything,' he protested, his chains jangling. 'Not a single thing. Really, I don't. I'm at the beck and call of any who enlist my services ...'

'*Tut-tut-tut*,' Tytugg clicked softly and shook his head. He traced the point of the pin lightly down the lugtroll's bulbous nose. 'I'm disappointed in you, Huffknot.' His voice grew harsh. 'I don't like being disappointed.'

'You've got to believe me!' the lugtroll pleaded.

'When you starts telling me the truth – the *whole* truth, Huffknot – then maybe I shall start believing you,' said the general. He turned and inspected the three small pots set out in a line on a trestle-table. He selected one at random, unstoppered it and sniffed the thick orange liquid inside. 'I wonder what this one does?'

Eyes wide and body quivering, Huffknot watched as the general poked the pin down inside the pot and withdrew it. A bead of orange clung to the sharpened point.

'Hold out your arm,' Tytugg demanded.

Huffknot did as he was told, the chain fixed round his wrist clanking as he moved. General Tytugg seized the arm, jabbed the pin into the skin and stood back to observe.

Almost at once, Huffknot felt the tiny pinprick burn, and he watched helplessly as his arm began to swell.

'Interesting,' said the general. 'Forgive me, Huffknot, but I thought you said the pots contained cosmetics – for the shryke-sisters. Feather-balm, you said. Beak-gloss. Cold cream . . .' He poked at the swollen arm. 'Yet it seems to work like . . . well, poison.'

Huffknot grimaced. 'I . . . I didn't know. She told me that . . .'

'*Who* told you?' General Tytugg demanded. Above and below, the hammerheads paused and looked round as his angry voice rose up above the general hubbub.

'I . . . I don't know her name,' Huffknot whispered.

Without a word, the general seized the second pot, pulled out the stopper and dipped the pin inside. This time, as he pricked the lugtroll's flesh, the skin developed an angry red rash that spread up his arm and down to his fingertips. And, as the pair of them watched, the whole area erupted in a mass of tiny pustules. Tytugg thrust the pin into the bottle a second time and held it close to Huffknot's face.

'Hestera,' he blurted out. 'Hestera Spikesap.'

'I knew it!' the general cried triumphantly. 'Hestera Spikesap . . .' He savoured the words. *'Hestera Spikesap –* the hag what ministers to that parasitic lardbutt, Vox Verlix.' He turned and called down to a hammerhead guard sitting on a wooden bench, hardening his cross-bow bolts in the fire. 'I owe you a barrel of woodgrog, Smutt,' he shouted. 'He *was* coming out of the Palace of Statues.'

The hammerhead looked up and grinned toothlessly. 'Sir,' he shouted back.

The general turned back to Huffknot. A thin-lipped smile spread across his leathery face, revealing an incomplete set of brown, jagged teeth. 'Looks like I've struck gold with you,' he said.

'But I don't know anything, believe me. I'm her slave. I have to do what I'm told,' Huffknot babbled. 'I was to deliver the pots to the shrykes, just as I told you, and return with a phial I would be given in return.'

Tytugg shuddered. 'Shrykes,' he muttered. 'One day, so help me, I'm going to wring every one of their scrawny necks. They've got it coming to them . . .' He looked up, eyes blazing. 'A phial of *what*?'

Huffknot shrugged. 'Your guards arrested me before . . .'

The general spat. 'Something to do with that Vox Verlix, no doubt,' he snarled. 'I've been meaning to pay that great fatsack another visit for quite some time.' He ran his fingers up and down his knife. 'Unfinished business, you might say. It's about time he learned who *really* governs Undertown.' He frowned. 'If I could just get into that rat-trap of a palace of his . . .'

He fell silent, deep in thought. Then he turned on Huffknot. His face was grim, his voice menacing.

'But of course!' he said, an evil smile playing on his lips. 'Hestera Spikesap's slave, you say. Well I'm sure *you* know your way round Vox's palace – where those traps are and how to avoid them. How, for instance' – Tytugg leered at the hapless lugtroll – 'a goblin who wanted to pay our so-called Most High Academe an unannounced visit might get into his personal chamber?'

'Unannounced visit?' said Huffknot. 'Personal chamber?' He trembled. 'I . . . I'm just a kitchen slave.'

General Tytugg turned away. He picked up the third pot and tugged the cork free. An acrid odour – like rotting oaksap and tildermusk – filled the air. The lugtroll blanched as the general plunged the pin into the black potion it contained. He stirred it three times, then turned back to the lugtroll and held the steaming pin inches from the bulbous nose.

'No, no!' Huffknot shrieked. 'Not that one! I beg you! Please! I'll tell you everything! *Everything!*'

Grasping his sword, Rook slashed desperately at the hideous gelatinous creature that reared up before him, its huge mouth writhing with tentacles. But it was no good. With a sudden beating of its belly-frill, the rubble ghoul surged forwards and swallowed him whole. It was like being smothered in scalding tar.

Rook couldn't cry out. He could barely breathe. He felt the tentacles attaching themselves to his face, his arms, his legs. He struggled, but could not move. The sword was wrenched from his fingers. Soon, his heart would stop and the suckers would start their work. He would be drained like the hanging carcass of a hammelhorn.

Helpless, he peered through the translucent body of the suffocating creature. He could just make out the towers of Undertown. With a sharp pang of despair, he thought how they looked farther away than ever . . .

All at once, there was a hiss, a shudder – and the rubble ghoul's mouth suddenly gaped in an involuntary spasm. Rook was spat out with such force that he was slammed into the rubble beside the spring. Something round and leathery almost hit him on the head as the creature spat again, and seemed to curl up into itself. Rook looked down. It was his water-bottle – empty now, and dry as a bone.

At that moment, the rubble ghoul let out a bloodcurdling screech and turned from purple to red, three jets of steam hissing noisily from its eyes. Its translucent body bubbled and popped, like water boiling in

a cauldron. A glass phial shot out of the writhing rubble ghoul and shattered on the rocks beside Rook.

'The hover tincture,' Rook murmured.

No librarian knight's equipment was complete without the antidote to the bite of the hover worm, the notorious Deepwoods predator. Here in Undertown, they were seldom encountered, and yet the small glass phial was considered a good-luck charm. Rook had good cause to thank it now. The antidote that acted against the horrific swelling caused by the hoverworm's bite was clearly fatal to the rubble ghoul.

With a small sigh, the creature flopped down onto a slab of rock. The last vestiges of moisture evaporated away. There was nothing left but a fine, dry membrane – with Rook's sword resting at the very centre.

Rook climbed to his feet and crossed over to the rock. Already the hot humid air was turning the remains of the rubble ghoul to dust. He stooped down for the sword, wiped the blade on his trousers and returned it to its sheath. Then, as he turned to leave, something caught his eye.

He stopped.

Not some*thing*, he realized, but some*one* – silhouetted against the sky just above him. Rook sank to his knees. He'd been hunted, almost died of thirst, been swallowed whole then spat out again, only to be cornered by . . . By *what*?

'I give up,' he murmured. 'I can't go on . . .'

The figure held out a hand. 'Varis would be very disappointed to hear that,' said a familiar voice.

·CHAPTER THREE·

THE SUNKEN PALACE

R ook could scarcely believe his ears. That voice! He
recognized that voice. Shielding his eyes with his
hand, he squinted up into the light. He saw an untidy
shock of fair hair, a turned-up nose, arched eyebrows
over glinting blue eyes . . .

'Felix?' he said. 'Is it you?
Is it really you?'

The figure reached for-
ward. Rook hesitated, then
grasped the outstretched
hand which gripped his own,
firmly, warmly, and pulled
him to his feet. There in
front of him, resplendent
in an array of bleached
white bone-armour and
grey muglump-leather
pelts, stood his old
friend Felix Lodd.

431

Attached to his belt were leather pouches and hide ropes. A curved, serrated knife hung at his side next to a sturdy crossbow slung through a faded grey holster. In the ashen dust of Screetown, this tall figure with his fair hair and bleached apparel looked almost ghost-like.

'I might look like a ghost,' laughed Felix, as if reading Rook's thoughts, 'but I'm real enough, Rook, my old friend.'

'Felix!' Rook cried, hugging him warmly. 'I thought you were dead! We all did. Even Varis. She said that nobody can survive for long in Screetown . . .'

'Much as I hate to disappoint my darling sister and all you learned librarians,' said Felix with a smile, 'it *is* possible to survive in Screetown – though not if you stand round a waterhole, chatting like two old washer-gnomes on laundry day.' He winked. 'Come, Rook,' he said, turning and effortlessly scaling a mound of rubble. 'Tonight you're invited to supper in the Sunken Palace!'

Rook scrambled up after him. 'Wait for me, Felix,' he gasped. 'Not so fast!'

Night was falling, and the shadows and the darkness were melting into one, yet Felix navigated his way skil-fully and confidently through the broken landscape. He clambered over rockfalls, skirted round gaping crevices and picked his way over uneven rocks and rubble, as agile and sure-footed as a lemkin.

Rook followed close behind – or as close as his stumbling, fumbling efforts allowed. Whenever he fell too far back, Felix would perch on a boulder or lean non-chalantly against a ruined pillar, smiling indulgently and waiting for him to catch up. The going was tough and Rook – hot, dusty and constantly out of breath – was beginning to flag.

'There are quite a number of us now,' Felix was saying as, once again, Rook caught up with him. 'We kowtow to no-one,' he told him, 'be they shryke, Guardian or goblin guard.' He smiled. 'We call ourselves the Ghosts of Screetown.'

'I can . . . can see why,' said Rook, fighting to catch his breath. 'But what do you actually *do* in this terrible place?'

Felix turned and continued, clambering effortlessly up over a jutting spur of broken rock. 'Hunt muglumps,' he laughed. 'Among other things.'

'Such as?' said Rook, wearily following him.

They reached a broad stretch of jagged rocks.

'Well,' said Felix, 'sometimes I organize raids with other ghosts to release those poor beggars in the Sanctaphrax Forest. We get them to Undertown, where you librarians take over, helping to shift them on to the Free Glades. Sometimes, to spice things up a little, I'll ambush a Guardian patrol – and the rest of the time I hunt and trap. All kinds of creatures, from feral lemkins in the ruins of Screetown, to muglumps in the sewers.' He paused and glanced back. 'Careful up ahead, Rook. It gets a bit tricky.'

Rook nodded grimly. He was doing his best.

They passed along a dark, narrow chasm, packed with shifting rubble to negotiate and awkward boulders to get round, and emerged at last beside a broad fluted pillar, cracked and lying on its side. Just beyond it, Rook saw a leaning statue, one arm – severed at the wrist – raised and reaching to the sky . . .

'I recognize this place,' he blurted out, disappointment in his voice. 'You mean, all this time, we've been travelling back the way I came.'

Felix nodded but said nothing. Reaching forward, he shouldered back a slab of rock and pointed down a narrow tunnel behind it. 'It's this way,' he told him.

Rook followed Felix into the dark tunnel and waited as his friend pulled the rock back into place.

'I'll lead,' Felix whispered. 'Put your hand on my shoulder. And don't make a sound.'

Rook did as he was told, shuffling forwards as Felix set off. The ground was bumpy and dropped steeply. Although his friend was steadying him, it was all Rook could do not to slip and pitch forwards. The air grew cooler, damper, and was laced with an acrid odour that grew more pungent with every step he took. Had he been on his own, he would have turned back there and then, but he was with Felix now and, for the first time since the terrible crash, he felt safe.

Beneath his feet came the edge of what seemed like a stone stair. Felix abruptly dropped away from him. Rook's hand grasped at nothing.

'Easy does it,' came Felix's voice, and Rook felt his friend's hand reaching back for him. He seized it gratefully and stepped down gingerly after him. A little further on, there was a second step; followed by a third . . . Then a long flight, which seemed to go deep

down into the rubble. The odour grew more pungent. 'What *is* that horrible smell?' he whispered.

'A ratbird roost,' Felix whispered back. 'And it's the best smell there is in Scree-town, believe me.'

As Felix spoke, Rook became aware of the sound of squeaky twittering far above his head and, when he looked up, it was as though the very rocks were squirming. There were thousands of the little creatures. Rook shuddered.

'No desirable residence is complete without a rat-bird roost,' said Felix above the rising clamour as the ratbirds raised the alarm. 'If anything unpleasant should come creeping along to pay us a visit, the ratbirds will soon let us know.'

It was darker than ever at the bottom of the stairs, but as the ground levelled out it became easier to walk. They seemed to be in some kind of ancient corridor. Felix increased his pace. Still holding on to him, Rook trotted along behind.

'Nearly there,' said Felix.

The next moment, they came to a thick curtain of animal hide, which Felix pulled aside to reveal a carved lintel set into the wall above a doorway. Rook peered in – and gasped.

He was standing in the entrance to a great chamber. Eyes wide, he followed Felix inside. Despite the dirty walls and blackened beams, the original grandeur of the place was still in evidence. There were marble pillars and a mosaic-tiled floor, and ancient lamps hung from the high moulded ceiling. Clearly this had once been the residence of someone wealthy – a prominent leagues-man, perhaps; or a successful merchant. Not that the contents of the room belonged to either.

There were dried muglump pelts, both large and small, covering every wall; and the implements that Felix must have used to slay them – curved swords, long thin javelins, and heavy nets, ringed with circular weights – hung from rows of great curling hooks. In one corner there were tusks, horns, skins and skulls; some stacked, some hanging, some clustered together in piles. In the other corner, set into an alcove above which a wall-torch flickered, was an ancient carved cistern. It was, Rook thought, similar to the Wodgiss-fonts the woodtrolls used in their celebrations – but made of stone, not wood. Into it – trickling from a crack in the rock – splashed a thin twist of crystal-clear water.

'Welcome to the Sunken Palace,' said Felix. He swept his arm around in a wide arc. 'A modest little palace, but I call it home,' he chuckled. 'But then I don't have to tell you, Rook, that when you've grown up in the sewers of Undertown, anywhere without a leaking roof is absolute luxury.'

Rook shook his head. 'It's amazing,' he murmured.

Felix clapped his hands together. 'Come on then, my old friend. You must be famished. Fetch me a pot of water from the cistern and I'll get a fire started.'

Rook happily did as he was told. He dunked the large pot into the cistern, filling it almost to the brim; then – holding it before him with both hands – staggered back across the dusty tiles, splashing water as he went, to the fireplace, where once huge logs would have burned.

Felix was there, down on his hands and knees. Having arranged the firewood – chopped-up beams, boards and pieces of furniture – he had unfastened one of the leather pouches attached to his belt and was setting out its contents on the hearth. There was a piece of flint, a short length of iron, oakbark dust and a ball of tinderwool.

As Rook watched, Felix teased a few strands of the orange wool from the ball and placed them down on a flat stone. Over this, he sprinkled the oakbark dust. Then, with the flint in one hand and the small iron bar in the other, he struck the two together. A bright spark dropped onto the oakbark and smouldered. Felix crouched down and blew gently. At first nothing happened. Then, with a puff of smoke and a soft crackle, the whole lot abruptly burst into flames.

'The trick is to get it into the firewood without disturbing the pile,' he murmured as he pushed the stone forward. The flames lapped at the twigs and branches.

He nudged the stone right into the centre. The wood caught. 'There,' he grinned. 'Now where's that water?'

'Here,' said Rook, and the two of them hefted the pot up, and hung its handle over the central hook.

With the fire blazing (it was Rook's job to keep adding extra pieces of wood from the pile by the wall) and the water coming to the boil, Felix gathered his ingredients from the hooks and shelves and busied himself with preparations for the meal.

He chopped, cut and tossed handful after handful of vegetables into the pot – diced roots and tubers, woodonions and pinegarlic, the sliced leaves of oaksprouts and barkgreens, and clumps of the succulent swamp-samphire which grew on the stagnant banks of the Edgewater River. He skinned and filleted three small

creatures – a snowbird, a rock-lizard and something that looked suspiciously like a piebald rat – cut them up into pieces and, having seared the flesh in the flames, tossed them, too, into the boiling pot, then added a cupful of barleyoats for thickening.

'And last but not least . . .' he murmured to himself, as he unclipped a second of the pouches from his belt. 'A little bit of seasoning.' He loosened the drawstring and thrust his fingers inside. 'Some woodpeppercorns, I think. A few dried dellberries, brushsage leaves . . .' He frowned. 'And just a hint of tripweed . . .'

'Oh, not tripweed,' said Rook. 'I hate it, remember? Pickled, dried, salted – it's all disgusting.'

Felix laughed. 'I've always loved it myself. But, all right, since it's you,' he said, 'no tripweed.' He crushed the seeds, berries and dried leaves he'd selected on a stone with the back of his knife, and dropped the whole lot into the steaming broth. A sweet, aromatic fragrance immediately filled the chamber, perfuming the dank air and making Rook's mouth water.

Frowning thoughtfully, Felix searched his belt for something else, opening and closing several other pouches. Rook watched, intrigued.

'Where is it?' Felix muttered. 'Ah, here it is! A corktug,' he cried as, with a flourish, he raised the bone-handled opener in the air. 'Let us have a goblet of winesap together, you and I, Rook, and toast our reunion!'

He seized a bottle from a rough lufwood crate, pulled the cork and poured out two goblets of the thick, dark amber winesap. He handed one to Rook.

'Try that,' he said.

Rook raised the goblet to his lips and sipped. A radiant smile passed across his face as the sweet fruity liquid coated his tongue and slid down his throat. A moment later, a warm glowing feeling coursed round his entire body. He took a second sip and shook his head. 'Delicious,' he said. 'The best I've ever tasted.'

'It should be,' said Felix. 'It was meant for General Tytugg. Drinks only the finest winesap, so he does.' He chuckled. 'Sadly for him, there was a little incident down in the boom-docks a couple of weeks ago and a whole consignment bound for the Hive Towers went missing . . .' He raised his glass and smiled at Rook. 'Here's to the Ghosts of Screetown!'

'The Ghosts of Screetown,' said Rook, raising his own glass high – before draining it in one go.

It was so good to see his best friend again. Rook felt a familiar ache in his chest when he recalled the Announcement Ceremony at which Felix had learned that he would never become a librarian knight like himself. He'd disappeared immediately afterwards without saying a word.

'They miss you, you know,' he said softly.

'Miss me?' said Felix, looking down into his goblet.

'Your father,' said Rook. 'And your sister, Varis. Did you never think of coming back? Or at least letting us know that you were still alive?'

Felix's face clouded over. 'Of course I did, Rook. Many's the time I considered returning to the sewers. But . . .' His voice faltered and he swallowed heavily.

'You have to understand. I was the son of the High Librarian, yet I wasn't picked to become a librarian knight! I let everyone down. My father and Varis. My tutors. Even you, Rook . . .'

'No . . .' Rook protested. 'You've never let me down, Felix . . .'

'You're a good friend,' said Felix. 'You tried your best to help me pass my exams – sitting up with me, night after night. But you know what I'm like with treatises and barkscrolls and all that stuff. I just wasn't cut out to be a librarian knight and I was too ashamed to admit it – so I ran away. And that's something I've had to learn to live with.' He shrugged. 'Besides, I love it out here. This is the life I was born to – not being locked away in some dank library, surrounded by fusty, musty books and barkscrolls – and fustier, mustier professors!'

'But how can anyone love Screetown?' said Rook. 'It's full of rotsuckers and rubble ghouls.' He shuddered. 'And worse.'

'Worse?' said Felix looking up.

'Far worse,' said Rook. 'I crashed near a great canyon north of here and disturbed the creatures living in it. I didn't get a look at them – but they sounded enormous, Felix. Huge scratching claws, leathery wings . . .'

Felix nodded. 'Interesting,' he said. 'This canyon, was it just below the great rock, close to where the Guardians lower their cages?'

Rook nodded.

'It's a bad place, Rook,' Felix told him. 'Usually I avoid it.' He paused thoughtfully. 'But these creatures of yours sound intriguing. I could do with a few new trophies to decorate the place.'

Rook's face broke into a smile. 'You're incorrigible,' he said.

'Yet never bored!' said Felix. 'But enough of me, let's see how our stew is coming along, and then, Rook, you must tell me about yourself. I want to know everything! Especially how a fine young librarian knight like yourself ends up slugging it out with a rubble ghoul down here on the ground in Screetown!'

While Felix stirred the thickening broth, Rook took another slurp of winesap. He shook his head. How *had* he ended up here? It was all so confusing.

'I can remember being on dawn patrol,' he said. 'I'd already checked round Screetown and was heading for the Stone Gardens, when something must have struck the *Stormhornet* – my skycraft – and me.'

Felix looked up from the bubbling pot. 'A Guardian harpoon perhaps?' he suggested.

'I wasn't close enough to the Tower of Night,' said Rook. 'Besides, it was more powerful than a harpoon; *much* more powerful. One minute I was riding the air, sails full and weights swaying . . .'

Felix nodded, his eyes betraying an envious longing to experience flight for himself. Rook's brow furrowed.

'The next,' he went on, 'noise. Deafening noise. And blazing heat. And blinding light. And the stench of burning spidersilk . . . I was thrown across the sky – still clutching onto the prow of the *Stormhornet*, trying desperately to keep her airborne.' He looked at Felix, his eyes filling up. 'We crash-landed. I . . .' He hung his head. 'I survived, but the *Stormhornet* . . . Oh, Felix, I carved her myself from a single piece of sumpwood. We . . .'

Felix stepped away from the fire and placed his hand on Rook's shoulder. 'There, there, old friend. I understand. You were given something precious – the gift of flight. And then it was taken away from you. It's the way I felt at the Announcement Ceremony all that time ago . . .'

Just then, there came a loud squawk and a flurry of flapping wings, and a snow-white bird with glinting eyes and one misshapen foot swooped down from the top of the stairs and landed on Felix's shoulder. It eyed Rook suspiciously.

'Is that a white raven?' gasped Rook. 'I thought they'd all left the Stone Gardens for good.'

'All except Gaarn here,' said Felix, tickling the vicious-beaked creature under its chin. 'He had a little accident when all the others left. I found him lying on the ground, little more than a fledgling; parched, half-starved and with a heavy stone crushing his foot. I nursed him back to health, and he's stuck by me ever since, haven't you, Gaarn?'

'Waaark!' it screeched. 'Felix Gaarn friends.'

Rook started back. 'He can talk,' he said, surprised.

'I taught him,' said Felix. 'I may not be able to fly like you, Rook, but Gaarn here is my skyborne pair of eyes. He sees all and reports his findings.' He paused. 'In fact, it's thanks to Gaarn here that I came to be out looking for a young librarian knight he saw stumbling through Screetown.'

'So that's how you knew where to find me!'

Felix nodded. 'I didn't know it was you though, Rook, old friend,' he said.

'Friend! Friend!' the white raven cawed.

Felix returned to the bubbling pot and stirred the stew with a long wooden ladle. He scooped out a piece of meat, chewed half and gave the rest to Gaarn. 'I think it's ready,' he said.

'Ready!' Gaarn confirmed.

'Are you hungry, Rook?' asked Felix.

'Hungry?' said Rook. 'I could eat a tilder!'

Felix laughed. 'So could I,' he said wistfully. 'But I'm afraid we'll have to make do with snowbird, rock-lizard and . . .'

'It sounds perfect,' Rook broke in. The stew smelled delicious. And if it did contain piebald rat, then he didn't want to know.

Deep down below Undertown, the sewer tunnels echoed to the soft, irregular *drip-drip* of water and the low murmur of voices. It was the end of the day and the professors and under-librarians were busy.

Fenbrus Lodd was deep in conversation with Alquix Venvax on the Lufwood Bridge. A gaggle of raft-hands shared a joke as they moored their vessels. Two guards high up on a jutting gantry exchanged watch. On the floating lecterns, chained in clusters to the heavier Blackwood Bridge, librarian scholars completed their arduous work for the day – putting the finishing touches to their scroll-scribing, capping their inkpots and calling down to the chain-turners to reel them in.

'Hurry up, down there!' came an irate voice. 'I've important business with the Professor of Light.'

'Coming, sir,' a large-eared lugtroll shouted back, as he scurried across the bridge, seized the winding-crank and began turning. 'At once, sir. Sorry, sir . . .'

Away from the Great Storm Chamber Library – dry and airy thanks to its wood-burners and wind-turners – the moist air of the tunnels and outer chambers was warmer than usual. It was as if the searing heat of Undertown above had permeated the sewers, making them clammy, sticky – and deeply unpleasant. Apart from the frisky piebald rats who seemed to revel in the higher temperatures, the sewer-dwellers – from the lowliest lectern-tender to the Professors of Light and Darkness themselves – were finding the atmosphere increasingly oppressive.

Just off the Central Tunnel, two junior librarian knights-elect returned to their sleeping chamber. As one, they slumped down on their hammocks.

'It's so hot,' said one.

'You can say that again, Kern,' came the reply. 'And all

these oil lamps don't help.' He flapped a hand lethargic-
ally in front of his face. 'Hot, smelly, smoky – and I swear
they create more shadows than they dispel . . .'

Further along the tunnel, an arched door led into a long,
vaulted sleeping chamber. The air here was thicker and
hotter than ever – and laced with the musty odour of
warm fur. A piebald rat scurried boldly across the damp
stone floor, making no attempt to conceal itself – as if it
knew that the occupants of the room were no threat. It
sniffed at the claws of a great hairy paw, twitched its
whiskers and sank two long, yellow teeth into the flesh.
Blood trickled down into its waiting mouth.

'Wuh!' grunted the creature, more from surprise than
pain, and kicked out half-heartedly.

It was a banderbear; a huge male with a thick scar

peeking through the
greasy, matted
fur across his
shoulder – one
of four bander-
bears, all huddled
together in the
corner of the
chamber. He
kicked again,
more viciously
this time, and
the piebald rat
scurried reluctantly
away.

'Wurra wollah weera-weer,' he groaned. *Now the vermin drinks my life-blood. My life here is dark indeed.*

His neighbour, a bony old female, groomed him gently – teasing the sewer-ticks from the creases of skin and crushing them between her front teeth. 'Wuh-wuh-wurruhma,' she whispered. *Patience. Soon the full moon shall fill your eyes once more.*

'Wuh?' grunted a third, and shuddered. *But when?* 'Weera-woor-uralowa . . .'

The fourth nodded, her strange facial markings gleaming in the yellow lamplight. 'Wurra,' she trembled. 'Wurrel-lurragool-uralowa.' *Your words are true. If he who took the poisoned dart has fallen, then what is to become of us?*

Just then, the doorflap flew open and a young librarian knight burst in, her tear-stained cheeks gleaming, her eyes red. 'Tell me it isn't true!' Magda Burlix blurted out.

The banderbears looked up.

'Please,' she said. 'Not Rook. It can't be.'

Wumeru, the banderbear female Rook had befriended on his treatise-voyage, climbed to her feet and lumbered towards her. 'Wuh-wuh-weeralah. Uralowa. Wurra-wuh,' she said softly.

Magda hung her head. She knew enough of the banderbear language to understand what Wumeru had told her. It only confirmed what she had overheard the High Librarian telling Alquix Venvax.

There had been reports of a young librarian knight losing control of his skycraft while out on patrol. They had plummeted to the ground. Now Rook had been officially listed as missing.

Magda shook her head, and wiped her eyes. 'I . . . I can't believe it,' she sobbed. 'I spoke to him only last night. In the refectory-chamber. He's the best flier we have. He'd never lose control of the *Stormhornet* . . . He . . .'

Wumeru wrapped her great furry arms around the stricken girl and hugged her warmly. 'Wuh-weera-lowaal,' she said. *Our hearts are also full.*

'Oh, Rook,' Magda murmured, her voice muffled by the thick fur. 'Rook.'

Behind her, the door-covering was drawn back a second time. Magda looked round to see Varis Lodd standing in the doorway, her face sombre.

'I see you've heard the news,' she said. She shook her head sadly. 'I had such hopes for Rook, my finest pupil. It is a terrible loss.'

Magda tore herself away from Wumeru's clutches. 'You talk as if he's dead,' she said. 'You've posted him as missing, Varis; *missing* in Screetown. Not dead.'

Varis stepped into the chamber and laid a hand on Magda's shoulder. 'Believe me, I know it's hard when we lose a comrade; a fellow librarian knight . . . The reports say he was seen struggling to control the *Stormhornet* as it plummeted to earth.'

'But nobody saw the crash,' Magda insisted. 'We don't know he's dead.'

Varis turned away. 'I only hope he didn't survive the crash,' she said quietly. 'Because if he did, there are many far more horrible deaths that await a librarian knight in Screetown.'

'No! No! *No!*' Magda shouted, clamping her hands over her ears and rushing towards the door. 'I won't believe it's true. He's not dead! He's not! *I* haven't given up on him, even if you have!'

Rook opened one eye and looked around. For a moment, he could make no sense of the sumptuous chamber he had woken up in. He was lying on a thick mattress of straw, weighed down by a tilderskin rug. Above him were elegant, fluted pillars, ornate oil-lamps, and gilded ceiling mouldings which glinted in the flickering light. From some way to his left, there came the sound of soft snoring as someone rolled over in his sleep – and everything came flooding back.

He had sat up far into the night talking to his old friend, Felix, telling him of his adventures on the Mire Road, in the Free Glades, and up in the skies above Undertown. He looked over at the figure next to the smouldering fire.

Felix was still asleep, his breathing soft and rasping, and a faint yet familiar smile playing on his lips. Felix had always enjoyed his dreams. Perched by his head on the corner of his pallet was Gaarn, his head tucked under his wing. Rook decided not to waken them. He wished he could go back to sleep but he knew he wouldn't be able to. Already he felt weighed down by the thought of what lay ahead.

They had planned it all the night before, over their bowls of steaming stew. Although it had pained him to leave Felix so soon after their reunion, Rook was still a librarian knight. He had to return to the Great Library and make his report on everything that had happened. After all, the librarians depended on their young knights to keep them informed of life above the sewers. He knew that if Felix helped him to get back to Undertown, he'd be able to find a pipe or an open drain – some entrance that would lead him down into the sewers.

'I know the sprawling underground network of tunnels better than I know the back of my own hand,' Rook had said.

'You always did, but I'll hate to see you go,' Felix had replied sadly. He sighed. 'But then I suppose if you must, you must. I can get you across Screetown, but you're forgetting one thing, Rook.'

'What?' he had asked.

'The Edgewater River,' Felix had replied darkly. 'If *river* is the right name for that curdled cesspit. You'll have to swim across it. The sewers are impassable between Screetown and Undertown. I've had to do it myself . . .' He had shuddered. 'I don't envy you, Rook. I don't envy you at all.'

Rook slipped quietly out from beneath the heavy covers, climbed to his feet and stretched. The winesap he'd drunk the previous night had left his mouth parched and claggy, and he crossed the tiled floor to the trickling cistern where he quenched his thirst with cold clear water. Behind him, Felix murmured something soft and indistinct; Gaarn ruffled his feathers – but the two of them slept on.

Rook splashed his face with water. Then, taking care to move quietly, he began to explore.

Although now a cellar, it was clear to Rook that the opulent chamber had previously been an upper storey of a magnificent building. The windows, now shut off with rocks and debris, must once have offered fine views over Undertown – before the crumbling Sanctaphrax rock had covered everything in rubble. The lofty ceiling – decorated with ornately carved league-shields and creatures in various poses – probably gave clues as to who might once have lived here, but it was too high up for Rook to inspect closely. One thing was certain, quite apart from being buried, the place had also suffered from a terrible fire.

The carved beams were charred, the floor tiles cracked, while the walls, he now saw, were blackened by smoke. It was only the hanging muglump hides that concealed the worst effects of the blaze.

Rook crossed over to the wall and ran his hand across its surface. His fingertips were coated with a powdering of soot, which he wiped away on the muglump-pelt to his right.

As he did so, pulling the spongy grey skin to one side, something on the wall behind caught his eye. He looked more closely and recognized the faint but distinctive shape of a painted sky pirate's tricorn hat. His curiosity aroused, Rook pulled a kerchief from his pocket and carefully wiped away the greasy coating of soot.

Below the tricorn hat was a face – a noble face, framed

by curling side-whiskers and a waxed beard. Fascinated, Rook kept wiping. A decorated greatcoat came into view. Were those mire-pearls stitched into the collar? he wondered; were they mire-gems set into the scabbard of his sword? And were those initials stitched into the hem of the garment?

He dabbed at the soot, taking care not to disturb the flaking paint beneath. 'W.J.' he murmured.

Intrigued now, Rook continued across the wall, pulling the great muglump skin away and laying it carefully aside. The proud sky pirate, he soon discovered, stood at one side of a family portrait. His wife stood to his left, tall and elegant. Beside them were six youths, of different heights but with similar faces, each one staring back intently at the artist who had painted them – staring back at Rook.

He continued working on the soot-covered wall, delicately removing every trace of it from their bodies. Their curious old-fashioned waistcoats and baggy breeches were revealed; their high buckled boots. They were standing, Rook discovered, on a tiled floor – the same tiled floor he was now kneeling upon. He exposed it all, little by little, until . . .

'What's this?' he murmured as a painted scroll began to appear directly below the feet of the sky pirate. Scarcely daring to breathe, Rook dabbed at it carefully. The paint was dark – almost as dark as the soot he was removing – but inside the curling frame, picked out in gold, were letters. One by one, Rook exposed them.

Wind Jackal.

Wind Jackal. So that was the name of this prosperous adventurer who had built himself such a fine palace in what was once one of old Undertown's more fashionable districts. Whatever had become of him? Rook wondered.

He returned to the wall, searching for further clues. There were similar plaque-like scrolls painted beneath each of the figures. The wife and mother was Hirmina. The youths, Lucius, Centix, Murix, Pellius, Martilius and, smallest of all, Quintinius. Beneath them all, like a ribbon flapping in the breeze, a painted scroll revealed that this was the *FAMILY ORLIS VERGINIX*.

It must have been so nice to be part of such a family, Rook thought, to have brothers to play with; to grow up in the busy bustle of old Undertown, free from the tyranny of goblins or Guardians. His gaze lingered on the portrait of the youngest son. There was something about the dark eyes and forthright set of the jaw that seemed oddly familiar.

'I wish I'd known you,' he mused softly.

Rook reached up and began cleaning the rest of the wall. Now that he'd started, he wouldn't be satisfied until the entire wonderful mural was revealed.

Above the open section of the great family chamber was the roof of the magnificent building it was housed in; a showy array of twisting spires and swollen minarets. All round it were other majestic structures; turrets and towers, mansions and palaces, forming a great townscape on the banks of the Edgewater River. A scroll, hanging from the beak of a painted caterbird, identified the area as *the Western Quays* – but this was the quays before they had been crushed by falling rocks.

Rook returned his attention to the top of the roof. There was something attached to the side of a minaret which, as he cleaned along it, revealed itself to be a rising length of chain. Link by link appeared as he removed the greasy soot, until he was stretching up as far as he could reach. Abandoning his task for a moment, he seized a nearby stool and jumped onto it. He resumed his feverish wiping – and gasped. For there before him, as the grime fell away, was the most perfectly executed painting of all.

It was an intricately detailed reproduction of a sky pirate ship, accurate to an astonishing degree. He could see every bolt, every lever, every knot of every rope which formed the criss-cross hull-rigging. The sails billowed. The mast gleamed. The brass plate, bearing the name *Galerider*, glinted in the sun. And Rook found himself staring up at the flight-rock wistfully . . .

Would such sky-flight ever again be possible in the Edge? he wondered.

'Waaaark!' came a loud screech, echoing round the chamber.

'*Whooooaa!*' Rook cried out as his legs trembled and the stool went over to one side.

'Six hours! Six hours!' screeched Gaarn.

Crash!

'What in Sky's name . . ?' came a puzzled voice from the far side of the chamber. 'Rook? What are you up to?'

Rook picked himself up off the floor, rubbed his aching head and righted the stool. Felix came running over to him – then stopped and looked up at the wall.

'Well I never!' he said. 'I never thought to clean the place up.'

'Beautiful, isn't it?" said Rook, standing back and admiring the wall-painting. 'It was underneath all that soot and grime. Look at the inscriptions, Felix. They're fascinating. We're standing in what was once the palace of a sky pirate captain called Orlis Verginix, also known as Wind Jackal. This is his wife. And those are his sons . . .'

'Yes, yes,' said Felix. 'History never really was my strong point. It's all so sort of *long ago*, if you know what I mean. It's the here and now that I'm interested in, not the past.'

'But the past moulds us, shapes us,' said Rook. 'Look,' he added, sweeping his arm around the great chamber, 'it's all around us.'

'If you say so,' said Felix, yawning. 'Now, how about breakfast? I'm starving!'

As they emerged, blinking, into the daylight outside half an hour later, Rook was struck by the intense heat of the shimmering air. It had been pleasantly cool and damp down in the underground chamber. Now, despite the earliness of the hour, it was stiflingly hot and humid.

With Gaarn perched on his left shoulder, Felix expertly charted a path through the rubble and ruins. Following behind, Rook braced himself for what lay ahead.

'There,' he heard Felix announce some time later as he

reached the top of a great mound of shattered stone. 'The Edgewater River.'

Rook climbed up beside him and peered ahead. Despite the heat, he shivered. The river looked un-inviting: thick and sluggish, with a dense swirling mist dancing on her oily surface. Together, he and Felix picked their way down to her banks. A rank odour, like stagnant vegetable matter mixed with stale perfume, permeated the air.

'Good luck, and give my love to my father and Varis,' Felix told him.

'Of course I will,' said Rook, then turned to face his friend. 'It isn't too late for you to come with me!'

'No,' said Felix, shak-ing his head. 'I . . . I can't go back. This is my world.' He jutted his square jaw towards the river. 'Go now, Rook,' he said. 'Swim hard and fast. Soon the river-mist will rise, and then you'll be spotted easily from the banks . . .'

'Oh, Felix,' said Rook, hugging his friend. 'Take care of yourself!'

Felix pulled away. 'We'll meet again,' he said. 'I'm sure of that.'

Rook nodded mutely, trying hard to stop the welling tears from trickling down over his cheeks. He turned away. The mist swirled; the turgid water slopped at his feet. Gaarn screeched a parting *farewell!* and took to the air.

'Yes, farewell, Rook,' Felix said, clapping his old friend on the back.

Rook glanced back. 'Farewell, Felix,' he said, his voice heavy with sorrow. 'You are a true friend.'

He looked away and took a step forward. Then another, and another . . .

CHAPTER FOUR

THE MISERY HOLE

Thick mud squelched and bubbled round his boots as Rook waded down the steeply shelving incline into the treacherous Edgewater River. He felt round his belt, checking that everything was tightly secured – not that there was much he could have done, even if something had not been. The brown water was up to his knees now; a step later and it was swirling around his waist. There was nothing for it. He would have to swim.

With his arms stretched out in front of him, Rook leaned forwards, kicked out with his legs and thrust ahead into the broad, sluggish river. The water felt warm and oily to the touch, and lapped lazily over the leather of his flight-suit.

Keeping his head up, he took long, powerful strokes, sweeping the viscous water behind him and leaving a stream of tiny bubbles in his wake. Sediment coiled up from the riverbed. The air about him smelled brackish and sweet; the water was gritty between his fingers. Stroke after stroke, he forged on to where he hoped the other side lay – though with the thick mist swirling round his head, it was not possible to be absolutely sure.

Rook had never liked swimming as a youth. The water flowing through the Storm Chamber Library had been too foul to venture into without a raft, and he had always avoided the sessions in the overflow-cisterns which his fellow under-librarians seemed to enjoy so much. Yet at the Free Glades, where the crystal-clear waters of the Great Lake had offered perfect conditions, he had grown to love it. Most mornings, he would get up early, dive in off the edge of Lake Landing and swim twice round the lake before breakfast.

'Come on in, Magda!' he remembered calling to his friend. 'The water's lovely!'

The same could not be said of the Edgewater River. And yet as the young librarian knight battled on – his breathing now regular and softly rasping as he slipped into an easy rhythm – he had to admit that the crossing was not as bad as he had feared. The river was warm, like a tepid bath. And while there was certainly a current pulling to his left, it was so weak that, as an experienced swimmer, he remained confident of making it to the other side without being dragged downstream.

More worrying was the thick mist. He couldn't see where he was going, nor how far he still had to swim.

And so he continued blindly, his arms thrusting forwards and sweeping back, his legs kicking, using the
direction of the current to guide himself across as best he
could. If he kept on like this, he told himself – slow but
steady – he was bound to reach the other side before too
long.

Towards the centre, however, the river began to grow
more choppy. It splashed in his face – warm and cloying.
And though he was immersed in water, he began to
sweat uncomfortably inside his flight-suit as he battled
against the increasing tug of the current. The odour of
the mist, coiling off the surface of the river, became
pungent, sickly; and when the twisting eddies lapped
against his panting mouth, its greasy feel and rotting
taste sent shivers of disgust rippling through his body.
His arms faltered, his legs grew heavy – yet he urged
himself on.

'Not far now,' he encouraged himself breathlessly. 'I'll
soon be back on dry land and . . .'

At that moment, his fingers brushed against something soft and slimy. His hand shrank back involuntarily.
He looked up. There was something there, bobbing, half-
submerged; something with matted patches of white
and black fur. Rook shuddered with disgust. It was a
dead piebald rat, washed out from the sewers; bloated

and stinking. The stench of its rotting body made him heave as it floated past, and for a moment he sank down beneath the water.

Splashing and spluttering, Rook broke the surface and gulped at the air.

'Idiot,' he muttered angrily. His squeamishness had made him careless. He could have been swept down-river.

Just then, and for the briefest of instants, the swirling mist thinned. Looking ahead, Rook caught a glimpse of the other side of the river. His heart sank. It still looked so, so far away – but turning back was not an option. He had to continue.

Rook struck off once more. The mist closed in around him. He struggled bravely on, keeping at right angles to the current as before, but unable to regain the smooth rhythm of arms and legs he'd got into earlier. Evil-looking clumps of matted weeds floated past him like rafts of broken limbs; unseen objects – some hard, some soft – brushed against him, both above the water and below. Were they mire-leeches squirming like maggots in the cloudy water below him? Was that a waterghoul lurking on the silty riverbed?

Rook tried to push such idle thoughts away, but at that moment – from high above his head – there came the chattering of a passing flock of snowbirds. They seemed to be mocking him.

He'll never make it, he thought he heard them trilling to one another. *He's going to drown! He's going to drown!*

For a second time, the sun burned through the mist –

not for long, but just enough for Rook to see that the far bank, though still horribly distant, was indeed closer than it had been before. He could make out tall workshops and warehouses, dock-workers with wherry-hooks and hard hats, and a swarthy goblin scurrying along the raised jetty, a long hooked pike clasped in his hand.

Again the mist grew thick. Rook trod water, fighting the persistent current whilst he got his breath back. Then he struck out again for the far bank. His legs seemed to be getting heavier and heavier, as though lead weights had been attached to his boots. Every stroke was an effort. Every kick used up a fraction more of his rapidly dwindling strength.

'Easy does it,' he told himself as he drove on through the treacly water. 'Slow and steady. One stroke after the other. Forward . . . back . . . forward . . . back . . .'

The next time the air cleared, it did not thicken up again. Instead the great snakelike coils of dense swirling mist were dwindling to wispy twists. Rook could now see the riverbank clearly. It was fringed with piers and jetties along which he could see figures shuffling to and fro. Although it was a relief to see that he had barely fifty strides to go, he was now seriously worried that someone might spot him.

With his head low in the water, Rook continued towards the bank. He moved slowly, carefully; pushing the water back with his arms without making so much as the tiniest splash. His legs, heavier than ever, dragged behind him. Not looking up for fear of catching the eye of some dockhand or goblin guard, he swam on as blindly as when the mist had still held him in its grip.

All at once, he felt his boots trail along the squelchy riverbed. The next moment, as he reached down, his searching fingers touched soft mud. Digging in, he pulled himself slowly into the shallows until he was lying half-in half-out of the water. If anyone noticed him, they should think he was simply something that had washed up on the shore. Slowly, cautiously, avoiding any sudden eye-alerting movement, he lifted his head and looked up.

He had been lucky. Very lucky. He was lying in the shadow of a raised platform which jutted out high above his head. It was supported on thick wooden pillars, the closest of which stood half-a-dozen strides or so to his right. He could hear heavy footsteps clomping across the boards above him and, peering closely, saw the broken images of goblins and trogs flashing past the gaps between them.

He'd done it! he thought gratefully as he pulled himself up onto dry land. He'd made it across the Edgewater River. Now he had to find his way back into the sewers. He tried to get to his feet – but found to his horror that he couldn't move his legs.

In a sudden panic, Rook rolled over and looked down. '*Aaeei* . . .' Terrified of giving himself away, he stifled the cry with his hands. Shaking with terror, he stared at his legs. Each had been swallowed up by a great bony fish, which clung tightly up to his knees, like a pair of angler's waders.

Their bodies were gaunt, like canvas stretched over a skeleton, their eyes cold and grey, their sucker mouths – pink and frothing – gripped round the tops of Rook's shins.

'Oozefish,' he breathed.

Rook knew all about oozefish. Petris Fillit's treatise on the subject was a classic of its type. It was housed on a floating-lectern in the Great Library, where disobedient under-librarians were forced to learn its two hundred and thirty-two pages off by heart as a punishment. Oh, yes, Rook knew all about oozefish. He knew how they attached themselves to prey too large to swallow whole; sinking it, drowning it, guarding it, and waiting for it to rot enough for their suckers to begin feeding. He knew that they lived both in the Edgewater River and in the Mire, sliding through mud and water with equal ease. He knew their mating rituals, their gill structure – and of the third lid their eyes possessed. But most relevant of all, he knew how to remove one, should it become attached.

Trying hard to stop his hand from trembling – and thanking the bad-tempered old professor who'd punished him for talking in class, Rook seized his sword, reached down towards his left leg and – taking care not to injure himself – plunged the tip of the blade into the fish's secondary gill, hidden behind its bulging blow hole. There was a soft squelching sound as the sucker instantly released its ferocious grip. The oozefish wriggled down off his leg, flapped wildly for a moment on the mud, then disappeared headfirst into it.

Encouraged, Rook tightened his grip and leaned forwards a second time – but something the first one had done must have alerted the other oozefish to danger, for before he could strike, the creature had already disgorged itself. With a writhing flip, it squirmed down into the soft white mud after its companion. Rook watched its bony tail retreat and the mud plop and fall still.

Still shaking, he climbed to his feet. Though wobbly, his legs seemed none the worse for being swallowed by disgusting oozefish. He took his bearings.

If, as he thought, it was the slave-workshops above his head, then the boom-docks – the obvious way into the sewers – were too far upstream. And he couldn't risk being seen heading up the riverbank. No, his best bet was to go into Undertown itself and find a drain large enough for him to squeeze down. Once he hit one of the main underground tunnels, he'd be back in the Great Library in no time.

He headed up the mudflats, keeping to the shadows, running from one wooden pillar to the next; pausing to catch his breath, before running on to the next. Gradually, the platform drew lower. The sound of pounding boots grew louder and was joined by raised voices; shouting, cursing and barking commands. Rook chewed into his lower lip nervously. The goblin guards were already out, overseeing the change from the night-shift to the day-shift of the work-slaves. It must be seven hours or thereabouts. Soon the whole place would be thronging.

Just then, a snarl and a howl echoed through the air. Rook froze. Not only were they armed, but the goblin guards had white-collar woodwolves with them.

Head down, he darted out from beneath the platform, over to a rear-floodwall and up an old rusty ladder bolted to its vertical side. The metal creaked and threatened to pull free of its moorings as he climbed. Rook felt vulnerable. Exposed. If anyone saw him . . .

No-one *will* see me! he told himself sharply. Just get a move on!

At the top of the ladder, he peeked over the top of the wall. Then, having checked that the coast was clear, he jumped up and made a dash for the nearest buildings – a jumble of rundown warehouses, workhouses and tall slatted lofthouses once used for drying sailcloth and seasoning wood. Between them was a network of dark, narrow alleys, like an intricate maze. Rook took a deep breath and entered.

He turned left. Then right. Then right again. He tried desperately to picture the layout of the place. But it was no use. Despite all the Undertown patrols he'd carried out, he simply could not get his bearings down here on the ground.

As he ran on, the high windowless sides of the buildings seemed to press in about him. It was so hot and close. Sweat poured down his face. It occurred to him that if anything should appear at the ends of the alley, then he'd be trapped. If only he knew the arrangement of streets and alleys of Undertown just half as well as he knew the tunnels and pipes of the sewers below . . .

Just then he heard something that told him *exactly* where he was: the squeaking of an unoiled crank being turned and the low babble of gossip. He paused and listened. The squeaking continued, followed by a *clonk* and a *splash*. Rook smiled. There was no doubt about it; although he couldn't see it, he must be within spitting distance of the Eastern Well. Many was the time he had flown past, noting both the gathering of goblin matrons who would cluster together, deep in conversation, as they filled their jugs and urns from the well-bucket – and the fact that the handle needed oiling!

He crept forwards and, guided by his ears rather than his eyes, squeezed himself into a long, narrow opening between the backs of two wood and stone buildings. The sound of the hushed voices grew louder as he slipped sideways along the gap, which grew narrower and narrower the further he went. At the end at last, he stopped and peered out cautiously from the shadows.

In front of him, just as he'd expected, was the Eastern Well – a tall, ornate structure which was sole source of water for an entire district – and the ancient goblin matrons clustered around it. He peeked out a little further, looking right, left and round the cobbled square. There was a main

drain with a barred gate entrance which lay down the street
on the opposite side, Rook remembered – but how could he
get to it? Should he work out some circuitous route, keeping to the narrow alleys? Or should he simply make a dash
for it across the square? After all, the goblin matrons
wouldn't do anything to stop him – *and* it would give them
something new to talk about.

He was about to risk it when he noticed one of the
matrons look up and murmur to her neighbour; and
then the two of them glance round. They'd heard something. The next moment, Rook heard it too – the rising
sound of heavy boots marching towards him.

It was a contingent of goblin guards!

Darting back into the narrow gap, Rook crouched
down – his knees grazing the stone wall as he did so –

and held his breath. Heart in his mouth, he watched as the first pair of armed guards stomped past the end of the passageway. Their breast armour, helmets and heavy weapons glinted in the early-morning brightness. Next, flanked by a second pair of goblins, Rook saw a ragged slave, head down and back bent, as he shuffled past. He was followed by others – twelve in all, Rook counted – each one yoked by the neck to the one behind. A final pair of goblins brought up the rear. Rook trembled and shrank back as far as he could into the shadows. To his horror, he had noted that they were not alone. Each one had a white-collar woodwolf beside him, straining at the leash.

Praying he would not be noticed, Rook watched first one goblin go past, struggling to control the vicious beast he was holding; then the other. At last, they were both gone from sight. Rook sighed with relief.

That had been close, he realized. Too close . . .

'What's that, Tugger?' the goblin's voice floated back. 'Did you smell something, boy?'

'And you, too, Ragger?' came a second voice. 'What's up? Is there something there?'

Rook's heart missed a beat. The wolves had caught his scent. *They knew he was there.*

Turning on his heels, Rook bolted back down the narrow alley, away from the terrible danger. As he scrabbled and stumbled, he shot a look back over his shoulder to see the goblins – their bodies black against the light at the end of the alley – bend down and fiddle with the wolves' collars. They were unclipping the woodwolves from their leashes.

Rook ran for all he was worth.

'He's getting away, Slog,' called one of the goblins.

'Oh, no he's not,' came the reply. 'Ragger, you go that way. Tugger, you go round there, boy. That's it! Head him off at the end of the alley!'

Heart pounding, Rook sped desperately along the narrow alleyway. He had to reach the other end before the wolves did. Twenty strides to go by his reckoning. Not far – but then woodwolves were renowned for their fleetness of foot. He could hear them yelping from his left and his right as they ran down alleys parallel to his own. His head filled with terrible memories from his childhood that he couldn't push away; memories of slavers, and woodwolves, and the last time he had seen his parents alive . . . The yelping grew more excited. Any second now, the terrible creatures would reach the end of the alley and cut him off . . .

'Come on, come on,' he urged himself.

As he neared the end, the passageway became comparatively wide. Rook sprinted the last ten strides, out onto a narrow street and down the alleyway opposite. Behind him, the two wolves met up and resumed the chase. Their excited baying twisted in the air, a discordant duet.

Rook needed to find a means of escape as quickly as possible; a drain that would lead him down into the sewers. A drain-cover! He had to find a drain-cover. And quick!

Sweat drenched his body and soaked his hair, which lay flat and wet against his head. The new day was proving to be the hottest and most humid so far. But he

couldn't stop. Drawing on reserves of strength he hardly knew he had, Rook turned sharp left at a junction and scurried down a dark alley which was full of early-morning merchants and punters, and lined with small workshops. The smell of hot metal and singed wood assaulted his nostrils as he barged his way through, past joiners and turners, past buzzing lathes and screeching circular saws.

'Oi! Watch it!' voices shouted out angrily. 'Watch where you're going!'

But Rook took no notice. Librarian knight though he was, he couldn't afford to be polite or thoughtful. Not just now. His one priority was to escape.

Suddenly this was made easier for him as the trogs and trolls began scattering before him, leaving a path for him to run down. At first he thought they must be clearing a way for him. The next moment, he realized what it was they were shouting as they dived for cover. His heart missed a beat.

'Woodwolves!' 'Woodwolves!'

Rook glanced back over his shoulder. He was hoping against hope that he was outrunning the terrible creatures. But as he saw the flashing eyes and slavering mouth of the first great woodwolf behind him, those hopes were dashed. It was gaining on him. Any second now, it would be snapping at his heels. He raced on – only to discover that the second woodwolf must have circled round to cut him off after all, because now it appeared in front of him at the far end of the alley. As their eyes met, it bared its teeth and snarled menacingly.

Without a second thought, Rook darted into the workshop to his left. A wizened woodtroll with a rubbery nose and a pronounced squint looked up from his lathe indignantly.

'What in bloodoak's name do you think you're doing?' he bellowed as Rook barged past him, sending spindles, table-legs and tools flying. 'I . . . *aaargh!* Woodwolves!'

'Sorry!' Rook called out. Shoving the door aside, he tore through into the back room of the workshop and dived outside, through the far window.

He landed, rolled over and jumped smartly to his feet. The woodwolves were in the room behind him, baying for his blood. Rook reached up, slammed the shutters to and bolted them into place.

There was a loud splintering crash and a howl of pain as the first, then the second of the woodwolves lunged at the wooden shutters. The hinges creaked and the panels buckled and bowed – but the shutters remained in place.

'Thank Sky and Earth for that,' Rook murmured as he took to his heels once more.

The woodwolves howled with rage and Rook heard them pounding back through the woodtroll's workshop to the alley. They weren't about to give up.

And neither am I, thought Rook determinedly.

He darted down an arched opening between two rather grand buildings opposite which – if his memory served him correctly – were Wheelwright's Mansion and the former Leagues' Meeting House. He was right where he wanted to be, at the edge of central Undertown. The place was fairly riddled with drains, both large and small. At the end of the covered passage, he emerged into a second square, far grander than the one housing the Eastern Well. To his left was the Central Fountain – its once glorious cascade of water now reduced to a low, stumpy-looking column. And to his right . . .

'Sky and Earth be thanked,' Rook murmured.

At last he had stumbled across a drain. He dashed towards it and crouched down. Set into the huge flag-stones it was one of the older variety, circular and latticed. He plunged his fingers down into the gaps in the cast-iron grille and tugged.

From the far corner of the square he heard the yelping arrival of the first woodwolf. The second one wouldn't be far behind.

Teeth clenched and legs locked, he grunted out loud with effort. There was the soft grinding sound of grit on metal, and the drain-cover came free. Rook pushed it aside and hurriedly lowered himself down into the dark-ness below.

The wolves, sensing that their quarry was about to escape, sprinted towards him. Rook felt round feverishly with his right foot for the first rung of the iron ladder he knew should be there somewhere, bolted to the inside of the narrow pipe – and found it. He shifted himself round, reached up and slid the drain-cover back into place, just in the nick of time.

The tunnel was plunged into darkness. Above his head, he heard the woodwolves scratching desperately at the metal grille and howling with frustration.

'Too slow,' he taunted softly.

As if the woodwolves themselves knew this to be true, they abruptly stopped their yammer and trotted away. Rook grinned with relief. Then, with a last look up at the pinpricks of light piercing the metal cover above his head, he began the descent. Rung by rung, he climbed down the vertical pipe which would bring him out into one of the great transverse tunnels, deep under the ground. With a bit of luck, he should arrive back at the Great Storm Chamber Library before . . .

'*Aaagh!*' he cried out, as his left foot slipped into thin air. The next rung was missing . . .

It all happened so quickly. His right foot slipped, his hands were torn from their grip, and the next thing he knew, he was tumbling backwards.

'*Unkh!*' he grunted as he landed with a sudden, heavy thud and the air was forcibly expelled from his lungs.

Where am I? he wondered. Then a horrible thought occurred to him. It couldn't be . . . It *mustn't* be . . .

Cautiously he opened his eyes to see – but the pitch blackness around him was giving nothing away. He felt round gingerly with his hands. He felt walls, round and rigid, and from the feel of it, made from woodwillow withies, woven together like . . . like a huge basket . . .

Rook groaned. He knew *exactly* where he was.

He was inside one of the traps set by the goblin guards

to capture those who tried to escape from Undertown. Misery holes, they were called. Like huge mudlobster-pots, they were set inside the sewer entry pipes beneath deliberately sabotaged ladders. He was a librarian knight: he should have known, been on his guard. Instead, he had blindly climbed down the ladder thinking he was safe.

Misery holes. He shook his head. The traps were well-named, Rook thought bitterly, and he, Rook Barkwater, had become their latest victim. It was little wonder, he realized, that the woodwolves had seemed so un-concerned when he'd escaped them. He'd been such a fool. They hadn't been chasing him at all, they were corralling him to the booby-trapped drain. They'd tricked him, and he had fallen for it, hook, line and sinker. But he wasn't finished yet.

He climbed to his feet and shook the plaited bars of the cage as hard as he could and tried to wrench them apart; he kicked and hammered at them; he drew his knife and tried sawing at the wood – but all to no avail. The misery hole was not about to release its quarry so easily.

'There must be *some* way out,' Rook groaned.

'There isn't,' came a little voice from the far side of the cage. 'I've already tried.'

Rook started with surprise. 'Who's there?' he hissed.

'M-my name's Gilda,' said the little voice tearfully. 'And I'm very frightened. I've been here *ages* and . . .' – she shuddered – 'soon . . . soon, they'll be coming for us.'

·CHAPTER FIVE·

NUMBER ELEVEN

Rook felt the hairs at the back of his neck tingle. There was such fear and despair in the small, childlike voice.

'Are you hungry?' he asked softly. 'I've got some dried dellberries. And a hunk of black bread . . .'

'Water,' said Gilda. 'Have you any water, sir? I'm so thirsty.'

'Yes, yes,' said Rook eagerly. He fumbled at his belt and removed his water-bottle. 'Here,' he said, reaching out towards the sound of the voice.

He felt a hand brushing his fingers as it seized the bottle, then heard the sound of slurping and swallowing. Rook smiled, glad that he'd been able to do something – however small – to help the poor creature.

'Thank you, sir,' said Gilda a moment later. 'Thank you kindly.'

Rook reached out a second time. He felt the water-bottle graze his fingertips; then, just as he was about to close his hand around it, it slipped from his grasp and

478

clattered on the bottom of the cage.

'Oh, mercy me, I'm sorry, sir,' Gilda cried out. 'Indeed I am!'

'It's all right, Gilda,' Rook assured her. 'Don't fret.'

He crouched down and, reaching into the pockets of his flight-suit – both right and left – pulled out a small rough stone from each. As he put them together on the palm of his hand, the whole cage was abruptly bathed in a warm yellow glow. Gilda gasped.

'Mercy me!' she exclaimed. 'Magic rocks!'

Rook smiled. 'They're sky-crystals,' he said. 'Given to me by the Professor of Light himself in the Great Library.'

'So you're a librarian?' said Gilda, her voice trembling with awe. Rook looked at her eager little face, eyes wide and astonished. The shadowy glow from the crystals shone on her pointed ears, her stubby waxen plaits, her broad nose . . .

'Why, you're a gnokgoblin,' Rook said.

'Indeed I am, sir,' said Gilda, 'a poor gnokgoblin from the Eastern Alleys. I was on an errand for my grand-mother, I was, sir, when those there goblins set their wolves on me. Just for fun, sir . . . Just for fun . . .' The little gnokgoblin buried her head in her hands and sobbed.

Rook placed a hand on her shoulder and squeezed it gently.

Gilda looked up, her face wet with tears. 'My grand-mother's a poor seamstress, sir, always has been. But these days, she's getting frail – and her eyesight is

failing. She relies on me for everything, so she does. Oh, mercy me, sir, if I don't return from my deliveries . . .'

'It's going to be all right, Gilda,' said Rook.

Another sob convulsed the little gnokgoblin and she grasped Rook's hand in hers. 'Oh those wolves, sir!' she shuddered. 'Howling, slavering, snarling . . . They chased me, sir. And . . . and I thought I was being so clever hiding beneath the drain-cover . . .' She breathed in noisily. 'And now *this*!' she wailed, the tears streaming down her cheeks.

'There, there,' said Rook. 'I know the feeling, believe me.'

'Oh, sir,' she sobbed, throwing herself forwards and wrapping her skinny arms around his neck. The basket swayed, and from far off in the system of tunnels, Rook heard the sound of squabbling ratbirds. 'But it'll be all right now, won't it, sir?' she said. 'You being a real living and breathing librarian knight with magic rocks and all.' Gilda's grip tightened.

'Of course it will,' said Rook uncertainly, patting her awkwardly on the back.

He glanced up at the inward-pointing spikes of the cage above his head; so easy to fall into, yet impossible to escape. They were well and truly trapped in the misery hole.

Gilda's sobs slowly subsided, and her grip loosened. She wiped her eyes on the back of her hand and sat back. 'What's it like there?' she asked in her small voice.

'What's *what* like *where*?' said Rook.

'The Free Glades,' said Gilda. 'You're a librarian knight, so you must have been there. What are they like? Are they as beautiful as they say? Granny says that everyone is free there, and safe. And no-one goes hungry, and no-one is ever beaten – that it's the most wonderful place in the world!'

'It is,' said Rook dreamily. 'Like a shining beacon in the middle of the dark Deepwoods – the most beautiful place in all the Edge. Glades with towering pinetrees and crystal lakes, and the night sky studded with a million dazzling stars.'

Gilda looked up at him shyly. 'Do you think that one day I might see it for myself?' she asked.

Rook leaned forwards, took both of her hands in his own and squeezed them warmly. 'I'm sure of it,' he said.

Gilda smiled happily, and nodded. 'Me, too,' she said earnestly. 'Now you're here, *everything's* going to be all right.'

Just then, from above their heads, there came a loud sound. Grinding. Metal on stone. Gilda gasped.

'It's them,' she whispered.

Rook nodded. He pulled himself up onto his haunches, quickly returned the sky-crystals to their separate pockets, and looked up. Far above, as the drain-

cover was slid aside, a thin sliver of light grew and grew
– like the moon going through all its phases, from new to
full, in a matter of seconds. The grinding noise set
Rook's teeth on edge. The next instant, a great head was
thrust down into the hole.

'What have we got here, then?' he muttered gruffly.
The light streamed over his shoulders and down into the
eyes of the prisoners below. 'Two, by the looks of things.'
He clapped his hands together. 'A good catch!'

'Haul 'em in, then,' came a second voice, high-pitched
and imperious, 'and let's take a closer look!'

Rook turned to Gilda. 'You'll be all right,' he said. 'I
promise.'

Gilda nodded, her eyes wide and trusting. 'Thank
you, sir,' she whispered.

Just then, the cage jerked and dropped down a couple
of strides. Gilda gasped. Rook clung onto her arm with
one hand and the plaited bars of the cage with his other.
From above there came a stream of violent curses and
the crack of a whip. The cage stopped falling.

'*Pull*, Krote, you great, useless lump,' demanded the
high-pitched voice impatiently. 'By Sky, I'll have you
boiled down to glue! PULL!'

The voice echoed angrily down the tunnels – where it
was answered by a chorus of ratbirds and piebald rats,
chattering and squealing in alarm. The cage jolted and
slowly began to rise. Gilda whimpered and gripped the
side of the cage firmly. Rook looked out through the bars
– at the sides of the rusting sewer-pipe sliding past and,
a little higher up, at the booby-trapped ladder. Finally,

with a bump, the cage came to a halt directly beneath the drain-opening.

A thin leather-covered pole was thrust into the cage, past the inward-pointing spikes, stopping inches from the top of Rook's head. With a click, it opened up, revealing itself to be a heavy umbrella-like object. With much heaving and grunting, the opened umbrella was pulled back out of the cage, springing open the inward-pointing spikes, like the petals of a vicious flower.

A huge hand reached in, grabbed Rook by the scruff of his flight-suit and lifted him bodily into the air – Gilda clinging to his knees. Rook found himself staring into the bloodshot eyes of a hulking great tufted goblin with hairy ears, a jutting jaw and pitted skin that showed the ravages of a hard life and many a savage battle. Dressed in heavy armour, he was still holding the drain-cover under his arm, making it look as light as a the lid of a barrel of woodale.

Behind him, Rook caught a glimpse of a tumbril, the covered wagon fashioned, like the cage, from wood-willow. Two weary prowlgrins were in harness and he could see the driver – a bony mobgnome, by the look of him, a pencil in one hand, reins in the other.

'What have we got, then?' chirped the mobgnome. He licked the point of his stubby pencil and raised his hand ready.

The tufted goblin looked the two of them up and down as they dangled from his fist. 'A big'un and a little'un,' he grunted, his voice deep and guttural.

'If you could be a *little* more specific, Krote,' said the

mobgnome, his voice laden with sarcasm.

Krote's heavy brow furrowed. 'Gnokgoblin,' he called back to the driver, who noted the details on a small scroll of bark.

'Male or female?' said the mobgnome.

'It's a girl,' said Krote. 'And the second . . .' He frowned, and turned his blunt, brutish face towards Rook, who grimaced at the smell – and feel – of the goblin's moist, malodorous breath. 'I's not sure, Mindip,' he said, as a stupid grin spread across his face, 'but I reckon we might've caught usselves a 'brarian knight.'

The mobgnome jumped down from the tumbril and hurried over. 'Are you sure?' he said. 'A librarian knight, you say? Here, let me see.'

Krote turned to his partner and dropped Rook and Gilda, who landed in a heap at the mobgnome's feet.

' 'Ere, take it easy, Krote, you great lummox! Gotta be careful with the merchandise. If he *is* a librarian, he'll be valuable, see?' Mindip crouched to inspect Rook as he lay, winded, on the greasy cobbles.

As the mobgnome's sneering face came close, Rook saw his chance. He leapt to his feet and drew his sword . . .

But the mobgnome simply laughed. 'Well, well, well,' he said. 'He *is* a librarian knight. No doubt about it! You handle him, Krote, there's a good fellow. I'll take care of the girl.'

Behind him, Rook heard the tufted goblin's low growl. Mindip flourished his evil-looking whip and lunged to Rook's left. There was a sharp *crack!* and Gilda cried out with pain as the end of the mobgnome's whip wound itself around her neck.

'Sir . . . help . . .' Gilda gasped, as the mobgnome tugged hard on the whip, tightening the grip round her neck and pulling her towards him.

Glancing round, Rook saw the tufted goblin raise his great arms. He readied himself.

'Sir . . . *urrrrrgh* . . .' Gilda gurgled.

It was no use. Rook knew he had to do something. Looking back hurriedly, he saw the helpless young gnokgoblin being dragged towards the tumbril by Mindip. At the same moment, Krote lunged. Rook leapt desperately out of his reach and swung his sword. It sliced through the leather whip, freeing Gilda, and caught the mobgnome, Mindip, a glancing blow on the backswing.

Blood spattered down onto the stone flags.

Krote paused to stare down at Mindip and, for a terrible moment, it was as though everything stood still. The next, the furious goblin raised his great head and roared as the mobgnome crumpled to the floor, gripping his belly.

'Mindip!' he bellowed. 'You hurt Mindip!'

His tufted ears trembled. The whites of his eyes turned red.

'Run, Gilda!' Rook cried, gripping his sword as firmly as he could.

Arms raised, the tufted goblin lunged again. He swung the heavy drain-cover through the air in a wide, whistling arc. Rook gasped as he saw the great lump of iron coming towards him. He was frozen to the spot . . .

Out of the corner of his eye, he glimpsed Gilda's green dress fluttering as she made a dash for it . . .

CLONK!

The drain-cover hammered into the side of Rook's head, the sword slipping from his grip and clattering on the cobbles.

There was a flash of intense brightness, a rush of cold – then darkness.

*

Rook woke up with a jolt. Where was he? he wondered. The jolting continued.

He was in motion, that much was certain, bumping and clattering over cobblestones; every movement jarring his body and making his head pound. He was in some kind of a cart. All round him he could hear the sound of soft moaning.

Slowly he opened his eyes. The light poured in. He was inside a tumbril, its wicker roof casting criss-cross shadows over its cargo.

'Mind the pot-holes, you stupid oaf!' came a shrill voice from up at the front. 'Every jolt is agony. I'm bleeding all over my new cloak – and it's all your fault, you useless sack of guts!'

'Sorry, Mindip. He was just a bit quick for me. But I got him in the end, didn't I?' came a gruff reply.

Rook pulled himself onto his elbows, his head throbbing so badly he wanted to cry out, and looked round. He found himself face to face with an old slaughterer lying beside him, his red hair streaked with grey. He shifted round. Apart from the slaughterer, there were others, their faces seeming to blur and smudge as Rook struggled to make sense of it all. There were a couple of waifs, their ears fluttering like woodmoths, a lumpen cloddertrog, snoring loudly, and a strange-looking individual with scaly skin, tiny flute-like ears and a rubbery crest that ran across the centre of his head and halfway down his back.

'E's woken up,' muttered a voice from the back of the tumbril.

'Yeah, poor beggar. Come round just in time to see his new home, innit? The Sanctaphrax Forest . . .'

'If the shrykes don't get to him first!'

Rook shuddered uneasily. Above his head, a solitary white raven circled in the sky, cawing raucously. Its wings looked to Rook like paddles, slicing through the dense, treacly air. It was hot; so stiflingly hot. He could barely breathe. And every time he moved his eyes, the pounding in his head grew more intense.

He raised his hand and touched round his left temple gently. The bone was tender and, when he inspected his fingers, he found them dark with congealed blood.

Outside the clattering tumbril, the streets were getting more and more busy. Peering giddily through the slatted sides, Rook could see merchants, traders and groups of armed guards. Some were standing in clusters. Most were streaming along the road in the same direction he was travelling. From up ahead, there came the hustle and bustle of a great crowd; the sounds of clattering, clanging, dull moans and raised voices, and every now and then a sharp klaxon blast that made Rook wince with pain.

'Left! *Left!*' shouted the mobgnome. 'It's *that* way!' He pointed.

The tufted goblin pulled on the reins, and the tumbril was driven through a low, narrow archway into a broad square, heaving with activity and louder than ever. Rook's head spun all the more. There was movement and colour, and loud noise that seemed to set the very air trembling. The tumbril abruptly lurched to a halt. The goblin turned round.

'Wake up, you idle bunch of sewer-rats!' he bellowed.
'We've arrived.'

The mobgnome climbed down, clutching his belly,
hobbled painfully round to the back of the covered
wagon and unlocked the door. The tufted goblin
appeared beside him – a heavy cudgel in one hand – and
reached inside. Rook looked on helplessly as his neighbour, the old slaughterer, was dragged out by the ankles.

Rook was next. The tufted goblin reached out towards
him – but he kicked the great hairy hand away. 'I can do
it on my own,' he muttered.

Yet as he pulled himself to
his feet and the blood
drained from his
head, he swooned
dizzily and stum-
bled over one
of the un-
conscious
waifs.

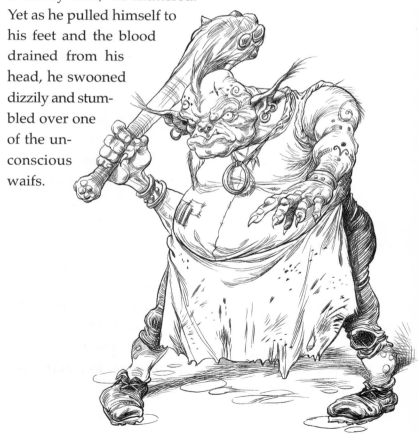

'If you weren't so valuable, I'd slit your throat right here!' snapped the mobgnome, wincing with pain and ticking off a name on his barkscroll ledger. 'Krote, get him out of there!'

The tufted goblin grasped the front of the young librarian knight's jacket and tugged. Rook lurched forwards, banging his head on the top of the doorway as he was pulled from the tumbril and set down on the ground. His legs were wobbly. His head throbbed.

'This way,' came a gruff voice as two flathead goblins seized him by the arms and frogmarched him away.

The cobbles blurred below Rook's feet as he was propelled to the centre of the square. All round him, the noise grew louder. There were shouts of anger and cries of despair, and the raucous screech of the klaxons blasting out intermittently. Suddenly the guards came to a halt.

'Here we are,' said the one to his left, his voice seeming, to Rook, to grow loud and soft as he spoke. 'A librarian knight.'

'Slightly damaged by the look of him,' added the other.

'Leave him with me,' came a third voice.

Struggling to focus, Rook stared ahead at the figure before him. It was a hammerhead goblin. His scarred face seemed to be expanding and shrinking; his eyes spiralling, the number of rings in his ears constantly changing. Abruptly, the flathead guards let him go and withdrew. Rook swayed back and forwards. He felt giddy, bilious. Everything was swimming before his eyes.

The hammerhead seized him by the arm and pulled him upright.

'One of Krote's catch, no doubt,' a voice was saying.

'I don't know what he does to them,' said another.

Rook looked up groggily. Someone was looming towards him, an arm raised. Rook trembled. Was that a dagger in his hand – a dagger still dripping blood? Was his throat about to be cut?

He tried to cry out but no sound emerged.

The dagger came down. Except it wasn't a dagger at all but a brush, dripping with crimson paint. It daubed at the front of Rook's flight-jacket, once, twice; leaving two vertical red stripes.

'Number eleven!' shouted yet another voice and Rook felt himself being bundled on.

Everything swirled and whirled about him as he was dragged forward. He became aware of a new noise – a creaking, jangling sound – and looked up to see a strange contraption hovering above him; in focus one moment, blurred the next. He tried hard to concentrate.

Glimmering in the dazzling heat, a series of great curved hooks hung at regular intervals along a length of chain which was attached to a wide circle of wooden uprights three strides high. A team of flatheads sat on a raised bench at the centre, turning sets of pedals with their feet. As the pedals went round, so too did the chain – taking the hooks with it.

All at once, a huge pair of hands grasped both of his arms at once, and Rook found himself being hoiked high up into the air. From behind him, close to his ear, there came the sound of tearing leather as a hook sliced through the back of his jacket. The sharp point grazed the back of his head. The next instant, the hands let him go and Rook found himself suspended from the hook, his feet dangling above the ground as the chain dragged him round.

All about him, the atmosphere was frenetic; a chaotic hubbub of screeched insults and dark curses; of jabbing elbows, sly dead-legs and the occasional thrown punch. Figures scurried this way and that, fighting to get a good position close to the wooden poles from which the chain hung.

Hands, claws, talons snatched, prodded and poked at Rook as he swung by. Just ahead of him, as the chain jerked momentarily to a halt, a crowd surged round a figure struggling on a hook. Rook could make out voices raised above the hubbub.

'Number nine. Lugtroll for sale. Strong in the shoulder and short in the tooth. Ideal for pulling any chariot, cart or cab. Fifteen gold pieces . . .'

'I'll take him!' cried a voice.

'Sold!' A klaxon sounded. 'To you, sir . . .'

The chain jerked on, swinging Rook with it like a badly laundered shirt on a washing line.

Another voice shouted out, 'Number ten. Who'll buy this flathead goblin? In his prime, he is; ideal for the toughest of construction work . . .' There was a flurry of activity and a chorus of excited shrieking, then, 'Sold!' The klaxon blast echoed round the square. 'Sold to the goblin with the eye-patch!'

Rook trembled. It was just a matter of time before he, too, was sold. His own slave-dealer – the flathead who had hung him up on the hook – was doing his best.

'Number eleven. Young, fit, strong. An academic. A *librarian knight*, no less! Top quality, I'm sure you'll agree!'

Saltflies were buzzing round Rook's head. They landed on his ears, his lips; they crawled round his eyes, lapping at the drops of sweat. Suspended from the hook, his leather flight-jacket tight beneath the arms, Rook was unable to bat them away. He wriggled and screwed up his face but the flies continued to torment him, seemingly aware that he could do nothing about it. He closed his eyes wearily.

'How about this one?' a screeching voice enquired, and Rook felt himself being sharply poked and prodded. 'What do you think?'

'I don't think so, mistress,' came the shrill reply. 'Won't get much sport out of it. Looks half dead already.'

Rook's eyelids fluttered. He saw two tall shrykes – one an elegant matron with purple plumage and a bone flail; the other, at the end of a leash, a drab shryke-mate. As she turned away, the matron thrust her beak in the air and sniffed.

'Come, Mardle,' said the shryke, tugging on the leash. 'Far too over-priced anyway.'

494

Rook shuddered, relieved that the fierce yellow-eyed creature with the sharp talons had moved away. But his relief was short-lived. As the bird-creatures moved on, they were replaced by a sinister figure in a black cloak with the white emblem of a screaming gloamglozer emblazoned upon it – a Guardian of Night.

'How much?' said a thin rasping voice.

'To you, sir, seventy-five,' a voice shouted back. It was the flathead slave-dealer who had hung him up on the hook.

'Thirty,' said the Guardian. 'He's damaged, and my master, the High Guardian of Night, likes his librarians fresh as a rule . . .'

'Sixty,' said the voice firmly. 'And that's my final offer.'

'Well . . .' mused the Guardian, his face buried in the shadows of his hood.

Rook felt an icy sweat break out on his forehead. Sold to the Guardians of Night. No, it could not be happening. Not this! Anything but this . . .

Suddenly his head lolled forward. It was all too much. His throbbing temples. The suffocating heat. The breathtaking tightness in his arms and chest . . . And all the while, the prodding and poking and pinching continued – though further away now. Further and further. As if it was happening to someone else, while he – Rook – was in his hammock, all wrapped up in a nice warm blanket . . .

'Seventy!' a voice called.

'Sold!'

Rook opened his eyes and looked round blearily. Beside the slave-dealer stood a stooped figure in an embroidered hooded cape; it had broad ears, doleful eyes and bony fingers which it held out before it like a wood-mantis. It reached forward and took Rook's hands in its own, one after the other. It scratched at the calluses on his palms, it picked at the nails, it scrutinized the fingers from every angle and fingered the leather cuffs of his flight-suit thoughtfully.

'Yes, he'll do,' the figure said. 'Have him delivered.'

The flathead nodded. There was a soft jingle as the gold coins were passed over and the flathead raised his klaxon.

'Number eleven!' he roared. 'Sold to Hestera Spikesap.' The klaxon bellowed loudly by Rook's ear.

The next instant, Rook was lifted from the hook and placed down on the ground. His legs threatened to crumple. Yet as he breathed in the air – unrestricted at last by the choking jacket – his head began to clear. Behind him, his place on the hook had been taken by a quivering nightwaif; his ears fluttering nervously, his waistcoat daubed with the number 14. As the chain pulled him away, the slave-dealer flathead went with him.

For a moment, Rook considered making a dash for it. But only for a moment. Before he could move so much as a muscle, he was seized by both arms and dragged away by the two hefty hammerheads who had answered the klaxon-call. They bundled him roughly through the crowd and delivered him to the chaingang-master – a leathery-skinned hammerhead with a clipboard and a whip – standing at the head of a line of slaves.

'Number eleven,' he noted, glancing at Rook's front and making a note of it. 'Full chain! Put him at the end.'

Rook was dragged along the row of dejected individuals – creatures from every corner of the Edge, now all yoked together with wooden collars and chains; fifteen in all.

As the wooden yoke clicked shut around his neck, he knew that that was it. He was no longer an individual. Someone had bought him and Rook Barkwater was no more. He was a mere number now. A bonded slave . . .

At the front of the line, the chaingang-master cracked his whip. 'Forward!' he roared.

The chained slaves set off, stumbling at first before getting into a slow, shuffling rhythm. On either side, armed guards marched beside them, barking commands and cracking their whips. Rook shuffled with the other slaves; his legs dragging, his head held rigid by the wooden yoke. Behind him, the sounds of the market receded; far in front, the great Sanctaphrax rock, with the jagged Tower of Night at its top, loomed in the sky.

Rook groaned. Once again – like a boulder-salmon battling against a formidable current – he was being

taken back the way he'd come. Worse than that, he now had no doubt as to where he was bound.

The Sanctaphrax Forest. It had to be.

His whole body was overwhelmed with fearful heaviness at the thought of what lay ahead. Like so many before him, he would be worked to death by the goblins in the Sanctaphrax Forest – for the scaffolding which supported the crumbling rock was as greedy for slaves to labour upon it as it was for the neverending supplies of wood that shored it up. Every pillar, every rafter and every cross-beam was stained with the blood of those who had perished there.

Rook fumbled desperately with the catch of the yoke, hoping to tease it open – but in vain. There was no escape. Ever since his decision to climb down into the sabotaged drain, his fate had been sealed. Already he could see the sluggish Edgewater River – and a large

flat-bottomed boat moored to a wooden jetty. A ferry-goblin with a long pole was seated on the bank, chewing on a straw as he waited idly for his doomed passengers.

It was hot and airless on the ground. Rook looked up into the cool, open sky, where once he had flown his beloved *Stormhornet* high above the streets of Undertown and looked down on tiny specks chained together far below. He had never, even in his darkest dreams, realized what it was to be one of those specks. He'd been too high up, exhilarated by the thrill of flight and the rush of the cool wind in his face, to imagine what it must be like down there . . .

And now I have become one of those specks, Rook noted glumly.

Lost in his own misery, he failed to notice that they had left the main road which led down to the river. It was only when the chaingang-master bellowed '*Halt!*'

that he realized they had ended up in one of the more affluent districts of Undertown. The buildings were tall, elegant and, though now past their best, still evoked the grandeur of their opulent past.

'This is the place,' barked the chaingang-master. 'Unyoke number eleven.'

Rook frowned. Number eleven? But that was him. Who *had* bought him?

The other slaves groaned miserably. A few jangled their chains.

'Be still!' bellowed the chaingang-master and cracked his whip threateningly.

The slaves fell silent.

The flatheads unlocked the yoke around Rook's neck and dragged him towards a small side door set into the wall at the foot of the towering building. Rook looked up; he recognized it at once.

The facade, though cracked and scarred, was ornately decorated, every jutting ledge, every curlicued plinth and every sunken alcove occupied by a statue. Scores of them; hundreds – continuing up as far as Rook could see.

The Palace of Statues. It looked different from down here on the ground; more imposing, more sinister – but unmistakable nonetheless.

'Move!' grunted one of the flatheads, and shoved him hard in the back.

Rook stumbled forwards, tripped over something lying in his path and ended up sprawling on the cobbles.

The first of the flatheads reached the small arched

doorway, raised his fist and hammered loudly. The second seized Rook by the hole in the back of his jacket, pulled him roughly to his feet and marched him to the door – but not before Rook had seen what had tripped him.

It was the remains of a statue of an ancient leaguesman, shattered from its fall from the crowded upper ledges. Its sightless, unblinking eyes met Rook's and he felt a familiar pang of pain deep in his chest.

You're just like me, he thought. I, too, have fallen to earth.

Even now, he could hear the grinding of bolts being slid across from inside the door. At the bottom. At the top. There was a soft click and the door cracked open . . .

· CHAPTER SIX ·

HESTERA SPIKESAP

The rusty hinges creaked mournfully as the door before Rook slowly opened. He peered into the darkness of the widening gap. Why had he been brought here to the ancient Palace of Statues?

All at once, a long, bony arm reached out from the shadows and a sinewy hand – all knobbly knuckles and jagged yellow claws – gripped him round the wrist, and tugged. Rook swallowed hard as he was dragged forwards.

Behind him he could hear whips cracking, guards bellowing, and the yoked slaves howling with dismay ... Then – as the door slammed shut with a loud *bang* – nothing.

Rook's breathing caught in his throat. A heavy silence closed in about him. It seemed to throb in his ears, oppressive and unnatural, with not a single sound from outside penetrating the stillness within; while after the glare of the daylight, his eyes struggled to adjust to the gloomy half-light of the vast, cavernous hall before him.

Compared with the unbearably hot, humid air outside in the street, the air in the hall was wonderfully cool. Rook felt the grip tighten on his wrist.

Before him, standing alone in the vast, gloomy space, was a thin, stooped and – judging by the deep wrinkles creasing his high forehead and the white tips to the whiskers on his ears – *old* goblin. Not that Rook was about to under-estimate him. The goblin might look a bit doddery, but he was obviously powerful – like leather, he had been toughened and strength-ened by the passing years.

'Number eleven, is it?' the goblin muttered, peer-ing at the daubed numbers on Rook's front. 'Number eleven! Well, Speegspeel had better get number eleven to the kitchen straight away. Speegspeel doesn't want any trouble, oh, no! Speegspeel does as he's told.'

The goblin motioned for Rook to follow him, and set off across the cool, marble floor of the entrance hall.

Rook kept close behind him. As his eyes grew accustomed to the dim, shadowy half-light of the hall which seeped in through the slats of the shuttered windows above, he saw statues – hundreds of statues, in various poses and numerous styles, lurking in every shadow. There were crowds of them all round the sides of the hall, on fluted pedestals and scalloped plinths, with countless others set into alcoves in the walls; there were statues along the balconies, statues lining the grand sweeping staircase and still more disappearing up into the shadowy heights far above his head.

Each one – like those balanced so precariously on the outside of the building – had once been a former leaguesman. Their wealth and status had been captured in stone. Close by was one – short and portly – who was clutching a length of carved rope, symbolic of the material which had made his fortune; another held a stone telescope to his eye; a third had a sculpted hammelhorn standing at his feet. All of them were dressed in marble finery with jewels picked out in the stone, fur-like collars, lacy ruffs and long sweeping cloaks carved from the gleaming white rock. And as he stared closer, so their unblinking eyes appeared to narrow; their mouths, to sneer.

'Oh, they watch old Speegspeel,' the goblin grumbled softly, pushing Rook in front of him. 'They watch, just waiting for the chance to topple over when he least expects it. But old Speegspeel's too clever. They won't get Speegspeel.'

He shoved Rook viciously in the back. Rook stumbled forwards, his footsteps echoing on the cold marble. He gazed up at the grey cloaked shapes of the statues around them and realized with a jolt that they were not cloaked at all, but rather festooned in thick, dusty cobwebs. They webbed every finger, veiled every face and hung down from every outstretched arm like lengths of tattered muslin.

As they approached the other side of the vast hall, Speegspeel motioned towards a small panelled door, set beneath a modest archway ahead. Two cobweb-shrouded statues stood guard on either side. Speegspeel stepped forward, fumbled with the door handle and, with difficulty, pushed the heavy wooden door open.

'Go on, number eleven.' The old goblin chuckled. 'It doesn't do to keep Hestera Spikesap waiting. Speegspeel knows! Oh, yes, he does!'

Rook stumbled inside and found himself at the top of a steep staircase.

'That's the way,' came Speegspeel's voice. 'Down those stairs, number eleven. Hestera's expecting you.'

The door closed and Rook heard the soft shuffle of the old goblin's footsteps receding. He peered down. The stairs disappeared far below him into a noxious, dark orange glow. Gripping the banisters tightly and trying to stop his legs from shaking, he started down the flight of stairs.

Down, down, into the sunken bowels of the palace Rook went. Beneath his feet the wooden stairs – simple boards set into the stone of the palace's supporting walls – were worn and slippery. They creaked and bounced and he had to take enormous care not to lose his footing. As he went deeper, so the air grew hotter and steamier, and filled with a strange odour that Rook was unable to identify. It grew increasingly pungent with every successive step he took; now sour, now metallic, now laced with acrid smoke which coiled up thickly and fuzzed the brightening orange glow.

As he neared the bottom of the stairs, he glanced back and was shocked to see just how far down the rickety open staircase he'd come. The top was swathed in darkness and he couldn't even see the little door. It was a wonder he hadn't broken his neck, he thought giddily as he went down the last few steps.

On solid ground at last, Rook looked round and gasped. He was standing in a vast, seething kitchen. Supported by an intricate brickwork structure of stout pillars and curved arches which criss-crossed above his head, the underground chamber wheezed and heaved with heat and noise, while the intoxicating fumes were stronger than ever. They seemed to be coming from the far side of the kitchen, where the orange-yellow glow was brightest.

Just ahead of him was a long table, its surface gouged and scorched by years of misuse, overflowing with a seeming chaos of utensils, equipment and convoluted paraphernalia. Ladles, spoons, mortars and pestles, stacks of trays and sheaves of paper; scales, scissors, phials of tincture and pots of oily creams; boxes, beakers, skewers and cleavers; rulers, funnels, candles and pipettes . . .

The jumble wasn't limited to the table. The floor around it was littered with crates and sacks, each one overflowing with Deepwoods' fauna and flora; everything from dried razorflit wings to shrivelled globes of pus-fungus. Bundles of herbs and leafy branches and bunches of dried flowering shrubs hung from every wall, every arch and every pillar, giving the whole place the appearance of a vast upside-down forest. There were cupboards and cabinets; their drawers bursting with dried lichens, mosses and various desiccated remains. Racks, stacks and rows of shelving, crammed full with countless bottles – both large and small – all filled to the brim, stoppered and labelled. Some contained bark-chippings, identified by spidery writing – *Lufwood, Leadwood, Lullabee, Sallowdrop, Blookoak* . . . Some contained berries; dried, pickled, steeped in oil; some had nuts, some seeds. Some contained leaves – from the tiny spiky grey foliage of the creeping woodthyme, to the vast heart-shaped leaves from the sweetly aromatic, yet deadly poisonous, black-bay.

Rook frowned. What was so dangerous a herb doing in a kitchen? he wondered. And as he moved slowly round, inspecting the shelves and cabinets more closely, he saw other suspicious ingredients.

A barrel of venomous rosy heartapples; a flagon filled with deadly scrapewortberries, half a dozen of which he knew could kill a fully grown hammelhorn . . .

This kitchen was a poisoner's paradise!

Just then, a thin, wheedling voice rang out. 'Who's creeping round my kitchen? Is that you, Speegspeel, my old loverly ... I've warned you about creeping round my kitchen, haven't I? Don't want another stomach-ache, do we, dearie?'

Rook's heart missed a beat. He screwed up his eyes and stared in the direction the voice had come from.

In front of him, set on dumpy legs against the black-ened back wall, he could see a gargantuan pot-bellied furnace, its glass door at the front seeming to wink at him like a great orange eye. Ornately handled bellows stuck out from a hole in the grate-cover at the bottom; a black, twisting chimney emerged from the top and dis-appeared into the wall high above. To the right of the furnace was a towering heap of logs; to its left, an even higher pile of uncut branches and trunks – together with the saws and axes to turn it from one to the other. And to the left of that, set into the wall ...

Rook gasped with amazement. Huge, luminous bell jars fizzed and bubbled above acid-yellow flaming burners, all connected by a seemingly chaotic jumble of interconnecting pipes and tubes which coiled and looped and doubled back on themselves before coming down in a neat row where they dripped slowly into a line of glass pots below them. Rook leaned forward and raised his fingers to the small brass spigot at the end of one of the pipes.

'Don't touch that, dearie,' wheedled the voice. Rook started back. 'Come over 'ere and let me look at you, my loverly!'

A short, wrinkled old crone stepped out from behind the forest of pipes and tubes. Rook recognized her at once from the market; a short, dumpy goblin with grey skin and heavy-lidded eyes. She was clothed in chequer-board livery, a stained pinafore, and a white cowlcap – the high, arched headgear favoured by goblin matrons – on her head. In one hand, she was clutching an opened bottle; in the other, a tiny measuring spoon. She glanced up at Rook.

'Hestera Sp . . . Spikesap?' Rook asked.

'That's right, dearie,' she told him. 'Wait a second. Can't you see I'm trying to concentrate?'

Returning her attention to the bottle, she tipped a level spoonful of red powder down the slender neck. Then another, and another, counting off as she did so. '. . . Six. Seven. Eight.' She stopped and returned the spoon to the small pot. Then, having corked the bottle and shaken it vigorously, she held it up to the light. The colourless contents had turned red. With a satisfied smile playing over her thin lips, Hestera picked up her quill, dipped it in the ink-well and wrote on the label – in the same spidery writing that Rook had noticed before – a single word: *Oblivion*.

'Oblivion?' Rook murmured.

'Never you mind about that, dearie,' Hestera said, putting the bottle to one side and bustling round the table. 'Let's have a good look at you, my loverly.' She dragged him to the light; pinched him and prodded him with her sharp little fingers. 'Wiry but strong,' she said. 'I think you'll do.' Her small eyes narrowed as she

509

twisted his head round. 'You've taken a nasty blow, dearie? Does your head pain you?'

Rook nodded.

Hestera reached up and placed the flat of her palm across his forehead. It felt oddly dry, like parchment – but pleasantly cool. She nodded, turned away, and Rook heard the sound of clinking glass, pouring liquids and the metallic clatter of stirring. She turned back, and held out a glass of frothing green liquid.

'Drink this, dearie,' she told him.

Rook stared nervously at the glass in her outstretched hand. What was in it? Nectar of rosy heartapple perhaps? Or scrapewortberry juice?

'Go on, my loverly,' said Hestera, thrusting the glass into his hand. 'It won't kill you.'

Slowly Rook raised the glass to his mouth and sipped. It tasted delicious – a tangy mix of flavour after flavour. Pineginger. Rocklime. Dellberry and anisleaf . . .'

'That's right,' said Hestera. 'Every last drop, dearie.'

As the liquid coursed round his body, Rook felt himself being reinvigorated and, by the time the glass was empty, not only had his head stopped throbbing but he had begun to feel fit and well once more. He wiped the back of his hand across his mouth and placed the glass down on the table.

'Amazing,' he said. 'What is it?'

'Just one of my little concoctions, my loverly,' said Hestera, testing his forehead for a second time. 'Feeling better, are we?'

Rook nodded. 'Much better, thank you.'

Hestera smiled, a nasty glint in her eyes. 'Good, then you can get to work and build up that fire!' She strode over to the pot-bellied stove. 'Look at it,' she said. 'It's glowing orange, dearie. *Orange!* It hasn't been touched for three days. Not since Huffknot went missing. And now it needs tending.' She wrapped her shawl tighter about her shoulders. 'My kitchen is growing cold. Can't you feel the chill, my loverly? Why, my teeth are beginning to chatter . . . Feed the furnace! Feed it until it glows white hot! Just the way I like it, dearie.'

Rook picked up a log from the pile and was just about to take it towards the glowing furnace when a voice inside his head spoke. *Not so hasty, my young furnace-keeper!* it said.

Rook froze. The log clattered to the floor. It was as if icy fingers were probing his brain, causing a stabbing pain behind his eyes and making it difficult for him to think clearly.

'I was just getting him to stoke up the furnace with a few logs, dearie,' Hestera protested indignantly. 'Where's the harm in that, Amberfuce? It's freezing in my kitchen. Tell him, Flambusia; *freezing!*'

The unpleasant chilled sensation in Rook's head abruptly stopped. He turned to see not one but two figures standing in the shadows behind him. One was a hulking great creature – possibly of cloddertrog-extraction, and made bigger still by the stacked sandals on her feet and winged hat upon her head. She was dressed in voluminous robes which fluttered and shimmered in the trembling heat. Before her, seated in a buoyant sumpwood chair, was an ancient-looking ghost-waif, hunched and shaking; his skin pale and mottled; his eyes dull and half-closed.

'My dear Hestera Spikesap,' he croaked, his drooping ears and limp barbels trembling. 'How many times must I remind you? We really can't be too careful. If you must go shopping at the slave auction, please, please, *please* bring your purchases directly to me!' His sunken cheeks sucked in and out alarmingly.

'I was going to, dearie,' said Hestera, pushing Rook towards the tiny waif. 'But he's only just arrived. And it's *so* cold – I thought he could feed the furnace first, and then . . .'

'No, no, *no*, Hestera!' The waif fell back in the chair exhausted, choking and gasping for breath. His companion, Flambusia, leaned round.

'Lawks-a-mussy!' she exclaimed. 'You're vexing your-self again. And what did I say about vexing yourself?' She pulled a cloth from her sleeve and mopped Amberfuce's glistening brow. 'Nursie said, don't! It isn't good for your constitution. And nursie knows best.'

The waif closed his eyes. His ears rippled strangely. His breathing became slower, more regular. 'You're right, of course, Flambusia,' he said at last, his words breathy and snatched. 'It's just . . .' He flapped a bony arm in Hestera's direction. 'This . . . this *creature*! She's a law unto herself . . .'

Hestera folded her arms. 'Well, he's here now,' she said sharply. 'What are you waiting for?'

'Bring him closer, Hestera,' said Amberfuce wearily.

'Go on, dearie,' said Hestera, shoving Rook in the back.

Rook stumbled across the tiled floor, and stopped in front of the buoyant chair. An unpleasant smell hung round the sickly-looking creature, a curious mixture of stale milk-rusks and antiseptic which grew stronger as Amberfuce leaned forward in his chair.

'Kneel,' he croaked.

Rook did as he was told. The waif grabbed him by the collar, pulled him closer and stared deep into his eyes. For a second time, Rook felt the icy tingling inside his head.

Let me in, whispered a voice. *Let me in, Rook Barkwater, librarian knight . . .*

The tingling grew more intense. Chilled, numbing; it was as if the icy fingers were searching his mind and reading his thoughts, turning them over like the pages of a book.

A librarian knight . . . Lake Landing . . . the voice inside his head said. *A skycraft; the Stormhornet . . . An approaching storm, a rippled lake . . .* The ancient waif closed his eyes, and his back arched as he threw himself back in the chair. *An under-librarian!* The voice was strong now, insistent. *A lectern-tender, a chain-turner . . . Deep, deep sorrow . . .* The waif gripped Rook's cuffs tight and pulled him closer. *Tears . . . Pain . . . Bad dreams . . .*

Rook shuddered.

Let's clear them all away, the voice inside his head told him. *Let them all go. Give them to me. That's the way. Let all those troubled thoughts disappear for ever . . .*

Rook's head swam as his memories slipped away, one by one, little by little. Soon there would be nothing left.

'No,' he groaned, jerking back and trying to push the numbing fingers away with his thoughts.

Don't fight me! Rook heard inside his head, and he felt the fingers tighten their grip as they continued their searching.

It was tempting to do as the waif had instructed. Anything to bring a hasty end to the terrible jarring of those ice-cold fingers, scraping and scrabbling inside his head. Yet, if he *didn't* fight . . .

His mind was already beginning to resemble a barren landscape of snow and ice. Impressions, thoughts, feelings – Rook seemed to see them staggering across the empty wasteland only to be seized by the probing fingers and frozen solid.

Must try to hide from the icy fingers, Rook thought. Must hide myself. Rook. Rook Barkwater . . .

Like a great searchlight, the waif's probing thoughts swept across Rook's mind, poking into nooks and crannies, prising open cracks and crevices and unlocking door after door after door, on down into the deepest of his most distant thoughts.

Still on his knees, Rook swayed back and forwards, his head lolling from side to side. It was so hot in the kitchen; stiflingly hot, the air laced with miasmic fumes from the furnace.

Yet inside his pounding head, it was cold – bitterly cold – as the icy fingers delved deeper, freezing every part of him.

I . . . am . . . Rook . . .

A blizzard wind seemed to whip away his memories and thoughts like so many snowflakes. Rook . . . I'm Rook . . . He ran away from the icy, probing fingers and fell into the arms of something soft, something warm; something from his earliest memories. A banderbear. *His* banderbear.

The great creature raised a warning claw to her lips, pulled him down into a mossy hollow and wrapped her arms around him. Rook curled up and hid himself away inside the huge creature's warm, furry embrace.

He couldn't be found now. He was safe. Secure . . .

With a jerky shake of his head, Amberfuce sat up straight. His eyes snapped open.

'Well?' said Hestera.

'Oh, I think you'll find he'll be compliant now,' the

waif said, as Flambusia mopped his glistening brow. 'His mind has been cleared. A blank slate, so to speak.' He frowned, and flapped the nurse away irritably. 'A fine mind it was, it must be said,' he remarked thoughtfully. 'A strong mind. It seems such a shame to take all those brave thoughts and noble memories from such an intrepid young lad. Still, Hestera, I'm sure you'll soon teach him afresh – particularly if you treat him as casually as all the oth . . . oth . . . others . . .' His words collapsed into a fit of coughing. He wheezed and gasped for breath.

Flambusia patted him gently on the back. 'There, there,' she said soothingly. 'You've been overdoing it again.'

'Medicine . . .' Amberfuce croaked. 'My . . . medicine . . .' The coughing resumed, louder than ever.

'At once,' said Flambusia, grabbing the buoyant chair and steering it away. Just before she disappeared from sight, she turned and flashed a smile at Hestera. 'I don't know where we'd be without your medicine,' she said.

As the two of them left, Hestera turned her attention to Rook. He was still on his knees, head slumped and eyes staring blindly ahead. She raised his chin with one hand and clicked her fingers with the other. 'I only hope Amberfuce hasn't gone too far,' she muttered. 'It wouldn't be the first time.' She stepped back. 'Stand!' she commanded.

Rook struggled to his feet. 'Yes,' he intoned obediently.

'Good, dearie,' muttered Hestera. 'Right, you've got to

work if you want to earn your daily gruel. To the furnace
with you. Stoke the fire! Stoke it up high!'

'Yes.'

'Very good,' said Hestera. She pulled on a heavy glove
and opened the door at the front of the furnace. A blast
of scorching, sulphurous air struck Rook full in the face.
He recoiled – but said nothing. 'Yes, very good, indeed,'
said Hestera. 'Amberfuce has done well. *Very* well.'

Rook stood before the furnace, stock-still, unblinking.
His mind was blank; so blank that he wasn't even aware
that he didn't know what to do next.

'The logs,' came Hestera's voice. 'Take the logs from
the pile and feed the fire.'

'Yes.'

He crossed over to the towering heap
of logs and seized the one closest to
him. It was large, unwieldy, and almost
twice his own weight. He
dragged it across the floor,
grunting and groaning
with effort. In front
of the furnace, he caught his breath
before reaching down, clasping the
rough bark and hefting the whole lot
up into the air. The log rested precariously on the lip of the circular
door-frame for a moment, threatening to fall back and crush him
– then keeled forwards onto the
glowing embers inside.

'That's it,' Hestera told him.
'Now pump the bellows
– up, down, up, down;
that's the way . . . Then
fetch another log. And
then another, and an-

other – and you keep on fetching them and feeding them
to the fire until I tell you to stop. Understand?'

'Yes, I understand.'

The work was back-breaking. Time and again, Rook
dragged the heavy logs across to the great furnace,
hoiked them up and tipped them in. With each one, the
fire blazed hotter and hotter. It scorched Rook's lungs
and skin. It singed his hair . . .

Yet inside his head it was all still a frozen wasteland
that the flames could not touch. Though his body was
suffering, his mind was unaware of anything beside the
sound of Hestera's voice.

'Another log!' she rasped. 'And hurry! You're slowing
down!'

'Yes, Hestera.' He doubled his efforts.

But in the emptiness within, something stirred – a tiny
movement in the snow as a buried speck of consciousness flickered. The banderbear's embrace warmed his
spirit.

Rook, it whispered. *You are Rook.*

He was curled up in a foetal ball, protected from the
arctic chill by the banderbear's reassuring embrace. The
waif's icy fingers had taken his memories, his thoughts,
his hopes and fears, his nightmares and dreams . . . But

there was one thing that had remained out of reach; that most important and precious thing of all. The seed of his existence, the essence of himself – in short, the knowledge of who he was.

Rook Barkwater.

He was still safe in the warm embrace of the banderbear that had once protected him as a child, lost and alone in the Deepwoods . . .

Rook stumbled and dropped the log he was dragging to the furnace. His head was spinning.

The ice was in retreat. Rook crawled from the banderbear's warm arms. The memories, the thoughts, the feelings; they were all beginning to thaw.

Suddenly, with a loud roaring in his ears and a flash of blinding light, everything came flooding back. *Who* he was. *Where* he was . . .

'That's enough for today, dearie,' said Hestera, eyeing him suspiciously. 'You can get to your bed.'

'Thank you,' said Rook, trying hard to conceal his relief. The stifling heat of the blazing furnace was getting to his racked and weary body now. He didn't know how much longer he could have kept going. With a huge effort – using every last reserve of strength – Rook hefted the log he was holding up into the fire and stood waiting for his next instruction.

Hestera slammed the great round furnace-door shut and secured the latch. She turned to Rook. 'You sleep over there,' she said, pointing back to the low table. 'Underneath.'

'Thank you,' said Rook.

He shuffled towards it, crouched down and, taking care not to knock the bump on his head against the table-top, crawled beneath. There was a mattress of woodchips and shavings strewn across the tiles – soft, warm, inviting. Rook lay down, curled up into a ball and breathed in the sweet, aromatic scent of the fragments of wood. His eyelids grew heavy; his body seemed to sink into the floor.

Hestera stood above him. 'Sleep well, little furnace-keeper and build up your strength,' she rasped softly. 'You'll need it. Today you have fed the fire . . .'

Rook wrapped his hands round his knees and pulled them up close to his stomach. 'Thank . . . you . . .' he whispered drowsily.

A darkness descended; the outside was switched off, sense by sense – and Rook slipped into a deep, dream-less sleep. Hestera chuckled unpleasantly.

'. . . But tomorrow you will feed the baby.'

·CHAPTER SEVEN·

FEEDING THE BABY

Early the following morning, Rook was rudely awoken by something hard and pointed jabbing into his back. His eyes snapped open.

For a moment, he was perplexed. He seemed to be lying on a pile of wood-shavings. The sharp, stabbing sensation struck him in the back a second time.

'*Ow!*' he cried out loud, and rolled over.

Peering down at him was a grey-skinned old goblin matron with a stick clutched in her bony hands, its sharp end pointed towards him. 'Look lively, my loverly,' she was saying. 'Get up. There's plenty of work to be done.'

At the sound of her shrill, wheedling voice, everything suddenly came flooding back. Speegspeel the butler, Hestera Spikesap the cook, and the sickly waif, Amberfuce, who had probed his mind and erased his past – or at least, tried to . . .

Mustn't give myself away, Rook cautioned himself as he crawled out from beneath the table and scrambled quickly to his feet. He looked round giddily. The furnace was glowing and the hot, stifling air shimmered like water. Hestera raised the stick and pointed to the table behind him.

'Victuals,' she said.

Rook turned. A place for one had been laid. There was a large bowl of steaming grey gruel with a wooden spoon sticking out of the middle, and a glass of what looked like the same liquid he had drunk the previous evening.

'Eat, drink – and be quick about it, dearie,' said Hestera. 'The furnace is getting low.'

With no stool or bench to sit down on, Rook had his meagre breakfast standing. The gruel tasted as unpleasant as it looked – smoky, salty and with a stale tang of mould about it – but by washing down each claggy spoonful with a slurp of the frothing green juice, he was able to sate his hunger and slake his thirst at the same time.

'Hurry up, dearie,' said Hestera impatiently. 'That furnace needs building up.' She shuddered and pulled her shawl tightly about her. 'My old bones are chilled to the marrow.'

What was she talking about? Rook wondered. The kitchen was scorching. His entire body was damp with sweat. He drained the glass, laid it down next to the half-empty bowl and turned to Hestera. 'Thank you,' he said expressionlessly.

'Better you thank me with deeds not words,' said Hestera. 'Stoke up that fire, dearie. Get it blazing white hot. White hot, d'you hear? As hot as it can possibly be, for today's the day we feed the baby.'

'Yes,' said Rook, taking care that his face betrayed not the faintest flicker of emotion. He turned away and headed for the great mound of logs, Hestera's words echoing in his head.

Feed the baby? he thought. What baby?

By the time Rook had dragged the first of the logs across to the furnace, Hestera had already opened the circular door. As he stepped in front of it, a blast of roaring heat struck him full in the face. He let out a soft, involuntary moan.

Hestera turned and gave Rook a long, searching look. Rook could feel her dark suspicious eyes boring into him. Struggling to remain impassive, he reached down, seized the log and thrust it into the furnace. Then he turned, crouched down and worked the bellows, just as Hestera had shown him – four sharp movements, up, down, up, down. There was a crackle and a hiss and the glow from the fire turned from a deep gold to pale, luminous yellow.

'*White* hot, remember, dearie,' said Hestera. 'More logs, more logs. And keep working those bellows!'

A dozen logs and a deal of back-breaking bellows-pumping later, Rook was relieved to hear Hestera declare herself satisfied at last. The pot-bellied furnace was creaking and juddering as the fire inside blazed more furiously than ever; blinding as the sun and lightning hot.

'Come over 'ere,' my loverly,' she said. 'Observe what I do.'

'Yes,' Twig croaked. His throat, parched and scorched,

felt as though it had been sandpapered; his legs felt weak and heavy. Yet as he left the furnace and headed into the shadows where Hestera was busy fiddling with a length of rope, he found that the air was cooler and his head began to clear.

'Unknot this for me, dearie,' said Hestera. 'I can't reach.'

Rook nodded obediently, stretched up to the wall-mounted cleat and detached the tangled coil of rope. He handed the end to Hestera who, without a word, fed the rope through her hands. From high above, there came a soft clatter and Rook looked up to see a large wooden bucket slowly descending towards them. When it was low enough, Rook reattached the rope to the cleat.

'Make sure it's tied securely, dearie,' said Hestera. 'That's it. Now come and have a look.'

Rook gave the rope an extra tug, then returned to the bucket, now suspended a couple of strides above the floor. Steadying it with one hand, Hestera reached in with the other and pulled out a small, red, bulbous object which glistened as she held it up to the light.

'It's an acorn,' she announced.

Rook frowned. With its red flesh, thin, slimy membrane and thick juice that oozed like blood, it looked like no acorn he had ever seen before. Nor did it smell like one.

It was, he thought, his nose wrinkling at the stale, metallic odour, more like a piece of offal – a hammelhorn liver, perhaps; or a tilder kidney.

'An acorn,' he repeated, trying to mask the surprise in his voice.

'But not just any old acorn, dearie,' said Hestera. 'This here is a *bloodoak* acorn. Harvested in the Deepwoods by woodtrolls, so they are, my loverly. And there's a tricky task, I can tell you! What with the bloodoaks eating all the flesh they can get their tarry-vines on and all, the harvesters often get harvested, if you take my meaning. You want to count yourself lucky you're here working for me.'

'Yes,' said Rook, his stomach churning.

'That's why they're so expensive,' she went on. 'I mean, it stands to reason. But you try telling that to that old tightwad, Amberfuce. Always moaning on about the price, so he is. But as I always tell him, if it keeps the master upstairs happy, then it's gold pieces well spent, and no mistake.'

Hestera carefully placed the acorn in the crook of her apron and, selecting another, held it up to the light. Rook watched queasily as she picked out four more of the quivering crimson blobs and placed them in her blood-stained apron. At last she turned to Rook.

'That should do, my loverly.' She pointed a blood-stained finger across to a rack of hearth-tools – tongs, brushes, shovels; a set of bellows and several small hatchets. 'Fetch me a shovel, dearie,' she said.

Rook did as he was told.

'No, not that one,' came Hestera's voice from behind him as he reached out. 'That one there with the long handle.'

Rook seized the shovel she wanted, and returned to Hestera.

'That's it, my loverly,' she said. 'Now, hold it out flat in front of me. That's the way. Now, we place them out on the shovel-tray, so.' She stared down at the half dozen acorns thoughtfully. 'Maybe one more,' she said at last, turning and retrieving a seventh acorn from the swaying bucket and placing it next to the rest. 'That's better. Now for the roasting. Follow me.'

Hestera headed back to the furnace. Rook went with her, holding the bloodoak acorns out in front of him. Hestera slipped on a pair of heavy gloves, reached up and pulled the furnace-door wide open. The heat blasted out.

'*Ooh*, lovely,' Hestera cooed. 'Nice and warm in my cold, old bones.' She turned back to Rook. 'Pass over the shovel,' she said. 'Careful, now.'

Rook stepped forwards, feeling himself wilt as the heat grew suddenly more intense. He handed over the precious load of bloodoak acorns and retreated.

'Pop it in like so,' said Hestera, plunging the shovel into the white-hot heart of the furnace. There was a hiss and the unmistakable smell of roasting meat. 'And now we wait,' she said. 'A couple of minutes ought to do it.' She turned back to Rook. 'Course, normally you won't be doing such a large batch, dearie,' she said. 'One acorn is enough for at least a hundred bottles of oblivion.'

'Oblivion,' Rook repeated.

'I was making some up when you arrived,' said Hestera, 'do you remember? Oh, no, of course you don't,' she added – thankfully before Rook could give himself away. 'I was forgetting. Silly old Hestera . . .' She picked at a splatter of crusted, blood-coloured sap on her apron. 'Oblivion,' she sighed. 'It's the master's little tipple. Keeps him happy, so it does. And it's all my own recipe,' she added, with obvious pride.

Rook remained still, impassive.

'I distil it from the finest vintage sapwine.' Hestera nodded at the chaos of pipes and tubes, burners and bell jars set into the wall to her right. 'I have some on the go the whole time,' she said. 'But it's my own secret ingredient that makes it so special. Powdered blookoak acorn. It's what gives it the kick the master likes so much . . . ' She pulled Rook close and her eyes narrowed. 'It's our little secret. You won't tell anyone will you, dearie?'

Rook could smell her fetid breath, sour and moist in his face. 'No,' he managed to say.

The goblin released her grip and pushed him away with a laugh. 'Course you won't, my loverly. After all, you're part of our little family now. You won't ever be meeting anyone else to tell Hestera's secret to, not ever again . . .'

She turned back to the furnace, pulled the shovel out and inspected the acorns. 'Hmm, half a minute longer, I think . . .' She thrust them back inside. 'Of course, we shan't be making oblivion today. Oh, no. Today we're going to feed the baby.'

'Feed the baby,' Rook repeated softly, but his mind was still racing from the impact of her words. Never meet anyone else . . . Not ever again?

Hestera pulled the shovel from the furnace a second time. 'Perfect!' she announced. 'Look at it closely, dearie. This is exactly the colour and consistency you should be aiming for, see?'

'Yes,' said Rook, looking down at the shovel. Where the seven slimy offal-like acorns had been, there now lay a single pile of powder; as fine as flour, as crimson as blood.

Hestera pulled the shovel clear of the furnace, pushed the door shut with her shoulder and headed back to the table, the charred handle clasped in her bony hands. 'As I say, normally I'd keep this in a jar until I needed it for the oblivion. But not today . . .'

'No, today we're going to feed the baby,' said Rook, relieved to hear his own voice was still flat and expressionless.

'That's right, dearie,' said Hestera. Her dark eyes glinted behind their hooded lids. 'At least, *you* are.' She rested the end of the shovel on the table-top. 'Now, grab a bell jar, my loverly, and brush all of the bloodoak powder inside. That's the way. Every last speck. And be quick about it! Timing is everything.'

Rook hurried to complete his task, trying his hardest to do exactly what Hestera had told him. Yet despite his best efforts, as he swept the soft bristles over the shovel, some specks of the red powder missed the bell jar and fluttered down to the damp floor. Hestera, thankfully, seemed not to notice.

When the shovel was completely empty, she turned and returned it to the rack. Rook picked up the bell jar and examined the vivid red powder inside. It was so bright it seemed almost to be pulsating . . .

'Put it down,' came a voice by his shoulder.

Hestera was back, a small pot clasped in her hands. She placed it down on the table next to the bell jar and unscrewed the lid. Curious, Rook peered inside. It was half-full of a pale sepia powder that glittered in the dim light of the kitchen.

'Phraxdust,' said Hestera.

'Phraxdust,' repeated Rook flatly, trying desperately to conceal a surge of excitement. He knew all about the stuff – that it came from stormphrax, that precious substance created in a Great Storm, so heavy in darkness that it had once been used to weight down the old float-ing rock of Sanctaphrax; that it was produced naturally and safely in the half-light of the Twilight Woods as the stormphrax broke down; that it could purify even the most polluted water . . .

'Ay, finest quality phraxdust, dearie,' said Hestera. 'Garnered by the shrykes in the depths of the Twilight

Woods.' She tapped the side of her nose. 'We have a little arrangement . . .' She bustled forwards and handed Rook a pair of tweezers. 'But we are wasting precious time,' she said. 'The bloodoak powder is cooling. See how the colour is growing dimmer. Add some phraxdust to it, dearie; then shake the whole lot up together.'

'Yes,' said Rook. He held the tweezers with his forefinger and thumb and dipped them into the pot. 'How much do I add?' he asked.

'For seven bloodoak acorns, seven pinches of phraxdust,' came Hestera's reply from the other side of the kitchen. Rook glanced round and was surprised to see that the old goblin matron had slipped away and was now crouched down behind a heavy bench, her white cap just poking up above the worktop. 'Go on!' she snapped.

Rook turned back to the powders, his heart clomping like a skittish tilder. What he was doing must be dangerous, he realized – otherwise, why would Hestera be shielding herself?

He leaned forwards and, with trembling fingers, took a tweezer-pinch of phraxdust and moved it over to the bell jar. Then, breath held, he opened the tweezers and a sprinkling of sepia fell onto the crimson powder inside.

Rook reached in for a second pinch. His palms were wet. Glistening beads lined his forehead, and as he leaned forwards once more, he struggled to focus on the bell jar. Sweat was running into his eyes; his head was throbbing.

'Take care not to drop any of the phraxdust, dearie,' came Hestera's wheedling voice.

Rook opened the tweezers and the tiny particles of phraxdust dropped. As they did so, a single speck broke away from the rest and swirled round in the scorching air-currents. Down towards the table-top it floated, then up again, spinning and glittering – now in lamplight, now in furnace-glow; then down again, floating past the edge of the table and hitting the floor with its traces of bloodoak powder . . .

BANG!!!

The explosion which ripped through the kitchen was as violent as it was sudden. It shook the floor, it rocked the heavy table, it seized Rook and tossed him back across the kitchen like a wet rag. He landed heavily by the wall, the tweezers still clamped in his grip.

'Careless, dearie! Very careless!' came a shrill voice. 'Jaspel was careless, and *he* didn't last long!' She wagged a bony finger at him reproachfully. 'I *told* you to take care!'

'W . . . what just happened?' stammered Rook, picking himself up. His nostrils quivered at a familiar smell – like wood-almonds; toasted wood-almonds . . .

'You must have dropped some bloodoak powder before, and then some phraxdust just now,' said Hestera matter-of-factly. 'Outside the bell jar, they're very unstable – any bit of moisture and . . . *bang!*'

Rook froze. It suddenly occurred to him that if moisture was the cause of the explosion, then his entire body was a detonator. Just one clammy finger; one bead of sweat, and . . . The thought of it made him sweat more heavily than ever. Suddenly he was like a sieve, dripping water from every pore.

'Hurry up!' said Hestera sharply. 'We must feed the baby. Carry on, dearie.'

Wiping his shaking hands as best he could on the front of his jacket, Rook hurried back to the table. He raised the tweezers, reached forwards gingerly and held his breath. Then, with his fingers trembling like a sallow-drop in a storm, he dropped the next tweezer-pinch of sepia phraxdust into the bell jar. He repeated this four more times.

'At last,' said Hestera. 'Now stopper it up and give it a shake.'

'Yes,' said Rook faintly. Feeling sick to the pit of his stomach, he reached forwards, seized the bell jar and held it up. The phraxdust formed a thin layer on top of the bloodoak powder. He pushed the cork into place.

'A good shake, mind,' said Hestera.

'Yes,' said Rook. He could feel the heat from the toasted powder warming his hands – his nervous hands; his *moist, clammy* hands . . . Eyes clamped firmly shut, he shook the glass jar vigorously. Nothing happened.

He looked up. The powders had mixed together.

Just then a tinkling sound echoed round the kitchen. It was coming from the wall behind the table, where a row of bells attached to coiled strips of metal were mounted to a board. Each one was identified by a small plaque beneath – *the Great Hall*, *the Banquet Hall*, *the Master's Chamber* . . . It was the one marked *Leagues' Chamber* that had just rung. The bell was still swaying.

'Quickly, dearie! Quickly!' said Hestera. 'Speegspeel is waiting. Bring the bell jar over here, my loverly, and I'll warm it up ready.'

Back at the furnace, Hestera placed the bell jar on the ledge of the door and waited till the powder inside was once again glowing a vivid red. Then, without saying a word, she removed it and hurried off, beckoning to Rook as she went.

He followed behind her as she crossed the kitchen to the opposite corner. There, half-hidden in shadow, was a carved stone head set into the wall and gurning hideously. It was huge, each bulging eye the size of Rook's head and the bulbous nose as large as a hammel-horn. Beneath it, the mouth was vast and snarling. Rook frowned. Hestera seemed to be aiming straight for it.

'Step inside and hold this close to you, dearie,' said Hestera, handing him back the bell jar. 'You're to take it up to the Leagues' Chamber at the very top of the palace. Speegspeel will meet you there. Don't keep him waiting.'

Rook nodded mutely. Hestera pulled a lever set to the right of the stone head, and the bared teeth opened.

Rook stared into the mouth. Inside was a small cupboard-like affair – oddly modest for so grand an entrance – with a length of rope hanging from above.

'It's a pulley-lift,' Hestera told him. 'It connects all the different palace floors. Go on, dearie.'

Despite the heat of the hot bell jar clasped to his chest, Rook shivered. He manoeuvred himself up into the small box-shaped compartment and sat cross-legged on the floor. The rope hung down before his face.

'That's the way, my loverly,' said Hestera. 'Seize the rope and pull. Pull with all your might. And don't stop till you reach the top. The bell jar mustn't be allowed to cool down. If it does, moisture could form on the inside of the glass – and if that happened . . .'

Rook swallowed noisily.

'But then, I'm sure a big strong lad like you won't have any problems. Not like old Gizzlewit. Stopped halfway up at the banquet hall, so he did. Horrible mess! Glass and guts everywhere!'

Rook swallowed again and hugged the bell jar tightly to his chest – anything to keep it warm.

'Go on, then, dearie,' said Hestera, her voice laced with impatience. 'Speegspeel's waiting, remember.'

Rook seized one side of the rope and pulled down hard. The pulley-lift juddered and he felt himself rising up. He pulled again. The kitchen disappeared – and with it the intense heat from the blazing furnace. Higher he rose, in a dark chimney-like space, pulling hand over hand in a regular rhythm. Sweat beaded his forehead and dampened his hair; the muscles in his stomach and

arms began to protest. But he mustn't allow the bell jar to cool. Rook drove himself on.

A dim light above his head grew closer, closer . . . All at once, Rook found himself staring out of a narrow opening into the statue-filled hallway. It was as cavernous and shadowy as he remembered. And as cold! Tightening his grip on the rope, he pulled harder than ever.

A moment later, he glimpsed an ornate reception hall with rugs on the floor, and numerous chairs and benches, each one covered with a ghostly dust-sheet.

He continued up. An upper landing flashed past; then, on the other side of a metal grille, a small library with books lining the walls and display cases in the centre of the room. His arms were throbbing now, each tug on the rope harder than the one before. He wanted to stop, to rest – but he knew he dare not.

A little further up, squinting through the hatch-like opening, Rook saw a grandiose room. The ceilings were tall and vaulted; a crystal chandelier hung low over a long, blackwood table laid out with gold cutlery and silver goblets.

Rook's body was aching; his head throbbed. And he was hot. So hot . . .

'The banquet hall . . . Gizzlewit!' he murmured weakly, and started back, horrified by sight of the misty clouds of breath twisting from his lips as he spoke.

He might be hot, but the banquet hall was freezing. Gizzlewit's terrible end flashed before his eyes.

Doubling his efforts, Rook pulled on the rope with all his might. The banquet-room hatch disappeared as the pulley-lift went back into the square chimney-like stack. For a moment the rope twisted and snagged and the lift slowed. Rook tugged all the harder. There was a slight jerk, and the ascent continued. Up, up, up he went, past a locked hatchway and on. It grew darker, mustier; sticky spiderwebs wrapped themselves round his hands and face. But he kept going. And as he did so, something occurred to him. Something wonderful. It was getting warmer . . .

With a jolt and a loud *clonk!* the lift came to an abrupt halt. Rook looked about him anxiously. It was darker than ever. Pitch black. He couldn't see his hands in front of his face.

Just then, he heard a soft sing-song muttering behind him. He twisted round and cocked his head to one side. The voice grew clearer. '*Keep to the black, not the white, if you want to keep your life,*' it was saying. Rook recognized the slightly hissing voice of the old goblin who had dragged him inside the palace. It was

Speegspeel. '*Keep to the black, not the white, if you want to keep your life.*'

Rook reached forwards, and his fingers closed round a small handle, which he twisted and pushed. The door remained shut. Trying hard not to panic, Rook paused, and listened.

'*Keep to the black, not the white . . .*' The rhyme broke off abruptly. 'Oh, he'd better be quick, so he had . . .'

'Speegspeel, I'm here!' Rook cried out. 'In the pulley-lift!' He rattled and shook the door, and banged upon it with his fist.

The goblin fell still and Rook heard the sound of hurried, shuffling footsteps approaching. There was the sound of jangling metal and a key being slid into a lock. The next moment, the door burst open, dazzling light flooded in and Rook found himself peering into the expectant face of the butler.

'Number eleven!' he exclaimed, relief splashing across his face. 'Oh, but he's a strong one, that number eleven. Speegspeel knew he would be.' His eyes narrowed. 'And have you got it? Did you bring me food for the baby?'

Rook opened the front of his jacket and pulled out the bell jar. Speegspeel clapped his hands together, making a sound like clacking wood. 'Excellent!' he hissed. 'Jump out, number eleven,' he said. 'Hurry now. Follow me.'

Rook swung his legs round and, holding the bell jar carefully, jumped down onto the floor. The staggering heat of the chamber wrapped itself around him like a suffocating blanket. He found himself standing in a magnificent rooftop chamber.

Above his head, a spectacular panelled-glass dome opened up onto the bright sky beyond. Some of the panes had been broken and lay glittering on the floor around a huge, ring-shaped table – crudely repaired with ropes and wooden splints – which filled the centre of the chamber. On the side nearest him lay a great stone head, its unblinking eyes staring down blindly at the wooden boards; while on the far side of the table, out of place in the rundown finery of the chamber, stood a rickety-looking structure some twenty strides or so high, at the top of which – like an egg in a nest – was cradled a large metal ball. It was there that Speegspeel was heading.

He circled the table, picking his way through the broken glass, and stopped at the foot of the scaffold. Rook stopped beside him, then watched curiously as the old goblin reached for a trumpet-like instrument some fifteen strides long which was leaning up against the wooden framework. With a soft grunt of effort, Speegspeel raised it up into the air, placing the flared bell at one end against the surface of the metal ball and the other end to his ear. His leathery skin creased as a smile spread across his face.

'Baby needs feeding,' he said. 'It's nearly full enough, but not quite . . .' He laid the ear-trumpet aside and turned to Rook. 'Follow me,' he said. 'Follow Speegspeel and we'll feed the baby.'

Rook tucked the bell jar under his left arm and followed the goblin up the tricky ascent. It looked difficult – and was even more difficult than it looked.

The wood was rough and splinters kept jabbing into Rook's fingers; the gaps between the struts were wide and awkward to navigate – particularly with the heavy jar threatening to slip at any moment. He clambered over a long, thick beam set at an angle and on up towards the criss-cross framework which supported the great ball, keeping pace with the goblin.

'We're almost there, number eleven,' Speegspeel called over his shoulder encouragingly.

Rook glanced down. The floor seemed miles below him already. He looked up again. He was level with the ball now. Close up, with its coppery gleam and segmented body, it looked like nothing so much as a giant wood orange, the impression completed by the long, stalk-like length of rope hanging down from a small hole in its underside. Just above, Speegspeel held out a hand.

'That's the way,' he said. 'Now right on up to the platform.'

Rook reached up, took the goblin's hand and pulled himself up beside him. He was standing on a rough, almost-circular platform which ringed the top of the ball.

'Look at baby,' Speegspeel whispered. 'Beautiful, isn't it?' He stroked it softly, feeling the smoothness of its burnished outer casing. 'The master designed baby. But Speegspeel, he made it. Just like master said. Beautiful baby. Beautiful big baby.'

Far above Rook's head, a white raven swooped across the sky on soft, padded wings. Its gimlet eyes bored down through the glass dome of the great statue-covered building.

'See the cap, number eleven? Set into baby's centre,' whispered Speegspeel. 'Remove it. Gently now . . .' Rook did as he was told. 'Now empty the bell jar into it. Every last speck. And quickly, before any nasty moisture gets into baby. We don't want that . . . Not yet.'

With fumbling fingers, Rook slowly tipped the jar up. Then with a deft flick he thrust the neck of the jar down into the hole in the copper casing. It was a perfect fit.

As the powder dropped down into the ball, Rook found himself looking through the glass bottom of the jar and into the so-called baby. It was almost full. He tapped the glass, and the last few specks of red powder dropped down inside. Then, in one movement, he pulled the empty bell jar away, slammed the cap back into place and tightened it.

'All done,' came Speegspeel's voice in his ear. The goblin was stroking the side of the huge ball with pride. 'We'll have the baby full up in no time. The master will be so pleased with us.'

Rook followed the goblin back down the scaffold. At the bottom, Speegspeel clapped him on the shoulder.

'The baby's fed,' he said, 'so you'd best be getting back. You don't want to cross old Hestera Spikesap. Speegspeel knows.' He rubbed a gnarled hand slowly round his stomach. 'Not if you don't want no mysterious stomach-ache,' he said. 'She's good at those. Mark old Speegspeel's words.'

Returning to the kitchen was infinitely easier than leaving it had been. The lift went down all by itself. All

Rook had to do was hold onto the rope to make sure it didn't go too quickly.

'*There* you are, dearie!' said Hestera as he reached the bottom. He climbed out through the stone mouth into the suffocating heat of the kitchen. 'I was wondering where you'd got to,' she said, dragging him back towards the furnace. 'It's got chilly since you've been gone. Stoke up the fire with logs, my loverly. Lots of logs.'

'Yes,' said Rook wearily.

'And get those bellows working again. I need to warm these cold, aching bones.'

'Yes.'

'And when you've done that, you'd better chop some more logs. We're running rather low.'

'Yes,' said Rook. He handed Hestera the empty bell jar and the cork and, with a sigh, marched off towards the heap of logs.

But despite his weariness, Rook's mind was racing; full of questions with no answers and wild speculations. What was *baby*? Why had it been built and what could it possibly be for? One thing he knew for certain; he had to find out. And, as an icy chill gripped him despite the heat of the kitchen, he realized that only one person would have the answers to these questions . . .

The master of the Palace of Statues, Vox Verlix himself.

·CHAPTER EIGHT·

VOX'S EYE

'More logs, dearie! The furnace is getting low,' came Hestera's wheedling voice.

'Yes,' said Rook wearily.

He'd slept fitfully the night before, his troubled dreams filled with complicated recipes for bloodoak acorns and phraxdust, and a fat baby, its burnished copper face twisted up with fiery rage as it screamed, *More! More! More!* Rook had awoken almost as tired as when he'd lain down to sleep. Now it was back to the endless toil in the stifling kitchen and he was really suffering.

As he hefted a great log up into the insatiable furnace, a spasm of weariness racked his body and it was all he could do to keep his eyes open. In the corner of the kitchen, seated on two vast carved rocking chairs, Hestera and Amberfuce's nurse, Flambusia Flodfox, were deep in whispered conversation.

'I gave him three drops of your lufwood tincture, just like you said, Hesty dear,' Flambusia was saying, nodding down at the waif who was dozing in his chair beside them. 'And it didn't seem to have any effect,' she added. 'I swear he's getting used to it, Hesty. I had to add a drop from your, er . . .' – her eyes narrowed and she leaned forwards conspiratorially – '*special* potion.'

'Oh, Flambusia!' clucked Hestera. 'I've told you, that is only for emergencies. Why, one drop too much and . . .'

'Hesty, dear, you know I'm careful. Besides, his constant nagging is so hard to take. But just look at him now.' The huge nurse smiled indulgently at the waif. 'Sleeping like a baby.'

Hestera caught sight of Rook out of the corner of her eye. 'Excuse me, Flambusia,' she said. 'I shan't be a minute.'

The old goblin matron bustled over to the table, poured a glass of the green liquid from a pewter jug and hurried across to the furnace. 'Here we are, dearie,' she said to Rook. 'Drink it all up now.'

Rook looked round blearily. Hestera placed the glass in his hands; he raised it to his lips. At the first taste, Rook felt charged with renewed energy and he gulped down the rest of the green juice greedily. It coursed through his veins, invigorating his body and clearing his head.

'Thank you,' he said.

Hestera was shaking her head in bemusement. 'My word,' she said. 'What a thirst! Why, you remind me of Birdwhistle . . . Poor, *dear* Birdwhistle . . .' she added wistfully. She reached forwards and squeezed Rook's upper arm with a bony thumb and forefinger. 'Feels good, doesn't it?' she said. 'Hestera's little potion's building you up nicely.'

'Yes,' said Rook. It was true; in the short time he'd been in Hestera's kitchen, the hard work and strange diet had certainly had an effect. He could *feel* it. He was definitely broader in the shoulders now; stronger in the arm.

'Come on, then, dearie,' said Hestera. 'Let's see you using those fine young muscles of yours. Stoke up the fire and get those bellows pumping.'

'Yes,' said Rook, keeping his voice flat and toneless.

Hestera turned away. 'Sorry about that, Flambusia, my loverly. Now, where were we? Ah, yes . . .' She rummaged in the folds of her apron and pulled out a small phial of brown liquid. 'Here's a little potion that should be helpful.' Her voice dropped. 'It should make that chesty cough of his just a little worse.'

'Thank you, Hesty dear,' said Flambusia, spiriting it away into the tiny bag which hung from her huge forearm. 'You're always so helpful . . .'

Ding! Ding! Ding! Ding! Ding . . .

The peace of the kitchen was shattered by the sound of insistent ringing. Flambusia stopped mid-sentence and Amberfuce stirred groggily and began coughing. Rook looked round to see the central bell – the one marked *the Master's Chamber* – jiggling up and down on its coiled ribbon of metal like a startled ratbird. Vox Verlix must be summoning someone to his chamber.

Great hacking coughs racked the waif's body as he slowly emerged from his stupor. Rook would have to watch his thoughts, he realized.

'The master calls,' Hestera announced. 'Flambusia, my loverly, I think you-know-who's awake.' She pointed at the waif.

'Oh, don't I know it, Hesty dear,' said Flambusia, tapping the side of her head and shaking it. She turned to the coughing waif. 'I heard you the first time,' she said. 'Don't you go getting yourself in a state . . . Yes, yes, I know the master wants us upstairs. I was just about to wake you . . .'

The waif fell back in his chair and motioned the nurse to take hold of its long handle. As the two of them set off across the kitchen, they passed Speegspeel sitting on a stool and gnawing at a hunk of meat. Amberfuce motioned for Flambusia to stop and fixed the goblin with a cold stare.

Speegspeel looked up wearily. 'What? What's that?' He sighed. 'Oh, they are demanding of poor old Speegspeel. Can't even let him have his lunch without disturbing him.'

The waif's huge ears twitched, but his stare was unwavering.

'All right, all right, I'm going. Speegspeel will be at the door to greet our visitor, don't you worry.'

Muttering under his breath, Speegspeel abandoned his half-eaten leg of hammelhorn, wiped his greasy fingers down his front, and set off towards the stairs. Flambusia followed him, with Amberfuce the waif directing her to hurry from his chair, whilst attempting to control his coughing.

The bell rang again, more insistently than ever.

'Coming, my treasure,' Hestera purred. She scuttled over to a large chest of cupboards, unlocked one of the doors and pulled out a bottle of oblivion. 'By Sky above and Earth below, he got through that last batch quickly,' she was saying. 'I shall have to make some more up.' She decanted the crimson liquor into a pewter jug with a hinged lid, then placed it on a silver tray.

Rook quickly turned away and busied himself with a log as she hurried back across the kitchen, the tray clasped tightly before her. He didn't want Hestera to see him slacking, or who knows? – he might just end up with a nasty stomach-ache. With a grunt of exertion, Rook hefted the log up onto his shoulders and, doubled over, staggered towards the furnace.

'You can stop doing the logs, dearie,' said Hestera hurriedly as she bustled past him. 'And follow me. I want you to take this up to the master, and mind you don't spill a drop!'

Rook let the log fall to the floor and straightened up. He followed Hestera back to the pulley-lift where she opened the bared teeth of the doorway.

'Look lively, my loverly,' she said.

Rook climbed into the pulley-lift and took hold of the rope. Hestera slid the tray in behind him. 'Ninth floor,' she said. 'And be quick about it. Don't keep the master waiting or you'll have me to answer to.'

'Yes,' said Rook quietly.

The teeth snapped shut and, in the darkness, Rook pulled hard on the rope. The pulley-lift lurched upwards.

'One,' he panted with exertion as he reached the entrance hall. He glimpsed Amberfuce, ears fluttering, gesticulating towards Speegspeel while Flambusia fussed by his side.

Two. The reception chamber. Sweat ran down Rook's back and his breathing was heavy and loud in the confined space. Three, the library; four, the banquet hall; five . . .

Rook's mind was racing. He'd been fortunate; uncommonly fortunate. There he'd been, wondering how to get to meet Vox Verlix – and now, thanks to Hestera Spikesap, he was about to come face to face with him. He tugged down hard on the rope. Six . . . Seven . . . Eight . . .

'Nine,' said Rook. He pulled the brake-lever. The lift came to a halt. Bathed in sweat, Rook was directly in front of the locked hatchway he'd seen the previous day. From inside came the sound of a ringing bell announcing his arrival, followed by whistling and wheezing and the *thump thump thump* of someone heavy lumbering closer.

There was a jangle of keys, a scraping of metal – and the door swung open. Rook found himself looking out into a vast, shadowy chamber, the candlelit air thick with woodjasmine incense. There were massive dark tapestries covering the walls. Thick rugs and plump silk cushions – one embroidered with a golden tilder – were strewn across the floor. And, in the centre of it all, stood a huge round table made from the whitest marble Rook had ever seen. The next moment, a gigantic figure loomed before him, blocking everything from view.

'Give it to me,' rasped a wheezing voice.

Rook picked up the tray and held it out. Two great podgy hands, studded with jewelled rings, seized the tray.

As Rook watched, the figure wobbled back from the hatch and into the candlelight. There, with shadows flickering across his vast, bloated features and the gold medallion of high office hanging from his neck, stood Vox Verlix himself. He grasped the jug of oblivion in one massive paw and took a long slurp before wiping his mouth on his sleeve. His eyes glazed over.

'You can go,' he mumbled.

Rook was about to say something when the door slammed abruptly shut.

From the other side came a loud burp and a high-pitched, wheezy laugh, followed by the sound of something big and ungainly stumbling into things and knocking them over. Rook hesitated, his ear pressed against the door. He listened and waited . . .

Finally he heard the sound of heavy snoring. He tried the door but it was no good. The hatchway was locked from the other side.

With a sigh, Rook took hold of the rope, released the brake and the pulley-lift began its long descent. Still, he reasoned as the various hatches flashed by, I know where Vox is now. The ninth floor. And even if the hatchway is kept locked, the pulley-lift isn't the only way to get to the master's chamber . . .

'Thank Earth and Sky you're back, dearie,' Hestera cried as he reached the bottom. 'What kept you so long? It's perishing down here.'

Rook climbed out into the searing heat of the kitchen. Hestera fussed about him. 'The fire, dearie,' she wheedled.

'You must see to the fire at once, before these cold old bones of mine seize up completely. How can I be expected to sort through my recipes in a freezing kitchen? Look lively, now.'

'Yes,' said Rook, and traipsed obediently off to the log he'd dropped earlier. Seizing it with both hands, he swung it up off the ground and into the furnace in one movement, then returned to the pile of logs for another.

Hestera, meanwhile, withdrew to a walk-in cupboard at the end of the kitchen, from which she emerged a moment later clutching a great sheaf of parchments and a large empty ironwood box. Struggling with the awkward load, she shuffled back across the kitchen and sat herself down on a chair in front of the furnace with a soft sigh of contentment. Then with the parchments laid out across her aproned lap and the box before her, she began sorting through the recipes, clucking to herself and muttering beneath her breath.

Rook fetched another log and tossed it into the furnace; and then another, and another – pumping the bellows vigorously after each new addition. The furnace glowed brighter. The kitchen grew hotter.

'That's the way, dearie,' Hestera murmured, her eyelids growing heavy. 'Nice and warm, just the way I like it.'

Rook smirked. The goblin was beginning to nod off. I'll give you nice and warm, he thought. I'll have this kitchen hotter than it's ever been before. He gave the bellows a good pump. Hestera's eyes flickered and closed.

Rook kept on feeding the roaring flames until the furnace was so full that he could fit no more inside. The blast was infernal, hotter even than the great industrial furnaces he'd seen in the Foundry Glade from where he'd rescued Wuralo and the other banderbears. How long ago that now seemed. Dripping with sweat, Rook pumped the bellows one last time.

Behind him, Hestera's head lolled forwards and several sheets of parchment slipped from her lap to the floor. A rasping snore echoed through the air.

Rook smiled. Hestera was fast asleep and he had his opportunity to sneak away. As he passed the snoring goblin, he stole a glance at the recipes strewn across the floor by her feet. *Tincture of Ear-ache. Melancholia Salve. Eyeblind Drops* and *Cramp Linctus* . . . The words were picked out in Hestera's spidery writing. He was about to leave when one parchment in particular caught his eye. *Stomach-ache Cordial*, it said.

He scanned the page. *Pour in the sallowberry vinegar and tildermilk and simmer until curdled . . . Allow to cool . . . Add a pinch of dried chundermoss if vomiting is required . . .*

Rook's top lip curled in disgust. In his studies in the Free Glades, Rook had received instruction from gabtrolls and oakelves who had dedicated their lives to the study of the properties of herbs and plants in order to create potions and lotions that would ease suffering and cure pain. But not Hestera Spikesap. The twisted creature was clearly using *her* arts to cause misery and pain. Rook stared down at the hateful 'recipes'. He would have liked nothing better than to sweep the whole lot up in his arms and stuff them all into the furnace . . .

But not now, he told himself, turning away. Now, he had to get out of the kitchen and find the ninth floor.

The sound of Hestera's snoring grew fainter as Rook crept stealthily away. Into the cooler shadows he went, leaving the scorching furnace and the wicked poisoner behind him.

He picked his way through piles of boxes and mountains of sacks, on past long, cluttered tables strewn with pots and pans, jars and glass vessels full of curious liquids. At last, the staircase was before him, its upper steps disappearing into the murky gloom, far above his head. Rook began climbing.

It was only when he was halfway up that a thought struck him. What if the door was locked?

At the top at last, he seized the handle gingerly and turned it slowly, slowly . . . then pulled. The door – thank Sky – opened, its ancient hinges protesting weakly. Rook slipped out through the gap, closed the door quickly behind him – and fell still.

There, on the other side of the huge entrance hall, shivering in the cold air, his back towards him, stood Speegspeel.

Rook edged forwards and peeked round the jutting leg of a dusty, cobweb-strewn statue. The ancient butler was standing alone by the front door, blowing into his hands. The statue tottered unsteadily and, seizing it with both hands, it was all Rook could do to stop it crashing over.

'Who does he think he is? High and mighty librarian keeping old Speegspeel waiting,' Speegspeel grumbled as he stamped his feet up and down and hugged his arms about him. 'Speegspeel's cold,' he muttered sullenly. 'And hungry ... Everybody puts upon old Speegspeel, so they do. Wouldn't even let him finish off his lunch ...' He turned back towards the door, slid a silver spy-hole across and peered out. 'Where *is* he?'

With Speegspeel's back turned, Rook emerged from behind the statue and tip-toed across the tiled floor as silently as he could, keeping close to its statue-lined fringes. Darting from statue to statue, Rook made for the great staircase ahead of him, rising up out of the gloom. He was halfway across the hall when the old goblin turned back again. Rook held his breath and froze, blending in with the statues around him.

'At everyone's beck and call the whole time,' the butler was complaining, 'and what thanks does Speegspeel get?' He sniffed and began pacing back and forth. 'A kindly word wouldn't come amiss now and again ...' He turned away.

From somewhere above him, Rook heard an ominous low creak. Instinctively he dropped to the ground and raised his arms protectively above his head.

CRASH!

The sudden loud noise tore through the great hall, and

around him the cobwebbed statues wobbled, as if in support of their toppled colleague that now lay shattered on the marble floor. The hall fell silent – until Speegspeel's voice cried out; a mixture of triumph and defiance.

'You'll have to try harder than that if you want to catch old Speegspeel!' he bellowed, raising a fist at the statues crowding the alcoves above him.

Rook peered round the plinth of the statue he was cowering behind. The butler kicked at the broken remains of the ancient statue.

'Thought you'd had me that time, didn't you? Waiting till my back was turned. But Speegspeel was too quick for you, wasn't he? Eh?' He chuckled as he headed across to the door leading to the kitchen. 'Now Speegspeel will sweep you up and tip you away. And good riddance!'

The goblin disappeared through the door. Rook seized his chance. Head down, he made a dash for the staircase and, taking the stairs two at a time, he bounded up the first flight and crouched down on the first landing in the shadow of a carved newel post. He looked back to see Speegspeel returning across the great marble floor, a heavy knotted broomstick tucked under one arm. Whistling tunelessly, the goblin set about sweeping the shattered statue into a neat pile.

'Important visitor,' he muttered to himself. 'Got to make the right impression . . .'

Turning away, Rook continued up the elegant staircase, dodging the bright beams of sparkling sunlight which sliced down at an angle from high windows; keeping to the shadows. All round him were the statues. They stood on plinths and platforms on every landing and lined the corridors which radiated away in all directions like the spokes of a great wheel. Hundreds of them, like a great stone army lurking in the gloom; watching, waiting . . .

They're just carvings, Rook told himself. Pieces of rock, no more.

The air was cold, but it wasn't only that which was making him shiver. As he passed them by, the statues creaked and seemed to whisper and sometimes Rook thought he caught them moving out of the corner of his eye – but when he turned to look, they were always standing as motionless as before.

At the sixth landing, the musty air was laced with the mentholated tang of embrocation. Rook heard the sound of distant coughing and Flambusia's disembodied voice – honeyed and sinister – as it echoed down the corridors.

'If you won't keep still, then I can't rub it in properly,' she was cooing. 'And then that cough of yours will never get better.'

Rook hurried on. He didn't stop again until he reached the ninth floor. Pausing for a moment to catch his breath, he looked round.

The landing he was standing on was quite different from the others he had passed. Unlike the patternless marble of the lower levels, the floor here was inlaid with an intricate pattern of tiles. As he looked more closely, he saw that they were not random abstract designs but rather countless creatures – some known, some unknown – all cunningly interlocked.

The ear of a woodhare-like creature formed the mouth

of an oozefish, whose dorsal fin in turn provided the space between the broad legs of a banderbear above it. A lemkin fitted together with a snicket, the dark jutting jaw of the one forming the edge of the white wing of the other; a daggerslash mutated into a razorflit; a muglump into a fromp. And so it continued all the way along the single broad corridor which led away from the landing. Just the one corridor, Rook noticed – unlike the other floors which had corridors leading off from the landings in all direction.

At the far end of the single corridor was a high window. A shaft of sunlight streamed through it, slicing along the length of the corridor, striking the crystal chandelier above Rook's head and sending rainbow-coloured darts of light flashing through the air in all directions. They spun and collided; they skidded over the white marble of the statues and sparkled on the tiled floor.

Halfway down the corridor, to his right, a magnificent doorway was set into the wall. The panelled door it framed was emblazoned with the same symbol of high office – a sun-like circle seg-mented by jagged bolts of lightning – which Rook had seen on the medallion hanging around Vox's neck.

'The Master's Chamber,' he whispered.

He had just set off down the hallway, keeping to the shadows close to the near wall, when a sudden clatter halted him in his tracks. He slipped back into the darkness of a cobweb-filled alcove that must once have housed a statue and watched anxiously. The noise had come from outside – most likely a statue falling down the front of the building.

As the noise died away, it was replaced by another, altogether closer: the low scraping sound of metal on stone. This was followed by a muffled *crunch*, and the silhouette of a goblin guard in battle-dress appeared at the high window. Rook shrank back further into the alcove and held his breath.

The goblin guard pulled the window open, balanced for a moment on the ledge, looking round – before jumping down onto the floor. As he dropped, the sunlight glinted on the serrated blade of the evil-looking scythe clenched between his teeth. He landed lightly, braced his splayed legs and looked round again. Then, glancing suspiciously about him, he advanced along the corridor, his bare feet pattering softly on the tiles.

Rook watched, horrified. It was clear the goblin had
only one thing on his mind.

Murder!

He swallowed heavily. The goblin was almost at the
door now. He could see the individual bristles of his
tufted ears; he could smell his unwashed body. The
goblin pulled the scythe from his mouth and gripped it
tightly in his hand. Then, with a final glance over his
armour-plated shoulders, he took a step forward and . . .

It all happened so quickly. The tile beneath the
goblin's feet clicked down as he stepped on it. At the
same moment, from up in the shadows of the high
ceiling, there came an answering click followed by a
hissing *swoosh* as a long pendulum swung down
through the air. The goblin never knew what hit him.
Before he could move so much as a muscle, the heavy
curved blade at the end of the swinging pendulum sliced
through him like butter, cleaving the would-be assassin
in two.

Rook stared open-mouthed, scarcely able to believe
what had just happened. The goblin was dead; his body
twin islands in a growing sea of blood. Rook tore his
horrified gaze away. Above his head in the shadows, the
deadly pendulum clicked back into place as – at exactly
the same moment – the tile did the same, merging seam-
lessly with the others in the treacherous mosaic.

'A booby-trap,' Rook trembled.

He stared at the floor. Each ornate shape now seemed
deadly. Any one of the tiles, Rook realized, could
unleash the hideous pendulum – or worse. He was

trapped, paralysed with fear, unable to take a step forwards or back. At his feet was a white tile – snowy white, shaped like the head of a gloamglozer. Its curling horns formed the underbelly of a black serpent coiled above it.

'Black serpent,' Rook murmured. 'White gloamglozer.' *White* gloamglozer. Black and white ... Something stirred in his memory: *Keep to the black, not the white, if you want to keep your life.*

It was Speegspeel. Rook had heard him singing the little tune over and over up in the Leagues' Chamber.

Keep to the black, not the white, if you want to keep your life ...

Emerging from the alcove, Rook stepped tentatively onto the black serpent, then a black hammelhorn, and from that onto a black lemkin, taking care to avoid the white halitoad between them. So far, so good. Trying hard not to look at the bloodied corpse, he skirted round the snow-white head of a huge rotsucker – via a black tilder and a second black lemkin – and arrived at last at the large, ornate door.

Rook put his ear to the carved wooden panel and listened. He could hear nothing; nothing at all. He reached forward, grasped the door handle and turned it. The door slid silently open and Rook slipped gratefully inside.

Rook found himself in the same opulent chamber he had glimpsed from the pulley-lift. Dark, shadowy and reeking of incense and musky perfumes, it was far larger than he'd imagined – a cavernous hall made to seem smaller than it was by the sheer number of items cluttered within it.

There was a forest of racks and stacks, each one bulging with sheaves of parchment; and tall stands with curling hooks sprouting from their tops, draped with sailcloth, silken ropes and lengths of fine material embroidered with gold and silver. On the floor were the fur rugs and plump satin cushions Rook had seen earlier; on the walls were dark tapestries – while dangling from the ceiling, like a library of hanging scrolls, were countless yellowed squares of parchment suspended from ropes and motionless in the still air.

They must be sticky, Rook realized, for on both sides of every parchment, there were countless creatures fixed to the surface: woodmoths, oakbugs, bees and wasps; snickets and ratbirds in various stages of decay; the skeleton of a dwarf-rotsucker, its parchment skin stretched over bony wings ... The traps, it seemed, caught every airborne intruder into Vox Verlix's chamber – though of the master himself, there was no trace.

Keeping to the wall, Rook continued round the chamber. And as he picked his way through the chaos, he began to look more closely at the rows of charts, blue-prints and diagrams – sepia ink on tilderhide and thick parchment – which hung from taut wire racks and cov-ered every flat surface. He recognized a detailed plan for the Great Mire Road, annotated with lengths and weights and detailed descriptions of how to sink the great pylons into the soft, shifting mud of the Mire. There were several cross-sections of the Tower of Night, each one subtly different from the one before – and a model of the design that had finally been chosen. And as he went further, he passed a table covered with set-squares and slide-rules, and piles of calculations detailing what was arguably Vox's most ambitious project: the Sanctaphrax Forest.

Next to a long workbench was an easel with a single yellowed piece of scroll pinned to a drawing-board. On it was a complicated design for something large and round with intricate internal chambers, covered with minute annotations. Rook recognized it at once.

'The baby,' he breathed.

His fingers traced the round form beneath which, underscored with an angry red line, were the words, *blast them all to open sky!*

So it was true what they said. Vox Verlix, the greatest engineer and architect there had ever been, was a bitter, broken creature. Rook looked around at the clutter. Vox had been betrayed by everyone he'd had dealings with: Mother Muleclaw, the shryke roost-mother who had seized the Great Mire Road when it was completed; Orbix Xaxis, who had ousted Vox from the Tower of Night and forced him to seek refuge in old Undertown; and finally General Tytugg, the goblin-leader Vox had himself hired to enslave Undertowners and force them to work on the Sanctaphrax Forest, but who instead had taken over Undertown and made Vox a virtual prisoner here in the Palace of Statues. The goblin assassin lying in the hallway was just the latest of many, Rook guessed, sent by the brutal general who made no secret of his contempt for his former master.

Ahead of him, Rook saw an ornate gilt frame fixed to the wall. He moved closer, expecting to see a painting of one of the former occupants of the chamber – perhaps even a likeness of Vox Verlix himself. Instead he found himself looking at a small, blackwood door. It was the entrance to the pulley-lift. He looked round. There was the satin pillow with the embroidered tilder; there, the thick fur rugs, and there, the round white marble table. Behind them, bathed in shadows, was what seemed to be a huge upholstered chair, a heavy throw in blues and purples draped over it and a long rope with a brass ring at its end, hanging down beside.

Rook looked more closely at the chair. It was moving up and down to the unmistakable sound of a soft rasping snore which grew louder and louder until, with a sudden sharp snort, it woke the sleeper up. Rook took a step backwards into the shadowy clutter. Just then the tasselled throw was tossed aside, and what Rook had taken to be a chair clambered to its feet.

'Vox Verlix,' Rook murmured, transfixed.

Vox looked round, bleary-eyed. He scratched his head, jiggled a fat finger in his ear and belched twice. 'That's better,' he muttered.

Rook remembered seeing a picture of Vox Verlix as a cloudwatcher apprentice; young, lean and with a glint of naked ambition in his steely gaze. The bloated drunkard he had become was unrecognizable. Rook watched him with a mixture of pity and disgust as he heaved his great weight across the floor.

He stopped at the table and looked up. Rook followed his gaze to a funnel-shaped contraption with mirrors, chains and levers suspended above him. With a loud grunt of effort, Vox reached up and pulled hard on one of the brass chains. A mirror tilted, and a broad beam of light fell upon the great marble table-top below.

Rook peered out from behind a rack of barkscrolls. Vox was looking down at the illuminated table, his face bathed in light. Rook eased himself forwards, craning his neck for a better view.

Vox reached above his head again, pushing a lever up and lowering a second chain. The image on the table-top shifted – and Rook stifled a gasp as he realized what he was looking at. It was Undertown and its environs. Somehow, Vox Verlix had designed a contraption to bring the view outside into this vast windowless chamber and, as he raised and lowered the sequence of chains and levers one after the other, the image on the vast circular table-top came sharply into focus.

'I can see you all . . .' Vox murmured gleefully. His sweat-drenched face was animated, the small beady eyes glinting coldly. 'There is nowhere to hide, for Vox's Eye sees everything! Everything! The end is coming, you puny woodants,' he cried. 'The end is coming – and only I can see it!'

Rook felt his pulse quicken. Then, curiosity winning over caution, he stepped up onto a padded footstool for a better look at the image on the marble table. There was the Undertown skyline; the Tower of Night; the Mire Road – and, arching above it all, a heavy, cloud-laden sky . . .

The stool wobbled. Rook lost his balance and lurched to one side, knocking into a tall vase which toppled and crashed to the floor.

Vox looked up, the expression on his face a mixture of fear and rage. 'Who's there?' he demanded fiercely.

Rook was about to step forward and introduce himself as Hestera's new assistant – as well as inventing some errand that would explain his presence, when . . .

'Say your prayers, Vox Verlix,' came a low, gruff voice.

Rook froze. The voice came from the shadows near the door.

Vox turned towards the voice. 'Show yourself,' he said, his own voice tinged with unease.

'As you wish, *Vox Verlix – Most High Academe*,' came the voice, spitting out the name and title with contempt. And as Rook watched, a goblin appeared from the shadows. Tall and heftily built, he was dressed – and armed – like the goblin guard Rook had seen in the corridor. He brandished a vicious-looking curved scythe with glinting jags, an evil grin playing round his scarred lips and blackened teeth. 'I come with a message from General Tytugg . . .'

'How . . . How *dare* you!' Vox blustered, his double chins wobbling indignantly. 'Get down on your knees when you address the Most High Academe of Sanctaphrax and all Undertown!'

The goblin's grin widened. 'They said you were fat,' he said, and made a show of running a callused thumb slowly along the curve of the glinting blade. 'I'm going to enjoy hearing you squeal,' he snarled.

'General Tytugg shall hear of your insolence,' said Vox imperiously. 'And you shall *both* regret it!'

Rook shook his head. Vox was in mortal danger and, for all his bluster, there was the unmistakable glint of panic in his deep-set eyes. Rook realized that it was up to him to do something. Slipping back into the shadows, he seized the first object he could find. It felt reassuringly heavy.

'Most High Academe,' the goblin laughed. 'Why, you nasty great big fat useless blubbery parasitic lardbucket!' He lunged at Vox with the scythe.

'Please!' Vox gasped. 'I'll give you anything.' A spasm of desperation flashed across his face. 'Anything at all!' He stumbled backwards, arms raised defensively. 'No, no, no . . .' he cried.

The goblin raised his scythe high in the air, slicing through the dancing particles of dust. The blade glinted. Vox froze.

'Now squeal for General Tytugg . . .'

'*Aaaiiieeeeee! Aaaiiieeeeee!*' Vox cried out with terror, screeching and squealing like a stuck woodhog. '*AaaiiiEEEEEEE!!*'

Rook leapt from the shadows, the heavy

lump of wood held above his head with both hands. The goblin's sword flashed. Vox toppled backwards. With a grunt of effort, Rook swung the wood through the air and brought it down on the back of the goblin's head with colossal force.

The heavy wooden object struck with a splintering crack. The goblin stiffened but remained standing. Rook swallowed hard. Goblins had skulls as hard as ironwood. He struck him again – a savage blow to the side of his head . . .

The goblin tottered where he stood, staggering slowly round in a circle. His eyes swam in their sockets, then shot abruptly upwards, leaving only the bloodshot whites showing. With a low groan the goblin fell backwards, stiff as a board, and crashed noisily to the floor.

Rook poked the body with his foot. The goblin was not dead – but he'd have a headache to remember when he finally woke.

'It's all right,' said Rook to the huge figure cowering before him. 'You're safe now.'

Vox lowered his arm and looked up. 'You . . . you saved my life,' he said. 'Who are you?'

'Rook Barkwater,' said Rook. 'Assistant to Hestera Spikesap.'

'Hestera's slave,' he sniffed. Grunting and groaning with effort, he rolled over onto his front and eased himself up into a standing position. 'I am grateful to you,' he said wheezily and extended a podgy hand. His eyes narrowed. 'What are you doing outside the hatch?'

'I . . . *errm* . . . Hestera . . . that is, Speegspeel . . .' Rook was floundering.

Just then there was a polite, distinctive knock at the door; three light taps, followed by a gap, and then three more. 'About time!' muttered Vox. 'Enter, Speegspeel!' he called out.

Rook watched the ancient butler do a double-take as he emerged from the shadows at the back of the room. His gaze jumped from face to face of the occupants of the room.

'Master,' he said. 'Number eleven. And . . .' He grimaced. '*There* he is!' he gasped. 'Old Speegspeel knew there'd be two of them. Always hunt in pairs, goblins, so they do – when they've got murder in mind. Saw the other one outside in the corridor – knew there'd be a second one somewhere hereabouts.'

'The slave-lad here laid him out,' said Vox, adding sharply, 'It's just as well *someone* around here has their wits about them.' He nodded towards the piece of wood still clutched in Rook's hands and chuckled; a sound like water gurgling down a drain. 'Fortunate indeed that I designed it to be strong.'

Rook looked down and was surprised to find himself holding a finely crafted scale-model of a tower. 'The Tower of Night,' he said softly.

'Ay, the Tower of Night,' said Vox. 'Built to withstand both hurricanes and cannon-balls . . .'

'And the most terrible place ever built upon a Sanctaphrax rock,' came a soft, cracked voice from over by the door.

Vox's eyes narrowed. 'I know that voice . . .' he whispered.

'Ah yes, Speegspeel was forgetting, master; what with all the palaver over goblin assassins, 'n all. Your visitor has arrived.'

As he spoke, a wiry individual stepped forwards from behind Speegspeel. Rook gasped.

The visitor was well-kempt, with trim hair and beard, polished cheeks and fine clothes; for all the world the successful merchant or money-lender. Yet the eyes told a different story; they, and the deep lines that etched his face. This was someone who had known great pain and terrible suffering; someone who had stared down into the yawning chasms of black despair. His gaze bored into Vox's eyes.

Vox looked back at him, puzzlement flickering round his eyebrows. 'You are the emissary from the librarians?' he began.

'You have changed since last we met,' the visitor said. He nodded towards the medallion of high office around Vox Verlix's neck. 'It was the night you stole that little trinket.'

Vox's mouth fell open; the colour drained from his cheeks. 'Cowlquape Pentephraxis,' he gasped in disbelief. His head shook slowly from side to side. 'No . . . No, it can't be!'

But it was, as Rook was only too aware. What could the true Most High Academe of Sanctaphrax be doing here in the Palace of Statues holding court with Vox Verlix?

'But you're . . . you're . . .' Vox paused.

'Dead?' suggested Cowlquape. 'As you can see, Vox, I'm very much alive. When you betrayed me to the Guardians of Night I expect you thought they'd kill me. But no, they kept me alive – if you can call being locked up on a stinking cell-ledge in the depths of the Tower of Night, living. I suppose they enjoyed knowing that while I lived, you could never be the true Most High Academe, despite your claims . . . But enough of this. I am, as we both know, here on behalf of the librarians to discuss important matters; *pressing* matters . . .' He stopped mid-sentence and stared at Rook, who was standing beside Vox – actually seeing him for the first time. His eyebrows arched with surprise. 'Rook,' he said. 'It can't be. But it is! Rook, my boy, what are you doing here?'

Rook grimaced sheepishly. 'It's a long story,' he said.

'You know this slave?' said Vox.

'Slave?' said Cowlquape. 'Rook Barkwater is no slave. He is a librarian knight; the most valiant of his generation – and the person who rescued me from the Tower of Night. It seems we *both* owe him our lives, Vox.'

Vox sighed. 'I thought he handled himself rather well for a mere kitchen assistant.' His narrowing eyes glinted. 'But Hestera bought him at the slave auction, which makes him *my* property . . .'

Cowlquape breathed in sharply. 'Times have changed, Vox,' he said, his voice level and firm. 'The tables are turning . . .' He looked down meaningfully at the unconscious goblin guard.

'Yes, yes, all right,' Vox blustered. 'Consider yourself restored to freedom by the Most High . . .' He caught Cowlquape's steely gaze and coughed awkwardly. 'Er . . . yes . . . well . . . Let's just say, you're free.' He turned to Speegspeel. 'Refreshments for our guests,' he said gruffly. '*Both* our guests.'

Rook's heart soared. He felt a wave of relief, as if a great weight had fallen from his shoulders. Free once more; he was free! Speegspeel nodded, neither his face nor his voice registering any emotion. 'Yes, master,' he said.

'And Speegspeel,' Vox added. 'Send Amberfuce up. I have a little job for him.'

'Yes, master,' Speegspeel repeated. He turned and started away.

'Oh, and one last thing,' Vox called after him. 'You'd better tell Hestera to visit the slave auction right away. We need another slave to help with the baby. Straight away, do you understand?'

'Yes, master,' said the old butler, shuffling off. 'Speegspeel understands.'

As the door clicked shut, Vox turned to Cowlquape. 'And now, old friend, we must let bygones be bygones, don't you agree?' he said. 'Come and look into Vox's Eye.'

·CHAPTER NINE·

THE TWO MOST HIGH ACADEMES

Cowlquape's sunken green eyes flashed with naked delight.

'Rook, my dear lad, I can't tell you how good it is to see you alive and well,' he said, clapping him warmly on the back.

Vox was over by the marble table, muttering to himself and swaying back and forth as he surveyed the sky.

'We heard you'd come down in Screetown,' Cowlquape continued. 'Naturally we feared the worst.' He smiled sympathetically. 'What happened to you?'

'My head's still spinning – I can't quite take it all in,' said Rook. 'Oh, Most High Academe, sir, I . . . I was beginning to think I'd never see another librarian ever again.'

Cowlquape reached forward and touched Rook on the arm reassuringly. 'Easy now, lad. You've clearly been through a lot. But I'm here now and it's all going to be fine, believe me.'

Rook nodded and sniffed and collected himself. 'I did come down in Screetown,' he said at last. 'Something struck the *Stormhornet* when I was on dawn-patrol – something loud and fiery . . .' His voice drifted away.

'And then?' said Cowlquape. 'How did you end up here?'

Rook shook his head slowly, suddenly lost to a series of fleeting images which flashed before his eyes: the rubble ghoul, the oozefish and woodwolves; the Sunken Palace and the misery hole; the tumbril ride to the auction-square . . . 'It's a long story,' he said at last, and smiled apologetically.

'And there'll be time enough to tell it back in the library, Rook, my lad,' said Cowlquape, nodding. 'But right now, I must attend to our fat friend over there. He sent a strange missive to the Great Library, requesting an urgent meeting with an emissary who could speak on behalf of the librarians. It was passed to one of our agents in Undertown by someone from the palace and our experts verified it as genuine.' His voice dropped. 'We had a hastily convened council-meeting, and it was agreed that I – as the true Most High Academe – should represent the librarians. Besides,' he added, 'I was intrigued to see what had become of my former colleague. It is many years since our paths last crossed . . .'

Just then, from the far end of the dark, cluttered chamber, Vox looked up from the Eye. 'Time is short,' he said peevishly. 'I thought I'd made *that* much clear in my message.'

'Oh, you did, Vox,' said Cowlquape, crossing the room and approaching the huge figure. 'You certainly did. What you didn't make clear was why.'

Rook watched with fascination as the two academics stood facing each other. One was morbidly obese, the other painfully thin. One was dressed in flamboyant, though stained, robes of embroidered satin and tasselled silk; the other wore a simple brown gown made of some rough, homespun cloth. Like chalk and cheese, they couldn't have been less similar.

Even the medallions which hung around their necks were different, for whereas Vox's was dull and worn, Cowlquape's one was highly polished and glinted as brightly as his amused eyes. Vox's gaze seemed fixated on it.

Cowlquape smiled. 'I see you've noticed the seal of Old Sanctaphrax,' he said. 'The librarians kindly replaced the one you stole.'

Vox glowered. Rook could feel the tension between them.

'Oh, Vox, Vox, what went wrong?' Cowlquape continued calmly. 'With your skills and my vision, we could have rebuilt Sanctaphrax. Together in partnership . . .'

'Partnership!' Vox blustered. 'You just wanted the glory while I did all the hard work. What was it you were always saying? Ah, yes,' he said, his voice taking on a mocking sing-song quality. 'Everyone's equal and we're all the same; earth-scholars and sky-scholars; professors, apprentices and even Undertowners.' He wagged a flabby finger at Cowlquape. 'A recipe for disaster. It would never have worked.'

'You never gave it a chance, Vox,' said Cowlquape sadly. 'You went behind my back and betrayed me to Orbix Xaxis and the Guardians of Night. Did you really think you could trust them?'

'I did what I had to do,' said Vox. '*Someone* had to assume the role of leader. A proper leader; a leader prepared to lead. It was what you never understood, Cowlquape. All those endless meetings and consultations; trying to keep everyone happy – yet satisfying no-one . . .'

'Someone like you, eh?' said Cowlquape softly. 'A traitor . . . A usurper . . .' He let the words sink in. 'Is it any wonder that things have come to this?'

'I . . . I . . .' Vox blustered hotly.

'You've destroyed everything, Vox. Everything . . .' he said. 'And the sad thing is, it could all have been so different. If you had trusted me as I trusted you, Vox, we could have built a better world together, you and I. And now look at you!' He sighed. 'You had so many wonderful talents, Vox . . .' He shook his head sorrowfully. 'And you've squandered them all. What a waste your life has been.'

Vox looked away, muttering under his breath, and reached for a jug of oblivion. 'You always were a pompous little creature, weren't you?' he growled. 'At least I didn't end up imprisoned for years on end.'

'No? Are you sure?' said Cowlquape evenly. 'Look around you, Vox. When did you last dare to leave this palace, with its barred windows and booby-trapped corridors? When did you last even venture beyond this chamber? You are as much a prisoner as I ever was.' He tutted softly. 'The bully being bullied . . .'

'They double-crossed me,' said Vox quietly. 'All of them. The shrykes, the Guardians, the goblins . . . But they'll soon be smiling on the other side of their faces.' His voice rose. 'For it's all coming to an end. That's what I want to tell you. Undertown is done for. Time is running out . . .' He stared at Cowlquape. 'And it's why I need the librarians. You're the only ones I can trust.'

Cowlquape looked puzzled. 'Undertown, done for?' he said. 'What do you mean, Vox?'

'I mean precisely what I say, Cowlquape,' said Vox, his voice growing louder still. 'Undertown is finished. Doomed! The whole sorry lot will be washed away, and with it all the back-stabbing traitors and treacherous infidels who have sought to destroy me!' He raised the jug, took a noisy glug of the bright red liquor and wiped his mouth on the back on his sleeve. 'A storm is coming!' he announced. 'A mighty storm!'

'A storm?' said Cowlquape.

'Yes, Cowlquape. A storm, the like of which has never been seen before. Can you not feel it in the air; the searing heat, the stifling humidity? Have you not noticed the formations of the clouds?'

Rook found himself nodding. Every day he had been noting the ominous changes in the weather.

'A storm to end all storms,' Vox continued, sweeping his massive arms round dramatically as his voice rose to fill the great chamber. 'No-one shall be spared. And I alone, Vox Verlix, know exactly when it will strike – down to the very second.'

'But how can you possibly know when . . ?' Rook began.

Cowlquape silenced him with a hand on his arm. 'Vox

Verlix was the finest cloudwatcher the College of Cloud ever produced, Rook, my boy,' he said quietly. 'If he says a storm is coming . . .'

'I do! I do say a storm is coming,' said Vox excitedly. He reached forward and seized Cowlquape by the sleeve. 'Look,' he said, tugging him sharply across to the round white marble table and pointing down at the illuminated image from outside laid out across its surface.

Cowlquape looked down. Rook, eager to see for himself, stood beside him and scanned the tabletop. Vox's podgy fingers spread across the sky.

'You see these clouds,' he said, taking a swig at the oblivion. 'Like giant anvils? They're growing all the time, merging, fusing together and gaining power with every passing day. I've consulted my cloud tables,' he continued, the drink staining his lips red. 'I've done the calculations. I alone know when the dark maelstrom will strike!'

Rook glanced at Cowlquape. The true High Academe was deep in thought.

'And when the dark maelstrom does strike,' Vox went on, 'there will be lightning and hail, and torrential driving rain will flood the sewers within minutes. If the librarians are to survive, then you must leave your underground chambers and flee. Leave Undertown, Cowlquape, and head for the Free Glades . . .'

Behind them, the unconscious goblin groaned softly. Again, Rook looked up at Cowlquape – but the old academic's thoughts were difficult to read.

'You're proposing that the librarians leave Undertown?' he said at last, his voice calm and even.

'You must, Cowlquape,' said Vox urgently.

'What, up and go – just like that?' said Cowlquape, fixing Vox with a level stare. 'Tell me, Vox,' he said. 'Just supposing we could get out of the sewers and somehow make it past General Tytugg's goblin guard, and then by some miracle also manage to get through Muleclaw's shrykes and cross the Mire to reach the Free Glades . . .' He paused. 'Why would you help us?' His eyes narrowed. 'What's in it for *you*?'

'For me?' said Vox, an air of injured innocence playing over his blubbery features. He breathed in wheezily. 'If I were to tell you,' he said, 'how you and all the librarians could get safely through Undertown and down the Great Mire Road, I would ask just one thing in return.'

Cowlquape shook his head and smiled. 'And what might that be, Vox?' he said.

Vox returned his gaze, his face deadly serious. 'That you take me with you.'

*

'So this is where you hide when you're not toadying up to the High Master,' came a sneering voice.

Xanth looked up from his desk and sighed. Mollus Leddix, the cage-master, stood in the doorway, his black hood pulled back to reveal his twitchy weasel-like features and small dark eyes. An ugly grin was playing across his face.

'Not that it'll do you much good. Not if the rumours are to be believed,' he added.

'What rumours, Leddix?' said Xanth wearily. He mustn't let the executioner get to him.

'Oh, the rumours that the High Guardian doesn't quite trust his favourite since he got back from spying on the librarians in the Free Glades. They say that all that Free Glade air turned his head, made him soft, unreliable . . .'

And I wonder who put those ideas into the High Guardian's head, Xanth thought bitterly – but he managed a smile as he looked up at Leddix. 'Oh, I wouldn't listen to those rumours, Leddix, if I were you,' he said. 'I'd be more worried about the rumour going round that a certain executioner was overheard hatching a plot with the Captain of the Nightwatch. Now if the High Guardian was to hear about *that* . . .'

'You wouldn't dare,' snarled Leddix.

'Just try me,' said Xanth, rising from his stool.

Leddix stepped back and laughed a thin, weasely chuckle. 'No need to be like that, Xanth,' he said. 'Mustn't let little misunderstandings get in the way of our duty. Talking of which . . .' He straightened up. 'A

fresh young librarian has been apprehended and the High Master has ordered an interrogation. Right up your street, I would have thought, Xanth,' he added, his voice oily and insinuating, 'given your special knowledge of the librarians and their ways.'

Xanth nodded, but said nothing. There it was again. The same underlying implication . . . He was not to be trusted.

Leddix beckoned for Xanth to follow him to the Interrogation Chambers and, as he did so, the executioner muttered, 'The High Master will be observing. And remember, Xanth, when you're finished with her, the prisoner is mine!'

They arrived outside an interrogation chamber deep in the lower recesses of the Tower of Night. A tall heavily-built Guardian – a cloddertrog with swarthy scarred skin and flowercabbage ears – opened the door and Xanth entered the small room. Leddix slunk away down the corridor, chuckling softly as the door swung shut.

In the corner, slumped against the wall, was a librarian knight, unmistakable in green flight-suit and light wood armour. The prisoner looked up, thick plaits falling across her face.

'Xanth?' came a small voice. 'Xanth?'

Xanth froze. The prisoner knew his name.

'Xa-anth?'

'Be silent, prisoner,' Xanth said in a low growl.

He needed time to think. The spy-hole on the opposite wall was open and the High Guardian was observing his every move. How Leddix would love it if he made a slip now . . .

Arms tied behind her back, the prisoner flicked the golden plaits off her face with a toss of her head. She was bruised and battered, with a black eye and one side of her lower jaw badly swollen. A trickle of dried blood ran from the corner of her mouth. She was a mess, certainly – yet Xanth recognized her at once. After all, having spent the best part of eighteen moons studying beside her at Lake Landing, how could he fail to?

'It *is* you, Xanth,' she said. 'I knew it was. It's me, Magda. Magda Burlix . . .'

Xanth stared at her impassively, his face betraying not a single flicker of emotion.

'Xanth?' said Magda. 'Don't you remember me?'

'On your knees!' shouted Xanth roughly. He was clammy and hot, sweat beading his forehead, his cheeks and the top of his shaven head. He'd liked Magda. She'd been good to him at Lake Landing when he'd broken his leg and . . .

No! he told himself sharply. He would have to deal with her as he would *any* prisoner. Orbix Xaxis was watching.

'I said, on your knees!' he snarled, and kicked her viciously in the side.

Magda struggled awkwardly to her knees, the tight ropes biting into her wrists. She looked up at Xanth, her eyes as wide as a tilder doe's, willing him to recognize her. But Xanth was having none of it. Refusing to meet her imploring gaze, he pulled a notebook from one pocket, a thin, sharp ironwood pencil from another; opened one, licked the other and started writing.

'Name,' he said quietly.

'Xanth,' said Magda, her voice breaking with emotion. 'You *know* my name.'

Xanth's scalp prickled. He could feel the accusing glare from the spy-hole burning into the back of his head. 'Name!' he repeated harshly.

'You know my name,' came the tearful reply. She sniffed. 'It's me, Xanth. Magda Burlix.'

Xanth scribbled it down.

'Position,' he said, a moment later.

'I am a librarian knight,' said Magda and, even though he didn't look up, he could tell from her voice that she was glowing with pride as she spoke. 'And as such, you know I can tell you no more – even unto death.'

'You were apprehended by our patrols on the banks of the Edgewater,' said Xanth quietly. 'What were you doing there?'

'I am a librarian knight,' Magda repeated. 'I can tell you no more, even unto ... *aarrgh!*' she cried out as Xanth slapped her hard across the face.

Her head dropped. Xanth stared down at her, his hand stinging, his head swirling with mixed feelings. Magda was brave and kind. She had been so good to him . . . But the High Master was watching and he mustn't allow his feelings to show, not even for an instant.

He breathed in sharply. 'What – were – you – doing – by – the – Edgewater – River?' he asked, enunciating every word crisply, coldly.

Head still lowered, Magda sighed. 'It can't do any harm,' she said. 'Not now. You're going to kill me anyway, so I'll tell you. I wasn't on librarian business, I was on my own. I was looking for Rook. Rook Barkwater – remember him?' she asked bitterly. 'He went missing. In Screetown. The librarians have given up on him. But I couldn't.' She looked up, her golden plaits trembling. 'And do you know why? Because Rook is my friend.' Her eyes narrowed to angry slits. 'But then you wouldn't understand, would you? Because you don't know what friendship is.'

She turned and spat on the floor.

Behind him, Xanth heard a soft *click* as the cover to the spy-hole closed. With a sigh of relief, he snapped the notebook shut and put the pencil back in his pocket.

He'd passed the test.

'My plan is simple,' said Vox, scanning the Undertown horizon. 'With the librarians' help, I intend to lure the goblin army and the shrykes into a trap of my own devising, leaving the way clear for us . . .' – he laid a podgy hand on Cowlquape's shoulder – '. . . to leave Undertown by the Mire Road unmolested.'

'And what is to be the bait in this trap of yours, Vox?' asked Cowlquape, his brow furrowed.

'Why, my dear Most High Academe, who do the shrykes and the goblins hate even more than each other?'

'The librarians!' said Rook, unable to contain himself.

'Your young friend is correct,' laughed Vox, his chins wobbling in the candlelight. 'I intend to inform both the shrykes *and* the goblins precisely how they might safely penetrate the Great Library itself . . .'

An excellent plan, master, a sibilant voice whispered in Rook's head.

Vox turned, along with Cowlquape and Rook. 'So good of you to join us, my dear Amberfuce,' he said. 'How's that cough of yours? No worse, I trust.'

The waif emerged from the shadows, followed by the massive figure of Flambusia Flodfox, a huge hand on the handle of the sumpwood chair. She blushed and rearranged Amberfuce's shawl fussily. The waif tutted and waved her away.

How may I be of service, master? The sibilant voice sounded again in Rook's head, and he shuddered.

Vox gestured airily towards the prone figure of the goblin, lying beside the marble table. 'I wish you to wash this wretch's mind clean, Amberfuce, and then place a little message in his pathetic brain . . . This message . . .'

Vox stared into Amberfuce's large dark eyes. The waif's ears twitched as he stared back.

Understood, master. Very cunning. Very cunning indeed . . . came the sibilant whisper.

'Yes, yes,' said Vox, turning back to the table. 'Get on with it, then!'

The waif's eyes closed and his head lolled back. At Rook's feet, the goblin flinched and shook his head. Spasms racked his body; his jaw clenched and unclenched; his eyeballs swivelled round in their sockets independent of each other – and Rook trembled, knowing exactly what the goblin was going through. Little by little, the waif was sifting through his thoughts; discarding ones he had no use for and replacing them with those of his master, Vox.

'It is time, it is time,' the goblin mumbled, his head lolling from side to side. 'General Tytugg . . . I have the secret route into the Great Library . . . It lies defenceless before us . . . Attack from the eastern entrance to the sewers and show no mercy . . . Death to the librarian scum!'

The waif glanced round at Vox who was standing

watching; a self-satisfied smirk played over his blubbery face. 'Very good, Amberfuce,' he said. 'Now the rest of it.'

Amberfuce nodded and returned his attention to the goblin, whose head jerked back so hard that his neck cracked.

'Dead,' he cried. 'Vox is dead . . . I killed him . . . With my own bare hands . . . I heard him squeal like a great fat woodhog . . . A mound of blubbery . . .'

'Yes, yes,' Vox interrupted testily. 'I think he's got the message, Amberfuce. Now send him back to the Hive Towers.'

Amberfuce concentrated. The goblin nodded, his eyes staring ahead, unblinking. 'Must return to General Tytugg,' he muttered. 'At once.'

The goblin climbed to his feet and, without another word, set off across the cluttered chamber. As the door clicked shut, Vox chuckled to himself unpleasantly.

'That's General Tytugg taken care of,' he said. 'Now

for the shrykes. I need someone to go to the court of the Shryke Sisterhood and tell that feathered monster, Mother Muleclaw, that the goblins have the Great Library within their grasp. It is vital that this someone convinces her that she has the goblins *and* the librarians at her mercy. I was thinking, er . . .' Vox's gaze fell on Rook. 'A runaway slave, perhaps? With nothing to lose? Prepared to sell his friends and comrades out for a pouchful of shryke gold?'

Cowlquape turned to Rook. 'You have been through so much, Rook, lad,' he said, his eyes glistening with emotion. 'Would you do this, Rook?' he said. 'Would you pay a visit to Mother Muleclaw? For the librarians? For me . . ?'

Rook swallowed hard. The thought of Mother Muleclaw and the court of the Shryke Sisterhood filled him with dread; just as impersonating a treacherous slave sickened him, and yet . . . He looked into Cowlquape's concerned, kindly eyes.

'I'd be honoured to,' he said.

·CHAPTER TEN·

THE ELEVENTH HOUR

i
The Hive Towers

It was steamy, smoky and scorchingly hot inside the cavernous Hive Towers. The rank air hummed with the odours of unwashed goblins, burning lamp-oil and boiling tripweed, and the smoke from the foul stinkwood logs which burned intensely in the central brazier, their acid-green flames lapping at a tilder turning on the spit above. Drips of fat oozed from the revolving carcass and fell hissing into the fire, and puffs of acrid smoke rose up to join the dense miasmic cloud writhing in the conical towers far above. The goblins themselves were listless and irritable. Tempers were fraying.

'Turn that spit faster, scum!' roared a goblin undermaster, and cracked his whip. The mobgnome slave cowered miserably and struggled to obey.

From the shadows of a far corner came a loud groan,

followed by a parched, rasping cry. 'Woodale! More woodale! I'm dying of thirst, here.'

'Me, too,' said another. 'It's so blasted hot.'

'Yeah, where's that accursed slave?' bellowed a third.

'Coming, sirs. I'm coming,' said a weary voice, and a dumpy mobgnome pulled away from the communal ale-vat, climbed down the rickety ladder propped up against it, and – a slopping jug of woodale clasped in her callused hands – scurried across the hall to top up the goblins' tankards.

High above them, on one of the jutting stanchions, a look-out guard was bellowing at his replacement. 'You're late!' he roared. 'Shryke-loving dunggrub!'

'Who are you calling a dunggrub?' the second guard shouted back, his face red with rage. 'You stinking woodhog!'

He shoved the first guard hard in the chest. The guard lashed back. A scuffle broke out. Meanwhile, below them on the sleeping platforms, a second fight was in progress. With teeth bared and fists flying, three hefty tufted goblin guards were rolling about, crashing into the sleeping-pallets and sending the laden guard-racks tumbling – and all, apparently, over some dispute about mattress straw.

Down on the first-storey platform, General Tytugg was well aware of the state of his troops. Tension was high; morale low. He knew that the problem was nothing to do with spits or shifts, or who had the biggest wad of clean straw, but rather the terrible airless heat – both inside and outside the Hive Towers – that was

driving each and every one of his goblin guard to distraction. He himself was suffering, and he paced up and down the platform, his brow furrowed, his fists clenched.

'Get out of my way!' The angry voice cut through the general hubbub. It was coming from the entrance gates, where a group of guards were clustered round a new arrival.

'Out of my way!' roared the goblin a second time and attempted to brush the crowd aside. 'I have important information for General Tytugg . . .'

'Clodwit?' bellowed a voice from above them. 'Is that you?'

The goblins turned as one, to see General Tytugg's furious face glaring down at them. 'Ay, sire,' Clodwit shouted back. 'I bear news!'

'Step aside!' the general roared. 'Let him through!'

The goblins did as they were told and Clodwit hurried through the gap in the grumbling crowd, wiping the sweat from his brow as he went. The general, having climbed down the steep flight of stairs from the platform, was waiting for him at the bottom. Head lowered, Clodwit approached and greeted him as goblinlore required, with one fist raised and the other pressed to his heart.

'Make your report,' said General Tytugg. 'And for your sake, I hope it's a good one, or you'll join that tilder over there on the roasting-spit.'

Clodwit smiled and looked up. 'Vox Verlix is dead, master.'

'Dead,' whispered General Tytugg, his eyes widening with pleasure. 'Are you sure?'

'Killed him with me own hands,' said Clodwit proudly, patting the sheathed scythe at his belt. 'Squealed like a great woodhog when I stuck the blade in, so he did . . . One, two, three, four . . .' He jabbed at the air, demonstrating where the blade had struck.

All round the cavernous Hive Towers, the news was spreading. Vox Verlix was dead.

Clodwit's face clouded over. 'Glitch was sliced in two outside the chamber,' he said. 'The place was booby-trapped, just like you said – but I sneaked in behind a slave and waited for my opportunity to strike!'

'You've done well, Clodwit,' said General Tytugg. 'Very well.' He clapped the goblin on the shoulders. 'Vox Verlix called himself my master,' he went on, 'just because he had once paid me for my services.' He hawked and spat, a great glistening ball that landed in the stinkwood fire with a hiss. 'But who's the master now, eh?' he said, and laughed unpleasantly. 'With Vox Verlix in his grave, Tytugg is the Master of Undertown!'

'And there's more, sire,' said Clodwit in a low voice, as a rising swell of cheering began to echo round the great towers. Tytugg listened closely. 'Before he died, Vox pleaded for his life. He said he could help the goblins defeat the librarians, master. He told me that there was a secret route into the sewers which leads directly to the Great Chamber; showed me where it was in exchange for his life.'

'A secret route!' Tytugg exclaimed, his eyes glinting. 'Where is this secret route?'

The goblin crouched down and began to draw in the dust of the hard mud floor. 'Here's the underground library chamber and here's the central tunnel,' he said, drawing first a circle, then bisecting it with a long, horizontal line. 'And the main entrances are here, here and here,' he continued, marking the ground with crosses to represent the Great Eastern and Western Entrances, and the broad pipes which emerged in the boom-docks. 'But according to Vox, there is another entrance here,' he said, stabbing at the ground just above the Great Eastern Entrance.

Tytugg he looked at the spot thoughtfully. 'There's a small sink-hole there,' he said. 'I thought it was blocked.'

'That's what they wanted us to think,' said Clodwit. 'Vox learned of it from a librarian slave he employs in his kitchen.'

'Cunning old woodfox,' chuckled General Tytugg, his uneven brown teeth gleaming in the light from the brazier. 'To think that it was there all the time.'

All round the Hive Towers, the watching goblin

guards were cheering Clodwit's success and the scatter of applause was turning to a loud, rhythmic clapping.

General Tytugg frowned. 'Secret or no,' he said, 'surely the librarians don't leave it unguarded.'

'Not normally,' said Clodwit, 'but Vox reckoned they're about to have one of their ceremonies. The true Most High Academe is to make an important announcement. Two nights from now. At the eleventh hour.'

'The eleventh hour,' Tytugg repeated, furrows creasing his scarred brow.

'Apart from a skeleton guard posted at the main entrances, Vox said that everyone will be down in the Great Library Chamber at that time,' said Clodwit. 'Trapped. Defenceless. They'll be like sitting ducks; just waiting to be picked off, he said.' The goblin frowned as the false memories jostled for position inside his head. 'He claimed he was going to tell his old friend and ally, General Tytugg, all about it – and let you take all the glory. He was on his knees, pleading for me to spare his life.'

The general gave a derisory snort. 'I'm sure he was,' he said. 'Did he say anything else?'

A cruel smile stretched the goblin's thin lips. 'No, master,' he said, fingering his scythe. 'Your name was the last thing he uttered.'

General Tytugg threw back his head and roared with laughter. 'Wonderful! Wonderful!' he roared. 'Vox Verlix is no more, and now I'm going to destroy the librarians as well. Once and for all! Even Mother Muleclaw and her scabby shryke-sisters haven't been able to penetrate the

Great Library. Truly I shall become the greatest ruler of all the Edge. "General Tytugg" shall be the last words *many* shall utter.'

Around the hall, the goblin guards were picking up on the latest snippets of information as the eavesdropped conversation between Clodwit and the general passed from one to the other. The thick, stifling air was becoming charged with excitement and expectation.

'Death to librarian scum!' someone shouted and a great cheer went up, so loud and so long it set the beams overhead rattling. The heavy hand-clapping grew louder and a chant started up, quiet at first, but growing louder with ever passing second as the goblins whipped themselves up into a frenzy of battle-rage.

'Ty-tugg! Ty-tugg! Ty-tugg! Ty-tugg . . .'

ii
The Great Storm Chamber Library

'Order! Order!' bellowed Fenbrus Lodd, trying to make himself heard above the agitated babble of voices echoing round the tall ceiling of the underground library chamber. He raised his heavy blackwood gavel high in the air. *'Order!'*

Despite the lateness of the hour, the Great Storm Chamber Library was packed – and in uproar. There were librarians everywhere; crowded together on the Blackwood Bridge, clinging precariously to the jutting gantries overhead, crammed into the floating buoyant lecterns and onto the bobbing rafts in the main water channel below. Every one of them was staring across at the old Lufwood Bridge where the council members were all assembled, standing before high-backed chairs laid out in a broad semi-circle. Every one of them was shouting.

'Never!'

'Heresy!'

'Blasphemy!'

The atmosphere had been charged ever since the Open Council Session had first been called. Now it was at fever-pitch. It had been strange to be summoned to the library so late; stranger still to be witnessing the High Librarians in open session. But strangest – and most disturbing of all – was what Cowlquape Pentephraxis, the true Most High Academe, had just proposed.

'Leave the Great Library?' shouted a middle-aged

librarian, spluttering with rage. His side-whiskers flapped and the tasselled mortar-board jiggled about loosely on his long, pointed head.

'Shame! Shame!' bellowed another indignantly.

'Over my dead body!' croaked an ancient research-librarian, the buoyant lectern he was wedged within dipping wildly as he brandished his bony fists at the row of High Council members before him.

Bang! Bang! Bang! Bang!

Fenbrus Lodd's gavel hammered down like a volley of heavy hailstones. Unchecked, the librarians continued to berate their superiors who, for their part, remained in dignified silence.

There was Alquix Venvax and the other senior professors, Varis Lodd, captain of the librarian knights, and the Professors of Light and Darkness, Ulbus Vespius and Tallus Penitax. In the middle of the curved line, standing before his especially high-backed chair, was Cowlquape Pentephraxis, true Most High Academe – and object of most of the assembled librarians' outrage and indignation.

He looked stooped, uncertain and oddly frail in the face of such obvious hostility. His brown robes trembled. Fenbrus Lodd, the High Librarian – standing apart from the others at the top of a tall, carved blackwood lectern – could feel the meeting was slipping out of his control. He slammed the heavy blackwood gavel down – *Bang! Bang! Bang!* – and bellowed furiously at the top of his voice.

'Order! *Order!* I will not have these disturbances!'

The raucous hubbub dropped a notch.

Bang! Bang! Bang!

'I shall clear this chamber if I do not have immediate silence,' he warned, his eyes blazing. '*Order! Order!*'

The din subsided further.

'The true Most High Academe wanted you here – professors, sub-professors, librarians, apprentices and under-librarians – to bear witness to what we, the High Council, debate this night; for our final decision affects us all. Such rabble-rousing behaviour is unfitting.'

The chamber became quieter still with only a low, intermittent murmuring breaking the silence. With a short nod of satisfaction, Fenbrus Lodd turned to Cowlquape.

'My apologies, Most High Academe,' he said. 'Pray, proceed.'

Cowlquape raised his head and faced the sea of hostile faces before him. He stepped forwards, scanning the crowd for the ancient research-librarian who had cried out.

'Ah, there you are, Surlix,' he said, his gaze fixing on the wizened individual in the buoyant lectern. 'Over your dead body, you say.' His soft voice was audible in every corner of the now silent chamber. 'I tell you, Surlix; I tell you all . . .' He glanced back at the row of librarian dignitaries. 'If we do not leave the Great Library Chamber, then it will be over *all* our dead bodies – for I have it on good authority that a mighty storm is imminent.'

'A storm? A storm?' the librarians muttered among themselves.

Bang! Bang! Bang!

'That is why it's been getting so hot, so humid,' Cowlquape continued. 'The storm is gathering. I have been shown the cloud charts. It will strike at midnight in two nights' time. If we have not left the Great Library before the eleventh hour, we will all surely drown.'

'What nonsense is this?' shouted a red-haired librarian, unable to keep silent a moment longer. 'We've weathered storms before!'

'Yes, that's what the sluice-gates are for,' one of the raft-hands shouted up from the flowing waters below.

'I, for one, refuse to leave the sacred library!' cried an angry voice. And a chant began somewhere to the left of the Blackwood Bridge, which soon spread. 'Stay! Stay! Stay! . . .'

Bang! Bang! Bang!

'This is no ordinary storm,' Cowlquape shouted above the rising din. 'It is a . . .'

Bang! Bang! Bang!

'Silence!' roared Fenbrus Lodd.

Cowlquape breathed in sharply. 'It is a dark mael-strom,' he said.

There was a gasp from all sides which rose up and echoed round the vaulted ceiling.

'A . . . a dark maelstrom?' said Fenbrus Lodd uneasily, looking round from his lectern. 'Are you sure?'

Cowlquape nodded earnestly. 'Vox Verlix, the greatest cloudwatcher there has ever been, showed me his calcu-lations. There can be no doubt about it – in two nights' time, the maelstrom will strike.'

'Vox Verlix!' shouted an angry voice. 'Why should we believe anything *he* says?'

Cowlquape raised his hand. 'Because he *needs* us. In exchange for taking him with us, he has worked out a plan to enable us to escape from the sewers and take this great library of ours to a new home in the Free Glades!'

Alquix Venvax pushed his steel-rimmed glasses up nose with trembling fingers. His lower lip, too, was trembling. 'But this is my home,' he said in a soft, quavering voice. 'I don't want to leave it.'

A murmur of agreement spread out across the crowded chamber like ripples on a lake. Fenbrus Lodd glared round darkly, raised his gavel and was about to bring it down when Varis suddenly sprang forward.

'The Free Glades is the most wonderful place in all the Edge!' she exclaimed. 'I know,' she added, 'for I have been there. It is a sparkling jewel in the Deepwoods; a beacon of light and hope for academics everywhere.'

The librarians listened intently. Varis Lodd was renowned both for her academic rigour and for her self-less bravery. If *she* thought moving to the Free Glades was a good idea . . .

'Just think of it,' she was saying. 'A new beginning in a place where learning is valued and academics are revered.' She turned round to face Alquix. 'You say that this place is your home. But look at it. Why should you have to remain down here in the sewers? In the *sewers*, for Sky's sake! Hiding away, too frightened to show your face above ground.' Her voice softened. 'When did you last feel the warm sun on your back, Alquix Venvax?' she asked. 'Or rain in your face, or the wind in your beard? When did you last see the stars?'

Alquix remained seated. 'It is true,' he murmured sadly. 'I miss all these things.'

'We are academics,' Varis continued, turning her attention to the crowd, now hanging on her every word. 'We have dedicated our lives to the pursuit of knowledge – knowledge of the Edgeworld. Yet we skulk down here, beneath the ground, in this dark, damp hole, cut off from the world we claim to hold so dear. Librarians, one and all, I second the Most High Academe's proposal. We should leave the sewers and build a new library in the Free Glades!'

A loud cheer went up. This time, Fenbrus Lodd made no attempt to quieten the librarians down, either with threat or gavel. His daughter's impassioned speech had not only won over the librarians but it had also persuaded him of the wisdom of Cowlquape's proposal.

He turned to Cowlquape, his voice thick with emotion. 'If you think we can trust the usurper, Vox Verlix, then, Most High Academe, that is good enough for me and . . .' – he looked around at his fellow council members – 'for all of us.'

Bang! Bang! Bang!

Fenbrus Lodd brought the great gathering back to order with his heavy gavel. 'There is much to do and two days is all we have,' he said. 'Panniers must be loaded. Crates and boxes must be filled. And everything must be packed up securely in waterproof tarpaulins and loaded onto the rafts and barges . . .'

Cowlquape looked at the High Librarian, grateful to him – and his daughter, Varis Lodd – for swaying the librarians in favour of his proposal. Now all he could do was hope, and pray to Earth and Sky that everything would go smoothly.

'Two days' time, at the eleventh hour,' he murmured to himself. It seemed so terribly close.

iii
The Court of the Shryke Sisterhood

As well as the tollgate towers, tally-huts and talon-shaped barriers – familiar landmarks, all – there was a new construction at the eastern end of the Great Mire Road. It stood tall and imposing, an immense ironwood pine, uprooted from the rich soil of the distant Deepwoods and transported whole to its current site. Here it had been erected, supported by myriad ropes and staves, its branches stripped, polished and bedecked with the ornate perches beloved by the Shryke Sisterhood.

The Roosting Tree towered above the Mire Road and, in its branches, the High Sisterhood were gathered, their screeching voices raised in increasingly raucous debate. Mother Muleclaw herself, resplendent on a suspended gilded throne, wound the plaited leash she was holding in and out of her talons as she listened closely.

'The verminous goblin scum are swarming round the Hive Huts like crazed woodants!' one of the shryke-sisters, a tall individual with gaudy plumage and gaudier gowns, was saying.

'They're up to something, sisters! The hammerhead guard is said to be gathering at the Great Eastern sewer entrance,' added a second sister, her tall purple crest quivering violently.

'Indeed,' commented a third. 'Tytugg's definitely up to something. I can feel it in my tail feathers!'

'Which is why I say we should attack now, sisters, and bathe our claws in goblin blood!' said the purple-crested one adamantly, talking louder to be heard above the shrieks and battle-screeches of the battalions of shrykes performing their drill-manoeuvres below. 'Attack, I say. *Attack!*'

'And I say again that we must wait, Sister Talonscratch,' interrupted an angular shryke perched opposite her. She shook her long, mottled face slowly. 'Tytugg is clever. We must send out our spies; we must curb our impatience until we are certain of his plans, sisters.'

'My dear *cautious* Sister Hookbill,' said Sister Talonscratch, her voice soft and honeyed, 'always pecking at the seeds on the ground rather than reaching for the fruits in the branches!'

'Indeed, *venerable* sister,' replied Sister Hookbill gently, her voice laced with the stirrings of impatience. 'As I peck at the seeds on the ground, as you so delicately put it, I hear the whispers in the forest – while the fruit-seekers risk breaking their fine feathered necks on untested boughs.'

Sister Talonscratch's eyes blazed. 'You squawk of untested boughs, Sister Hookbill,' she said sharply, her feathers ruffling menacingly, 'when there is goblin blood to be tasted!'

'Sisters, sisters,' said Mother Muleclaw. Her hanging-throne swung from side to side. 'Calm yourselves. We need clear heads and sharp eyes in these dangerous times . . .'

Just then there was a loud disturbance below as a party of shryke guards approached the Roosting Tree. The entire circle of sisters spun round indignantly.

'A thousand apologies, sweet sisters,' said one of the guards.

'But we found *this*,' said the second, dragging a bedraggled youth by the scruff of the neck. Throwing him down roughly onto the boards at the base of the tree, the guard squawked up to the roost-mother above. 'Caught him snooping around by the tally-huts at the Mire Gates, your supreme Highness.'

The shrykes squawked and clucked with rage. The youth raised his head nervously and looked up. There was a loud *crack* as the first of the guards struck him on the shoulder with her bone-flail. 'How dare you cast your gaze upon the shryke-sisters!' she screeched. 'Librarian filth!'

The youth lowered his head. 'I . . . I'm sorry,' he said. 'But I must speak with . . .'

A second *crack* sounded, as the other guard brought her flail down heavily on his back. 'You will only speak when spoken to!' she shrieked.

'Let the librarian speak,' clucked Sister Hookbill. 'Seed-pecker that I am, I sense we might learn something from him.'

'He dared to meet our gaze!' shrieked Sister Talon-scratch. 'I say we tear out his liver and gorge on it!'

'Enough!' commanded Mother Muleclaw as her yellow eyes fell on the cowering figure of the youth. She lowered her hanging-throne. 'What business does a librarian knight have at the tally-huts?' she said. 'Speak, wretch, or my sister here shall feast on your liver!'

Keeping his head down, the youth replied, 'My name is Rook Barkwater,' he said. 'I am a librarian knight no longer. I spit on their rules and restrictions. Sewer rats, the lot of them! I seek the freedom of the Deepwoods and I'm prepared to sell out every last one of them to get it!'

The clucking grew louder. Mother Muleclaw's yellow eyes narrowed. 'Stand up,' she said. 'Explain yourself.'

Rook did as he was told, taking care to keep his gaze fixed firmly on the floor below him. He didn't want to feel the searing pain of the bone-flail again.

'They accused me of forging my treatise and stealing barkscrolls,' he said, his voice little more than a murmur. 'Lies, all of it. And for that, they shall pay dearly.'

The shrykes fell still. Mother Muleclaw leaned forwards, pressed a vicious talon against the underside of his chin and jerked his head upwards. Rook found himself staring into the cold, unblinking eyes of the formidable creature.

'Pay dearly?' she said. 'How, pray?'

'The librarians are in great danger, if they only knew it,' he said with a bitter smile. 'The goblins have discovered a secret passageway into the Great Library and they intend to attack and take it for themselves.'

'You see!' screeched one of the shrykes. 'I *told* you Tytugg was up to something!'

Mother Muleclaw silenced her with a flap of her taloned hand. 'Why should we believe you, librarian scum?' she growled.

'Because I hate the librarians, and with the gold you shall pay me for the information I give you, I can buy a passage back to the Deepwoods,' said Rook, head still bowed. 'Fifty gold pieces is all I ask. A cheap price for the chance to destroy the goblins and the librarians at a stroke . . . And I know the shrykes understand the value of a good spy. I could be even more useful to you once I reach the Free Glades.' He paused. 'For the right price.'

'Go on,' said Mother Muleclaw, leaning forward in her roost throne. Around her, the other sisters had fallen quiet.

'First the gold,' said Rook, looking up and meeting her gaze.

For a moment, Mother Muleclaw said nothing. Then, with a savage jerk of the plaited leash, she yanked her puny shryke-mate up beside her. Rook noticed the leather coffer strapped to his back.

'Stand still, Burdle,' snapped Mother Muleclaw as she pushed a key into the lock of the coffer and turned it. 'Fifty, you say,' she said, and thrust her hand inside. She counted out the coins. 'There,' she squawked and tossed the gold to the floor at Rook's feet. 'There's thirty. That's *plenty*. Unless you *want* to see the colour of your own insides . . .'

Rook crouched down and began stuffing his pockets with the gold pieces. As the final coin clinked down beside the others, he climbed to his feet.

'The goblins will attack from the east,' he began, 'and I can show you an entrance from the Great Western Tunnel that will lead you straight to the Great Storm Chamber Library. Attack at the right moment and you will trap the goblins *and* the librarians.'

Mother Muleclaw clucked excitedly. 'Tell me when to attack and you shall be escorted along the Mire Road in my own personal carriage!' she said.

Rook smiled, his gaze as unblinking as that of the shrykes themselves. 'Attack in two nights' time,' he said. 'At the eleventh hour!'

·CHAPTER ELEVEN·

XANTH FILATINE

X anth stood by the window of his study looking out at the new day dawning, his head in turmoil. It was hotter than ever that morning, with the atmosphere so still that, although the window was wide open, not the faintest breath of fresh air penetrated the stifling room.

Mopping his glistening brow, he surveyed the huge, dark, anvil-shaped clouds which lined the horizon with a mounting sense of dread. They were vast and dense, their horizontal upper reaches silhouetted against the heavy blood-red sky. Xanth shuddered. Was this the storm the Guardians had been awaiting for so long? It looked so menacing, so evil . . .

At least, Xanth thought, if the storm *did* strike, the air might clear and the temperature drop. It had been so hot the night before that he'd barely slept a wink, tossing and turning beneath sweat-drenched covers, his dreams troubled and disturbing.

Far below him, Screetown was stirring. Further off, the lights of Undertown were going out, one by one, and on the narrow streets between the clutter of rundown buildings he saw Undertowners and goblins – as tiny as woodants – going about their daily business. Further still and he could just make out the signs of activity at the end of the Great Mire Road.

He pulled a telescope from the folds of his gown and focused on the tally-huts, the gateway towers – and the writhing mass of the bird-creatures clustered together in groups on the great platform beneath the towers and the curious tree-like construction which had sprung up a couple of days earlier. What was more, he realized as he switched his attention to the road itself, there were more arriving all the time. Like the clouds, the entire shryke army seemed to be advancing on Undertown.

The Eastern Roost must be almost deserted, he thought. But why? Did they also sense an impending storm?

Just then, a white raven flew past the window, cawing loudly. Xanth lowered the telescope and watched as the creature flapped past the Tower of Night, over Screetown and on towards the Stone Gardens.

Xanth sighed wistfully, wishing that he, too, could fly away from the dark evil tower. He no longer belonged here. Perhaps he never had . . .

If he *could* fly, however, it wouldn't be to the Stone Gardens. No, if Xanth had wings, he would head off in the opposite direction; to the Deepwoods. He smiled to himself. Maybe Leddix was right, after all; maybe the Free Glade air had turned his head . . .

He'd flown there, of course, in the Free Glades; soaring above the Great Lake on the *Ratbird*, the skycraft he had built with his own hands. He sighed again. How differently things might have been if that maiden flight hadn't ended up with him crashing into Lake Landing and breaking his leg . . .

Xanth turned away from the window, crossed the stone floor and sat down on the stool at his desk. He had work to complete. A barkscroll lay before him, half-translated from the ancient tongue of the first academics. He picked up his pencil and read over the last sentence.

Et syth thit lyghtninge bleue slamme to thit steyne strykenard, yereby to makke sund.

And his transcription.

And so the blue lightning strikes the stricken stone, thereby making it . . .

'*Sund*,' he murmured. 'Healthy? Well? . . .'

His mind – already muzzy with the airless heat and

lack of sleep – began to wander. And as he traced his fingers over the pattern of whorls and knots in the surface of the wooden desktop, he remembered Oakley Barkgruff, the kindly woodtroll who had helped him carve his skycraft from the great slab of sumpwood; what a thrill it had been to feel the wood beneath his hands take on the shape of a ratbird . . .

And the slaughterer, Brisket, scarcely older than himself, who had taught him everything he knew of sail-setting and ropecraft. How he'd loved those intricate rope-knots and the subtle shapes of a billowing sail . . .

And, most of all, Tweezel, the ancient spindlebug who had shown him how to varnish his craft – and with whom he had spent so many indulgent hours, sipping aromatic teas and listening to the wise old creature's stories. Even now, he could recall that thin, reedy voice telling him of far-off days when the spindlebug had walked the streets of old Sanctaphrax . . .

Then there was Parsimmon, the Master of the Lake Landing Academy; and Varis Lodd; and his fellow students, Stob Lummus, Rook Barkwater . . .

And, of course, Magda. Magda Burlix; the librarian knight he had interrogated so cruelly the day before, acting as though he didn't know her, and sealing her fate.

'Oh, Magda! Magda! Magda!' he cried out, slamming the pencil down on the table and pushing the barkscroll away. He couldn't work. Not now.

The stool scraped loudly on the stone floor as he pushed it back and climbed to his feet. He began pacing the small room, to and fro from bed-pallet to window

and back again, rubbing his hands over his shaven scalp
and muttering under his breath.

'I've tried so hard to be a good Guardian. Nobody can
say that I haven't. Obedient. Loyal. Ruthless ... And
then *you* come along, Magda, stirring up all kinds of
stuff I thought I'd forgotten about. Why did you have to
get caught? Eh, why *you*?' His face hardened. 'Sky blast
you!'

Yet even as he cursed her, Xanth knew it wasn't
Magda's fault that he was feeling the way he did. He
clutched at his head. How had it ever come to this?

Back at the window, he glanced across at the Palace of
Statues. It had been many long years since Orbix Xaxis
had first taken him into his confidence, flattering him,
tempting him and finally luring him away from Vox
Verlix whom he'd been serving as a young apprentice.

Whenever he could, Orbix had taken Xanth aside.
'There could be an excellent future in the Tower of Night
for a quick-witted lad such as yourself,' he would tell
him. 'You could go down in history, my boy, as the one
who healed the stricken rock and returned Sanctaphrax
to its former glory.'

Though alarmed by the mask and dark glasses which
concealed Orbix's face and muffled his voice, Xanth had
listened keenly, his heart thumping with excitement.

Then one cold morning, as Vox struggled with the construction of the Sanctaphrax Forest, Orbix had gone
further. 'Vox Verlix is finished, I tell you,' he'd said softly.
'And those arrogant buffoons, the librarians, will never
manage to find a cure for the rock with their poultices

and potions. *We* are the future.' His voice had dropped to a gruff whisper. '. . . The Guardians of Night, are

the true heirs of the sky-scholars,' he'd said. 'Join us, Xanth. Join us.'

And he had. That night, in the darkest hour just before day-break, he had stolen away from his quarters and met with Orbix Xaxis's shadowy fol-lowers on the upper gantries of the tower. There he had joined the breakaway faction of Guardians, signing his name to the Oath of Allegiance with his own blood.

Xanth turned away and crossed the room slowly, the painful memories com-ing thick and fast.

Before the blood on the parchment was even dry, Orbix had whisked him away and quizzed him relentlessly about every aspect of Vox Verlix's apart-ments in the tower, the layout of corridors and staircases, the exact timing of his daily routine, the movements of his palace guards – and of Vox himself . . .

Three days later, Orbix Xaxis had launched his attack, massacring all those loyal to Vox Verlix, who had fled for his life; seizing the Tower of Night for himself and declaring himself its High Guardian.

Xanth sat down heavily on the corner of his bed-pallet, knees clutched tightly to his chest, and began rocking slowly backwards and forwards. Although he hadn't realized it at the time, he'd been used . . . Used . . .

From deep down in the bowels of the tower, he heard muffled thuds as doors were slammed, one after the other, and in between, the intermittent wail of desperate voices. The prisoners were being fed. Each time a door was unlocked for their daily ration of gruel and water to be pushed inside, mournful cries escaped the atrium and echoed up into the higher reaches of the tower. Xanth put his head in his hands. Soon the terrible prison stench, wafting out through the opened doors, would also fill the air.

Prisoners! Yes, under Orbix Xaxis, there were many prisoners; captured librarians, Undertowners and denounced Guardians accused of plotting against him. Nobody was safe. Xanth had earned his new master's trust by interrogating prisoners. He was, he realized guiltily, good at it; getting them to talk through a mixture of brutality and kindness.

It was how he'd first met Cowlquape, the hapless Most High Academe, betrayed by Vox to Orbix Xaxis, who had imprisoned him. The High Academe was free now, but Xanth couldn't help missing him – after the initial interrogation, he had grown to like and admire the resilient old academic.

Cowlquape it was who had buoyed him up so many times over the years when his spirits were low: with no-one else to talk to, Xanth had often crept down to the dungeons to hear the professor talk of his love for the Deepwoods. He had held Xanth spellbound with his stories of that mysterious place, far from Undertown, with its exotic fauna and flora, and tales of the tribes and forest-folk that dwelt there. And when the opportunity had arisen for Xanth to travel there himself, he'd seized it – though he had been too ashamed to tell Cowlquape that he was travelling there as a spy for the Guardians of Night.

Despite the sultry heat of the small chamber, Xanth shivered with a mixture of sadness and remorse. He *had* left the sinister tower and travelled to the Free Glades. And there, for the first time in his life, he had tasted happiness, just as Cowlquape had promised he would. But in the end, he had had to return. He'd had no choice. At risk of being unmasked as a spy, he'd had to flee back to the Guardians. It had broken his heart to leave, and on his return it had been too painful to see Cowlquape. Never again did Xanth visit him in his cell. So far as he knew, the old professor did not even know that he had returned.

Now, of course, the tables had been turned. Cowlquape Pentephraxis, former Most High Academe of New Sanctaphrax, was free, while *he* . . .

Just then, Xanth heard the soft clinking of chains. He jumped to his feet and hurried to the window. It was one of the terrible cages, empty now, being raised up from the deep ravine below.

Xanth turned away and slammed his fist down onto the desk. If he'd had his doubts about the High Guardian before – with his tortured prisoners, his summary executions and his fanatical hatred of the librarians – now that Orbix had begun feeding the poor, helpless librarians to the terrible rock demons, Xanth knew that his master had gone beyond the bounds of brutal tyrant. The so-called Purification Ceremonies were nothing more than an excuse for the High Guardian's twisted sport. Orbix Xaxis was a madman, a maniac. A monster.

Returning to the window, Xanth paused. By daylight, the approaching clouds looked darker and more imposing than ever. Perhaps this time, after decades of drought, the Edge was about to be struck by a mighty storm – with driving rain, thunder and lightning . . .

Lightning!

Despite himself, Xanth felt a shiver of excitement. *Sacred* lightning. The lightning which every Guardian believed would strike Midnight's Spike and so pass down through the crumbling Sanctaphrax rock, healing it as it went.

What if Orbix was right? Xanth wondered anxiously. What if a storm did break, and the lightning did strike, and did heal the Sanctaphrax rock? What then? The power struggle between the warring factions of shrykes and goblins, Guardians and librarians was in the balance at the moment – as it had been for many years.

But if the Guardians of Night *were* to cure stone-sickness, then all that would change at a stroke. The Guardians would both govern New Sanctaphrax *and* take control of the sky, as buoyant flight-rocks began once more to grow in the Stone Gardens.

And, if *that* happened, then who would become the most powerful figure in all the Edge? Why none other than the High Guardian himself, Orbix Xaxis! Did he, Xanth, really want that to happen?

Thud! Thud! Thud!

The three heavy blows at the door echoed round the small study-chamber and brought Xanth out of his reveries with a start. The door burst open.

'You're wanted up on the Upper Gantry, now,' said a surly-looking guard gruffly. 'Come with me.'

As Xanth stepped into the corridor, the rank odour from the dungeons made him grimace. Poor creatures, he thought. And Magda was one of them; down there in the putrid depths, perched on her jutting prison-ledge. Alone. Frightened . . .

Oh, Magda, he thought sorrowfully as he followed the armed Guardian up the flights of stairs to the High Guardian's quarters. I should thank you, not curse you, for stirring such memories and doubts and emotions. Ever since returning from the Free Glades, I've tried desperately to keep my feelings under control, but you . . . you, Magda, have brought them flooding back. I cannot stay in this evil place. I must leave – and somehow take you with me.

*

Xanth's footsteps echoed round the High Guardian's sumptuous stately chamber as he made his way across the polished leadwood floor. The place was as luxurious as his own study was austere. It was crammed full of priceless items, all plundered from the ruined palaces of Screetown.

There were gilt framed mirrors and intricate tapestries, sparkling with gold and silver thread, on every wall; ornate vases, candelabras and dancing figurines on shelves, plinths and podiums, and in tall, elegant glass-fronted cabinets. Huge turquoise and magenta porcelain urns stood in every corner, a crystal chandelier hung overhead, while at the far end of the room, on either side of the gantry-doors, stood two ferocious banderbears, carved from the same heavy leadwood as the floor – and looking for all the world as though they were rearing out of it.

'There you are, Xanth,' came a steely, yet slightly muffled voice and a sinister black-gowned figure appeared between them.

'High Guardian,' said Xanth.

'Join us,' said Orbix, turning away.

At the far end of the gantry, crouched down beside the ceremonial cage like a great woodcrow hunched over carrion, was Leddix. He looked up, but his sallow face was impossible to read.

'Come closer,' snapped Orbix.

Xanth approached. The mask clamped over the High Guardian's mouth hissed ominously; the dark glasses reflected Xanth's own anxious face back at him.

'I've had my doubts about you, Xanth,' Orbix said. 'You may have noticed. Ever since you returned from the Free Glades . . .' His voice trailed away.

Xanth swallowed nervously.

'But my doubts were clearly misplaced,' Orbix continued. Xanth tried not to show his relief. 'When I saw you kicking that librarian scum, I knew that the rumours about your loyalty were . . . were . . .' He glanced round at Leddix. 'Were less than well-founded.'

'By the Oath of Allegiance, I did my duty as a Guardian of Night,' said Xanth solemnly.

'Indeed, indeed,' said Orbix. 'You acted admirably.' He stepped forwards, clapped an arm around Xanth's shoulder and steered him towards the balustrade at the end of the broad, jutting gantry. Behind him, Xanth heard Leddix – sullen and disgruntled – muttering under his breath.

'The Great Storm is almost upon us,' said Orbix, nodding towards the towering stacks of cloud before them. 'We must be ready for it.' He pulled Xanth round and drew his muzzled face close. 'I want you to prepare Midnight's Spike. Clean the cogs, oil the levers, check the winding-chains. At the precise moment the storm breaks, the spike must rise smoothly up to its full extent to receive the healing power of the lightning bolt. Nothing must go wrong, do you understand?'

Xanth nodded dumbly.

The High Guardian relaxed his grip on Xanth's shoulder, and from behind the muzzle came a muffled grunt of satisfaction. 'I know you will not fail me.' He straightened up. 'Go now. See to the spike.'

'Sir,' said Xanth. He turned away and headed back towards the gantry-doors.

Orbix turned his attention to his cage-master. Behind the muzzle, his breathing was rasping and heavy. 'Leddix,' he hissed. 'I trust everything is in place.'

'Yes, High Guardian,' said Leddix, giving a small, cringing bow. 'The tunnel between the ravine and the sewers has been completed. I supervised it myself.'

'And have you inspected the bait?' he said.

Leddix nodded enthusiastically. 'Such sweet, tender young flesh, High Guardian,' he simpered. 'They're really going to go for her, I can promise you that.'

Orbix strode over to the balustrade and stared down for a long time as if deep in thought. Leddix hovered behind him.

'They'll tear her to shreds,' he said keenly. 'How they'll cheer from the upper gantries. It'll be the best Purification Ceremony yet.'

The High Guardian turned and regarded the cage-master. Behind his muzzle, unseen by Leddix, his lip curled. 'Leddix, Leddix,' he said, his voice dripping with contempt. 'You have understood nothing. This will be no ordinary Purification Ceremony. I don't intend this young librarian to be torn to shreds for the mere delectation of the upper gantries . . .' He paused, and beneath his mask, the rasping breathing quickened.

'You don't, High Guardian?' said Leddix, a puzzled disappointment in his voice.

'No, you fool!' snapped Orbix. 'Why do you think your work gangs have been labouring day and night these past months, digging a tunnel between the ravine and the sewers? Why do you think we've been nurturing the rock demons, feeding them only the sweetest, most tender librarian flesh? Simply to keep you and your bloodthirsty cronies on the upper gantries entertained?'

Leddix shrugged uneasily.

'Of course not!' Orbix sneered. 'I intend her to flee down the tunnel we have so kindly provided. She will run for her life, run to the Great Library – and after her, snapping at her heels and shrieking for the succulent flesh, will come the pursuing rock demons.'

His voice became louder. Leddix seemed almost to shrink into himself.

'They'll infest every tunnel,' the High Guardian told him. 'Every nook, every cranny. They'll run amok, driven into a frenzy of bloodlust by the scent of all that tender librarian flesh around them; a scent they have grown to love so well. There will be no escape! Not a single librarian will survive!'

Leddix bowed low. 'A stroke of genius, High Master,' he said, his voice oily, fawning. 'Truly the Guardians are blessed by your inspired leadership.'

From behind the mask there came a thin, cackling laugh. 'Tomorrow at noon, when the sun is at its highest, the last and greatest Purification Ceremony of them all will begin.'

· C H A P T E R   T W E L V E ·

THE GREAT LIBRARY FLEET

The ceiling fans, their blades whirring like agitated woodmoths in moonlight, were having little effect in the Great Storm Chamber Library. Rather than cooling the stifling atmosphere, their frantic beating seemed to be making the air even hotter. Below them, on the library bridges and numerous gantries, the librarians – their clothes damp and their faces glistening with sweat – worked with grim determination.

Groups of conical-hatted professors hurried over the bridges and along the long, winding sewer tunnels, clutching boxes and crates and huge bundles of barkscrolls. Under-librarians, their robes flapping behind them, were racing up and down from the jutting gantries overhead to the channels of water below with heavy rolls of waterproof oil-cloth slung between them. The lectern-keepers, marshalled by the bridge-masters' barked commands, were expertly winding in the skittish buoyant lecterns, one after the other. They were chained together in vast bobbing bunches, waiting to be attached to the huge vessels which were taking shape on the water below as hundreds of barge-hands and sewer-rafters feverishly lashed their craft together to form a fleet of five massive flat-bottomed ships.

Above them, on the Lufwood Bridge, the Council stood poring over barkscroll blueprints and library inventories. There was Fenbrus Lodd the High Librarian, short and gruff, his shock of curly white hair forming a glowing halo round his head. And Varis Lodd, his daughter, captain of the librarian knights, looking curiously cool and collected in her leather flight-suit despite the heat; her green eyes darted here and there, missing nothing. Beside her, deep in conversation, were the Professors of Darkness and of Light; Tallus Penitax in heavy dark robes, and Ulbus Vespius, his cloak glowing white in the shadows.

Behind them all, the aged figure of Alquix Venvax hopped from foot to foot, unable to contain his agitation at the sight of his beloved library being packed up and entrusted to the treacherous waters of the Edgewater River. It was all proving too much for him.

'This is madness!' his querulous voice rang out above the clamour all round. 'Madness! We shall all drown and this great library we have fought and died for will be lost for ever!' His voice cracked with emotion as tears streamed down his face. 'Please, there must be another way . . .'

The council turned and Varis sprang to the old

professor's side as he crumpled to his knees. Below them, an uneasy silence fell as under-librarians, professors, barge-hands and sewer-rafters suddenly stopped what they were doing and looked up at the group on the Lufwood Bridge.

'There is no other way, Alquix, my old friend,' came an equally frail voice – though unlike the old professor's, this one had a calm, steely determination about it that cut through the stifling air and echoed round the Storm Chamber. The council stepped aside as Cowlquape, the Most High Academe, in full regalia, stepped up to the balustrade of the Lufwood Bridge and spread his arms wide.

'I know there are many amongst you who are loath to leave this great library of ours,' he said, addressing the crowd.

There were murmurs and whispers from the upper gantries and barges below.

'It has been our refuge and haven against those who have sought to destroy us for so long. The sewers have kept us safe, it is true, but now, as the dark maelstrom approaches, they will flood, and all we have fought and died for will be lost. So we must leave this place we've called home, the only place many of you have ever known, and make this perilous and terrible journey. Remember . . .' – Cowlquape's voice rose to a crescendo – 'the Storm Chamber will soon be no more. But with your help, my dear brave librarians, the Great Library will live on!'

There was utter silence. All eyes were on the Most

High Academe. Above, the monotonous whirring of the ceiling fans seemed louder than ever. Suddenly Fenbrus Lodd stepped up beside Cowlquape and raised a fist.

'Long live the Great Library!' he roared.

'The Great Library! The Great Library!' The words rang out as the librarians took up the chant; professors throwing their conical hats in the air, under-librarians banging on the wooden boards of the gantries and the barge-hands hoisting their oars above their heads.

At last Cowlquape raised his hand and the cheering subsided. 'Thank you, brave librarians. Now back to work, all of you,' he commanded. 'The eleventh hour approaches.'

Everyone returned to their tasks with renewed vigour. The five great vessels were nearing completion. Each was broad and flat, braced with thick ironwood staves in the middle, and tapering to a long thin point at either end. The prows were fitted with anchor weights and grappling-hooks, while each stern had been raised high with a platform for

the helmsman. Rows of benches lined the sides, already bristling with oars. In the centre of each boat, the lecterns were being loaded, jostling and clashing together as the nets being used to restrain the buoyant wood were strapped into place.

'The work is going well,' said Fenbrus Lodd, turning to Varis who was busy overseeing the storage of the fragile skycraft onto the fourth barge with the Professors of Light and Darkness.

She looked up. 'Yes, Father,' she said, 'though I'd be happier leading a squadron in the air than trusting myself to the water. Besides, the fleet should have airborne cover.'

'It's far too dangerous,' said the Professor of Darkness, shaking his head. 'Even for you, Varis.'

'Tallus is right,' said the Professor of Light. 'With the storm about to break, no skycraft would last five minutes out there.'

'And we'll need them later,' the Professor of Darkness reminded her. 'Once we have left Undertown . . .'

'*If* we ever leave!' interrupted Fenbrus. 'All this discussion! For the love of Earth and Sky, hurry it along, all of you. Varis, you heard the professors. No skycraft! We'll just have to hope and pray that we meet no resistance on our way to the Mire Gates.'

'You shall not, I promise,' a voice rang out.

Unnoticed, a cloaked figure had emerged from the shadows of the tunnel at the far end of the Lufwood Bridge, and stepped into the frantic atmosphere of the Great Storm Chamber. Now the figure strode boldly forwards onto the bridge and pulled back the hood that masked his face.

'Rook!' Fenbrus exclaimed. 'I can't tell you how good it is to see you, lad!'

'And for me to see you, High Librarian,' said Rook. 'I have much to tell.'

'Make your report,' said Fenbrus Lodd. 'For everything depends on it!'

The council gathered round the white-faced youth, Cowlquape offering him a lufwood stool.

'Don't crowd him,' Fenbrus Lodd said, as he climbed down from the lectern. 'You there,' he gestured to an under-librarian. 'Get the lad some water.'

'Sit,' said Cowlquape, placing a hand on his shoulder, 'and catch your breath, that's the way.'

Rook sat down shakily and tried to suppress a shudder. 'It was terrible,' he began. 'I'd almost forgotten how truly monstrous the shrykes are. The stench, the noise – and the way their unblinking eyes bore into you.' He shuddered again. 'I could have sworn that they saw right through me . . .'

'You've been very brave, Rook,' said Cowlquape gently. 'You're safe now.' He paused. 'And if they had seen through you, you wouldn't be here.'

Rook nodded and managed a smile. 'I stuck to the story Vox gave me, about hating librarians and wanting to betray them . . .'

'Shrykes understand treachery,' Varis broke in. 'They find it easy to believe.'

'I told them where and when to attack the library, just like we agreed . . .' Rook continued, looking round at the faces of the High Librarian and the Professors of Light and Darkness uneasily.

'Now there is truly no going back,' said Fenbrus, looking askance at the worried face of Alquix Venvax, who shook his head sadly. The Professors of Light and Darkness exchanged glances.

'And Mother Muleclaw believed you?' the Professor of Darkness asked.

'She did when I demanded fifty gold pieces,' said Rook. 'And offered me safe passage down the Mire Road in her own personal carriage into the bargain when I gave her the details. She thinks she has a spy who will continue working for her – so let me live, thank Sky.'

'Like I said,' Varis muttered, 'shrykes understand treachery.'

Cowlquape turned back to Rook. 'So you think the path down the Mire Road will be clear?' he said.

'Yes, I'm sure of it,' said Rook. 'As I was leaving, I saw vast numbers of armed shrykes streaming in from the Eastern Roost. The entire shryke army is massing. They plan to swarm down into the sewers at the eleventh hour, leaving only fledglings and puny shryke-mates guarding the Mire Gates.'

'We can handle them,' said Varis firmly.

Cowlquape leant forward and rested a hand on Rook's shoulder. 'This is excellent,' he said. 'I had my doubts, but Vox's plan seems to be working.'

'The fat barkslug,' muttered Fenbrus Lodd darkly.

'You have served the Librarians well, Rook,' Cowlquape continued. 'Refresh yourself and then make your way down to the jetties. There is a place on one of the boats for you.'

Rook smiled. Although he would have willingly done anything asked of him to help with the grand exodus, he was exhausted. And though proud to have played his part in Vox's plan, he was relieved that it was now over.

Varis stepped forward and wrapped an arm around his shoulder. 'Come, Rook,' she said. 'Let's go and find you something to eat.'

Just then, there came a plaintive yodel from the far end of the Lufwood Bridge. 'Wuh-wuh, Ru-wuh-uk, Uralowa. Wurra!'

Rook recognized it at once. *Welcome back, Rook, he who took the poison-stick. We have missed you.*

'Oh, banderbears!' he cried.

There was Molleen, an old female, the light glinting on her gappy smile and chipped tusk as she grinned at him lopsidedly. And Weeg, the huge shambling male with the ugly scar across his shoulder. And Wuralo, dear Wuralo, the female with the curious markings which encircled one eye and crossed her snout, that he had rescued from the Foundry Glade – taking a poisoned arrow to the shoulder for his pains. And last but not least, there was Wumeru, his friend. How many moons had passed since that first Deepwoods encounter . . ?

Forgetting how weary he had been feeling only moments before, Rook dashed towards them, arms outstretched, and fell into Wumeru's tight embrace. The others clustered round them, hugging tightly, and forming a huge moss-speckled dome of fur.

At the middle of it all, scarcely able to breathe, Rook smelled the warm, comforting odour of musty fur. It calmed his anxiously beating heart and brought back vivid memories, both good and bad. Of banderbear slaves. Of the great convocation. And of a single banderbear female who, years before, when he was a small orphaned child, lost and alone in the dark Deepwoods, had found him and cared for him until one of his own kind had come to take him away . . .

'My friends . . .' he mumbled, struggling to free himself from their powerful arms. 'Wurra-wuh, meerala!' *My heart sings loudly to be with you again!*

'Wuh-wuh!' 'Wurra-weeg!' 'Larra-weera-wuh!' The banderbears were all speaking at once.

Wumeru silenced them with a slight tilt of her head.

'Wuh-wella-loom,' she said gravely. *Our hearts are glad to be with you, too.* 'Weera-wullara.' *But they also grieve that we must leave you.*

Rook stepped back. 'Leave me?' he asked, touching his chest with an open hand and tilting his head. 'Why must you leave when we have only just been reunited?'

Wumeru held out a vast paw and clasped Rook's face, drawing it close to her own. He could smell her sweet breath, and see the sorrow in her eyes.

'Wurra-weeg, wurra-woolah,' the banderbear said softly. *We must take the fat one to the Mire Gates. It has been agreed.*

'It's true,' said Varis, appearing at Rook's side. 'As part of our agreement, you know we must take that great oaf, Vox, with us. The banderbears have agreed to go to the Palace of Statues and carry him to safety in a specially constructed bower. It will be dangerous, but we gave our word, as librarians.'

'Wuh-wuh wooralah,' Rook said softly. *This mission is perilous. No-one would blame you for refusing.*

'Wurra-weeg!' said Wumeru sharply, her teeth bared. 'Wurroo-leera!' *Our own hearts would break with shame.* Varis smiled. 'They won't let us down, Rook,' she said. 'And Sky willing, we'll all meet up again at the Mire Gates.' She motioned to the banderbears who, each in turn, embraced Rook, then left the bridge.

Rook turned to see a tall, ornate bower standing in the shadows of the tunnel. It had a wide padded bench, surrounded with plush curtains, all mounted on a carved frame. Two broad, varnished poles stuck out from the sides; one at the front, one at the back.

The banderbears bent down, seized a length of pole each in their great clawed paws and, on Varis's command, lifted the bower up in the air.

'Wuh-wuh, weeralah-loog-wuh,' muttered Molleen, smiling bravely. *Light as a feather, even for an old bag of bones like me.*

Rook smiled back. They were so brave, all of them. The librarians were fortunate indeed to have the help of such noble creatures. He could only hope that Molleen would be able to carry the bower as easily when it bore the weight of that great, bloated mountain of flesh, Vox Verlix.

'Wuh-wuh!' he whispered, his hand brushing lightly against his chest and forehead. *Fare you well.* There were tears welling in his eyes.

Fare you well, Rook, came the banderbears' reply as they set off along the tunnel. *And soon may the moon shine down brightly on our next meeting.*

Rook swallowed hard, but the painful lump in his throat remained. They would meet again, he told himself.

Wouldn't they?

Fenbrus took his arm and guided him from the bridge. 'You have done well, Rook Barkwater,' he said kindly. 'Eat well, then take your place on a bench in one of the great vessels, next to your old professor, Alquix Venvax. He needs a steady shoulder to lean on. Go, and Earth and Sky blessings be upon us all in the Great Library fleet!'

·CHAPTER THIRTEEN·

THE CLODDERTROG GUARD

As Xanth Filatine climbed down the narrow ladder from the flimsy spike-ledge at the very top of the Tower of Night, the tooled-leather box slipped from his shoulder. It knocked against the side of the ladder with a loud *clunk*.

'Gloamglozer blast you,' Xanth muttered under his breath as he paused and lifted it back onto his shoulder.

The box was heavy. Inside it were spanners and steel-brushes and an oil-can with a long, slender spout, as well as numerous more delicate instruments – a spindly plumb-line spirit-level to ensure the vertical ascent of the spike; a ratchet-grip used for aligning the teeth of the many interlocking cogs; and most important of all, a calibrated barometric astrolabe made of brass, the readings from which Xanth had to record faithfully and pass on to his master. The High Guardian's instructions had been clear.

Nothing must go wrong.

With a grim smile tugging at the corners of his mouth, Xanth wiped a hand over his sweaty brow and continued down the ladder. He realized he was panting.

Xanth had been up at the crack of dawn that morning, and though it was still early, the air was already hot and humid. It sapped his strength, leaving his body weary and making it difficult to concentrate.

He glanced round as he descended, pausing for a moment to take in the best view – aside from a skycraft saddle – in all of the Edge. He saw Undertown swarming, not with Undertowners, but with battalions of goblins. Reports had reached the tower that a curfew had been called, and the goblins were marching through the deserted streets and congregating in a large square to the east of the city. Far off in the opposite direction, he could just make out the shrykes also amassing in huge numbers, the colourful battle-flocks seeming to glow in the hazy light. And beyond all of this, he could see the great stacks of cloud beginning to coalesce to form a vast wall of swirling darkness.

Reaching the bottom of the ladder, Xanth stepped down onto the lookout-platform and opened the toolbox. He searched its contents for a moment before removing a metal bar, pointed at one end and with the metal head of a gloamglozer decorating the other. He examined it briefly, turning it over in his hand, the same grim smile playing on his lips. Suddenly a gruff voice spoke, making the hairs at the back of his neck stand on end.

'Who goes there?' it demanded.

Xanth spun round – slipping the metal implement into his pocket as he did so – to find himself confronted by a hulking cloddertrog guard, one hairy ham of a hand hovering near the handle of the great curved sword which hung at his belt. The cloddertrog's small red eyes narrowed and his nostrils flared.

Xanth glared back at him. 'It's me,' he retorted crossly. 'Xanth Filatine. You challenged me on my way up, you great oaf!'

'Password,' grunted the cloddertrog, his face betraying not a hint of emotion.

Xanth sighed. '*The rock demons screech,*' he intoned in a bored voice.

The cloddertrog guard's gruff voice grunted back the response mechanically. '*For soon they will be free.*'

'Satisfied?' said Xanth. 'Made absolutely sure it's the same Xanth Filatine you challenged half an hour ago?'

The cloddertrog's small eyes stared back, hard and stony. He made no move to let Xanth pass. 'Rules is rules,' he grunted. 'Even for a librarian-loving pet of the High Guardian . . .'

'What did you say?' thundered Xanth, his violet eyes blazing. 'I have the authority of the High Guardian of Night!'

'Rules is rules,' muttered the guard, a slight quiver in his voice.

'I could have you thrown into the foulest dungeon-ledge in the tower, you insolent wretch – and don't think I wouldn't,' Xanth continued, his eyes boring into the cloddertrog's. 'Go on, take a good look at this face and remember, the next time you show such insolence, you'll be seeing it from the other side of a dungeon peephole. Understand?'

The cloddertrog looked down at his heavy iron-shod boots, and moved to let Xanth pass.

'Understand?' the youth repeated.

'Yes,' said the guard in a low growl.

'That's better,' said Xanth, sweeping past, and dis-appearing from view down the winding staircase.

The cloddertrog stared after him. 'Xanth Filatine,' he growled, spitting out the youth's name. 'I'll remember your face, don't you worry about that.'

The tower was swarming with black-cloaked Guardians. They were on the gantry-landings, keeping watch, and on the jutting weapon platforms, tending to the harpoon-turrets and swivel catapults, in constant readiness for any attack. It seemed to Xanth, as he made his way down the winding staircase from Midnight's Spike, that just like the goblins and the shrykes, the Guardians of Night, too, were massing. Why, the entire guard seemed to have been turned out today.

'Step aside!' he barked time and again as he barged his way down the great tower. 'Make way! I'm on important business for the High Guardian!'

Past the spy-turrets and guard-decks he went, and down past the great gantry with the sinister feeding-cage glinting at the far end. The bars of the cage seemed to tremble in the hot, shimmering air. He was indeed on important business, he thought bitterly, but not for the High Guardian, Sky curse him. Right now, his master was probably laughing to himself behind that evil metal muzzle as he anticipated the Purification Ceremony scheduled to take place at noon.

But it wouldn't – not if he, Xanth Filatine, could do something about it. Magda, his friend, would not end up as bait for the rock demons, he would see to that! But time, Xanth realized, his pulse quickening, was not on their side. The minutes were ticking by.

'Move aside!' he shouted, barging his way through a group of Guardians, standing on an open landing.

As he hurried down lower still, the tower broadened and the single stairway became one of many. The air grew heavier and more oppressive, laced now with the scent of newly sawn wood and the odour of unwashed bodies. He passed Orbix Xaxis's living quarters, studies and stores, guardrooms and interrogation chambers, coming at last to the point where the tower divided up into an outer and inner section. The rooms and chambers formed the outer shell to the tower, with gantries of various lengths and widths protruding from their windows, while an inner wall encased the cavernous

central atrium which housed the terrible prison-ledges.
Xanth was sandwiched between the two of them, on a
high, rectangular landing dimly lit by cowled oil-lanterns.

'Password,' demanded a tall flathead goblin, stepping
from the flickering shadows.

'*The rock demons screech*,' said Xanth, catching his
breath with difficulty. The air down here was stifling.

'*For soon they will be free*,' the goblin intoned. 'Pass,
Guardian.'

Without so much as a backward glance, Xanth
continued on his way. The further down he went into the
shadowy depths, the hotter and more pungent the
atmosphere became. Eerie sighs and moans penetrated
the air from the other side of the wall.

Half walking, half running, Xanth entered the maze of
narrow walkways and rickety flights of stairs zigzagging
off in all directions around him. Each staircase led to a
door set into the inner wall. Behind
one of these doors was Magda
Burlix – and Xanth knew
exactly which one. It
was a cell he knew
well, for it

had once belonged to
his old friend, Cowlquape.
Now, however, it was set
aside for the librarian victims
of the evil Purification Ceremony.

Arriving at the bottom of a familiar sloping flight of stairs, Xanth ran headlong into two hefty flathead guards standing in front of a low, studded door. One of them stepped forward, a heavy club in his hand, while the other lowered the crossbow he was carrying and pointed it at Xanth's chest.

'Halt, who goes there?' said the first.

'Xanth Filatine,' came the breathless reply. 'On important business for the High Guardian.'

The guard frowned. 'Password?' he said.

Xanth tutted impatiently. '*The rock demons screech*,' he said.

'*For soon* . . .'

'Yes, yes, just get on with it,' snapped Xanth with all the bluster he could manage. 'Orbix Xaxis himself has sent me here. He wishes to interrogate the prisoner personally.'

The guards exchanged glances, and the one with the crossbow shook his head uncertainly. 'Orbix Xaxis, you say,' he said slowly. 'We haven't been told anything . . .'

'Are you challenging my authority?' said Xanth, his voice dropping to a low, menacing growl. 'If you are, I shall make sure that the High Guardian hears of your insubordination.'

The guards exchanged looks again. Xanth seized his chance, brushing the club and crossbow aside as he strode between them. Before him stood the door to the cell, the names of its former occupants carved into the thick, dark wood. *Cowlquape Pentephraxis* was at the top; below it others, librarian knights who had paid the ultimate price for their steadfast loyalty to the Great Library. *Torvalt Limbus, Misha Blix, Estina Flembel* . . . And there, at the bottom of the terrible list, the name he had been hoping to see.

Magda Burlix.

He slid the bolts across, top and bottom. Then, ignoring the troubled muttering of the guards behind him, he straightened up, grasped the handle firmly and pushed the door open. It struck the back wall with an echoing thud.

Xanth stood in the doorway, reeling giddily. He would never get used to the yawning chasm which opened up before him – nor the appalling stench of sewage and death. Prisoners, perched on nearby ledges, who had heard the door being opened, fell to their knees, clasped their hands together beseechingly and pleaded with this newcomer to set them free.

'Have mercy, sweet master!' they cried, their eyes staring imploringly.

'Release me!' cried a one-eyed lugtroll.

'This is all a mistake! A terrible mistake!' wailed a grizzled former professor, his spangled robes hanging in filthy tatters.

Xanth tore his gaze away from the hapless prisoners and looked down the narrow open-staircase to the jutting ledge. There, sitting motionless in the middle – her face turned away and her long plaits hanging down the back of her flight-suit – was Magda.

'You stand when a Guardian enters!' Xanth barked, as he descended the flight of stairs.

Magda looked round wearily.

'Get up, scum!' he ordered, in a hard cold voice. 'And come with me. The High Guardian wishes to interrogate you further.'

Magda turned away but made no move to stand up. Xanth strode across the ledge and prodded her roughly with his boot.

'I said, get up!' he repeated. Magda didn't move. With a grunt of irritation, Xanth bent down, grabbed her by the arms and dragged her to her feet.

'Aaagh-*ow*!' Magda cried out, as Xanth twisted her arm round behind her back. 'You're hurting me!'

'Shut up, Sky curse you,' Xanth hissed in her ear, 'and do exactly as I say.'

At the top of the stairs, he shoved her roughly through the doorway, past the guards, and bundled her on up the next flight of stairs. Only when he reached the top and the guards were out of sight did he relax the upward pressure on her arm. He leaned forwards.

'Just keep walking,' he whispered into her ear. 'Don't say a word.'

Outside the open cell door, the two guards turned to one another.

'I don't like this one little bit,' said one, his finger stroking the trigger of his crossbow. 'What do you think old muzzle-face is up to?'

'Dunno,' said the other. He tapped the club down in his open palm; once, twice, three times, before thrusting it decisively into the sheath at his belt. 'I don't know about you,' he announced, 'but High Guardian or no

High Guardian, I'm going to find Leddix. After all, as cage-master, the librarian is *his* prisoner, strictly speaking.'

Meanwhile, in the dark walkways above, Xanth and Magda had come to an abrupt halt.

'I'm not going another step!' Magda said, turning on Xanth.

Xanth released her. 'Magda,' he said softly, 'I'm trying to save your life.'

'Save my life?' said Magda, breathless with disbelief. 'You struck me, remember? You called me librarian scum . . .'

'I'm sorry,' said Xanth brusquely. 'But I had to. I was being watched. If they'd suspected anything, I'd have joined you in the ceremonial cage as rock demon bait. I still might, if we don't hurry,' he added.

'You almost broke my arm!' Magda complained, rubbing her throbbing elbow.

'Magda, *please*,' said Xanth. 'When they realize you've escaped, they'll sound the tilderhorn alarm and then we'll be done for. We'll have the whole tower-guard after us. I'm telling you, we must get out of here as quickly as we possibly can.'

'But why should I trust you, Xanth?' Magda persisted obstinately, her green eyes flashing with anger. 'You betrayed the librarians at Lake Landing. You serve the High Guardian of Night. You lie. You deceive.' She shook her head. 'Why should I believe anyone who wears the sign of the accursed gloamglozer emblazoned on his front?'

Xanth looked up, his violet eyes full of sorrow. 'It is true,' he admitted. 'I have done many bad things. Terrible, unforgivable things. Yet you – *you*, Magda – you awoke in me memories of a better life, and with them the dream of leaving this place – for ever. Come with me, Magda, and I shall make sure you get back to the librarians.' His voice faltered. 'It is time I made amends for the terrible crimes I have committed.'

Magda's mouth pursed as she searched the shaven-headed youth's face. 'You'll get me back to the librarians?' she asked. 'Promise?'

Xanth smiled. 'I give you my word,' he said.

Magda held out her hand, and Xanth took it gratefully.

'We'll take the baskets used by Guardian patrols heading into Undertown,' he explained. 'The Eastern baskets. They'll bring us down close to the Edge, not far from the Stone Gardens. I know a path that'll take us to Undertown without having to venture through Screetown . . .'

'Come on then,' said Magda, striding ahead. 'What are we waiting for?'

'Not that way,' said Xanth, halting her in her tracks. '*This* way!'

With Xanth in front and Magda following close behind, the pair of them made their way through the labyrinth of staircases and walkways. Xanth never faltered for a moment – now taking a right-hand turning, now a corner to the left, now continuing straight on – without a second thought. Down here, close to the base of the tower, there seemed to be almost no Guardians at all – which wasn't surprising, Magda thought, as the air was so foul that breathing it was almost intolerable. Xanth turned sharply to his right and hurried down a long narrow corridor with light streaming in from the far end.

'This is it,' he said. 'The Eastern Gate.' He stopped abruptly and grabbed Magda's arm. 'I almost forgot,' he whispered. 'The baskets are guarded.'

Magda watched, bemused, as he reached up and pulled the black hooded gown over his head. Underneath it was a second gown, identical in every detail. Magda looked at the garment with distaste as Xanth held it out to her.

'It's for you,' he said. He nodded toward the green flight-suit. 'Make you a little less conspicuous.'

Magda pulled the heavy gown – still warm from Xanth's body-heat – over her head. She tugged at the cuffs and smoothed the material down, shuddering uneasily as her hand passed over the symbol of the screeching gloamglozer, now emblazoning her own chest.

'Raise the hood,' Xanth said, doing the same. 'And when we're outside, let me do all the talking.'

Together, the two of them stepped out, wincing involuntarily at the daylight, so blindingly bright after the subdued lampglow within the tower. At the far end of the long, broad gantry were half a dozen baskets, each one suspended from overhead pulley-wheels mounted at the top of jutting struts, three on each side. A single guard – a wizened gnokgoblin – looked up as they marched towards him.

He was dressed in a black gown the same as their own

– but several sizes too big for him. Pushing his sleeves halfway up his scrawny arms, he gripped his sword.

'Password,' he said.

'*The rock demons screech*,' said Xanth.

'*For . . . for soon . . .*' The gnokgoblin frowned, a look of confusion flitting across his features. 'Very good,' he said, his voice quavering as if in fear of a repri-mand. 'Business in Under-town, Guardians?'

'That's no concern of yours,' said Xanth, striding past him, Magda at his heels.

The gnokgoblin moved aside, stumbling over the trail-ing hem of the gown as he did so. Xanth was already at the baskets. He climbed into furthermost one and helped Magda in after him.

Xanth took up a position on the raised winding-stool and unhitched the chain from the mooring-cleat. 'Hold tight,' he whispered to Magda. He let the links of the chain slide through his hands and slipped his feet into the winding-pedals.

The gnokgoblin watched them from the tower entrance. Once he had been fierce in battle, fighting alongside flatheads and hammerheads twice his size, and often taking the greatest trophy. These days, though, battles were no more than distant memories. His bones were old and his muscles shrivelled. Too weak to fight and too blind to operate the gantry weapons, he'd been appointed a basket-guard. It was one of the lowliest positions in the Tower of Night – yet it had its compensations. Leddix paid him well to keep his eyes and ears open.

The gnokgoblin smiled as the two Guardians disappeared from sight. *Business in Undertown*, indeed! Approaching the edge of the landing, he gave a long, low whistle.

Below, Magda gasped as the basket dropped down, concerned at the alarming way it twisted and lurched. Although she had countless flights to her name, there was a world of difference between being airborne in her beloved *Woodmoth* – the skycraft she had created with her own bare hands and which obeyed her every flight-command – and being suspended in this creaking basket from a disturbingly rusty-looking length of chain.

The lower they dropped, the closer the diseased Sanctaphrax rock came. At one point, Magda could have reached out and touched the crumbling rock – and would have, were it not for her fear of setting the unstable basket rocking. The porous rock was riven with cracks and fissures and huge boulder-shaped chunks threatened to break away at any moment. A small, grey creature with long twitching ears caught her eye as it scampered over the pitted surface in a flurry of dust and was gone.

'We'll soon be level with the Sanctaphrax Forest,' said

Xanth. The winding-pedals creaked softly as they turned.

Magda nodded. A moment later, the dark and damaged rock gave way to the vast wooden cross-beams and pillars constructed to support it.

'The Sanctaphrax Forest,' she whispered, her voice trembling with awe.

No wonder they called it a forest, Magda thought. Half the Deepwoods must have been cut down to build it. As she stared at the great vertical pylons thrusting up from the ground like mighty tree-trunks, and the chaotic jumble of branch-like struts and supports, transoms, rafters and beams, it seemed that *forest* was exactly the right word for the place.

A dark forest. An endless forest. A *living* forest . . .

It was almost as if the very spirit of the Deepwoods themselves had been transported here along with the trees that had been felled.

The so-called *forest*, she knew, served a dual purpose. Originally, it had been constructed to prevent the stricken rock from crushing Undertown below. The endeavour had not been entirely successful – as the ruins of Screetown bore terrible witness; yet, thanks to the vision of Vox Verlix and the endless backbreaking toil of the slave-workers, damage had been kept to a minimum. The other purpose was altogether more contentious. As everyone knew, the Guardians – in stark contrast to the librarians – believed that the rock must be kept from touching the ground if the coming lightning bolt was to heal it. It had been the cause of their terrible rift and the reason why the Guardians still hated the librarians.

Magda turned to Xanth. 'So you believe in the sacred lightning bolt, do you?' she said. 'Curing stone-sickness.'

Xanth hesitated and looked up. The basket turned around again. 'As a Guardian, I do,' he said, 'though my studies at Lake Landing with the librarians left me less certain . . .' He shrugged and resumed the long descent. 'Maybe none of them are right,' he said a moment later. 'Maybe there really is no cure for stone-sickness, in the sky *or* in the Deepwoods.'

Magda shook her head. 'As a librarian knight, I have to believe there is a cure out there in the Deepwoods somewhere. But what I don't understand is why the Guardians hate us so much for believing that. After all, we all want the same thing, don't we?'

Xanth looked away. 'I used to believe that, Magda. But the minds of the Guardians have been poisoned by sky-watching and envy. It is not only the stone that is sick. I only wish I had realized that sooner,' he added softly.

The basket lurched to one side, then righted itself. Magda swallowed nervously and gripped the sides of the basket till her knuckles went white. As the basket slowly turned, she found herself staring into the shadowy depths of the great wooden structure and heard a curious *whiffling* noise, like air passing through a narrow opening. She turned to see a bat-like creature with hooks on its wings and a long rubbery snout soaring through the criss-cross shadows and coming in to land on a tatty nest, one of many lined up along the broad crossbeam. It was a dwarf-rotsucker.

The breathy whistling sounds grew louder, and Magda realized that the creature was not alone. Dozens of others, their leathery wings wrapped tightly round them, filled the shadows behind it. An acrid smell of droppings made her nostrils quiver. This was clearly a regular roosting spot for the whole flock; a place they came to every morning, to rest up in the dark shadows and wait for nightfall – the creature she had watched must have been a straggler . . .

With a lurch, the basket dropped further and the dwarf-rotsuckers disappeared. A new sound filled the air. The sound of hard toil. There was sawing and chopping, and the shifting rhythm of numerous pounding hammers – and underlying it all, a constant low moaning: the sound of despair.

'Right, now try again,' bellowed a deep, throaty voice. 'And this time, put your backs into it!' A whip cracked and the moaning grew louder. 'Lift it higher! *Higher!*'

'Slave gang,' Xanth muttered grimly. 'The work on the forest never stops.'

The slave-master's furious voice echoed up through the air. 'Imbecile!' he bellowed and the whip cracked louder than ever. 'Do that again, and I'll snap your scrawny neck!'

Magda shuddered.

Xanth continued turning the winding-pedals steadily, and as the basket dropped Magda found herself face to face with the slave gang itself. She gasped and clapped her hands to her mouth.

Magda knew, of course, that the life of a slave was

harsh, particularly those assigned to work on the Sanctaphrax Forest. Nothing, though, could have prepared her for the sight of the group of pitiful unfortunates before her.

There were a dozen or so of them in all, from every part of the Edge. Beneath the grimy skin and matted hair, she could make out mobgnomes, gyle-goblins; a cloddertrog, a lugtroll, a pair of flatheads . . . Here, however, as slave-labour in the Sanctaphrax Forest, their backgrounds counted for nothing.

Wearing nothing but filthy loin-cloths, the hapless slaves were balanced precariously on rickety scaffolding and flimsy boards, their arms raised, struggling under the weight of the massive ironwood crossbeam they were attempting to push into place. Magda watched them, tears welling in her eyes. Their straining muscles were like knots of rope; their protruding bones, like sticks – for if there was one thing that the slaves had in common, it was this. They were all being starved to death.

'There's nothing you can do,' said Xanth softly.

Magda's face crumpled. 'I know,' she said. 'That's the worst thing of all.'

The moaning rose and fell in waves as the slaves tried, again and again, to raise the heavy crossbeam high enough.

'Higher! Higher!' bellowed a voice, and a great hammerhead goblin with a horned brass helmet and heavy leather armour stepped out of the shadows. He cracked his whip. 'Half a stride more!' he roared, urging the slaves forward.

Just then there was a muffled cry and Magda saw one of the gyle-goblins stumble and fall to his knees. Moaning loudly, the other slaves wobbled precariously, desperately trying not to let go of the ironwood beam. The hammerhead slave-master strode forward furiously, seized the quivering gyle-goblin by the scruff of his neck and raised him high up into the air.

'I warned you!' he hissed. 'You're more trouble than you're worth.'

He twisted the terrified gyle-goblin round and gripped him tightly in the crook of his elbow. He turned to the others. 'You're going to have to work even harder now!' he bellowed.

He seized the goblin's head and wrenched it sharply to the right. There was a dull crack.

Magda let out a cry of horror.

The hammerhead spun round and glared at her. 'Guardians, eh?' he sneered.

Magda looked down, grateful for the hooded gown which concealed her tear-stained face.

'Greetings,' Xanth called back, easing up on the winding-pedals for a moment. 'It is good to know that the welfare of the sacred Sanctaphrax rock is in such competent hands. The High Guardian himself shall hear of your excellent work.'

The slave-master tossed the limp body of the dead gyle-goblin off the platform and placed his hands on his hips.

'So long as old muzzle-face keeps paying, then we'll look after his precious rock,' he snarled. A crooked smile, all broken teeth and dark intent, flashed across his face. 'Perhaps *you'd* like to lend a hand . . .'

Xanth said nothing. He turned the winding-pedals with renewed vigour.

Magda could not speak. The condition of the slaves, condemned to labour until they dropped, had shocked her to the core; while the casual brutality of the slave-master played over and over in her mind. Although the moaning of the slaves soon faded away as the basket dropped lower, their memory would linger on so long as she lived.

'Magda,' said Xanth, turning to the young librarian. She didn't stir, lost in her own thoughts. 'Magda! We've arrived.' The basket touched down on the ground with a soft thud and Xanth secured the brake-lever before any more chain could unwind. He jumped down from the winding-stool and climbed out of the basket. 'Magda,' he said a third time, grasping her shoulders tightly with both hands. 'We've almost made it. The worst is over.'

'For us, maybe,' said Magda bleakly.

With Xanth's help, she climbed out of the basket and looked about her distractedly.

'Looking for something?' came a gruff voice.

Magda started back with surprise. Xanth spun round to see a cloddertrog guard standing before him, his thick heavy arms folded in front of him.

'*The rock demons screech*,' he said.

The guard eyed him dismissively, a sneer playing over his mouth. 'I recognize that face,' he said with an evil leer. He unfolded his arms and drew a heavy club from his belt. Vicious studs glinted in the heavy sunlight.

'Step aside this instant!' Xanth commanded, his voice breaking with outrage. 'I am Xanth Filatine, following orders given to me by the High Guardian himself. If he were to find out . . .'

Just then there was a stirring from the shadows behind him and a wiry individual with lank hair and weasely features stepped from the shadow. 'The High Guardian will find out soon enough,' came a thin voice.

'Leddix,' said Xanth, the colour draining from his cheeks.

'Surprised to see me, eh, Xanth?' the cage-master asked. 'Did you not realize that I have been having you watched?' He chuckled softly. 'I've been waiting for this moment for a long time, my treacherous friend. A very long time . . .'

'You're . . . you're making a big mistake, Leddix,' said Xanth. 'I'm warning you.'

'*You* warning *me*?' Leddix said, his face creasing with amusement. 'Oh, but you're a slippery one, Xanth Filatine. Sucking up to the High Guardian; poisoning his mind against me with your traitorous lies.' His expression hardened. 'But now I've got you, like a fat oozefish wriggling at the end of a line . . .'

'How *dare* you!' said Xanth with all the cold fury he could muster.

Leddix clicked his fingers and the cloddertrog guard leapt forward, his club raised and swinging.

'Watch out!' Magda cried.

But too late. The heavy studded club struck Xanth hard on the back of his head with a sickening crunch. The last thing Xanth saw was Leddix's goading smile, cruel in victory. Thin lips. Brown teeth. Dead eyes . . .

Then nothing.

·CHAPTER FOURTEEN·

AMBERFUCE

Nobody but a waif could understand how difficult it was, thought Amberfuce bitterly. His barbels quivered as he drew a circle in the thick dust that coated the crowded medicine stand beside his buoyant chair.

Needs dusting!

His icy thought cut through the muddle in his nurse's huge head.

'Ooh,' came a screech from the room next door, accompanied by the sound of a glass stopper being dropped. 'How many times must I tell you, Ambey, dear?' Flambusia called out. 'Nursie doesn't like you barging into her head!'

'Sorry, Flambusia,' whispered the waif in a pathetic voice.

Not even Flambusia – big, beautiful Flambusia, who nursed him, soothing his aches and easing his pains – not even *she* understood how difficult it was being a waif. All those thoughts in all those heads; whispering, moaning, shouting, without a moment's respite . . .

Eighty years ago, in the dark marshy waiflands, far off in the furthest reaches of the known Edgelands, it had been so different. Amberfuce's eyes glazed over and a smile set his barbels quivering. He remembered the delicious silence that had surrounded him as a waifling; so empty, so comforting – and broken only by the occasional whispering of another ghostwaif out there somewhere in the endless distance.

Amberfuce sighed.

Like so many before him, he'd been drawn to Undertown, lured by the promise of a better life and riches beyond imagining. Most found only misery and despair. But not Amberfuce.

The waif's smile widened and his eyes twinkled.

He had found employment. There was always employment to be found for a clever waif who was good at keeping quiet and listening. Amberfuce had kept his huge ears open and had soon secured himself a lucrative position in the School of Light and Darkness, snooping on the gossiping academics for his master, an ambitious High Professor.

Long dead now, Amberfuce thought darkly.

The professor had been the first of many masters, all interested and ready to pay for what he overheard in the gabbling, gossiping, endlessly noisy old Sanctaphrax. So many thoughts! So much noise!

Amberfuce leaned across to scratch at a dry, flaky patch of skin itching at the back of his knee.

He'd soon learned though; learned how to blot out the incessant babble and listen selectively. It had been hard.

Many waifs were driven insane after a few years in Undertown. But not Amberfuce. He was made of sterner stuff – and besides, he had his medicine.

A cough racked his frail body as he surveyed the rows of dusty bottles, nestling on the medicine stand. The large jars contained his tinctures; potent concoctions which soothed his poor, tired ears. The tall slender vessels were filled with salves and balms. And then there were the embrocations, greasy and black – how he enjoyed Flambusia's rough hands applying them . . .

Amberfuce chuckled throatily – and collapsed into a fit of coughing which, this time, showed no sign of abating.

'Oh, dearie-dearie me!' said Flambusia, bustling into the chamber, her heavy stack-heels clacking on the marble tiles. 'Can I never get a moment's peace and quiet?'

She hurried across the floor to the quivering waif, unstoppering a squat blue pot as she went. A pungent whiff of eye-watering sagemint and woodcamphor filled the air.

'Now, shirt up for Nursie,' Flambusia said calmly, 'and let's rub a little vapour embrocation into that chest of yours.'

She opened his gown and tugged at his undershirt with one hand then, dipping the other into the jar, she loomed in above the waif. As her plump, deliciously rough fingers worked the embrocation into his pallid, mottled skin, Amberfuce could feel his lungs being soothed. The coughing eased. He sat back in his chair, eyes closed.

He could make out Flambusia's thoughts in the background; fussy, cluttered and . . . what was that?

He stopped himself probing – he knew how she hated that – and tried to think of something else.

Professors! What a noisy squabbling rabble they were, the whole lot of them, with their petty grievances and niggling dislikes . . . But then he had met Vox Verlix, a junior professor in the College of Cloud; tall and opinionated, a braggart and a bully, never happier than when throwing his weight about. Young and callow though Vox was, Amberfuce had sensed something about him – something beyond the naked ambition, the base desires . . .

The waif smiled. It was Vox's mind – his brilliant, unfathomable mind – that had fascinated him. He had known at once that he could really *work* with this professor and that is exactly what he had set about doing.

'That should do you for now,' Flambusia announced, pulling the waif's undershirt back down and straightening his gown. 'Now don't you go getting yourself all excited again,' she chided him. 'You know it's not good for you.'

'Tea,' Amberfuce murmured, his eyes fluttering open for a moment. 'I'd like some nice herb tea.'

'Presently,' said Flambusia, turning away. 'Nursie's a bit busy at the moment. You get some rest, Ambey, dear.'

Amberfuce nodded resignedly, and closed his eyes again.

Ah yes, those early days as Vox's assistant . . . They'd

certainly been eventful. There had been the Mother Storm, and the loss of old Sanctaphrax, and the birth of the new rock. What times they'd been! Amberfuce rocked backwards and forwards in the buoyant chair.

Vox had ingratiated himself with the young fool of a High Academe, Cowlquape Pentephraxis. He'd pretended to believe in all that academics-and-Undertowners-being-the-same nonsense. And all the while, he, Amberfuce, had been listening and reporting back to Vox so that when the opportunity arose, the pair of them had been ready and waiting.

Stone-sickness had taken hold of the Edge, the new Sanctaphrax rock had begun to crumble and the leaguesmen's once mighty fleet had been decimated by the failing flight-rocks. Undertown and New Sanctaphrax had been in turmoil, and Cowlquape in despair. Vox had come up with a brilliant plan – the construction of a vast single tower on the Sanctaphrax rock, to replace the smaller buildings that the various squabbling schools and academies had built. The earth-scholars – their numbers increasing and influence growing – could have the lower levels for their Great Library. From there they could continue to search the Deepwoods for a cure for stone-sickness. The sky-scholars could inhabit the upper levels, establishing laboratories and workrooms and, most importantly, supervising the building of a mighty spike. This, they believed, would harness the power of any passing lightning and heal the stricken rock beneath.

It had been a masterly plan. Vox's plans always were.

Yet it was he, Amberfuce – negotiator, manipulator, deal-breaker – who, as always, had been charged with putting it into effect.

The smile on the ghostwaif's pale face broadened. He had been clever; very clever. He had persuaded the most important leaguesmen of Undertown to use their few remaining ships to carry one last cargo of Deepwoods timber into the city. Then, when the tower's construction had consumed the last of this, he had organized gangs of Undertowners to tear down entire districts to furnish the rest. And of course, while acting for Vox, Amberfuce had been careful to skim off fees and commissions for himself. The work had almost bankrupted the academics, but the Tower of Night had been completed.

From the ante-chamber, there came the sound of liquids being poured and the clinking of a spoon stirring. Amberfuce opened his eyes and glanced round hopefully – but there was no sign of Flambusia, with or without the herb tea. Ahead of him was the window, with the fuzzy outline of the tall, imposing tower seeming almost to mock him from behind the billowing lace curtain.

'Ah, me, the Tower of Night,' he murmured ruefully. 'Our first great masterpiece.' His voice was soft and rasping. 'How did it go so wrong?'

Looking back at it, of course, it was perfectly obvious. The earth-scholars had hated the tower from the start, and the Knights Academy had split into sky and earth factions. Once the library had been established, those knights sympathetic to the ideals of the earth-scholars had joined them. Together, they became known as the librarians. They had been opposed by the sky-scholars, who had gathered under the leadership of a wall-eyed, pasty-faced individual by the name of Orbix Xaxis. They had called themelves the Guardians of Night.

Librarians and Guardians; the two sides had prepared themselves for a showdown.

Amberfuce chuckled. He'd never heard such a hubbub! Such dark thoughts and high emotion! He'd told Vox to side with the Guardians – and had taken a nice fee from Orbix into the bargain.

What a night that had been! thought Amberfuce, sitting back in his buoyant chair. *The Night of the Gloamglozers*.

In their new black uniforms, emblazoned with the screeching evil creatures, the Guardians had launched their attack. All those openly loyal to Cowlquape had been swept from power, many paying with their lives – while the Most High Academe himself had disappeared.

Vox, Amberfuce remembered, had declared himself the new Most High Academe, and made him – Amberfuce – his chancellor. It made him tremble just to think of it. A small ghostwaif from the Deepwoods, High Chancellor of New Sanctaphrax and Undertown!

Where was his herb tea? he wondered, looking back towards the ante-chamber and strumming his fingers impatiently on the arms of the buoyant chair. What was taking Flambusia so long?

Of course it hadn't lasted. The Guardians had seen to that.

'Accursed ingrates!' Amberfuce wheezed bitterly.

He should have seen it coming, of course. He should have read Orbix Xaxis's dark thoughts more carefully but, drunk on power, he'd become negligent. It was more by luck than judgement that, on that fateful night when Orbix had made his move and sent Guardians to throw Vox and his chancellor from the high gantry to their deaths, he had been alert . . .

Orbix had wanted the tower all for himself and had planned to slaughter the increasingly obstructive

librarians, always carping and complaining, and blocking his plans. It had been Amberfuce who, sensing that
they might yet prove of use, had sent the librarians
word, just in time – and together they had all fled to
Undertown.

Vox and Amberfuce had taken refuge in the Palace of
Statues which, with the collapse of the great merchant
leagues, had been abandoned and was lying empty. That
was when Amberfuce had first moved into his precious
little chamber . . .

The waif sighed wearily. Where *had* all the years gone?

At first, the pair of them had prospered in the Palace
of Statues. Vox, the new Most High Academe, had been
accepted by the Undertowners and, with his chancellor
Amberfuce in charge of trade and taxes, the gold had
soon been flowing in. The Guardians of Night had kept
themselves to themselves, holed up in the Tower of
Night and waiting for their blessed storm. A queasy
equilibrium seemed to have been established.

But Amberfuce had known that it couldn't last, for
Undertown was all but cut off from the Deepwoods.
Dealings with the sky pirates had continued for a while
longer, but soon – as their sky ships also fell prey to the
relentlessly advancing stone-sickness – business in
Undertown had ground to a halt. Panic-buying turned to
looting. Mobs had taken to the streets. The economy had
been on the verge of total collapse . . .

With noon approaching and the sun high in the sky,
the motes of dust in the chamber fluttered like particles
of gold in the shafts of light streaming in from outside.

Amberfuce felt a tickle in his throat and put his handkerchief to his mouth to filter out the dust, cursing
Flambusia for being such a poor housekeeper. The whole
chamber needed a good clean. Time was when he would
have done it himself – removing every medicine bottle
and tincture pot and dusting them with fastidious care.
But not now . . .

Amberfuce sighed, and closed his eyes to the
neglected room. Vox! he thought. What an incredible
talent for invention he had possessed!

He recalled Vox's face when he'd come to him late one
night, his hair all sticking up, and his eyes burning with
excitement. He'd pulled a roll of parchment from a tube
and flattened it out on Amberfuce's desk, to reveal the
blueprint for a long complicated construction, mounted
upon stilts.

'It's a kind of bridge. It'll extend all the way from the Deepwoods to Undertown. I'm going to called it the Great Mire Road,' Vox had explained, his hands flapping about animatedly. 'Just think of it, Amberfuce. It will be Undertown's connection with the riches of the Deepwoods. I've already enlisted the help of the librarians. They're only too delighted to restore our links with the Deepwoods. We'll need their expertise with wood – you know what they're like; they know everything, from which acorn sprouts in summer, to which part of the ironwood log is strongest . . .'

'I hate to pour cold water on this brilliant scheme of yours,' Amberfuce had replied. 'It's all well and good building a bridge across the Mire, but how do you propose to get through the Twilight Woods?'

'The shrykes!' Vox had exclaimed, his eyes blazing. 'We'll do a deal with the shrykes! They're immune to the effects of the Twilight Woods. They can build a road through them to connect with our bridge! And then, Amberfuce, the riches of the Deepwoods will be in our hands.'

'And in the claws of the shrykes,' Amberfuce had added darkly.

'You can do a deal, Amberfuce,' Vox had replied. 'If anyone can, *you* can.'

Vox was right. Amberfuce had done a deal with the leathery, golden-eyed old bird, Mother Feathergizzard. As roost-mother of the vast nomadic shryke flock, she had agreed – admittedly, for a high price – to construct the Great Mire Road through the Twilight Woods.

Thereafter, in return, she would be allowed to tax that part of the road.

Everything had gone perfectly, Amberfuce remembered. The Twilight Woods stretch of the new road had been finished within six months, enabling fresh timber to be brought in from the Deepwoods so that the librarians and Undertowners could work on the longer section which crossed the Mire. It had taken three years to complete. Mother Feathergizzard had taken her tax – both in gold and in kind – and Amberfuce, as ever, had skimmed his own fee off the top.

'Ah, happy days,' he sighed, his voice muffled by the handkerchief. 'Happy days.'

It was only when the final section of the road had been put into place, joining the easternmost point of the road to the westernmost end of Undertown, that Vox had discovered just how high a price he had had to pay for the shrykes' help. The first wagons had just begun to roll when a shryke army had swarmed down the road and seized the whole Great Mire Road for themselves.

Still, it could have been worse, Amberfuce conceded. The shrykes had taken control of the road to the Deepwoods, it was true, but at least he and Vox had still had the citizens of Undertown to squeeze for taxes. And squeeze they had. Amberfuce had become richer than ever, forcing the dealers and merchants to pay duty on the Deepwoods' materials the moment they entered Undertown; then again before they could take their merchandise – fine cloth, tools and weaponry – from the workshops of Undertown back out of the city. By the time they had paid off the shrykes as well, there had been barely any profit left. No wonder they had always been complaining.

Amberfuce had listened to the mutterings, the threats and curses. The mood had grown ugly. There had been talk of rebellion; of revolution; of the Undertowners rising up and overthrowing Vox. And at the head of this mob – inciting an uprising and sowing the seeds of discontent – had been the librarians, Sky curse them!

Amberfuce's brow furrowed. The librarians had been useful in building the Mire Road certainly, but afterwards they had begun getting above themselves. What was more, still believing in all the nonsense Cowlquape had preached about Undertowners and academics being equal, they had proved themselves to be as dangerous as they were foolish. They had had to be stopped.

Amberfuce gazed from the window at the Tower of Night on the crumbling rock, propped up by the scaffolding of the Sanctaphrax Forest.

It had been a good bargain. Even now, he still believed that. Amberfuce had overheard talk of a great meeting being held at the Chantry Palace; the grand riverside building the librarians had made their headquarters. The leading Undertown merchants would be there, as well as the entire librarian faculty. It was too good an opportunity to miss. The traitorous vermin could be destroyed in one fell swoop . . . But they would need an army of ruthless killers to carry out the deed.

Amberfuce turned away from the window. 'Orbix Xaxis and the Guardians of Night,' he muttered. Yes, it had been a good bargain. He'd convinced Vox of that.

'The sacred rock is sinking,' he remembered his master saying at that fateful meeting between him and his enemy, Orbix Xaxis. 'But I can stop it before it touches the earth. Just think of it, Orbix,' Vox had said. 'The thing you fear most; the sacred rock touching the ground – and I'm offering to prevent that.'

'How?' the voice had rasped from behind the metal muzzle.

'By designing a great cradle of wood – the Sanctaphrax Forest – to hold the sacred rock in place. You know I can do it, Orbix . . . If I so choose.'

'And if you build such a thing, what price would I have to pay?' Orbix had growled.

'Oh, you'll enjoy this,' Vox had chuckled, his three chins wobbling – for he had been growing fat even back then, Amberfuce remembered. 'All you have to do is slaughter the whole librarian faculty and their cronies, the merchants. I trust you can handle that, Xaxis, my dear fellow.'

Amberfuce shivered. Xaxis *had* handled that. His Guardians had surrounded the palace where the librarians had been holed up three nights later, and there had been a mighty slaughter. The streets around the great building had run red with librarian blood, and yet . . .

There always seemed to be an *and yet*, Amberfuce thought bitterly.

And yet, some librarians had managed to fight their way out and had disappeared down into the sewers, where they had remained, like piebald rats, to this very day.

'Sky bless the librarians,' smiled Amberfuce; for even now, they had their uses . . .

'Soon be with you, sweet'ums,' Flambusia called from the ante-chamber. 'The pot's just coming to the boil.'

Amberfuce coughed weakly. Herb tea was just what he needed to soothe his parched throat. He looked around. Now, did he have everything he needed? It would be a long journey . . . Yes, it was all here. Flambusia could sweep all his medicines into that great bag of hers in two seconds. Dear, sweet Flambusia. Of course, she must come with him. He couldn't possibly leave *her* behind. Oh, no! Though there were plenty of others he would be glad to see the back of . . .

General Tytugg for one.

Amberfuce remembered his first meeting with the wily old hammerhead thug. He'd been introduced by Amberfuce's business partner, Hemuel Spume of the Foundry Glade. Hemuel looked after the Deepwoods side of Amberfuce's operation – and highly profitable it had become, too.

'Meet Tytugg,' Spume had smiled. 'He's visiting Undertown from the Goblin Nations, and I think he might be just what you're looking for.'

Amberfuce had looked at Tytugg's battle-scarred face,

ears ragged with sword cuts; tattooed arms and dented armour. He'd been impressed.

Needless to say, getting rid of the librarians hadn't been quite the answer to their problems that Amberfuce had hoped. In fact, even without the librarians' influence, the population of Undertown had proven maddeningly unco-operative – and the Guardians had been demanding that work on the Sanctaphrax Forest begin at once. There had been walkouts and pay-demands and a downing of tools. It had all been bad for business.

Of course, Vox hadn't seemed to notice. He had been working on his drawings and blueprints, absurdly happy to have another great project underway. No, it had been down to Amberfuce, as usual, to make Vox's plans a reality. There had been only one thing for it . . .

A small tingle ran down the waif's puny back. 'Slavery,' he whispered.

Since the Undertowners hadn't been prepared to work voluntarily, they had to be made to work. They'd had it too easy for too long. Amberfuce had decided to turn them into slaves. To do that, though, he had needed slave-drivers; an army of slave-drivers.

'*I* have an army,' Tytugg had said, 'out in the Goblin Nations. And none of your rabble of tufteds and long-hairs either. These are trained hammerheads and battle-hardened flatheads. But I warn you, Mister High Chancellor, sir,' he'd added darkly. 'We don't come cheap.'

'Oh, there'll be plenty of money for all of us,' Amberfuce had laughed. 'Just get your army to Undertown and

I promise you healthy profits for your trouble.'

Over the next few weeks, hammerhead and flathead goblins had travelled down the Great Mire Road in twos and threes, disguised as tinkers and tailors, trappers and traders, and merchants of every description. The shrykes had never suspected a thing. The ghostwaif chancellor had been there to receive them all in Undertown, ticking off the numbers. Soon, there had been a great army of the goblins dispersed in every part of Undertown, laying low – until Amberfuce had given General Tytugg the signal to act.

The waif rocked in his chair, rubbing his long spidery hands together as he thought of it. *The Week of Blood!* Over the next seven days, every single Undertowner had been systematically rounded up. Those unable to work – the elderly, the infirm – had been slaughtered on the spot. The rest had been enslaved. They were to be forced to work on the Sanctaphrax Forest – but first, there had been mass graves to dig . . .

Amberfuce yawned. 'Ends and means,' he muttered, nibbling at a fingernail, more ragged than the rest. He smirked to himself. Vox had been happy with the way things had turned out. And he, Amberfuce, had made a mint!

And yet . . .

There it was again. Amberfuce stopped his rocking and let his hands fall limply in his lap. If only Tytugg hadn't been so greedy. He should have detected that greed in the goblin general when they'd first met. It had spoiled everything. Instead of being happy sharing the profits from the sweatshops and foundries, and supplying the Sanctaphrax Forest workforce, General Tytugg had wanted it all.

He had simply cut Vox and Amberfuce out of the loop. Then he had maintained the Forest *and* run Undertown single-handed. There had been rumours – Amberfuce had heard them – that Tytugg had wanted Vox's chain of office so that he could declare himself Most High Academe.

The cheek of it! he thought indignantly. An uncouth hammerhead from the Goblin Nations, Most High Academe! It was absurd! But he also knew Tytugg wouldn't stop until Vox, and he, were dead. Amberfuce shook his head. Those two goblin assassins had come perilously close . . .

And so, it had come to this. Vox was a prisoner in the Palace of Statues with a handful of faithful servants to watch over him and a series of traps and murder-holes to keep the goblins at bay. That might be all right for Hestera the poisoner, besotted with her master; and old

Speegspeel, stupid but faithful – but not Amberfuce. He had a fortune salted away with Hemuel Spume in the Foundry Glade, and no way to get to it.

Vox was finished. Undertown was finished. It was high time he looked out for himself.

Just then, Flambusia bustled back into the room, a steaming glass of herb tea held in one hand, a plate of wafer-biscuits in the other. She placed them both down on a tall, slender table and pulled Amberfuce's buoyant chair over beside it.

'There,' she said. 'Herb tea and a little treat. But first you've got to be good and take your special medicine.' She pulled a small glass bottle from her apron, unstoppered the cork and poured out a spoonful of dark red liquid. Then, having returned the bottle to the apron-pocket, she stepped towards him. 'Open wide!' she chirped.

I don't think so, Flambusia. Amberfuce's icy thought entered the nurse's head. *I need to keep my thoughts clear. So, no special medicine, not today. Understand?*

'Ambey, dear,' the nurse protested. 'Stop it, you know I don't like it when you . . .'

Understand, Flambusia? The waif's eyes narrowed and the barbels at the corners of his thin mouth quivered. *Clear away the clutter. Empty your mind . . . completely . . .*

Flambusia dropped the spoon and sank to her knees with a whimper.

Give me the medicine. The waif's thought numbed the inside of Flambusia Flodfox's head. She held out the bottle and a thin, spidery hand took it. *Now pack up the rest of my bottles – carefully, mind. Then take me to Speegspeel. I have one last little errand for him.* He looked at the medicine bottle in his hand and laughed, darkly.

The nurse's huge head nodded dumbly.

'Excellent,' Amberfuce said, smiling. 'And Flambusia, my sweet . . .' The nurse hesitated, her eyes blank and stony. 'Do hurry, for time is short.'

SLAD, SLASHTALON
AND STYX

i
The Goblin Army

'It's time, Slad, the phalanx is forming!' The gruff voice was followed by a booted prod to the legs. The swarthy hammerhead goblin looked up to see his comrade, Dunkrigg, staring down at him. 'Look sharp!' he grunted.

Slad sat up. 'I must have nodded off,' he muttered. He pulled himself stiffly to his feet and, still groggy from his short nap, reached for the heavy curved shield and distinctive horned helmet of the elite hammerhead guard. He strapped the helmet in place between his wide-set eyes and raised the shield to his shoulder. 'I'm ready,' he said.

Dunkrigg nodded.

Around them, packed into the large gloomy square,

were goblins of all shapes and sizes – squat, stocky gnok-goblins in simple armour; hefty flatheads carrying heavy clubs; tufteds and long-haired goblins armed with curved bows and bristling quivers of arrows; ridge-browed and lop-eared goblins, and saw-toothed goblins with their distinctive carved stabbing spears. Each one was inked, branded or ringed with the specific marks of his individual tribe: each one was ready for battle.

At their head, the hammer-head guards formed up into the awesome battle phalanx, two hundred wide and three hundred deep, their shields overlapping and forming an impenetrable wall.

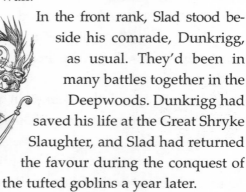

In the front rank, Slad stood beside his comrade, Dunkrigg, as usual. They'd been in many battles together in the Deepwoods. Dunkrigg had saved his life at the Great Shryke Slaughter, and Slad had returned the favour during the conquest of the tufted goblins a year later.

They were hammerheads. They lived for battle. Here in Undertown, however, life was far less dramatic. Here it was endless drill and the tedium of long hours in the Hive Towers, with only the occasional skirmish with a runaway slave or an errant factory-master to

look forward to. Tonight, however, would be different; tonight their enemy would have nowhere to run and nowhere to hide.

'Librarian scum,' growled Slad.

In front of him, the phalanx leader looked across to where General Tytugg stood on a raised stone plinth, waiting for an order. The general raised his curved sword.

'*Phalanx!*' he roared. '*Advance!*'

Slad grunted with approval as he fell into step with the others. No more drill, no more patrols, no more unsatisfying skirmishes. Finally the great battle they'd all been promised was about to begin. As the phalanx strode noisily out of the square and down the broad thoroughfare, Slad raised his head proudly. He liked the feel of his muscles, powerful and strong, as he marched. How they tingled, how they clenched; how they longed to be tested out in brutal armed-combat. He liked the weight of his armour, the solid tramping of his boots – and the fact that there were so many of them marching in step that the very ground trembled. Most of all, though, he liked the effect the great army was having on the inhabitants of Undertown.

As they marched past the ramshackle buildings, setting doors rattling and tiles falling, Slad caught sight of innumerable Undertowners woken from their sleep, peeking furtively from behind shuttered windows. Their faces were shot with confusion, with fear, with horror . . .

Slad chuckled to himself. This was more like it! Just like the old days, he felt invincible!

The phalanx turned left and was soon heading into a second square, smaller than the one the goblins had assembled in, and dominated by a huge arch. An open channel, running round the square and bubbling with water, flowed through the arch and cascaded down into the deep shaft beyond like a waterfall. With the sculpted flames on top of the arch and the rows of bars sealing the front, this was the infamous Great Eastern Entrance to the sewers beneath Undertown. The phalanx came to a halt in front of it.

'I don't understand, Slad,' Dunkrigg whispered from beneath the cover of Slad's raised shield. 'It's certain death to enter the sewers through the Great Eastern Entrance. Everybody knows that.'

Slad nodded. It was true. The barred entrance led through to a vertical drop where a torrent of water

poured down into a vast black tank – the so-called
Drowning Pool. Many goblins had perished there in an
attempt to enter the sewers – and the few who had made
it to the other side had been summarily dispatched by
the librarian guards. Not one of their number had ever
got through.

'So, what are we doing here?' hissed
Dunkrigg.

Slad shook his head. 'Don't know,
'Rigg, mate,' he said.

Just then General Tytugg strode up
from the rear, accompanied by a cowering goblin. They stopped in front
of a low trough behind which was a
tall curved obelisk, ornately carved
and with a dark plaque screwed
into the front.

Slad watched, bemused, as the
general motioned to the goblin,
who walked forward.
What was he up to?

Without saying a word, the goblin reached up and pressed the plaque firmly with both hands. There was a soft *click*, a grinding of stone on stone and the curved obelisk swung round to reveal a long dark shaft beneath it. The general motioned to the phalanx leader, who approached and received his orders before returning to the hammerhead guard.

The leader spoke to the front rank in a low voice tinged with urgency. 'The secret route into the sewers lies open to us at last,' he said. 'But the librarians are ingenious. The entrance is so narrow that we must enter it in single file. You, the front rank of the guard, have the honour of going first!'

Slad licked his lips and stepped forward, Dunkrigg behind, followed by the rest of the phalanx's front rank. At the entrance to the shaft, the phalanx leader thrust a blazing torch into Slad's hand.

Slad crouched down, shield over his shoulder, and gripped the torch firmly. Then, having kissed the carved bone amulet he wore at his neck for good luck, he stepped into the darkness. Instead of the ladder he was expecting, he found himself on a steep metal chute and, for a moment as he hurtled downwards, the flames of the torch flickered and threatened to go out.

After several long, unnerving seconds, his boots landed with a heavy thud on the floor below, and the flame once again flared brightly. Slad raised the torch in his hand, straightened up and stepped cautiously forwards. He was, he saw, in a vast underground vault with dark tunnels leading off in various directions.

Behind him, he heard the roaring of the water cascading down into the drowning-pool. In front, guarding the tunnel, was a large crossbow on a raised metal platform.

It seemed to be unmanned – but you could never be sure . . .

Slad moved cautiously forwards, plunging the flaming torch into every dark corner and shadowy alcove he came to. He didn't like this dark, dripping, subterranean cavern. It was no place for him, a hammerhead guard. It was a place for sewer rats – both piebald *and* academic . . .

'There's no point hiding,' he growled. 'I'll sniff you out wherever you are.'

Just then something moved to his left. He heard it, and saw it out of the corner of his eye. Drawing his sword, he spun round, lunged forwards – and sliced off the head of a scrawny piebald rat. Slad breathed out noisily and grinned with relief.

So far as he could tell, the place was deserted. He kicked the dead rat out of the way – just as Dunkrigg thudded down the chute behind him.

'It's all clear!' Slad called out over his shoulder, his voice echoing round the cavernous vault.

Almost at once, a third hammerhead appeared, followed by another, and another, as goblin after goblin slid down into the underground chamber. All round, the chamber soon echoed with coughs and grunts and shuffling of boots as the other goblins entered the vault and took up their positions; gnokgoblins, flatheads, tufteds, saw-tootheds . . . They hurriedly reformed themselves into their individual battalions and the phalanx rapidly resumed its shape.

Slad grinned. The battle was very close now. His temples throbbed with the blood coursing through his veins; his heart was beating wildly. Yes, it was just like old times. Beside him, he could sense a similar excitement in Dunkrigg who, eyes blazing, was licking his lips and clutching his shield with a white-knuckled grip.

Finally, the last of the goblin army passed through the narrow entrance and into the great vault. General Tytugg strode to the front, drew his sword and raised it high. He threw back his head as if to shout yet, when it came, his order to move was little more than a whisper.

'Phalanx, to battle!' His sinister words hissed round the glistening walls. 'Death to the librarians!'

ii
The Battle-Flocks

Perched high up on a jutting stanchion, Sister Slashtalon scratched at the feathery tufts beside her beak; with the weather so hot, the parasitic woodfleas were more active than usual. Her eyes, yellow and unblinking, bored down into the back of the armed goblin below her – one of the skeleton guard General Tytugg had left on the Undertown side of the Mire Road gateway.

He must have been gambling on the shrykes not noticing what he and the rest of his goblin army were up to, Sister Slashtalon thought, hissing with delight. He had gambled wrong.

Just then, behind her, she heard a low whistle. It was Sister Feathermane. She had reached her position at the bottom of the left tower. An answering call announced that Sister Beakscreech was also ready.

With a loud shriek, Sister Slashtalon launched herself off the stanchion of the Great Mire Gates and landed in goblin-controlled Undertown. The flathead guard spun round, a look of surprise etched into his brutal features. One hand flew to his sword; the other to his knife. Neither found their mark. Sister Slashtalon saw to that.

In one graceful move, she leapt up into the air and kicked out with her taloned feet. The razor-sharp claws slashed through the goblin's belly, ripping it open. Then, as he stumbled forwards, hands vainly grasping at his spilled guts, she struck him again. His neck snapped and his head was left hanging on by a knot of stringy tendons.

To her left and right, Sisters Feathermane and Beakscreech had dispatched their own guards with the same ruthless efficiency. More goblins were coming, swords drawn and clubs swinging – but it was already too late. Sister Slashtalon had unchained the great Mire Gates and pushed them open. A vast army of the bloodthirsty shrykes came pouring through and overwhelmed the hapless guards.

Mother Muleclaw – resplendent in purple and gold, sitting astride a huge, ornately-decorated prowlgrin – was at the head of the mighty flock. As the goblins were cut down all round her, she pulled on the reins and turned her prowlgrin round.

'Come, sisters!' she screeched. 'Tonight we shall feed on goblins' hearts and librarians' livers! You all know what you must do. Forwards, sisters! Forwards!'

Sister Feathermane gathered her battle-flock around her, as did Sister Beakscreech, and the pair of them set out towards the southern boom-docks. With low whistles and guttural clucks, Sister Slashtalon assembled her own battle-flock. They were to take the northern route to the boom-docks, seeking out and destroying any goblins they encountered on their way, for there must be none left who

might later try to cut them off. Having taken a final headcount of her squadron and issued last-minute instructions, Sister Slashtalon set off, while behind her the mighty Mire Gates were secured once more.

A motley collection of fledglings, their feathers still drab and downy, cowered in the shadows and chirruped their encouragement. Beside them, the weedy shryke-mates jangled their thin silver chains and squawked feebly.

Keeping close together, the squadron of shrykes left the Mire Road platform and entered Undertown itself. Once they hit the network of roads, they divided into smaller groups. At the head of each junction they came to, they split up again, inspecting the darkened narrow alleys and twittens in pairs – keeping in touch with each other with their reedy whistles and muted shrieks then reuniting at the far ends. Road by road, alley by alley, they inspected the whole area. Apart from the cowardly Undertowners peering out from the windows of their dilapidated dwellings, the shrykes saw no-one.

This part of Undertown, at least, was clear of any goblins. Sister Slashtalon was prepared to stake her life on it.

Their mission complete, the patrol-squadron headed along a narrow path between tall, wooden buildings which led down towards the Edgewater River. From there, where the West Wall of the city met the river, they made their way to the boom-docks.

Up ahead, Sister Slashtalon could see the other brightly coloured battle-flocks already milling about on

the muddy banks beside the jutting pipes; some dry,
some gushing water. And coming closer, she could make
out Mother Muleclaw herself, still perched atop her
battle-prowlgrin. As she got within earshot, Sister
Slashtalon realized the roost-mother was already
addressing the flock.

'... treacherous ... Do not stray ...' she was saying, her
words whipped away by the rising wind. Sister Slashtalon
trotted closer; the words became clearer. 'For the pipes are
not to be trusted,' Mother Muleclaw was saying. 'Some
lead to dead-ends. Many are booby-trapped ...'

Sister Slashtalon nodded. As one of the High Sisterhood, she had been present when that traitorous youth ...
What was his name? Rook ... When he had come amongst
them ...

She remembered his description of the sewer pipes
only too well. He'd explained how, in a system modified
by the librarians themselves, the pipes were operated by
a series of valves, each one opening or closing a different
sluice and directing the water in ever-changing routes. It
had kept them safe for years ... Not a single shryke had
ever breached this simple, yet deadly, defence.

The youth had told them something else, however.
Something crucial. Something which, even now, made
Sister Slashtalon's eyes glint with anticipation. He had
told them how, at ten hours that night, the librarians
would all be in the Great Storm Chamber Library,
attending some ceremony or other. From that moment
until the conclusion of the meeting, the valves would
remain untouched. Those already open would stay

open; those shut would stay shut. The shrykes would therefore be able to proceed safely through the network of pipes with no fear of being washed away and drowned. All they had to do was find a way through.

Sister Slashtalon raised her head and sniffed the air. The musty odour of fusty librarian emerging from the pipes made her tongue quiver. A smile passed across her face.

At Mother Muleclaw's screeched command, the shryke squadrons and battle-flocks proceeded into the pipes – keeping to the dry or almost dry ones. There was a gentle trickle coming from the pipe Sister Slashtalon led her shryke-sisters into. Although she hated the way the water swilled round the feathers between her claws, she knew that the running water would help lead them to their goal.

On into the pipes she took them, now left, now right, her keen eyesight and unerring sense of smell helping her to navigate the labyrinth of pipes. As she went, she heard water coursing through other pipes close by; fast gushing water that no-one could ever withstand – water that, if the valves were to change, would drown them in an instant and flush them back down to the mudflats of the boom-docks.

As she passed yet another of the valved-junctions – the torrent of water roaring behind it – Sister Slashtalon clucked, grateful that the treacherous youth's information had proved reliable. They were making good progress – as were all the shryke battle-flocks. One by one, they were emerging into a vast sub-chamber situated at the far western end of the Central Tunnel. Some were already beginning to explore the pipes and channels which led from it.

Mother Muleclaw raised her feathered arms and hissed for silence. 'Wait, sisters,' she called. 'Wait!'

Sister Slashtalon – about to try a tunnel for herself – paused, and fought down the disappointment which rose within her. Wait? When they were so close? It was almost too much to expect of them. Why, she could smell the librarians so clearly. She could almost *taste* them! Their plump, fatty hearts . . . Their tangy livers . . .

'We must not forget ourselves, sisters, for at the eleventh hour, the goblins will strike,' Mother Muleclaw continued. 'And we must let them. We shall let the predators catch their prey; for then, when they are done, the predators shall themselves become prey. *Our* prey! And we shall gorge upon them all!'

iii
The Guardians of Night

Orbix Xaxis, the High Guardian of the Tower of Night, was taking his time all right. The noon deadline had come and gone, and still the Purification Ceremony had not taken place. Now night had fallen, and Styx – a stocky gnokgoblin with tufted hair at his ears and a scar which passed down his cheek and over his jutting chin – was beginning to flag. Almost ten hours he had been waiting at his post, waiting for the signal to be given for the ceremonial cage to be lowered. Ten hours! He was beginning to wonder whether it would take place this day at all . . .

Just then – as far below him an Undertown bell rang out nine hours – Styx noticed a movement at the gantry-doors, and Orbix strode onto the gantry, his black gown flapping behind him. He sat up straight as the master stormed towards him. Behind the muzzle and dark glasses, it was impossible to tell what the High Guardian was thinking but the gnokgoblin didn't want to give the impression that he had been slacking.

'I asked for you, specially, Styx,' Orbix announced. 'I

want the cage descent to be as smooth and silent as
possible. Make sure everything's set accordingly.'

'Sir,' muttered the gnokgoblin, leaning forwards in
the raised seat at the top of the cage winching-gear. He
reeled in a length of surplus plaited rope and checked
the balance-weights.

Behind him, Leddix emerged onto the gantry, followed by two pairs of hefty flathead guards. Styx turned. Between the guards were the prisoners; two of them. One was a girl – pale and drawn, with sunken eyes and quivering lips, her plaits hanging limply onto her shoulders. The other was a youth. Thin. Wiry. Bruised. He was rubbing the side of his shaven skull tentatively. Styx recognized him; he was one of the High Guardian's special advisers. What was his name?

'Courage, Magda,' Styx heard him muttering as, flanked by the hulking guards, the two of them approached the cage. 'Don't give them what they want. You're better than they are, remember that!'

Orbix Xaxis turned towards them. 'You think so?' he sneered, and pushed his muzzled face into the youth's. 'You have disappointed me, Xanth,' he said, his voice hissing behind the muzzle. 'Disappointed me more than you will ever know.' He nodded towards Magda and tutted dismissively. 'It is a shame you have allowed your head to be turned by this librarian scum.'

Xanth lowered his head but said nothing.

'Yet even now, you still have a sporting chance. For it is the sweet meat of the librarians that the rock demons crave. If you ditch the girl, you might still manage to escape.' He chuckled. 'What will you do, Xanth? Abandon her and save yourself? Or stay with her and be eaten?'

Still Xanth remained silent.

Orbix grunted with irritation. 'Put them in the cage,' he cried. 'Let the ceremony begin.'

The pale girl and thin youth were bundled into the barred contraption which swayed precariously as the door was slammed shut and locked. The gnokgoblin's nostrils twitched.

Fresh meat, he thought. The rock demons *will* be happy.

The High Guardian raised his arms. 'Hail, the Great Storm!' he bellowed. 'Lower the cage!'

Styx seized the winding-levers and started turning. After an initial jolt, the cage began to go down, travelling slowly, smoothly and in complete silence – for, at the High Guardian's instructions, Styx had plaited strips of cloth into the winding-chain to muffle the tell-tale clanking sound of the cage's long descent. The rock demons should not be alerted too soon.

'Hail, the Great Storm! Hail, the Great Storm!' the chanting voices of the High Guardian, the cage-master and the four Guardians rang out.

Styx shuddered. He knew he had to be careful. Not only must the cage descend in silence but he also had to calculate the exact moment to apply the brakes. Too soon and the prisoners would drop down through the air. Too late and the cage could crash against the side of the canyon. Either way, the rock demons would be alerted before the prisoners had a chance to make a run for it. And that, as Orbix Xaxis had stressed, his eyes blazing behind the dark glasses, must not happen.

'Must get it right,' Styx murmured anxiously. 'Mustn't mess up.'

Leddix had whipped him so soundly the last time he'd made a mistake, he'd thought the flayed skin on his back would never heal. If he got *this* wrong . . .

'Hail, the Great Storm! Hail, the Great Storm!'

'Gently does it,' Styx whispered to himself, trying not to be distracted by the Guardians' chants as the cage below him began to swing in the rising wind. 'Mind that rock there. That's the way . . . A little lower. Just a little bit more . . .' He pulled the brake-lever and, as he looked down into the canyon below, sighed with relief. The cage had come to rest against a slab of rock, not fifty strides from the dark, jagged hole in the side of the canyon. 'Perfect,' he breathed.

Orbix, leaning over the balustrade, a telescope raised, monitoring the situation for himself, turned to the gnokgoblin. 'Open the cage,' he told him.

Styx reached up above his head, uncleated the plaited rope and tugged it hard. He heard a soft *click* below him and looked down to see the cage door swing open. Then as he continued to watch, scarcely daring to breathe, he saw the two figures emerge. They paused. They looked around, and for a moment Styx thought that they were about to split up . . .

'Come, Demons of the Deep,' Orbix Xaxis intoned. 'Come, now . . .'

Apparently deciding to stick together after all, the two ant-like figures set off, leaving the cage behind them. They can't have noticed the hole in the rock,

Styx noted, for they were heading away from it. He mopped his brow fretfully. It would be him who got the blame if anything went wrong . . .

The next moment, he noted something else; a tumbling of rocks; a wailing and screeching. Dark shapes were emerging from the depths of the canyon and slithering upwards towards the light.

The two figures must have noticed them too, for all at once, they were running. What was more, they had changed course. Abandoning their attempt to scale the side of the canyon, they were heading straight for the entrance to the tunnel.

'Excellent,' Orbix Xaxis purred, and Styx thought he could detect a smile behind the High Guardian's muzzle and dark-glasses. 'Run, run, as fast as you can,' he whispered.

'Hail, the Great Storm!' Orbix Xaxis cried out as, at the very same moment Xanth and Magda disappeared into the tunnel, a distant flash of lightning lit up the sky beyond the Edge. 'Hail, Demons of the Deep. Rid the Sky of its polluters, one and all!'

At that moment, the first of the dark shapes reached the shadowy hole. It paused, and sniffed round suspiciously. Others arrived behind it; a dozen, twenty, fifty . . .

Styx looked down to see the rock demons pouring into the tunnel. Their screeching had taken on a high-pitched intensity which, for all the torrid heat of the night, made the gnokgoblin's spine tingle icy-cold. Despite himself, he couldn't help hoping that the young couple might escape. Librarian or no, nobody deserved such a terrible fate.

He felt a hand on his shoulder. It was the High Guardian of Night himself, Orbix Xaxis. 'Well done, Styx,' he purred from behind the metal muzzle. 'With your skilful cage-craft, you have sealed the librarians' fate.'

·CHAPTER SIXTEEN·

THE STONE HEAD

R ook gripped his seat in anticipation. His old professor, Alquix Venvax, should have been sitting next to him, but his place was empty. Rook hadn't seen him since just before embarkation.

The barge gave a lurch to the right, then to the left. They were almost out of the sewers. Ahead, the other four barges of the Great Library fleet had already emerged from the sewer pipe into the strong current of the Edgewater River. Rook could just make out their crews rowing frantically against the current, bobbing and weaving in their desperate attempt to get up-river.

Although he had seen what had happened to the others, nothing could have prepared Rook for the sudden jolt as the choppy water struck the port side of the boat. It lurched violently, sending the cargo sliding to one side, the barge creaking and groaning in protest. Rook was soaked with water.

'Cut the buoyant-lectern net!' the barge-master cried out.

Several librarians jumped forwards, knives drawn. The net was cut and the lecterns were set bobbing about in the air above them. The vessel righted itself. Then, back in their positions, the librarians picked up their oars and brought the boat slowly round in the water until it was pointing upstream – all to the accompaniment of the barge-master's bellowed commands.

'Pull! Pull! Pull!' he shouted. 'Ten degrees to port . . . And pull! *Pull!*'

Slowly but surely, the barge began to make progress up the Edgewater River, following the rest of the fleet. It was hard work, though – for it wasn't only the currents the librarians had to contend with as they battled upstream, but also the strong headwind which tugged at the bobbing lecterns and threatened to drag the heavy barge back towards the endless falls at the Edge itself.

'*Pull! Pull! Pull!*' the barge-master commanded.

Rook breathed in deeply and looked around. The lights from the opposite bank glinted back at him. The fleet was keeping to the centre of the river where the

water was deepest. No-one wanted to run aground. Far, far ahead, the lofty towers of the Mire Gates were just visible. Rook felt a hand on his shoulder and looked up to see the Most High Academe looming above him.

'I see you have a spare seat,' he said. 'Do you mind if I sit?'

Rook shrugged. 'It was Alquix's place,' he said, 'but I lost sight of him as we boarded.

Cowlquape shook his head sadly. 'I feared as much, Rook, my lad,' he said, sitting down beside him.

'What?' Rook asked.

'He couldn't bring himself to leave his beloved library,' said Cowlquape simply.

'You mean he stayed behind, even though . . .' Rook felt tears sting his eyes as he thought of his kindly old professor.

'Yes, even though the eleventh hour approaches,' said Cowlquape. 'The goblins will already be entering the sewers. And the shrykes won't be far behind. Just thank Sky that *we* managed to get out in time.'

Rook nodded glumly and the pair of them stared up into the threatening sky. The dark clouds were writhing and squirming in the broken moonlight. 'We will make it, won't we?' he asked, turning to the Most High Academe.

Around them, the librarians groaned as they pulled on their oars to the barks of the barge-master.

Cowlquape continued gazing up at the sky. It was growing darker. 'According to Vox's calculations – he showed them to me himself – the dark mael-strom will strike at the eleventh hour precisely.'

Rook felt his stom-ach lurch uneasily, but it wasn't the motion of the barge that was unsettling him. There was something else nagging at the back of his brain. Something important that he couldn't quite put his finger on.

'Finest cloudwatcher the College of Cloud ever pro-duced,' Cowlquape was saying. 'Vox had it all. That's why I made him my deputy all those years ago. If Vox says the eleventh hour, then the eleventh hour it will be.'

'PULL! PULL! PULL!' The barge-master's cries grew ever more insistent.

'The Tower of Night, the Mire Road, the Sanctaphrax

Forest,' Cowlquape's hand gestured across the Undertown skyline. 'Say what you like about the fat wretch, but he's certainly left his mark.' The old professor looked down at his seal of office and fiddled with it distractedly. His eyes clouded over. 'Unlike some I could mention.'

Now it was Rook's turn to place a hand on the Most High Academe's shoulder. 'Don't do yourself down,' he said. '*He* left his mark on Undertown; *you* left your mark on people's hearts. I know which is more important.'

'Sky bless you, lad,' said Cowlquape, looking up with a smile. 'There were times in the dungeons of the Tower of Night when I doubted that.'

Rook shook his fist. 'Tower of Night, *pah!* Mire Road, *pah!*' He laughed, and Cowlquape joined in as Rook continued, 'Sanctaphrax Forest, *pah!* Vox's baby – *pah!*'

Cowlquape stopped laughing. 'Vox's baby?'

'Yes,' laughed Rook. 'His latest project – a great big sphere full of bloodoak acorns and phraxdust.'

'Phraxdust,' Cowlquape gasped, the colour draining from his face.

'It's horrible stuff,' Rook went on. 'I had a bit of an accident with it down in Hestera Spikesap's kitchen. A couple of specks of dust, a drop of water and *BANG!!* The explosion was colossal.'

'And he's packed a whole sphere full of the stuff,' said Cowlquape weakly. 'Sky above, suddenly it all makes sense. The fireballs, Rook! It must have been one of those that knocked you out of the sky. Vox has clearly been experimenting for quite some time.' His voice dropped. 'But I didn't think that even Vox Verlix was capable of such a thing. He's mad! Quite mad!'

'I . . . I don't understand,' said Rook unhappily as a wave of guilt washed over him. He'd had his own part to play in the feeding of the baby. But what exactly had he done?

'Don't you see, Rook?' said Cowlquape. 'If this "baby" of Vox's, packed full of phraxdust and bloodoak acorns, is as explosive as you say . . .'

Rook nodded.

'Then setting it off,' Cowlquape continued, 'could well trigger . . .'

'The dark maelstrom,' whispered Rook.

The lightning crackled as the clouds advanced. Far above in the sky, a white raven wheeled round and round.

'So *that's* how he could predict when it would strike,' Cowlquape murmured. 'Because he himself always intended to set it off. I've been such a fool, Rook, blinded by sky-charts and calculations . . .'

'It's not your fault,' said Rook. 'It's mine for not recognizing how dangerous Vox's baby actually was, and warning you all.'

'No, Rook,' said Cowlquape, rising from his seat. 'You couldn't be expected to know that. Few of us have ever been able to read Vox's dark mind, and those of us who have tried have failed miserably.'

Cowlquape collapsed, head in his hands, moaning softly. Rook leaped to his feet.

'What is it, Most High Academe?' he asked urgently. 'What is it?'

Cowlquape looked up, his face as pale and haggard as Rook had ever seen it. 'Vox insisted that the bander-bears carried him to the Mire Gates by ten hours,' he said, 'even though the maelstrom he predicted was due to strike at the eleventh. I thought nothing of it when I looked at those accursed charts and calculations, but now . . .'

'Now we know that he has the power to *cause* the dark maelstrom himself, and that we – the librarians – have arranged for him to be carried to safety!' Rook gasped.

'Yes,' said Cowlquape, gazing at the dark sky and fast flowing Edgewater. 'There's nothing to stop him launching his baby, creating the dark maelstrom, and destroying us all right now!'

'Oh, but there is,' said Rook grimly. There was steel in his voice. 'I'll stop it being launched – or die in the attempt.'

He jumped up from his seat and hurried to the side of the barge. He raised his arms.

'I'll meet you at the Mire Gates!' he called back. 'Earth and Sky willing!'

'No, Rook!' cried Cowlquape. 'I can't ask you to do this.'

'I must!' Rook cried, and he dived into the swirling Edgewater River.

Far above his head, the white raven let out a raucous shriek, turned in the air and soared off across Undertown.

'Good luck, lad!'

Cowlquape's quavering voice floated across the choppy surface of the river as the library fleet continued battling up-river towards the safety of the Mire Gates. Rook gritted his teeth. He'd need all the luck he could get.

He struck out for the far shore, praying that he might avoid the treacherous oozefish this time. After a few minutes his boots sank into the slimy bottom of the riverbed. Steadying himself and leaning into the current, Rook waded towards the bank. He emerged, quivering with exhaustion – yet there was no time to rest.

With a last glance back at the distant fleet, he dragged himself to his feet and up the muddy slope. In the distance, he could see the jagged outline of the Palace of Statues.

The shoreside buildings came closer, their lamplit windows showing him the way as the sky darkened. Rook darted down one of the narrow alleys. The palace, he calculated, must be some way to his right. He took a sharp turning, then another, and raced across a deserted square. At the far corner, he went through a narrow arch onto a broad, stately thoroughfare – and cried out with joy.

'Thank Sky!'

Looming up before him, the Palace of Statues was bathed in shadows and light. Pools of golden lampglow poured from every window, casting the statues on the balconies and the plinths on the walls outside in sharp relief. And from the top of the building a vast, circular beam shone up through the glass dome of the Leagues' Chamber, like a great chimney of light against the swirling clouds above.

'Just a little further . . .' Rook panted. 'Just a little bit more . . .'

At the palace at last, Rook dashed up the marble steps and hammered at the heavy oakwood doors with his fists. The thudding echoed loudly through the building inside, then faded away. There was no answer.

Rook groaned. Of course there was no answer, he realized. That was Speegspeel's job and, even as he stood there, locked outside, he knew that Speegspeel was high above in the Leagues' Chamber, preparing to launch the baby.

Darting back down the steps, Rook scurried round the building, checking the palace walls with every step he

717

took. It was only when he reached the back of the building, that he saw what he was looking for.

One of the statues at ground level had toppled to one
side and was leaning against the sheer, windowless reaches
of the lower wall. So long as it didn't slip, he should be able
to climb up it and onto the balcony above its weathered
head. From there, he judged, looking up, it shouldn't be too
difficult to find a route right to the very top.

The statue jolted as Rook climbed onto it. It was
slippery and unstable. Up over the statue's huge stone
knees he went, across to its waist and, using a fold in the
leaguesman's carved robes as a foothold, pulled himself
up onto the shoulders. From there he reached up again,
grabbed the bars of the balcony balustrade above his
head and hoiked himself up.

Below him, there was a loud *crash* as the massive
statue keeled over and smashed on the paving beneath.

Rook wiped his brow and looked up. Through the
thickening mist, he saw the statues. Hundreds of them.
In alcoves, on ledges, lining jutting buttresses and clinging to the sides of the wall . . .

He jumped across to the statue to his right, climbed up
over the stone body and onto a narrow ledge above it.

So far, so good.

He climbed up two more statues, arriving hot and
sticky on a narrow flying buttress where he paused for
breath. The mist had grown thicker still and swirled
round in the rising wind, which whistled through the
limbs of the statues and plucked at Rook's fingers as he
continued to climb.

Up, up, he went. There were still four storeys to go till he reached the Leagues' Chamber at the top of the palace. *Simenon Xintax. Farquhar Armwright. Ellerex Earthclay.* The plaques at their feet gave names to the statues he was climbing up: leaguesmen, all of them.

The stone knife and chisel clutched in his hands made Leandus Leadbelly – a former master of the Gutters and Gougers – particularly easy to climb. And yet, as Rook stood on top of his angular hat of high office, he was overwhelmed by a sense of sudden unease. The next moment, something happened.

The head moved.

Rook cried out, jumped up, and just managed to grab hold of the jutting leg of a pale yellow statue above his head. He heaved himself up onto the narrow ledge it was mounted upon, and looked back down, his heart hammering in his chest, as the leaguesman's head fell.

From behind, he felt something shoving him in the back. Something cold. Something hard . . . It was the pale yellow statue! What else could it be? And it was trying to push him off the ledge!

Arms flailing wildly in the air, Rook scrambled to one side and seized the arm of the neighbouring statue. Behind him, the pale yellow statue toppled forward and hurtled to the ground. At the same moment, there was a sharp *crack!* and the arm Rook was clutching came away in his hands, pitching him off-balance again.

With a cry of horror, he twisted round. He let go of the broken arm and, pinning himself back against the wall, peered down at the falling piece of carved stone as it

turned over and over in the thick air. There was a splintering crash as it landed and, as the mist cleared for a second, Rook saw the shattered arm lying amongst the broken pieces of the other statues he'd dislodged.

He breathed deeply and steadied himself, then looked up at the stretch still to go – and the statues he needed to climb to get there.

'They're not dead leaguesmen, they're statues,' he told himself, continuing the climb. 'That's all. Just lumps of stone.'

The mist swirled round his head, a noxious sulphurous brew that made his eyes water and his throat sting. At last, he reached a statue so near to the top that, once he had scaled it, he was able to climb across to the roof itself. Pulling himself up over the carved balustrade, he landed on the safety of the vast flat roof of the Leagues' Chamber itself.

He peered down through the windows of the glass dome. He saw the wooden scaffolding; he saw the circular platform with the spherical baby resting in the narrow cradle. But where was Speegspeel?

He hurried round the dome to where the panes of glass had been smashed. Looking down into the chamber, he saw a shattered circular table with a great stone head at its centre. His blood ran cold as the dead stone eyes met his. He was looking into the carved stone face of Vox Verlix himself.

Just then he heard the butler's rasping voice ring out. 'Time for baby to fly the nest. Old Speegspeel knows. He won't let the master down, oh no. Now's the time. The tenth hour . . .'

Rook peered down to see the butler approach the cradle and insert a funnel into the spherical case. The goblin reached for the water-bottle at his side, unplugged it and prepared to pour its contents into the funnel . . .

Rook bit his lip. One drop of water, that was all it would take – and baby would be launched into the sky.

'NO!' Rook bellowed, and jumped through the glass roof's jagged opening. He fell down through the air, legs pedalling wildly, and landed heavily on the shattered table.

Speegspeel swung round with a snarl, water-bottle in one hand, a knife in the other. 'What's old Speegspeel got to deal with now?' he growled. 'The kitchen slave, isn't it?' His red eyes narrowed.

Rook crouched and grasped the stone head at his feet. 'Drop the water-bottle, Speegspeel,' he commanded.

Speegspeel hesitated, then moved towards the funnel. Rook swung his arm in an arc and let go, grunting with effort. Vox's stone head flew through the air and smashed into the hapless goblin with a sickening crunch. Speegspeel crumpled to the floor with a whimper, the contents of the water-bottle emptying by his side.

'The statues got old Speegspeel,' he rasped. 'They got old Speegspeel in the end.'

His eyes fixed on those of the stone head for a moment, then glazed over to return their lifeless stare. Rook picked himself up and stumbled over to the cradle. He laid a hand on the smooth metal side of Vox's baby and looked down at the funnel jutting out from the casing. The hot, humid air was stifling. A drop of sweat fell from the tip of his nose and pattered on the inside of the funnel.

Rook stumbled back. 'What have I done?' he gasped.

As he spoke, there came an ominous rumble and a series of urgent clicks and creaks as the whole scaffolding seemed to shift about. Rook looked up anxiously. The next moment, there was a loud *crack*, and the horizontal beams which had kept the spring-mechanism closed, shot upwards with incredible force – and the baby was hurled from its cradle into the air, through the glass dome in a shower of falling glass, and on up into the night sky above.

For a moment, the air quivered with intense silence. Then . . .

A flash of blinding light and . . .

BANG!!!

The shock waves that followed the light struck with a battering rush of roaring wind. Roofs were torn away, buildings fell, statues plunged – and Rook was picked up and tossed back across the chamber . . .

As the dust finally settled, Rook scrambled to his feet. Dazed and frightened, he looked back at the sky through the hole in the glass dome. The light in the sky had shrunk in size, yet curiously seemed to be sucking everything inside itself as it grew smaller and more intense. Finally – as bright and tiny as a dazzling star – it disappeared completely, to be replaced with a spot of blackness as intense as the light it had followed.

Like a blot of ink, the dark spot grew and grew, spreading out across the sky. It turned the clouds black and cast the land below into absolute darkness. Huge fat raindrops began to fall. They landed heavily – all over Undertown, in the courtyard of the Palace of Statues,

through the broken panes of glass in the dome . . .

The next moment it was as though the sky had turned to a mighty river. The rain became torrential, cascading from above. It was, Rook thought as he scurried for cover, like being beneath a great waterfall.

Down below him, he saw that the courtyard was already awash with water, like a great lake lapping at the fallen statues. And if it was this bad here, what must it be like for the library fleet on the Edgewater? Would any of them make it to the safety of the Mire Road?

'Earth and Sky protect you,' he murmured softly. He turned towards the door and waded across the flooded chamber. 'Earth and Sky protect us all!'

CHAPTER SEVENTEEN

BLOODBATH ON THE BLACKWOOD BRIDGE

The High Guardian gripped the balustrade of the upper gantry and craned his bony neck upwards. From inside his metal muzzle came the sound of sniffing.

'It is time,' he murmured. 'It is time.'

Even now, as he stood surveying the boiling cauldron of the sky, the rock demons would be infesting the sewer-tunnels in search of librarian flesh. The sewers would be cleansed, and the Great Storm would come to heal the sacred rock.

'It is time.' Every muscle in Orbix's body tensed.

Below, the jutting gantries were crowded with silent Guardians gazing up at the heaving sky. Above them, the great swirling cloud banks that had circled Undertown for months had merged into one monstrous formation like a vast and mighty anvil. The air was so thick and heavy that even breathing had become difficult.

Suddenly a low moan rippled through the crowded gantries. Orbix looked down. A great fireball was slicing through the thick air, arcing up over Undertown and heading for the centre of the mighty anvil.

From inside the metal muzzle, there came a gasp. 'Sky be praised,' he breathed.

The fireball disappeared into the midst of the swirling cloud and, for a moment, there was an unearthly silence. The air burnt the High Guardian's lungs as he took a rasping breath.

Suddenly, from the very heart of the anvil, a cataclysmic explosion ripped across the sky – first dazzling white, then black as pitch. Deafened by the tumultuous percussion of the mighty thunderclap, Orbix raised his arms up high.

'Hail, the Great Storm!' he screeched.

'Hail, the Great Storm! Hail, the Great Storm!' The chorus of voices echoed round the Tower of Night. 'Hail, the Great Storm!'

All round, the black cloud fizzed and crackled with tendrils of lightning which zig-zagged off in all directions, a network of fiery veins, dazzling and jagged. As each individual lightning-bolt faded, so the deafening thunder rumbled across the sky, like a mighty hammelhorn stampede.

'Midnight's Spike!' Orbix Xaxis bellowed above the barrage of noise. He looked up from the upper lookout-platform at the figure of Mollus Leddix, poised on the spike-ledge, waiting for the command. 'Raise the spike!'

Leddix raised his hand in assent, and crouched down next to the winch-mechanism. Observing him from below, Orbix was struck in the face by a huge raindrop. As he wiped it away with his sleeve, another clanged against his muzzle – followed by another, and another.

Within moments, the rain had become torrential and the anvil had flattened out into a huge swirling disc above the Tower of Night, like the wheel of some huge wagon. Tendrils of lightning flickered and crackled round its rim.

'Hail, the Great Storm!' shouted the Guardians excitedly. 'Hail, the Great Storm!'

There was no time to lose. The healing power of the lightning had to be harnessed. Orbix brought a fist down heavily on the balustrade.

'Faster, Leddix!' he bellowed. 'Faster!'

Leddix cursed beneath his breath as he worked the winch-mechanism. This should have been that pasty-faced whelp Xanth's job, not his! The spike rose slowly from its oiled sheath and up into the boiling air.

Leddix fought to catch his breath.

'Nearly there,' he gasped. 'Nearly . . .'

Clang!

The spike was fully extended, the winch-mechanism straining beneath his hands. Leddix reached out for the deadbolt, hanging from a hook beside him. His hand grasped at thin air.

'What's this?' he yelped, straining to keep the winch handle from spinning back with his other hand while he felt around beneath the hook. 'It can't be . . .'

The deadbolt – long, pointed at one end and decorated with the gleaming head of a gloamglozer at the other – was gone. Leddix threw his head back, the rain splashing against his snarling face.

'Sky curse you, Xanth Filatine!' he roared.

Unable to hold the heavy mechanism for more than a moment without the deadbolt, Leddix's arms gave out. The winch-handle slipped from his sweating hands and rattled noisily back. Above him, the spike slid slowly down into the sheath.

Clang!

The sky crackled and flashed. The muzzled figure of the High Guardian appeared on the spike-ledge, his arms flailing in a demonic fury.

'I said, raise the spike! Leddix!' he screamed above the deafening thunderclaps. He grasped the cowering cage-master with claw-like hands and thrust his muzzle into his white face.

'C . . . c . . . can't,' Leddix whimpered. 'The . . . the . . . deadbolt . . . G . . . g . . . gone!'

'Then so are you!' the High Guardian's voice rasped through his muzzle. The claw-like hands tightened their grip as the High Guardian raised the struggling Leddix high above his head, and threw him from the Spike-Ledge. The cage-master's scream was drowned out by another huge clap of thunder.

'*Hail, the Great Storm! Hail, the Great Storm!*' Below, the Guardians' cries were reaching fever-pitch.

Above the great tower, the clouds were swirling like a vast cauldron of inky stew stirred by a great ladle. The lightning bolts converged, twisting together into a knot of fizzing light.

'*Hail, the Great Storm . . .*'

There was no time to winch the spike up from its sheath, Orbix realized, but he could not let the storm simply pass by. With a howl of rage and desperation, he leaped onto the top of the winching-mechanism and stood up, arms outstretched.

At that moment, the storm exploded with a sudden blinding flash. A single lightning-bolt – coiled and charged – hurtled down from the raging maelstrom above. It sliced through the black air like a mighty spear.

'Hail, the Great Storm!' Orbix cried out. 'Hail . . .'

The lightning struck – and with such violence that the Tower of Night shook from top to bottom, sending walls crashing and gantries falling. Guardians toppled, screaming, from their perches through the blue, flashing air. And as the mighty power of the lightning held everything momentarily in its deadly embrace, the wooden tower smouldered, the diseased rock it stood upon crackled and oozed – and from high above, Orbix Xaxis, High Guardian of the Tower of Night, let out a terrible unearthly scream . . .

*

'Do you think we've lost them?' Magda whispered.

Xanth knelt beside her in the small sewer pipe above the Southern Transverse. 'I'm not sure,' he said. 'I . . .' He hesitated. 'I think so.'

He was drenched in sweat. There had been times, with the rock demons scuttling after them, when he'd thought they wouldn't make it. But Magda, Sky bless her, had been as diligent about her sewer studies as everything else. She'd sought refuge in the narrowest, most awkward pipes in the system whilst their bigger pursuers had shrieked their frustration in the larger pipes behind. And now they'd emerged, just as Magda had promised they would, above the Southern Transverse, just in sight of the Central Tunnel and the entrance to the Great Library itself.

'What's that?' whispered Xanth.

Magda frowned. She'd noticed it too. From up ahead, there came a low, regular, pounding noise, overlaid with a strange jangling, like the clatter of metal. They both listened. Xanth turned to Magda, his face ashen grey.

'What *is* it?' he whispered.

Magda shook her head nervously. They couldn't go back – not with the rock demons behind them. She seized Xanth's hand and together the pair of them advanced towards the end of the transverse tunnel. Water trickled past beneath their feet.

At the junction with the Central Tunnel, they stopped again and peered out. Pouring from the mouth of a steeply sloping pipe ahead, into the Central Tunnel itself, were goblins – flatheads, tufteds, longhairs and, massing at the east doors of the Great Storm Chamber Library itself, the metal-clad ranks of the hammerhead guard.

'A goblin army?' Magda gasped, her hand shooting up to her mouth in horror. 'At the door to the Great Library?'

'Goblins to the front, rock demons behind,' Xanth whispered. 'We're trapped!'

Magda crumpled to her knees, her head in her hands. Silent sobs convulsed her body. 'It's over, Xanth.' Magda's voice was thick with tears. 'I can't go on.'

'But you must,' came a frail voice behind them. Xanth spun round, his fist raised – but Magda grasped his arm as an elderly librarian stepped out of the shadows.

'Alquix? Is that you?' Magda rushed to the professor and embraced him, her sobs returning.

'There, there,' said Alquix kindly, stroking her head. 'I feared we had lost you, just like Rook, but now I find you have returned – just as he did.'

Magda's sobs ceased, and she drew back. 'You mean Rook is alive?'

'Yes, my dear young librarian,' said Alquix. 'And not only is he alive, but thanks to him, our Great Library has been saved from these barbaric hordes.'

'I . . . I don't understand,' Magda began, but Alquix silenced her with a raised finger.

'There'll be time enough for explanations when you join the librarians at the Mire Gates,' he told her. 'But you must hurry. Already the sewers are beginning to flood.'

Xanth looked down at his feet. It was true. In just the short time they'd been standing in the narrow tunnel,

the trickle of water at their feet had turned to a steady stream. Alquix stepped up to the pipe's entrance and peered out.

'You there, lad,' he said, addressing Xanth directly for the first time. 'Do you think you and Magda here can make it across the Central Tunnel to that small culvert over there? It will take you to a little sewer grate up in East Undertown.'

Xanth looked. 'But the goblins!' he said. 'We'll be in plain view of the library entrance . . .'

'You leave the goblins to me, lad,' Alquix told him. 'Just make sure you both make it to the Mire Gates. The library has need of brave young librarians if it is to make it to the Free Glades.'

'Alquix, no!' Magda embraced the old professor again. 'We can't leave you here.'

Alquix pushed her gently away. 'I am old,' he said, smiling sadly. 'I've spent the best part of my life there in the Storm Chamber Library. Why, I helped build the Blackwood Bridge with my own hands before you were born. I cannot leave it, even now.' Tears were streaming down the librarian's face. 'Now, go!'

With that, he pushed past them and strode down the Central Tunnel towards the library entrance, raising his staff as he did so and bringing it clanging down against the walls.

'Long live the Great Storm Chamber Library!' he roared at the massed ranks of goblins before him.

Behind him, unnoticed, two figures – one hunched and supported by the other – slipped across the Central Tunnel and into a small culvert on the other side.

'Seize him!' General Tytugg's command rang out from the doors to the Great Library, which were being pounded by a huge battering-ram.

A phalanx of tufted goblins surrounded the old librarian, their razor-sharp spears at his throat. A thick-set hammerhead guard barged his way through the crowds still pouring into the Central Tunnel and seized Alquix, lifting him bodily above his head and carrying him back towards the library doors. Tytugg smiled as Alquix was dumped roughly at his feet.

'Our first librarian,' he sneered, turning to the ranks of sweating hammerheads, the huge battering ram poised to strike the library doors raised high above their heads.

'The rest of his kind are cowering behind these puny doors. We shall reunite him with them! He shall be our battle banner!'

He clicked his fingers and two flathead standard-bearers leaped forwards and grabbed Alquix roughly, strapping the frail figure to a long carved pole with a hover worm crest.

'Attack!' roared the general as the old librarian was hoisted high above the seething mass of goblins.

The hammerheads surged forwards, swinging the battering ram with incredible force against the library doors, which splintered like matchwood.

'Victory to the goblins!' Tytugg roared.

'Victory to the goblins!' the great army roared back as it poured into the Storm Chamber Library. 'Victory to the goblins!'

In front, the hammerhead guard marched forward, their shields interlocking in a solid wall, Alquix held high on the hover worm standard in their midst. They thundered across the Blackwood Bridge as, above and below them, the tufteds and longhairs swarmed onto the gantries and over the Lufwood Bridge, their ranks bristling with spears and crossbows.

Tytugg and his captains stepped through the shattered gates and surveyed the scene.

'I don't understand it,' the general muttered. He looked up at Alquix. 'Where are the librarians?'

A thousand goblin eyes turned to the old librarian. For a moment there was utter silence. Then Alquix's thin, reedy laugh rang out.

'They are safe!' he cackled. 'The library has been saved! Long live the Great Library . . .'

Just then, there was a blur of movement from one of the jutting gantries overhead and a flash of yellow and blue whistled down through the air. Then another. And two arrows buried themselves in the old librarian's heart.

Dumbstruck, the goblins stared at their standard in disbelief as Alquix's head slumped and blood poured down his chest.

'Shryke arrows,' the standard-bearer roared, brandishing a fist at the upper gantry opposite. 'And they came from up th . . .'

Before he could finish his words, a brightly tufted arrow embedded itself in his neck. He fell to his knees, blood gurgling from the gaping wound . . .

'What treachery is this?' General Tytugg's voice echoed round the great chamber. 'Take out the shryke scum on the gantries!'

As if responding to the general's commands themselves, shrykes suddenly appeared on every upper gantry, helmets and breastplates gleaming. They screeched loudly, raised their bows and the air hissed with the sound of flying arrows. At the far end of the

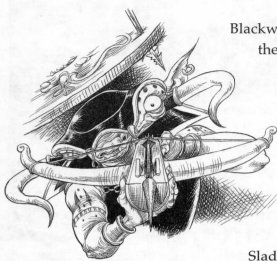

Blackwood Bridge, Slad the hammerhead fell to his knees and pulled the crossbow round from his back.

'Cover me,' he hissed to his comrade.

Dunkrigg raised his shield.

Slad primed the crossbow and looked through the sight. The plump gaudy chest of a brightly-coloured shryke appeared behind the cross of the viewfinder. Slad smiled and squeezed the trigger.

The bolt found its mark. The shryke's chest exploded in a flurry of feathers and blood. The bird-creature toppled off the gantry, hurtled down through the air and landed with a sickening *crunch* on the Blackwood Bridge.

'First blood!' Slad cried. He raised his crossbow a second time, taking care to remain behind Dunkrigg's shield as a volley of shryke-arrows flew in from all sides.

He ratcheted the bow-string back. He took aim. He pressed his finger gently against the trigger, and . . .

All at once, the great doors at the west end of the bridge flew open. Slad gasped. In front of the phalanx of hammerheads, pouring in through the west doors, were shrykes. Hundreds of them. Each one armed to the teeth and massing into flailing, screeching battle-flock formations.

From behind the shield wall, Slad braced himself and drew his sword; a magnificent two-handed hookblade.

'By Sky, old Cleave-in-Twain, you shall drink shryke blood tonight!' he said.

Around him, the other hammerheads in the phalanx drew their serrated blades and muttered battle oaths of their own. In front, the battle-flocks surged forwards like a cresting wave about to break on the solid bank of shields. The shrykes were armed with bows and arrows, pikes, whips and flails – but Slad knew it was their glinting beaks and gleaming talons he had most to fear from.

The shryke wave hit the shield wall and recoiled with a deafening howl, splatters of vivid shryke blood showering the front ranks. Here and there, ahead of Slad, hammerheads sank to their knees with low groans and the same look of shock and slow astonishment as they discovered that the blood pouring down over their breastplates was their own; their necks talon-slashed.

'Come, Dunkrigg,' growled Slad, advancing to plug the gap. 'Here they come again!'

Another battle-flock broke against the hammerhead phalanx – and tore it apart.

Slad found himself staring into a pair of yellow eyes as, either side of him, his comrades' severed heads shot high up into their air and their bodies crumpled to the floor, staining the Blackwood boards red. Dunkrigg lunged forwards, his shield deflecting the razor-sharp talon that was inches from Slad's throat.

With a roar of rage, Slad swung Cleave-in-Twain at the huge shryke battle-sister looming over him. The brightly plumed shryke swerved left and Cleave-in-Twain beheaded her flail-swinging companion behind.

From over his shoulder, Slad heard Dunkrigg groan and he turned to see his comrade's breastplate punctured and spurting blood. The shryke battle-sister's beak dripped with his blood as she rounded on Slad.

'NO!' he howled, blind with fury. He swung Cleave-in-Twain so hard and so fast that he sliced the bird-creature in two before her deadly beak could strike again.

He glanced down at Dunkrigg, his friend. He was already dead. Now Slad wanted revenge.

'*WHOOOAAAAA!!!*' he roared, striding forward.

With a piercing shriek, Sister Slashtalon leaped up and lashed out with her heel-talons. An expression of utter bewilderment spread across her flathead opponent's lumpen features as he looked down to see his breastplate sliced in two, blood pouring from it. Sister Slashtalon stepped forwards and savagely shoved him with her pike. The goblin keeled over the balustrade of the Blackwood Bridge and into the rapidly rising water.

'More! More!' she growled, a loop of drool hanging from the edge of her beak. The hunger was coming upon her.

Out of the corner of her eye, she saw a flash of steel as a long-haired goblin swung a great ball-and-chain at her head. Sister Slashtalon drew back and spat, venomously.

The green bile splattered into the long-haired goblin's face with a soft hiss. 'My eyes!' he screamed. 'My eyes!'

Slashtalon brought her beak sharply down, splitting the goblin open from sternum to stomach. With a jerk of her head, she plucked out the still-beating heart and swallowed it whole. Yes! Sister Slashtalon shuddered, her feathers standing on end; the hunger *was* upon her!

A huge hulk of a hammerhead goblin stormed towards her. His entire body was covered in blood; the blood of others. Sister Slashtalon reared up, talons bared, and stood her ground.

Slad's eyes were rolling; froth bubbled at the corners of his mouth. He stared at the vicious, blood-spattered bird-creature through a raging haze of crimson.

'*WHOOOAAAAA!*' he roared, hurling himself at the shryke, Cleave-in-Twain clasped in his bloodied hand.

Slashtalon leaped for-wards, all four sets of talons slashing at once.

They met in mid-air at the very centre of the Blackwood Bridge with a horrifying *crash*.

At the east doors, the remnants of the hammerhead guard had clustered round Tytugg. At the west doors, the ragged remains of the battle-flocks squawked and flapped around Muleclaw's banner. On the bridge itself, the mounds of dead covered the boards and, in places, rose above the balustrades. Below, the central sewer was fast flooding; the Lufwood Bridge was already submerged and goblins and shrykes alike clung to the lower gantries as the waters rose.

Slad's roar and Slashtalon's shriek intermingled as, for a moment, they stared into each other's eyes. Cleave-in-Twain was embedded in Slashtalon's gizzard as deeply as her talons had sliced into Slad's throat. Slowly, gently, the hammerhead and the shryke-sister sank to their knees where they remained, motionless, in their deadly embrace.

An eerie silence fell across the Blackwood Bridge.

High above the bloodbath, dark creatures appeared at the cracks in the vaulted roof and crawled through into the chamber. There, black against the white stone, they clung on upside down and sniffed the rich air, their eyes glowing. Calling to one another, they were joined by more, and more; pouring in through every crack and spreading out across the ceiling.

Suddenly, as if to some unheard command, the entire flock of rock demons launched itself from the ceiling as one and spiralled down through the air on leathery wings.

Across the bridge, goblin stared at shryke, and shryke at goblin. They all looked up as, like a black curtain falling on a red stage, the rock demons landed.

CHAPTER EIGHTEEN

THE GHOSTS OF SCREETOWN

Past rows of statues Rook ran, hurtling down the palace stairs two at a time. From outside came the distant crash of stone against stone as the deluge stripped the outer walls of their statues. He thudded down onto the final landing, skidded round – and stopped dead in his tracks. Hestera Spikesap was hurrying across the marble hallway below, heading for the staircase.

Rook took a step back and knocked into a statue which rocked on its base, then toppled forward, taking three of its companions with it.

'Hestera! Look out!' he shouted as the statues hurtled down towards the marble floor.

The old goblin didn't look up. Nor, as the statues shattered on the floor in front of her, did she miss her stride. She reached the stairs and began climbing. Rook noticed that she'd lost her bonnet. Her balding, scabby scalp glistened and her clothes were wet.

'I'm coming,' she crooned, as if soothing an infant. 'I'm coming, my sweetness . . .'

She brushed past Rook, her small red eyes looking right through him, and continued up the staircase. In her arms, she cradled a large red bottle, with a label marked *Oblivion: Special Vintage.*

Without looking back, Rook raced down the last flight of stairs to the marble hallway, almost losing his footing on the wet, slippery floor. Water was bubbling up from the kitchen door and spreading across the hall. Sodden recipes, pots, pans and potion bottles bobbed on its surface. Rook looked down as a green bottle marked *Retching Cordial* floated past.

He splashed across to the great woodoak door and seized its handle. From behind it came the sound of hissing which, as he pulled, grew to a mighty rushing roar.

A torrent of water rushed into the hallway from the street outside, knocking Rook back across the floor and drenching him to the skin. Above him, the statues on the staircase were toppling in twos and threes, splashing into the swirling water. Rook staggered to his feet and fought his way back to the door and out into the street.

The rain was like nothing he had ever seen before. It was torrential, a deluge; falling so hard and so fast that it resembled myriad silver wires, strung out taut between the ground and the boiling clouds overhead. And, as the tempestuous wind thrashed and spun, so the raindrops merged to form rippling, shifting sheets of water which slapped at the sides of the buildings and slammed down into the rising floodwater below.

'Sky guide and watch over me,' Rook muttered grimly as he waded through the ankle-deep water.

The rain forced him to lower his head protectively as it hammered down on his skull and shoulders, and ran down the back of his neck. Raising an arm against the battering downpour, he tried to take his bearings. Undertown had been transformed, its streets and alleys now deep canals of swirling, muddy water. In the distance he could just make out the towers of the Mire Gates peeking up above the muted skyline.

Had the library fleet made it? he wondered.

As he battled through the flooded streets, he became aware of other shapes, blurred and indistinct through the shimmering curtain of rain. They were ahead and behind him, in the alleys and lanes on either side; all moving along in a growing procession in the same direction as himself.

'Undertowners,' Rook murmured.

Just above his head, a whirring noise made him look up. A white shape, a blur of movement, shot from one

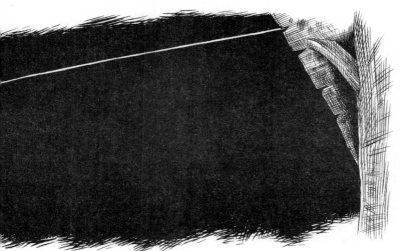

sloping roof to another on the other side of the street. A piercing whistle cut through the roar of the rain and was answered by three more from further up the street.

Rook waded on, finding a brief respite from the lashing rain behind the massive forms of a party of cloddertrogs.

'The Mire Gates – we'll be safe there, Duldug,' one called to his neighbour. 'The Ghosts of Screetown'll guide us, don't you worry.'

'What did you say?' Rook cried out, unable to conceal his excitement.

The cloddertrogs ignored him, pressing on through the downpour, and Rook was jostled from behind as other Undertowners brushed past him impatiently. He was in the middle of a vast crowd now and had to struggle to stay on his feet as it surged forwards. Just to one side of him, a gnokgoblin, a young'un in her arms, stumbled and let out a cry as she lost her balance.

Before Rook could do anything, a white figure swept down from a rooftop opposite. It landed with a splash, and grabbed mother and child. Rook could make out a bleached muglump-leather jacket, patched and mended, a white ratskin hat and a grappling-hook clutched in a white, bony hand.

'Run along now and take care,' the figure said, setting the gnokgoblin safely down.

'Bless you, sir,' murmured the gnokgoblin. 'Bless you.'

Rook stared open-mouthed at the figure before him. 'You're . . . you're one of them . . .' he spluttered, fighting against the force of the crowd. 'A ghost of Undertown.'

For an instant, the figure turned towards him and Rook saw the weather-beaten face of a mobgnome with piercing blue eyes looking into his own.

'Just keep moving, lad,' the mobgnome smiled, sending the grappling-hook arcing through the air with one graceful sweep of his arm. As the hook clanged onto a rooftop, the ghost pulled the rope taut and swung up through the air as if fired from a catapult, riding its springing recoil.

'Wait!' Rook called. 'I have a friend, Felix. Perhaps you . . .'

The ghost disappeared over the rooftops.

'. . . know him.'

Ahead, the street opened up into a square and, through the flapping sheets of torrential rain, Rook could see the Mire Gates looming up before him. The huge crowd was streaming into the square from all corners of Undertown. Groups of cloddertrogs, families of gnokgoblins, artisans and merchants; former slaves – all guided by the whistles of the ghostly white figures who

stood out against the black silhouettes of the rooftops all around.

A cloddertrog matron, swathed in a black raincloak, paused for a moment to check that her brood of young'uns was keeping up. A fearful-looking lugtroll – a gash down one cheek and nursing a swollen arm – hurried past her, muttering under his breath, 'Curse you, Tytugg. Curse all hammerheads!' Behind him came a stooped rheumy-eyed gnokgoblin who was being guided by her granddaughter, a youngster with stubby waxen plaits, a broad nose, and clutching a wrapped sword to her chest.

At the square, the Undertowners jostled against the Mire Gates, causing them to sway back and forth – and from behind them came the trilling and squawking of shryke-mates and fledglings.

As Rook eased himself through the seething crowds, he craned his neck to get a better view. He had to get to the jetty that lay just on the other side of the Mire Gates – for there, where the Edgewater River met the mudflats of the Mire, he hoped against hope that he would find the library fleet, safe and waiting for him.

From overhead came whirring sounds followed by sharp thuds as grappling-hooks struck the wood of the Mire Gates. In an instant, high up at the top of the gates, the white Ghosts of Screetown appeared. They stood there for a moment, swaying slightly before dropping down, as one, on the other side.

For a moment, the cheers of the Undertowners mingled with the piercing shrieks and cries of shryke-mates and fledglings. Then the huge gates slowly swung back.

Rook was carried forward as the crowd burst through the gates and spread out across the vast wooden platform beyond. He looked up and gasped at the sight of the Mire Road snaking out into the endless white mudflats before him.

Here on the other side of the gates, the rain was merely a light drizzle and the Undertowners broke up into excited groups; some dancing little jigs of celebration, some hugging each other, while others simply slumped to their knees and gave thanks. To his right, Rook could see a walkway winding down from the platform to the Edgewater Jetty.

He glanced back, and his heart lurched in his chest as he saw the Undertown skyline crumbling beneath the swirling black cloud of the dark maelstrom and its impenetrable sheet of rain. In the far distance, despite the deluge, the Tower of Night blazed like a mighty torch, the flames fed by great forks of lightning which crackled about it. It was a scene out of a nightmare; a nightmare that he, Rook, had unwittingly brought about.

For a moment, he forgot about the library fleet and sank to his knees. He had fed Vox's baby, the terrible fireball, with his own hands. Worse than that; it was he – *he*, Rook Barkwater, who had done everything to prevent it – who had triggered the dark maelstrom. His fists pounded the boards of the Mire Road with a mixture of fury, misery and despair. Above him, a white raven swooped low and hovered, letting out a raucous cry.

'Waaaark!' it screeched. 'Rook. Greetings!'

Rook looked up as the white raven landed beside him.

'Gaarn,' he said, managing a weak smile. He wiped his eyes. 'Is Felix with you?'

'Never far behind!' came a familiar voice and Felix – tall, powerful, clad in white muglump leather – strode across the platform, flanked on either side by Ghosts of Screetown.

'Oh, Felix!' Rook cried, and leaped to his feet. 'So much has happened since we last met!'

'So it has, Rook, my friend,' laughed Felix, clamping an arm round Rook's shoulder. 'Undertown is finished. Our future – yours and mine, and all these brave souls' – lies out there.' He gestured with a sweep of his arm. 'In the Free Glades!'

A cheer went round the crowd that had gathered about them.

'But you don't understand,' Rook said miserably. 'This is all my fault. I could have prevented this terrible storm, but I failed. Not only that, but . . .' He bit his lip as tears welled up again.

Felix patted Rook's shoulder, a look of concern clouding his features. 'I can't pretend I understand you, Rook, but I can see this has hit you hard. It can't have been easy down there in the sewers when this storm struck. Did any other librarians make it out alive?'

Rook started back. The librarians! He spun round and started running towards the walkway that led to the Edgewater Jetty. 'They made it out of the sewers in a fleet of library barges, and onto the Edgewater,' he called back over his shoulder. 'I said I'd meet them here at the Mire Gates, if . . .' – he stopped and slowly turned round – '. . . we survived.'

Felix turned to the white raven which now nestled in its familiar position on his shoulder. 'Gaarn,' he said. 'Go, seek and return!'

With a cry, the white raven launched itself into the air and wheeled round, heading off towards the dark skies over the Edgewater.

'Come, Rook,' said Felix, pointing towards the walkway, his voice choked. 'You have an appointment to keep.'

Rook looked down from the balustrade and shuddered. On his sky-patrols, he was used to seeing the sluggish Edgewater snaking its way through the channels of mud. Tonight, however, it had grown so broad and so deep that it raged and frothed below him, threatening at any moment to pluck the support-beams away and hurl the whole jetty into the perilous waters.

Sick with worry, Rook scanned the river, the bank, the raised walkways – *everywhere*; desperate for some sign of the missing library fleet. Surely they should have made it by now! Gripping tightly hold of the balustrade, he leaned out, neck craned, scanning the curve of the river . . .

'And they're all out there?' asked Felix, the choking sound still in his voice. 'The whole council? Varis . . ? And my father?'

'Yes,' said Rook. 'The two of them were both in the fourth barge.'

They looked out at the furious waters in silence. Above them, on the Mire Gates platform, the ghosts were organizing the Undertowners for the great exodus down the Mire Road. Felix looked over his shoulder, then back at the Edgewater. Beneath their feet, the jetty shuddered.

'You know,' he said, slowly. 'We haven't got long, Rook. This jetty's giving way and the Mire Gates will follow. If we don't set off soon, we'll all be lost . . .'

'Just a little longer,' Rook pleaded. 'After all, it's your sister and father out there, Felix. You're acting as if you don't care!'

Felix looked down at his feet, the muscles in his jaw flexed and unflexed. 'All I've ever wanted,' he said quietly, 'is for my father to be proud of me, Rook. And now, just when I might have proved myself to him at last, he is lost out there. Don't you think *I* want to wait longer?' His fist slammed against the balustrade.

'I'm sorry,' said Rook. 'It's just . . .'

'I know, I know,' said Felix, clearing his throat. The jetty lurched again. Above them, shouts rang out and a group of ghosts marched down the walkway, escorting two struggling black-robed Guardians.

'We found these two by the Mire Gates, Felix,' the mobgnome ghost reported. 'Shall we slit their throats and dump them in the Edgewater? It'd be kinder than letting the Undertowners loose on them.'

The Guardians stopped struggling as Felix stepped forward and pulled down their hoods.

Rook gasped. 'Magda! And . . . Xanth!'

'Release them, Lemlop,' said Felix. 'This one's got a flight-suit on beneath her robes – she's a librarian, you fool! And this one . . .'

'I can vouch for him,' Magda said boldly, her eyes flashing.

'You can?' said Rook.

'He saved my life, Rook.'

'Felix,' said the mobgnome ghost urgently. 'We've got to get out of here . . .'

'I know, Lemlop,' said Felix, turning to go.

Reluctantly, Rook turned away from the balustrade, his head hanging. Magda fell into step beside him as they mounted the walkway to make their way back to the Mire Gates platform.

'Rook, what's happened? Where is everybody?' she said. 'There are rock demons loose in the sewers and a goblin army in the Great Library. We were expecting to meet the library fleet here . . .'

'I was, too,' said Rook. 'Oh, Magda . . . The librarians . . .'

'*Librarians! Librarians!*' A cry went up. Above them, the crowd of Undertowners thronged the Mire Gates platform, shouting and pointing excitedly.

Rook turned to follow their gaze. 'It's them!' he exclaimed. 'It's the Great Library Fleet! They've made it!'

The first great barge rounded the bend in a flash of oars, a clatter of bobbing buoyant lecterns and the regular cries of the barge-master urging the librarians on. A white raven flapped above it, cawing loudly. The second barge came into view, followed by the third, the fourth, the fifth – and Rook saw that they had all been lashed together with long ropes.

So typical of the librarians, he thought. All of them had to make it to safety – or none.

Hurrying back down the rickety steps of the walkway, Rook raised his cupped hands to his mouth and bellowed across to the approaching barge. 'Throw me your tolley-rope!' he shouted. 'Quickly, there isn't much time!'

No reply came, but the barge shifted direction. It was heading straight for the jetty.

'Stroke! Stroke! Stroke!' The gruff cry of the barge-master echoed over the roaring of the water.

The Ghosts of Screetown hurried down the steps onto the jetty and, as the fleet came alongside, they grabbed the coils of tolley-rope tossed to them and tied them securely to the mooring rings which lined the sides.

One by one, the librarians disembarked. They looked utterly exhausted. Silent and dazed, their muscles throbbing with pain, they staggered onto the jetty, which threatened to collapse at any moment. As Fenbrus Lodd stepped out of the fifth barge, the wooden pillars set into the mudflats below creaked loudly and the landing-platform trembled.

'Unload the barges!' he roared, above the weary chorus of moans and groans. 'As quickly as you can!'

The librarians set to it, helped by the ghosts and a contingent of large cloddertrogs who, with their powerful bulk, made short work of the task. Rook, together with Magda and Xanth, who had discarded their black robes, tossing them contemptuously into the swirling waters of the Edgewater, all pitched in. As the final skycraft and buoyant lecterns were being carried on to the Mire Gates platform, the jetty collapsed and disappeared, along with the empty barges, back into the inky blackness of Undertown.

The whole council, flanked by Felix's ghosts holding burning torches, was now gathered in the centre of the platform. Tallus Penitax, the Professor of Darkness, stood beside Ulbus Vespius, the Professor of Light, and beside them, Varis Lodd. Cowlquape – looking older and more haggard than ever – sat in the centre, on an ornately carved trunk. Next to him stood the High Librarian, Fenbrus, his arm raised for silence.

'My dear librarians!' His voice had lost none of its power or authority. 'Earth and Sky be praised we have made it this far. A long journey still lies ahead of us, but we are indeed blessed to be able to share its dangers with the good people of Undertown. And for this, we, and they, have to thank, the ... *errm* ... I believe they're known as ... the Ghosts of Screetown! And their leader ...'

A huge cheer went up from the Undertowners as Felix stepped into the torchlight.

'Ah, yes,' said Fenbrus, 'their leader, who is . . . What is your name, my brave young fellow?'

Felix's eyes met his father's.

Fenbrus blinked. His mouth fell open . . . 'Felix? . . .' the High Librarian spluttered.

Felix smiled, a look of eager anticipation on his face. He held out his arms to embrace his father.

A tear trickled down the High Librarian's cheek. 'I . . . I . . . I don't know what to say . . .' His face coloured with embarrassment. He cleared his throat noisily and patted Felix stiffly on the shoulder.

There was an awkward silence. Felix's face fell.

Was that it? he wondered. The reunion he had, for so many years, both dreaded and longed for . . . A pat on the shoulder!

Varis rushed forwards and embraced her brother, but he didn't seem to notice, his eyes still fixed on his father's face – and a look of hurt and disappointment on his own.

'My dear librarians, Undertowners and ghosts,' Fenbrus's voice rang out, strong and clear, once more. 'Our journey shall be long and difficult but, if we all work together and look out for one another, at its end we shall have earned the right to a fresh start, not as librarians, or Undertowners, or ghosts – but as Freegladers, one and all!'

Rook joined in the chorus as, all around, Undertowners picked up their belongings, librarians shouldered backpacks and commandeered shryke wagons, and ghosts with flaming torches prepared for the long march down the Great Mire Road.

Rook, Magda and Xanth fell in behind Felix. His dark expression suggested he didn't want to talk. They made their way silently towards the front of the mighty procession. As they pushed through the empty shryke tally-hut and out onto the Mire Road itself, Rook breathed in sharply with astonishment, then let out a cry of joy.

Ahead of them, a short distance away, was Vox's bower, carried by his banderbear friends.

'Weeg! Wuralo!' Rook called. 'Wumeru! Molleen! Weera-lowa. Wuh-wuh weega!' *Your burden is great. Let others take it now!*

But something was wrong. The banderbears didn't respond to his yodelled greeting, but instead continued their slow, shambling march up the Mire Road.

The curtains of the bower twitched. *All's well, my friends,* an icy voice sounded in Rook's head. *Let us go on our way . . .*

Rook turned to Felix and grabbed him. There was a

glassy look in his friend's eyes. 'All's well,' he was mumbling. '. . . Go on their way . . .'

'NO!' shouted Rook. He grabbed Felix's grappling-hook and threw it at the bower. It snagged on a wooden upright and Rook felt the rope pull taut as he lashed the other end to a Mire Road balustrade.

The banderbears continued carrying the bower, straining against the rope until – with the sound of splintering wood – the upright came away. The banderbears collapsed onto the wreckage of the bower, crushing the frame and snapping the carrying-poles in two. Rook came running up, followed by Magda, Xanth and Felix.

'I don't know what came over me,' Felix said, shaking his head.

'I think I do,' said Rook, 'but I'm not sure I understand it. You see, this is the bower Cowlquape sent to carry Vox to safety . . .'

The banderbears were clambering to their feet, shaking their heads in turn and yodelling softly.

'Weega-wurra-loora,' murmured Wumeru, her fingers fluttering. *A dark forest dream has lifted like a mist.*

'Wuh-wuh, wugeera. Luh-weeg,' added Molleen, with a shudder. *My mind now comes back to me. Before are only windswept echoes.*

Rook patted the backs of the banderbears reassuringly. 'Weg-weeg. Weegera, weera, wuh-wuh,' he yodelled, and touched the tips of his fingers to his chest. *Do not fear. No harm has come of your sleepwalking, friends of my heart.*

'Vox?' came a querulous voice behind them. 'Is that you, Vox? We kept our side of the bargain, yet *still* you planned to destroy us! Shame on you!'

The frail figure of Cowlquape, followed by the High Council, marched forward to join them round the wreckage. Cowlquape stopped and looked from the banderbears to the bower and back again.

'Oh, dear,' he said, a smile coming to his lips. 'There seems to have been an accident. Is anyone hurt? No? How about you, Vox?'

Cowlquape pulled aside the length of heavy curtain that was covering a great quivering bulge. There, sitting cradling a dazed-looking ghostwaif in her massive fleshy arms, was the figure of Flambusia Flodfox.

'Speak to me, Ambey, dear,' she clucked. 'Speak to me!'

Rook walked over to the Mire Road balustrade and untied the rope. He looked back at Undertown, almost totally obscured by the terrible dark maelstrom. It was all over, he thought, but the heavy weight that had been pressing down on his chest for days seemed to have lifted.

He was with his dearest friends again; Felix, Magda, the banderbears, even Xanth – and ahead lay the greatest adventure of his life.

He gripped the balustrade tightly for a moment, his knuckles white. Was that the Palace of Statues crumbling in the distance?

Relaxing his grip, he turned back to the others, a smile on his face. Undertowners, librarians and the Ghosts of Screetown filed past in an endless procession down the Mire Road. Rook's gaze followed them.

'Freegladers,' he murmured.

*

'Amberfuce,' said Vox, his voice barely more than a whisper as the awful truth dawned.

'I gave him some of my special medicine, and he got Speegspeel to slip it in your oblivion, dearie.' Hestera smiled. 'Then he took your bower. Flambusia begged me to go with them,' she said, 'but I told them I'd rather stay.' She smiled again, her face creasing up into unfamiliar folds. 'I wouldn't leave you, my sweetness. Not ever.'

The palace shuddered as yet another buttress crumbled into the surging torrent below. The whole west side of the building was now gone, and the wind and rain howled through the massive cracks opening up in the walls.

'Betrayed,' Vox murmured. He slumped to the floor and held his head in his hands. 'Betrayed!' A huge sob wracked his bloated body.

Hestera crouched down beside him, and rested a hand tentatively on his arm. Above them, the ceiling cracked, and the dripping water turned to a steady stream. Vox's sobbing suddenly stopped. He looked up, his small eyes narrowed to mean, murderous slits.

'*You*,' he muttered. '*You* gave Amberfuce some of *your* special medicine . . .'

'That's right, my sweetness,' said Hestera, uncorking the bottle marked *Oblivion: Special Vintage*.

'You mean,' spluttered Vox, 'you *knew* of his plans – and you didn't tell me!'

Hestera grabbed Vox by one wobbling, fleshy jowl and squeezed with an iron grip.

'*Ooowww!*' Vox screamed, his fat hands attempting to slap the goblin away.

'Of course I didn't tell you, my sweetness,' Hestera crooned, jamming the bottle into Vox's gaping mouth.

Vox's hands stopped flapping as Hestera held the glugging bottle firmly in place. His eyes dulled and closed; his head lolled to one side. The crack travelled from the ceiling, down the wall and snaked across the floor. The great chamber shuddered.

'It's what I've always wanted. A dream come true, Vox, my loverly,' said Hestera, cradling his massive head in her apron and rocking gently from side to side. 'You, my sweetness, all to myself.'

FREEGLADER

THE DEEP WOODS SETTLEMENTS

THE FOUNDRY GLADE

THE GOBLIN NATIONS

THE EASTERN ROOST

THE SILVER PASTURES

THE
FREE GLADES

THE SLAUGHTERERS
CAMP

THE IRONWOOD
GLADE

SOUTH
LAKE

WOODTROLL
TIMBER YARDS

THE GREAT LAKE

LAKE LANDING

WAIF GLEN

NORTH
LAKE

LULLABEE
ISLAND

NEW
UNDERTOWN

CLODDERTROG
CAVES

THE FREE GLADES

INTRODUCTION

A monstrous pall of swirling cloud hangs over the Edge, obscuring everything below. At its centre, a mighty storm fizzes and crackles with a deadly, destructive energy.

Like some evil demon, this dark maelstrom is devouring its prey, the once great city of Undertown. Yet even as the city crumbles and is washed away by the seething torrent the stormlashed Edgewater River has become, hope lives on in the hearts of the Undertowners – the cloddertrogs, gnokgoblins, lugtrolls and all those others who had once thronged the busy streets – fleeing down the disintegrating Great Mire Road. Led by the Most High Academe, Cowlquape Pentephraxis, and the librarian knights, their tethered skycraft bobbing behind them, they dream of a new life in that beacon of freedom and knowledge nestling in the far-off Deepwoods, the Free Glades.

Ahead of them lies the Mire, a treacherous wasteland of bleached mud and seething blow-holes, which is home to a host of fearsome creatures that prey on the weak and unwary. And then beyond that, beckoning from afar, the Edgelands, a place of swirling mists, where demons, spirits – and even the terrible gloam-glozer – are said to torment those who venture into its barren landscape.

Further still lie the Deepwoods themselves, with their swarms of snickets, packs of wig-wigs, poisonous plants and venomous insects. Bloodoaks that would swallow you whole, and reed-eels that would bleed you dry. Rotsuckers, halitoads, logworms . . . Not to mention the primitive tribes that live there – the skulltrogs and gahtrogs; brutal, speechless creatures that hunt in packs and devour their kill while it is still warm.

But there is no going back. Not now. Every one of the fleeing Undertowners understands this to be true. For many, this is the beginning of the greatest adventure of their lives.

In this, they are not alone, for Undertown is not the only place to be affected by the dark maelstrom. At the far end of the Mire Road, the remnants of the Shryke Sisterhood of the Eastern Roost realize that their lucrative trade with Undertown is over. They, too, must seek a new life, but instead of hope, there is bloodlust and vengeance in their hearts.

News of the great disaster is also reaching the villages of the Goblin Nations, never slow to spot and exploit the weaknesses of others. Talk in the tribal huts, with their heaped skulls and dangling skeletons, is of war and conquest.

And they are not the only ones with grand designs. In the smoky, fiery hell that is the Foundry Glades, Hemuel Spume is hard at work on plans of his own. He is waiting impatiently for his business partner to join him. When he does, Hemuel Spume has a surprise waiting for him. He permits himself a thin smile.

'I'll give them Free Glades,' he mutters scornfully. 'Long live the Slave Glades!'

As the dark maelstrom grows and spreads, the vast multitude of Undertowners struggles on along the Great Mire Road, and all the while driving rain beats against them mercilessly, chilling them to the bone and dampening their spirits.

They are fighting a losing battle. Ahead, sweeping across their path, bordering the Edgelands, are the beguiling yet treacherous Twilight Woods, a place that none but a shryke might journey through unscathed. All round them, the road is collapsing . . .

They must seek help, or perish.

*

The Deepwoods, the Stone Gardens, the Edgewater River. Undertown and Sanctaphrax. Names on a map.

Yet behind each name lie a thousand tales – tales that have been recorded in ancient scrolls, tales that have been passed down the generations by word of mouth – tales which even now are being told.

What follows is but one of those tales.

PART 1

FLIGHT

· CHAPTER ONE ·

THE ARMADA OF THE DEAD

'What are we going to do?'

Deadbolt Vulpoon turned from the cabin window and glared at the thin quartermaster who had just spoken.

'The storms over Undertown are growing, if anything,' said a cloddertrog in a bleached muglumpskin coat.

The other sky pirates at the long table all nodded.

'And there's nothing moving on the Mire Road,' he added. 'All trade has stopped dead.'

The nodding turned to troubled muttering.

'Gentlemen, gentlemen,' said Deadbolt, resuming his seat at the head of the table. 'We are sky pirates, remember. Our ships might no longer fly, but we are *still* sky pirates. Proud and free.' His heavy hand slammed down on the table so hard, the tankard of woodale in front of him leaped up in the air. 'And no storm – dark maelstrom or not – is going to defeat us!'

'I repeat my question,' said the thin quartermaster with a supercilious sniff. 'What are we going to do? There are over thirty crews in the armada. That's three hundred mouths to feed, three hundred backs to clothe, three hundred purses to fill. If there is no trade on the Mire Road, then what shall we live on? Oozefish and mire water?' He sniffed again.

'No trading, no raiding,' said the cloddertrog.

Again, the assembled sky pirates nodded in agreement.

Deadbolt Vulpoon grasped the tankard and raised it to his lips. He needed to collect his thoughts.

For weeks, the dark clouds had gathered on the far horizon at the Undertown end of the Great Mire Road. Then, two days ago, the huge anvil formations of cloud had merged into the unmistakable menacing swirl of a dark maelstrom.

Sky help those caught underneath, he'd thought at the time.

Now Undertown was lost from view and the Mire Road was deserted. A great shryke battle-flock had disappeared in the direction of Undertown just before the storm struck, and then the remaining shrykes from the tally-huts had retreated back to the Eastern Roost . . .

Deadbolt took a deep draught from the tankard and slammed it back on the table. 'I have sent out another raiding party,' he announced with a confidence he didn't feel. 'And until we get to the bottom of this, I for one don't intend to panic.'

'Raiding party!' snorted the thin quartermaster, pushing his chair noisily back and climbing to his feet. 'To raid what?' He paused. 'I hear there's opportunities opening up in the Foundry Glades, and that's where my crew are headed. And you're all welcome to join us!'

He strode from the cabin.

'Gentlemen, *please*,' said Deadbolt, raising a hand and motioning to the others to remain seated. 'Don't be hasty. Think of what we've built up here in the Armada. Don't throw it all away. Wait until the raiding party returns.'

'Until the party returns,' said the cloddertrog as the sky pirates got up to leave. 'And not a moment longer.'

As they trooped out, Deadbolt Vulpoon climbed to his feet and returned to the window. He looked out through the heavy leaded panes at the Armada of the Dead beyond.

What exactly *had* they built up here? he wondered bitterly.

When stone-sickness had begun to spread through the flight-rocks of the sky ships, he and the other sky pirates had read the writing on the wall. They came together and scuppered their vessels, rather than letting sky-sickness pick them off one by one.

The hulks of the sky ships had formed an encampment in the bleak Mire, and a base from which to raid the lucrative trade along the Great Mire Road. It wasn't sky piracy, but it was the closest thing to it in these plagued times. And sometimes, when the mists rolled in and the wind got up, he would stand on his quarterdeck and imagine he was high up in Open Sky, as free as a snowbird . . .

Vulpoon looked at the grounded vessels, their masts pointing up so yearningly towards the sky, and a lump formed in his throat. The ships still bore their original names, the letters picked out in fading gold paint. *Windspinner*, *Mistmarcher*, *Fogscythe*, *Cloudeater* . . . His own ship – the *Skyraider* – was a battered and bleached ghost of her former glory. She would rot away to nothing eventually if she didn't raise herself out of the white mire mud.

But that, of course, could never happen, for the flight-rock itself at the centre of the great ship was rotten. Unless a cure for stone-sickness was discovered, then neither the *Skyraider*, nor the *Windspinner*, nor the *Mistmarcher*, nor any of the other sky pirate ships would ever fly again.

Thick, sucking mud anchored the great hulls in place, turning the once spectacular sky vessels into odd-shaped buildings, made all the more peculiar by the additional rooms which had been constructed, ruining the lines of the decks and clinging to the sides of the ships like giant sky-limpets.

What future lay ahead for him? he wondered. What future was there for any of the those who called the Armada of the Dead home?

Deadbolt reached for the telescope that hung from his breast-plate. He put it to his eye and focused on the distant horizon.

He could see nothing through the impenetrable black

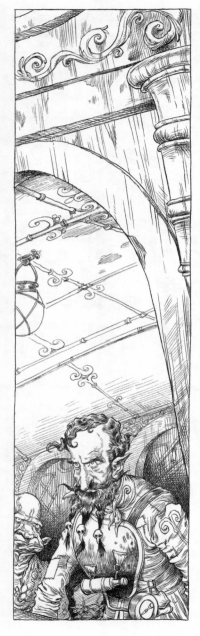

clouds – either of Undertown or of the Great Mire Road. Even the distant Stone Gardens, normally silhouetted against the sky, were covered with a heavy pall that obscured them completely.

Deadbolt Vulpoon sighed. He lowered the eye-glass and was about to turn away when something caught his eye. He returned the telescope to his eye and focused the lens a second time. This time his efforts were rewarded with a clear picture of seven, eight . . . nine individuals tramping towards him. It was the raiding party.

Back so soon? he wondered, a nagging feeling of disappointment settling in the pit of his stomach.

Two of the sky pirates were holding up poles, at the top of which was a large brazier-cage. The burning lufwood charcoal it

contained blazed with a bright purple light which illuminated the treacherous Mire, ensuring that no one
inadvertently stumbled into a patch of sinking-sand,
stepped on an erupting blow-hole, or stumbled into a
fearsome muglump . . .

As the raiding party came closer, Vulpoon leaned out
of his cabin window. 'Any luck?' he bellowed.

Yet even as he cried out he knew the answer. The sacks
slung across their shoulders were empty. The raid had
yielded nothing.

'There's nothing to be had at all,' a tall mobgnome
with an eye-patch shouted back.

'The road's deserted,' added another. 'The shrykes
must have headed back for the Eastern Roost.'

'We found these two halfway across the Mire,' said a
third, a lanky flat-head with a large ring through his
nose. 'Claimed they were on their way to see us. Nothing
but a few trinkets on either of them.'

Deadbolt Vulpoon noticed for the first time the two
strangers in their midst. Both were young. One of them
was dressed in librarian garb, the hood of his cloak
pulled up against the cold Mire wind. The other – taller,
tougher-looking – was clothed in bleached muglump
skins. He raised his head and returned Vulpoon's gaze
boldly.

'What can we do for you, lad?' said Vulpoon.

'My name is Felix Lodd,' came the reply. 'As for my
business, that is between me and the leader of the great
Armada of the Dead.'

For a moment Vulpoon hesitated. The youth was

impudent. He could have him locked up until he learned
a few manners – and yet he had spoken admiringly of
the Armada . . .

'Bring them up,' he ordered.

'And there was a battle, you say?' said Deadbolt
Vulpoon.

They were in the captain's cabin, the assembled sky
pirates seated at the long table. The youth in the
muglump skins stood before them, his hooded companion behind him.

'Yes, a great and terrible battle,' said Felix, nodding.
'Vox Verlix . . .'

'Vox Verlix, ruler of Undertown!' interrupted the thin
quartermaster who, on hearing of the raiding party's
return, had delayed his departure. 'Is that slimy skyslug
still around? Swindled me out of a whole consignment
of bloodoak timber once, he did. He was busy building
that tower of his on the Sanctaphrax rock. Swore I'd get
my revenge!'

Deadbolt raised his hand to silence him. He turned
back to Felix. 'What about Vox Verlix?' he asked.

'Organized the whole thing, by all accounts,' said
Felix. 'Tricked the goblins and the shrykes into going
down into the library sewers, then triggered a storm to
drown the lot of them.'

'So *he's* responsible for the dark maelstrom!' Deadbolt
shook his head. 'I might have known. Typical academic
– always meddling with the sky.'

'Yet it was also to be his undoing,' said Felix.

'You mean he's dead?'

'Almost certainly,' said Felix. 'I saw his palace collapse as the maelstrom closed in.'

'Pity,' said the quartermaster, his teeth glinting unpleasantly in the yellow lamplight. 'I've been looking forward to slitting his gizzard.' His right hand, poised as if holding a dagger, slashed through the air. 'Like so,' he said and his cruel laughter, echoing round the cabin, was joined by the others seated about the table.

'Undertown is destroyed,' said Felix, and the laughter stopped abruptly. 'Utterly destroyed. We managed to escape . . .'

'Who is "we"?' asked Deadbolt, leaning forward in his chair.

'Undertowners, young and old; librarians from the Great Library in the sewers, and . . .' He paused. 'And those I command – the Ghosts of Screetown.'

A low murmur went round the table. Suddenly the youth's confident, almost impudent, manner made sense. Even out here in the Mire they had heard of the Ghosts of Screetown – so called because of their bleached white, ghostly appearance – who were a band of fearless hunters and fighters from the worst part of Undertown.

'So, you're the leader of the ghosts,' said Vulpoon, trying to disguise the awe in his voice.

'Since when does a ghost need help?' interrupted the quartermaster in a sneering voice. 'I mean, after Screetown, surely the Mire can hold no terrors for you – if you *are* who you say you are.'

Felix took a step towards the quartermaster, his eyes

blazing. 'I do not ask help for the ghosts,' he said. 'I ask it for the Undertowners and the librarians who, even as we speak, are back there in the black mists of the Mire Road. They cannot return. They must go on, but the way is perilous.' He took a long, slow breath. 'But you know the Mire,' he said. 'By going through the Edgelands, we can avoid the Twilight Woods. But first, we must get across the Mire. For that, we need your help . . .'

'And if we do help you,' said Vulpoon, 'what's in it for us?'

Felix smiled. 'Spoken like a true sky pirate,' he said impudently.

Deadbolt Vulpoon felt himself redden with sudden anger. 'What's left for you here?' the youth continued. 'Without Undertown and the Mire Road trade, you'll rot away here like these precious ships of yours. Join us, and you can build a new life in the Free Glades . . .'

'And what's to stop us simply raiding you?' Vulpoon interrupted gruffly.

'Try that,' said Felix hotly, 'and the Ghosts of Screetown will cut you down, and the mire mud will run thick with treacherous sky pirate blood.'

'You march in here, insulting sky pirates and our sky ships,' said Vulpoon, his eyes blazing and fists clenching. '*And you expect us to help you!*'

The librarian stepped forward and lowered his hood for the first time. The others fell still and looked at him.

'Once, Deadbolt Vulpoon, *you* needed help,' he said, his voice low, the words quick. 'You were locked up in one of the roadside shryke cages. I gave you food to eat

and water to drink. Do you not
remember? You *said* you would
never forget,' he added softly.

The sky pirate captain looked
stunned for a moment before
breaking into a huge grin that
made his face wrinkle up and his
eyes disappear.

'You!' he boomed, striding
across the cabin. 'That was
you!' Roaring with laughter,
he clapped Rook on the back
warmly. 'Barkwater, isn't it?'

'Yes, sir. Rook Barkwater,'
he said. 'And now it is
my turn to ask for help
from you.'

'Rook Barkwater,' Vulpoon repeated, shaking his head
in amazement. 'Of all people!' He turned to the other sky
pirates. 'This lad saved my life,' he said. 'I cannot refuse
him what he asks. We shall help the Undertowners.'

'He didn't save *my* life,' snorted the thin quartermaster.

Deadbolt's face darkened. He reached out and
grasped the quartermaster by the collar with a huge
hand, and twisted. 'You were ready enough to quit the
Armada before,' he roared. 'This way, you get to enjoy
the Free Glades rather than the filth of the Foundry
Glades. Say "no", and I'll snap your scrawny neck,
Quillet Pleeme, by Sky I will!'

'There'll be no need for that, will there, Quillet?' said the cloddertrog in the bleached muglumpskin coat, loosening Deadbolt's grip.

The quartermaster shook his head weakly.

'The ghost is right,' the cloddertrog said. 'The Armada is finished. There's nothing for us here. We're with you, Captain.'

'To the Free Glades!' roared Deadbolt, releasing the quartermaster and clapping Rook on the shoulder once more.

Rook smiled. 'To the Free Glades!' he replied.

·CHAPTER TWO·

EXODUS

'**B**y Sky, lad,' gasped Deadbolt Vulpoon, pausing at the top of the mud dune to catch his breath, 'that's a dark maelstrom all right. The darkest, blackest, most accursed I've ever seen, and no mistake.'

Rook scrambled up beside him, the claggy white mud pulling at his mud-shoes and mire-poles like hungry oozefish. 'And it seems . . .' he panted, 'to be spreading.'

Deadbolt hawked and spat with disgust. 'This is what you get when you tamper with nature,' he growled. 'Cursed, meddlesome academics! They can't leave anything alone!'

In front of them, a thick, dense line of low mesanumbic cloud – flat at the top and with great billowing forms beneath – was advancing from the direction of Undertown and steadily engulfing the Great Mire Road, like a huge logworm swallowing its prey.

Felix appeared at Rook's shoulder, his pale face stained purple by the lufwood light of the brazier he was carrying. 'We can rest later,' he said tersely. 'Time is running out.' He shook his head. 'I only hope they'll have the sense to get off the Mire Road before the storm catches them.'

There were purple braziers all around them now as the sky pirates of the Armada breasted the ridge and gazed down at the white plains below. Far ahead, the Great Mire Road loomed out of the boiling cloudbank and wound its way across the wilderness on spindly legs like a half-swallowed thousandfoot.

'Allowing for heavy carts and young'uns,' said Deadbolt Vulpoon, scanning the horizon, 'these Undertowners of yours should be approaching the Twilight Woods tally-huts, give or take a span or two. That's half a day's hard mud-marching from here. Judging by the speed of that storm we should reach them just before it does!'

'Well, what are we waiting for?' said Felix, clapping Deadbolt on the back and smiling for what, to Rook, seemed the first time in days. 'I'll take a mud-march over a stroll in Screetown any time.'

Deadbolt's eyes twinkled. 'We'll see, my lad,' he chuckled, 'we'll see.' He turned to the sky pirates. 'Armada, advance!' he bellowed, his voice booming across the tops of the dunes. 'And look lively about it!'

Each crew raised its brazier-cage in assent, and the great mass of sky pirates slipped and slithered down the far side of the dunes and strode out across the sucking mud towards the imperilled Mire Road.

Rook would never forget that march across the vast Mire plain. Each crew tramped on in single file, following

the brazier-carrier at its head, chanting in unison, a dirge-like marching song.

'*One 'n two 'n three 'n four; mud in the eye to old Muleclaw!*'

The slap of mud-shoes on mire mud beat out the rhythm.

'*Five 'n six 'n seven 'n eight; chase her back to the Mire Gate!*'

Before long, Rook found himself joining in, his eyes fixed on Deadbolt's brazier-cage in front of him. Soon his breathing was harsh and heavy, and sweat was running down his face. But the steady beat of the mud-shoes and unwavering rhythmic chant drove him on.

He was dimly aware of the cawing of white ravens swirling in angry flocks overhead, and occasionally the shuddering thud of a nearby blow-hole exploding, sending a tall, glistening column high into the air and spattering the entire party in hot, clinging mud. After the third such shower, Rook, like the sky pirates in front of him, didn't even flinch, but trudged mechanically on. The mud clung to his boots, weighing them down and making every step he took more difficult than the one before. Up ahead, he heard Deadbolt's booming commands.

'Bear west, you mudlubbers! Close up the line, *Windjammer*! Hold steady, *Fogscythe*!'

As he closed his eyes and willed himself on, Rook began to imagine that he was part of a real armada, up there in the wide open sky, high above the cloying mire mud, and that Deadbolt Vulpoon was back on the quarterdeck of his sky ship, marshalling his sky pirate fleet.

It wasn't long though before this daydream was drowned out by the sound of his own rasping breath and the blood hammering in his temples. His legs felt like hull weights, his head seemed lighter than air and, as he stared ahead, Deadbolt's brazier light swam before his eyes as if under water. On and on they marched, the pace never flagging.

'*One 'n two 'n three 'n four; Tytugg's goblins at the door . . .*'

Rook stumbled and felt the rope secured round his middle jerk him upright.

'*Five 'n six 'n seven 'n eight; leave that hammerhead to his fate . . .*'

Rook stumbled again, this time falling to the ground and sprawling in the soft mud.

'*Halt!*' came Deadbolt's command. 'Loose the ropes!'

Rook felt hands untying the rope. He tried to get to his feet. How long had they been marching? Hours? Days?

'I'm . . . sorry . . .' he gasped. 'I . . . can't . . .'

'Sorry, lad?' Deadbolt's voice boomed at his ear. 'There's no need to be sorry. Look.' Rook raised his head and wiped the caked mud from his eyes.

There, in front of them, towering above the mire mists, was the Great Mire Road, beyond it the jagged treeline of the Twilight Woods. Gathered at the balustrades above the sky pirates, the Mire Road teemed with a vast multitude of Undertowners, cheering and brandishing flaming torches.

It was getting dark – and not only because night was approaching, Rook realized with a jolt. The vast billowing form of the dark maelstrom was on the far horizon to the east, and looming ever closer.

The Undertowners must have noticed it too, for as Rook gazed back, too exhausted to move, he saw them climbing over the balustrades and clambering down the ironwood-pine struts of the Mire Road onto the mud below. All around, the bustle of feverish activity became more desperate, and the air grew thick with urgent cries and screeched demands. He scanned the balustrades for any sign of his friends, the banderbears, but it was impossible to pick them out in the milling throng.

The librarians were busy manhandling great crates, stuffed with barkscrolls and treatises, off the precarious walkway and down onto the mud below. The Undertowners, too, were hurriedly evacuating the Mire Road, with those still up on the wooden structure lowering bundles of belongings and livestock and cradles bearing mewling young'uns carefully down into the upstretched arms of those far below. And all the while, the Ghosts of Screetown – distinctive in their white muglumpskins and bone-armour – hurried between them all, marshalling, corralling, shouting commands and offering help wherever it was needed.

Groups of lugtrolls and woodtrolls were working together on makeshift shelters and tents. A band of cloddertrogs were securing their bundles of belongings to long stakes, driven into the mire mud, whilst beside them, librarian knights expertly tethered their bobbing skycraft to heavy mooring-poles. Directly ahead, a large family of gnokgoblins was helping one another down from the road, their meagre possessions strapped to their backs.

Rook felt a hand under his arm lifting him to his feet, and found himself looking into Felix's smiling face.

'Not bad mud-marching for a librarian!' he laughed, though from the way he looked – mud-spattered and red-faced – Felix was just as exhausted as Rook himself. 'Looks like we got here just in time,' he added, pointing to the storm that was coming closer with each passing minute. 'But if they don't get down off the road in double-quick time, we might as well not have bothered.'

'So those are your Ghosts of Screetown,' said Deadbolt, standing hands

on hips and whistling through his teeth. 'Mighty fine bunch, and that's the truth. Handy with those ropes as well.'

'They could do with some help,' said Felix, turning to the sky pirate captain, 'if your crews are up for it after our little stroll.'

'By Sky, you're an impudent young pup!' laughed Deadbolt, and flourished his brazier-cage. 'Armada!' he barked. 'To the Mire Road! Let's get this rabble out into the Mire and hunkered down. There's a storm abrewing, or hadn't you mudlubbers noticed?'

The sky pirates instantly sprang forwards and began clambering up the struts of the Mire Road, slinging ropes and grappling-hooks up to those above, and attaching pulleys and slings to their tether-ropes. Soon, a steady flow of Undertowners was descending safely to the mud, and a vast encampment began to form all round Rook.

'Get clear of the road!' came Felix's clear voice. 'You don't want to be under it when the storm strikes!'

'Secure those prowlgrins!' Deadbolt's voice thundered. 'And overturn those carts for shelter!'

Even as he spoke, a heavy gust of wind snatched his words and carried them off. Rook looked about him. He must find the librarians and make his report. Unlike Felix, he was a librarian knight, and under orders from the Most High Academe, Cowlquape Pentephraxis.

As he started to make his way through the bustling throng of Undertowners, pitching tents and overturning carts, and even digging shallow holes in the mire mud,

Rook felt a wave of exhaustion break over him. He was about to join a cloddertrog family under a hammelhorn cart when a familiar voice called out.

'Master Rook. I trust you have done the library a good service.' Fenbrus Lodd strode towards him, his bushy beard bristling in the growing wind. 'The sky pirates have agreed to guide our Great Library across this desolate wasteland?'

Rook nodded. 'Yes, High Librarian,' he replied. 'Captain Vulpoon . . .'

'And that son of mine, why is he not with you?' interrupted Fenbrus, irritatedly.

'He's . . .' began Rook.

'I'm here, Father,' said Felix appearing, flanked by two of his ghosts.

'So you are,' said Fenbrus haughtily. 'So you are. Now, Felix, I want you and those ghosts of yours to secure the Great Library over there.' He pointed with his staff to a large throng of librarians who were hauling several huge carts, complete with protesting hammelhorns, into a rough circle. 'There are still a number of library carts on the road and time is running short. We must not lose them.'

Felix smiled grimly. 'There are still Undertowners up

on the road, father,' he said.
'My ghosts are helping them
first . . .'

'But the Great
Library!' blustered
Fenbrus, growing red in the
face. 'I must insist that you . . .'

'I don't take orders
from you!' thundered Felix,
sounding to Rook's ears not
unlike his father.

A crowd was gathering
round, listening in to the
heated words between the father and son.

'The library carts must be secured,' said Fenbrus Lodd
stubbornly, his eyes blazing. 'Not a single scroll must be
lost.'

'Nor must a single Undertowner perish!' countered
Felix hotly.

'Now, now,' came a quavering yet authoritative voice,
and Cowlquape himself stepped between them. 'If we all
work together, we shall be able to ensure the safety of
both the library *and* the Undertowners,' he said.

From behind him, there came a loud snort and everyone turned to see Deadbolt Vulpoon standing there, his
hands on his hips and a scornful look on his face.

'That's the last of the Undertowners off the road,' he
said grimly, 'but how you expect *any* of this rabble to
make it across the Mire with you lot bickering like this is
beyond me.'

'We were rather hoping,' said Cowlquape, approaching the sky pirate and bowing his head in greeting, 'that
you might be able to help us, Captain . . . err . . .'

'Vulpoon,' said Deadbolt. 'Captain Vulpoon.'

A trace of a smile flickered across Cowlquape's face.
'Ah, yes. Captain Vulpoon. I met your father once a very
long time ago – and in circumstances quite as perilous as
these, if my memory serves me right.'

'You must tell me about it sometime,' said Deadbolt,
returning his smile. 'But right now, you all need to get
everything and everyone secured if this here storm is to
be weathered.' He nodded towards the huge flat-topped
cloud formation boiling up overhead. 'After that' – he
was shouting now, to be heard above the roaring wind –
'we can talk about getting across the Mire.' He smiled
darkly. 'That is if there's any of us left to get across.'

Felix stepped forward. 'You heard the captain!' he
roared. 'Jump to it!'

The crowd dispersed, battening everything down and
hurriedly disappearing into holes and tents, and under
the upturned carts.

'Secure those hammelhorns!' Deadbolt bellowed,
striding off towards a group of slaughterers. 'We'll have
need of them soon enough!'

Fenbrus rushed after him. 'The library carts, Captain.
Don't forget the library carts!'

As the High Librarian's voice was swallowed up by
the rising howl of the wind, Cowlquape turned back to
Felix and Rook. 'You've done very well,' he said. 'Both of
you. I was unsure whether you'd be successful. After all,

I've come across enough sky pirates in my time to know how stubborn and wilful they can be . . .'

'Sounds like someone I know,' said Felix with a sigh.

Cowlquape nodded understandingly. 'You must try and understand your father,' he said. 'His dream is to recreate the Great Library in the Free Glades . . .'

'I know that,' said Felix, and again Rook heard the mixture of emotions in his voice. 'Him and his accursed barkscrolls! And what are they anyway? Bits of paper and parchment. It is the Undertowners – the *Freegladers* – who are important.'

'Of course, Felix,' said Rook, the wind almost drowning out his voice. 'But we are librarians. The barkscrolls are like living things to us.'

Felix didn't seem to hear him. 'I must see to the ghosts,' he said, turning on his heels and striding away.

Rook shrugged sheepishly at Cowlquape, and was about to run after Felix when he felt a tap on his shoulder. He turned, to see two of his best friends, Xanth and Magda, standing there, huge grins spread across their faces.

'It *is* you, Rook!' Magda exclaimed. 'We hardly recognized you under all that mud!'

Rook smiled back. 'Am I glad to see you two!' he said.

The heavy rain started as darkness fell, whipped into lashing sheets by the driving wind. Huge hailstones followed, and heart-stopping crashes of thunder. The Mire Road writhed, creaking and groaning like a dying monster as its timbers gave way, one by one. From inside their makeshift shelter, Rook huddled between Xanth and Magda.

'Do you think it's ever going to stop?' he said miserably.

Magda sighed. 'I wonder if the weather's ever going to be the same again.'

The shelter had been fashioned from an upturned cart and heavy bales of straw, covered with a tarpaulin staked down in place. So far it had kept the worst of the storm out, but at any moment Rook expected the terrible wind to rip the cart from over their heads and scatter the bales.

'So you're to fly with the Professor of Light,' said Rook, trying to keep his mind on something else. The librarian knights were masters of flying their delicate, wooden skycraft, made of buoyant sumpwood and powered by huge spidersilk sails. Since stone-sickness had put paid to the great sky ships, these tiny craft were the sole means of flight in the Edge.

'Yes,' said Magda, managing to smile. A crack of thunder broke overhead. The ground trembled. 'The plan is for Varis Lodd and her flight to head directly to the Free Glades to summon help, while the Professor of Darkness leads a flight high over the Twilight Woods section of the Mire Road in case shrykes are massing there to attack.'

'And you?'

Magda tried to sound brave. 'The Professor of Light is to lead us to the Eastern Roost to check on the shrykes there,' she said. 'There are rumours of a Hatching.'

Rook shivered. The words 'Eastern Roost' brought back such terrible memories. 'Aren't you afraid of going back to . . . that place?' he asked.

'We've got no choice,' said Magda simply. 'But at least this time I'll have *Woodmoth* with me – and the Professor of Light. He's one of the best librarian knights we have.'

'I wish I had *Stormhornet*,' said Rook with a sigh, remembering his lost skycraft, wrecked in a crash in Screetown. 'Then I could go with you, instead of having to stay with the footsloggers.'

'If it's good enough for Felix Lodd, it's good enough for you and that's a fact,' said Magda, trying to make light of it, but Rook could tell she, too, was upset by the fact that they wouldn't be flying together.

'*I'm* not even welcome amongst the footsloggers,' said Xanth darkly.

'What do you mean?' said Rook.

'I'm a traitor, Rook,' said Xanth, 'or had you forgotten? I served the Guardians of Night. I plotted and spied. Because of me, brave librarian knights were murdered. Because of me, *you* almost perished in the Foundry Glades.'

'All that's behind us now. The Guardians of Night are no more,' said Rook, 'destroyed by the dark maelstrom back in Undertown. And besides, you've changed, Xanth. *I* know. And I'll tell anyone else who wants to know as much.'

'And so will I,' said Magda. 'You rescued me from the Guardians, Xanth. I'll never forget that.' She tried to smile encouragingly.

Far above their heads, the storm seemed to be reaching a new intensity.

'You don't see the look in the librarians' eyes,' said Xanth bitterly. 'The look of distrust, the look of hatred. They look at me and see a traitor and a spy.'

Magda put an arm round Xanth. 'But inside, Xanth, your friends can see plainly . . .' she said softly, 'you have a good heart.'

Outside, a huge thunderclap broke and the little cart shook until its wheels rattled.

CHAPTER THREE

MUD-MARCH

Shortly before dawn, with feathers of light dancing on the horizon, the wind died down, the torrential rain eased off at last and an eerie silence descended over the mudflats of the Mire. Rook rubbed his eyes and looked round blearily, as disturbed by the unearthly stillness as he had been by the tumultuous storm that had raged through the night.

He rolled over and, leaving Xanth and Magda to sleep on, crawled to the edge of the shelter and attempted to push the tarpaulin back. But it was stuck fast, held in place by something pressing against it from outside. Grunting with effort, Rook pushed hard. There was a soft *flummp!* and the tarpaulin abruptly flapped free. Rook poked his head out of the gap he had created.

'Earth and Sky,' he murmured.

The vast encampment, with its upturned carts, battened-down tents and hastily constructed shelters, was now just a series of gently undulating mud-dunes stretching off into the distance as far as the eye could see.

Here and there, one of these dunes would erupt into life as its occupants dug their way out – just as Rook had – only to pause and look around with the same bemused expression on their faces.

'Rook?' Magda's sleepy voice called out. 'Is it over? Has the storm passed?'

'Come and see for yourself,' Rook called over his shoulder. 'It's incredible.'

Magda's head appeared next to his own, followed by Xanth's. They peered out across the bleached plains, shocked and bewildered.

'Look!' Rook exclaimed, pointing at the flat, muddy horizon.

'What?' said Magda, who was already scooping handfuls of mud aside and squeezing out of the hole on all fours. 'I can't see anything.'

'Exactly!' said Rook, following her. 'The Great Mire Road! It's gone!'

Xanth scrambled after them. All around, other mud-dunes were coming to life as the Undertowners emerged from their shelters into the blinding light of the white mud and early morning sky.

'You're right,' gasped Xanth, following Rook's gaze.

Where the Mire Road had towered over them the night before, now there was only a low ridge of mud, punctured here and there by splintered beams and pylons, like the ribs of a giant oozefish. Wreaths of acrid smoke began to coil up into the sky as braziers and cooking-fires were lit, and the air filled with the sounds of scraping and scratching as everyone struggled to rid themselves and their belongings of the clinging mud.

Xanth and Magda seized a couple of pieces of broken wood and began shovelling at the drifted mud-dune surrounding the hammelhorn cart. But it was hard going, with the wet mud constantly sliding back into the areas they had cleared.

'Come on, Rook,' Xanth panted. 'We could do with a hand here.'

But Rook did not hear him. He was staring at the remains of the once impressive feat of engineering, lost in his thoughts. So, this was the end of the Great Mire Road; a road he, Rook, had travelled as an apprentice librarian . . .

The image of Vox Verlix's fat face hovered before him – Vox Verlix, the greatest architect and builder the Edge had ever seen. The Great Mire Road had been his masterpiece, the greatest of all his mighty projects. But, like the Tower of Night and the Sanctaphrax Forest, it too had been wrested from him by others, leaving the former Most High Academe angry and bitter. And so, like a petulant child breaking its toys, he had brought down the power of the dark maelstrom on Undertown and destroyed his precious creations – and destroyed himself in the process.

Rook shook his head and turned away. Vox Verlix, Undertown, the Great Mire Road – they were all in the past. There was no turning back. Now, the homeless Undertowners and librarians had to look to the future, Rook realized, a future that lay far away across this desolate wasteland . . .

'Head in the clouds as usual!'

The sound of the voice snapped Rook out of his reverie. In front of him stood Varis Lodd, Captain of the Librarian Knights, resplendent in her green flight-suit. Rook bowed his head in salute.

'Captain,' he greeted her.

Varis laid a hand on his shoulder. 'I wish you could come with us, Rook,' she said kindly. 'But our loss is the library's gain. Keep the barkscrolls safe until our return, Rook, and you'll have completed a task every bit as important as ours.'

Rook nodded and tried to return her smile.

'Now, where's that friend of yours?' Varis looked past Rook and, as her gaze fell on Xanth, Rook noticed her jaw tighten and her eyes glaze over.

Xanth looked up and must have seen her expression too, for he stopped shovelling mud and stared down dejectedly at his boots.

'Xanth!' Magda laughed, still shovelling furiously. 'Don't give up! You're as bad as Rook . . .' She stopped when she saw Varis and straightened, bowing her head. 'Captain,' she said.

'The flight awaits, Magda,' said Varis, pointedly ignoring Xanth. 'Say goodbye to . . . your friends, and report for duty.'

Magda nodded solemnly. She turned and hugged Rook, then Xanth. 'Take care of each other,' she said

urgently. 'Promise me.'

They promised. Xanth's face was ashen white; his voice, barely more than a whisper.

'It'll be all right, Xanth,' said Magda. 'Rook and I will speak up for you in the Free Glades, won't we, Rook?'

Rook nodded earnestly.

'Now, come and see me off,' she said, trying to sound cheerful.

'I'll stay here,' said Xanth. 'You go, Rook. I'll finish digging the cart out.'

Magda gave him another hug, then turned to Rook. 'Here goes,' she said, and strode off after the Captain of the Librarian Knights.

Rook followed them through the gathering crowds, the buzzing hum of excitement in the air growing louder as they neared the tethering-posts. Heavy stakes had been driven down into the mud and the skycraft lashed securely to them. Now they were being untied, and the great flocks of skycraft were bobbing about in the early-morning air. Two squadrons were already prepared, with scores of young librarian knights seated astride their skycraft and waiting for the signal to depart.

Rook watched Magda climb onto her *Woodmoth*, unfurl the loft and nether-sails, realign the balance-weights and unhitch the flight-ropes. At the sight of her, he felt a heavy weight pressing down on his chest, turning to a dull ache. He swallowed hard, but the pain remained. Beyond the excited crowd he spotted Varis Lodd and the Professors of Light and Darkness, the three of them already hovering in the air, one at the head of each squadron.

As the last librarian knight climbed aboard his skycraft, Varis Lodd flew up higher, bringing the *Windhawk* round. She raised an arm and gave a signal.

Free Glades Flight, depart, she motioned in the signalled language of the librarian knights.

At her command, and as silently as snowbirds, some three hundred or so skycraft soared up into the sky as one. They hovered expertly overhead, securing and setting their sails, and adjusting the flight-weights that

hung beneath each craft like jewelled tails.

Twilight Woods Flight, depart. The Professor of Darkness silently gave the command, and the three hundred hovering craft were joined by three hundred more.

Eastern Roost Flight, depart. It was the Professor of Light's turn to give the signal; a right arm crossed to the left shoulder, three fingers outstretched. The air seemed to tremble as the squadron of librarian knights under his command – including Magda herself – rose up from the ground.

Like a vast and silent array of exquisite insects, nine hundred skycraft filled the sky above Rook's head.

'Oh, *Stormhornet*,' he murmured, his heart breaking. 'How I miss you.'

A sudden gust of wind seemed to galvanize the skycraft as, one by one, their sails filled like blossoming flowers and they moved off.

Rook followed their path, his mouth dry, his chest aching, as the skycraft caught the stronger currents high in the sky and began to gather speed. All around him cheers went up as the Undertowners and librarians saluted the librarian knights.

But as the skycraft grew ever more distant, the cheers fell away and the mood of the crowd changed. They were on their own now, out here in the vast muddy wilderness. Rook sighed. He felt the same.

Of course, he knew that the skycraft would be no use in the swirling, howling winds of the Edgelands that awaited them. He knew it made sense for the librarian knights to go on ahead to scout for danger and bring help from the Free Glades. He knew they all planned to meet up again at the Ironwood Stands. He knew all of this – but still, he couldn't shake off the feeling of having been abandoned.

In the distance, high above the Twilight Woods, the vast flock split up into three; one section swooping off to the north, one to the south, and the third continuing due west in the direction of the Deepwoods. Soon they were lost from view and, with a low murmur, the crowd began to disperse.

Rook turned and made his way back to Xanth as, all through the encampment, the Undertowners began to prepare for the long march ahead. From his left he heard commands being issued and he spotted Deadbolt Vulpoon striding through the encampment, barking into a raised megaphone.

'Mud-shoes and mire-poles for everyone!' he instructed. 'And eye-shields. Those without should improvise. There's plenty of timber to be had from the old Mire Road.'

There was a feverish scramble for scraps of wood and, all over the encampment, trogs and trolls, goblins, ghosts and librarians – all aided by the sky pirates – began lashing lengths of wood to the soles of their boots, cutting down sticks to the right length and fashioning eye-shields that would, they hoped, protect them from the dreaded mire-blindness.

'Batten down all crates and boxes!' Deadbolt's amplified voice continued. 'Charge your brazier-cages with lufwood, and fix runners to the bottoms of every cart and carriage!'

Again, there was a scramble for wood, and the air was soon echoing with the sounds of chopping and sawing and hammering as every vehicle had its wheels removed and stowed, to be replaced with long, curved runners which, Earth and Sky willing, would glide effortlessly over the treacherous mud.

'Those with prowlgrins, put them in harness!' Deadbolt's voiced boomed as he continued marching through the bustling encampment. 'Those without will

have to strap themselves in. Always pull! Never push!'
He caught sight of a herd of hammelhorns standing
forlornly in a shallow pool. 'And hammelhorns may *not*,
I repeat, *not* be used for pulling the sledges. They'll only
sink. They must be tethered together and led.' He
paused and stood looking round, his hands on his hips.
'*And get a move on!*' he roared. '*We depart at midday!*'

Rook found Xanth sitting on the remains of the
hammelhorn cart, which had been completely stripped
of wood for mud-shoes. He was surrounded by four
huge mountains of shaggy, mud-caked fur, and smiling
broadly.

'I can't understand a
word they're saying,'
he laughed as Rook
ran up.

'Wumeru!' Rook
shouted out in delight.

The banderbear
turned. 'Wurrah-lurra!
Uralowa leera-wuh!'
she roared, her words
accompanied by arm
movements, curiously

delicate for one so large. *Greetings, Rook, he who took the
poison-stick. It is good you are back with us.*

'Wuh-wuh!' Rook replied, his hand lightly touching
his chest. It was good to hear his banderbear name again.
'Wurra-weeg, weleera lowah.' *Greetings, friend. Together
we shall face the journey ahead.*

'Wurra-weeg, wurra-wuh!' the other banderbears joined in, clustering around Rook in an excited group. There was Wuralo, who he'd rescued from the Foundry Glade; Weeg, with his great, angry scar across one shoulder, and old Molleen, her single tusk glinting in the low sunlight as she tossed her head animatedly about.

'What are they saying? What are they saying?' said Xanth excitedly, joining the throng.

'They're saying,' laughed Rook, 'that they've been searching the camp and have been trying to ask you if you'd heard of me – but you didn't seem to understand a word they said. Molleen here thinks you seem rather stupid, but that it isn't your fault – it's because your hair's so short!'

Xanth burst into laughter, and the banderbears yodelled in unison.

'Tell her,' said Xanth, 'that I'll grow my hair just for her.'

As the sun rose higher in the milky sky, the chaos of the Mire encampment gradually took on a semblance of order. Every cart was laden, every backpack stuffed full; at Fenbrus Lodd's command, the prowlgrins had been harnessed up to the sledges carrying the precious library crates.

An hour earlier, following Deadbolt Vulpoon's orders, the Undertowners had started to rope themselves together in groups of twelve. Now, they were all taking up the positions allocated to them by the sky pirates in a huge column, with the family groups and the Great Library at the centre, the sky pirates themselves at the head and the Ghosts of Screetown bringing up the rear. Roped together, Rook, Xanth and the banderbears were just behind the last of the huge library sledges, its jostling, slavering team of fifty prowlgrins raring to go.

Felix called to them from towards the back of the column. 'Good luck, Rook! Make sure those great shaggy friends of yours don't step on any prowlgrin tails!' His laughter boomed out across the Mire.

Rook smiled. He wished he could be as brave and cheerful as Felix.

Just then, Deadbolt Vulpoon strode past, his sword held high and the megaphone clamped to his mouth. Rook raised his scarf to shield his eyes from the dazzling whiteness ahead, his stomach turning somersaults. High above his head, a great flock of white ravens circled noisily, the furious cawing echoing off across the endless Mire, and reminding Rook just how far they had to go.

'ADVANCE!!' Deadbolt Vulpoon's voice boomed as he strode out ahead.

The column began to shuffle forward – front first, then further and further back down the lines, until every single individual in the vast multitude was in motion. Rook fell into step, Xanth and the banderbears marching beside him. Up ahead, families of gnokgoblins and lugtrolls marched, their makeshift mud-shoes slapping on the mud, keeping them from sinking.

Yet the going was tough for all that.

Soon, many were struggling – from frail old'uns, their aged limbs protesting, to young'uns, thin and under-nourished, yet too big to be carried. Behind them came the library sledges, with Fenbrus Lodd and Cowlquape Pentephraxis walking alongside them, the High Librarian anxiously checking and rechecking the ropes, the runners, the prowlgrin harnesses . . .

'Nothing must be lost,' he was muttering. 'Not a tome, not a treatise, not a barkscroll.'

They all tramped on resolutely through the afternoon and into the evening. Dark clouds gathered overhead once more, and Rook pulled his collar up against the rising wind.

From up ahead, Deadbolt's voice boomed. 'Keep marching! There can be no stopping, you mudlubbers! Close up the gaps!'

It was almost completely dark when the rain first started – big, fat drops that spattered down on the mud-flats. Within seconds, it had become torrential, bucketing down on the Undertowners for the third time in as many nights.

'We keep on!' Deadbolt's voice called out above the hiss and thunder of the howling wind and battering rain.

His words were passed back down through the lines of the drenched multitude, growing more despondent with every repetition.

'We keep on?' muttered a gnokgoblin matron desper- ately, glancing back at her family, roped behind her, barely able to keep going.

A cloddertrog to her left, bathed in purple light from the brazier-cage he was carrying, nodded grimly. 'We keep on,' he said.

Rook himself was struggling. He was hungry, and

the icy rain had chilled him to the bones. On either side of him, the banderbears panted noisily, while behind him – pulling on the tether-rope that bound them together – Xanth slipped and slid on his unfamiliar mud-shoes.

A curious numbness seemed to grip both Rook's body and his mind. He was no longer thinking of where he was going. The future no longer existed; nor did the past. There was only this, here, now. One step after the other, trudging across the endless reaches of the Mire.

One step. Then another, and another . . .

The night passed in a stupor of mud, sweat and shivers, and a cold grey light began to dawn. Despite Deadbolt's best efforts, the pace had slowed to a painful crawl, with small pockets of stragglers beginning to fall behind. If this continued, he knew the column would soon cease to be a column at all, and become instead a disorganized rabble, impossible to lead.

At last there came the command everyone had been waiting for.

'HALT!' bellowed Deadbolt. 'We rest for one hour! No more! Any longer and we'll all be muglump bait – that is, if the mud-flows don't get us first.'

With a collective sigh, the column stopped marching, and the long lines of Undertowners broke up into small groups, huddled together against the biting wind. Sitting between Molleen and Wumeru, Rook and Xanth escaped the worst of it – but were still both chilled to the bone.

'I never thought I'd say this,' said Xanth, smiling

weakly, 'but I almost miss Undertown. How can anybody call this desolate waste home?'

Rook didn't answer. He was gazing past Xanth at the
treeline in the distance.

'The Twilight Woods,' he murmured.

From the cold, icy mud of the Mire, the twinkling light
of the Twilight Woods was hypnotic. Warm, inviting
glades sparkled, fabulous clearings shimmered; nooks
and crannies, sheltered from the bitter winds, beckoned
seductively.

Xanth put his arm on Rook's shoulder. 'Don't even
think about it,' he said sternly. 'That path leads to death
. . . A *living* death.'

Rook looked away and shook his head. 'I know, I
know,' he said. The Twilight Woods! That beautiful,
seductive, terrible place that robbed you of your mind
but not your life, condemning you to live on for ever as
your body decayed. 'It's just that . . . it looks so . . .'

'Inviting,' Xanth said grimly. 'I know that.' He
shivered as a blast of icy wind hit him. The next
instant he was up on his feet and waving wildly.

'Molleen! No!' he cried out. 'Molleen! *Come back!*'

Rook leaped up. The old banderbear had torn free of her tether and was stumbling across the mudflats, her eyes fixed on the Twilight Woods ahead.

'Weeg-worraleeg! Weera wuh-wuh!' Rook shouted desperately. *Come back, old friend, that is death calling you!*

Wumeru, Wuralo and Weeg's anguished yodels rang out. *Come back, old friend! Come back!*

But the old banderbear ignored them. And she wasn't alone. Up and down the column, individuals were cutting the ropes that bound them to their groups and dashing towards the alluring glades of the Twilight Woods.

Deadbolt's voice boomed from the front of the line. 'Column fall in, and advance if you want to see another dawn! Advance, I say! And keep your eyes looking up front, you mangy curs!'

Ahead of them, the library sledges lumbered forwards. Rook, Xanth and the banderbears broke ranks as one, and made after Molleen, only to be jerked back by

the rope that secured them to their sledge. Rook tore at the rope feverishly.

'Molleen, wait!' he shouted. 'We're coming to get you!'

'Fall back in line!' roared a voice in Rook's ear. Deadbolt Vulpoon, his face like thunder, loomed over him. 'Fall back in line or I'll run you through!' He brandished a serrated-edge sabre menacingly. 'And don't think I won't!'

Rook stopped, tears stinging his eyes. 'But Molleen,' he said, his voice breaking. 'She's our friend, we must . . .'

'You follow her and you'll all be lost,' said Deadbolt firmly. 'There's no saving her, believe me, lad.'

The library sledge pulled the rope taut as Rook fell back into line. The others followed, the banderbears moaning softly, Xanth shaking his shaven head.

'Sky curse it!' Deadbolt thundered. 'This is all my fault. I took us too close to the treeline, then took pity on you mudlubbers and allowed you to stop. Well, there'll be no more of it. We march on! Or we die!'

With that he was off, striding back down the column, barking orders left and right. Rook shut his eyes, and concentrated on putting one foot in front of the other. The plaintive yodels of the banderbears rang out across the white mudflats as, in the distance, the shuffling figure of Molleen disappeared into the Twilight Woods.

They marched on all through that dismal grey morning and on into a rain-sodden afternoon. Few spoke; even the chants of the sky pirates up in front tailed off, and the only sounds were the barks and yelps of the prowlgrins and the relentless *slap, slap, slap* of mud-shoes on mire mud.

The grey afternoon gave way to the dim half-light of evening, and the wind grew stronger once more, pelting them with heavy rain that stung their faces and soaked them to the skin.

'That's the Edgeland wind,' called back the librarian on the library sledge. 'We must be getting close!' He cracked the whip and urged the yelping prowlgrins on.

The rope round Rook's middle jerked taut, forcing him to quicken his pace. All round him, the air was filled with curses and moans as the marchers struggled to keep up.

Suddenly, rising above it all, there came the noise of squelching mud, and a curious *plaff-plaff* sound. Rook looked up. To the left of the column, a cluster of low mud-dunes seemed to be approaching, rising and falling in a slippery rhythm as they did so.

'MUGLUMPS!'

The cry went up from the back of the column, where the Ghosts of Screetown had obviously spotted the danger.

The rope suddenly tugged Rook violently to the right as the librarian on the library sledge battled to control the panicking prowlgrins. Ahead, the four other sledges were in equal trouble. The low shapes were gathering and, from their path, it was obvious that the closely harnessed packs of prowlgrins were their intended prey.

Felix and his ghosts appeared out of the gloom on all sides. Fenbrus Lodd, Cowlquape beside him, shouted desperately to his son.

'The library sledges! Felix!' he screamed. 'They're after the sledges!'

Rook was running now, with Xanth and the bander-bears dragged behind him, as the library sledge careered across the mud.

'Cut yourselves loose!' shouted Felix to Rook and the other librarians. 'And follow the braziers of the sky pirates!'

With a grunt, Rook tore at the knotted rope round his middle and slid to a halt as it fell free.

'There!' shouted Xanth, beside him. He pointed.

Ahead, Deadbolt stood on a mud-dune, waving a flaming purple brazier over his head as if possessed. 'Rally to me, Undertowners!' he roared. 'Rally!'

The huge library sledges slewed and skidded away to the right, the yelping screams of the prowl-grin teams drowning out the cries of their drivers. The mud-dunes seethed and boiled with the low, flapping shapes of the half-hidden muglumps in pursuit.

Panting, Rook reached Deadbolt, who was now surrounded by a huge crowd of mud-spattered and bewildered Undertowners. Xanth and the banderbears came lumbering up behind him.

'There lie the Edgelands, Sky help us! We'll regroup there!' shouted Deadbolt above the howling winds, and pointing to a low, grey ridge in the middle distance. 'Mothers and young'uns first!'

The Undertowners surged forwards across the glistening wind-flattened expanse of mud ahead, all eyes fixed on the distant ridge. Every one of them was driven by a desperate, half-mad frenzy to get out of the clinging mire mud and onto dry land. Rook was jostled and bumped as Undertowner after Undertowner barged past.

'You heard him!' Xanth shouted. 'Come on. We're nearly there, Rook!'

But Rook shook his head. 'I'm a librarian knight,' he said in a low voice, his words almost lost in the gusting wind. 'My place is with the library.'

He turned back towards the library sledges. Xanth and the banderbears hesitated. It was obvious from their eyes that they shared the Undertowners' mire-madness. Every fibre of their beings longed to be rid of the terrible white mud.

'And our place is with you,' said Xanth.

They turned and fought their way through the crowd, and back out into the Mire. The library sledges, like huge lumbering beasts, were away to the right, and had halted their mad dash. Now they seemed marooned, their tops bristling with librarians like hairs on a hammelhorn. As they approached, Rook could see why.

Felix and the ghosts were busy cutting the traces that harnessed the prowlgrin teams, while his father waved his hands in the air wildly, from on top of one of the sledges.

'Stop! Stop!' he was bellowing, but Felix ignored him as he cut through another tilderleather strap.

The slithering mounds had congregated in a flapping, slurping reef round the sledges, kept at bay for the moment by brazier-wielding ghosts – but inching closer by the second.

Rook stopped. If they went any further, they risked straying into the midst of the muglump pack. He shook his head miserably. There was nothing they could do; they were helpless spectators. He sank to his knees in the cold white mud. How he hated the oozing filth that seemed to cling so, pulling you down, smothering the life out of you, until you were so weary you just didn't care any more . . .

All at once, the mire mud erupted in front of him. Felix had cut the last harness and given the signal. With piercing screams, the prowlgrins – all two hundred and fifty of them – stampeded out across the mudflats.

The mounds closed in around them. Up out of the mud, the muglumps reared, in plain sight at last. Rook stared, transfixed with horror. The last time he'd seen a muglump was with Felix, in the sewers of old Undertown – but that sewer-dweller seemed tame compared to these monsters. The size of a bull hammelhorn, with six thick-set limbs and a long whiplash tail, each muglump slithered through the soft mire mud just below

the surface, breathing through flapped nostrils.

Now, with a bone-scraping screech, they pounced on the hapless prowlgrins and, in a frenzy, tore them limb from limb with their razor-sharp claws. Soon, the mire mud was drenched in prowlgrin blood as the muglumps feasted.

'Let's save this library of yours!'

Felix's booming voice pulled Rook away from the horror. He was helping the librarians down from the sledges, organizing them into teams and picking up the traces.

'We don't have much time,' said Felix, motioning to the ghosts to join them. 'They'll be back for us soon.'

'Come, librarians!' Cowlquape's voice rang out. 'We must all pull together!'

Rook, Xanth and the banderbears ran over the mud to join the librarians who, when they saw the huge figures of Wuralo, Weeg and Wumeru, gave a cheer.

'Thank Sky we've got you,' said the prowlgrin-driver, greeting them. 'If you and your friends here could set the pace, we'll try to keep up!'

They picked up the traces and tether-ropes, and each sledge, drawn by a team of ghosts and librarians, resumed its journey across the wastes towards the thin grey ridge in the distance, now twinkling with purple lights. Behind in the gathering dusk, the snarls and grunts of the muglump feast spurred them on.

One step after the other, Rook thought grimly. One step. Then another, and another . . .

·CHAPTER FOUR·

THE EDGELANDS

It was dark as the exhausted librarians dragged the last library sledge up out of the Mire and onto the flat, rocky pavement of the Edgelands. They were greeted by Undertowners, young and old, who held out flasks of warming oakapple brandy and bowls of broth. There were small braziers ablaze, groups huddled round them for warmth, and clusters of muddy-cloaked Undertowners who'd simply lain down and fallen asleep where they'd stopped.

Rook rubbed his eyes and looked about him. To the south were the Twilight Woods, their hypnotic golden glow bright and enticing in the darkness. To the north, the Edge fell abruptly away into the bottomless void. Trapped between the two, the vast multitude of Undertowners, librarians, sky pirates and ghosts prepared to sleep, while all around them miasmic mists writhed and swirled – now thinning to show the full moon glinting on the rocky pavement, now thickening and obliterating everything from view.

Rook accepted a bowl of warm broth from a gnok-goblin matron, and stumbled over to a brazier where the banderbears were being patted on the back by some library scroll-scribes and lectern-tenders. Xanth hung back with that unhappy look in his eyes that Rook noticed whenever his friend was near librarians.

All around them, the night was throbbing with activity as the Undertowners pitched their tents, raised their wind-breaks and got their stock-pots bubbling. Food was bartered; meat for bread, woodale for water. Young'uns were settled down for the night. And while they slept, their elders worked on, preparing themselves for an early start the following morning – and post-poning the moment when they too would have to turn in for the night.

It was reassuring working together; safety in numbers, so to speak. They all knew that when asleep, every single one of them would be alone. That was when the Edgelands was at its most dangerous, when the misty phantasms filtered into their dreams and nightmares . . .

The fires were stoked and restoked, and the brazier-cages were filled to the brim with their supplies of lufwood. Hammelhorns were fed and watered. The mud-clogged runners were removed from the sledges and the wheels returned to their axles. And amidst it all, Rook noticed, a brisk trade in good-luck charms was establishing itself, with the trolls, trogs and goblins vying for business.

'Amulets! Get your bloodoak amulets here!' a stocky woodtroll was calling, a bunch of carved red medallions on thongs clasped in his stubby fingers. 'Guaranteed to repel every dark-spirit and empty-soul!'

'Leather charms!' shouted a slaughterer. 'Bone talismans. Ward off wraiths and spectres. Keep the gloamglozer himself at bay.'

'Bristleweed and . . . *slurp, slurp* . . . charlock pomanders,' cried a gabtroll, her long tongue lap- ping at her swaying eyeballs. 'Bristleweed

. . . *slurp, slurp* . . . and charlock pomanders.'

'I don't think we'd have made it without your friends here,' said a sprightly-looking under-librarian by the name of Garulus Lexis, clapping Rook on the back.

Rook smiled and passed on the librarian's thanks.

'Wug-weeghla, loora-weela-wuh,' said Wumeru. *His words warm my heart, but my stomach remains empty.*

'Well, we'll soon see to that,' laughed Garulus when Rook had translated, and he bustled off, returning a few moments later with a sack of hyleberries and a large pot of oak-honey. 'Enjoy!' he said, as the banderbears tucked delightedly into their feast.

Xanth sat down quietly next to Rook and drew his cloak about him.

'Does your ... er ... friend need anything?' said Garulus, nodding at Xanth, a look of mild contempt on his face.

'Nothing, thank you,' said Xanth.

The other librarians round the brazier exchanged glances.

Rook gave Xanth his bowl. 'Here, finish this, Xanth,' he said. 'I've had my fill. Go on, it's good.'

Xanth accepted the bowl with a thin smile and drained its contents. The librarians ignored him.

'Well, *now* what are we to do?' Ambris Loppix, an assistant lectern-tender asked. 'Without the prowlgrins, the library carts are all but useless.'

'I don't know about you,' said Queltus Petrix, an under-librarian, 'but I just about broke my back pulling the blasted thing through the Mire even *with* the help of young Rook's friends here.'

They all nodded.

'We can't take it with us, and we can't leave it behind,' said Garulus, shaking his head sadly. 'After all, what are librarians without a library?'

'There *is* something you could do,' said Xanth quietly. The librarians all looked at him. 'A way to get every barkscroll across the Edgelands and to the Free Glades,' he went on.

Ambris snorted and Queltus turned away. Garulus pushed his half-moon spectacles back onto the bridge of his long nose. 'And what, pray, is that?' he said, contempt dripping from every word.

'Every Undertowner could carry a scroll. There are thirty thousand scrolls, aren't there?'

'Yes,' said Garulus uncertainly.

'And there are at least thirty thousand of us – Undertowners, ghosts, sky pirates, librarians . . .'

'And one Guardian of Night,' said Garulus, fixing Xanth with an icy stare.

'No, listen . . .' Rook began, jumping to his feet. But before he could speak further, the gaunt figure of Cowlquape, Most High Academe, stepped into the brazier light, flanked by Felix and Fenbrus Lodd, doing the rounds of the librarian camp fires.

'It is a *brilliant* idea,' he said with a gesture of the hand that they should all remain seated. 'If we entrust one scroll to each one of us, librarian and Undertowner alike, then we all become a *living* library, and we can cast off these cumbersome carts.'

'But the lecterns . . .' began Fenbrus.

'We can build more lecterns, my friend,' said Cowlquape. 'It is the barkscrolls, and the knowledge they contain, that is precious. Xanth, here, has remembered that, when some of us have been in danger of forgetting it.'

Fenbrus coughed loudly, and his face reddened. Felix beamed and winked slyly at Rook.

'We shall unload the carts at dawn and distribute the library. Felix, can you and your ghosts supervise?'

Felix nodded.

'Now,' said Cowlquape sternly, looking round. 'Fenbrus has something to say to you. Please listen carefully, and pass it on. It could mean the difference between life and death to us out here in the Edgelands.'

Fenbrus stepped forwards, coughed again, and cleared his throat. 'Tomorrow, we venture through the Edgelands,' he began, 'and as your High Librarian, I have consulted the barkscrolls to learn what I can of what lies ahead. Make no mistake,' he said gravely, looking at each of them in turn, 'we are about to enter a region of phantasms and apparitions, where your ears and eyes will deceive you. Out there on the barren rocks, the Twilight Woods are on one side and the Edge itself on the other. If the wind blows in from the Edge side, we shall be travelling through heavy cloud and fog. The danger then is of losing our sense of direction and plunging over the Edge and into the void.'

Rook shuddered. All eyes were glued to Fenbrus.

'On the other hand, if the wind changes and blows in from the Twilight Woods, then the madness of that place will infect the Edgelands and, most likely, will infect us too.'

'And if that happens?' asked Garulus.

'Hopefully,' said Fenbrus, 'it will not last long, but our only defence is to rope ourselves together in pairs, and to talk to each other. For the great danger is to sink into a waking dream without even realizing it. If your partner falls silent, you must wake him instantly, or the phantasms will take hold and he will be lost for ever.' He paused. 'I intend to partner my son, Felix, here.'

He coughed again, and Felix smiled.

'And I was hoping,' said Cowlquape, 'that you, Garulus, would do me the honour . . ?'

Garulus nodded. Rook felt a hand on his shoulder.

'Would you, Rook . . ?' Xanth mumbled as the other librarians left to spread the news.

'I'd be honoured,' said Rook, smiling.

'And then, Xanth?' said Rook. 'What happened then? We've got to keep talking, remember.'

'I know, I know,' said Xanth wearily. 'But I'm so tired.' He sighed. 'And then I became his assistant. Me, assistant to the High Guardian of Night himself, Orbix Xaxis! It all seems like a dream to me now . . .'

No one had slept well that night on the rocky pavement. The ground beneath them was too hard, and it was cold, with the howling wind slicing through the air like ice-scythes. Long before the sun had even risen, everybody in the vast multitude had already packed up their belongings and tethered themselves together in lines, ready for the daunting journey ahead. Felix and the Ghosts of Screetown had ushered them to the five great library carts and, as they'd walked past, each in turn had been handed a barkscroll, a treatise, a tome; one tiny part of the whole library.

Now, as the sun rose slowly – creamy-white behind the dense, swirling mist – they were marching on, their elongated shadows stretched out in front of them. A low babble of voices echoed above the clatter of cartwheels as the pairs of Undertowners indulged in feverish conversations, anxious that none of them should fall prey to the Edgelands' phantasms.

In their midst, the librarians marched, with Rook and Xanth still deep in their own conversation.

'And that metal muzzle he wore,' said Rook, chuckling. 'What was all that about?'

Xanth smiled weakly. 'Orbix Xaxis was a creature of many superstitions,' he said. 'He only bathed by the full moon. He never ate tilder if there was an "r" in the month. And he believed that the air was still full of the "vile contagion" which had brought stone-sickness to the Edge.'

'He blamed the librarians for stone-sickness, didn't he?' Rook added. 'Believed we'd brought it back from the Deepwoods. Is that why he killed so many of us?'

'He was mad, I realize that now,' said Xanth, his face drawn and tense. He shuddered. 'Oh, those accursed Purification Ceremonies of his. I dread to think how many Undertowners and librarians were sacrificed to the rock demons. And for what?' He shook his head, leaving the question hanging in mid air. 'Orbix Xaxis was mad all right, Sky curse his wicked soul . . .'

'Xanth,' Rook gasped, looking round uneasily, half expecting to see the spirit of the High Guardian himself emerging from the mists. 'Careful what you say, here of all places.'

The wind that had been howling continuously since they first stepped on to the rocky pavement had now died down, and a heavy swirling fog had descended like a white blanket.

'This reminds me of when I was a young'un,' said Rook, still endeavouring to keep talking, despite the cold, suffocating mist that tightened about them. 'There was this old forgotten cistern in the sewers. I'd lower myself into it, pull the top shut over my head and spend hours there, tucked up and hidden, with only a lantern and a smuggled treatise for company . . .' He frowned. 'Xanth?' he said, concerned that his friend was letting his mind stray. 'Are you listening?'

'Oh, yes,' said Xanth, his voice dull.

Behind them, Ambris Loppix's voice could clearly

be heard. 'They say he hand-picked the captured librarians for that master of his.'

'I heard that he actually enjoyed listening to their screams. Called it "singing", he did,' replied his partner.

'Do you know how they celebrate Wodgiss Night in a woodtroll village?' said Rook, trying to drown out the sound of the librarians' conversation. 'It's in my barkscroll, *Customs and Practices Encountered in Deepwoods Villages*.' Rook patted his knapsack, where the barkscroll he'd been entrusted with was safely packed.

Xanth made no response.

'First of all, there's this huge procession,' said Rook, 'with drums and trumpets, and everyone wears these fantastic exotic head-dresses . . .'

'And then he became a spy . . .' Ambris was saying.

'And the young'uns all get their faces painted,' said Rook. 'Like animals. Some are fromps, some are lemkins, and there is even one done up like a vulpoon, in a feathered suit and a strap-on beak . . .'

'Betrayed *hundreds* of apprentice librarians on their way to the Free Glades, apparently . . .'

Rook turned and glowered at the librarians – though tethered as he was, there was little he could do to shut them up.

'Execution's too good for him, that's what I say,' replied Ambris's partner.

'They'll know what to do with him in the Free Glades, the stinking traitor . . .'

'Don't listen to them, Xanth. They don't know what

they're talking about,' said Rook, still glowering at the librarians.

'I'm sorry, Rook, I just can't stand it any more,' Xanth said tremulously. 'They're right. I'm no good. I'm rotten . . .' His voice trailed away.

Rook turned back to his friend. 'You're *not* rotten, Xanth. You're . . . Xanth? What are you doing? Xanth! *Xanth!*'

His friend had vanished, the rope that bound him hanging limply from the main tether.

'No, Xanth,' Rook shouted, struggling to loosen his own binding. The rope fell away behind him as he dashed off after his friend. 'Xanth. Xanth, wait! Come back!'

Behind him, Rook heard the banderbears yodelling in alarm, and the librarians bellowing at him to come back. But he couldn't abandon his friend. He just couldn't.

Up ahead, he caught a glimpse of a misty figure through the thickening fog – but almost at once, it was gone again. Like a snowbird in an ice-storm, the shaven-headed youth had disappeared.

'XANTH!' Rook roared.

But there was no reply save his own muffled echo.

'XAAAAANTH!!'

As the desperate cry faded away, Rook realized that he could hear nothing. Nothing at all. It was as if the vast multitude of Undertowners, librarians, ghosts and sky pirates had simply vanished along with his friend. Suddenly, he was alone, lost in the swirling mists of the Edgelands, the treacherous Twilight Woods on one side, the Edge on the other – and no one to talk to.

The wind began to pick up again, but it had changed. Now, instead of lifting the fog, it swirled into eddies and ripples. And as Rook stumbled on over the greasy stone, trying his best not to twist his ankles in the cracks and fissures, he began to hear voices.

Lots of voices. Wailing and keening and whispering softly.

'Sweet dreams, Master Rook,' they seemed be saying, the innocent words belied by the cold, menacing hiss. 'Sweet dreams . . .'

CHAPTER FIVE

THE SEPIA STORM

Rook stumbled on, sweaty and scared, trying hard to shut out the whispering voices – but it wasn't easy. No matter how hard he pressed his hands to his ears, how loudly he hummed, how vigorously he tried to engage in conversation with himself, they would not be silenced. They would not be still.

'Xanth!' he cried out, his own voice carried off on the warm wind sweeping in from the Twilight Woods. 'Xanth, where *are* you?' He paused, removed his hands from his ears and cocked his head to one side, hoping against hope that this time his friend would reply. The air echoed with a thousand voices; high, low, angry and sad – every voice in the world it seemed but the one he longed to hear.

'Oh, Xanth,' he murmured. 'Not all librarians are like Ambris Loppix. Why did you listen to him?'

'Once a Guardian, always a Guardian!' the voices seemed to hiss back at him. 'He betrayed others. Now he's betrayed you.'

'It's not true!' Rook shouted back at the swirling, sparkling air. 'Xanth's changed. He's one of us now!'

'One of us, one of us,' taunted the chorus of voices, and Rook glimpsed a black shape out of the corner of his eye. He spun round, to be confronted by a tall figure in a black gown and a metal muzzle.

'Orbix? Orbix Xaxis?' Rook gasped, his conversation with Xanth flooding back to him. 'No, it can't be, I must be . . .'

'Dreaming?' a cold, cruel voice hissed through the muzzle. The white gloamglozer emblazoned on the black gown fluttered in front of him.

'You're not real,' said Rook, backing away, his feet slipping on the greasy rock.

'Aren't we, young librarian knight?' hissed the

voice. 'Are you quite certain of that?' The gowned figure cackled with laughter, and waved a bony claw-like hand.

As if in response, spectres and phantasms loomed out of the shadows, each one with a gloamglozer of its own emblazoned across its chest. They doubled in number, and doubled again, and again and again, until all around him, everywhere he looked, they were all Rook could see. It was as if he'd wandered into a mighty army of Guardians of Night.

'We are real enough,' the voices sounded about him, mocking, jeering. 'As real as your blackest thoughts!'

'As real as your darkest fears!'

'As your deepest nightmares!'

The countless images of the gloamglozers smiled as one, their great fangs glinting savagely, their eyes flashing. The muzzled figure raised his clawed hand and beckoned slowly.

Rook felt a terrible, numbing fear welling up deep inside him. It spread out from his chest, along his arms and into his fingertips; it coursed down his legs, making his knees tremble, and sinking to his toes. He tried hard to fight it, but it was no good. Like a lemkin, held by the murderous stare of a predatory halitoad, he was paralysed. There was nothing he could do. Even his face seemed frozen as the fear travelled up his spine, over his scalp . . .

'No, no, no,' Rook muttered, unable even to blink. 'Remember what Fenbrus said. This is one of those waking dreams. But that's all it is. A dream, that's all . . .'

'That's all! That's all! That's all!' jeered a thousand cackling voices.

Rook could bear it no longer. He threw back his head and screamed like a wounded animal.

'Xanth! Xanth! *Xanth!*'

His cries drowned out the jeering voices and, for an instant, the black figures seemed to shrink back into the swirling mists. At the same moment, the fear that held him released its grip and, without a second's thought, Rook was up and running across the slippery pavement as fast as his legs could carry him.

'I've got to get out of here! I've got to get out of here!' he shouted, as he ran blindly through the swirling mist.

'Out of here! Out of here!' cackled voices behind him, driving him on.

This way and that Rook ran, slipping and stumbling, terrified of falling yet too frightened to stop, until – imperceptibly at first – the thick grey mist seemed to thin out and take on a golden tinge.

All at once, Rook came to an abrupt halt. Ahead of him, the jagged skyline of the Twilight Woods crackled with electric blue filaments as, high in the air above, boiling black clouds swirled in a gathering whirlwind. The glow from between the trees brightened and faded as a warm, slightly sickly mist blew in from the woods and into his face.

Was he awake or asleep? Was it dreams or illusions that surrounded him? Could he even be sure that it was the Twilight Woods he could see before him now, and not simply something else his feverish imagination had conjured up. Certainly, it *looked* like the Twilight Woods, and with the seductive whispers and wheedling cries floating in on the rising wind, it *sounded* like it too. What was more, it had never seemed more inviting.

Rook took a step forward, and then stopped. 'That way lies death,' he reminded himself. 'Living death.'

He was about to turn and go back into the swirling mists of the Edgelands Pavement when, high above the gold-drenched trees, the sky tore itself apart with a deafening *crack*, and the air blazed dazzlingly bright. Rook looked up to see a huge, zigzag lightning bolt break off from the base of the dark, spinning cloud and hurtle down into the woods below.

He gasped as a blast of scalding air hit him full in the face. The air filled with the scent of toasted wood-almonds. Eyes wide open, mouth agape, Rook watched the blinding lightning turn to crystal as it pierced the glow of the woods, solidifying in an instant to a zigzag crystal spear which continued down behind the trees to the earth below. He shivered, awestruck by the incredible sight. A Great Storm, born of the dark maelstrom and drawn to the Twilight Woods like a moth to a flame, had discharged its colossal electric charge in the form of a mighty lightning bolt, deep at its centre.

'Stormphrax,' Rook breathed.

There was a distant echoing *thud* as the point of the frozen lightning bolt plunged deep into the twilit ground. The rock beneath Rook's feet trembled and he fell to the ground. It was as if the Twilight Woods – itself astonished by the lightning strike – had taken a sudden

intake of breath, sucking back the mist it had previously been blowing out across the Edgelands. And, as the mist disappeared into the Twilight Woods, Rook found himself being sucked after it and had to claw at the rocky pavement to prevent himself toppling head over heels into the deadly glades in front of him.

The next moment, and as abruptly as it had begun, everything suddenly fell still. Rook released his grip on the rock surface and climbed gingerly to his feet. As he looked round he saw that, for the first time since he'd set foot in the Edgelands, the thick, swirling mist had gone and he could see the pavement of rock stretching away into the distance on either side and in front.

There was no sign of the Undertowners . . .

But wait! Rook's heart missed a beat. Yes! There, in the distance, by a great rocky crag, was a figure, waving frantically.

'Rook!' Xanth's voice echoed across the flat, rocky expanse. 'Rook! Look out!'

'Xanth!' Rook shouted joyfully, and began running towards the far-off figure.

'Look out!' came Xanth's voice again. 'Behind you!'

Rook glanced back over his shoulder, from where there came a rumbling, rolling sound that was growing louder by the second. The next instant, a great, boiling blanket of sepia dust – rushing and roaring like a torrent of floodwater – burst out of the Twilight Woods and spread across the rockland.

It was heading straight for him. Even as he went to turn away, Rook knew that there was no point trying to flee. He could never outrun the oncoming storm. Having breathed in, the Twilight Woods was now expelling the full force of the lightning that had just struck it, in one mighty roar. Transfixed, Rook stared at the sepia-coloured storm surging across the rock towards him; closer, ever closer . . .

'*Aaaiiii!*' Rook cried out as it scythed his legs out from under him, sending him crashing to the ground and jarring his elbow painfully as he landed.

The turbulence tightened its grip around him, roaring and whistling and tugging at his clothes. He found himself being blown over and over, unable to stop, as – like a great, glowing tidal wave – the storm swept him across the rocky pavement towards the Edge itself.

All round him as he rolled, the dust sparkled brightly, like a maelstrom of tiny stars. It filled his eyes, his ears, it seeped in through the pores of his skin and, every time he inhaled, he breathed the glittering fragments and particles deep down into his lungs.

'Must . . . stop . . . myself . . .' he groaned, flinging his arms and legs out, trying in vain to stop the storm sweeping him on any further. But it was no good. The rock was too slippery, and the storm too strong.

All the while, the Edge was coming closer, flashing before his eyes as he continued to roll, a gaping nothingness where the rocky pavement simply stopped and the Edgelands fell away into the bottomless void beyond.

Bruised and battered, Rook was losing the battle. He was dizzy, he was dazed. Ahead of him, as he was driven on inexorably towards the Edge, he thought he

glimpsed the gloamglozer
– and not some fancy emblem stitched
to the front of a robe either. This was the
real thing. Huge. Imposing . . .

Yes, there it was again, looming out of the glittering dust-storm ahead, its great horned head raised in
evil triumph. It was as if the terrible creature had come
to gloat; to stand at the very Edge itself and watch him,
Rook Barkwater, tumbling helplessly into the empty
nothingness.

Rook knew then that he was done for.

'Rook! Rook!'

Rook trembled. It even knew his name.

'ROOK!'

Beneath him now, the last few strides of rocky
pavement were rolling past. In front, the void yawned.
Rook clamped his eyes shut and hugged his arms to his
chest. There was nothing, nothing, that he could do to
save himself.

With a lurch, and a gasp, he felt the rock suddenly disappear from beneath him.

Falling. He was falling. This was it. He'd tumbled over the Edge and . . .

'*Unkhh!*'

With a heavy jolt, his fall was broken. Something tightened round his middle, pinning his arms to his side and leaving him gasping for breath. Bewildered, Rook looked down, to see a rope! He was dangling from a rope above the endless emptiness beneath, with the torrent of dust-filled air cascading over the Edge to his left like a mighty waterfall.

The next moment, he felt himself being yanked upwards, backwards through the air. His back slammed hard against the rock. Hands seized him by the shoulders, rolled him round and dragged him up over the lip of rock and onto solid ground. Then they released him.

Wriggling round awkwardly, Rook managed to loosen the rope and slip free. He climbed shakily to his feet, his stomach churning, his ears ringing. Looking up, he found himself standing in the shelter of a great angular crag of rock, carved and weathered by the Edgeland winds into a monstrous hunched form.

'The gloamglozer,' Rook whispered.

The brightly glowing sepia storm was swirling round it on both sides as it poured out over the Edge. Xanth, he saw, was standing beside him, bent double and panting noisily. Straightening up slowly, he put his hands on his hips and took a long, deep breath.

'Thank Sky the mist cleared when it did,' he said at length, 'or I'd never have spotted you.' His face clouded over. 'Oh, Rook, I'm so sorry I ran off . . .'

Rook silenced him with a wave of his hand. 'Just thank Sky you were top of the class at ropecraft,' he said. 'And that this rock was here to shelter behind . . .' His voice faded away. He was feeling increasingly light-headed, and his arms and legs were beginning to ache. 'It's strange,' he said softly, 'but I think I know this place.'

The pair of them looked out. Even as they had been speaking, the great waves of dust-laden storm-ripples were losing their power, the sepia storm exhausted. And as the roaring softened, the torrent shrank to a trickle and the sparkling light grew dim.

'Come on,' said Xanth quickly. 'There's still a chance we can catch up with the others . . .'

He stopped and stared at Rook, who had dropped to his knees and was peering cautiously down over the cliff-edge.

The wind had abruptly changed direction, and was driving in from beyond the Edge once more, icy cold and heavy with moisture. From below, there came eerie sounds of chains clanking and something *tap-tap-tapping* against the rock-face, while behind, the northerly winds howled through the cracks and crevices of the huge, monstrous-shaped rock.

Despite the dull pain behind his eyes that made it so difficult for him to focus, Rook was more certain than ever that he knew where he was. He leaned over a little further and . . .

Yes, there they were; the great mooring-rings driven

into the rock that he
remembered seeing
once before. Most
were empty, some
bore ropes or
chains, while
from others,
there hung the
shattered
remains of
sky pirate
ships that had
been destroyed
where they were
moored, swaying in the storm
winds like great, bleached skeletons.

'I do know this place, Xanth,' he called back hoarsely.
'Wilderness Lair, it's called. The mighty sky pirate fleets
used to take refuge here, clinging to the cliff-face like
rock-limpets.'

Xanth made no reply.

'It's the place where the *Skyraider* was moored,' Rook
went on. He was finding it difficult to catch his breath.
'You remember the *Skyraider*?' he added, turning to see
whether Xanth was paying attention.

His friend was staring at him, his eyes wide.

'Captain Twig's sky pirate ship,' Rook said slowly,
softly. 'The one that launched the attack on the Tower
of . . .' His voice faded away completely. 'Xanth?' he
said. 'Xanth, what is it?'

'It . . . it's . . .' Xanth faltered. He looked Rook up and down. 'You're . . .'

Rook gasped. He could see for himself now. Climbing shakily to his feet, he raised a hand to his face. Then the other. Both were glowing. As were his arms, and his chest, his body, his legs . . .

'Xanth,' he breathed, as the glowing grew more intense, 'what's happening to me?' His head was spinning. His legs turned to jelly. 'Xanth . . .'

He saw his friend running towards him, his arms outstretched, his face creased with concern. Inside and outside, the light grew brighter; dazzling him, blinding him, till he could take no more.

'Help me,' he whispered, his last words as he crumpled to the ground in a curled and glowing heap.

Xanth crouched down and put an ear tentatively to Rook's chest. His heartbeat was so faint, Xanth could hardly hear it.

'I'm so, so sorry, old friend,' he said, scooping Rook up in his arms and heaving himself to his feet. 'This is all my fault.'

He turned and began the long, arduous journey across the Edgelands rock, the heavy burden weighing him down and making every step an ordeal.

'By Earth and Sky, Rook,' he swore, stumbling on across the rocky pavement, 'enough brave librarian knights have died because of me. I shan't let *you* become one of them.'

·CHAPTER SIX·

DUSK

i

The Palace of the Furnace Masters

Hemuel Spume rubbed his spidery fingered hands together and smiled a thin-lipped smile. He always enjoyed this time of day.

The furnace fires had been freshly stoked for the night shift and the tall chimney stacks were belching out thick clouds of acrid smoke that stained the early evening sky a brilliant red. Exhausted lines of workers were tramping off to the low open-sided huts to snatch a few hours of much-needed sleep amid the unceasing din of the drills and hammers coming from the metal-working shops. An undercurrent of low, muttered complaints filled the air as the night workers jostled each other to reach their benches and forges.

The Foundry Master was standing in the upper gallery of the Counting House, a tall, solid wooden tower at the western end of the magnificently carved

857

Palace of the Furnace Masters. The mullioned windows were grimy with soot, both inside and out, yet this did little to mar the splendour of the view outside.

As far as the eye could see, the rows of blackened chimneys pointed like accusing fingers up at the blood-red sky. Beneath them, the glowing furnaces seemed to stare back at Hemuel, like the eyes of a thousand forest demons, throwing grotesque shadows across the huge timber stacks that fed them. Everywhere there was noise, bustle and industry, just the way he liked it – and never more so than now, as dusk was falling. With the changing of the shifts, the clamour of activity in the Foundry Glades was reaching a crescendo, before settling into the night-time cacophony of hammer-blow, foundry-clatter and furnace-blast.

Hemuel traced a bony finger through the soot on the window, and pushed his steel-rimmed glasses up his long nose. It hadn't always been like this. Oh, no. When he – Hemuel Maccabee Spume – had first come to the Deepwoods all those years ago, the Foundry Glade had been an insignificant forest forge, turning out trinkets and cooking pots for itinerant goblin tribes and the odd band of wandering shrykes. The ambitious young leaguesmen back in Undertown had said he was mad to bury himself out here in the Deepwoods, but Hemuel knew better . . .

The corners of his eyes crinkled with amusement as he thought back to those early days. So much had changed since then, and almost all for the better – at least, for him.

Stone-sickness had put an end to sky-flight, changing

the patterns of trade in the Edge for ever. No longer could the heavily-laden league ships transport the man-ufactured goods of the Undertown workshops out to the Deepwoods and return with precious timber and raw materials; no longer could the sky pirates prey upon the wealthy merchants and traders. After stone-sickness had struck, *all* cargo had to travel overland. And that – as Hemuel Spume had taken note – was a costly enterprise.

Once the shrykes had taken control of the Great Mire Road, the Undertown leagues had been forced to pay them high taxes for the right to trade with the Deepwoods. Costs of their products had soared and, as a result, the Undertowners had priced themselves out of business. Hemuel Spume had seized the opportunity to fill the gap in the market. The Foundry Glade – independent of the shrykes' greedy influence – had grown and prospered.

Soon it wasn't just one glade but many, spreading through the boundless Deepwoods like a fungus. Its influence increased. Why, without the success of the Foundry Glades, the Goblin Nations themselves would never have grown to their present size. And what's more, whether they liked it or not, they were now totally dependent on the knowledge and skills of Hemuel Spume's Furnace Masters.

Yes, times were good, Hemuel Spume had to admit, but you couldn't stand still. On no, not for a moment. Once you did that, you became complacent.

After all, look what had happened to the shrykes at the Eastern Roost. They'd sat back and grown rich on the

Undertown trade, putting all their eggs in one basket, so to speak. And now, if the reports he had received from his business partner were to be believed, they, along with Undertown itself, were finished.

As Foundry Master, Hemuel Spume wasn't about to stand still. He had great plans, monumental plans; plans that would change the face of the Deepwoods settlements for ever. Territory, riches, power: he wanted it all.

He turned and surveyed the ordered rows of leadwood desks stretching off before him down the dark hall. At each one, hunched over and spattered with black ink, sat a scribe. There were mobgnomes, lugtrolls and all manner of goblins, all furiously scribbling, accounting for firewood quotas, ore extraction, smelting rates and workshop output. The air buzzed and hissed with a sound like mating woodcrickets as five hundred quills scratched and scraped at five hundred pieces of coarse parchment.

The sound was punctuated by the dry rasping cough peculiar to the Foundry Glades. Foundry-croup, it was called. Most who breathed the filthy, smoke-filled air suffered from it. The scribes, up in the Counting House gallery, got off relatively lightly – unlike the slaves who worked the foundries. Two years they lasted on average, before their lungs gave out.

Hemuel Spume made it a habit always to wear a gauze mask when he inspected the foundries. At other times, he kept to the high towers and upper halls of the palace, where the air was considerably cleaner. Nonetheless, even he was prone to the occasional coughing fit. It simply couldn't be helped. Feeling a tell-tale tickle in his throat, he reached into a pocket of his gown and pulled out a small bottle, which he unstoppered with his spidery fingers and put to his lips.

As the pungent syrup slipped over his tongue and down his throat, the tickling stopped. He returned the stoppered bottle to his pocket, removed his glasses and polished them fussily with a large handkerchief.

Thank goodness for Deepwoods medicines and the gabtrolls who dispensed them, he thought. He, personally, had ten of the stalk-eyed apothecaresses at his sole disposal. How his sickly business partner would enjoy that, he mused.

'Excuse me, Foundry Master, sir?' came a tentative voice.

Spume looked up, replacing his glasses as he did so. An aged clerk, Pinwick Krum, stood before him, an anxious frown on his pinched face.

'Yes, yes,' Spume snapped impatiently. 'What do you want?'

'The latest consign-ment of workers has arrived from Hemtuft Battleaxe,' Krum replied.

Spume's eyes narrowed. 'Yes?'

'I'm afraid there's only five dozen of them,' came the reply. 'And they're all lop-ear goblins . . .'

'Lop-ears!' Spume cried, his face redden-ing and a coughing fit threatening to explode at any moment. 'How many times do I have to tell him? It's hammer-heads we need, or flat-heads – goblins with a bit of life in them – why, those lop-ears are nothing but slack-jawed plough-pushers!' He poked his clerk in the chest. 'Battleaxe is not to be paid until we've tried them out. If they're no good, he doesn't get a single trading-credit, do you understand?'

'Yes, sir,' said Krum, his voice laden with weariness.

Hemuel Spume turned, rubbed a hand over the sooty window and peered out into the darkness. Below him were five chained columns of abject goblins, their heads bowed and bare feet shuffling, being led by guards through the filthy encampment, one after the other.

Lop-ears they certainly were, the curious tilt of their crooked ears accentuated by the number of heavy gold rings which hung from them – but Spume was relieved to see that the majority were pink-eyed and scaly goblins, fierce in battle and hard workers, rather than the indolent low-bellies that Battleaxe had tried to fob him off with before.

'*Humph!* Better than the last lot, I suppose,' he said peevishly. 'But nowhere near enough.'

'I know, sir,' said Pinwick Krum, wringing his hands together ingratiatingly. 'But what is one to do?'

Spume slammed his fist down on his desk, causing the great mass of scribes to look up as one, consternation on their brows and nervous coughs in their throats.

'This is intolerable,' he shouted. 'Absolutely intolerable. The furnaces have to be fed! Now, more than ever. I will not allow everything we have built up here to be jeopardized by a lack of labour. Doesn't *anyone* want to work these days?' He poked the shrunken clerk hard in the chest again. 'I want three hundred new workers,' he said. '*Good* workers! *Hard* workers! And I want them by this time next week at the latest. Do you hear me?'

'Yes, sir. But . . .'

'Hammelhorns butt, *Mister* Krum,' Spume interrupted. 'You are not a hammelhorn, are you?'

'No, sir. B . . .'

'If Hemtuft Battleaxe wants our goods, then he has to pay for them!' he shouted. 'And our price is goblin labour! And it's just gone up, tell him. Now, get out!'

Pinwick Krum turned and left, muttering quietly

under his breath as he went back down the lines of coughing, quill-scratching scribes, and over to the side door. Hemuel Spume watched him going, an unpleasant smile playing over his thin lips.

'Three hundred, Krum. Don't disappoint me,' he called after him. 'Or I'll have you put on double stoking-duty in the leadwood foundry. You won't last five minutes.'

As Krum shut the door quietly behind him, Hemuel Spume returned his attention to the window. Although the sun had only just set, the thick pall of smoke that hung permanently overhead had already thrown the Foundry Glades into darkness. The tail-end of the column of lop-ears was being checked in at the slave-huts.

'Sixty measly goblins,' he muttered. It was barely enough for five foundries, and he had *twenty*-five to fill.

Hemuel Spume shook his head. With the projected rate of expansion, even if Pinwick did manage to secure a deal for three hundred goblins, a month later they would need another three hundred, and three hundred more the month after that . . . It was simply unsustainable.

He raised his head, and stared off past the great Foundry Glades to where the distant Deepwoods lay. There, far off to the north, lay the Free Glades. Hemuel Spume smiled, his small, pointed teeth glinting in the lampglow.

'The Free Glades,' he purred. 'That so-called beacon of light and hope . . .' His lips twisted into a sneer. 'And a limitless supply of slaves.'

ii
The Great Clan-Hut of the Long-Haired Goblins

'So that's the great Hemtuft Battleaxe, is it?' Lob asked, peering over the heads of the goblins in front of him, struggling to get a good view.

'Doesn't he look fine in that shryke-feather cloak of his!' commented his brother, Lummel. 'They say he plucked each feather himself from a different shryke-sister.'

'Shut up, back there,' a voice hissed angrily. 'Some of us are trying to listen.'

Lob and Lummel fell silent. As a rule, their older brothers would have attended such an important assembly, but all six of them had recently been dispatched

to the Foundry Glade as slave-labour, and what with harvest-time fast approaching and all, there had been no one else to send to report back. The last thing either of them wanted to do was get on the wrong side of a hefty great hammerhead at their very first Meeting of the Clans.

'Sorry, Master.' Lob touched his bonnet deferentially and nudged his brother to do the same.

The hammerhead ignored them.

Lob and Lummel Grope were low-bellied goblins of the lop-ear clan. In their straw harvest-bonnets and characteristic belly-slings, they stood out amongst the warlike goblins all around them, and both felt more than a little overawed.

They were standing at the centre of a vast crowd that had assembled outside the great open-sided clan-hut of the long-hairs; a crowd packed with goblins of every description, all crushed together so tightly it was difficult even to breathe. Flat-heads and hammerheads, pink-eyed and scaly goblins; long-haired and tufted goblins, snag-toothed, saw-toothed and underbiter goblins; all were represented.

Inside the clan-hut, on a raised stage, sat Hemtuft Battleaxe of the long-hair goblin clan, leader of the Goblin Nations. Preening his shryke-feather cloak, the grey-haired Battleaxe looked down from his carved wooden throne, placed as it was on top of a pile of skulls of deceased clan elders. On the platform before him stood the leaders of the four other clans, their heads bowed in supplication.

Rootrott Underbiter, clan chief of the tusked goblins, was the first to look up, his two massive canines glinting, his yellow eyes impassive. As leader of one of the larger clans, there was a look of sullen insolence on his face, despite his thin, twitching smile.

Next to him stood Lytugg, leader of the hammerhead clan, and granddaughter of the old mercenary, General Tytugg of Undertown. For one so young, she boasted an impressive array of battle scars as befitted the leader of the most warlike of all the goblin nations.

Beside her, sat the old, hunched figure of Meegmewl the Grey, clan chief of the lop-ears, as sharp-witted as he was ancient. Although the least warlike of the major clans, the lop-ears were the most numerous by far, and Meegmewl was not to be underestimated.

Nor, for that matter, was Grossmother Nectarsweet the Second, clan chief of the symbites. She spoke for the gyle, tree, webfooted and gnokgoblins of the nations – the symbites who were responsible for such a rich array of products, everything from gyle-honey and dew-milk, to teasewood rope and lullabee grubs. Her five chins wobbled in a languid ripple as she raised her huge head and met Hemtuft's gaze levelly.

Hemtuft Battleaxe waved a hairy hand. As leader of the long-hairs and most senior of the goblin clans, his word was law. He knew though that, without the support of the other clans, the Goblin Nations would disintegrate and return to the roving, warring tribes they had been before. And that was something no one wanted.

'I understand, of course I do,' he said, as the crowd around the clan-hut jostled closer, trying to catch every word. 'Your lop-ear clan has paid a heavy price in supplying the labour to the Foundry Glades, and yet it is a price we must pay for the spears, the ploughs, the cooking-pots, and everything else that none of us would do without.'

'Say the word, and my hammerhead war bands could overrun the Foundry Glades like that,' said Lytugg, with a snap of her bony fingers.

Hemtuft shook his head. 'Lytugg, Lytugg. How many times must we go over this?' he said wearily. 'It is point-less to use force against the Foundry Glades. Hemuel Spume and the Furnace Masters would die before they revealed the secrets of their forges and workshops to us. And then where would we be? In charge of a lot of use-less machinery that none of us could operate. No, if we are to succeed, we must pay the price the Foundry Master demands of us . . .'

The skeletons of the old clan chief's predecessors, hanging from the rafters of the huge thatched roof, clinked like bone wind-chimes in the breeze.

'But why must *we* pay it alone,' Meegmewl the Grey croaked, turning his milky eyes to the ceiling.

'Because there are so many of you,' retorted Rootrott Underbiter nastily.

'. . . And not a single hammerhead or flat-head shall stoke a furnace!' Lytugg snarled fiercely. 'We are war-riors!'

Around Lob and Lummel, the hammerhead and flat-head goblins cheered and brandished their hefty clubs and spears.

'But things can't go on like this!' Grossmother Nectarsweet's big, wobbly voice proclaimed, silencing the cheering.

'And nor shall they!' Hemtuft roared, getting to his feet and spreading his arms wide, until, in his feathered cloak, he resembled a large bird of prey. 'For if we attack the Free Glades and enslave them, then never again will goblins have to be sent to work the foundries.

*Slave*gladers will go in their stead!'

Lob and Lummel turned to one another, eyebrows raised. All round them, the crowd exploded with noise, and a chant got up.

'Slave Glades! Slave Glades! Slave Glades!'

'There has never been a better time for this, our greatest battle!' General Lytugg's voice rang out above it all. 'The shrykes are all but done for! Undertown is no more! With help from our friends in the Foundry Glades, we shall launch an attack on the Free Glades while they are vulnerable and in disarray; an attack the like of which the Edge has never known. No one will withstand the might of the Goblin Nations.'

Lob shrugged. Lummel lowered his eyes. They both knew that it hadn't been Freegladers who had sent their brothers to be worked to death in the Foundry Glades: Hemtuft Battleaxe and the other clan chiefs had seen to that.

'We shall be victorious!' bellowed Lytugg, and a mighty roar echoed round the great hall.

Lob and Lummel were feeling increasingly out of place in the midst of all the grimacing faces and frenzied cries. What was wrong with farming? That was what they wanted to know. After all, everyone had to eat. Instead, all their neighbours seemed to have but one thing on their minds the whole time. War!

Flaming torches were lit and waved in the warm evening air as the crowd began to break off and return to their villages.

'To victory!' roared Hemtuft Battleaxe after them. 'And the Slave Glades!'

iii
The Hatching Nurseries of the Eastern Roost

'Look at the little darlings! Always hungry!' hissed portly Matron Featherhorn to her gaunt companion, the elderly Sister Drab. The pair of them were making their way along the central aisle of the great hatching-hut, inspecting the nursing pens as they went.

As they passed them by, the shryke juveniles in each enclosure scuttled towards the barred gates and craned their necks towards the two elders, screeching loudly for food. Only two days had passed since they had hatched out from their eggs, yet already they were more than half their fully-grown size.

'They certainly are, my dear,' Sister Drab replied, nodding approvingly. Her eyes narrowed and glinted coldly. 'It won't be long now.'

The pair of them reached the end of the hall, where a complicated wood and rope construction of cogs, pulleys and connecting-rods was anchored. The penned shrykes grew louder. Matron Featherhorn jumped up and seized a heavy lever which, with the weight of her swinging body, slowly lowered. There was a hiss overhead as tank-valves opened and a torrent of warm prowlgrin entrails poured down into the feeding pipes.

All round, the hatching-hut exploded with frantic scratching and squawking as the juveniles scurried across the pens – crashing into one another in their greed – clamped their beaks round the feeding pipes and waited impatiently, their eyes rolling and stubby wings flapping.

Matron Featherhorn turned her attention to the winching-wheel, and there was a loud *clunk* as she seized it tightly, pulled it sharply to the right and released the entrails down the pipes. The juveniles sat back on their haunches – their eyes instantly glazed with contentment – as the meat sluiced down their necks and into their stomachs.

Matron Featherhorn watched their bellies swell. 'That should do for now,' she said at last, tugging the wheel back the other way.

The flow of entrails abruptly ceased. The bloated shrykes flopped to the floor on their backs and closed their eyes.

'That's it, my pretties,' Sister Drab hissed. 'Sleep well; grow tall and strong

and fierce.' She turned to Matron Featherhorn. 'Soon we shall have a new battle-flock to feast on the entrails of our enemies.' She shook her head. 'And a new Sisterhood and roost-mother in fine plumage!'

The old matron fiddled with her mob-cap uncertainly. 'I only hope you're right, Sister Drab,' she said. 'With Mother Muleclaw and the Sisterhood lost in Undertown, we are sorely in need of new flock leaders.' She clucked unhappily. 'After all, we're getting too long in the beak to take *that* responsibility on, eh, sister?'

Sister Drab sighed. With her eyes dim and her tawny feathers grizzled with grey and white, she had thought her days of decisions and responsibility were long since past. In her prime, High Sister Drab had been an important figure in the Shryke Sisterhood, second only to the roost-mother herself. Yet, when they had moved to the Eastern Roost, she had been happy to relinquish power, unable as she was to adjust to the new permanent settlement.

Now, everything had changed again. With the battle-flocks, the entire High Sisterhood *and* Mother Muleclaw herself, all massacred in the sewers of Undertown, apart from a shifty gathering of useless shryke males, there was no one left in the Eastern Roost but a small flock of hatchery matrons and a handful of venerable elder sisters like herself. It had been left to them to tend to the mighty clutch of eggs – their future battle-flocks, high sisters and roost-mother.

They had stayed up through the stormy night, assiduously adding and removing layers of straw and down to the great nests, ensuring that the eggs remained at a constant temperature. They had slaughtered and gutted the prowlgrins and filled the feeding-tanks ready. And when the time had come for the great Hatching itself, they had raised their voices as tradition decreed and screeched their greetings to the newly-born fledglings;

'From shell to air,
From yolk to feather;
Gorge and grow strong!'

The hatchlings had lost their downy fluff within hours of being born, and were fully fledged by their third meal. There was every type of plumage, from striped and speckled beiges and browns, to the gaudiest of purples, reds, blues and oranges – the feathers pointing to the future mapped out before them all, be it forming warlike battle-flocks or creating a new High Sisterhood. Now, with the new flock growing taller and stronger as they slept, even as she watched, it was indeed – as Matron Featherhorn had just reminded her – left to her to start making decisions once again.

'Ah, sister,' Sister Drab replied at length. 'It is as I always suspected. We shrykes are nomads, wanderers. We were never meant to settle down in one place.'

'But the Eastern Roost . . .' Matron Featherhorn began.

'The Eastern Roost is unnatural,' Sister Drab interrupted. 'A shryke nest should never be settled. She paused. 'Oh, I concede it worked well enough when we could control the traffic on the Great Mire Road. But now that the road has been destroyed, and Undertown with it, there is no longer any reason for our great city to exist.'

Matron Featherhorn's beak dropped open.

'Yes, sister,' the gaunt shryke elder continued. 'I know my words come as a shock, but the time has come for us to leave the Eastern Roost. We have become soft here, pampered and indolent. We must pack everything away, saddle up the prowlgrins and return to the treetops. We must go back to our old slaving ways – after all, such a way of life saw us prosper for hundreds of years.' She flapped an arm towards the future battle-flocks. 'And with these little darlings, we shall soon prosper once more, sister, and for hundreds of years yet to come.'

The grizzled matron shivered, and tightened the shawl around her shoulders. 'Slaving, you say,' she said. 'Slaving's no longer the easy life it once was. Times have changed, venerable sister. The Deepwoods tribes have organized themselves. There are the Goblin Nations, made strong by their alliance with the Foundry Glades. And then, the Free Glades . . . They stand and fight together, not like the old days when scattered villages were easy prey. Are you suggesting we attack any of these?'

Sister Drab tutted and shook her head. 'No,' she replied. 'At least, not yet, cautious sister,' she replied. 'We are too few in number. But there is another target. A moving target, many of leg and soft of underbelly, flee-ing this way from a ruined city . . .'

'The Undertowners!' Matron Featherhorn shrieked excitedly.

'The very same,' came the reply. 'I have spies out searching for news of their progress, and have high hopes . . .'

Just then, there came the sound of furious squawking from outside the hatching-hut. Sister Drab and Matron Featherhorn exchanged glances before scurrying back down the aisle, past the slumbering juveniles, and out onto the jutting balcony outside.

High above their heads, the air was filled with hundreds of insect-like craft, slowly circling the Eastern Roost. Mother Featherhorn looked up. 'Librarian patrol,' she muttered.

Sister Drab nodded. 'It seems we are not the only ones to have sent out spies.' She leaned over the balustrade.

Far below her, at the foot of the rows of hatching-huts, a gathering of aged sisters, greying matrons and scrawny shryke males were standing round the central platform, pointing up at the sky and chattering nervously. Beside them, at the battlements, the Eastern Roost's defences stood idle.

'Don't just stand there!' Sister Drab shrieked furiously. 'Do something!'

The shrykes sprang instantly into action; priming the air-catapults, aligning the sights, setting the lufwood balls ablaze . . .

At least, that is what they were attempting. But the tasks were as unfamiliar as they were testing. This was guard work; work that, in the past, all of those gathered on the platform had either been excused or excluded from. Now, however, the guards were gone, and with no one to defend them, it was up to the so-called 'roost-minders' to defend themselves, and more importantly, their precious charges in the hatching-huts.

'FIRE!' Sister Drab screeched – and threw herself to the ground as a purple fireball whistled past her head, singeing her ear-feathers as it went.

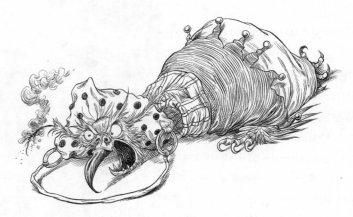

It was not the only fireball to be misfired. Half a dozen of them slipped ignominiously from their firing-bowls and had to be doused with water before they set fire to the walkways and platforms themselves. Others flew feebly out in a low arc before flopping down into the forest beyond.

Yet there were some – not many, but a few – that were perfectly launched.

'Yes, yes, yes!' Sister Drab hissed excitedly as, looking up from the floor, she saw four, five . . . six of the flaming purple fireballs speeding up into the sky and hurtling into the swirl of distant librarian skycraft.

There was a loud *bang* and an explosion of sparks as one, then two more of the skycraft were struck and began spiralling down, down, through the sky. Two of them fluttered off towards the Deepwoods. The third, however, out of control, was heading straight for the Roost.

Sister Drab climbed to her feet and rubbed her taloned hands together in anticipation. 'Come on, my lovely,' she whispered. 'Come to Sister Drab.'

Like a wounded snowbird, the skycraft flapped and fluttered down to the ground and landed with a soft clatter on the boards of the central platform. Its rider struggled – but the tangle of tethers and ropes which had prevented the hapless librarian from ejecting over the relative safety of the Deepwoods, continued to bind fast. The shrykes gathered round in a circle, lances prodding and flails swinging.

'Careful!' shrieked Sister Drab. 'Don't kill it!'

Squawking with disappointment, two of the shrykes sliced through the ropes and dragged the librarian from the ground.

'And the rest of you, resume firing!' Sister Drab screeched.

Matron Featherhorn turned to her. 'It seems we might not need to rely on those spies of yours after all,' she said.

'True, true, sister,' said Sister Drab, her neck ruff rising menacingly. 'First we shall pluck this librarian, then we shall skin it slowly, until *all* of our questions have been answered. For I tell you this, Matron Featherhorn,' she said, her voice rising to a screech, 'the Undertowners' whereabouts will be revealed – even if I have to read the prisoner's steaming entrails to find them!'

·CHAPTER SEVEN·

THE IRONWOOD STANDS

Rook noticed the breathing first. It was slow and regular. In and out, it went. In and out. In and out . . . Then he became aware of soft, moss-scented fur pressed against his cheek and the loamy odour of warm breath in his face. He felt great muscular arms enfolding him, cradling him gently.

This is a dream, Rook told himself. An old familiar dream – a dream from my childhood.

He was a young'un, little more than a toddler, and he was being rocked to sleep by a crooning banderbear, safe and secure in her Deepwoods' nest. The air was filled with the sound of a familiar lulling voice that rose and fell as he rocked softly back and forth, back and forth . . .

It was a beautiful dream. Rook felt safe and protected. His head ached and his limbs felt dull and heavy, but the nest was warm and the yodelled song was soothing. He didn't want to wake up. He wanted to lie there for ever, his body warm and his head empty, yet even as he had this thought, he knew the dream couldn't last. He'd have to wake up and face . . .

What, exactly? With a jolt, Rook realized he didn't know. He struggled to collect his thoughts.

There was Undertown, and the dark maelstrom pouring down, flooding the streets, washing everything away . . . The Mire Gates, the Undertowners fleeing, and then . . .

And then . . .

Nothing. His mind was a blank. The banderbear's soft yodel filled his head, and the gentle rocking continued. Slowly, Rook opened his eyes.

Moss-stuffed leafy boughs, curved and secured above his head, forming a familiar shelter.

It was a *banderbear* nest.

'Can it be real? Or am I still dreaming?' Rook croaked, his throat feeling as dry as dust.

'Ssh-wuh-ssh,' came a voice.

Rook's eyes focused on the kindly face of a banderbear. 'Wumeru,' he whispered, as he recognized his oldest banderbear friend. 'Is that you?'

'Wurra-wooh. Uralowa, wuh-wuh!' the banderbear whispered, gently stroking his temple with her thumb. *This is no dream. You are safe now, friend who took the poisonstick. But you need to rest.*

'Meera-weega-wuh,' Rook replied, his hand movements languid and slow, before stabbing at the air. 'Wuh! Loora-weer? Wellah-wuh?' *But how did I get here? I can remember nothing!*

Wumeru's ears fluttered as she replied, her voice gentle, her gestures animated. *The stubble-headed one says he saved you from an Edgeland storm and brought you back to us, here in the Deepwoods . . .*

'Deepwoods?' Rook murmured uncertainly, his voice faltering. 'Stubble-headed one . . ?'

Wumeru nodded over her shoulder and Rook became aware of another figure, hanging back in the shadows of the nest. The banderbear grunted and the figure came forward and crouched beside them. It was a youth. He looked concerned. His skin was sallow, his eyes sunken, his hair shaven close to the skull.

'Rook! Are you all right?' he asked, staring anxiously into Rook's oddly pale – almost glowing – eyes.

Rook stared back, his mouth open, bewilderment flickering in his eyes.

'Rook, it's *me*,' said the youth. 'Xanth. We've made it to the Deepwoods, old friend.'

Rook frowned, and racked his brains. 'Xanth?' he said at last, a memory flickering at the back of his mind. 'Xanth Filatine? I . . . I haven't seen you since we trained together in the Free Glades . . . You ran away . . . They . . . they said you were a spy, Xanth; a traitor . . .'

Rook's head began to spin, and with it, the shaven-headed youth's face seemed to fade back into the shadows. Wumeru resumed her gentle rocking as Rook's head slumped against her soft fur and he drifted into a dreamless sleep.

The banderbear waved a huge paw at Xanth, who had hesitated by the nest's entrance. 'Wuh!' she grunted, and though Xanth could speak not a word of the curious banderbear language, he was left in no doubt that his presence in the nest was not wanted.

Then again, his presence was not wanted outside either, he thought bitterly.

He crawled out of the banderbear nest, which was expertly camouflaged on the forest floor with mosses and ferns, and straightened up. All around him, the massive trunks of the Ironwood Stands rose up, their uppermost branches lost in the clouds blowing in from the Edgelands close by. On their lower branches – each one as wide as the Mire Road and heavy with pine-cones

the size of hammelhorns – the Undertowners were setting up camp.

Xanth had been lucky to find them, he knew that. Carrying Rook on his back, he'd stumbled across the Edgeland Pavement through the thick swirling air. Just when he thought he could go no further, the mists had thinned and he'd glimpsed the tops of the mighty iron-wood pines, dark giants looming out of the fog. With one last gigantic effort, he'd forced himself to continue and had dropped down from the hard rock of the pavement onto the soft, springy floor of the Deepwoods themselves.

When he stumbled into the camp, already forming in the Ironwood Stands, the banderbears had taken Rook away and he'd been left to face the stony faces of the librarians, who whispered behind their hands. Snubbed by them and uncertain what to do for the best, Xanth had turned away and sought out the banderbears. They had allowed him to help them construct their nest, but begrudgingly – and he could tell by their whispered grunts that they, too, blamed him for luring their friend into danger back in the Edgelands.

And now, evening was falling here on the edge of the mighty Deepwoods. Unwilling to stray far from the banderbear nest, Xanth sat himself down heavily on a rock close by. He leaned forwards, his shoulders hunched, his head held in his hands.

'Sky above and Earth below,' Xanth groaned miserably, the palms of his hands rubbing over his rough, stubbly scalp. 'What *am* I to do?'

'Now, now,' came a voice, and Xanth felt a bony hand clapping him on the shoulder. 'What are you doing down here on the ground, eh? You should be up in the trees, getting yourself ready for the long night ahead.'

Xanth looked up to see Cowlquape Pentephraxis smiling down at him kindly.

'Cheer up, lad,' said Cowlquape. 'Things are never quite so bad as they seem.'

Xanth winced. He knew the old professor meant well, but the words stung. 'Aren't they?' he said glumly.

Cowlquape's gaunt face creased with concern. 'The Edgeland mists can cause madness, Xanth,' he said. 'You can't be blamed for that. And besides,' he added, nodding towards the concealed nest, 'you did a brave thing carrying young Rook to safety.'

Xanth's eyes welled with tears. 'Try telling *him* that,' he said. 'There's something wrong. The storm's changed him. He hardly seems to know me. He called me a spy . . . a traitor . . .'

Cowlquape squeezed Xanth's shoulder reassuringly, and sat himself down next to the youth. 'Give him time,' he said. 'He needs to rest.'

'But his eyes . . .' Xanth blurted out. 'They were dazzling, and such a strangely piercing blue . . . And his skin; his whole body – it was *glowing* . . .'

'I know, I know,' said Cowlquape. 'The treetops are buzzing with talk of it. Caught in a sepia storm, I believe you said?'

Xanth nodded.

'I, myself, once saw something similar,' the High Academe mused.

'You did?' said Xanth.

Cowlquape nodded. 'The ways of the Sky are strange indeed,' he said. 'I was a young apprentice in old Sanctaphrax, when I met a young sky pirate captain who'd been caught by a great storm. He was found in the Stone Gardens, glowing every bit as brightly as young Rook there.'

'What happened? Did he recover?' Xanth asked.

'The glow died away after a few days,' said Cowlquape reassuringly. 'His strength returned and, eventually, one stormy night high on a balustrade in old Sanctaphrax, he got his memory back.' He shook his head. 'We can only hope that the same is true for Rook.'

Xanth gasped. 'You mean he might *never* properly remember who I am?' he said anxiously.

'What the Sky inflicts,' said Cowlquape, spreading his arms wide as he climbed to his feet, to indicate the Deepwoods around them, 'the Earth can often heal.' He smiled. 'Come on, now. You can't spend the night down here on the ground. It's far too dangerous . . .'

Xanth shrugged miserably.

'I've got my hanging-stove going,' Cowlquape continued. 'We could share a spot of supper together. What do you say?'

Xanth glanced round at the banderbear nest, then back at Cowlquape. He smiled. 'Thank you,' he said. 'I'd like that very much.'

*

The Ironwood Stands – where the vast multitude of fleeing Undertowners had set up camp – stood out from the
surrounding trees, their angular tops plunging through
the rest of the forest canopy like arrowheads.

Once, the stands had been a familiar landmark both to
league ship masters and sky pirate captains. These days,
following the arrival of stone-sickness and the
subsequent scuppering of all those old vessels, it had
become just as familiar a sight to the brave young
librarian knights who had mastered flight in their small,
wooden skycraft – which was why it was the obvious
place for the Undertowners to wait for the return of the
librarian knight squadrons.

The ragtag army of Undertowners, librarians, sky
pirates and ghosts could then proceed to the Free
Glades, with the librarian knights flying protectively
overhead.

'Keep up,' Cowlquape said urgently as he and Xanth made their way across the bouncy forest floor to the base of a huge ironwood tree. 'Night is falling, and it's not safe for us down here on the ground.'

They passed a herd of hammelhorn, clustered in a large circle – tails touching, horns facing outwards – to form an impregnable wall. They were sound asleep. Cowlquape reached for a dangling rope-ladder that was secured to a huge branch above and began to climb. Xanth quickly followed him.

Covered lamps and hanging-lanterns were attached to the trees all around them, illuminating the broad, sweep-ing branches. The air was filled with shouts and whistles. Ropes and pulleys were being used to hoist the boxes, bags and chests up from the ground. Hammocks and cooking-braziers swung from overhead hooks; and the huge branches bristled with sleeping bodies, four, five, sometimes six abreast.

As he continued up the tree after Cowlquape, Xanth was a little dismayed to find that he was surrounded by librarians. Earth and Sky forgive him, but he would have preferred to be in one of the neighbouring trees where others were setting up camp. Families of amiable mobgnomes, gnokgoblins and woodtrolls; gangs of rowdy cloddertrogs, parties of good-natured slaughterers – all of them taking help and instruction from the gruff sky pirates and the energetic ghosts, who were leaping between them from branch to branch, tree to tree, their rope lassoes and grappling-hooks never still.

Xanth could feel accusing glares boring into his back, and hear hateful whispers. And when they arrived at the Most High Academe's hanging-stove, Xanth's heart sank.

'How's it coming along, Garulus?' said Cowlquape.

The under-librarian looked up. 'Almost done, sir,' he said. He stirred the stew, raised the wooden spoon to his lips and sipped. '*Mmm*,' he murmured thoughtfully, 'tad more salt, perhaps.' He held the spoon out to Cowlquape. 'What do *you* think, sir?'

'I'm sure it's marvellous,' said Cowlquape. He ushered Xanth forward. 'Let the lad try a bit.'

Garulus's eyes narrowed. He dipped the spoon into the bubbling stew, filled it and held it out. Then, just as Xanth was about to take a sip, Garulus tipped the spoon forward, spilling the stew all down Xanth's tunic.

'Oh, dear. How *clumsy* of me,' Garulus muttered.

'Why, you . . .' Xanth stormed, his eyes blazing, his fists clenched. This was the final insult.

Garulus trembled and leaped behind Cowlquape. 'High Academe! You saw, it was an accident!' he appealed from behind Cowlquape's back.

Xanth glared back at Garulus, his teeth bared, his dark eyes black.

'Look at him, High Academe. He's an animal – a wild animal!' Garulus's voice was high-pitched and quavery.

'Now, now,' said Cowlquape calmly, laying a restraining hand on Xanth's shoulder and dabbing at his tunic with a handkerchief. 'You've had a hard day, Xanth. You're tired. And look, no harm done.'

'Once a Guardian of Night, always a Guardian,' hissed Garulus, growing bolder. 'It'll all come out at the Reckoning, you wait and see.'

'That'll be all, thank you, Garulus,' said Cowlquape, fixing the under-librarian with a cold stare.

Garulus tutted and shrugged his shoulders. 'As you wish, High Academe, but I'd be careful if I was you . . .'

'Yes, yes,' said Cowlquape, waving him away to a rope ladder. 'Don't you worry, Garulus. Xanth and I are old friends, aren't we, Xanth?'

Glancing over his shoulder, the under-librarian left them, and Cowlquape crossed to the hanging-stove and dished up two bowls of steaming stew.

'Old friends?' said Xanth, when they were seated cross-legged on blankets beside the warm hanging-stove, eating. 'You mean I was your jailer in the Tower of Night.'

Cowlquape smiled. 'You might have been a Guardian, Xanth, but even back then in that terrible prison, I could tell you had a good heart. You visited me, took the trouble to talk to me, to learn all you could of the Deepwoods and the knowledge they contain . . .'

'But I was still your jailer,' said Xanth bitterly, putting down the bowl, his stew untouched. '*And* I spied for the High Guardian of Night. The librarians know that, and will never accept me.'

'You must wait for the Reckoning,' said Cowlquape, 'in the Free Glades.'

'The Reckoning?' said Xanth, his dark eyes troubled.

'At the Reckoning, someone must speak up for you,'

said Cowlquape, finishing his stew and placing the bowl aside. 'I only wish that "someone" could be me,' he added, 'but even though I know you have a good heart, I only knew you as a Guardian, so my testimony would do you more harm than good, I'm afraid. No, you need someone who has witnessed you doing good . . .' He looked up and smiled. 'Now, finish your stew. Look, you've hardly touched it.'

'I'm not hungry,' said Xanth. It was true. At the mention of the Reckoning awaiting him at the Free Glades, his appetite had left him.

'Then get to your hammock, lad,' Cowlquape told him. 'You look exhausted.'

'I am,' said Xanth, turning to go.

'And don't worry,' Cowlquape called after him. 'Everything will look brighter after a night's sleep.'

Xanth nodded, but made no reply. That was easy for the Most High Academe to say. And as he lay in his hammock, staring up through the branches above his head at the marker-beacons blazing at the tops of the trees, he couldn't help worrying. What if Rook never regained his memory? And where *was* Magda? He turned over and pulled the blankets round him. Perhaps the Most High Academe was right, he thought as he drifted off to sleep; things *would* look better in the morning.

Xanth slept lightly through the night, his dreams punctuated by the night-noises of the Deepwoods. The shriek of razorflits, the squeal of quarms, the distant yodelling of banderbears communicating with those nesting below him on the forest floor. At sun-up, he was roused by the raucous chattering of a flock of bloodsucking hacker-bats, vicious creatures with large, violet eyes and tube-like proboscises, roosting upside down in a nearby tree – along with the cries of the cloddertrogs and flat-heads who were beating sticks and shouting in an attempt to scare them off . . .

Xanth rolled over in his hammock, and looked round at the curious tree-encampment, strung out in the high branches of the ironwood pines. The sun, dappled against the rough bark and pine-needles, was bright and warm after the previous day's overcast gloom. Xanth smiled. Tomorrow had indeed turned out to be a brighter day, just as Cowlquape had said it would. Perhaps it would also be a better day . . .

'Skycraft approaching from the east!' bellowed a voice high above him, as one of the look-outs spotted an incoming squadron.

All about him, as Xanth climbed from the hammock, the Ironwood Stands abruptly exploded into activity, with all eyes turning to inspect the sky.

'They're coming from the Twilight Woods,' someone shouted.

'It must be the Professor of Darkness,' bellowed some-one else.

On a branch some way above Xanth, Fenbrus Lodd passed Cowlquape his telescope. 'They're right,' Xanth overheard him saying. 'It's Tallus all right. Let's hope he brings good news.'

Shielding his eyes against the sun, Xanth watched the

distant rash of dots grow larger. Closer they came, the light blazing on their bulging sails and swinging weights, turning expertly as they swooped down through the air, preparing to land. Soon, across the entire Ironwood Stands, the uppermost branches filled with skycraft – sending the hackerbats flitting off at last, screeching with fear and indignation.

'Over here!' Fenbrus called across to the Professor of Darkness, who had manoeuvred his own skycraft down low amongst the trees and was looking for a place to land. 'And welcome back, Tallus! What news do you bring?'

'Nothing,' came the reply as the Professor of Darkness touched down. He dismounted. 'Whatever the shrykes are doing, they're not in the Twilight Woods.'

Fenbrus frowned. 'Curious,' he said, rubbing his beard thoughtfully. 'Being immune to its effects, I was quite convinced that they would launch an attack from there . . .'

'Maybe they sensed that a Great Storm was on its way,' said the professor. 'You know how sensitive the bird-creatures are to the weather. And I'll tell you this, Fenbrus, nothing – not even the shryke-sisters – could have survived the after-shocks of that terrible explosion of lightning as it struck.'

'You saw it happen?' said Cowlquape.

The Professor of Darkness nodded. 'Everything,' he said. 'From the advancing swirl of cloud, to the release of the bolt of stormphrax lightning. Quite awesome,' he said, 'though nothing compared with what came afterwards. A gigantic, glittering sepia storm that pulsed outwards in all directions, through the Twilight Woods . . .'

Cowlquape shook his head sagely. 'And poor Rook, unsheltered on the rocky pavement of the Edgelands, must have taken its full force,' he said softly. 'It's a miracle he survived.'

Xanth, who was standing on a ledge to the right, busying himself with the rolling up of his hammock and packing of his bags, listened carefully. If it was as bad as they were suggesting, then maybe Rook would *never* fully recover.

'A truly remarkable experience,' the professor went on. 'It was only a shame that Ulbus wasn't there to witness it for himself. As Professor of Light, he would have found it uniquely interesting . . .'

'Skycraft approaching from the south!' two look-outs bellowed in unison, and all around them, Undertowners and librarians began to wave and cheer.

'Perhaps that's him now,' said Fenbrus, raising his telescope and focusing in on the second squadron of skycraft approaching the Ironwood Stands. He frowned a moment later. 'No it isn't,' he said. 'It's my daughter.'

Three hundred more skycraft swooped down into the

branches to be greeted with a rising swell of cheers and cries and whoops of delight. As Varis came closer, heading straight for the tallest tree in the Ironwood Stands, where Cowlquape, Fenbrus and Tallus Penitax were all assembled, Xanth swung his belongings onto his back and started down to the forest floor. Perhaps Rook had woken up feeling better this new day . . .

'Good news,' Varis Lodd announced excitedly, as she jumped down from the *Windhawk*. 'Greetings, Most High Academe.' She bowed her head. 'Greetings, High Librarian.'

'Yes, yes, daughter,' Fenbrus frowned. 'Forget the formalities. What *is* the news?'

'Help is at hand,' she said. 'Even as we speak, the Freeglade Lancers are on their way!'

'But this is tremendous news,' said Cowlquape, excitedly.

'Excellent, Varis,' added Fenbrus. 'You have done well. Very well, indeed. The Freeglade Lancers – finest fighters in the Deepwoods!'

'Finest, until now, father,' came a voice, and Fenbrus and the others turned to see the muglumpskin-clad figure of Felix on a branch of the next tree. He was standing with his hands on his hips, surrounded by the Ghosts of Screetown.

'Oh, Felix,' said Varis. 'This isn't a competition.'

Felix glanced at his sister, and then at his father. Fenbrus coughed awkwardly and looked away. Felix smiled ruefully. 'Isn't it?' he said. He turned to his companions. 'Ghosts!' he called out. 'Help the

Undertowners down from the trees and spread the good news.' He glanced back at his father. 'The Freeglade Lancers are coming! We're saved!' he added sarcastically, and then was gone.

Down on the forest floor, Xanth was searching for the banderbear nest. It was so cleverly camouflaged that, even now in the daylight, he was having trouble spotting it. Suddenly, from behind him, a few strides away, there came a yodel and Xanth spun round to see Wumeru emerging from a thicket with Rook in her arms. Barely able to contain himself, Xanth rushed up to them.

'Rook! Rook!' he began.

Rook opened his eyes and stared at Xanth. The startling blue intensity of his gaze chilled Xanth to the bone.

'Xanth Filatine,' Rook mumbled. 'I remember now. You betrayed librarian knights on their way to the Free Glades, then ran away to the Tower of Night before you were unmasked . . .'

Xanth hung his head, tears stinging his eyes.

'Oh, Xanth, you were my friend. How could you have done it? How *could* you . . .'

Rook's eyes closed again. Xanth stretched out a hand, but Wumeru shook her great head, and he stepped back to let her pass. What now? Xanth thought.

Just then, high above, fresh cheers broke out. Xanth's heart gave a leap. The third squadron of librarian knights – those who had set off under the leadership of the Professor of Light, Ulbus Vespius – must be returning from their foray to the Eastern Roost. Xanth craned his neck back and searched the skies.

Of course, Magda should be amongst them. Magda would speak up for him, even if Rook couldn't!

Soon, the air around the crowded Ironwood Stands was buzzing as the last three hundred skycraft hovered round, searching for landing spaces. High up near the top of the trees, the Professor of Light dismounted and strode towards the waiting welcoming-committee, all eager for his news. Bowing in turn to Fenbrus, Tallus and Varis Lodd – and Deadbolt Vulpoon and Felix Lodd, who had joined them – he addressed himself directly to Cowlquape.

'I bring bad news,' he said grimly.

'From the Eastern Roost?' said Cowlquape.

'Yes, sir,' said the professor. 'There has been a great Hatching – the biggest battle-flock I've ever seen!

Thousands of them, flooding out of the hatching-huts, and heading this way. They're young, but fully-grown, sleek of feather and sharp of beak and claw – and with a frenzy of blood-vengeance in their hearts.' He shook his head. 'I've never seen anything like it.'

'And how far off are they?' asked Cowlquape.

The Professor of Light shrugged. 'Half a day on prowlgrin-back,' he said. 'Maybe more, maybe less . . .'

Cowlquape took a deep intake of breath. He turned to Fenbrus. 'We can't risk breaking camp,' he said. 'The Undertowners must remain up in the trees.'

Fenbrus frowned. 'Are you sure?' he said. 'If they're heading for the Ironwood Stands, shouldn't we get as far away from here as we can?'

'On foot, we wouldn't stand a chance,' said Cowlquape. 'There are too many old'uns and young'uns among us. Why, we'd be picked off like the ripe fruits of a woodsap tree. No, our only hope is to wait for the Freeglade Lancers.'

'But what if the shrykes get here first?' asked Fenbrus.

'Then we must defend ourselves,' said Varis. 'There are the librarian knights, the ghosts, the sky pirates . . .'

Deadbolt nodded in agreement. 'We're well used to

combat with the scraggy bird-creatures,' he chuckled, and gripped the handle of the great curving sword at his side. 'It'll be a pleasure to dispatch a few more.'

'All right,' said Fenbrus Lodd, at last. 'But no fighter must carry a barkscroll. They must hand them over to a librarian or an Undertowner up in the trees for safe-keeping – until after the battle. Not a single item from the sacred Great Library must be risked in combat.'

'You and your barkscrolls!' snorted Felix, turning away. 'If we lose this battle, father, there will be no barkscrolls, no Great Library! And the shrykes will make slaves of all those they don't slaughter!'

As news of the battle-flock spread through the Ironwood stands, a numb panic gripped the Under-towners, one and all, as their thoughts turned to the awful possibility of their having to come face to face with the cold, bloodthirsty bird-creatures.

Xanth, still anxiously searching the skies, left the forest floor and climbed up into the trees once more. High into the upper branches he went and, as the pilots of the Eastern Roost flight landed, one after the other, he rushed after them, grabbed them by the arms and asked them all the same question.

'Have you seen Magda Burlix? Have you seen Magda Burlix?'

Most of the librarians merely shook their heads. Either they hadn't seen her or, more often, they had no idea who she was. Xanth was becoming increasingly desperate.

Then, seeing a rather rotund individual landing his

skycraft on a branch of the next tree along to his right, he leaped across the yawning gap – with no thought of the danger. The librarian looked at him curiously.

'Magda?' said Xanth breathlessly as he climbed to his feet.

The librarian finished tethering his skycraft. ''Fraid not,' he said. 'The name's Portix.'

Xanth frowned impatiently. 'Have you *seen* her?' he said. 'Magda. Magda Burlix.'

The librarian shook his head and turned away. Xanth was about to leave when a gaunt individual appeared from the shadows, the tethers of his own moth-shaped skycraft wrapped round his hand.

'Magda Burlix, you say,' he said. 'Are you a friend of hers?'

Xanth nodded keenly. 'I am,' he said. 'We were in Undertown together.'

The gaunt librarian stepped forwards and clapped his free hand on Xanth's shoulder. 'Bad news, I'm afraid, young fellow,' he said. 'She was shot down over the Eastern Roost. I'm sorry to have to tell you, she hasn't made it.'

·CHAPTER EIGHT·

BLOOD FRENZY

In the forest clearing, a grazing tilder doe looked up, startled, ears twitching. Her fleshy pink nostrils sniffed nervously at the air. She could sense something approaching – something dangerous.

All around her, other Deepwoods creatures were similarly uneasy. Up in the branches, fromps coughed their warning alarm while roosting hackerbats and snowbirds chattered and chirruped. A panic-filled family of lemkins, trembling in the long grass, tried hard to remain still and not give themselves away. But it was no use. Abruptly, terror got the better of one of the nervy youngsters.

'*Waa-iiii – kha-kha-kha-kha-kha . . .*' it shrieked, breaking cover and bolting across the forest floor in a streak of blue, followed quickly by all the rest.

The fromps followed suit, leaping away from tree to tree. The hackerbats and snowbirds took to the sky. Halitoads and razorflits, woodboar and weezits, and all the other creatures that had been poised, ready to run, scurry, slither or flap off at the first sign of danger – they each erupted from their hiding-places and fled.

For a moment, the forest clearing was a frantic, screeching, snorting, dust-filled place; a noisy blur of panic. Out of it sprang the tilder doe, her legs like coiled springs as she bounded through the air and skidded off into the surrounding forest. The next moment, the clearing fell still.

It was quiet, empty and hushed like the moment of tranquillity at the end of a storm, or that instance of stillness just before dawn. The air was motionless. Nothing stirred . . .

The next moment everything changed, as a single shryke exploded from the vegetation, the sunlight in the clearing flashing down on her tawny feathers and glinting on her bone-flail. Then another. And another. Then thousands as, like a great wall of fire driven on by hurricane winds, the vast shryke battle-flock sped past on powerful legs.

Some were brown, some were grey, some were a drab mixture of the two; some were striped, some were spotted, some mottled, some flecked; some had neck-ruffs, some had crests. All of them had razor-sharp beaks and rapier claws – and, as if these were not enough to strike fear into the hearts of their enemies, the shrykes also carried fearsome weapons: lances, maces, pikes and flails, curved scythes, serrated swords . . .

'Kaaar-kaaar! Kut-kut-kut!' a piercing call sounded from the treetops as a shryke-sister with red and purple plumage appeared, leaping from branch to branch on the back of a prowlgrin.

'Keer-keer-keer!' Her call was answered by her sisters in the treetops all round.

Like a swarm of snickets, the battle-flock veered off in answer to the treetop calls, never easing up for a moment as they thundered on through the forest. High above, clinging on tightly to the prowlgrin-reins, the noble Shryke Sisterhood – several hundred strong, with gaudy plumage and flamboyant battledress – guided the battle-flock towards their distant goal.

At their head, resplendent in tooled gold armour, the young roost-mother – Mother Muleclaw III – threw back her fearsome head and gave a piercing shriek.

'Kut-kut-kut-kaaaar!'

Red and yellow, purple and blue, her luxuriant plumage gleamed in the early morning sun, her neck-ruff and tail-feathers flapping as the grey prowlgrin she sat astride leaped on through the forest. Below her, the battle-flock increased its pace.

Some way behind her, also on prowlgrinback, Sister Drab, Matron Featherhorn and the shryke elders trotted across the clearing, pulling a large group of tethered shryke-mates behind them.

'It's good to be on the move again,' squawked Matron Featherhorn.

'Indeed, sister,' agreed Sister Drab, giving a vicious tug on the leashes in her clawed hand. 'See how the Deepwoods tremble before us! Nothing can stand in the way of a battle-flock with its blood up!'

'The little darlings!' clucked Matron Featherhorn. 'Hard to believe they were hatchlings such a short while ago. Oh, and look at Mother Muleclaw!' She cooed with pride.

Sister Drab nodded. 'A natural roost-mother,' she said. 'I knew it the moment she hatched. Why, she'd killed and eaten the others in her clutch before her shell was even cold. Magnificent!'

'I can't wait to see her in battle,' said Matron Featherhorn.

'Patience, sister,' replied Sister Drab. 'We shall be there soon enough and, if the librarian knight spoke correctly, the Undertowners will be at our mercy!' She closed her eyes and smiled with pleasure.

Oh, how that captured librarian knight had screamed and shouted and begged for death, writhing beneath her probing talons as she'd extracted every last bit of information. Then, when she'd got everything she wanted, how the hapless creature had turned tack, begging for mercy instead.

And she *had* been merciful, she remembered. Rather than linger over the flayed, tortured body longer than she'd needed, she had torn out the heart with a single stab of her beak and swallowed it while it was still beating. Delicious! The librarian had lived just long enough to see it.

Sister Drab looked up ahead as she cantered on and, as the forest thinned for a moment, she glimpsed the unmistakable shape of the mighty Ironwood Stands, rising up out of the forest canopy and silhouetted – dark and imposing – against the pinky-yellow sky in the distance.

'Not far now,' Sister Drab clucked contentedly. 'Not far. I can almost taste the blood on my tongue!'

Preparations had been made and now an eerie silence hung in the air. High up at the very top of the tallest ironwood pine, Felix Lodd and Deadbolt Vulpoon were deep in conversation.

'Do you think it'll work?' said Felix.

'It's *got* to work,' said Deadbolt, 'or we're dead meat, the lot of us, and that's a fact!'

'Dead, or slaves,' said Felix bitterly.

'Oh, if the shrykes triumph, there'll be very few slaves, believe me,' said Deadbolt, ruefully stroking his beard.

Felix raised an eyebrow.

'It's a young battle-flock, according to your Professor of Light,' the sky pirate said.

'He's not *my* Professor of Light,' said Felix.

'Maybe not, lad,' he said, 'but that doesn't alter the

fact that these shrykes are newly hatched. They're ill-disciplined and inexperienced. Once they go into battle, they'll get the blood frenzy, and the only way to stop them will be to kill them. You mark my words.'

Deadbolt raised his telescope and looked back across the Deepwoods for any trace of the approaching shryke battalions.

'See anything?' Felix asked.

The sky pirate captain shook his head and snapped his telescope shut. 'Not yet,' he said darkly, 'but they're on their way.' His eyes narrowed, and his nostrils twitched. 'I can *smell* the scurvy creatures . . .'

Far below, on the forest floor, Xanth felt a heavy hand on his shoulder and turned to see a cloddertrog sky pirate looming over him. The pirate wore a

THE BATTLE OF THE LUFWOOD MOUNT

THE LUFWOOD MOUNT

UNDERTOWNERS

LIBRARIAN KNIGHTS

SKY PIRATES

GHOSTS

SHRYKE BATTLE FLOCK

THE IRONWOOD STANDS

muglumpskin coat and carried a heavy poleaxe.

'Librarian, is it?' he asked, scrutinizing Xanth. 'You lot are with the Undertowners at the lufwood mount. The shrykes are on their way – or hadn't you heard?' he added sarcastically.

'I was looking for my friend, Rook Barkwater . . .' said Xanth, nodding towards the empty banderbear nests in front of them. 'But he seems to have left.'

'Rook Barkwater?' said the cloddertrog. 'Isn't he that librarian knight who got caught in the sepia storm?'

'Yes,' said Xanth. 'The banderbears were tending to him in this nest . . .'

'If he's with banderbears then he'll be safe enough,' said the cloddertrog. 'It's yourself you ought to be worried about, out here in the open with a shryke battle-flock due at any moment. You should be with your librarian friends.'

Xanth shook his head sadly. 'The librarians aren't my friends,' he said. 'In fact, I don't seem to *have* any friends.' With a sigh, he slumped down on the forest floor.

'Well, you can't sit round here feeling sorry for your-self,' said the cloddertrog. 'Here, you can join me if you like,' he added, and held out a massive hand. 'Henkel's the name. Captain Henkel of the *Fogscythe* – currently without a crew, on account of them having run off to seek their fortunes in the Foundry Glades with a scurvy cur by the name of Quillet Pleeme. *Pah!* But that's another story . . . Come on, if you're coming.'

Xanth smiled, and was about to reach up and take

Henkel's hand, when he
noticed an oil-cloth bundle
resting against the moss-
covered side of the
abandoned nest. He
reached over and
picked it up.

'What have you got
there?' asked Henkel,
peering down as Xanth
carefully unwrapped the package.

'It's . . . it's a sword,' said Xanth.

'And a mighty fine one at that. Can't leave it lying
around here,' said Henkel, as Xanth got to his feet. 'Best
hold on to it for now, lad. You can look for its owner
later. Anyway, if you stick with me, you'll have need of
it . . .' he stuck out his massive hand again '. . . friend.'

This time Xanth clasped it and shook it warmly.
'Friend!' he replied.

'Keer-keer-kaaaaarrr!' screamed Mother Muleclaw,
spurring her prowlgrin on through the branches.

Below her, the shryke battle-flock surged forwards,
shrieking and screeching in reply. Ahead of them stood
the Ironwood Stands, their branches heavy with the
hunched figures of Undertowners huddled round burning stoves. It was almost too good to be true. They were
at her mercy, and she, Muleclaw – beautiful, strong,
hungry Muleclaw – would show them none!

Foam flecked her long, curved black beak. She opened

it, threw back her head and spat a trailing arc of bile high into the air. Her bright yellow eyes flashed, their dark pupils fully dilated. A mist was descending in front of them; a red mist.

She must taste blood! She must taste it now, and gorge! And gorge! And gorge . . .

From below her, a volley of flaming arrows flew up from the bows of the jostling flock and into the tops of the massive ironwood pines. One by one, the resinous tips of the huge trees caught fire and blazed like gigantic torches. Below, on the branches, the Undertowners remained motionless, as if rooted to the spot, their hanging-stoves twinkling in the fading afternoon light.

With a grunt, the roost-mother's prowlgrin launched itself from the topmost bough of a copperwood and onto the end of one of the massive branches of an ironwood pine. She was followed by her roost-sisters, shrieking with savage glee.

'Kut-kut-kut-kaaaaar!'

'Keer-keer!'

'Kut-kut-kut-kaaaaarrr!'

Below, the main body of the battle-flock flowed round the massive trunks of the Ironwood Stands in a screeching feathered flood. Thousands of piercing yellow eyes turned upwards in eager anticipation.

They didn't have long to wait. Mother Muleclaw and the shryke-sisters were spreading out through the branches, slashing and swiping with their claws and bone-flails from astride their leaping prowlgrins. The bodies of the Undertowners fell like ripe fruit, down into the seething mass below.

'Kaaar! Kaaaar! K-k-k... Ki? Ki? Ki-i-i-i!'

The expectant shrieks of the battle-flock changed abruptly to indignant, high-pitched whistles. What was this? Not flesh and blood, entrails and guts, but ... Wood . . . Cloth . . . Bundles of moss and sacking!

The shrykes tore at the stuffed effigies in frustration. Mother Muleclaw pulled up her prowlgrin with a vicious tug on its reins and seized a figure slumped beside a hanging-stove.

'Kiii-kiii-i-ai-ai!' she screamed as she recognized it for what it was; a stuffed dummy in a woollen shawl, its hastily carved wooden head grinning back at her mockingly.

Suddenly, on the branch above, a shryke-sister gave a strangled scream and plunged past Muleclaw, her throat skewered by a crossbow bolt. The roost-mother's eyes swivelled round. They were under attack!

'KAAAAAR!' shrieked Mother Muleclaw in a frenzy of rage and frustration as, the next moment, the sky around the Ironwood Stands filled with librarian skycraft.

They swooped in close, firing blazing arrows and heavy bolts, before swerving away. The shryke-sisters were easy targets and fell in twos and threes, then fours and fives, and then dozens, as the skycraft swarmed about the ironwoods like angry woodhornets. Down on the forest floor, the battle-flock erupted into a frenzy as the bodies rained down and they began gorging themselves on their fallen sisters.

And still the librarian knights swooped in, loading, firing and reloading, until not a single prowlgrin-mounted shryke-sister remained in the blazing Ironwood Stands.

Below, the frenzied battle-flock seethed. They had tasted blood at last – but not nearly enough. Suddenly, clambering down the massive trunk of an ironwood tree like a gaudy feathered beetle, Mother Muleclaw appeared. Her prowlgrin dead, her armour battered and her gaudy silks singed, she halted above the heads of her flock, with her talons embedded in the rough bark.

'Kut-kut-kaaaaii!' she shrieked, and all eyes turned to her.

She waved a claw towards the forest where a trail, marked by discarded bundles of belongings, led away. Her yellow eyes flashed. Above them, the skycraft soared up and away over the trees.

'Kaaaar!' Mother Muleclaw screamed. '*KAAAAAARR!*'

*

'It's gone quiet,' Gilda whispered to her companions. 'What do you think's happening now?'

Turntail, an elderly mobgnome, squeezed her hand warmly. 'The lull before the storm,' he said, his voice soft and wheezy. 'By Sky, if I were only fifty years younger, I'd show those disgusting bird-creatures a thing or two. I'd crack their skulls and split their gaudy gizzards open, so I would. I'd . . . I'd . . .' He collapsed in a fit of hacking coughs.

'Quiet, back there!' came an urgent voice.

The mobgnome pulled away and tried to stifle the cough with his hands. Gilda patted him on the back. Rogg, a grizzled, one-armed flat-head who was sitting with them, pulled a bottle from his belt, unstoppered and wiped it, and handed it across.

'Sup that,' he said gruffly.

Turntail held it to his lips, slurped, swallowed – and gasped for breath, his eyes streaming. 'What . . . is . . . it . . ?' he rasped.

'Firejuice,' said Rogg. 'Like it?'

'It's . . . it's . . .' the mobgnome began. 'The most disgusting drink ever to have passed my lips.'

Rogg snorted. 'Stopped you coughing though, dinnit?'

Behind them, a high-pitched voice spoke up. 'I wouldn't mind a drop of firejuice myself,' he said. The others turned to see a wizened old lugtroll, pale and trembling, wrapped up in a tattered scrap of blanket. He smiled toothlessly. 'Warm these palsied bones of mine a tad,' he said.

Rogg passed the bottle back. 'Just a drop, mind,' he said. 'Don't want you keeling over.'

Gilda nodded. Although the journey from the Ironwood Stands to the lufwood mount had been little more than a few hundred strides, it had severely tested several in their small party. Gilda had had to support Turntail the whole way, while Rogg had ended up carrying the lugtroll under one arm, and a portly gabtroll and her babe-daughter under the other.

Still, at least Gilda hadn't had to carry the sword any longer. Wrapped in its oil-skin cloth, it had been an awkward bundle – though she'd kept it safe all the same, carrying it all the way from Undertown and into the Deepwoods. It was the least she could do for the brave young librarian who had lost it when he'd rescued her from slavers in old Undertown. She'd feared he was dead, but she'd kept the sword with her all the same, just in case . . . And then she'd spotted him! She could hardly believe it.

Oh, he'd changed all right. He was sick, she could see that clearly. He was carried right past her in the arms of a huge banderbear. His eyes were closed and he was moaning softly, but it was definitely him; *her* brave young librarian.

The banderbear had disappeared inside a nest with him, and Gilda had been too frightened to follow. The creature had looked so big and fierce, and the poor librarian so ill. She decided it would be best not to disturb him, so she'd propped the precious bundle by the entrance where they'd be sure to find it. She'd planned to go back to make sure – but then news of the shryke attack had broken and everyone was suddenly

running around in a terrible panic, gathering up everything they could carry . . .

That was just this morning. Gilda looked around at
her companions. Together, like all the other
Undertowners – old and young, rich and poor – they
had struggled gamely on, heading westwards, away
from the ironwood pines and on through the dense
Deepwood forest.

Twice, they had come to places where the trees had
been felled by teams of ghosts and sky pirates – two vast
concentric circles which ringed the lufwood-covered
crag – and had had to pick their way over the jumble of
fallen branches and logs. Finally, they had arrived at the
top of the mount; tired, weak and frightened.

They'd made camp there, along with the thousands of
other Undertowners. Below them, the lufwood-covered
mount had soon echoed with the sound of sawing and
chopping as the ghosts and sky pirates erected makeshift
barricades to protect them. Then, as the afternoon light
had begun to fail, the librarian knights had taken off and
flown back towards the Ironwood Stands.

Gilda had marvelled at the sight. How proud and
brave they'd looked! Then, along with the others, and
hardly daring to breathe, she had listened for the tell-tale
sounds of battle.

When the first furious shryke scream had echoed
through the trees, everyone had fallen silent, and as the
mighty battle had raged at the Ironwood Stands, they
had all listened carefully to every crack, every cry, every
distant screech, scream and wail. The more suspicious

among them had stroked their amulets and whispered prayers and incantations that the brave librarian knights would prevail and that the Undertowners, in their concealed fastness, might survive.

Now it was quiet again, with the stillness more terrifying even than the noisy battle. As the sun set, the librarian knights arrived back, and as the moon rose, the sky glowed red in the distance where the Ironwood Stands blazed. The librarians, ghosts and sky pirates took to the barricades in the darkness below the lufwood mount.

Slowly, whispered rumours of the slaughter of the shryke roost-sisters filtered up to the Undertowners, and low murmurs filled the night air. A battle had been won, so it seemed, yet the roost-mother lived on. The battle-flock still had a leader and, having regrouped, was heading towards them.

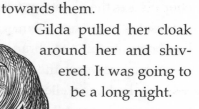

Gilda pulled her cloak around her and shivered. It was going to be a long night.

*

Xanth was glad he was standing next to Henkel. With the whole shryke army on its way, he felt better knowing that the hefty, battle-scarred cloddertrog was at his side, mighty poleaxe in hand. Xanth looked down at the sword in his own hand. It was certainly magnificent, with a polished pommel, an ornate handle and a blade so sharp it could split a hair lengthways.

He looked up at the cloddertrog, his eyes gleaming. 'It's fantastic, isn't it?' he said.

'Certainly is,' said Henkel. 'Some kind of ceremonial sword by the look of it. Though I daresay that won't stop it slicing a shryke or two in twain.' He laughed throatily. 'Try it out, lad.'

Xanth parried and lunged and swung the sword round in wide sweeps, before jabbing at the air in a succession of short sharp movements. It was so well-shaped and perfectly balanced that it seemed almost to move by itself, slicing through the air like an agile ratbird in flight.

'Excellent, excellent,' said Henkel. 'It could have been made for you. And I'll tell you this, lad, if . . .'

The cloddertrog stopped and his eyes narrowed. Around him, the sky pirates stopped talking and scanned the treeline. They were behind the second ring of barricades, constructed from the trees cut down in front of them.

'Open ground,' Deadbolt had growled. 'It'll stop them coming at us from the treetops.'

Ahead of Xanth, across the cleared forest, he could see

the first ring of barricades. These were being defended by Felix and the ghosts. He could just make out the helmeted figure of the leader of the ghosts as he signalled to his companions to prepare for the onslaught they all knew was coming.

Xanth heard Henkel's gruff voice. 'Hold your ground, lad,' he told him.

Xanth gripped the handle of his sword and prayed that he might be brave. The night air was still, the only sound, the odd cough or muttered curse from the ranks of sky pirates lining the log barricade. All eyes were focused on the ghosts at the first barricade across the clearing.

Then Xanth heard it. A blood-curdling scream that sent shivers coursing down his spine. It was followed by another and another from the dark shadows of the treeline.

'Here they come,' muttered Henkel. 'Sky protect us.'

Suddenly, a huge wave of screaming bird-creatures, crested with a glittering

array of pikes, war hammers and bone-flails, broke through the trees and smashed into the first barricade. Xanth gasped. Everywhere, the ranks of ghosts splintered into individual fights as first in one place, then another, shrykes broke through their defences. The whiplash cracks of ropes cutting through the air and wrapping themselves round feathered necks sounded all down the line as the ghosts fought desperately to hold back the tide.

But it was hopeless, Xanth could see that, and his stomach gave a sickening lurch. There were just too many of the shrieking, frenzied shrykes.

Every instinct told him to turn and run away, now, before the evil flood of feathers and fury swept *him* away. Henkel must have seen the look on his face, for he turned to Xanth and laid a huge hand on his shoulder.

'Steady, lad. This is the hardest part, waiting for the storm of battle to break. Trust in that sword and stay close.'

Xanth nodded and tightened his grip on the handle of the sword. Sharp and bright as it looked, could it really stop one of those evil shrieking bird-creatures? He was about to find out.

'Fall back, Ghosts!'

Felix's shouted command sounded above the din of battle, and suddenly the air filled with whipcracks as ropes shot over Xanth's and the sky pirates' heads and wrapped themselves round tree branches behind them. In an instant, hundreds of white-armoured ghosts launched themselves out of the midst of the thrashing,

flailing shrykes and flew through the night air, landing behind the second barricade.

Xanth gasped. He'd never seen anything so spectacular.

'Very pretty,' Henkel growled. 'Now the real fighting begins!'

At the first barricade, the battle-flock screeched with frustration as the shrykes saw their enemy escape from their clutches. They swarmed over the log wall and surged forward across the cleared ground.

Xanth could see the eyes of the approaching bird-creatures flashing, bright yellow, their sharp beaks and talons glinting in the moonlight.

'Fire!' came Deadbolt Vulpoon's booming command, and a deadly volley of crossbow bolts spat from the ranks all around Xanth.

The first wave of shrykes screamed and fell beneath the clawed feet of those following, but the huge battle-flock hardly checked its pace.

'Fire!' came the command again. 'Fire!'

Each volley of missiles cut swathes through the feathered ranks – but still the shrykes continued towards them.

'Here they come!' bellowed Henkel as the wave of shrykes threw themselves on the barricades. Xanth gagged as the stale odour of rancid entrails and shryke waste tainted the air. All round him, the terrible feathered creatures burst over the barricade and fell upon the sky pirates, their eyes blazing, their beaks gaping. Beside him, Henkel swung his poleaxe in a low, horizontal sweep, decapitating three screaming shryke guards. Xanth thrust his sword out in front of him and felt a jolt run through his arm as first one shryke, then another, ran onto the point and skewered themselves through their hearts.

'Well done, lad, well done,' Xanth heard Henkel shouting across to him as he withdrew his sword, sticky with shryke blood. There was a roaring in his ears and he felt as if his heart was about to explode. 'Watch out!' Henkel roared. 'Behind you!'

Xanth turned, to be confronted with a huge, muscular

shryke, with flecked brown and cream plumage, swing-ing a spiked ball the size of his own head through the air towards him.

He leaped back, ducking as he went, and brought the sword round in a sharp uppercut, severing the shryke's arm, sending the ball and chain spinning back through the air before embedding itself in the creature's neck. Thick, dark blood gushed down her front as she fell, gurgling and twitching, to the ground.

He had scarcely a moment to catch his breath when three orange-feathered shrykes with scythes came at him. Desperately, Xanth parried their blows and ducked out of the way of stabbing beaks and claws. Sweat was pour-ing down his face as he gasped noisily, his lungs burning and his limbs aching.

'*Urrghh!*' he cried out as a claw-hammer glanced off his shoulder and he fell to one knee.

Suddenly, the shrykes in front of him exploded in a shower of blood and orange feathers and Xanth looked up to see Henkel, bloodied poleaxe in hand, looming over him.

'Run!' he roared.

Xanth didn't need telling twice. He leaped to his feet and dashed after the cloddertrog, who cleared the way with massive swings of his poleaxe. They were joined on all sides by bloodied, feather-spattered sky pirates, as they dashed up the steep wooded slopes of the lufwood mount towards the summit. Behind them, the ghosts covered their retreat by swinging through the trees and raining down burning lufwood darts into the battle-flock's path.

At the summit, they were greeted by the ashen faces of thousands of Undertowners, huddled together in abject terror. Around them, the librarian knights had spread a thin defensive line, their skycraft firmly anchored to the rocky crag. It was clear by the grim looks on their faces, that this was where they were going to stand and fight.

Xanth saw the imposing figure of Fenbrus Lodd standing, arms folded defiantly, next to the stooped Most High Academe, Cowlquape. Varis Lodd and the Professors of Light and Darkness stood guard round them, their crossbow quivers bristling and their swords unsheathed.

Deadbolt Vulpoon came stamping up to them, his beard red with shryke blood, and his greatcoat cut to ribbons. 'We held them as long as we could,' he growled, bowing his head to Cowlquape. 'And that son of yours and his ghosts are making them pay for every step of the mount they climb,' he added, turning to Fenbrus. 'He's a good 'un, and no mistake.'

Fenbrus Lodd looked grave. 'This is where we make our stand,' he said. 'If the Great Library is to perish, let it be here on the lufwood mount over our dead bodies.'

'It most likely will be,' said Deadbolt darkly. 'For they're in a blood frenzy now, just as I feared.'

Xanth sat down on a rock next to Henkel and tried to catch his breath. A pale moon shone down and bathed everything in silvery light. All round, there was the sound of quiet sobbing and stifled moans.

'You did well back there, lad,' said Henkel, wiping his bloodied poleaxe on his muglumpskin coat. 'I was glad to have you by my side, friend.'

'And I you, friend,' said Xanth, managing a smile.

'Come,' said the cloddertrog. 'The night is not over yet.'

The sky pirates joined the librarian knights defending the summit of the lufwood mount, and before long, the white figures of the ghosts came whistling through the trees on their long ropes and added to their number. Dark clouds drifted across the moon and a chill wind got up as an eerie silence fell over the crowded mountain top.

'What are they waiting for? Why don't they attack?' whispered Xanth.

They could hear the shrieks and calls of the battle-flock in the trees below them. 'They're gorging on the dead,' said Henkel simply. 'And when they've fin-ished . . .' he surveyed the treeline with weary eyes 'then they'll come for us.'

They hadn't long to wait. The calls of the shrykes abruptly grew louder, with one piercing shrieked cry loudest of all.

'KAAAAR-KAAAAR-KAAAAR!!'

It sounded through the lufwood trees of the mount.

'Kut-kut-keer-keer!' came answering shrieks from all around.

Suddenly, the air was alive with feathered arrows whistling out of the trees and into the defenders. One grazed Xanth's cheek and sent him cowering to the ground. When he looked up, the battle-flock had broken cover and was advancing towards them.

They no longer swarmed in a shrieking, surging tide, but instead, were walking slowly and deliberately up the rocky slope. Their feathers dripped with blood; their claws and beaks were crimson and their eyes glowed a deep, throbbing red.

Xanth stared at the bloody spectacle, mesmerized. There was nothing anyone could do to stop this terrible onslaught, he realized miserably. They were all doomed.

As the huge circle of shrykes closed in on the Undertowners and their defenders, the piercing call sounded again.

'KAAAAR-KAAAAR-KAAAAR!!'

The huge shryke roost-mother pushed through the flock and raised a dripping claw. This was it! The final gorging!

Then all at once, there came the clear, sweet sound of a tilderhorn calling out from the forest below, followed by a low rumbling like distant thunder. The roost-mother paused, her claw still raised high. What was this?

'Kiii-kiii-kiii.' Small, yelping cries spread through the battle-flock behind her, which changed to shrieking calls of panic a moment later.

From behind them, out of the forest, a great, bristling, writhing creature was attacking and driving the startled shryke battle-flock into a confused jostling heap. As Muleclaw turned, the creature seemed to split up into hundreds of individuals, each with a spike, stabbing and goading the shrykes from every angle.

Xanth looked up. Around him, all eyes had turned

towards the sounds of distress coming from the back of the battle-flock. Suddenly, an armoured lancer on an orange prowlgrin burst through the shrykes, followed by twenty more. Green and white chequerboard pennants fluttered from their lances; red banderbear badges emblazoned their white tunics.

'The Freeglade Lancers!' the shout went up.

Soon, everywhere Xanth looked, lancers on prowl-grins were breaking through the shrykes and scattering them in confusion.

'KAAAAR-KAAAAR-KAAAAR!' shrieked Mother Muleclaw as she saw her battle-flock disintegrate and fall back in a frenzied, flapping panic.

Behind her, Xanth gripped the magnificent, razor-sharp sword, took a deep breath and swung it through the air.

'KAAAAR-KAA . . . K . . . *urrgh!*'

The roost-mother was dead before she hit the ground, her magnificent plumed head with its curved black beak separated from her gold armoured body.

'Henkel! Henkel!' Xanth cried, turning back in triumph. 'I did it! I got her! I killed . . .'

He stopped and fell to his knees. Henkel stared back at him with unseeing eyes, a thin trickle of blood dripping from the corner of his mouth, his body slumped forward in a half-sitting, half-crouching position and a barbed, feather-flighted shryke arrow protruding from his chest.

'Hey, you there! Yes, you!' came an angry voice. Xanth turned, to see Felix Lodd standing over him, his eyes blazing. 'Where did you get that sword?'

Sister Drab and Matron Featherhorn tramped back through the forest, their shryke-males still on leashes clasped in their shaking hands. It was dark and cold, with the moon lost behind rain-drenched clouds that had swept in from the north.

'Our darlings!' wept Matron Featherhorn. 'So young, so inexperienced. They couldn't help themselves . . .'

'It was the blood frenzy,' said Sister Drab, shaking her head. 'That I should have lived to see the day a battle-flock turned on itself, and shryke gorged on shryke.'

'There was nothing you could do, sister,' said Matron Featherhorn, her eyes streaking. 'Nothing *any* of us could have done. Their blood was up. They couldn't help themselves. With Mother Muleclaw dead up there on that accursed mount, there was no one left to control them.'

'Curse the Undertowners!' spat Sister Drab. 'And curse the Freeglade Lancers! To think we had victory within our grasp . . .'

'What is there for us now?' asked Matron Featherhorn. Behind her, the males warbled and twittered feebly.

Sister Drab turned and looked at her companion, her gaze cold and unblinking.

'Our finest battle-flocks destroyed in Undertown. Now our fledgling army killed in the Deepwoods. We have nothing left, dear Matron Featherhorn,' she said bitterly. 'The age of the shrykes is over.'

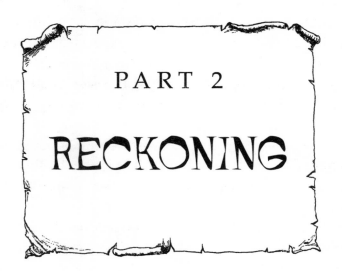

PART 2

RECKONING

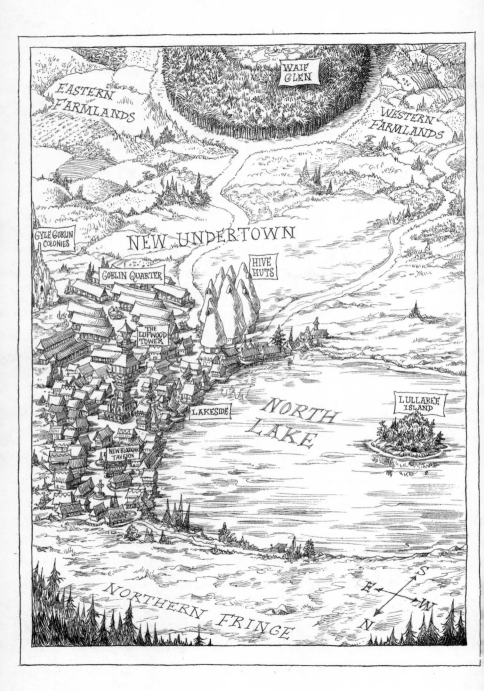

·CHAPTER NINE·

NEW UNDERTOWN

The sun shone down on the Free Glades. Never before had the streets of New Undertown thronged with quite so many revellers as that evening in late summer, when the new turned out to celebrate the arrival of the old. After their long and dangerous journey, the vast multitude from old Undertown marvelled at their new surroundings.

Every ornately carved building on every thorough-fare, from grand avenue to narrow alley, was festooned with flags and streamers, and multi-coloured bunting criss-crossed overhead. Long lines of twinkling lanterns – yellow, pink and white – had been strung up through-out the town, from the elegant Lufwood Tower at its centre to the cowl-shaped Hive Huts to the south. They zigzagged along each street, they lined the bridges, they ringed the squares; down to Lakeside they went, gleam-ing and glinting from every market stall and reflected in the deep, still waters of North Lake.

As the golden light of the setting sun dimmed, the

lanterns seemed to glow brighter than ever, flickering on the happy faces of the Undertowners, new *and* old. Some were laughing, some were singing, some were dancing – everything from whirling goblin jigs and rowdy trog stomps, to a hopping lugtroll line that snaked its way through the streets. A band of musicians played alongside it on pipes, drums and a vast stringed instrument carried by four and played by three more. Through the centre the winding chain of dancers went, past the Lufwood Tower and down to Lakeside, where the street-stalls were overflowing with food and drink.

'Woodale! Get your woodale here!' bellowed a ruddy-faced mobgnome from behind a trestle table which bowed in the middle under the weight of a large and heavy barrel.

'Goblets of winesap!' called a gnokgoblin matron from a neighbouring stall.

A group of lugtrolls – young and old, and all weary after their long journey from old Undertown – compared

what was on offer, before pausing in front of a gabtroll's barrow. One of them – a young male in a ragged cloak – leaned over a steaming vat and breathed in deeply.

''Tis oakmead, sir,' said the gabtroll softly. 'Spiced and honeyed, with just a hint of nibblick.' She picked up a tankard and a ladle and poured a little of the warm liquid out. 'Would you care to try some?' she said.

The lugtroll took the tankard and sipped. It was delicious. 'How much?' he asked cautiously.

'How much?' the gabtroll replied, her eyeballs bouncing about on their stalks in amusement. 'This is the Free Glades. All for one, and one for all.' She swept her arms round in a wide arc. '*Everything's* free. All that you poor, dear old Undertowners can eat and drink.'

The lugtrolls looked at one another, smiles breaking out on their faces. Back in the filth and misery of old Undertown, they'd had to scratch a living hauling firewood for the leagues' forges. The work was hard and the days were long, and the only payment was a meagre

supper of grey gruel and black bread. Yet here in New Undertown, the air was sweet and everywhere they looked they were greeted by happy, smiling faces.

'Thank you, mistress gabtroll,' the young lugtroll proclaimed gratefully. 'Thank you a thousandfold.'

'So it's oakmead all round, is it?' the gabtroll said, her tongue slurping noisily over her eyeballs as she ladled out the drinks. 'To your very good health!' she announced. 'And welcome! Welcome one and all.'

In every part of the throbbing town, as was happening throughout the Free Glades, from the southern meadowlands to the northern fringes, from the eastern woodtroll villages to the western shores of the Great Lake, the newcomers were being greeted and feted like long-lost friends and relations.

'Toasted pine-nuts,' cried a mobgnome from a kiosk close to the waterside as she spooned the salted delicacies into barkpaper cones. 'Candied woodsaps, jellied dellberries . . .'

'Tilder sausages and black bread,' shouted a slaughterer nearby. 'As much as you can eat.'

As the sun sank and the moon rose, the streets grew fuller and fuller. Groups of colourfully dressed cloddertrogs streamed in from the cliffside caves in the south-east to greet their ragged, weary compatriots newly arrived from the over-crowded, rundown boomdocks of old Undertown, and it wasn't long before they were all carousing noisily, drunk on traditional tripweed beer.

Columns of woodtrolls and slaughterers trooped

northwards together to New Undertown to join in the festivities, joined on their way by gaggles of gyle goblins, sweeping in from the east. And they all came together, old Undertowners, New Undertowners, grinning and bowing, slapping one another on the backs and shaking each other's hands. They talked and they sang and they shared what they had, from tales of their pasts to plates of tilder sausages. And the cry went up in every single corner of the town, a thousand times or more.

'Welcome to the Free Glades! Welcome, indeed!'

Down on a small wooden jetty jutting into North Lake, two flat-head goblins were sitting close to one another, idly flicking bits of gravel into the water and watching the ripples spread and interlock.

'I never thought I'd ever see you again, Gorl,' said one, her eyes filling up with tears.

'Nor I you, Reda,' came the reply, as he squeezed her hand tightly.

'When they took you away . . .' she sobbed. 'When they chained you up and marched you off to the Sanctaphrax Forest, there was nothing left for me in old Undertown. So I came here and made a new life for myself. But I never forgot you. I always . . .'

'I understand,' said Gorl, 'but that was *old* Undertown. It's all in the past. The important thing is that we're together again.' He looked round. Far to his left, the Ironwood Glade stood out against the starry sky. Behind, the glow of the lights, the smells of the food and drink, the sounds of music and dancing and laughter

continued, all reminding him of where they now were. He smiled and pulled her close. 'And we're Freegladers, now.'

Reda remained still, smiling to herself as she felt his strong arms wrapping themselves around her.

Back at the Lufwood Tower, a small procession was making its way through the cheering crowds to the foot of the grand sweeping staircase that led up to the first-floor platform, which was bedecked with garlands of flowers and forest fruits. There, waiting patiently, stood the Free Glade Council, all three of them.

Parsimmon, High Master of Lake Landing, a short gnokgoblin in shabby robes, peered over a large bunch of woodlilies, a huge smile on his wizened face. Next to him, on a high stool of carved lufwood,

Cancaresse of Waif Glen stood on tiptoe, her huge translucent ears quivering expectantly. Next to them, Hebb Lub-drub, the mayor of New Undertown – a low-belly goblin – looked huge, his embroidered belly-sling festooned with a gleaming chain of office.

As the procession drew closer, the prowlgrins' feathered collars fluttered and the ceremonial bells attached to their harnesses jangled loudly as the carriage they were drawing jerked to a halt at the foot of the stairs. The door opened and the stooped figure of Cowlquape Pentephraxis climbed out, followed by Fenbrus Lodd and his daughter, Varis. With each new appearance, the crowd cheered. Last to emerge from the carriage were the Professors of Light and Darkness, their gowns – one black and one white – flapping in the rising breeze.

As the five of them climbed the steps, one after the other, towards the garlanded platform, so the gathered crowd clapped their hands and stamped their feet and roared with approval. At the top, Cancaresse held out a tiny hand to Cowlquape in greeting. Her soft melodious voice sounded in the minds of everyone watching.

'Welcome, friends. The Council of Three has become the Council of Eight. It is time for all of us to rejoice – as Freegladers!'

'Freegladers!' roared a red-faced cloddertrog to a nightwaif, throwing his beefy arm around the weedy creature's narrow shoulders. 'There's no such thing as *old* Undertowners and *new* Undertowners, any more. We're all Freegladers now!'

'Indeed,' chirped the nightwaif. 'Freegladers, one and all – and,' he added, his huge, batlike ears fluttering and swivelling to the left, 'if I'm not very much mistaken, the New Bloodoak Tavern has just broken open a fresh batch of woodale barrels to celebrate!'

'It has?' said the cloddertrog, hoisting his new friend up onto his shoulders. 'Then let us go and share a tankard or two, you and I.'

They had indeed broken open a fresh batch of woodale at the New Bloodoak Tavern. They'd needed to. Mother Bluegizzard, the old shryke matron who ran the place, had been so busy that she had been forced to assist her serving-goblins as they rushed round topping up tankards and keeping the drinking-troughs full. With the ale flowing so freely, the atmosphere was rowdier than normal, with laughter and singing and clapping and the *clatter-clomp-crash* of dancing on the tables echoing from every window.

'More woodale, gentle sirs?' Mother Bluegizzard asked – a laden tray balanced on the crook of her arm and her spectacular blue throat feathers fluffed up with exertion – as she squeezed her way through the swaying crowd to the table where a group of new arrivals was sitting.

'A friendly shryke with foaming woodale?' said Felix Lodd, swapping his empty tankard for a full one. 'The Free Glades is truly a wondrous place!'

'Wondrous indeed!' said Deadbolt Vulpoon, following suit. 'Thank you, gracious madam. This old sky pirate will be forever in your debt!'

At the other side of the table, Wumeru, Wuralo and Weeg were given fresh beakers of frothing dellberry and woodsap juice. Although there was nothing in their refreshments to affect their mood, the three of them had already got so caught up in the atmosphere of the place that whenever a song went up, they yodelled along with the rest, swaying from side to side, their great hairy arms raised above their heads.

Mother Bluegizzard looked at them all benevolently. They were an interesting bunch, these old Under-towners; the confident young ghost with his twinkling eyes and shock of blond hair, and the grizzled old sky pirate, with his charming manners. And those bander-bears! They'd alarmed her when they'd first lumbered in, but they were so gentle and good-natured, the old bird-creature had quite taken to them. And then there was the quiet young librarian with the startling blue eyes, who was smiling at her now as she offered him the tray. He seemed a little lost, and didn't say much, and the banderbears fussed over him as if he was their cub.

The librarian took a tankard of woodale from the tray, and Mother Bluegizzard turned away to check on her other customers.

In the corner, Bikkle, her scraggy shryke-mate, was collecting the tankards and sweeping up. He was a drab little creature, but he was *her* drab little creature and she loved him.

'Two more tankards over here,' a voice whispered in Mother Bluegizzard's head. She looked across the crowded room and saw the tavern waif flapping his huge ears at her. She winked back at him and approached the two drinkers he was pointing to with his long, spidery fingers.

'Mother Bluegizzard, you're a marvel!' laughed Zett Blackeye, a small tufted-eared goblin, as she took his empty tankard and replaced it with a full one.

His hefty sidekick, Grome, a cloddertrog in a battered leather cap, grunted his approval as she handed him his drink. 'No one ever goes thirsty at the New Bloodoak, eh, Mother?' he boomed.

'Our trough's getting low!' came a chorus of voices behind Mother Bluegizzard, and she turned to see her regulars, Meggutt, Beggutt and Deg – comrades from General Tytugg's army, who had deserted together and made the perilous journey to the Free Glades – beckoning to her.

'If you fine sirs will excuse me,' she clucked to Zett and Grome, and bustled over to where the three goblins squatted at their drinking trough. 'Same again, lads?'

The three goblins nodded eagerly and Mother Bluegizzard rolled a fresh barrel across the floor and leaned it against the rim of the trough.

'Ready?' she asked.

Three heads nodded and she pierced the wooden barrel with a razor-sharp talon, releasing a foaming stream of ale into the trough. The three heads went down and the air filled with the sound of heavy slurping.

'You're welcome,' said Mother Bluegizzard cheerfully, wiping her claw on her apron. 'Now, how about another tot of woodgrog, Captain?' she chuckled, turning to a tall, gaunt figure with a thick matted beard.

He was another one of her regulars. The Mire Pirate, they called him, but as he never spoke, no one knew his real name. He'd turned up in New Undertown more than a dozen years earlier and had soon found his way to the Bloodoak, where he had been a regular ever since. Certainly he looked like a sky pirate and from his

bleached skin, it was clear he'd spent much time in the Mire, hence his nickname. And yet, to Mother Bluegizzard, it was his eyes that were the most mysterious thing about him.

Misty and unblinking, those pale, staring eyes somehow managed to give the impression that they had seen sights that no one should ever witness – though, since she'd never heard him utter a single word, it was impossible to tell for sure.

Over in the other corner, the festivities were livening up.

'A toast!' cried Deadbolt Vulpoon, rising a little unsteadily to his feet. 'To us!' he proclaimed, raising his tankard. 'Free-gladersh!'

'Freegladers!' cried Felix.

'Fr-uh-gl-uh-wuh!' yodelled the banderbears.

Deadbolt turned to them as he fell back into his seat, his eyes twinkling mischievously. '*Wuh-wuh-wuh*,' he grunted. 'I can't unnerstan' a wor' you say!'

Wuralo and Weeg chortled to themselves. Wumeru nodded and gave an airy wave of her left arm. 'Weela-wuh, wurra-yoola-wuh,' she murmured.

'Wha' she say? Wha' she say?' said Deadbolt, turning to Rook.

Rook smiled, his eyes softly glowing. 'She said, "The woodale has loosened old Tanglebeard's tongue. Soon he will be yodelling!"'

The sky pirate roared with laughter. 'Why not,' he said. 'It don't seem too hard.' Throwing back his head, he bellowed out loud, 'Wuh-uh-uh-wuh-ooooo!'

Felix turned to him, his hands clamped over his ears. 'What on earth was *that*?' he said.

'Wasn't it obvious?' said Deadbolt, pointing into his empty tankard. 'I'm thirsty!'

Felix laughed. 'Woodale all round! And more squashed fruit for our hairy friends here!' he added, winking over at Fevercule, the tavern waif.

Deadbolt got to his feet and pulled each banderbear in turn to theirs. 'Now, here's a language we can all share!' he laughed, and began dancing an unsteady jig.

Rumbling with deep laughter, the banderbears joined in.

Felix turned to Rook, his eyes twinkling, and frowned. 'Rook?' he said. 'Are you all right?'

His friend was pale and the rings beneath his eyes were darker than ever.

'It's just that I get so tired,' Rook said, sitting back in his chair. 'And yet I can hardly sleep. Thoughts and half-remembered images race through my mind in a jumble. I can remember some things as if they happened yester-day, but others are a complete blank . . .'

'Do you remember this?' asked Felix, pulling a sword out from beneath his cloak.

'My sword . . .' said Rook slowly, frowning as a lost thought hovered at the edge of his memory. 'But it's . . . it's the one you gave me,' he said, 'all that time ago. Back in the underground library. I remember losing it in old Undertown . . .'

'And yet I found it in the Deepwoods,' said Felix, 'in the possession of one Xanth Filatine – the same Xanth

Filatine who led you astray in the Edgelands. Claims he found it.' He snorted. 'A likely story! He and his Guardian of Night friends probably looted it, and he's too ashamed to admit it.' He shook his head. 'He's a bad lot, that one, and no mistake,' he said. 'Didn't I tell you to watch out for him?'

'Xanth Filatine,' Rook repeated. 'I remember him from our time together at Lake Landing . . . He was unmasked as an agent of the Guardians of Night . . . But after that . . . nothing.' He looked up at Felix. 'Where is he now?'

'Don't worry about him,' said Felix gruffly. 'He's being taken care of.'

'I don't understand,' said Rook.

'He's being held in the Gardens of Light beneath the Ironwood Glade,' said Felix. 'And that's where he's going to stay until his Reckoning. And from what I hear, there are plenty who intend to speak out against him when the time comes, myself included . . .'

'Rook Barkwater!' exclaimed a voice. 'As I live and breathe. Rook Barkwater!'

Felix and Rook turned to see a stout individual standing behind them, his hands on his hips and a huge grin on his face.

'Don't tell me you don't know who I am!' he said, sounding hurt. 'It's me, Stob. Stob Lummus.'

'Stob Lummus,' Rook repeated thoughtfully.

'They told me at Lake Landing that I'd find you here,' he said, 'and here you are!' He leaned forwards and pumped Rook's arm up and down. 'It's so good to see you.'

'It's good to see *you*, too,' said Rook, struggling to make sense of the jumble of memories clattering about in his head. 'Lake Landing ... We were apprentices together, weren't we? You, me, Magda, and Xanth ...'

The smile faded from Stob's face. 'They told me of your trouble, Rook,' he said. 'A sepia storm. Is it true that that traitor, Xanth Filatine, led you into it on purpose?'

'I ... I ...' said Rook. 'My memory, it's ...'

'I understand, old friend,' said Stob, patting him on the back. 'A good dose of pure Free Glade air and you'll soon be on the mend ...'

'Hammelhorn,' Rook blurted out. 'You carved your skycraft in the shape of a hammelhorn.'

'That's right,' said Stob, nodding enthusiastically. 'Mine was a hammelhorn, Magda's was a woodmoth and yours was a stormhornet.' He frowned. 'And Xanth's was a ...'

'A ratbird,' said Rook.

Felix snorted. 'That figures,' he said darkly.

They were joined by the banderbears, who now supported a sleeping Deadbolt Vulpoon between them. Stob shook their paws, one after the other. 'Welcome to the Free Glades. Welcome, indeed!' he said to each in turn, pausing when he came to Deadbolt. He looked questioningly at Rook.

'Don't mind him,' laughed Felix, getting up. 'He's been warmly welcomed enough for one evening. Come, we'll find cosy hammocks waiting for us in the Hive Huts.'

Just then, the entrance doors flew in. Everyone inside the tavern fell still, the chaotic hubbub of loud voices and raucous song instantly replaced by the sonorous chanting of low voices.

'*Ooh-maah, oomalaah. Ooh-maah, oomalaah. Ooh-maah, oomalaah . . .*'

All eyes fell on the line of oakelves – seven in all – as they marched in, and wound their way round the crowded room. Their turquoise hooded robes were stained by the juice of lullabee trees and rustled slightly as they walked.

'The Oakelf Brotherhood of Lullabee Island,' Fevercule's whisper sounded in Mother Bluegizzard's head.

The one at the front swung an incense-burner on chains to and fro, to and fro, filling the air with sweet aromatic smoke, while at the back the last oakelf in the line rang a heavy bell, over and over, like the tolling of a death-knell.

'*Ooh-maah, oomalaah. Ooh-maah . . .*'

'To what do we owe this unexpected pleasure?' clucked Mother Bluegizzard, trying to disguise the peevishness in her voice. These oakelves certainly knew how to spoil a party.

The procession brushed past her and made for the corner of the room. The Mire Pirate's unblinking eyes followed it. All at once, the oakelf leading the small procession stopped in front of Rook Barkwater and lowered his hood. His face was as brown and gnarled as the trees the creatures had taken their names from. The chanting softened to a low, ululating drone. Above it, the oakelf spoke.

'We come in search of the one who was touched by the sepia storm,' he said, his voice frail and cracked.

He reached out with the censer and swung it, sending wreaths of smoke coiling round Rook's head. The young librarian knight's pale blue eyes gleamed more brightly than ever.

'Come with us,' said the oakelf, as the chanting grew louder once more. 'To Lullabee Island.'

·CHAPTER TEN·

LULLABEE ISLAND

'Lullabee Island?' said Rook, taking the oakelf's outstretched hand and finding himself looking into eyes so black that it was like staring into the depths of open sky itself. Twinkling there were lights, as bright as the stars, as full as the moon; yet as he looked more closely, he realized that it was his own eyes – eerily glowing – which were reflecting back at him.

'You are tired, yet cannot sleep?' asked the oakelf.

'Yes,' said Rook.

'Your head is full of thoughts and memories,' the oakelf continued, 'and yet you can find no peace?'

'Yes,' said Rook, his eyes glowing more brightly than ever.

'Then come with us to Lullabee Island. My name is Grailsooth, and these . . .' He waved a hand to indicate the others, and Rook was aware of the disconcerting gaze of six more pairs of dark eyes. 'These are my fellow brothers from the lullabee grove there. We have dreamed of you, Rook Barkwater, and have come to offer you what help we can.'

The silence in the tavern was broken by the clatter of a beaker of woodgrog as it slipped from the old Mire Pirate's hand and clattered to the floor.

'I'll come with you,' Rook said, his voice hardly more than a whisper.

He stood up and the oakelves turned to go. Felix jumped to his feet, followed by the banderbears on either side of him, low growls in their throats.

Deadbolt slid to the floor and began to snore softly.

'Rook!' Felix's voice was imploring. 'You're not well. You can't just disappear off to some grove on some island in the middle of the night . . .'

'Calm yourself, gentle sir,' clucked Mother Blue-gizzard, laying a restraining talon on Felix's arm. 'These are the Oakelf Brotherhood. They spread peace and heal-ing throughout the Free Glades.' All round the tavern, heads nodded. 'Their ways might seem strange to you and me, but no harm will come to your young friend in their care, I can promise you that.'

The banderbears looked at each other, their ears flut-tering, then stepped aside and bowed their heads. The oakelves' turquoise robes rustled as they shuffled in single file towards the door, Rook following after.

'You don't have to go with them,' Felix called out as his friend reached the door to the tavern. 'Just say the word and . . .'

Rook turned and smiled. 'It's all right, Felix,' he said, his voice weary and hoarse-sounding. His pale blue eyes were glowing so brightly that Felix gasped. 'Perhaps they can help me.'

'Would you like us to come with you?' Felix persisted, starting towards him. 'We can if you want.'

Mother Bluegizzard's ruff sprang up around her throat and she shook her beak at Felix. 'No, no, gentle sir, that just won't do. Only those invited can set foot on Lullabee Island. Everybody knows that. Now why don't you all have another drink, and let them take care of your friend?'

Wumeru took Felix gently by the arm and guided him back to his chair. 'Wuh-wuh,' she muttered softly.

Felix stopped. He couldn't understand the great lumbering beast, but he knew that she, as Rook's oldest, most trusted banderbear friend, would not allow anything bad to happen to him. If her instincts were to trust these oakelves, then who was he to disagree? He looked back. At the far side of the room, the door to the New Bloodoak Tavern swung open, the column of oakelves – Rook among them – walked out, and the door slammed shut behind them.

In the corner, the Mire Pirate, who had climbed from his seat and was watching the young librarian knight intently, a puzzled frown lining his brow, abruptly sat down once more.

The next moment, as if nothing at all had happened, all round the New Bloodoak Tavern, the revellers at every table took up where they had left off – every table, that is, expect for the one where Rook's friends had been sitting.

'Well, if we can't go with him to this Lullabee Island,' Felix murmured, as Deadbolt let out a loud snore, 'then the least we can do is go down to the lake shore and wait for him to return.' He shook his head. 'Though something tells me it's going to be a long night.'

In the corner, the Mire Pirate stared at the Ghost of Screetown as Mother Bluegizzard flapped towards him, a beaker of woodgrog in her claws.

Outside on the busy street, Rook Barkwater found himself being encircled by the group of oakelves, all chanting softly once more as they made their way slowly through the town. Down the bustling side-alleys they went, towards North Lake. Being so much taller than the oakelf brothers, he could see all round. They were surrounded still by the vast celebrating crowds of goblins, trogs, trolls and waifs, all dancing, singing, laughing and joking – and yet, as he continued, Rook noticed something strange.

Although he could see the revellers' lips moving, he could hear neither their song nor their laughter; their whoops, their yells, their happy cries. Only the low, ullulating chant of the oakelves reached his ears, filling his head with its deep, dark sounds.

'*Ooh-maah, oomalaah. Ooh-maah, oomalaah. Ooh-maah, oomalaah . . .*'

He paused for a moment where he stood, and shook his head, trying to clear it of the hypnotic chant – only to be gently urged on by the ring of oakelves around him. Down to the water's edge they went, turning right onto a lamp-lined path that hugged the lake, the dark, slightly

ruffled surface of the water to his side. Past the jetties
they continued, lines of pink and yellow lanterns strung
out along them; past the fishing cabins and reed-stalls;
past reunited families and friends, and couples strolling
arm in arm along the waterside promenade.

And gradually, as they continued, the twinkling lights
of New Undertown receded behind them. In their place,
reflected in the water – sometimes crystal clear, sometimes blurred and fuzzy, as the wind rose and fell – was
a sprinkling of stars and the huge, silver face of the full
moon. The number of individuals out walking
diminished and the amount of woodland and shrubbery
increased until the empty path, no more than a small
track now, disappeared into the trees.

Dark and overgrown, with the moonlight blocked out
by the dense overhead canopy, the only light in the forest
came from the circle of oakelves' robes as they glowed
about him, a soft, luminous turquoise. And still the
oakelves went on, picking
their way through

the woods, before cutting down through the under-growth to the lake.

Rook was entranced. The soft chanting, the fragrance of the incense and delicate blue-green shade all seemed to wash over him, through him, outside and inside. And as they approached the water's edge, the full moon laid out across its velvety black surface like a huge piece of silver, Rook realized that he was growing increasingly sleepy. His legs felt like lead and he could barely keep his eyes open.

'Step lightly, Master Rook,' said the oakelf with the swaying censer. 'I shall hold the side steady for you.'

For a moment Rook was confused. Then, looking down, he saw the small coracle which had been lashed to a twist of knotted root just above the surface of the water. The bobbing vessel was small, almost round, made of a plaited frame of woodwillow and sallowdrop, and clad in pitch-sealed tilderskin.

Once he, the largest of the group, had stepped across and settled himself down on the bench at the blunt end of the coracle, the others climbed in after him. It was a tight fit, and Rook was aware of the warmth of the bodies pressed in about him as the oakelves picked up their paddles, pushed off from the bank, and began propelling the little boat slowly across the moonlit lake.

The water splashed softly, the coracle dipped and swayed, and all the while the oakelves kept up their low, sonorous chanting. It was only as they drew close to Lullabee Island that Rook realized it wasn't the only music he could hear. Ahead of him, coming from

somewhere in the centre of the island, was more music – similar to that of the chanting oakelves, though a thousand times sweeter.

Rook's eyes closed and his head began to nod.

'Not yet, Rook Barkwater,' Grailsooth's voice sounded in his ear. 'Not just yet.'

Suddenly he heard a grating noise as the bottom of the coracle scraped against the loose gravel below them. He shook his head groggily and stifled a yawn. The oakelves abruptly stopped their chanting, and six of them jumped down into the water and began dragging the little boat up onto the shore.

Grailsooth took Rook gently by the arm. 'This way, Rook Barkwater,' he said.

Together, they headed away from the banks of the lake. The undergrowth grew thicker, the number of trees increased and between the trunks and branches, Rook noticed a pale turquoise light glowing in the distance and lightening the sky.

'Not far now,' Grailsooth murmured, turning and smiling at him.

Rook smiled sleepily. As he went further into the woods, the sapwoods and various willows began to give way to lullabee trees – massive specimens, with broad, bulbous trunks, spreading branches and huge leaves. Music filled the air – plangent chords and interweaving harmonies – as a warm wind passed lightly through the air. And, as the full moon shone down upon them, the leaves gave off a fine, glowing mist that cast the whole forest in a pool of deepest turquoise.

'It's so . . . so beautiful,' Rook murmured softly.

'It is welcoming us,' said Grailsooth.

'Welcoming us?'

'The lullabee groves are the most ancient and mysterious places in all the Deepwoods,' he said. 'And the grove here on Lullabee Island is the most ancient and most mysterious of them all.' He smiled and placed a hand on the young librarian knight's shoulder. 'And it is welcoming you, Rook Barkwater, for here you shall find rest.'

'But . . . but why *me*?' Rook muttered, as all round him, the music switched to soft glissandos, which rippled through the shifting shades of turquoise light.

'The Brotherhood dreamed of you,' said Grailsooth. 'You have suffered much.'

'The sepia storm?' said Rook, frowning, as the memories came back to him. 'In the Edgelands?'

'That, too, was in our dreams,' Grailsooth nodded. 'You were touched by the passing storm, as others have been touched before you . . .'

'And you can help me?' asked Rook, a tremor of unease tingling inside his skull.

The oakelf glanced round at him. 'That, Rook Barkwater, is for you to discover,' he said.

They continued through the lullabee grove towards the centre, where the oakelves gathered in a circle. Rook looked round him at the curious clearing in the trees. High above his head, the leaves glowed and hummed, filling the air with the most glorious chorus of musical sounds. And there, as the wind parted the great leaves,

he saw several dusty-grey sacklike objects hanging from the branches, glittering slightly, dangling down into the misty turquoise air, and turning slowly. Although he had never seen one before in real life, he recognized them at once from his studies in the Great Library of the underground sewers.

'Caterbird cocoons,' he gasped.

'Indeed,' said Grailsooth. 'The caterbirds have been hatching here for longer than any of us can imagine. Why, some of these cocoons are thousands of years old. While others,' he added, and pointed to a cocoon dangling from a branch to his left, 'are still to hatch.'

Rook's jaw dropped in amazement. 'You mean, that's a caterbird about to hatch?' he said.

'Perhaps,' said Grailsooth. 'But probably not in

my lifetime or, who knows? Not in yours either . . .' He shook his head sagely. 'A caterbird hatching is a rare thing indeed, Rook Barkwater, witnessed but once in a hundred years, perhaps longer. And yet, in this place, as you can see, it has occurred many, many times.'

Rook looked about him, awestruck. There was so much to take in; the entrancing music, the unearthly light, the sparkling cocoons which had been added to, one after the other, down the centuries.

The branches and the huge leaves glowed a shimmering turquoise and swayed gently to and fro as if in a breeze, yet to Rook, the air seemed unnaturally still. Grailsooth's huge dark eyes followed Rook's gaze, and he smiled.

'The caterworms are feeding on the lullabee leaves, filling the grove with their music,' he said.

Rook frowned. 'Caterworms? Where?'

'They are in the trees – all around us, Rook Barkwater. They are glisters. You see them only as light. It is they who weave themselves into cocoons and emerge as . . .'

'Caterbirds!' breathed Rook.

'Indeed,' said Grailsooth, and nodded to his companions, who melted away into the trees. 'And now, the time has come . . .'

All around, the music of the lullabee trees grew to a rousing crescendo.

The time for what? Rook wondered, suddenly feeling the weariness overwhelm him once more.

As if reading his thoughts, Grailsooth took him by the arm and pointed up into the trees to one of the caterbird cocoons. 'Time,' he said, 'to sleep in a cocoon. You will dream the dreams of the all-knowing caterbirds. You will see yourself through their eyes and, Sky willing, find peace . . .'

Rook realized he was trembling. See himself? Find peace?

'Go now,' said Grailsooth gently. 'Climb the lullabee and crawl into the caterbird cocoon. There, sleep will come to you and you will rest.'

As Grailsooth looked on, Rook did as he was told. He climbed the great knobbly trunk of the lullabee tree, shinned his way along a broad branch and lowered himself into the cocoon. It was soft and downy, giving slightly beneath his weight as he curled up inside it. Within seconds, he felt his arms and legs relax and his breathing became regular and heavy.

His eyes flickered for a moment as he realized that he was about to fall asleep in the cocoon of a caterbird. How strange, and yet how natural it felt. His eyes flickered again before shutting completely.

A soft, rasping snore mingled with the music of the glade as Rook drifted into a deep, dream-filled sleep.

CHAPTER ELEVEN

Cocoon Dreams

Rook was standing in a magnificent chamber, its walls decorated with murals and rich tapestries; the floor, a swirl of delicate mosaics. There was a fire roaring in the grate. Huge ironwood logs, nestling in a crimson bed of glowing embers, crackled and hissed as the yellow and lilac-white flames danced over them. And as they burned, so they shifted, and bright orange ash showered down.

Before the fireplace, the firelight flickering in their faces, were four boys. They had short, dark, wavy hair. One wore glasses. All of them shared the same fine, angular features and bright, darting eyes. They were laughing. The youngest was telling the others of some exploit or other, while they gently teased him.

As Rook watched them, his heart seemed to effervesce with happiness, as though thousands of tiny bubbles were filtering through it. So this was what it felt like to be part of a large family, surrounded by brothers.

There were two other boys in the chamber – older and

taller – practising their sword skills with tipped foils. A woman in an ornate gown and lace collar sat in an armchair to the right of the fireplace, the expression on her face as she surveyed her brood a mixture of amusement and pride; while on the far side of the room, a tall, dark-haired sky pirate stood by the window staring out. His beard was plaited and his moustache waxed. He wore a breast-plate of gleaming black, and a heavy sabre hung at his side. How imposing he looked, Rook thought – and strangely familiar, as if he'd seen him somewhere before.

As the fire crackled, the swords clashed and the laughter continued, Rook looked about him. To his left, the wall was covered with a spectacular mural. It was a townscape, with tall, elegant towers and magnificent palaces, and a river running through it all. In the sky above was a swirling flock of ratbirds, a sky pirate ship, and a great caterbird flapping endlessly across the shimmering blue heavens; while in the foreground, staring ahead, were eight figures. A mother and father; six brothers.

Rook took a few steps towards the wall and raised a hand to touch its painted surface. As he did so, the paint seemed to blister and boil, the colours turning dark and the image of the family disappearing before his eyes.

Smoke – suddenly, there was thick dark smoke coiling up from the floor.

Rook could hear terrified screams and calls for help. He turned and ran blindly across the tiled floor, desperately searching for a way out amidst the thick blanket of choking smoke.

The next moment, everything was in flames – the rugs, the tapestries, the curtains, the chairs. And the smoke grew denser, and the heat more intense.

Rook was shouting now, with all his might, but no sound came out. He sank to his knees, the acrid smell of the smoke in his nostrils and the roar of the flames in his ears. Sadness overwhelmed him, like raindrops pouring down a window-pane. It was as if he could touch it, smell it. He was racked by silent sobs.

Then everything went black . . .

Rook's body felt light, like a fragment of soot or a burnt ember. He was being blown away on a cool wind, a speck amongst the ashes of the terrible fire which had now burned itself out. He was floating, high above the roofs, towers and minarets of a great city. He peered down.

Far below, there was someone on a rooftop amidst the smoking buildings. It was one of the brothers. The youngest one. Crouched beside a shattered skylight, tears streaming down his cheeks, he hugged his knees closely to his chest and rocked slowly to and fro, to and fro . . .

Rook flew on, light as air, in and out of huge tumbling clouds. And as he did so, he felt an elation growing; a wild, exhilarating excitement!

Suddenly, he was on a sky ship in full sail, its deck rolling and bucking as the mighty ship sliced through the clouds. He clutched the stout lufwood mast to steady himself and looked up at the aft-deck.

There, standing proudly in the elegant clothes of a sky

pirate, was a lad with dark wavy hair. Beside him stood the sky pirate captain with the plaited beard and waxed moustache. He was leaning over the youth, guiding and advising him, as the lad – his eyes gleaming and his mouth smiling – steered the sky ship, turning the wheel and adjusting the flight-levers.

As he watched, Rook felt the father's love for his son, and the bond between the two. A heavy lump swelled in his throat and his eyes misted with tears . . .

Rook shivered. He was no longer on the sky ship in Open Sky, but inside a tall, draughty building. Looking up, he saw a long, curved staircase, twisting away into dark shadows. Halfway up – a tray clasped in its front claws – a huge, translucent spindlebug slowly climbed the stairs. Rook could see the blood pumping through its veins, the three bulbous lungs rising and falling, the two hearts slowly beating as, eventually, the creature reached a landing and approached a large ironwood door.

It knocked and waited – one, two, three, four, five seconds; Rook counted them – before seizing the handle and entering.

A girl with dark plaits and large green eyes looked up and smiled as the spindlebug approached with its tray. She was at a table, making a vast mosaic picture out of thousands of pieces of coloured crystal. Standing beside her, looking out of place and ill at ease, was a young sky pirate of about Rook's age, with dark wavy hair. He kept glancing over towards the balcony windows, where Rook glimpsed the backs of a sky pirate captain and a tall academic, the two of them deep in conversation.

Out beyond them, past the ornate balcony balustrade, Rook could see a magnificent skyline. To the left, a dome-shaped building with a huge bowl at its top, rose up from the rows of spiky towers around it, whilst in the distance, a mighty viaduct set upon a series of gigantic arched supports snaked through the city. To the right, twin towers, their upper ramparts topped with curious spinning, net-like minarets, stood out black against the billowing clouds.

'The mist-sifting towers of the School of Mist,' breathed Rook.

There was no doubt about it. He'd seen them in the ancient barkscrolls. Somehow, he was standing looking out over old Sanctaphrax . . .

Rook shivered again, this time violently. It was suddenly icy cold, and he was in a great circular space, buildings towering above him on all sides. Snow was falling. It fluttered down in large feathery flakes, covering every walkway, every rooftop, every road. Giant icicles hung from the eaves and sills. Looking up, Rook saw the youth again, at the top of what seemed to be the tallest tower of them all, so high above the ground it made Rook reel with dizziness just to watch him.

With one hand he gripped the balustrade; with the other, the hand of a girl as she dangled precariously over the edge. Clouds of condensation billowed from her lips, as she screamed and Rook could see her mouth forming three little words, over and over.

'Save yourself, Quint!'

But the snow got thicker and heavier, a great white blinding blizzard, until all at once it obliterated everything from sight . . .

Then Rook heard sobbing. Quiet, muffled sobbing. The dappled sunlight dazzled him for a moment but, as he shielded his eyes and looked around him, Rook realized that he was in the Deepwoods, and that the sobbing was coming from a stooped figure on a path, just ahead of him.

His instinct was to approach and ask what the matter was. But something made him hang back. The figure seemed so distraught, so inconsolable as it hugged a small bundle and swayed backwards and forwards, its heavy hooded cloak flapping. Just then, a tall sky pirate brushed past him and approached the figure. Rook heard sharp words and urgent whispers, and the sobbing grew louder.

Suddenly, the sobbing figure knelt down, and placed the bundle gently at the foot of a tree, before straightening up. Its hood fell back and Rook glimpsed a gaunt, dark-eyed face. The sobbing stopped. The sky pirate held out a hand and the cloaked figure took it and, as Rook watched, they walked silently away, not once looking back. Curious, Rook approached the foot of the tree and looked down at the bundle. He gasped.

It was a baby! A small baby, wrapped up in square of cloth, intricately embroidered with the picture of a lullabee tree. Its dark eyes stared back at him.

A sound made Rook look up, and with a jolt of surprise, he noticed a wooden cabin nestling in the branches of the tree above. Its circular door was opening. In the trees all around him, other small, rounded cabins were secured to the upper branches, purple smoke coiling from pipe-chimneys, and lights appearing at windows.

A stocky woodtroll-matron emerged from the door and climbed down the lufwood tree, huffing and puffing. Reaching the ground, she let out a shriek of surprise, before picking the bundle up. Rook felt a warm surge of love replace the icy chill in his chest. Before him, the woodtroll mother cradled the foundling, whispering sweet lullabies and tickling him under his chin. The baby cooed with delight . . .

The light faded and Rook was in the depths of the Deepwoods once more, tramping on through the night, his legs aching and his feet hurting. He was alone and without hope.

Suddenly, he felt a hand on his shoulder, and he found himself looking up into a kind, gentle face. It was the cloaked figure, but instead of the sky pirate with her, she was surrounded by young'uns of every description. Mobgnomes, cloddertrogs and red-haired individuals who hadn't yet turned termagant; woodtrolls, lugtrolls, gabtrolls and goblin young'uns from each major tribe; hammerhead and long-haired, lop-eared and tusked.

They were happy, and so was she, her eyes burning with joy. Rook found himself laughing and dancing in the sunlight in the midst of the throng of young'uns. They were beside a lake – one of three, stretched out in a line – with a towering cave-studded cliff behind them and a tall, imposing ironwood glade far to their left. And as they danced in a big circle – laughing and singing – the cloaked figure looked on, a huge spindlebug by her side . . .

The sounds of laughter faded and were replaced by beautiful music and turquoise light.

He was in a lullabee grove, not in a cocoon high in the branches, but on the forest floor. Suddenly, all round him, he could hear thrashing and tearing and muffled cries. And he looked up to see a majestic bird standing on one of the branches, high above his head. Beside it, the cocoon from which it had just hatched swayed emptily in the gentle breeze.

It was a caterbird.

It preened its violet-black feathers and scratched at its snowy white chest with long, jagged talons for a moment. Then, turning its head to one side, it looked

down, and fixed him with a long, unblinking stare.

Rook stared back at it and felt his head begin to spin under its hypnotic gaze . . .

The next moment, Rook became conscious of beating wings, and the air whistling past. To his right and left, huge black wings pumped up and down, up and down, driving him on through the air. Below him, the forest canopy flashed past – greens, blues, yellows – an ocean of foliage.

He was a caterbird! It was *his* wings beating; *his* beak open wide and *his* strange echoing cry.

Looking back over his shoulder, he saw a sky ship, with its billowing sails and sparkling varnished masts and hull soaring through the air behind him. And no wonder, he realized a moment later, for it was attached to a rope tied around his middle.

He was pulling the magnificent sky ship across the sky!

He opened his beak and gave another triumphant cry. The young sky pirate captain at the helm waved and shouted in reply. Rook turned back and flapped his wings, soaring ahead, resplendent against the sparkling sky.

But wait! What was that up ahead? A vast, swirling vortex of cloud and wind was hurtling towards him, and there was nothing he could do. He and the sky ship were heading straight for it.

The next instant, the vortex enfolded them and Rook felt himself falling, no longer a bird, but a librarian knight once more, his arms flapping uselessly in the rushing air. Down, down he fell; down into inky darkness . . .

Flames flickered around him. Lamps gleamed. He was sitting at a long table, spiky, red-haired slaughterers jostling him from either side, and a huge brazier of burning leadwood in front of him. The table groaned with tilder sausages, hammelhorn steaks, latticed tarts and huge, dripping pies. Tankards of woodale were raised and toasts loudly proposed. The warm air was full of delicious smells and hearty laughter. A sky pirate was getting married to a pretty slaughterer lass, and this was their wedding feast.

Rook slapped the table delightedly and joined in the singing. The woodale was delicious and the brazier fire wonderfully warm, and Rook felt his head begin to swim . . .

The sounds of merry-making faded. It was quiet in the slaughterer village, the hammocks overhead bulging with sleeping bodies. On the other side of the clearing, Rook could see the sky pirate captain pacing outside one of the leadwood cabins.

All at once, the thick hammelhornskin which hung across the doorway was swept apart, and a slaughterer matron emerged, her shock of red hair damp and sticking to her forehead. In her arms, she held a small baby, which she handed gently to the waiting captain.

'Your daughter, Captain,' she said, smiling.

And as the sky pirate captain raised the child high up in the air, waves of joy flooded Rook's heart.

He wanted to shout and dance and jump in the air! But the village was so quiet, he was afraid he'd wake the sleepers overhead. He was about to get up to run over to the captain – but the trees abruptly faded and the light turned from the crisp blue of dawn to the golden glow of dusk . . .

Rook was back in the Free Glades, on the edge of New Undertown, the Lufwood Tower dark against the glowing sky. A young couple with a young'un beside them were seated at the front of a prowlgrin-drawn cart, their belongings at the back, secured beneath a bulging tarpaulin.

A sky pirate stood beside them; a tall, heavily-built individual with a thick beard and dark, doleful eyes. Clearly agitated, the pirate was waving his arms around, remonstrating with the young couple, trying to stop them from leaving the Free Glades and setting out on their journey. He seemed desperate.

'It isn't safe,' he kept saying. 'The slavers are out.'

But they wouldn't listen. Instead, the young couple smiled indulgently, bounced the young'un on their knees and told him to 'kiss goodbye to Great Uncle Tem'.

As they rode away into the sunset, the sky pirate stared after them, tears streaming down his face – a face Rook was sure he'd seen somewhere before.

The sun set and the moon rose, and Rook felt his stomach give a sickening lurch . . .

It was the old dream, the nightmare that had recurred all through his childhood from as long ago as he could remember. Now, it was back again – and with all its familiar horror.

First came the wolves – always the wolves. White-collared, bristling and baying, their terrible yellow eyes flashing in the dark forest.

His father was shouting for him to hide; his mother was screaming. Rook didn't know what to do. He was running this way, that way. Everywhere were flashing yellow eyes and the sharp, barked commands of the slave-takers.

Rook whimpered. He knew what came next, and it was worse – far worse.

He was alone in the dark woods. The howling of the

slavers' wolf-packs was receding into the distance. Alone in the vastness of the Deepwoods – and something was coming towards him. Something huge . . .

Suddenly Rook felt the panic and terror leave him, to be replaced by a feeling of peace. He was in the huge, soft, moss-scented arms of a great banderbear, who hugged him to herself and yodelled gently in his ear . . .

Rook opened his eyes, the warm, safe feeling of the banderbear's enfolding arms lingering. He was inside the caterbird cocoon, the soft woven fibres holding him as securely as the rescuing creature of his dreams.

Sitting up, he felt wonderful. His head was clear and, for the first time in weeks, he felt fully rested; charged with a strength and energy he could feel coursing through his body. As he crawled towards the opening in the cocoon and stuck his head out, the images were already fading away, like water slipping between his fingers. He struggled to make sense of them as he looked around.

An early morning mist hung over the grove as Rook climbed down the gnarled trunk of the lullabee tree. On the ground, he stretched luxuriantly.

'I trust you slept well, Rook Barkwater,' Grailsooth's voice sounded beside him.

'Better,' said Rook, smiling back at the oakelf, his eyes no longer glowing unnaturally blue, 'than I have ever slept before!'

CHAPTER TWELVE

Passwords

i
The Foundry Glades

As the sun sank low in the sky, a ragged band of sky pirates struggled to the crest of yet another densely forested ridge. Their leader, a weasel-faced quartermaster in a torn and muddied greatcoat, unhooked a telescope from his belt and put it to his eye. In front of him, the endless Deepwoods stretched away to the golden, cloud-flecked horizon.

You might as well put your telescope away, Quillet Pleeme, a quiet, sibilant voice sounded in the quartermaster's head. *It might have served you well in the Mire, but it is almost useless here in the Deepwoods.*

The quartermaster turned, anger plain on his thin, sharp features. Beside him, gasping for breath, stood a huge matron – a cloddertrog – with a small, frail-looking ghost-waif strapped to her back. The waif's barbels quivered as he fixed the quartermaster with an unblinking stare.

'If you have something to say, Amberfuce,' said Quillet Pleeme, 'then say it out loud, instead of sneaking into my head.' Ever since he and his sky pirates had hooked up with the sickly waif and his huge nurse back in the throng of Undertowners in the Mire, the odious creature had been listening in to his thoughts.

'Apologies,' whispered Amberfuce meekly. 'But I simply wanted to point out that sight is less important than the other senses here in the Deepwoods.'

The other sky pirates joined them on the ridge, sweating profusely and blowing hard from the long climb. There was a heavily tattooed flat-head goblin, three thin, ill-looking gnokgoblins, a long-haired goblin and a couple of mob gnomes, all of them wearing heavy sky pirate coats festooned with weapons, canteens and grappling-irons. Together they had formed the crew of the *Fogscythe* before they had deserted their captain – a cloddertrog in a muglumpskin coat – and followed Quillet Pleeme.

Amberfuce, the waif, had promised them all riches beyond their wildest dreams, for they – every last one of them – were going to be Furnace Masters in the Foundry Glades. Amberfuce had promised them, and he would deliver on his promise because he knew someone; a very important someone.

That someone was Hemuel Spume, the head of the whole Foundry Glades. All they had to do, Amberfuce had explained, his eyes twinkling, was to escort him and his nurse to the Foundry Glades and then sit back and reap the rewards from a grateful Hemuel Spume.

How difficult could that be?

The sky pirates had soon found out. Sneaking away from the multitude of Undertowners as they trudged through the Mire had been easy. Even with Flambusia Flodfox, Amberfuce's nurse, carrying the ghostwaif on her back, complaining loudly and slowing them down, they'd made good progress. They were used to the Mire and mud-marching, and once they'd crossed back over the shattered Mire Road, they'd arrived at the southern Edgelands in less than a day.

The Edgelands had been unpleasant, and all of them were plagued with visions and nightmarish apparitions – especially the ghostwaif, before Flambusia had given him some of her special medicine. But again they'd made good progress, and the journey really did seem to be as straightforward as Amberfuce had said it would be. And then they had entered the Deepwoods.

They'd lost Brazerigg to a logworm almost at once, and the gnokgoblins had come down with pond-fever soon after, forcing them to pitch camp for a week. Now their provisions were running out, and the way ahead lay over endless forest ridges which stretched off as far as the eye could see.

'There must be an easier route,' Myzewell the flat-head had moaned on the third day of hard climbing and bone-jolting descents.

The way to riches is never easy, my friend, Amberfuce's sibilant whisper had sounded in his head.

Now, on the fourth day, here they all stood, tired and hungry, at the top of yet another ridge with the Foundry Glades still nowhere in sight.

'Where now?' Quillet Pleeme snarled, snapping his telescope shut.

The ghostwaif closed his eyes and sniffed the air, his huge, paper-thin ears quivering. 'I can hear clinking and clanking,' he whispered. 'Grinding and hissing, hammering and howling. I smell molten metal and furnace smoke.' He stretched out a long thin finger. 'Over there, just beyond the next ridge, my friends . . .' His hand trembled, and a harsh cough racked his tiny body.

'That's what you said two days ago,' snarled Myzewell the flat-head.

'There, there, Amby, dear,' fussed Flambusia, throwing a blanket over her shoulder. 'You wrap up warm, and don't go getting into a bother.'

Quillet shrugged and turned to the other sky pirates. 'We've come this far. What's another hill or two, between friends? Come on, you scurvy curs! Look lively!'

Cursing beneath their breath, the sky pirates began the long descent into the growing dusk. As Myzewell started after them, Quillet pulled him back and, glancing up ahead at the figure of Flambusia disappearing down the slope, whispered in his ear.

'I've had enough of this. I, for one, think the waif's lost. One more ridge. If we get to the top and we don't see furnace chimneys, then we cut our losses and return to the Mire.'

'But what about the waif and his nurse?' growled Myzewell.

'We ditch them. We'll travel more quickly, and there'll be two less mouths to feed.' The quartermaster drew a hand across his throat in a cutting motion. 'Wait for me to give the word,' he whispered. 'And mind you keep your thoughts clear, or the waif'll suspect something.'

'And the word?' said Myzewell, giving a sharp-toothed grin.

'"Goodbye",' said Quillet quietly.

Five, hard, scrambling, bone-jarring hours later, the sky pirates wearily approached the crest of the next ridge. The slope had been heavily forested, with sharp thickets of razorthorns amid dense stands of greyoaks and flametrees. Several times, as the thorns ripped their coats and the branches scratched their faces, Quillet and Myzewell exchanged dark looks. At last they reached the top, and Quillet's mouth dropped open.

It was the smell that hit them first. Thick, acrid and choking smoke, mixed with a sulphurous metallic stench. Then the low insistent roar of the furnaces and the sound of thousands of hammers on metal. Looking down, Quillet could see the glowing fires of the Foundry Glades twinkling through the drifting wreaths of smoke.

Amberfuce turned to the open-mouthed quarter-master, a slyly knowing look on his face. *You have something to say, perhaps?* he asked, his sibilant voice hissing in Quillet's head. *No? Well then, let us make our way to my good friend Hemuel Spume's palace without delay.*

As they made their way down the hill towards the glades below, the noise and smell and choking smoke grew more and more intense. Ahead of them, the trees thinned until they found themselves picking their way through a forest of tree-stumps. The air grew hot and sooty, and instead of tall forest trees, the glowing metal foundry chimneys towered over them, belching out smoke.

Amberfuce pulled his scarf up over his mouth. His breath was coming fast and wheezy. Flambusia fussed with him anxiously, reaching up every few steps to pop a cough-lozenge into his mouth.

They approached the first furnace they came to, and Quillet's beady eyes narrowed. A long line of workers snaked from the huge timber stacks on one side of the furnace to its open fiery mouth on the other. With heavy groans of exertion, they fed the flames with an endless supply of logs passed by hand down the line, while overseers patrolled, cracking heavy tilderleather whips. The sky pirates looked at one another.

'Poor creatures,' muttered Stegrewl, the long-haired goblin.

'Oi! You, there!' came a rough voice. 'Stop right there!'

They turned to see a phalanx of burly flat-head goblin guards bearing down on them, a large, battle-scarred captain at their head.

Amberfuce tapped Flambusia on the shoulder, motioning her forward, but before he could speak, Quillet Pleeme had pushed past her and addressed the captain face to face.

'Greetings!' he said, bowing his head in salute. 'We are sky pirates who have risked our lives to escort Chancellor Amberfuce of old Undertown safely to the Foundry Glades . . .'

The captain delivered a swift blow to the quarter-master's midriff that sent him tumbling to the ground, doubled up and gasping for breath. 'Silence, scum!' he roared, raising his sword.

My dear captain . . . er . . . Hegghuft, is it? Amberfuce's honeyed tones sounded inside the guard's head. *I can tell you are a warrior of great distinction. One of my great friend Hemuel Spume's most trusted captains. He will be pleased when I tell him of your . . . er . . . diligence.*

The waif pulled his scarf down to reveal a sickly, ingratiating smile.

The goblin stared back at him and slowly lowered his sword.

'Now if you would be so kind as to take me to your master . . .' Amberfuce said out loud, fighting to stifle the cough rising in his throat.

The captain nodded slowly, then turned to his guards. 'Take their weapons,' he ordered, indicating the sky pirates before turning back to the waif. 'This way, Chancellor,' he growled.

They made their way through the Foundry Glades, past furnaces bigger and more terrible than the first, barging through scurrying workers and their bullying guards, until at last ahead of them, the palace loomed into view. They hurried across the front courtyard, in through the gates and – still accompanied by the goblin guards – up a broad staircase to the third floor. In front of them, a huge metal-plated door swung slowly open and a stooped individual with steel-rimmed glasses and long side-whiskers appeared, flanked on either side by palace guards.

'Amberfuce! Amberfuce!' he cried, peering up at the ghostwaif slumped on Flambusia's back. Can it really be you? After all these years!'

'Hemuel, my dear friend,' said Amberfuce, looking down. He pursed his lips with irritation. 'Get me down, Flambusia,' he said. 'Now!'

The nurse reached up, lifted her charge out of the sling on her back and plonked him down with just a touch more vigour than was absolutely necessary. 'There,' she said, smiling sweetly.

Amberfuce collected himself. 'It's been far too long, Hemuel,' he said, breathlessly.

'Indeed,' said Spume. 'But I've made great progress here in the Foundry Glades while you've been holed up in Undertown.' He smiled, revealing a row of jagged yellow teeth, and rubbed a forefinger and thumb together. 'Your investments have done very well. We're expanding, Amberfuce, expanding beyond our wildest dreams. I've got the goblins just where I want them, and the Free Glades in my sights. And now you're here, Amberfuce, old friend, to share in this great venture.'

'Wild prowlgrins couldn't have kept me away,' said Amberfuce excitedly, his barbels quivering. 'We must speak in private, right away.' He tapped the box clutched to his chest. His voice dropped. 'I think you'll find what I have here of interest.'

'Oh, but of course,' said Hemuel Spume. 'Follow me.'

He turned away. Amberfuce followed, Flambusia stooping over him, mopping his sweaty brow with her handkerchief as she went.

'What about us?' said Quillet Pleeme, peevishly. 'Aren't you forgetting something? You promised that your friend here would make us Furnace Masters . . .'

Hemuel Spume stopped and spun round on his heel. 'Furnace Masters?' he said, a ghost of a smile playing on his thin lips. He looked at the ghostwaif, who smiled back at him. 'Oh, Amberfuce, you naughty old thing! Sky pirates as Furnace Masters? Whatever next! You knew I'd never agree.'

Amberfuce nodded. 'Yes,' he whispered, 'but *they* didn't know that.'

'You said you'd have a word!' Quillet Pleeme pleaded, his voice a thin whine. 'A word, you said. A word . . .'

'Oh, I have a word,' said Amberfuce nastily. 'Perhaps you recognize it?'

Quillet, Myzewell and the sky pirates stared back at the ghostwaif as the guards seized them by the arms.

'Goodbye!'

Hemuel Spume smiled. 'Some do very well here,' he said, 'if they work hard. Guards, take them away!'

As the cursing and moaning faded behind them, Hemuel Spume led Amberfuce and Flambusia to the back of the great hall. He paused by a small door, and waved Flambusia away.

'If you'd be kind enough to leave us, my dear,' he said.

'But . . . But . . .' cried Flambusia outraged. 'His medicines! His embrocations! His . . .'

'Flambusia *never* leaves my side,' said Amberfuce, his barbels quivering with agitation.

Hemuel flashed the same thin-lipped, yellow-toothed smile as he turned the handle, pushed Amberfuce inside the ante-chamber and slammed the door in Flambusia

Flodfox's pink, indignant face. Locking it, he turned to
Amberfuce.

'First things first,' he said. 'You wanted to speak to me
in private . . .'

'Yes, yes,' said Amberfuce. 'But I didn't mean without
Flambusia . . .'

Hemuel steered the ghostwaif over to a small table.
'Forget the nurse for a moment,' he said, 'and show me
what's in that box!'

Amberfuce laid the box down, pulled a key from
around his neck and opened it. Inside, there were
wads of folded paper. He pulled

one out at ran-
dom, opened it
up and spread it
out on the table.
He cleared his
throat.

'As the right-
hand waif to Vox
Verlix, the most
brilliant mind in old
Undertown, I had access
to his private chambers.
When I sent word
to you that I was
coming, I prom-
ised I'd bring
s o m e t h i n g
special with me.'

'Indeed you did. But just *how* special?' said Hemuel Spume, his eyes glinting.

'This,' said Amberfuce with a little chuckle, 'is one of Vox Verlix's blueprints. Everyone knows the Sanctaphrax Forest, the Tower of Night, the Great Mire Road . . .' He shrugged. 'Yet they were but a few of his ideas. He worked on others, too. Many others.' He removed a second blueprint and spread it out over the first; then a third . . . 'Catapults, log-launchers, flaming slings . . . His mind was never still. And this . . .' He took a fourth blueprint from the box and spread it out carefully on top of the others. 'This is the finest of the lot.'

'So I can see,' said Hemuel, his eyes glinting wildly as he pawed over the detailed design. 'Wonderful! Wonderful!' he breathed.

'I knew you'd be pleased,' said Amberfuce.

'I couldn't be more pleased,' said Hemuel. 'And now, in return, I have a little surprise for you.'

'A surprise?' said Amberfuce, coughing with excitement. 'What . . . sort of . . . sur . . .' The coughing grew worse. 'Oh, Flambusia!' he gasped. 'I need Flambusia!'

From behind them, there came a muffled hammering on the door and the sound of Flambusia's outraged voice, demanding to be let in.

'You don't need her, believe me,' said Spume with a smile, as he led the frail ghostwaif over to the far side of the ante-chamber, and opened a second door.

Amberfuce looked through into the room on the other side. His eyes widened, his cheeks coloured – and his cough magically melted away. 'Hemuel,' he gasped.

'Have I died and gone to the Eternal Glen?'

The Foundry Master chuckled as he ushered the waif inside the room, where a score of gabtroll apothecaresses immediately surrounded him, each one bearing kneading-rods, birchwood-twigs, rough flannels and spicy, aromatic massage-oils.

'I'm putting my own personal attendants at your disposal. Enjoy!'

'Amby?' Flambusia wailed bleakly.

The ghostwaif was gently laid out on a raised table.

'Amby?'

But Amberfuce didn't reply. Doused in oils and ointments, unguents and salves; rubbed, kneaded and stroked, a radiant smile spread across his face. His eyelids fluttered for a moment, then closed.

'AM-BY!'

'Not now, Flambusia,' he purred happily, as he submitted to the wonderfully rough, firm hands. 'Not now.'

ii
The Goblin Nations

'But why must the lop-ear clan always bear the heaviest burden?' Meegmewl cried out indignantly.

The old grey goblin had heard some things in his life, but to demand a consignment of a thousand goblins a month was outrageous, even for Hemuel Spume. With the harvest not yet in, it would mean hunger in the clan's villages at the very least.

'Because, old goblin, my flat-heads and hammerheads are warriors,' said Lytugg fiercely. 'They're willing to act as guards, but as for operating the foundries and furnaces . . .'

'And that goes for my lot, too,' snarled Rootrott Underbiter. 'We tusked goblins are prepared to make sacrifices, don't get me wrong.' He drained his tankard and slammed it heavily down on the table. 'We're ready to fight, of course we are, but as for those accursed Foundry Glades, enough is enough!'

Hemtuft Battleaxe shifted forward in his chair, adjusted his feathered cloak and cleared his throat. 'We need those "accursed Foundry Glades", as you put it,' he said, fixing the tusked clan chief with a cold stare. 'I don't believe we have any choice in the matter.' His eyes darkened. 'Now, more than ever before, it is vital to keep them well supplied with labour.' He looked round. 'I take it we're all agreed on that, at least.'

The other clan chiefs nodded cautiously.

Sensing that his hastily convened closed-meeting was shifting in his direction at last, Hemtuft seized the advantage. He looked sternly at the clan chiefs, one after the other: Lytugg the hammerhead, her red eyes blazing; Rootrott Underbiter the tusked goblin, scowling; Grossmother Nectarsweet the symbite, her huge chins glistening with drops of woodale, and Meegmewl the Grey, shrunken and frail, yet defiant even now . . .

'There are great plans afoot in the Foundry Glades,' Hemtuft said. 'Plans that will bring the clans untold wealth and prosperity in the future – if only we are

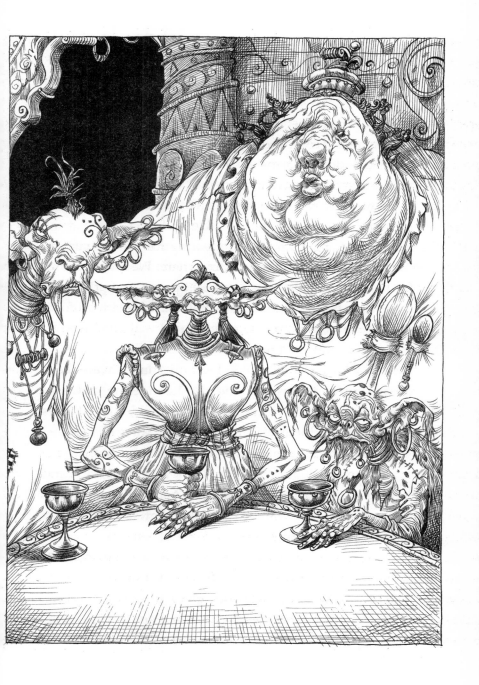

prepared to make a sacrifice now . . .'

As he spoke, a dumpy black-eared goblin matron went round the table, topping up the goblets. Knowing how challenging the meeting would be, Hemtuft had got in extra woodale specially. The five of them present were already on their second barrel.

'What are these plans you speak of?' Meegmewl asked. 'Plans that demand so much of my clan brothers.'

Hemtuft Battleaxe looked grave. 'You must trust me, Meegmewl the Grey,' he said. He looked askance at the black-eared goblin matron retreating from the chamber. 'There are Free Glade spies everywhere! We must be careful. All I can say is that Hemuel Spume is working on something big; something that will take a huge workforce to bring to fruition, but something that will guarantee us victory! He calls it "the glade-eater".'

For a while, no one spoke. The only sounds were those of sipping and slurping, and the hammering down of pewter tankards on the ironwood tabletop. It was Rootrott Underbiter who first broke the silence.

'Glade-eater, eh?' he said. 'I like the sound of that.' He smiled unpleasantly. 'I'll give you old'uns, the sick and the lame, and that's my final offer. As for my finest tuft-eds and black-ears, they're needed for battle. The Furnace Masters aren't getting their sooty hands on *them*!'

A murmur of agreement went round the table. Hemtuft nodded sagely. 'I'll send our third-borns,' he said. 'They never make the finest warriors anyway.'

'No hammerheads, but I can spare some flat-heads,' said Lytugg. 'Strictly for guard-duty, you understand.'

'Good,' smiled Hemtuft. 'How about you, Nectarsweet?'

'I suppose I can spare a colony or two of gnokgoblins,' she replied, the rolls of fat beneath her chins bouncing about as she spoke. 'But I need my gyle goblins, every one of them. They're my babies . . .' Tears sprang to her tiny eyes.

'Yes, yes,' said Hemtuft, turning to Meegmewl. 'You heard the sacrifices the other clans are prepared to make,' he said sternly. 'Now it is the turn of the lop-ear clan.'

Meegmewl sighed. 'I've already sacrificed too many a pink-eye and grey,' he said. He shook his head. 'The mood in the clan villages is turning ugly . . .'

'Pah!' said Lytugg scornfully. 'Is the great clan chief, Meegmewl the Grey, frightened of his own goblins?'

Meegmewl looked down at the table. Hemtuft laid a hand on his shoulder.

'What about your low-bellies, old friend?' he said, smiling. 'They're a good-natured, docile lot – and there's plenty of them. I'm sure Lytugg can lend you some of her flat-heads to round them up.'

Lytugg nodded.

'Ah, yes, the low-bellies,' said Meegmewl quietly. He sighed again. 'I suppose you're right, though I don't like it. I don't like it at all. Good-natured, docile creatures they may be, but even a low-belly can be pushed too far.'

Hemtuft raised his goblet. 'To the glade-eater!' he roared.

*

'Now, friends of the harvest, let us gather round the table and each say our piece.'

'It's not a table!' someone shouted. 'It's a hay-cart!'

'Move over!'

'Who are you pushing?'

Lob and Lummel Grope were attempting to bring a meeting of their own to order. Having attended Hemtuft Battleaxe's great assembly of the clans in the long-hairs' open-sided clan hut, they knew more or less what to do. The trouble was, no one else did.

'Friends,' said Lob, in a loud whisper. 'Please! If we all speak at once, no one will be heard.'

'S'not fair, so it isn't and that's a fact,' said an old low-belly, scratching his swollen stomach through the grubby fabric of his belly-sling.

'S'always us,' another piped up, his straw bonnet jiggling about on his head. 'An' I for one have had enough of it.'

'I've lost a father, two brothers, eight cousins . . .' broke in a third heatedly.

'No one cares a jot about us . . .'

The babble of voices rose, with everyone trying to speak at the same time and no one able to hear anyone else. It was punctuated by occasional knocks on the barn-door, as others arrived to join the meeting. Lummel raised his hand to restore order. The last thing they wanted was to get into a shouting match and attract the attention of a flat-head patrol. But feelings were running high.

Word of Hemuel Spume's latest demands had gone round the Goblin Nations like wildfire, and it wasn't only the lop-ears in the western farmlands who were protesting. Goblins from all over were covertly whispering, one to the other, that enough was enough, and the meeting in the old wicker barn was getting larger and more unwieldy all the time.

'Who goes there?' bellowed a low-belly with a stubbly chin and a pitchfork, menacingly raised as yet another visitor knocked on the door.

'A friend of the harvest,' came the hissed reply. 'Let me in.'

The door was unbolted and pulled back. The new-comer – a young tufted goblin with a jagged-toothed sabre and an ironwood shield – poked his head inside.

'Enter, friend,' the low-belly guard said. 'But leave your weapon outside.'

The tufted goblin did as he was told and went in. A moment later, the guard was admitting a sick-looking tusked goblin, and a trio of garrulous gnokgoblins.

'Friends . . .' Lob shouted, his call lost among the rising cacophony of voices.

'I mean, we've only got half the harvest in,' someone was complaining. 'Are we expected to leave the rest in the fields to rot?'

'It just don't seem to occur to them that we all gotta eat!'

'War, war, war – tha's all they ever seem to talk about.'

'Friends, one and all!' Lummel called out. 'We must band together . . .'

But no one heard him. Of course, it didn't help that each and every one of the gathered goblins was tucking in to the woodapple cider that they had discovered was being stored in the barn. In the end, it was an old tusked goblin who took it upon himself to impose some kind of order on the proceedings. He strode to the front, where Lob and Lummel were now standing on top of the hay cart, and bellowed for quiet, before collapsing and calling for a swig of cider.

Shocked, the gathering of goblins fell silent. All eyes turned to the front.

'Thank you, friends,' said Lob, humbly. He turned to face the expectant crowd. 'We have all lost loved ones to the Foundry Glades,' he began.

'And soon the flat-head guards will come for us,' Lummel continued. 'Low-belly, gnokgoblin, long-hair and tusked, young and old, frail and sick!'

The crowd murmured, heads nodding. 'But what can we do?' called out a gnokgoblin.

'We must work together,' said Lob.

'We must help each other,' said Lummel.

A muttering got up in the crowd as the two brothers' words sank in. They made sense, and the goblins started offering help to one another, suggesting places where those who were on the lists for the Foundry Glades might safely be concealed. As the noise began to rise once more, Lummel raised his hand for quiet.

'We all know what this is about,' said Lob, as the noise abated. 'The clan chiefs want a war against the Free Glades, a war that'll make them rich. That much is clear. But why should *we* fight the Freegladers? Do not all of us have friends and relations who live among them?'

A murmur of assent went round.

'What quarrel have the Goblin Nations with the Free Glades?' Lummel added. 'Why, their mayor is a goblin. A low-belly goblin! Hebb Lub-drub is his name.' He paused, to let the words sink in. 'A low-belly goblin, mayor of New Undertown.' He shook his head. 'Do any of us here want to help destroy such a place?'

For a moment there was silence. Then, tentatively at first, but with growing conviction, voices from all round the old wicker barn answered.

'No . . .'

'No . . .'

'No!'

Lob and Lummel looked at one another and grinned. It was a start. A good start.

iii
New Undertown

As darkness fell, Mother Bluegizzard – fresh from her afternoon nap – flapped round the tavern, a long flaming taper in her claws, lighting the lamps and greeting her faithful old regulars as she went. It was only when she got to the far corner that she realized one of them was missing.

She nodded towards the empty table. 'No Mire Pirate again tonight?' she asked.

Zett shrugged. 'Doesn't look like it,' he said.

'Haven't seen him all week,' added Grome, scratching his great hairy chest with all fingers as he spoke.

Mother Bluegizzard frowned, her neck ruff trembling. 'Most peculiar,' she commented. 'I wonder where he's got to.'

Meggutt, Beggutt and Deg poked their heads up out of their drinking trough, one after the other.

'We ain't seen him, neither,' they said. 'Not hide nor hair.'

The old bird-creature lit the last lantern and blew out the taper. 'I hope he's all right,' she said. 'Place doesn't seem the same without him.'

The others all nodded. None of them had ever heard the old Mire Pirate utter so much as a word, yet his empty table seemed to make the tavern even quieter than usual. Even Fevercule had no idea. They returned to their drinks.

In fact, if any of the regulars had bothered to look,

they'd have discovered that the Mire Pirate wasn't far from the Bloodoak Tavern at all. The dishevelled old sky pirate, with his great bushy beard and haunted eyes, was standing on a small hill screened by lufwood trees, but with a clear view of the North Lake jetty below. He'd been coming to this exact same spot for a week now, standing and staring, as silent as a statue, through the long moonless nights until dawn broke above Lullabee Island. Then, each morning, he'd turn and trudge silently away, only to return the next night.

This night was no exception. The Mire Pirate stood on the secluded hill top and stared over at the island in the lake and waited. He waited as the moon rose, clouds drifted across the sky and the hawkowls hooted. He waited as the

moon sank and another dawn broke. He was just about to turn away and trudge back to New Undertown once more, when a distant splash made him hesitate.

As he watched, a small coracle bobbing on the water made its way from the island to the jetty. He raised a hand to his mouth, as if stifling a cry, and was about to descend the hill when he noticed a small group hurrying towards the North Lake jetty below.

The Mire Pirate checked himself and waited.

'There he is!' shouted a youth in a bleached muglump-skin jacket, and the three banderbears beside him yodelled out across the water.

The *splash-splash* of the paddles increased as the coracle approached the shore. With the help of its crew of turquoise-clad oakelves, a librarian climbed from the little boat and onto the jetty.

'Rook!' Felix exclaimed. 'At last! There you are!'

'Good morning, Felix!' Rook smiled, clasping his friend's hand and shaking it vigorously.

The banderbears yodelled and gesticulated in delight. The oakelves smiled and, without saying a word, pushed off from the jetty and began the journey back to Lullabee Island.

'All week, we've been waiting,' said Felix. 'All week! I was beginning to wonder if you were *ever* going to return! But, my word!' He let go of Rook's hand and stared into his face. 'It seems to have done you the power of good, by the look of you, Rook!'

'A week?' said Rook, shaking his head in disbelief. 'I've been asleep in the caterbird cocoon for a whole week!'

'Caterbird cocoon?' said Felix. It was his turn to look amazed. 'So that was the miracle cure, was it? Why, those clever old oakelves. We were right to trust them after all, weren't we, fellas?'

The banderbears yodelled their agreement.

'Now, we're wanted at Lake Landing, Rook,' said Felix, clapping him on the back. 'Absolute hive of activity it is. But you'll see what I mean when we get there.' He laughed and pulled Rook after him. 'Come, it's a fine morning for a stroll and you can tell us all about the dreams you had in this caterbird nest of yours – a whole week's worth!'

As the small group made off, the old sky pirate emerged from behind the lufwood trees. He watched them for a moment, his pale eyes misted with tears. His lips moved and in a voice deep and gravelly from lack of use, he whispered one word.

'Barkwater.'

·CHAPTER THIRTEEN·

TEA WITH A SPINDLEBUG

Despite the early hour, the Gardens of Light were far from still. Spindlebug gardeners with long rakes and stubby hoes patrolled the walkways between the fungus fields, tending to the pink, glowing toadstools. Milchgrubs, their huge udder-sacs sloshing and slewing with pink liquid, grazed contentedly. Slime-moles snuffled round their pits, trying to find any uneaten scraps from their last feed; while all round the illuminated caverns, crystal spiders and venomous firemoths strove to keep out of one another's way.

Up above, in the Ironwood Glade, there was no moon and the sun had not yet risen. Apart from the occasional snorts and cries of the prowlgrins roosting in the branches of the tall trees, the place was silent. The fromps and quarms were sleeping, and the predatory razorflits had not yet returned from a night of hunting.

Suddenly, breaking the stillness and illuminating a

patch of dark forest floor with light, a column of several dozen gyle goblins appeared. They were fresh from a successful foraging trip collecting moon-mangoes – large, pink-blushed fruits that ripened at night and had to be picked immediately if their succulent flesh was not to turn sour. Walking in single file, the gyle goblins made their way to the centre of the Ironwood Glade where a well-like hole in the ground was situated. They stopped, swung the baskets down and, one after the other, tipped their contents down the hole.

'That's the gardens fed. Now let's fill our milch-pails and take them back to the colony,' one of them commented.

'Honey for breakfast, deeee-licious!' said another, her heavy eyelids fluttering.

Far underground, as the first load of moon-mangoes landed on the giant compost heap below, a gaunt youth glanced over from the raised ledge he was ambling along. The glowing light played on his short cropped hair. A second load tumbled down through the air, followed by a third and a fourth. The youth looked up and focused wistfully on the long tube they were emerging from, high up and inaccessible in the domed ceiling, far above his head. As he watched, half a dozen firemoths fluttered round the bottom of the tube, and disappeared in, heading for the forest outside.

'I wish *I* could leave,' he murmured.

But that was not possible. There was only one way in and out of the Gardens of Light large enough for those who dwelt underground – and that was guarded at all times. He had no choice but to remain under the ground, roaming the paths and ledges, always bathed in the same unchanging pink light. Close to three weeks he had spent down there already, yet he'd only seen a fraction of the sprawling Gardens of Light, with their winding labyrinth of walkways and glowing tunnels, stalagmites and stalactites, fungus beds and drop-ponds.

Crossing a small bridge of opalescent rock, he heard the sound of steady chomping and looked down to see a brace of slime-moles in a steep-sided pit below him, chewing contentedly on fan-shaped fungi. A couple of glassy spindlebugs – heavy trugs swaying from their fore-arms – were passing along the walkways, dropping food down into the pits. One of them paused for a moment.

'That's right. Tuck in, my beauty!' it said, as one of the slime-moles below wobbled over and began devouring the fungus. 'Will you look at that.' The spindlebug

nudged his companion. 'Her slime-ducts are bulging!'

'Just as well,' replied its neighbour. 'The rate those young apprentices get through mole-glue! Filling their varnish pots every few minutes . . .'

'I know, I know,' said the first one, tutting. 'It's not as though we're made of the stuff.'

'No, but *they* are!' said the second one – and the pair of them looked down at the slime-moles as they squirmed about, leaving trails of gleaming, sticky goo in their wake, and trilled with amusement.

The youth walked on. A herd of huge, lumbering milchgrubs being herded down to the great honey-pits for milking crossed his path. Shortly after that, a librarian apprentice – his eyelids puffy with lack of sleep – came hurrying towards him, an empty bucket clutched in his hand.

'Run out of mole-glue, eh?' the youth asked.

'Uh-huh,' came the gruff reply, and the librarian knight scurried past, his head down and eyes averted.

The youth sighed. Everyone knew who he was and why he was there – and no one, it seemed, wanted to be caught talking to him.

He climbed higher, up a bumpy ramp and onto a narrow ledge which hugged the arched wall. There were caves leading off it. Some were empty, some were being used for storage; from one, there came the soft murmur of voices.

Scratching his stubbly head, the youth paused for a moment and looked in. Half a dozen young librarian knights were sitting on low stools, each one bent over a pot balanced on a small burner, stirring vigorously. There was a familiar smell, like singed feathers and burnt treacle. One of them noticed him, looked up, frowned and looked away.

The youth turned, and headed sadly off. No one wanted anything to do with him.

Then, just as he was rounding a jutting rock, he caught sight of an old spindlebug tap-tap-tapping its way along a broad ledge on an upper level. The creature was huge – far bigger than any of those who were tending to the fungus beds or slime-moles. In one of its front arms it carried a tray. In the other, a walking stick to help support its immense weight. Both the size and the yellow tinge to the outer casing indicated that the spindlebug was ancient.

As the two walkways converged, the creature came closer, the glasses and tea-urn on the tray clinking together softly. 'Up so early,' it said as it approached, its voice high and quavery.

The youth shrugged and pulled a face. 'I can't sleep well down here,' he said. 'It's always so light. I never know whether it's day or night . . .' He sighed miserably. 'I miss the sky, the clouds, the wind on my face . . .'

The spindlebug stopped before him, and nodded. 'You're here to prepare for your Reckoning,' it said. 'Use this time to reflect on your life, to contemplate your deeds and . . .' It coughed lightly. 'And your *mis*deeds. The time to leave will come all too soon.'

'Not soon enough for me,' the youth snorted. 'Stuck down here in this prison . . .'

'Prison, Xanth?' the great, transparent creature interrupted. 'You, of all people, speak of prisons!'

Xanth visibly shrank at the spindlebug's words, and when he spoke, his voice had lost its arrogant bravado. 'You're right,' he said quietly. 'And I'm sorry. I know I can't compare this place to the Tower of Night . . .' He shook his head miserably. 'Oh, Tweezel, when I think of the years I spent serving the Guardians of Night; the evil I did, the misery I caused . . .'

Tweezel nodded. 'Come now,' he said gently. 'Let us go and share a spot of tea together, you and I. Just like we used to do. Remember?'

Xanth's looked up into the spindlebug's face and saw his own reflected in the creature's huge eyes. Yes, he remembered the times he'd spent drinking tea and listening to the spindlebug's stories as a librarian knight apprentice. How he'd loved those quiet moments they'd shared, but his memories of them were poisoned by the knowledge that even as he'd smiled and sipped the fragrant brew, he'd been an imposter.

'Are you sure?' he said.

'Certainly I'm sure,' said Tweezel, his antennae trilling. 'Follow me.'

Keeping close to the ancient spindlebug, and ignoring the muttered comments and angry glares from the apprentices they passed, Xanth followed him down the ledge and in through a narrow opening in the wall. Beyond the doorway, the space opened up to reveal a cosy, if rather cramped, chamber, furnished with a squat table and low benches. Tweezel ushered Xanth to sit down and placed the tray down on the table in front of him, knocking his arms and elbows on the walls as he did so.

'My, my,' the ancient creature commented. 'I swear this place gets smaller every day.'

Xanth smiled. Clearly it was Tweezel who had grown rather than the tea-chamber which had shrunk, and Xanth found himself wondering just how old the spindlebug actually was.

Quietly, methodically, the spindlebug placed one of the glasses under the spigot of the ornate wooden tea-urn and turned the tap. Hot, steaming, amber liquid poured out, filling first one, then the other glass. Next, he added crystals of honey with a set of silver tongs, and a sprig of hyleberry blossom. As Xanth watched the familiar ritual, remorse and guilt welled up within him.

Tweezel noticed his tortured expression. 'You are not the first to have felt guilt,' he said. 'And you certainly will not be the last.'

'I know, I know,' said Xanth, fighting back the tears. 'It's just that . . .'

'You wish you could undo the things you have done?' said Tweezel as, with a slight incline of his head, he handed Xanth the glass of tea. 'Change the decisions of the past? Put things right? Lift the heavy weight of guilt that is pressing down on your chest?' He fell still. 'Try your tea, Master Xanth,' he said.

Xanth sipped at the tea, and as the warm, sweet, aromatic liquid slipped down his throat, he began to feel a little better. He set the glass aside.

'Guilt is a terrible thing if you hide from it,' the spindlebug said. 'But if you face it, Xanth, accept it, then perhaps you can start to ease the pain you are in.'

'But how, Tweezel?' said Xanth despairingly. 'How can I face up to the terrible things I've done?'

The spindlebug crouched down on his hind quarters, and sipped at his own tea. He didn't speak for a long time, and when at last he did, his voice was croaky with emotion. 'Once, a long, long time ago,' he said, 'there was a couple – a lovely young couple – who were very close to me. *They* had to do a terrible thing . . .'

Xanth listened closely.

The spindlebug's eyes were half-closed, and he rocked backwards and forwards very slightly as he remembered a distant time. 'It all began in old

Sanctaphrax, when I was a butler in the Palace of Shadows to the Most High Academe himself. Linius Pallitax was his name, and he had a daughter, Maris. Delightful young thing she was,' he said, his eyes staring dreamily into the middle distance. 'Heavy plaits, green eyes, turned-up nose, and the most serious of expressions you ever did see on the face of a young'un . . .'

He paused and sipped at his own tea. 'Hmm, a touch more honey, I think,' he murmured. 'What do you think, Xanth?'

'It's delicious,' said Xanth, and drank a little more.

Tweezel frowned. 'One day, a sky pirate ship arrived,' he said. 'The *Galerider*, it was called, captained by a fine, if somewhat unpredictable, sky pirate by the name of Wind Jackal. I remember coming to inform my master of his imminent arrival, only to discover that he – and his son – were already there.'

'His son?' said Xanth, who was beginning to wonder where exactly the story was going.

'Aye, his son,' said Tweezel. 'Quint was his name. I remember the very first time I clapped eyes on him.' He frowned again and fixed Xanth with a long, steady gaze. 'In some ways, he was not unlike you,' he said. 'The same guilty tics plucking at his face; the same haunted look in his eyes . . .'

Xanth hung on his every word.

'Of course,' Tweezel went on, 'it all came out later. He told me the whole story,' he added, and smiled. 'I've a good ear for listening.'

'So what happened?' said Xanth.

'What happened?' Tweezel repeated. 'Oh, how cruel life can be. It transpired that, apart from his father who had been away at the time, the poor lad had lost all his family in a great and terrible fire. His mother, his five brothers, even his nanny – they had all perished in the flames. Somehow, being the youngest and smallest, he had managed to squeeze through a tight hole and had fled across the rooftops to safety.' He paused. 'He was full of guilt for being the only one to survive.'

'But he'd done nothing wrong!' Xanth blurted out.

'That's exactly what I told him,' said Tweezel. 'But I don't think he was ever able to accept it – which possibly explains what happened later . . .'

'What?' said Xanth.

'I'm coming to that,' said Tweezel calmly. 'Time passed, and Quint and Maris became friends.' He smiled. '*Close* friends. Inseparable, they were. Maris nursed her father when he became ill and Quint took up a place in the Knights' Academy. They were happy times, exciting times! I often think about old Sanctaphrax, and that long cold winter . . .' The spindle-bug's eyes closed completely, and he seemed to have fallen asleep.

'Tweezel?' said Xanth. 'Tweezel? Maris and Quint . . . What happened to them?'

The spindlebug opened his eyes and shook his huge, glassy head. 'Many, many things,' he said. 'They got married, they set sail on a sky ship captained by a brutal rogue by the name of Multinius Gobtrax . . .' He shuddered.

'And?' said Xanth, struggling to contain himself.

'They were shipwrecked,' said Tweezel simply. He took Xanth's glass and topped it up with tea. 'I never quite got to the bottom of exactly what took place out there in the skies above the Deepwoods. Quint wouldn't talk about it, and poor Maris couldn't talk about it. There was a storm, that much I know. And, in the tumultuous wind and rain, Maris gave birth to a son on board the sky ship. Then . . .' The great creature's eyes misted over. 'Oh, my poor mistress,' he said, his voice quavering with emotion. 'Even now I find it hard to think about what happened.'

'What?' said Xanth.

'They had to make a terrible decision,' said Tweezel. 'They were stranded in the middle of the Deepwoods with a new-born baby, and Gobtrax and the rest of the crew refused to take it with them. Quint and Maris both knew the young'un would never survive the journey on foot back to Undertown.'

Xanth's jaw dropped. 'What did they do?' he murmured.

'They found themselves near a woodtroll village. They knew that woodtrolls feared and distrusted sky pirates – but a foundling might just stand a chance,' said Tweezel. 'So they left the young'un there and set off for Undertown.' He shook his head. 'Maris never spoke again.'

'That's terrible,' said Xanth.

Tweezel nodded. 'The guilt, Xanth; it was the guilt that almost killed them both. I came the moment I heard that they'd made it back to Undertown. And a sorry sight they were, too. They were both half-starved and Maris had come down with a fever. Nothing but a bag of bones, she was. I found them in lodgings above a tavern – the Bloodoak Tavern, run by an avaricious old bird-creature by the name of Mother Horsefeather. Quint, by this time, was calling himself by his sky pirate name – Captain Cloud Wolf . . .'

'What did you do?' asked Xanth.

'The only thing I could do,' said Tweezel. He placed his empty glass down gently on the tray. 'I packed up my belongings and left Sanctaphrax at once. After all, since Linius Pallitax my master had died, there was precious little to keep me up there. Besides, I had known the young mistress since *she* was a baby. I nursed her back to health, though it was touch and go for a few weeks, I can tell you.'

'And Cloud Wolf?' said Xanth.

'Cloud Wolf set sail in a sky pirate ship of his own,' Tweezel explained, 'with money lent to him by Mother Horsefeather. He hated leaving Maris, but he'd promised her that if they made it back, he'd return to the Deepwoods to find their child. I think he realized what a terrible thing they'd done. Of course, Mother Horsefeather was only interested in the lucrative cargoes of timber Cloud Wolf would bring back.'

'Did he find the baby?' said Xanth.

Tweezel shook his head. 'No,' he said sadly. 'Voyage after voyage he made, each time returning with a heavily-laden ship – but without the one thing he'd actually set out for. And all the time, I could see the guilt eating away at him. It got so bad that eventually he couldn't bear to see the look in Maris's eyes when he returned empty-handed. At last, he just stayed away from the tavern.' Tweezel sighed heavily.

'When Maris finally recovered from her fever,' he went on, 'she had changed. She, too, was racked with guilt, that much was plain to see in her face. And, like Cloud Wolf, she set out to do something about it. Each night, she would leave the tavern by the backstairs and roam Undertown, looking for young'un waifs and strays with no parents of their own, and bring them home with her.

'The first one, I remember, was a young gnokgoblin whose parents had disappeared in the Mire. Then a pair of slaughterers. Then a young mobgnome lass who had had to run away from her violent uncle . . .

'And yet, despite the good she was undoubtedly doing, Maris was never truly at peace. Her terrible loss weighed too heavily on her heart, and she yearned to go back to the Deepwoods.'

'To search for her lost child?' Xanth asked.

'I thought that, at first,' said Tweezel, 'but I think there was more to it than that. I think she wanted to face up to her guilt, and ease it by trying to put right the terrible thing she'd done. If she couldn't find her own abandoned baby, then she would find and care for those abandoned by others. I think *that's* what she yearned to do.'

'And did she?' said Xanth, feeling the weight of his own guilt tugging at his heart.

'Let me finish my story,' said Tweezel, 'and you can decide for yourself.' The spindlebug took a long, slow breath that set the papery tissues of his lungs fluttering inside his chest. 'It was a cold and stormy night when we all set off – Maris, myself, and our little family of Undertown orphans, on foot . . .'

'On foot!' said Xanth, amazed.

'Certainly,' said Tweezel. 'We were in no hurry. And as we travelled, across the Mire, through the treacherous Twilight Woods – led blindfolded by a shryke-mate, Dekkel, his name – and into the Deepwoods themselves, we picked up waifs and strays every step of the way. Through woodtroll villages, slaughterer encampments and gabtroll clearings we wandered, attracting more and more young'uns wherever we went – orphans with no future, drawn to our growing band, because no one else would have them. And you should have seen Maris!' Tweezel's antennae trilled at the memory. 'She was radiant. Like a mother to them all!

'Of course, it was dangerous,' Tweezel continued, his eyes narrowing. 'The Deepwoods is a treacherous place at the best of times, even for well-armed sky pirates – though I like to think that my own considerable know-ledge of the place helped us survive. There were flesh-eating trees, bloodthirsty carnivores, slavers with wolf-packs and innumerable shryke patrols. Many was the time we had to take to the trees, or hide out in hollows, until the dangers had passed. And that's the way it would have continued if we hadn't found what we were looking for . . .'

'And what *were* you looking for?' asked Xanth, intrigued.

'A home, Xanth,' said Tweezel, a smile playing on his face. 'A home.'

'Where?'

'Can't you guess, Master Xanth?' The spindlebug trilled with pleasure. 'I remember it as if it was only yesterday. We emerged from the dark depths of the forest into the most beautiful place any of us had ever seen.

'There was a wide expanse of grassy slopes, strewn with flowers and fruit bushes, which led down to a crystal clear lake, one of three stretching out in a line. In the centre of one was a small island, the lullabee trees growing upon it filling the air with a soft, turquoise mist. To our left was a tall cliff, studded with caves and rising out of the forest like a vast, curved edifice; to our right, on the other side of the lakes, an ironwood stand, with trees so tall and straight, it seemed as if they were skewering the clear blue sky, high above our heads. The sun was shining. Birdsong filled the air, joined at once by the sound of laughter and singing as the young'uns gambolled down the grassy slopes to the water's edge.

'And when I turned to my mistress, Maris, I could see by the look in her eyes that our long trek was over. We would wander no more.'

Xanth gasped. 'It's the Free Glades, isn't it?' he exclaimed. 'You'd found the Free Glades!'

'Indeed we had,' said Tweezel. 'Indeed we had. That first night, we camped out beneath the stars. No creatures disturbed us; no tribes attacked. It was as if we were surrounded by an invisible mantle that kept us safe from danger.

'The following morning, we began to explore the area. It was, for the main part, uninhabited, but we discovered first that there were oakelves living on the island of lullabee trees, and later that a colony of spindlebugs dwelt in caverns beneath the Ironwood Glades.'

'Spindlebugs!' said Xanth, and chuckled.

'To our eternal good fortune,' said Tweezel, nodding. 'I was able to persuade them to take us in, and we stayed with them until we had constructed the first buildings which were to become New Undertown.' He paused. There were tears in his great eyes. 'And that's how it all began, Xanth. From such simple and humble beginnings . . .'

Xanth could feel a lump forming in his own throat once more.

'Soon others came, and stayed. Everyone who arrived at the Free Glades immediately felt at home. Slaughterers and woodtrolls established villages to the south, while cloddertrogs, inspired to give up their nomadic existence, started living in the eastern caves. Even passing goblins decided to stay, and settlements sprang up all along the eastern banks of the lakes . . .'

'And Maris?' asked Xanth. 'What happened to her?'

The spindlebug cocked his head to one side. 'Ah, Maris,' he said, and smiled. 'She was the mother of the Free Glades and, I think, as she saw the young'uns grow and settle down and have families of their own, she found the peace she had searched so long for. And when, some years later, she died, she was as happy as I had ever seen her – even though she had never again set eyes upon her son . . .'

'So the Free Glades made her well,' said Xanth thoughtfully, speaking as much to himself as to the great spindlebug. He stared down bleakly at the half drunk glass of tea, cold now, before him. 'She found peace,' he murmured.

'For many, the Free Glades have been a place of healing,' Tweezel broke in. 'To those who are lost or abandoned or mired in their own unfortunate pasts, it can be a place of sanctuary and rebirth.' He paused. 'Of course, the first step is to confront the guilt you carry, not hide from it . . .'

Xanth flinched. 'Is that what I've been doing?' he said. 'Hiding from my guilt?' His face paled. 'But if I face it, will I really be able to live with it? Or will it destroy me and . . ?' He fell silent, unable to put the terrible thoughts into words.

Tweezel leaned forwards. 'That,' he said, 'is what we'll find out at your Reckoning.'

CHAPTER FOURTEEN

THE NEW GREAT LIBRARY

As they walked through the lush farmland that stretched before them, Rook glanced back over his shoulder. New Undertown, with its narrow cobbled streets, bustling squares and thronging lakeside, had almost disappeared from view. The mighty Lufwood Tower poked up above the gently undulating hills and the tall, irregular pinnacles of the gyle goblin colonies to the west glimmered in the morning sun – but the roofs of the Hive Huts were lost from view, and Lullabee Island to the east was no more than a distant memory.

At the top of a low hill, criss-crossed by small fields and edged with copperleaf hedges, Rook stopped, threw back his head and let out a great, joyous shout.

'Oh, Felix,' he laughed. 'I can't tell you how good it is to feel the sun on my back and the wind in my face, and to be surrounded by all this.' He spread his arms wide.

Felix laughed in turn. 'You mean sour cabbage and glimmer-onion fields?' he said.

Several low-belly goblins looked up from the field next to them, where they were pulling large red turnips, and doffed their harvest-bonnets in greeting.

'No,' said Rook. 'I mean . . . well, yes, *all* of it. The Free Glades, all around us. Isn't it wonderful!'

'Well, it certainly beats Screetown, I'll give you that,' said Felix. 'Now, if you've quite finished disturbing the peace, let's get a move on, or we'll never get to Lake Landing!'

They set off again down the hill. Ahead of them, the three banderbears – who had out-paced them – were waiting patiently for their two friends to catch up. They seemed distracted, Rook noticed, their small ears quivering and their noses twitching as they cast longing glances at the Deepwoods' treeline far in the distance.

'Wuh-woolah, weeg wullaah!' Rook called as he approached. *Forgive me, friends, my feet are slow, but my heart is light!*

'Wella-goleema. Weg-wuh,' Wumeru replied, turning from looking into the distance and falling into step. *It's good you are recovered.* 'Wug-wurra-wuh. Wuh-leera,' she yodelled softly in his ear. *We will wait for you as long as you need us, friend.*

Ahead of them, to the east, the impenetrable wall of thorn-oaks that surrounded the mysterious Waif Glen stood out, dark blue and black against the bright cloud-flecked sky. They continued past fields of gladewheat and blue barley swaying in the breeze before, once more, coming to a halt. Before them, the lake shimmered in the morning sun, the huge silhouette of the Ironwood Glade on its far shore mirrored in its glassy surface.

'It takes my breath away,' said Rook. 'It always did.'

'It's spectacular,' replied Felix, 'I'll give you that.'

To the east, the woodtroll villages in their clumps of lufwood trees were stirring. A long line of hammelhorn carts, laden with logs, was already snaking out from the timber yards in their midst and making for the near shore of the Great Lake and the tall tower on the large wooden jetty which jutted out into its waters.

'Lake Landing,' breathed Rook as he gazed down at the Librarian Knights' Academy, where he had learned about the secrets of sky-flight so long ago – or so it seemed to him. 'It's hardly changed . . .' he began. 'But what's that?'

Felix followed his friend's gaze and smiled. 'I was wondering when you'd notice,' he said. '*That* is my father's pride and joy. The new Great Library of the Free Glades – or rather, it will be when it's finished.'

Rook stared at the massive construction, wondering how on earth he had failed to see it immediately. It was tall and round and had been built on the end of a wooden pier directly opposite Lake Landing. Although clearly, as Felix had pointed out, there was still work to be done, with scaffolding enclosing its upper reaches, the library was already an impressive building. What was more, it looked familiar.

'But I've seen this somewhere before,' said Rook.

'Not another of your cocoon dreams, Rook,' said Felix, with a smile.

Rook shook his head. He'd told Felix about the strange dreams he'd had on Lullabee Island as they'd walked, but this wasn't one of them.

'No,' he said. 'This building is an exact copy of the Great Library of old Sanctaphrax! I remember seeing drawings of it on barkscrolls . . .'

'Barkscrolls, eh?' said Felix. 'Once a librarian, always a librarian, eh?' He nudged his friend. 'Well, come on if you're coming. My father's waiting to see you.'

As Rook and the banderbears followed Felix down the track leading to the Great Lake, the already massive building grew larger. The main circular wall stood some eighty strides or so tall. Above it, the roof soared up into the air like a vast pleated cone, with flying buttresses and jutting gantries sticking out from it on all sides, their horizontal platforms constructed as landing-decks for the skycraft which buzzed all round.

At first sight, with the noise and the bustle, the whole area looked like one of utter chaos. But as Rook stared, he could see that there was an order to everything taking place, with everyone working together, all under the bellowed commands of the goblin foremen and librarian overseers.

From the south-east, the long line of hammelhorn carts, driven by woodtrolls and laden with felled trees, came trundling down the dirt track from the timber yards to the lakeside, where they deposited their loads in huge piles. Cloddertrogs and flat-head goblins were stripping the branches and bark from them and sawing the logs into broad planks. Gnokgoblin tilers crawled over the great wooden roof, hammering lufwood and leadwood shingles into place in neat lines and intricate patterns. Slaughterers and mobgnomes with cranes were tying ropes round the bundles of prepared timber and winching them up to the top, where joiners and carpenters were constructing the gantries.

'It's amazing,' Rook gasped, as he strode closer. 'There's so many of them, and they're working so quickly.'

'Yes, when these Freegladers set about building some-thing, they don't waste any time,' said Felix, obviously impressed. 'You should see my father, Rook. I've never seen the old barkworm happier! Talking of whom . . .'

They were approaching the huge ironwood doors of the new library, and the din of hammering, sawing and shouted commands up above was almost deafening. The entrance was full of Undertowners, laughing and joking and congratulating one another.

'You made it, Hodluff!' exclaimed a gnokgoblin, clapping a cloddertrog on the back. 'I lost sight of you at the lufwood mount. Are your young'uns safe?'

'Yes, Sky be praised,' said the cloddertrog. 'We've all settled in a beautiful cave, and we've come to hand over our barkscrolls.'

'Me, too!' laughed the gnokgoblin joyfully.

In the midst of the throng stood the portly figure of Fenbrus Lodd himself, the High Librarian, a huge smile on his heavily bearded face.

'Friends, friends!' he was booming. 'Welcome to the new Great Library. Find a librarian and hand over your barkscrolls for cataloguing, and may Earth and Sky bless you all!'

Rook approached him and gave a short, respectful bow. 'Rook Barkwater,

librarian knight,' he said. 'Reporting for duty.'

'Ah, Rook, my boy,' said Fenbrus, his eyes lighting up. 'So it is, so it is – and looking so much better, I'm pleased to see.'

'Oh, I am better, sir,' said Rook. 'Fully recovered.'

'Excellent,' said Fenbrus. 'Then you can begin straight away. As you can see, we have a steady stream of barkscrolls returning to us, all needing to be catalogued . . .'

'But,' began Rook, 'I was hoping to return to sky-flight, with the librarian knights . . .'

Fenbrus frowned. 'But I understood that you lost your skycraft in old Undertown,' he said.

Rook nodded, a lump coming to his throat as he remembered the *Stormhornet* lying smashed in the rubble of Screetown.

'Then you'll have to speak to Oakley Gruffbark the woodmaster about carving a new one. He's busy carving a likeness of yours truly up above the main entrance as we speak . . . In the meantime, you can be of use here in the library.' He beamed happily. 'Isn't it magnificent?'

Rook nodded.

'Speaking of which, Rook,' said Fenbrus Lodd. 'I hope the barkscroll *you* were entrusted with is safe.'

Rook reached inside his shirt, and pulled out the leather pouch into which he'd pushed the roll of parchment. He held it out.

'Excellent,' said Fenbrus, giving it a loving examination. '*Customs and Practices Encountered in Deepwoods Villages*. Perhaps you'd like to start by cataloguing it yourself,' he said. 'It'll give you a chance to appreciate what we've built here.'

Rook nodded a little reluctantly. Library cataloguing was not what he'd had in mind when he left Undertown for the Free Glades – though he was, it was true, intrigued to see the building beyond the entrance he was standing in.

As he entered the cavernous, vaulted chamber of the new Great Library, Rook's heart missed a beat. It was even more impressive from within than without. Tall tree-pillars stood in lines, hundreds in total and each one with a little plaque at its base. Rook looked up into the shadowy roof space, where the tree-pillars divided and sub-divided into branchlike sections, each one housing a different category. This was where the scrolls were stored, high up in the well-ventilated, pest-free upper reaches.

The whole place was a hive of activity. At ground level, and up on raised platforms around the walls, research was already in progress, with bent-backed academics poring over treatises and scrolls and labouring over work of their own. In the central areas, the activity was more frenetic, with innumerable librarians scaling the tree-pillars, winching themselves along the branches in their hanging-baskets and loading up the clusters of leather tubes where the individual barkscrolls were stored.

Taking his cue from the signposts dotted about at the junctions, Rook hurried to the far side of the library where, in the Deepwoods' section, he found a tree-pillar

with a plaque marked *Social Behaviour*. He started climbing, taking the rungs two at a time, right up to where the first fork occurred. Already, he was high above the library floor. He forced himself not to look down.

Historical/Legendary were the words on each of the forks. He took the former. *Past* and *Present* were the next choices. He dithered for a moment, before taking *Present*. Then *Societal* and *Individual*. Then *Nocturnal* and *Diurnal* ... And so it went on, defining and redefining the treatise in his hand increasingly specifically. When the forking branches became too thin and weak to support his weight, he climbed into one of the hanging-baskets and, grabbing a rope, winched himself across.

He was now high in the upper rafters of the huge domed roof and could feel a gentle, modulated breeze on his face. All around him, the barkscrolls in their holders rustled like leaves in a forest. Finally, he arrived at the woodgrape-like bunch of leather tubes.

Most were still empty, though a couple had already been stuffed full with scrolls. Just to make certain he had found the right place, Rook pulled one out and inspected it. '*Practices and Customs in Deepwood Village Life*,' he read. The subject matter was almost identical.

He had done it!

Pushing his own scroll into the adjacent tube, he began the long descent to the ground. To his surprise, he had found the whole process exhilarating, and when he reached the floor, his heart was racing.

'My word, lad, that was quick,' said Fenbrus Lodd as he arrived back. 'I can see you're going to make a first-rate scroll-seeker!'

Rook smiled. 'I suppose so,' he said quietly. 'Until I can fly again.'

'Yes, well, go and find Garulus Lexis,' Fenbrus went on. 'He'll assign you a sleeping-cabin in the upper gantries. They've just been completed. Quite spectacular views and you'll be able to watch your knight friends on sky patrol.' He paused and gazed over Rook's shoulder. 'Are those banderbears with *you*?'

'Yes,' said Rook, looking across at his three shaggy friends standing waiting for him, their ears fluttering as they listened to what was being said. 'They've been with me ever since I became a librarian knight . . .'

'That's as may be,' said Fenbrus sternly. 'But bander-bears are creatures of the forest. They certainly don't belong in a library. Surely you can see that?'

Rook noticed the banderbears' eyes light up. Wumeru stepped towards them, her great clawed arm raised.

'Wulla-weera. Wuh,' she yodelled. *We hear the Deepwoods calling us, yet for you we would stay, friend.*

Rook trembled. 'You brought me here,' he said to Wumeru. 'I am indebted to you – to *all* of you. You've done so much for me. Now, it is plain that I must do something for you . . . Let you leave . . . Oh, Wumeru!' he cried, and fell into the great creature's warm, mossy embrace.

'Loomah-weera, wuh,' the banderbear replied, scratching his back gently with her claws. 'Wurra-moolah-wuh.' *Farewell, my friend. The moon will shine on our friendship for ever.*

'Wuh. Uralowa, wuh-wuh!' the others chorused. *You shall sleep in the nest of our hearts, he who took the poison-stick. Farewell!*

Tears in his eyes, Rook watched as the three great shambling banderbears left the library behind them. Weeg, with the great scar across his shoulder; Wuralo, with her curious facial markings, whom he had once rescued from the Foundry Glades, and Wumeru – dear Wumeru; the banderbear he had first befriended all that time ago in the Deepwoods. How he loved all of them. Now they were going. Rook swallowed away the painful lump in his throat and waved.

'Farewell,' he called. 'Farewell!'

'I think it's time *I* was heading off as well,' came a voice from his left. 'Back to New Undertown.'

Rook spun round to see Felix lurking in the shadows behind the great ironwood doors. Fenbrus had his back to them and was surrounded by a fresh crowd of happy Undertowners.

'What are you doing there?' Rook hissed.

'Didn't want my father to see me,' said Felix. 'He keeps trying to rope me into working in this boring old library of his. Says I need to settle down. Me! Settle down!' He laughed and edged towards the door. 'Say hello to the old barkworm from me, and tell him that his ever-loving son is busy with his ghosts and sky pirate friends in New Undertown.'

'But Felix!' protested Rook. 'Do you have to leave right now?'

'Sorry, Rook.' Felix shrugged his shoulders and grinned. 'Said I'd meet Deadbolt at the Bloodoak. Must dash! Have fun up there in the rafters!' he laughed, and with that he was gone.

Rook turned and wandered back into the library, all of a sudden feeling very alone. His banderbear friends had left, returning to a life in the Deepwoods. Now Felix, too, had gone – back to the bustle of New Undertown. And here he was, Rook Barkwater, on his own.

He looked up. The reading gantries were crowded with librarians; the rafters above, full of baskets swinging backwards and forwards. And as he looked, Rook knew in his heart of hearts that this wasn't the life for him, and never could be. No, he needed to get out there, into the clear, sunlit air of the Free Glades.

Mind made up, he turned and strode through the library doorway. Pausing in front of the lufwood scaffolding outside, Rook peered up and squinted. And sure enough, high above his head was the familiar short, stocky figure of Oakley Gruffbark, the master carver who had taught him everything he knew about carving a skycraft.

Crouched down on a narrow platform laid out across the scaffolding, a chisel and mallet in his hands, the old woodtroll was busy carving a massive likeness of Fenbrus Lodd from a single block of wood. Although only half complete, the head – with its corkscrew hair, thick beard and intense stare – was already unmistakable.

Pausing just for a moment to catch his breath, Rook began scaling the scaffolding that criss-crossed its way up the front of the building. Compared with the roof-beams and swinging baskets, climbing the lufwood scaffolding was easy.

As he emerged on the platform beside Oakley, the woodtroll turned. His bright orange hair, twisted into the traditional tufts Rook remembered so well, was flecked with grey and white now. Otherwise, he looked no different. Neither, it seemed, did Rook, for Oakley recognized him at once.

'Rook Barkwater of the *Stormhornet*!' he cried. 'I never forget an apprentice, or their skycraft. Well, I declare! And how is life treating you, lad?'

'All right,' said Rook, 'although I'm afraid I lost the *Stormhornet* on patrol over old Undertown.'

The woodtroll tutted sympathetically. 'I'm sorry to hear that. It's a terrible loss,' he said softly. 'Like losing a part of your self.'

'Yes,' said Rook, tears welling up in his eyes at the memory.

Oakley laid his tools down, turned his back on Fenbrus Lodd's half-finished beard and clamped his large, leathery hands around Rook's shoulders.

'Now, tell me truthfully,' he said, looking deep into Rook's eyes. 'A loss like that takes time to get over. Do you think you're ready to start carving a new skycraft?'

'Yes, yes,' said Rook. 'I've made up my mind. I want to return to the skies as soon as possible.'

Oakley nodded. 'Well, Rook, you know what you have to do. There are no short cuts. You must go to the timber yards and select for yourself a large piece of sumpwood. Choose carefully and think long and hard before you first put your chisel to the wood, because that's the thing with carving – it can't be rushed. It has to . . .'

'Come from the heart,' Rook finished for him.

'Precisely,' said Oakley. 'You know the score, Rook Barkwater.' He gestured back at the carving of Fenbrus. 'With a bit of luck I should be finished with the High Librarian here in the next week or so. I'll come and look in on you then, and see how you're doing.'

'Thank you,' said Rook. 'I'll start straight away!'

*

Two weeks later, Rook's carving was not going well. Although he had selected the best, finest-grained piece of sumpwood he could find in the woodtroll timber yards, he could still not decide what to carve. Each time he put his chisel to the wood and raised the mallet, his mind was filled with images of the stormhornet. And yet try as he might, he couldn't see the curves and arches of a stormhornet – or any other creature – in this piece of sumpwood. And if he couldn't carve the prow, then he couldn't make a skycraft. And if he couldn't make his own personal skycraft, then he couldn't fly. And if he couldn't fly, then he couldn't rejoin the librarian knights. He was stuck staring at this lump of wood – and there was no sign of Oakley Gruffbark.

Finally, Rook left the workshop in the timber yards and returned to the library to look for him. He found the old woodtroll still hard at work on his carving, high above the ironwood doors of the new Great Library. Not only was the High Librarian's beard finely chiselled and minutely rendered, but now the head and shoulders had outstretched arms and lovingly carved fingers.

'Can't help it, lad,' said Oakley, catching the disappointment in Rook's eyes when he told him he was too busy to help him. 'The wood is our master. It tells us what lies within. And this here wood demanded arms held out in greeting.' He stroking the carving gently. 'And two solid legs as well before I'm finished.'

Rook sighed. He knew that in the meantime, he had no choice. He reported back to the High Librarian, who was most understanding.

'The main thing is to keep busy,' Fenbrus said, patting him on the back. 'You're a fine scroll-seeker, Rook – just made for the roof timbers!'

So Rook had returned to cataloguing and fetching barkscrolls high up in the new library, frustrated and longing more than ever to take to the sky outside.

It was late one cool, sunny evening when, following yet another long day's filing, Rook was walking down the wooden jetty at Lake Landing. Halfway along, he paused, crossed to the side and leaned over the balustrade, looking at the rippled water below him.

It wasn't that he was unhappy at the library. He enjoyed working with the scrolls, reading for long hours on the platforms and mastering the baskets until he could reach even the farthest corners of the high dome. It was just that he missed sky-flight so much. Each evening, as the librarian knights returned from patrol, he'd see them from his sleeping-cabin – Varis and the Professors of Light and Darkness at the heads of their squadrons. And he'd feel his heart breaking as they swooped down through the air. He longed to join them – but the carving simply wouldn't come.

'Hey, Rook!' called a voice from up ahead, breaking into his thoughts. 'Is that you?'

Rook looked over to see the familiar, stout figure of his old friend Stob Lummus silhouetted against the sinking sun. He acknowledged him with a wave, but stayed where he was. It was Stob who came to him, stopping beside him and looking out across the water.

'Haven't seen you for a while, Rook,' he said at length.

'Keeping you pretty busy at the new Great Library, I hear. Nearly all the barkscrolls have been handed back. A wonderful achievement, I must say! You must be very proud.'

Rook nodded. 'I am, Stob. But what I really want is to fly again.'

Stob chuckled. 'Do you remember *my* first attempt at flight?' he said. 'Ended up steering the old *Hammelhorn* straight into an ironwood pine. Just over there, if I remember correctly. I was never really cut out for skyflight.' He paused. 'I enjoy what I do now . . .'

'You're Parsimmon's assistant, aren't you?' said Rook. 'Keeping all those young apprentice knights in order, I hope.'

Stob laughed again. 'Doing my best, Rook,' he replied.

There was another long pause. Rook liked Stob, but he was tired and fed up and didn't feel much like talking.

'Talking of apprentice knights, looks like our old classmate, Xanth, is getting his come-uppance,' said Stob finally. 'I never trusted him. Something deceitful in his eyes . . .'

Rook shrugged. 'I feel sorry for him. All the librarians tell such terrible stories about him, but I only remember him as an apprentice here at Lake Landing . . .'

'It'll all be sorted out at the Reckoning,' said Stob. 'The Free Glades will be better off without his sort.'

They stared out across the lake in silence.

'I was really sorry to hear about Magda,' said Stob, breaking into the stillness again. 'Now she *was* a true friend. I'll miss her.'

'Me, too,' said Rook glumly. 'Looks like it's just you

and me now, Stob – and neither of us flying. Fine librarian knights *we* turned out to be!'

The sun dropped down beneath the horizon, and the pink and orange light spread out across the surface of the lake like shimmering oil. The wind dropped. The water fell still. Out of the silence, Rook heard a low humming sound, and turned to see the red and black striped body of a stormhornet flying low over the lake.

'A stormhornet!' said Stob, breaking the silence. 'Wasn't that . . ?'

'Yes, thanks for reminding me,' said Rook. He turned to his erstwhile friend, seeing him properly for the first time. He had grown paunchy, and deep lines were etched into his face down the sides of his mouth. Yet he looked happy for all that – a contented schoolmaster. 'Oh, Stob,' he groaned. 'How I envy you!'

'*You* envy *me*?' said Stob, surprised.

'Yes,' said Rook. 'You're obviously happy teaching here at Lake Landing – whereas I . . .' He paused.

'You want to fly again,' said Stob. 'Yes, I know, you told me. So what's stopping you?'

Rook brought his fist down on the balustrade in frustration. 'Everything, Stob! Everything! I can't carve another skycraft, it just won't come. And Oakley Gruffbark can't help me. And Fenbrus Lodd – he wants me to stay at the library. I'm stuck there from dawn till dusk . . .'

Just then, echoing across the water, came the insistent sound of trumpeting tilder horns, followed by the clatter and clomp of heavy footfalls. Rook looked up. There, bathed in lantern light and golden twilight glow, he saw

a great troop of prowlgrins galloping along the edge of
the lake. Surcoats flapped and pennants fluttered and
the polished armour of the riders glinted brightly.

'Earth and Sky,' Rook breathed. 'Who are *they*?'

Stob looked at him surprised. 'You really don't get out
much, do you?' he said. 'They're the Freeglade Lancers,
of course. That's the dusk patrol. Make a pretty fine
spectacle in this light, don't you think?'

'The Freeglade Lancers,' Rook repeated, awestruck.
'Heroes of the Battle of Lufwood Mount . . .'

Stob looked at his friend. 'Rook, are you feeling all
right?' he asked, concern plain on his plump features.

'They're magnificent!' said Rook. 'Magnificent!'

·CHAPTER FIFTEEN·

CHINQUIX

Late the following morning, Rook set off. He had swapped his librarian robes for the green leather flight-suit of a librarian knight, a kit-bag strapped to his shoulders and his sword at his side. All round him, as the sun rose higher in the sky, it was business as usual on the banks of the Great Lake. Cloddertrogs and mobgnomes, flat-heads and slaughterers; they were all hard at work, endeavouring to put the finishing touches to the magnificent new library before the current spell of good weather broke.

Rook, however, was leaving it all behind. He'd spoken to Felix the night before, and Fenbrus Lodd earlier that morning. Felix had been his usual self, full of enthusiasm and encouragement.

'Freeglade Lancers, eh, Rook?' he'd laughed. 'Not bad for a bunch of tree hoppers, and they *did* get us out of a tight spot at Lufwood Mount. Good luck to you!' He'd raised his tankard to the rest of the regulars in the New Bloodoak. 'To Rook's new career!'

Fenbrus Lodd's response, of course, had been quite different. The High Librarian had tried to persuade him to stay – though there was nothing he could say to change Rook's mind. There was a jaunty spring now in the young librarian knight's step, a joyful whistled tune on his lips and, as he strode off along the lakeside, his spirits soared.

He passed the lines of woodtrolls on hammelhorn carts, still arriving from the east with their cargoes of felled trees, and departing the same way with rubble and rocks and off-cuts of timber.

Gradually, the sounds of hammering and drilling, carving and sawing, the shouts and the cries, all faded away. Water splashed softly against the muddy banks where reed-ducks and rockswans nested, and sleek young fromp-pups playfully scampered and tumbled.

Reaching a narrow track, Rook left the water's edge and headed up through windgorse and woodfurze towards the Ironwood Glade. Far ahead, he could see its dark, imposing trees swaying gently in the breeze and heard the distant sound of their needle-like leaves hissing like running water.

Soon after, the undulating land went down into a deep dip and, with the thorny shrubs rising up all round him, the glade disappeared from view, the hissing stopped and another sound filled the air – the sound of happily singing voices. Rook continued and, as he rounded a corner in the twisting track, he saw a large band of gyle goblins before him, heavy pails of pink honey swinging from their clenched fists, coming from the opposite direction.

'Morning, Freeglader,' the gyle goblins greeted him warmly as they drew nearer.

'Good morning, Freegladers,' said Rook, returning their greeting with a smile.

The gyle goblins clustered round him and a couple of them politely offered him some of their raw honey to drink.

'We prefer it boiled up in our mother's cooking-pots,' said one. 'Nice 'n' warm.'

'But you might like it as it is,' said another, offering him a beakerful. 'Sweet and refreshing.'

Rook took the beaker and sipped at the pink liquid. It was indeed delicious – and far more refreshing than he would have thought possible. 'Thank you, thank you,' he said, grinning at the gyle goblins each in turn. 'It's marvellous.'

'You're most welcome, friend,' came the reply.

The gyle goblins continued on their way and Rook waved after them. Alone once more, he turned and resumed his journey with renewed energy and, as he climbed the slope on the far side of the dip, his thoughts returned to Fenbrus Lodd and the meeting they'd had early that morning.

'You're absolutely sure this is what you want to do,' the High Librarian had pressed him. The pair of them had been standing in Fenbrus Lodd's study inside the library, the hushed purr of academic activity softly echoing all about them. 'The Freeglade Lancers do an excellent job patrolling our borders, but they're a rough and ready lot, you know.'

Rook had laughed. 'Unlike the librarian knights, you mean?' he said.

'Yes, well, we've got some pretty interesting characters in our ranks as well, I grant you,' Fenbrus had said. 'But that aside, Rook, there's a great future waiting for you here in the Great Library if you would only accept it. You've got the skills to make a superb librarian; the perseverance, the agility and accuracy – why only yesterday, my assistant Garulus Lexis was saying what a terrific start you've already made as a scroll-seeker.' His brow had furrowed as he surveyed the youth warmly. 'The Great Library *needs* bright young academics like you, Rook.'

'I . . . I'm very flattered, sir,' Rook had said, his cheeks reddening, 'really I am. And I love the library, of course,' he'd added, looking out through the study door at the magnificent roof timbers, bedecked with hanging barkscrolls. 'And yet, I . . . I need something else . . . I'm a librarian knight who has lost his skycraft. Perhaps by joining the lancers I can serve not only the librarians but all Freegladers.'

'By Earth and Sky, you sound just like Felix,' Fenbrus had said, his eyes twinkling. 'Can't seem to get him to leave the ghosts and join us in the Great Library. But I had such high hopes of *you*, my lad. Still,' he'd said, shaking his head resignedly, 'I can see I'm not going to change your mind.' And he'd reached out, seized Rook by the hand and pumped it heartily up and down. 'I shall miss you, lad, but I wish you all the very best. The library's loss is the Freeglade Lancers' gain. And remember, there'll always be a welcome for you back here at the library, any time you choose to return. Any time at all!'

'Thank you, sir,' Rook had said and was about to leave, when Fenbrus had told him to wait just a moment longer.

He'd hurried over to his desk, pulled a drawer open and rummaged about noisily inside it, returning a moment later with a roll of parchment, which he'd handed over. Rook had looked at it, curious.

'Open it up, lad,' Fenbrus had said, his eyes gleaming excitedly. 'Given your chosen career, I think you might find it quite helpful.'

'*On the Husbandry of Prowlgrins*,' Rook had read out loud. '*A treatise by . . .*' He'd stopped, then smiled. '*Fenbrus Lodd . . .* So this is . . .'

'My very first treatise, that's right, Rook,' Fenbrus had said. 'Keep it safe and return it to me one day – possibly with additions of your own. After all, you did say you enjoyed treatise work. And if you're not going to be a scroll-seeker, then we'll get you working as a scroll-*writer*, eh?

Go on, then. Get out, before I change my mind and have you assigned to quill-sharpening duty.'

The High Librarian had sounded gruff, but Rook had noticed the moistness in his eyes. Despite his bluster and stern manner, Fenbrus Lodd has a kind heart, Rook thought, as he struggled up the overgrown slope – I wonder why he never lets his own son see it?

Reaching the top of a ridge at last – red-faced and out of breath – he looked up and saw the towering trees of the Ironwood Glade just before him. He stepped forwards and entered the huge stand of trees. It was like entering a gigantic, windowless hall. The temperature dropped and the sounds of the Free Glades outside became muffled.

Stepping gingerly over the glade floor, his feet sinking into the thick mattress of pine needles, Rook looked down. Somewhere far below him lay the Gardens of Light, where Xanth Filatine was being held.

Poor Xanth, he thought. Nobody seemed to have a good word to say about him, and yet . . . No, it was no good. Try as he might, Rook couldn't remember anything about his friend's betrayal so long ago.

From high above his head, as he plunged deeper into the shadow-filled coolness of the glade, he heard sounds – the soft whinnying of countless prowlgrins; the low buzz of voices. And looking up into the tall trees, their huge branches criss-crossing, not unlike the roofbeams of the library, he saw that he was below the Prowlgrin Roosts. Hundreds of the creatures perched overhead – snuffling, nuzzling, resting and preening; some gnawing on bones, some wandering from branch to branch. And amongst them in the half-light, Rook could just make out individuals, with chequered green and white at their necks and red figures emblazoned on their chests.

'The Freeglade Lancers,' Rook murmured.

He started up the nearest ironwood pine, finding handholds and footholds in the rough bark and climbing at an angle, crossing from branch to branch, as he made his way up the close-growing trees. It was just like climbing the roof timbers at the new Great Library, only on an altogether bigger scale. Soon, he was far above the ground and all around him, in place of barkscrolls, were prowlgrins of all ages and sizes.

They ambled this way and that freely, purring contentedly as they grazed on the tilder-carcasses which hung from heavy hooks, and sometimes snorting loudly as, in a sudden display of activity, they launched off from one branch with their powerful back legs and grasped hold of the next with the long claws of their stubby forelegs. Clearly used to the lancers in their midst, none of them paid Rook any attention.

Nor, at first, did the lancers themselves. Those who were not asleep in hammocks, slung from the overhead branches, were busy with their duties. Some sat cross-legged, sharpening their ironwood lances with notched jag-knives. Some polished their breast-plates and limb-guards with tilder grease. Others – in twos and threes – were grooming their prowlgrins, brushing their fur and oiling their great paws.

Most of them, Rook noticed, were gnokgoblins, small,

wiry creatures whose close relationship with the great roosting beasts was similar to that of the gyle goblins and spindlebugs in the Gardens of Light below. But there were a smattering of others – mobgnomes, lop-eared goblins, slaughterers . . . It was, in fact, a slaughterer who first noticed Rook. Looking up from the broken harness he was busy repairing, he caught sight of the young librarian.

'Well, well, if it isn't a librarian knight,' he said. 'And what can we humble lancers do for you?'

Others looked round to see who their comrade was talking to.

'Greetings, Freeglader,' Rook said. 'If you could take me to see your captain . . .'

'Captain, eh?' said one of the gnokgoblins. 'And what would you be wanting with him?'

'Certainly don't get many librarian knights around here,' said his companion. 'I thought you lot preferred being up in the sky.'

''S safer up there, innit?' said the first gnokgoblin, raising his eyebrows and provoking laughter from the others.

Rook's face reddened. 'I . . . I want . . . I wanted . . .' he stammered.

'Spit it out, lad,' said the slaughterer. 'Stone me, I thought you librarian knights were meant to be good with words – what with all them barkscrolls and that . . .'

'Come on, now, you lot, cut it out,' came a gruff voice.

'Captain Welt,' said two of the gnokgoblins as one.

Rook looked round to see a short yet heavily-built

gnokgoblin swinging down on
a rope from a higher branch
and landing squarely beside
him. He had dark eyes, a low
brow and a deep scar that
crossed his cheek, clearly
made by the knife that had
left one of his ears half the
size of the other.

'In't there something useful
you could be getting on with, eh,
Grist, Worp, Trabbis?' he asked,
turning from one gnokgoblin to
the other, 'rather than joshing the
lad here? And as for you,
Ligger,' he added, turning
to the slaughterer, 'I dis-
tinctly remember telling you to
skin those tilders before the prowlgrins got their teeth
into them. We need the pelts!'

'Yes, Captain. Sorry, Captain, sir,' said Ligger, and
hurried off.

The gnokgoblin captain turned to Rook. 'Well, son?'
he said. 'Why *are* you here?'

The gnokgoblins busied themselves, while listening
closely.

'I want to join the Freeglade Lancers,' Rook replied,
trying to ignore the smirks of the gnokgoblins watching
and listening from the surrounding branches.

'Do you now?' said the captain. 'Can you ride?'

'I . . . I have ridden a prowlgrin before, sir,' said Rook. 'I'm sure, with a little practice . . .'

'Practice!' the captain snorted. 'I'm sure with a little practice, *I* could fly a skycraft, but that wouldn't make me a librarian knight. What makes you think you could make it as a Freeglade Lancer?'

'It's just that . . . well . . .' Rook began, his face falling. 'I lost my skycraft – crashed over Screetown – and I can't seem to carve a new one, and I've been stuck in the library in the meantime. And . . . and then I saw you out on patrol the other evening. And I talked to Felix about it, and *he* said . . .'

'Felix?' said Captain Welt, his good ear twitching. 'Felix *Lodd*?'

'Yes, sir,' said Rook.

'Felix Lodd of the Ghosts of Undertown?'

Rook nodded. 'Felix said I could do a lot worse than join the Freeglade Lancers, especially after what you did at the Battle of Lufwood Mount.'

'Did he now?' said the captain, nodding sagely. Behind him, Rook could hear the eavesdropping gnokgoblins murmuring to one another. They were all clearly impressed.

'Well, why didn't you say so before?' said Captain Welt. 'Any friend of Felix Lodd is welcome to join us, and Sky knows we could do with new riders. We lost a lot of good lancers at the lufwood mount.' He shook his head for a moment, then reached forward and slapped Rook on the back. 'String your hammock up over there,' he said. 'Grist and Worp'll sort you out – and report to me tomorrow morning at eight hours. Understood, Lancer?'

'Understood, sir,' said Rook happily.

Rook slept well. The cool night air suited him so much better than the stuffy atmosphere inside a sleeping cabin; it always had. He was woken at sunrise by Ligger the slaughterer, who had prepared a breakfast of smoked rashers of tilder and pine-hen eggs for himself, Rook, and the three gnokgoblins, Grist, Worp and Trabbis. The five of them were soon hunkered down on the broad branch, tucking in.

'So, Worp tells me you're an Undertowner,' Grist was saying, as he chewed the salty fried meat.

'I was brought up in the Great Library in the sewers of old Undertown,' Rook nodded. 'But I was born out here in the Deepwoods, so I'm told.'

'Told?' said Worp. 'Don't you know?'

'Let the lad enjoy his breakfast in peace,' Ligger interrupted, and gave Rook a nudge. 'Don't mind them. Gnokgoblins are nosy – you can tell that just by looking at them!'

The three gnokgoblins laughed so hard, Rook thought they might fall off the branch if they weren't careful.

'It's all right,' he reassured Ligger. 'I don't mind. I'm an orphan. My parents were killed by slavers when I was little, and the librarians took me in and raised me.'

'Undertowner, librarian, gnokgoblin or slaughterer – it's all the same,' said Worp, wiping his mouth on his sleeve. 'We're all Freegladers now.' The others all nodded. 'Though for a moment back there, I didn't think we'd make it,' he said quietly.

'You were at the Battle of Lufwood Mount?' asked Rook, putting down his plate.

'We all were,' said Ligger.

'We lost some good lancers that day,' said Grist, shaking his head grimly.

'Them shrykes had the frenzy upon them,' said Worp and shuddered. 'The hunger . . .'

'If the roost-mother hadn't been killed, we'd have lost a whole load more,' said Trabbis.

'You're not wrong there,' said Worp and the others nodded earnestly.

'I saw it happen,' Ligger said, 'just as Vanquix and me made it through to the Undertowners' lines. Never saw the like of it in all my days. This young lad stepped up – shaved head, big flash-looking sword. Sliced her head off in one blow, he did! Right in front of us. The whole shryke flock just went crazy – turned and started attacking each other.' He shuddered at the memory of it. 'So where were you?' Worp asked Rook. 'Head in the clouds?'

'Well, sort of,' said Rook, smiling. 'But not in the way you mean . . . I'd been struck by a sepia storm, way out in the Edgelands. I was half dead. My banderbear friends took me away from the mount before the actual battle began. They made their own way to the Free Glades, taking it in turns to carry me. I remember very little about it . . .'

'A friend of banderbears, eh?' said Ligger, obviously impressed.

'Fine, noble creatures,' the gnokgoblins were all agreeing, when all at once a tilder horn sounded, the rasping cry echoing round the glade.

'Eight hours already,' said Ligger. 'Time to muster.'

The gnokgoblins hurriedly finished the rest of their breakfast and drained their mugs. Ligger grabbed Rook by the arm.

'Come on,' he said. 'You've got an appointment with Captain Welt.'

The next two weeks were among the most challenging of Rook's life. Despite his training as a librarian knight, nothing could have prepared him for what followed. Instead of the elegant arts of ropecraft, sail-setting and flight practice, Rook learned the bone-crunching techniques of branch-riding and iron-wood jousting.

Gripping on to a slender lower branch with his legs, and dodging the incoming iron-wood pine-cones, he had to remain in position as the branch was bounced up and down by ropes, tugged and jerked by bellowing lancers. Time and again he was unseated, and fell down onto the soft pine needles below, only to climb back onto the branch

and resume the seemingly neverending practice.

And as if that was-
n't bad enough,
every day there were
the endless tilts at the
quintain, with the
heavy ironwood lance
clasped under one arm
while the other was
strapped to his side.
Suspended from a branch in a narrow rope-swing and
pushed, Rook swung to and fro, hitting the target and
being hit in equal measure by the quintain's pivoting
padded arm. At night – despite the others sniggering at
the bookish former librarian in their midst – he read
from Fenbrus Lodd's treatise, soaking up every word
and learning all about the prowlgrins
he had yet to ride.

In the third
week, he was
introduced to
the creatures

at last and instructed how to clean and groom them, how to file their claws and oil their leathery feet. He patted them on the sides of their great heads and tickled them with his fingertips, just the way the treatise had taught him to. He learned about tack; the harnesses, saddles and reins, and the heavy bits that were held between their great, gaping mouths which enabled them to be controlled.

Ligger and the gnokgoblins all had prowlgrins of their own, on whom they lavished great care and attention. They were tame – sleek grey, brown, orange and black creatures who had formed strong bonds with their riders. But there were also others – some young and unbroken; others ownerless since the loss of their Freeglader riders. These, Rook and the other new recruits looked after. It was at the end of that third week that Captain Welt himself came up to Rook at the close of yet another gruelling day.

'I've had my eye on you, Rook Barkwater,' he said. 'You're a quick learner and no mistake. I think the time's come for you to choose a prowlgrin of your own. Ligger,' he said, turning to the slaughterer. 'Take him with you to the central-corral. Tomorrow, he'll ride beside you on patrol.'

'Thank you, sir,' said Rook, breaking into a broad smile. It was the moment he'd been waiting for.

He and Ligger set off at once, cutting through the Ironwood Glade, towards the great central roost, chatting excitedly as they went. As they got closer, the air grew musty and Rook could hear the sounds of whinnying and snorting as the roosting creatures sensed their approach. They were greeted by the roost-marshal, Rembit Tag, a small, muscular gnokgoblin with thick, black hair.

'We've been sent by Captain Welt,' Ligger announced. 'Rook here needs a prowlgrin mount.'

'Does he now,' Rembit said, eyeing Rook up and down, gauging his size and weight. He selected a saddle for him and handed it over. Then, turning, he nodded towards the herd. 'I'd go for one of the large greys,' he said. 'Not too much spirit, but dependable.'

Rook looked. They were a mixed flock. There were the large brown, grey and black prowlgrins, with thick, muscular hind-legs and tiny front paws. Then the slightly smaller, but more skittish, orange prowlgrins – sleek and fast, but harder to handle. Rook stepped forwards, and walked amongst them, patting them, stroking and tickling them. The prowlgrins purred and nuzzled against him. Rembit was impressed.

'They like you,' he said. 'You seem to have a natural way with them.'

Rook nodded. *The prowlgrin has forty-three places receptive to stroking, patting and tickling: the eyebrow, the middle digit of the toe* . . . Fenbrus's treatise intoned in his head.

There was one prowlgrin he'd noticed, perched on a branch some way off from the others. Unlike them, with their yellow eyes and plain coats, this one had eyes of bright, piercing blue and a skewbald pattern of dark brown patches on snow-white fur.

The white, spotted prowlgrin – exceptionally intelligent,

but temperamental. Rewards careful handling, but easily ruined by a heavy hand . . .

'What about that one?' he said.

'Ooh, no,' said the marshal. 'You don't want that one. It was ridden by Graze Flintwick, a flat-head. Cut down in the Battle of Lufwood Mount, he was. Won't let anyone else near it. I only keep it out of respect for old Flintwick . . .'

But Rook was intrigued. There was something about the way the prowlgrin with the beautiful markings skittered about, its gaze flickering anxiously, that caught his eye. Passing through the more docile prowlgrins which nuzzled against him as he went, he approached the skewbald creature slowly. Ligger and the marshal went with him.

'What's his name?' said Rook.

'Chinquix,' Rembit replied. 'But believe me, he can't be ridden. In fact, I'm amazed he's allowed you to get this close.'

Rook nodded and, with his head lowered, but eyes holding the gaze of the nervous beast, moved towards it. 'Chinquix,' he said softly. 'It's all right, lad.'

Approach a nervous prowlgrin from the side, maintaining eye contact at all times, and blowing softly . . .

The prowlgrin reared up and let out a yelp of distress.

'Yes, yes, I know,' Rook whispered. 'Steady now. Steady . . .'

Keep hands at one's side, and head lowered . . .

'I really can't advise this,' Rembit began, but Ligger took his arm and stilled him.

. . . Introduce oneself to the prowlgrin by means of smell . . .

Rook stepped closer to the creature. He licked his fingers and traced them gently round the prowl-grin's flaring nostrils, whispering as he did so.

'Chinquix, Chinquix . . .'

As he did so, the prowl-grin breathed in. It stopped pawing the ground and seemed to listen. Rook smiled softly and, still holding the great creature's nervous gaze, he leaned forwards and blew softly.

The prowlgrin blew back and its bright blue eyes softened. The yelping sound subsided, and in its place, rumbling from deep down inside its throat, came a low, contented purr.

'Good lad, Chinquix,' said Rook, throwing the saddle over its back and tightening the straps under its belly, tickling and stroking it all the while. 'Good, good lad!'

'Well, I never,' said Rembit. 'Most incredible thing I've ever seen. Where on earth did you learn to do that?' he asked.

Rook turned towards the marshal, only to find Chinquix nuzzling against him, greedy for more attention. He patted the barkscroll in his top pocket. 'Just something I read,' he said.

Rembit shook his head. 'If I hadn't seen it with my own eyes . . .'

Behind him, Ligger had mounted his own prowlgrin, an orangey-brown beast by the name of Belvix. He trotted over to Rook.

'Very impressive,' he said. 'Now, let's see how you get on in the upper branches.'

Rook didn't need telling twice. Steadying his prowl-grin, he swung himself into the saddle and gave the reins a small flick. Almost immediately, Chinquix bounded into the air, and Rook found himself racing through the branches, the blood coursing along his veins. Not since *Stormhornet* had he felt such exhilaration.

'I'm alive, Chinquix!' he cried, his voice echoing round the Ironwood Glade. '*I'm alive!*'

·CHAPTER SIXTEEN·

CANCARESSE

Inside the tall, dense ring of spike-briars and milkthorn trees, their curved thorns sharp and forbidding, Waif Glen was bathed in the pale yellow light of early morning. Everything had been made ready.

The winding gravel paths were newly raked, the pools and waterfalls clear, the rockeries tidy, while the ornamental evergreen trees with their small, dark, waxen leaves, had been freshly clipped into intricate, angular shapes. Arbours and alcoves had been prepared for those who would soon sit in and walk around them. At the centre of the garden was a circular lawn of fragrant herbs, recently mown, out of which towered an ancient gladewillow, its mighty branches falling like a golden curtain to the ground.

Cancaresse the Silent, Keeper of the Garden of Thoughts, stood in the shadows beneath the glade-willow, her shimmering robes hanging loosely from her bony shoulders and the tips of her long, spidery fingers pressed together in concentration . . .

They were coming, that much was certain. As her large, papery ears fluttered, she could hear them – all the ones who had been summoned to the Reckoning, plus those others who, for their own reasons, desired to be present.

Even now, her waif attendants were helping the visitors to navigate the seemingly impenetrable wall of thorns that kept the sounds of the outside world at bay. She sensed their amazement as the path through the treacherous thorn trees and briars opened up before them and felt their jolt of unease as they noticed the various waifs – ghostwaifs, greywaifs, flitterwaifs, nightwaifs – staring back at them from out of the shadows. One by one, they began to appear, emerging from the thorny wall of undergrowth and blinking into the light.

Welcome, she said, her soft

voice cutting through the cluttered thoughts in their heads.

Keeping largely to themselves, the visitors moved round the garden, unknowingly seeking out the places where they felt most comfortable. Some contemplated their reflections in the deep, limpid pools, some sat beneath the swaying sallowdrop trees, while others continued walking, lost in contemplation, their footsteps crunching softly in the gravel. And, as more and more individuals joined the slowly growing number, the sounds of their thoughts filled Cancaresse's head.

She trembled, her frail body quivering at the jumble of voices as they hummed and buzzed like woodbees. Already though, as the calming atmosphere of the garden took hold, they were beginning to quieten down; to be stilled and soothed and steered to clear, uncluttered thought.

A faint, inscrutable smile plucked at the corners of her mouth as she slowly parted the gladewillow curtain and cast her gaze round the garden. Normally, there would be a troubled cloddertrog or two soothing their anger by the pools, or a solitary gyle goblin easing his melancholy on the gravel paths. But on days like this – Reckoning Days – it seemed as if all of the Free Glades had turned up, their heads filled with noisy thoughts.

As they moved around, Cancaresse began to listen in to them, one after the other. Some had dark thoughts, full of anger and blame. Some had sympathetic thoughts, full of sadness, whilst the majority had minds buzzing with the inquisitiveness and gossip-fed interest of the casual onlooker. Cancaresse moved swiftly over these and concentrated on only the strongest emotions she could sense coming from the various corners of the garden.

There was a young sunken-eyed librarian knight brooding by the healing-pools. And there, a fussy under-librarian delicately sniffing a sallowdrop blossom to ease his pain. And over on the straight gravel path, the High Academe himself, head down and hands clasped behind his back, while in the wicker arbour there lounged a tense and fidgety ghost, his muglumpskin jacket bright against the dark evergreen bushes behind him. A little way beyond, two Freeglade lancers edged their way round the waterfalls of memory. Their thoughts intrigued her – she would get to them in due course.

A soft, scent-laden breeze wafted across the manicured lawns and neatly clipped bushes. Cancaresse paused. Her ears trembled and twisted round.

'Aah,' she sighed.

Behind her, standing in the deep shadows by the gnarled and knotted trunk of the gladewillow, was the object of all their thoughts: a youth with short cropped hair. He was pale and looked anxious, like a startled lemkin – but then, she thought, who wouldn't at his own Reckoning?

She closed her eyes for a moment and breathed in, her frail body quivering as she did so. It was time to begin.

She stepped through the curtain of gladewillow leaves and made her way across the lawn and onto the gravel paths, stepping so lightly that her feet made no sound.

She wandered unnoticed, mingling with the visitors, seeking out those whose emotions ran deepest . . .

In front of her, kneeling on the marble surround of a pool, was the sunken-eyed librarian knight, his thoughts as deep and dark as the water he was staring into. There was pain and hurt in his thoughts, and a rage so strong, it made her papery ears flutter with its intensity. She approached him, and laid her spidery fingers against his chest.

Show me, she spoke inside his head.

The youth unbuttoned his flight-jacket and hitched up his undershirt. A jagged scar crossed his ribs. Cancaresse reached out and traced a finger along the angry red line, staring deeply all the while into the youth's eyes.

Yes, she said, her voice full of sadness and regret. *Yes, I see. An ambush – in the terrible city of the bird-creatures . . . Your friends, so young, so brave, hacked to pieces, one after the other by the vicious shryke-sisters. The blood, the screams, one, two, three, four – and now it is your turn . . .*

She shuddered, her tiny body quivering as it felt the librarian knight's pain.

A slash of a razor-sharp claw . . . And then you're running, running! Running!

Cancaresse closed her eyes and probed deeper into his memories.

Cowering in the shadows of a walkway; watching, waiting, praying that the shrykes won't find you. The terror. The pain.

The sound of the bird-creatures' triumphant cries . . .
'Betrayed by their own! Betrayed by their own!'

She opened her eyes and stared into the librarian
knight's face, the memory of the shrykes' taunting
screech still fresh and raw.

'Thank you, Xanth!' the shryke's voice cackled. *'Xanth
Filatine!'*

Cancaresse let her thin arms fall limply to her side. She
turned and walked away from the pool and across the
gravelled paths, leaving the youth to his brooding. There
were others whose thoughts she must hear. She crossed
the scented lawn and wandered through the sallowdrop
trees, their branches heavy with yellow and white
blossom, stopping in front of the fussy under-librarian.
She regarded him with large unblinking eyes.

He was slight, but spritely-looking, with half-moon
spectacles which had slipped down over the bridge of
his long, thin nose. His thinning hair had turned to a
shade of grey, yet from the way the bright sun
glinted on it, Cancaresse could see that once it
had been as red as copperwood leaves. Inside
him, the waif sensed a hole, a gap –
something missing that could never
be replaced.

Tell me, she said. *Open your thoughts
to me.*

She leaned forwards, reached up and
placed her hands on either side of his head, and gasped
as his pain washed over her.

Your son. Cancaresse's heart ached. *Your poor, dear son*

. . . Artillus, rosy-cheeked, ginger-haired. Your pride and joy. You told him not to wander off in the sewers; you told him it wasn't safe, but he didn't listen . . . So young, so impetuous . . .

The waif shuddered.

You only found out the true horror later . . . A sky patrol high over old Undertown saw it and reported back . . . Captured by Guardians, dragged into the Tower of Night and . . . and . . .

The pain was almost too much to bear. Cancaresse trembled.

Your son, and another young prisoner, lowered in a cage from the tower, into the ravine below . . . A ravine full of hideous creatures – rock demons . . . They didn't stand a chance. She shook her head. *Sacrificed by the High Guardian of Night and his young deputy – interrogator of all prisoners brought to the Tower of Night . . . Xanth. Xanth Filatine . . .*

Cancaresse moved away, leaving the stricken underlibrarian to the thoughts that time might soften, though never heal.

Ahead of her on the gravel path, she saw an elderly academic dressed in simple, homespun robes, staring into space. His eyes were green and kindly, yet behind them the waif detected years of pain and torment, with every line on his wrinkled face telling its own tragic story. Despite all this, Cancaresse could sense that the Most High Academe, Cowlquape Pentephraxis, was not a bitter man – indeed his thoughts about the youth were kind and warm. And yet, behind them, deeper down . . .

The waif took his hands in her own, and squeezed them lightly. Cowlquape's thoughts echoed inside her head.

So, she said, *you consider him a friend?*

A smile passed over the High Academe's thin lips. Cancaresse smiled in turn.

Yes, a friend. So many, many hours talking together of the Deepwoods . . . Its mysteries and wonders . . . Of your adventures there with the great Captain Twig . . . Oh, how Xanth loved to hear you speak of them!

The waif frowned.

But what is this? In what dark, fetid place do you two friends sit talking?

An involuntary shudder ran down the length of her spine.

A prison! A terrible prison, deep in the bowels of the Tower of Night . . . How you suffered . . . The stench, the filthy rags, the lice and ticks . . . Year after year, on a jutting ledge in the darkness . . . And . . . The key in the lock . . . The heavy door opening . . . Your jailer entering . . .

Xanth. Xanth Filatine!

As the waif pulled away from Cowlquape, he had already immersed himself once more in the colour and grandeur of the Deepwoods – the place which, throughout his long years of incarceration, he had returned to in his thoughts time and time again. There was a smile on his lips and a dreamy look on his face. The Most High Academe was truly happy.

But what of the youth? Cancaresse sighed.

Xanth Filatine had clearly done much to be ashamed

of. He had been a spy, a traitor, a torturer, a jailer . . . He had caused great suffering and pain, strong emotions that flowed through the thoughts in the garden.

The waif paused in her tracks, and looked round. There, to her right, was the youth in the muglumpskin jacket whom she'd noticed earlier. He looked more fidgety than ever now, pacing up and down beside the wicker arbour.

Ah, the bold young Ghost of Screetown, Cancaresse thought. *Let me see now what he has to say.*

She stole up beside him and took him by the hand. The frenetic pacing slowed. The youth turned and looked deep into her eyes, and as he did so, Cancaresse felt a hot rush of anger boiling up in his thoughts.

Your best friend, Rook, betrayed by this Xanth creature! . . . Once a Guardian, always a Guardian . . .

It was so hot and fiery inside the ghost's head that Cancaresse felt almost as though she were passing her fingers over a flame . . .

He lured him off into the Edgeland mists — he was almost killed thanks to him. Then he steals Rook's sword . . . The sword you gave him! Typical of a Guardian, and no more than you'd expect of Xanth Filatine!

Cancaresse dropped the hot-blooded ghost's hand and sighed. It seemed that Xanth Filatine really was no good. All around her she was aware of the thoughts of the Freegladers.

Worthless traitor!

You can see the evil in his eyes.

The Free Glades are better off without his sort!

She brushed them away, as if swatting troublesome woodmidges, and walked on. When she reached the waterfalls of memory, she stopped and gazed at the cascading water. And as she did so, Tweezel's thoughts came back to her.

She had taken tea with the great spindlebug the previous evening, just as she always did before a Reckoning, in order to benefit from his wisdom.

'I have looked into his heart,' the old spindlebug had told her. 'There is a lot of guilt there. Guilt that grows like a great mushroom, but only because it has the soil of goodness to grow upon. Beneath the guilt, I believe Xanth Filatine's heart is good.'

Cancaresse's thoughts were suddenly interrupted by a high-pitched cry of joy, and she turned from the waterfall to see a gnokgoblin young'un come bounding past her, a delighted look on her face. She rushed towards one of the two Freeglade lancers who were standing to one side of the flowing water, and threw herself into his arms.

'Rook! Rook!' she squealed. 'It *is* you!'

'Gilda!' cried the Freeglade lancer. 'Gilda from the misery hole in old Undertown! I can't believe it! You made it to the Free Glades!'

The pair hugged each other delightedly. Cancaresse approached and held out her long-fingered hands.

What joy! What delight! her voice sounded in both their

heads at the same time. *Come, take my hands and share it.*

The Freeglade lancer and the gnokgoblin each took Cancaresse's hand, and the three of them walked together.

Two friends re-united! A joyful reunion . . .

She looked down at the little gnokgoblin, who smiled up at her. *You have suffered, little one . . . First the misery hole . . . And then the long journey to the Free Glades. But you carried something with you . . . A sword . . . A sword that belongs to Rook, the librarian knight who risked his own life to save yours in old Undertown! You kept it safe on your journey, and then . . . Oh, little one! You didn't want to disturb him! You left it outside the banderbear nest in the Deepwoods . . .*

Cancaresse felt Rook's hand tighten around her own. She looked up into his eyes.

Yes, Rook! Her voice was light and joyful in his head. *Xanth didn't steal your sword. He found it! And that's not all . . .* Her eyes narrowed as she gazed at him. *Your thoughts are hidden deep . . . Confused and blasted by the sepia storm . . . But I can bring them back within your grasp . . . Yes . . . There it is . . .*

The Edgelands . . . You, in a sepia storm, being swept across the rocky pavement towards the Edge itself . . . A hand reaching out, grasping yours and pulling you back to safety . . .

Xanth's hand, Rook. Xanth Filatine!

Rook frowned. 'Yes,' he whispered softly. 'I remember.'

And there is more, the waif continued. *At great risk to himself, he picked you up, cradled you in his arms, and carried you back across the Edgelands and through the Deepwoods. He did not rest until he had delivered you safely to the banderbears.*

'Yes, yes,' said Rook. He remembered it all now; every terrible step of the long journey. 'He rescued me,' he murmured. 'Xanth Filatine. He saved my life.'

Cancaresse smiled and let go of his hand. *He has been a faithful friend to you. Now enjoy this happy reunion.*

She smiled as Rook took Gilda's hand, and the two of them strolled across the scented lawn. Behind her, she was aware of another voice – hard, callous, and yet with a tender edge to it. She turned and gazed into the eyes of the second Freeglade lancer, a short, stocky slaughterer with spiky flame-coloured hair.

So you were at Lufwood Mount? she asked.

The slaughterer nodded, and she sensed the pain and loss of brave comrades.

You saw the slaying of the roost-mother ... A shaven-headed youth with a fancy sword ... Bravest thing you ever saw ... Turned the tide of battle ... A hero ... Xanth Filatine!

Cancaresse left the Freeglade lancer gazing at the waterfall and wandered off through the garden once more. The sun had climbed to its highest point in the sky and was beating down warmly, shrinking the shadows in the gardens. The time had come, the waif realized, to hear from Xanth Filatine himself. She crossed the lawn, drew back the gladewillow curtain and beckoned to the youth to join her.

Xanth emerged from the shadows and stumbled out into the brilliant sunshine, his shoulders hunched and his eyes screwed up against the light. As he drew close, Cancaresse sensed his unhappiness and uncertainty, and the power of his conflicting emotions. There was guilt, remorse, hurt and unhappiness. He was alone – shunned and despised.

She placed her hand on his shoulder. He turned, and looked at her with his dark, haunted eyes. And as their gaze met, everything changed. It was as though a dam had been breached, and she was suddenly drenched in a torrent of thoughts that poured out over her.

I served a terrible master for years, loyally carrying out his evil plans. It was wrong, it was wrong; I know it was wrong – but I was so young . . .

But no! This is no excuse. This cannot take away the horror of what I did.

Cancaresse nodded.

I betrayed them. I betrayed so many. My hands are stained with blood that I can never, ever wash away.

Cowlquape gave me hope of escape with his stories of the Deepwoods, and yet the only way to get there was as a spy for the Guardians of Night! How many valiant apprentice librarians must have died because of my treachery! And then I was unmasked and fled, like the coward I was, back to the Tower of Night!

Oh, if only I could have stayed in the Free Glades, where, for the first time in my life, I had encountered enduring friendship – Rook, Magda, Tweezel . . . But it was impossible . . . I let them all down. Each and every one of them. How can I ever undo the wrong I have done?

He paused, a haunted, despairing look in his eyes. Almost at once, the torrent of thoughts, pent up for so long, gushed forth once more.

I tried! Earth and Sky know, I tried, but to what avail? I was a traitor. A spy. A curse on all who came close to me and trusted me. Yet, I did try, you have to believe me . . .

Cancaresse nodded again, slowly.

Back in the tower, I could see more clearly than ever how wicked the High Guardian of Night truly was. I did everything I could to stop the madness.

My heart was full of joy when Cowlquape was rescued from the Tower of Night – and how I wished I could go with him . . . Yet, I knew I could not. I had to stay and do everything I could to lessen the evil my master was doing.

That was my punishment.

I did what I could for those who fell into the Guardians' clutches. I tried so hard to rob the cages of their sacrifices – to find excuses in my interrogations to set them free. Yet Leddix, the executioner, would often whisk them away . . .

Oh, but how the loss of those I couldn't save sickens me to the very bottom of my heart . . .

Cancaresse nodded. She could feel his pain clearly. The youth fell to his knees in the middle of the sunlit lawn and buried his face in his hands. Sobs racked his body and, from all corners of the garden, Freegladers gathered round. The moment of Reckoning had come at last. All eyes fell on the tiny figure of Cancaresse the Silent, Keeper of the Garden of Thoughts.

Friends, her soft voice sounded in a thousand minds. *I have looked deep within many minds, shared deep sorrows and terrible pain . . .*

She looked round at the faces in front of her; at the librarian knight with the terrible scar, the grieving under-librarian and the care-worn High Academe.

I have also felt loyalty, bravery and friendship, the waif continued.

She noticed Rook and the slaughterer nodding, and Felix, the ghost, looking ashamed.

I have weighed the good and the evil Xanth Filatine has done, and though the scales are more finely balanced than at first I thought . . . She looked down at Xanth, sorrow plain in her eyes. *I'm afraid, Xanth, that . . .*

The youth stared back at her, his face a stark white in the brilliant sunshine.

'Stop! Wait!' A voice broke the silence.

A gasp went round the Garden of Thoughts as a newcomer suddenly burst through the crowd of Freegladers.

'But you were shot down!' cried one.

'We thought you were dead!' called another.

Magda Burlix, her flight-suit torn and grimy, limped towards Xanth and the waif. 'Forgive me, but I must speak with you,' she said urgently.

Cancaresse stepped towards the young librarian knight, her great veined ears fluttering. *Tell me what you know,* she said.

The librarian knight knelt before her, and the waif placed her long thin hands on Magda's head.

He rescued you from the Tower of Night, she said, her soft voice resonating in the heads of everyone present. *He risked his life guiding you through the sewers and back to the safety of the librarians even though he knew they hated him and would shun and despise him ... He did this with no thought of reward — only that you might live ...*

Cancaresse looked up.

The moment of Reckoning has come, she said silently, and around the garden, every head nodded.

She turned to Xanth and raised her arms, the palms of her hands turned upwards. Her robes shimmered in the midday sunlight.

'Welcome, Xanth Filatine,' she said. 'Welcome, Freeglader.'

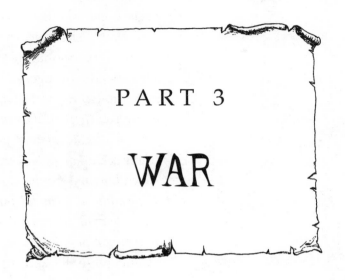

PART 3

WAR

NEW VILLAGES

WESTERN FARMLANDS

LOP-EARED GOBLIN VILLAGES

TUSKED GOBLIN VILLAGES

TREE GOBLIN COLONIES

GREAT LOG ROAD TO FOUNDRY GLADES

WEB-FOOTED GOBLIN COLONIES

THE GREAT LONG HAIRED GOBLIN VILLAGE

FLAT HEAD GOBLIN VILLAGES

HAMMER HEAD HIVE HUTS

EASTERN PASTURES

LONG HAIRED GOBLIN VILLAGES

THE GOBLIN NATIONS

CHAPTER SEVENTEEN

GLADE-EATER

'**A**aagh!' the low-bellied goblin cried out in agony as he fell heavily to the filthy foundry floor. He curled up into a ball, but the blows kept coming.

'Ignorant, clumsy, half-witted oaf!' the flat-head guard bellowed, punctuating each word with lashes from his heavy whip.

'Forgive me! Forgive me!' the low-belly whimpered. The whip cracked louder than ever, tearing into the skin at his back and shoulders, drawing blood. '*Aaaagh!*' he howled. 'Have mercy on this miserable wretch . . .'

The guard, a brawny flat-head with zigzag tattoos across half of his face and over both shoulders, sneered unpleasantly – though he did at last stay his arm.

'Mercy?' he snarled. 'Another accident like that and I'll finish you off for good. I've got quotas to meet, and I'm not gonna meet them with no-good slackers like you. Y'understand me, huh?'

The low-belly remained curled up and motionless, too frightened to speak in case he incurred the goblin's violent wrath once more. It wasn't his fault he'd stumbled. It was blisteringly hot in the metal foundry, and he was parched, and weary, and so weak with lack of food he could barely see. His head was swimming, his legs had turned to rubber. And when the moulds were full of the glowing molten metal, they were *so* unsteady . . .

'*Understand?*' the flat-head guard roared.

'Yes, yes, sir, he understands,' said a second low-belly goblin, scurrying to his brother's side. Taking him by the arm, trying not to touch the raw, open wounds on his back, he helped him to his feet. 'Sir, it won't happen again, sir. I give you my word.'

The flat-head spat with contempt. 'The day I take the word of low-belly scum like you is the day I hang up my hood and whip,' he sneered. 'Get that mess cleared up!' he roared, nodding down at the floor where the spilled molten metal had solidified into a huge, irregular lump. 'And you lot,' he added, cracking his whip at a small group of gnokgoblins over by the ore-belts. 'Give 'em a hand.'

Warily eyeing the guard's whip, with its three tails, each one tipped with a hooked spike, the gnokgoblins approached. Then, together with the low-bellies, they tugged and heaved the huge lump of metal, grunting loudly as they did so, gradually shifting it over the floor through the smoke-filled foundry.

All round them, the place throbbed with ceaseless noise as the enslaved workforce toiled in their individual groups, stripped to their waists, their grimy, sweaty bodies gleaming in the furnace-glow. There were hefters and stokers, smelt-lackeys and mould-navvies – each one of them cowed, half-starved and racked with foundry-croup – working at the feverish pace dictated by the slave-driving guards.

With military precision, logs were turned to heat in the main furnace, ore was turned to iron in the smelting-vats, and the long, heavy moulds – suspended on chains from ceiling-tracks high above – were filled with brightly glowing molten metal and steered towards the cooling-bays. It was raw materials to finished product in less than an hour.

And what a finished product! Huge, curved scythes which, once expertly hammered, honed and polished, were set aside in long racks, waiting to be taken off in hammel-horn-drawn carts to the assembly-yards.

Fighting against the intense, choking heat that was driving them back, the group of hapless goblins struggled on towards the smelting vat.

'One – two – three ... *Heave!*' cried one of the gnokgoblins.

Groaning with effort, they all clasped the huge lump of metal and pushed it up, up, over the lip of the pot-bellied vat, and down into the molten metal within. It landed with a splash, a hiss and a puff of acrid smoke, before rolling over and melting like butter in a fire. The poor low-belly who had spilt the molten metal in the first place slumped to the ground.

'Get up,' the other urged him, glancing anxiously round to see whether the flat-head goblin guard was paying them any attention.

'Can't, Heeb,' came the reply, little more than a grunt.

'But you must,' his brother insisted. 'Before he accuses you of slacking again.' He shook his head grimly. 'I can't lose you, too, Rumpel. Not after the others . . . Rudder, and Reel. You're all I've got left. You *must* get up . . .'

'*Pfweeeep!*'

A shrill steam-whistle blasted loudly, cutting through the thick, noisy air of the foundry and signalling the end of the shift. The rhythmic hammering and teeth-jarring screech of the sharpening-rasps abruptly ceased, as the goblins downed tools and shuffled away, leaving their posts empty for the next shift. Soon, only the roar of the furnace remained.

'Thank Earth and Sky,' Heeb murmured. 'Come, Rumpel,' he said, taking his brother by the arm a second time. 'Let's get out of here.'

Rumpel struggled to his feet and, without a word, let himself be led from the foundry, stumbling clumsily like a hobbled hammelhorn. His head was down, his ears were ringing, his back felt as though it was on fire.

Outside – as the line of exhausted goblins brushed past those arriving for work – the sky was the colour of congealed gruel and a soft, cold drizzle was falling. At first, it soothed the vicious, blood-encrusted weals in the low-belly's flesh. It wasn't long though before what had started as cooling, after the blistering heat of the foundry, became bitterly cold as Rumpel's feverish body was chilled to the marrow.

'C . . . c . . . c . . . can't t . . . t . . . take it no m . . . m . . . more,' he stammered, his teeth chattering and body shaking. And as the caked smoke in his lungs began to loosen, so his frail, bony body was racked once more with the hacking cough that tormented every one of the Foundry Glades slave-workers.

Heeb looked round at his brother. The pair of them were making their way across the glade to the hovel that had become home to them and seventy others. He noted the deathly pallor to his skin, the dark charcoal-grey rings beneath his eyes, and the rheumy, unblinking stare – as if his gaze were already fixed on the world beyond the unceasing cruelty of this one. It was an expression he had seen before – in the faces of his other brothers, Reel and Rudder, shortly before they had died.

'Hang on in there, little brother,' Heeb said softly. 'I'll get those wounds dressed, we'll have something to eat, and you can rest up.' He smiled weakly. 'It's going to be fine, you'll see,' he added, only wishing that his words were as easy to believe as they were to say.

Ahead of them now, bathed in the fine, grey rain, were the slave-huts. Their own – a rundown, ramshackle hovel – was situated slap-bang in the middle of the row. The ground had been churned up, and they had to drag themselves on those last few strides through thick, claggy mud that clung to their tattered boots. There at last, Heeb helped Rumpel up the three wooden steps, lifted the latch and pushed the door open.

A blast of stale, fetid air struck them in the face, a mixture of rotting straw, running sores and unwashed bodies. The two of them stumbled inside.

'Shut that door!' someone bellowed, before his voice gave way to a thick, chesty cough, which was soon joined by several others, until the whole hut was echoing with loud, febrile coughing.

'Shut up! Shut up!' a voice kept shouting from the far end. 'Shut that infernal row!'

Heeb steered his brother down the central aisle of the hut towards the place where they slept – two wooden pallets covered with rank, mildewed straw. Forgetting for a moment the cuts and weals on his back, Rumpel fell down onto the makeshift bed – only to cry out and roll over the next moment.

'Shut up!' the voice came back with renewed vigour. 'I'm trying to sleep here!'

'Shut up yourself,' someone else shouted back and a

heavy clod of earth was lobbed at the complainer. 'If you can't sleep, then you haven't been working hard enough!'

With everyone on different shifts, there were always some trying to sleep while others were coming and going; eating, drinking, muttering to themselves . . . dying.

Heeb knelt down beside his brother, pulled a small pot from his trouser pocket and unscrewed the lid. The sweet, juicy smell of hyleberry salve wafted up – though the pot was almost empty. Licking the grime from his finger as best he could, Heeb scraped out the dregs of the salve from the corners of the pot, top and bottom.

'Lie still,' he said, and proceeded to smear the pale green ointment around the worst of his brother's wounds. Rumpel flinched, and moaned softly when the pain got too much. 'You've got to hold on a little bit longer,' Heeb told him, as he massaged the salve into the skin. 'We're almost done now. It's almost over . . .'

'Al . . . almost o . . . o . . . over,' Rumpel repeated, every syllable a terrible struggle.

'That's right,' said Heeb encouragingly. 'The catapult cages have been completed. *And* the step-wheels and lance-launchers. And the boiler-chimneys. And the long-scythes will soon be ready as well.' He tried to sound cheerful. 'Won't be long now before we're finished . . .'

'F . . . fi . . . finished . . .' grunted Rumpel.

'Glade-eater? Pah!' said Heeb. 'Goblin-crippler, more like!' He shuddered as he replaced the lid on the small pot. 'You stay there, bro',' he said gently. 'I'll get us something to eat.'

He climbed wearily to his feet, grabbed his and Rumpel's mug and bowl, and shuffled off towards the gruel-pot at the end of the slave-hut, which bubbled slowly under the watchful eye of a web-foot trustee. Heeb groaned. The fact that his brother was in a worse state than himself did nothing to lessen his own exhaustion. His cheeks were hollow, his eyes were sunken and his ribs stuck out like bits of kindling. Like his brother and the other low-belly goblins, he had little need for the belly-sling that hung loosely at his front – for just like them and all the others in the slave-hut, he was slowly being worked to death.

The gruel was grey and slimy and smelled of drains, and as it was ladled into his and his brother's bowls, Heeb couldn't help heaving. He filled the mugs with dirty water from the barrel and returned to the sleeping pallet.

'Here we are,' he said, placing everything down and pulling out a spoon from his back pocket. 'Do you want me to feed you?'

Rumpel made no reply. Heeb wasn't even sure he'd heard him. Lying on his side, he was simply staring ahead, his breathing rasping and irregular.

Heeb swallowed anxiously. 'Don't die on me,' he whispered softly. 'Not now. I couldn't bear it.' Tears welled up in his eyes. 'I told you, Rumpel, it's almost over. They've almost finished. Trust me, it's not long to go now. Not long . . .'

*

Lummel Grope dropped his scythe, stood up straight and stretched. 'Earth and Sky, but this is backbreaking work, Lob,' he said, and he reached inside his belly-sling to scratch the great, round, hairy stomach it supported.

'You can say that again,' said Lob. He pulled his straw bonnet from his head and mopped his brow on his sleeve. 'And thirsty work, to boot,' he added.

Lummel picked up the half-empty flagon by his side, pulled the stopper out with his teeth, and took a long swig of woodapple cider. 'Here,' he said, handing it over to his brother.

Lob wiped the top with the palm of his hand and did the same. '*Aaah!*' he sighed. 'That sure hits the spot.'

The two brothers were in the middle of a blue-barley

field. Half of the crop had already been scythed down and gathered up into neat, pointed stooks. The other half was still waiting to be cut and bundled. It was over-ripe, with the heavy ears of barley showing the first signs of spoil-bloom, and no matter how hard the two low-bellied brothers worked, both of them knew it could never be fast enough.

'If only it weren't just the two of us,' Lummel grumbled.

'I know,' said Lob, nodding sadly. 'When I think back to last year . . .' He shook his head miserably. 'I just hope and pray the others are all right.'

Lummel took the flagon back, and tipped another mouthful of cider down his throat.

'Rumpel, Rudder, Heeb, Reel . . .' Lob's eyes welled with tears at the thought of their absent brothers. 'Dragged off to those accursed Foundry Glades like that . . .' He swung his arm round in a broad circle that included the farm-holdings owned by their neighbours, their fields as full of uncut blue-barley as their own. 'The Topes, the Lopes, the Hempels . . . Half of them already gone, and the other half waiting to be rounded up and carted off with the rest . . .'

'And we'll be next, you mark my word,' said Lummel. 'Any time now those flat-heads'll be back. And this time, it'll be to send us off to war.'

'And it won't just be us low-bellies, neither,' said Lob. 'No one's going to be spared this time round. Gonna send us all off to fight, so they are. And then what's to become of the harvest? You tell me that.'

Lummel nodded sagely, and the two brothers stood in

the field, side by side, passing the flagon back and forth as they surveyed the sprawling patchwork landscape of fields, villages and settlements spread out before them.

The Goblin Nations had come such a long way since its beginnings as a single gyle goblin colony, with tribe after tribe from all the major clans settling down as neighbours. Peaceable symbites had arrived first; as well as the gyle goblins, there were tree goblins, web-foots and gnokgoblins, settling round the dew ponds and in the Ironwood Stands. But later, others had joined them – warrior-like goblins who, despite their traditional rootlessness, had become increasingly attracted to this more stable and reliable way of life.

Tusked and tufted goblins, black-ears and long-hairs, pink-eyed and greys – they had constructed nondescript huts at first, often clustered round a totem-pole carved from the last tree left standing when a patch of forest was cleared. Later, some individual tribes had branched out – both geographically and architecturally – building towers and forts, round-houses and long-houses. Even some groups of flat-heads had seen the advantages of settling down and had taken land for themselves where they'd erected their own distinctive wicker hive-huts.

The two brothers stared ahead in silence at the scene. In the middle distance, the jagged Ironwood Stands where tree-goblins dwelt and long-hairs trained were silhouetted against the evening sky. Due south and east, the flat-heads' and hammerheads' wicker hive towers broke the distant horizon where, even now, dark forbidding clouds were gathering.

Further to the north, beside the mist-covered web-foots' dew ponds, the pinnacles of the gyle goblin colonies glinted in the rays of the sinking sun, while far to their right, in the partially cleared forest areas, they could see smoke spiralling up out of the chimneys of the huts in the new villages – some not yet even blooded – where the latest tribes and family groups to arrive had begun to settle.

Lob's face tightened with anger. 'Why can't the clan chiefs just leave us in peace? Why must we go to war? Why, Lummel, why?'

Lummel sighed. 'We're just simple low-bellies,' he said, slowly shaking his head. 'The mighty clan chiefs don't concern themselves with the likes of us, Lob.'

'It's not right,' said Lob hotly once more. He nodded round at the blue fields, the barley swaying in the rising easterlies. 'Who's gonna harvest that lot, eh? No one, that's who. It'll just get left to spoil in the fields.'

'S'already starting to turn,' said Lummel.

''Xactly,' said Lob. 'And what's there gonna be to eat on those long, cold, winter nights then? You tell me that!' He took the flagon back from his brother, drained it and wiped his mouth on the back of his hand. 'One thing's for certain, those high and mighty clan chiefs won't go hungry.'

'You're right, brother,' said Lummel. 'They'll be feasting in their clan-huts while we do the fighting and dying in this war of theirs.'

'Clan chiefs!' said Lob, his voice heavy with contempt. He spat on the ground. 'We'd be better off without them.' He picked up his scythe, turned his attention to the waiting barley and began cutting with renewed vigour. 'What you and I need, brother, are the friends of the harvest . . .'

'Lob,' said Lummel, his voice suddenly hushed and urgent.

'You heard what was said at that meeting,' Lob continued, scything furiously. 'There's a whole load of goblins like us, from every tribe and all walks of life who think just the way we do . . .'

'Lob!'

Lob paused and looked up. 'What?' he said. 'It's true, isn't it? . .'

And then he caught sight of what his brother had already seen – a long line of scrawny web-footed goblins tramping through the fields towards them from the north-east under heavy armed guard. They were dripping wet from head to toe. Clearly, the flat-head guards had interrupted their sacred clam-feeding and dragged them out of the water without even allowing them to return home for a change of clothes. The thin, scaly creatures looked lost and forlorn away from the dew ponds and the giant molluscs they tended that lived in their depths.

Lob gasped. 'By Earth and Sky,' he whispered, his voice trembling, 'if they're picking on harmless symbites now, then no one in the Goblin Nations is safe any more.'

'Oi, you two!' one of the flat-head guards bellowed across the blue-barley field. 'Get over here and join the ranks at once.'

Lob and Lummel looked at one another, their hearts sinking. The moment they had both been dreading had arrived, and much earlier than their worst fears. Where were the friends of the harvest now?

'Look lively!' shouted the flat-head. 'You're in the army now.'

'But . . . but the harvest,' Lob called back. 'We haven't finished bringing it in . . .'

'Forget the harvest!' the flat-head roared, his face blotchy crimson and contorted with rage. 'Let it rot! A richer harvest by far awaits us in the Free Glades, and all *you* have to do to reap it is to follow in the tracks of a glade-eater!'

Flambusia Flodfox was down on her knees, her large head lowered and her great rear raised. She was feeling more sorry for herself than she had ever done before in her life. She'd lost weight on her meagre, tasteless diet of black bread and barley gruel, her chest was bad, her joints were swollen, her hands had been chafed red raw and her corns were playing up. To crown it all, she hadn't seen Amberfuce for days.

To her right stood a metal pail, filled with cold water

and overflowing with soapy suds. Time and again, as she shuffled forwards on her inflamed knees, she plunged a big, bristly brush into the water and scrubbed vigorously at the muddy marks on the white marble floor, muttering under her breath as she did so.

'Oh, if only they'd let me see him,' she complained, her voice weak and peevish. 'Why, if Amby knew just how they were treating me . . .'

Just then she heard a noise. She paused, and pushed a greasy hank of hair back, revealing the puffy, red-rimmed eyes behind. From behind her, the heavy clomping of boots came closer.

Muddy boots, most like, she thought miserably. And then I'll have to scrub the whole floor all over again.

Not that Flambusia was about to complain out loud. She'd tried that once – and still had the angry welts across the backs of her legs to prove it. That Foundry Master was a tyrant all right. The footsteps approached and passed her by without stopping.

Casting a sideways glance round, she saw that there were two of them. Hemuel Spume was one, his longcoat hissing as it glided over the floor, the purifiers on his angular hat wreathing his head in aromatic smoke. He ignored her completely. Beside him

was his esteemed

visitor, in whose honour she, Flambusia, had been ordered to scrub the marble floor spotless. Hemtuft Battleaxe, he was called, a savage-looking long-haired goblin with a long feathered cloak that swept back behind him as he and Hemuel hurried up the stairs beyond – leaving, just as she'd feared, a trail of muddy footprints behind them. A moment later, she heard an upper door slam.

Bang!

Flambusia looked up, an expression of utter misery in her rheumy eyes. 'Oh Amberfuce, my love,' she moaned pitifully. 'What are they doing to you up there?'

Upstairs in the treatment room adjoining his bed-chamber, Amberfuce the Waif, once High Chancellor to the Most High Academe of old Sanctaphrax, was still not absolutely convinced he hadn't died and gone to the great Eternal Glen. The last thing on his mind was his former nurse. In fact he wasn't thinking of anything except his own pleasure. Even when Hemuel Spume knocked on the door and entered, with Hemtuft Battleaxe close on his heels, it was as much as he could do to open his eyes and raise a thin, spidery hand in greeting.

The soak-vat – or 'cooking-pot', as his attendant gabtrolls called it behind his back – was, to Amberfuce's mind, the most wonderful contraption ever invented. It was round and squat, fashioned from burnished copper and filled with warm liquid. Amberfuce sat inside it on a small stool, only his head protruding from the top.

There was a series of pipes attached to the outer shell of the vat, delivering hot water, silken balms and salves and purified air – which bubbled through the fragrant, oily liquid inside – from the bottom, and removing the cooled overflow from the top. And as if that were not enough, the team of gabtrolls – their tongues slurping constantly over their eyeballs in the steamy room – were fussing about Amberfuce's head, stroking his ears and temples, massaging his cranium and rubbing sweet-smelling unguents into his skin.

Hemuel approached him, the stocky goblin following close on his heels. Amberfuce's eyelids fluttered as he struggled to concentrate on the visitors to his room.

Leave us a while, he told the gabtrolls, speaking directly inside their heads.

The gabtrolls did as they were told, putting down their sponges and loofahs and vials of aromatic oils, and withdrew. Hemuel Spume stepped closer.

'You're looking so much better, dear friend,' he said, a smile tugging the corners of his tight mouth as he looked round the steamy room, scented candles with misty haloes burning on every surface. He pulled off his steel-rimmed glasses and wiped the steam from the inside of the glass. 'I trust the gabtrolls are taking extra-special care of you, as I ordered.'

'They're wonderful, wonderful,' Amberfuce gushed. 'I haven't felt so good in years.'

'You've earned it,' said Hemuel. 'Those blueprints were invaluable.' He raised his arm, and gestured to his companion. 'I've just been showing our esteemed visitor here how well our work is progressing,' he explained.

'Indeed,' said Hemtuft, nodding gravely. 'Most impressive . . .'

I see, said Amberfuce, his soft voice hissing inside the long-haired goblin's head.

Hemtuft winced. He despised waifs at the best of times, with their soft, weak bodies and insidious thoughts. And this one – pampered and sibilant – was a particularly unpleasant specimen. Then again, as Hemuel Spume had explained, he'd stolen the plans from Vox Verlix which had made everything possible, and the goblin general made a note to himself to keep his contempt and disgust reined in.

'My army is assembled,' he told them both. 'The Goblin Nations are ready to march!'

To march? The waif's voice sounded contemptuous. *Don't you mean to follow, General?*

For a second time, Hemtuft winced. He would never get used to the way the frail-looking creatures would invade thoughts, and he resented the waif's tone – but he tried to mask his anger as he turned to Hemuel.

'The axes of the long-hairs are sharpened,' he said, 'the swords and scythes of the hammerheads and flat-heads whetted. The lances of the lop-ears are oiled, the quivers of the pink-eyes are full and the clubs of the tusked and underbiters all freshly studded. We are ready!'

Hemuel Spume smiled, a twinkle in his eye. 'As are my glade-eaters,' he rasped.

·CHAPTER EIGHTEEN·

SUNSET IN THE FREE GLADES

'Good luck, Blad,' said Felix, raising his tankard to the ruddy-faced slaughterer in the muglumpskin jacket who was seated beside him. 'Here's to your new life in the Silver Pastures!'

'The Silver Pastures!' echoed the other ghosts clustered round the huge, circular table in the Bloodoak Tavern.

'Though why you'd want to spend your days chasing after herds of hammelhorns beats me ... Stupid great creatures!' laughed a mobgnome named Skillet, nudging his wiry gnokgoblin companion. 'Skut and I are off to the southern fringes to trap fromps.'

'That's not all you'll trap if you're not careful,' said Brove, a lugtroll, darkly. 'That's hammerhead country, so they say. The forests up there are crawling with them.' He shook his head and tapped his bone breast-plate. 'Once I take this off, it's the quiet life for me. Got a nice little cave in the northern cliffs picked out, I have, a small plot to grow tripweed, and a hammelhorn cart to take it to market . . .'

'Well, now I've heard everything!' Felix burst out, clapping the lugtroll on the back. 'Brove Gloamcheek, the toughest troll in all of Screetown, scourge of the Guardians of Night, is about to become a gardener!'

The whole table exploded with laughter and the ghosts raised their tankards once more.

'To fromp trapping!'

'To tripweed!'

'To Brove the gardener!'

The locals sitting round the tavern turned and looked at them with a mixture of curiosity and amusement. Meggutt, Beggutt and Deg toasted the rowdy group before plunging their heads back into their drinking trough. Zett Blackeye smiled a gap-toothed smile and his hefty cloddertrog sidekick, Grome, raised his drinking-pail in salute. Only the old sky pirate in the corner ignored the ghosts and sat instead staring into his goblet of sapwine with pale, unblinking eyes.

Draining his tankard in one huge gulp, Brove turned to Felix. 'So what about you?' he said. 'Once we're disbanded, there'll be no one to listen to your muglump-hunting stories . . .'

'Or to lead raids on the Tower of Night . . .' chipped in Blad.

'. . . Or to swim 'cross the Edgewater in the middle of the night,' added Skillet.

'In full bone-armour!' Skut reminded him.

'Happy days,' said Brove, and put his tankard down on the table.

An awkward silence fell over the ghosts as they each remembered their former home; the rubble-strewn, demon-haunted desolation of Screetown, so different from the peaceful tranquillity of the Free Glades. None of them liked to admit it but, despite the dangers and hardships they'd had to endure, they were going to miss their former lives as ghosts – and none more so than their young leader, Felix Lodd.

Felix peered into the depths of his tankard thought-fully before breaking the silence. And when he did, his voice was raw with emotion. 'My father wants me to join him in the new Great Library.' He shrugged. 'He says it's my duty to the librarians – and to him . . .'

'Felix Lodd, a librarian,' said Skillett, his face cracking into a broad grin. 'Who'd have thought it?'

The others laughed – though a little uncomfortably. They could sense their leader's inner turmoil and unhappiness.

Felix shrugged again. 'Still, if it'll make the old bark-worm happy . . .'

Suddenly, the heavy ironwood door burst open with a loud *crash* that made the roof timbers of the New Bloodoak Tavern shake, and in strode Deadbolt Vulpoon, followed by a stream of sky pirates.

'Well, lads, look what old Deadbolt's found, skulking in the woods of the western fringes,' he said, nodding over his shoulder.

The two sky pirates behind him wrestled with a

hulking figure in an iron collar attached to a chain. The acrid smell of rotting meat and dank vegetation was unmistakable. The figure stopped struggling and straightened up, ear and chin rings glinting in the lamplight. Two bloodshot eyes surveyed the ghosts from beneath heavily tattooed brow-ridges. An upper lip curled in disdain, to reveal two rows of sharp, pointed teeth.

Felix rose to his feet. 'A hammerhead,' he said with awe.

Though the sky pirates on either side of the goblin were big, strapping individuals, beside the hammerhead they looked decidedly small. Luckily for them all, the goblin's wrists were tied securely behind his back and his legs were hobbled by a short length of stout chain.

'A *warrior* hammerhead,'

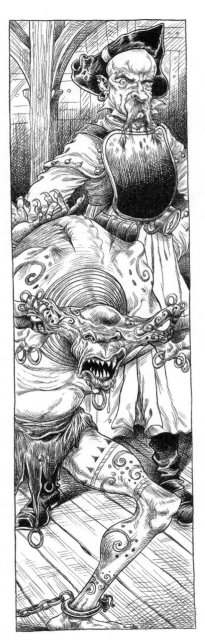

said Deadbolt proudly, ignoring the murderous look the goblin gave him. 'Fresh from the Goblin Nations. Armed to the teeth and looking for trouble. We were fromp trapping when we surprised his war band.'

'What did I tell you?' said Brove to Skillet. 'Dangerous thing, fromp trapping.'

Skillet swallowed uneasily.

'War band?' said Felix with surprise.

'That's what it looked like to me,' said Deadbolt. 'They weren't carrying their birthing-bundles or their weaving-rods, just weapons – and plenty of them! They were looking for trouble all right.'

The goblin sneered and fell to his haunches, his eyes darting round the tavern.

'His mates turned and disappeared into the woods as soon as they saw us.'

'*They ran away?*' Felix could hardly believe it.

The goblin spat on the floor and leered up at him. 'Run now, fight soon,' he said in a low, guttural voice.

'When?' said Felix, dropping to his knees and staring into the goblin's face. '*When* will the hammerheads fight?'

'Soon,' said the hammerhead, his smile revealing his jagged white teeth once more. 'Hammerheads fight *soon*.'

'That's as much as we could get out of him,' said Deadbolt with a wave of his arm. 'He must have been at the woodgrog, because when his mates fled, they left him curled up under a sapwood tree, snoring his head off. Speaking of which, where's Mother Bluegizzard? I'm parched!'

'Woodgrog!' said the hammerhead, licking his lips. 'Teg-Teg want woodgrog!'

'I think he's had enough!' said Mother Bluegizzard, flapping over with a heavily-laden tray, her mate, Bikkle, hiding behind her skirts. 'Now, if you wouldn't mind, please remove your visitor, Captain Vulpoon. He's upsetting my regulars!'

'Take Teg-Teg here to the Hive Huts,' said Deadbolt. 'And see about getting him a bath,' he added. 'He smells worse than a halitoad!'

As the sky pirates bundled the great hammerhead out of the tavern and the door slammed shut behind them, everyone in the Bloodoak let out a sigh of relief. Meggutt, Beggutt and Deg resumed their drinking, thirsty after all the excitement. Zett and Grome exchanged glances, while in the corner the lone sky pirate looked back down at the table before him.

'Earth and Sky, wouldn't fancy meeting someone like him on a dark night,' said Skillett, draining his tankard and catching Mother Bluegizzard's eye for a top-up.

'Me neither,' added Blad.

'Maybe not,' said Deadbolt Vulpoon, as he and the remaining sky pirates joined the ghosts at the table, 'but I have the horrible feeling we're going to. You heard him. "Fight soon", he said, and I for one believe him.'

Felix's eyebrows drew together darkly. 'You reckon the hammerheads you disturbed were snooping then?' he said.

'No doubt about it,' said Deadbolt darkly. 'And they didn't want to be seen either. Scouting out our defences, if you ask me.'

Felix frowned. 'How many did you say there were?'

'At least two hundred,' said Deadbolt grimly. 'And we found evidence of many more. Camp fires, clearings and old hive-huts, freshly used' – he wrinkled his nose – 'by the smell of them. I reckon we've got half the Goblin Nations out there, just waiting for the chance to attack.'

Felix leaped to his feet, his eyes blazing. 'Well, what are we waiting for?' he said, the excitement plain in his voice. 'We must warn the Freeglade Council at once and prepare for war!'

'Good luck with that!' said Deadbolt with a snort. 'You know what these Freegladers are like. So long as there's crops in the fields and timber in the yards, they're happy. Even the librarians are more concerned with that library of theirs than anything else.'

'Then it's up to us!' said Felix with a triumphant smile.

He looked round the table, his gaze fixing momentarily on each of his ghosts. 'You're going to have to put those plans of yours on hold, lads,' he said. 'Blad, the Silver Pastures will have to wait. Skut and Skillet, it's goblin fighting not fromp trapping for you. And Brove, forget the gardening and hang onto your bone-armour. You're going to need it!'

'Aye, Felix,' he said.

'And as for me,' he said, his eyes blazing brightly. 'It looks as if the librarians will just have to get along without me for the time being.' He raised the tankard which Mother Bluegizzard had just refilled. 'Forget the Ghosts of Screetown,' he said. 'Here's to the Ghosts of New Undertown!'

*

All clear to the west, the young skycraft pilot signalled, before swooping down low and fast, skimming over the long, pale green grass of the Silver Pastures and soaring back, high into the air.

Steady, Xanth! his companion signalled back, adjusting her sail with a deft flick of her tolley-rope and rising up beside him.

'Still trying to impress the tilderherders, I see!' Magda shouted across to Xanth with a smile.

'Just enjoying the *Ratbird* again!' Xanth shouted back, patting the carved prow of his skycraft. 'It handles even better than I remember,' he added, laughing out loud as, with a skilful twitch of the loft and nether-sail ropes, the spidersilk sails billowed and the little craft soared up high above his flight partner.

'We're not here to enjoy ourselves! We're on patrol!' Magda called after him, stroking the carved prow of the *Woodmoth*. It was true, it was exhilarating to be back in the air. After the shryke fireball had torn through her spidersilk sail and sent her spiralling out of control to slam into the forest floor, she had feared *Woodmoth* would never fly again. But she'd picked herself up and, pulling the stricken skycraft behind her, had trudged for days through the Deepwoods. It had taken weeks to recover from that terrible journey, not to mention to repair the *Woodmoth*. And now, here they were once more, soaring through the clear Free Glades air.

High above, Xanth tugged on the hanging-weights and swooped back down through the sky, panicking a herd of tilder grazing below him, and sending them galloping off across the grasslands. In the distance, several slaughterers on skycraft waved in salute and gave their characteristic whooping calls. There was nothing a seasoned tilderherder appreciated more than skilful flying. Xanth waved back and swooped round in a slow arc to rejoin his companion.

Come on, Magda signalled, trying not to smile. *Let's head back. We need to make our report.*

Xanth nodded and followed her as she set a full sail. Below them, the vast grasslands of the Silver Pastures shimmered in the morning light and great herds of bellowing hammelhorns grazed beside skittish runs of leaping tilder.

Beyond the Silver Pastures, the rolling green canopy of the Deepwoods stretched out seemingly for ever. Far, far away were the tiny specks that marked the beginning of the Goblin Nations, and on the distant horizon the inky smudge of the Foundry Glades glowered like a bad dream. Here in the bright sunshine, all was peace and tranquillity. Xanth caught Magda up and signalled across to her.

Race you back to Lake Landing!

Magda made no reply, but from the way the *Woodmoth* abruptly darted off through the air in the direction of the Free Glades, it was clear that she had not only seen his challenge but had also taken him up on it. Like two snowbirds in a windstorm, the skycraft streaked across the sky.

Past the look-out tower they went, leaving the Silver Pastures behind them; over the spiky tree-tops of the forest ridges and down towards the Free Glades. Far below them, the great northern cliffs dotted with cloddertrog caves came into view. A moment later, New Undertown appeared, with the three lakes spread out before them, their still, deep waters reflecting the midday sky like burnished mirrors. And as they flew on, they were joined by other librarian skycraft as patrols flew in from every direction towards Lake Landing.

The Great Lake came closer and Magda eased off, letting the loft-sail go slack. *It's OK!* she signalled. *You win! If Varis sees us racing, we'll be for it!*

Xanth brought the *Ratbird* round and gently steered it

in. The pair of them landed amongst many others on the
thronging platforms of Lake Landing.

'Timid lemkin,' whispered Xanth in Magda's ear as
they secured their skycraft.

'Show off!' she responded and stuck out her tongue.

The dozens of skycraft, tethered to jutting mooring-
bars, bobbed around in the warm breeze that was getting
up, while the gantries and flying-walkways were filled
both with those librarian knights who had just landed
and those who were about to take off. Magda and Xanth
headed off along the jetty to where a cluster of young
librarian knights had assembled and were deep in loud,
animated conversation with each other. As they joined
them, so too did Varis Lodd, striding up from the
direction of the refectory tower, her green flight-suit
gleaming in the bright sunlight.

'Librarian knights!' she said, her voice sharp-edged
and commanding. 'Stop gabbling like a bunch of
woodgeese and make your reports!'

The librarian knights snapped to attention, eyes facing
forwards and divided into twos. All raised their hands
and signalled their reports with crisp precision.

Movements to the south. Suspected flat-head party.

Varis nodded, her eyes narrowing.

Forest fires near the Foundry Glades. Spreading this way.

Varis nodded again, her face stony and expressionless.

*Fired upon over the southern fringes. Grey goblins' barbed
arrowheads. No casualties.*

Varis moved along the line, nodding curtly as each
librarian pair reported in turn. There had been goblin

sightings, recently deserted clearings and glowing camp fires all round the borders of the Free Glades.

'And you two?' Varis's voice, stern and strident, cut through the silence.

Magda and Xanth, who'd been nudging each other and trying to make one another giggle, looked up guiltily. Magda raised her left hand and signalled the wide arc of the Silver Pastures, while Xanth circled his thumb and forefinger and bowed his head.

'All quiet in the Silver Pastures, eh?' Varis gave a thin smile. 'At last, some good news. Though with all that fancy flying and racing, I'm not surprised you two didn't notice anything. Thank goodness for the slaughterer herders. At least *their* reports are reliable!'

Magda and Xanth both reddened as all eyes turned to them.

'Librarian knights, dismissed!' Varis barked, and the ranks broke up and headed for the refectory tower.

'Xanth!' Varis's hand was on the librarian knight's shoulder. As she drew him to one side her voice became low and confidential. 'Talking of herders' reports,' she said, 'a certain slaughterer tells me that your flying this morning was the finest he'd ever seen.'

Xanth's face reddened once again, but this time he was smiling.

'If things are as bad as I suspect, your flying skills will soon come in useful.'

'They will?' said Xanth.

'Yes,' said Varis, smiling in turn. 'As my flight marshal.'

*

'Steady, boy,' Rook whispered as he felt Chinquix quiver beneath him.

The branch the prowlgrin was perched on seemed impossibly slender, but Rook had learned to trust his mount's judgement completely. In all their exhilarating treetop gallops through the Deepwoods, the powerful skewbald prowlgrin had never put a foot wrong. And in contrast to its bigger brown and orange cousins, Chinquix was fast and quick-witted. Rook had only to touch the reins or squeeze his legs with the slightest pressure for the prowlgrin to respond instantly.

But there was more to their bond than simply *mount* and *rider*. Whenever Rook appeared in the roost, Chinquix's blue eyes would light up and his thin, whiplash tail would thrash the air excitedly. Then Rook would tickle Chinquix just above his nostrils and the prowlgrin would close his eyes and let out a low rumbling growl of contentment.

'What is it, boy?' whispered Rook, leaning forward in the saddle. Chinquix's nostrils were quivering as he sniffed the air. 'What can you smell?'

Rook scanned the horizon. To his right, the undulating ocean of leaves continued into the distance; before him, a similar view was interrupted in several places by iron-wood stands, the stately pines reaching up high above the rest – while to his left . . .

He gasped. His jaw dropped and his eyes widened, unable to believe what they could see.

'What in Sky's name?' Rook murmured.

For two long days, the troop of Freeglade Lancers had been out on patrol. They'd started off far to the north-west of the Free Glades, and had gradually made their way eastwards, skirting round the outer fringes and making occasional forays deeper into the forest. Up until now, they'd discovered nothing untoward. In fact, if anything, the forest had seemed quieter than usual, and on that first night spent in his swaying hammock, Rook had slept better than he had done for years.

The following morning, however, the deep sonorous calls of giant fromps from distant ironwood stands had woken them, and the troop had set off to investigate the cause of the disturbance. As they rode, leaping through the upper branches, their lance pennants fluttering, they had passed Deepwood creatures fleeing through the forest below.

Now, Rook could see why. Beneath him, Chinquix gave a low growl of alarm. Other riders joined Rook, high up above the leafy canopy: the gnokgoblins Grist, Worp and Trabbis, Ligger the slaughterer, and Captain Welt himself.

'Earth and Sky!' the captain exclaimed. 'What is *that*?'

Rook shook his head. Countless trees had been felled, leaving a bald swathe of scorched earth through the forest. Beyond it was a second track, even broader than the first, and thick with chips of wood – all that remained of the magnificent lufwoods, leadwoods and lullabees that had until so very recently been standing there.

'The trees have been decimated,' cried Grist, pulling

on the reins and steadying his prowlgrin.

'Razed to the ground,' added Worp.

'Flattened and incinerated,' gasped Ligger.

'And scythed,' added Ligger. 'Look at these saplings. They've been sliced right through.'

Grist turned to Captain Welt. 'Goblins?' he asked.

But the captain shook his head. 'No goblin work party I've ever seen could clear the forest like this,' he said. 'It takes weeks to fell an ironwood stand, yet look . . .'

The lancers looked where Welt was pointing. The stumps of the mighty pines stuck up from the devastated forest floor like the gap-toothed smile of a gabtroll. All round them lay the charred remains of twenty or so huge fromps, still clutching branches in their great curved claws.

'And we heard the fromps calling just this morning,' the captain said grimly.

'So, who or what did this?' asked Ligger, his red face anxious and drawn.

'It beats me,' said Welt.

'Well, whatever it was,' said Rook, pointing down the tracks to smoke on the horizon, 'it's heading straight for the Free Glades!'

As evening fell over New Undertown and the sky turned from gold to deepest copper, the lamps of the Lufwood Tower were lit, one by one, until the whole magnificent building was ablaze with flickering light. High in the tower, on the open platform just below the roof, the Council of Eight had gathered. Garlands of

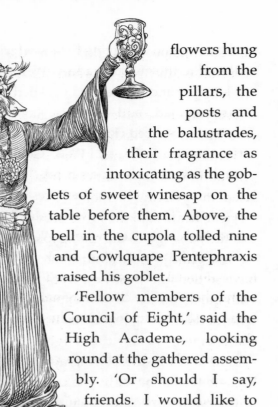

flowers hung from the pillars, the posts and the balustrades, their fragrance as intoxicating as the goblets of sweet winesap on the table before them. Above, the bell in the cupola tolled nine and Cowlquape Pentephraxis raised his goblet.

'Fellow members of the Council of Eight,' said the High Academe, looking round at the gathered assembly. 'Or should I say, friends. I would like to propose a toast.'

Parsimmon, the Master of Lake Landing, and Fenbrus Lodd, the High Librarian, exchanged knowing glances. The Professors of Light and Darkness picked up their goblets with a smile, while stony-faced Varis Lodd took hers in both hands. Hebb Lub-drub, Mayor of New Undertown, looked embarrassed and clicked his fingers for his empty goblet to be refilled, while Cancaresse, Keeper of the Gardens of Thought, fluttered her huge ears as she raised her tiny thimble of winesap.

'Hebb informs me that the harvest has been gathered

in,' Cowlquape proceeded, 'that the grain-stores, the beet-houses, the fruit-lofts and milch-barns are all full to bursting . . .'

Everyone raised their goblets to the low-belly goblin, who smiled delightedly.

'While Parsimmon, here, reports the largest graduation of apprentices from the Lake Landing Academy in living memory!'

'Hear, hear!' said the Professors of Light and Darkness together, bowing to the gnokgoblin master.

'And Cancaresse reassures me that the Undertowners have settled into their new lives here in the Free Glades with great success.' Cowlquape smiled at the tiny waif, who nodded in agreement. 'But perhaps our greatest achievement here,' the High Academe continued, spilling a drop of his winesap as he raised his goblet high above his head, 'is the completion of the magnificent new library under the guiding hand of Fenbrus Lodd. To the Great Library!'

'To the Great Library!' chorused the Council of Eight as one, and drained their goblets.

But wait . . . Cancaresse's soft voice sounded in everyone's head. *One of our number does not share our happiness* . . . The waif turned to Varis Lodd, her ears fluttering like paper. 'You are troubled?' she asked quietly.

Varis nodded. 'There are disturbing reports coming in from the forest fringes all round the Free Glades,' she said, putting her goblet down on the table.

'Reports?' said Cowlquape with concern. 'From whom?'

'From my librarian knights, from the sky pirates *and* from the ghosts . . .'

'*Pah!*' interrupted Fenbrus Lodd. 'The ghosts, indeed. That's just that son of mine out looking for trouble . . .'

'No, father.' Varis's voice was stern. 'I believe there's more to it than that. I believe that the Free Glades are in great danger . . .'

Just then, there came a clattering sound followed by a loud whinny, and a powerful skewbald prowlgrin appeared on a buttress below and launched itself up onto the platform balustrade, scattering the garlands of glade-lily and pasture-violets. A Freeglade lancer slipped from the saddle and thudded to the floor, where he knelt in front of the Most High Academe, his head bowed and his breath short and panting.

'Rook!' said Cowlquape. 'Rook Barkwater, is that you?'

'I . . . I bring . . . urgent news . . .' Rook gasped, gulping in lungfuls of air, 'from Captain Welt . . . of the Lancers . . . He sent me on ahead . . . Chinquix was the fastest . . .'

'Yes, yes,' said Varis. 'What news, Rook?'

'The Free Glades . . .

are in . . . great . . . danger,' he panted.

'Danger?' said Cowlquape, 'from what?'

'From that!' said Rook, leaping to his feet and gesturing towards the distant horizon.

Cowlquape and the council crossed to the balustrade and peered out at the reddish glow in the distance.

'From the sunset?' said Cowlquape. 'I don't understand . . .'

'Sunset!' Rook interrupted, his voice breaking with emotion. 'Believe me, Most High Academe, sir, that is no sunset!'

·CHAPTER NINETEEN·

INFERNO

'Rook Barkwater reporting back!' the young lancer cried out as he tugged at the reins of his powerful skewbald prowlgrin.

Captain Welt acknowledged him with a nod of the head and a barely perceptible smile. Behind him, the massed ranks of the Freeglade Lancers – five thousand strong in all – stretched out across the meadowlands of the southern fringe. They wore green and white chequerboard collars, white tunics emblazoned with the red banderbear badges and, with their long, glittering ironwood lances raised, resembled nothing so much as a gigantic bristle-hog basking in the evening light.

'Captain,' Rook began, and patted Chinquix, who was panting and snorting, his great pink tongue lolling out of the corner of his mouth as he sucked in huge gulps of air. 'The Council of Eight send their compliments to the Freeglade Lancers and their illustrious leader . . .'

'Yes, yes, Rook, lad,' interrupted Captain Welt. 'You and Chinquix here have made excellent time getting back from the Lufwood Tower. Don't waste it now with empty greetings. What exactly did the council *say*?'

Rook took a deep breath. 'The librarian knights are taking to the air,' he told him, 'and the ghosts and sky pirates are organizing the defences of New Undertown, but . . .'

'But?' said Welt, his low brow creased and his dark eyes boring into Rook's.

'But they need time to evacuate the villages of the woodtrolls and slaughterers to the cloddertrog caves in the northern cliffs . . .'

'Then we shall buy them that time!' said Welt, glancing round, 'if necessary, with the blood of the Freeglade Lancers!'

Behind him, the lancers roared their approval and thrust their ironwood lances high in the air. Rook smiled.

'You've done well, Rook, lad,' said Welt, wheeling Orlnix, his orange prowlgrin, round on the spot. 'Now find your troop and fall in. We've got a long and bloody night ahead of us!'

He spurred his mount and trotted out along the edge of the meadowlands in front of the lancers. All eyes turned to the treeline in the distance. Above the jagged silhouettes of the copper-elms and gladebirch trees, the sky was an angry crimson, as columns of smoke rose up from the depths of the forest all along the southern fringes of the Free Glades.

Rook found Ligger the slaughterer, and Worp, Trabbis and Grist the gnokgoblins, sitting grim-faced astride their prowlgrins in the centre of the line. There was no time for greetings. An ominous rumble, like rolling thunder or the growl in the throat of a monstrous beast, was rising up from the forest in front of them, growing louder and louder as the light faded.

'By Sky,' Ligger murmured, his lance trembling in his hand. 'What *is* that?'

Beside him, Grist shook his head. Worp and Trabbis exchanged troubled glances. The next moment a loud splintering crash rang out across the meadowlands as a dozen or so towering copper-elms on the fringes of the glade abruptly toppled to the ground. An instant later, from a couple of places further to the right, more trees creaked and splintered and crashed to the forest floor.

The line of trees in front of the massed ranks of lancers now looked suddenly ragged. The ominous rumbling became a deafening roar as, out of the gaps in the treeline, in a flash of flame and screech of metal, came first one, then two, then four huge metallic monsters, heaving themselves out into the meadowlands.

The first was like a giant bat-tering-ram, with a long, curved metal spike pro-truding from its front. The next had long whiplash chains that spun round and round,

encircling   everything
before it and tearing
it from the ground,
while the third had
sweeping   scythes
that slashed through
the air – now high,
now at ground-level – cutting down everything that stood
in its way. Each infernal machine was propelled by a
mighty lufwood-burning furnace, and as the energy of
the buoyant wood was converted into power by screeching chain-belts and pulleys, so thick, black, spark-filled
smoke billowed from the furnace chimney above.

Rook looked at the terrible machines, one after the
other, his stomach sinking. From beside him, he could
hear Ligger whisper the same three words over and over.

Sky protect us. Sky protect us. Sky protect us . . .

With a deafening crash, two more of the
hulking glade-eaters burst
through the tree-
line, one hurling
massive rocks from
a three-armed cata-
pult; the other firing
blazing logs.

'Stand firm,
F r e e g l a d e
Lancers!' Captain
Welt commanded.

The rows of lancers did as they were told, holding their skittish prowlgrins steady while struggling hard to stop their lances from shaking as the blazing logs and massive rocks landed in their midst. As the machines crashed forwards, they scorched a path across the meadowlands every bit as pulverized as the tracks through the Deepwoods. And trailing behind – shields up, weapons at the ready and keeping to the smoking tracks – marched phalanx after phalanx of the goblin army; hammerheads, flat-heads, huge tusked goblins and small greys, lop-eared, long-haired and tufted, all tramping in the twake of the glade-eaters.

Rook wrapped the reins around one hand and gripped his lance tightly. He bent down and whispered to Chinquix. 'Easy now, lad.' His voice quavered. 'Wait for the command.'

Just then, Captain Welt's bellowed cry pierced the air. 'CHARGE!!'

The full moon's reflection in the glassy surface of the Great Lake barely rippled as, with the faint sigh of wind on spidersilk, nine hundred skycraft rose into the air from the great wooden platform of Lake Landing. Silent as moonmoths, their sails billowing, the craft climbed high above the black silhouette of the Academy Tower and hovered for a moment. Then, as silently as they had risen, the swarm of skycraft separated into three and streaked off across the sky – one to the east, one to the west and one to the south.

Xanth Filatine set his nether-sail and swooped down

in a wide arc round the three hundred skycraft of Varis
Lodd's squadron. He signalled as he went.

Keep in formation, Grey Flight . . . Close up on the right,
Green Flight . . . Steady, Centre Flight, follow the flight-
leader's course!

The flights – each a hundred skycraft strong – fell into
graceful arrowhead formations and followed Varis Lodd
as she set a course for the southern fringes. Xanth
checked his hanging-weights and swooped down to join
the leader of the Grey Flight, who looked up with a smile.

Looking good, Flight Marshal! Magda signalled.

So are you, Grey Leader, Xanth signalled back. *Just keep*
close when we get to the meadowlands.

Magda nodded, and Xanth peeled away to circle the
squadron again. As he marshalled the stragglers back
into formation, the moon appeared from behind the
swiftly moving banks of cloud and shone down brightly,
glinting on the carved and varnished heads of the
individual skycraft. To the north, Xanth could see the
Professor of Light's squadron, now just distant specks,
flying low over the farmlands towards New Undertown.
To the east, the Professor of Darkness's squadron skirted
over the tall, tree-covered bluffs beyond the woodtroll
villages.

Xanth checked his equipment for the hundredth time
as the squadron flew high above the waif glen and the
glistening lakes, and over the spiky treetops of the ironwood pines. His crossbow was in the holster strapped to
his leg. It was oiled and loaded. The bolts hung from his
flight-harness, sixty in each quiver, thorn-tipped and

razor-sharp. His stove glowed from the saddle hook to his right, and the pinesap darts were strapped to his back along with a gladebirch catapult and a sack of rock-hard ironwood pellets for good measure.

That should do for the time being, he thought, but just in case . . . He slipped his hand inside his tunic and felt the handle of a sharp straight dagger. He had no intention of being taken alive.

It was quiet up so high in the air, away from the hubbub of Lake Landing. Only the single thrummed note of the wind whistling through the taut string of his crossbow broke the silence – now loud, now soft – as the wind rose and fell.

Some way beyond the Ironwood Glade, at Varis Lodd's signal, the entire squadron bore round and headed west. Below them now, Xanth spotted the fringes of the Free Glades picked out in the moonlight as farmland gave way to meadowland. He saw at once that all was not well. The forest had been sliced through in broad swathes, the great glowing scars extending out across the meadowlands like slime-mole trails. Along these tracks, at least twenty in number, the torches of the innumerable goblin hordes pouring into the Free Glades glittered like marsh gems.

But that was not all.

As Varis signalled for the squadron to hover and Xanth dropped down in the air to gather in the strays, he could see, at the head of each glowing trail, a huge furnace, its fiery mouth belching heat and sparks, its chimney spewing forth thick smoke.

Squadron! Varis signalled. *Prepare for attack in flight formation, on my command . . .*

Xanth tensed in his saddle as he steered the *Ratbird* round and joined the hovering Grey Flight, already busy setting their sails with feverish intensity. *Good luck, Magda!* he signalled across to the *Woodmoth*.

Good luck, Xanth! See you on the other side! Magda gestured back with a sweep of her arm.

Just then, far below, came the sound of a tilder horn sounding a charge, and a great spiky formation of Freeglade Lancers hurtled over the meadowlands towards the glowing furnaces. Varis sped across the sky in front of the squadron, her clenched fist held straight ahead in the unmistakable signal.

ATTACK!!

Up ahead of them, Lob could see the tall chimney of the glade-eater spewing out the acrid, black smoke that caught in their throats and made their eyes stream. The

furnace glowed purple-blue as the goblin crew fed it with
huge lufwood logs under the steady crack of a flat-head
overseer's whip. Beside him, Lummel stumbled and
almost lost his long-handled scythe as he tried to regain
his balance on the churned up, splinter-strewn ground.

'Careful, brother.' Lob held out his hand to help him.
'That's a good scythe, that is. You don't want to go throwing it away!'

From the rear, a flat-head goblin let out a throaty roar.
'Close up in the ranks, you symbite pond-slime!' And the
air rang out with the sound of a bullwhip cracking and
anguished whimpers of pain.

The web-footed goblins behind them – some three
thousand strong – were suffering cruelly at the hands of
their flat-head captains. Most were armed only with nets
and fishing-spears, and were being horribly tormented
by the burning sparks that blew back from the huge
glade-eater they were forced to follow. They tried to fall
back, to protect themselves, but the flat-heads were
having none of it.

'Keep up close to the glade-
eater!' they roared,
cracking their whips.
'You can bathe your
scabby scales at

the lakeside in New Undertown by sunrise!'

As Lob and Lummel stumbled forwards, the wind changed and blew the furnace smoke out of their faces, and for almost the first time since their hellish march had begun, they could see clearly. Ahead of them, New Undertown gleamed in the moonlight. There were tall buildings with crystal windows and spiky turrets, broad avenues lined with lights, stretches of water, fountains and statues, gardens and parks, the like of which none of the low-belly or symbite goblins dragooned into marching on the place had ever seen or even dreamed of before.

'Hive-huts, look,' whispered Lob.

'And webfoot wicker-huts,' Lummel whispered back.

'And look at that dome there. I ain't never seen nothing so tall and grand and beautiful . . .'

'. . . And deserted,' Lummel interrupted.

Lob looked round and frowned. It was true. Despite the smells of woodale and perfume still lingering in the air; despite the lamplight, the open windows, the chatter of pet lemkins and distant lowing of hammelhorns, there was no sign of any New Undertowners. The taverns were empty. The streets were deserted. It was as though the whole place had been abandoned.

'Where's everyone gone?' whispered Lob.

Lummel shrugged. 'I don't know,' he whispered back. 'Perhaps they heard we were coming and ran away?'

Ahead of them the glade-eater gave a screeching roar as the Furnace Master thrust full power onto the drive-chains, and the monstrous machine trundled forwards onto the cobbles of New Undertown.

'To the Lufwood Tower!' roared the flat-heads on either side of Lob and Lummel. 'New Undertown is ours!'

They surged forwards, waving their bullwhips in the air, forgetting the low-bellies and web-feet in their eagerness to follow the glade-eater. Suddenly, as Lob and Lummel looked on open-mouthed, the cobblestones beneath the huge machine gave way and the glade-eater disappeared into the ground with an almighty *crash*!

For a moment there was a stunned silence as everyone stood rooted to the spot, a cloud of dust billowing over them and turning them white as it settled. The flat-head goblins in front looked like statues, Lob thought; big, ugly, startled statues. He started to laugh.

Suddenly something whistled past his nose with the sound of an angry woodwasp. It was followed by another, and another. At first Lob thought they had disturbed a nest or a hive, until he saw the statues crumple in front of him, crossbow bolts embedded in their chests like red badges.

He looked up and, with a lurch of his stomach that threatened to burst his belly-sling, he saw that the rooftops of New Undertown had sprouted white-clad figures in muglumpskin armour, swinging ropes and bristling with crossbows. Suddenly he became aware of Lummel bellowing in his ear.

'Lob! Lob! Snap out of it and run!'

Without another thought, he dropped his long-handled scythe, turned on his heels and ran as fast as his legs could carry him back to the comparative safety of the treeline. Behind them came a deafening explosion as the furnace of the glade-eater exploded. Burning lufwood logs shot up from the sunken pit and blazed a trail across the sky.

Catching up with Lummel, Lob slumped to his knees on the forest floor. 'What now?' he wheezed, panting for breath.

His brother shrugged as he looked round. 'Maybe we can go home,' he said.

'Not so fast,' came a low growl and the low-bellies looked up to see a phalanx of hammerhead goblins glaring down at them from the forest shadows. Their captain stepped forward, his brow rings jingling, his lips set in a contemptuous curl. 'The battle,' he snarled, 'is only just beginning.'

At the sound of the tilder horn, Chinquix leaped forwards – his muscular rear-quarters propelling him up half a dozen strides into the air and down again. All round, flashes of orange and brown bounding across the meadowlands told Rook that his friends were following. In front, the huge shape of a glade-eater raced up to meet them, its forward platform bristling with spears.

With another huge bound, Chinquix leaped past the rumbling machine as the air filled with the hum of serrated spears. Rook stood high in the saddle and gripped his ironwood lance tightly as they came down in the midst of the following goblins. A jolt ran down from his elbow to his shoulder as the lance struck

something solid – and then Chinquix was back in the air with another huge leap.

Rook looked down and noticed that the lance was dark with blood. Behind him, there were gaping holes in the ranks of the goblins – but with the scattered corpses of prowlgrins, too. He twitched on Chinquix's reins and the powerful creature bounded forward as another glade-eater reared up in front of them. Rook gripped his lance with all his might and felt Chinquix's powerful legs tense once more as they prepared to spring.

The glade-eater roared, the air black with smoke, as Rook and Chinquix sailed up to meet it. He felt his lance buckle as it struck the metal side of the furnace, then shatter. Chinquix's reins snapped out of his grasp and the stirrups were ripped from his feet as Rook felt his prowl-grin fall away beneath him. With a deafening *clang*, Rook hit the burning hot metal of the furnace and rebounded from it with a soft hiss, before falling back to land in the soft meadowland grass with a bone-jarring thud.

Struggling for breath, he leaped to his feet and drew his sword. The glade-eater trundled past belching flames and sparks, and Rook found himself confronted by a war band of powerful long-haired goblins in ornate tooled armour, wielding huge double-bladed axes.

With a savage roar, a massive black-haired goblin, his beard glinting with rings and his blue eyes flashing, swung a copper-coloured axe at Rook's head. Although his helmet crest deflected the blow, Rook was knocked back down to the ground. The goblin towered above him, hate blazing in his eyes.

'Death to the Freeglader scum!' he screamed, raising his axe. '*Unnnkhh!*'

The blue eyes glazed over suddenly as an ironwood pellet embedded itself in the goblin's forehead with an audible skull-splitting crack.

Rook tore off his shattered helmet as, overhead, skycraft flashed past, their riders raining down a deadly shower of bolts, flaming darts and ironwood pellets.

The long-hairs scattered, swinging their mighty axes above their heads with howls of rage.

Rook climbed to his feet. The Freeglade Lancers' charge had cut a swathe through the goblin army, but at a terrible cost. All around, desperately wounded prowl-grins thrashed about amid heaps of goblin dead. What was more, the charge had failed to halt the glade-eaters, which trundled on ever deeper into the heart of the Free Glades. And, as Rook looked, fresh goblin war bands swarmed out of the Deepwoods and along the scorched tracks.

Suddenly, a flash of white in the corner of his eye, made Rook spin round. And there beside him stood Chinquix, his nostrils quivering and the veins in his temples throbbing with exertion.

'Chinquix! There you are!' Rook cried, leaping into the saddle as the long-hairs regrouped and came on again. Rook raised his sword and urged Chinquix forward, a defiant cry on his lips.

'*FREEGLADER!!*'

*

Xanth pulled on the flight rope and climbed high above the meadowlands of the southern fringes. The squadron was regrouping flight by flight, the holes in their formation a testament to the desperate fight they'd been in. He looked back over his shoulder and shook his head ruefully. The charge of the Freeglade Lancers had been truly magnificent – more so, even, than the Battle of Lufwood Mount.

But at what cost?

All along the southernmost borders of the Free Glades, orange, black and brown corpses lay amidst heaps of bodies, marking the course of the lancers' charge. It had cut through the advancing columns of the goblin army, but had failed to stop the advance of the monstrous glade-eaters. Even now as he looked, Xanth could see the fiery furnaces glowing as they cut a swathe through the Timber Yards to the east.

The librarian knights had done what they could to help the lancers, flying down low over the goblin army time after time until their quivers were empty and their missiles spent. And they'd paid dearly for their persistence. Green Flight was down to two dozen craft, Centre Flight had lost fifty and Grey Flight . . .

Xanth let out his loft-sail and urged *Ratbird* forward. The remnants of the Freeglade Lancers had fallen back towards New Undertown, their sacrifice buying time for the woodtrolls and slaughterers to find safety in the caves of the northern cliffs. Now the librarian knights had to look after their own.

Xanth gathered speed and caught up with the tattered

scattering of skycraft that, at first, he had taken to be stragglers, but now saw – as he approached – were actually all that was left of Grey Flight.

Your Flight Leader? he signalled to a librarian knight who was struggling with a torn nether-sail. *Where is she?*

The librarian gestured ahead. There, at the head of no more than twelve skycraft, Xanth saw the unmistakable prow of the *Woodmoth*, a figure slumped low in its saddle.

'Magda!' he called out. 'Magda! Are you hurt?'

Magda looked up with dull, glazed eyes, her face black with soot – except for white tear-streaks. *I'm fine, Flight Marshal*, she signalled. *But look what they've done to my Flight.*

She slumped forward again, and they flew on together in silence towards Lake Landing as the thin light of dawn rose behind the dark treeline. Or, at least, what the librarian knights of Varis Lodd's depleted squadron took to be the dawn. It was only as they approached the Ironwood Stands and dropped lower to skim over the Great Lake and down to Lake Landing that they realized their mistake.

There was a glow in the sky all right, but it didn't come from the dawn. Instead, a red tinge lit up the drawn and weary faces of the librarian knights as they approached the lake.

'The Great Library!' gasped Varis Lodd, raising her arm to signal the following skycraft to hover.

In front of them, on the lake shore opposite Lake Landing, the new library blazed like a lufwood torch. All round it, a mighty goblin army danced and howled as a dozen mighty glade-eaters shot burning logs into the inferno. On the library steps, the bodies of librarians were piled high, their robes smoking as the burning embers of the blazing new library showered down on them.

Varis put her head in her hands. 'Father, father, father,' she sobbed.

The librarian knights clustered round, hovering uncertainly, unnerved by their leader's breakdown. But when Varis looked up, her eyes were blazing and her face was a mask of stone.

They haven't got to Lake Landing yet, she signalled. *The sight of the Great Library burning has proved too much of an attraction . . .*

Her eyes glinted with a fierce hatred.

Flight Marshal! She turned to Xanth. *Take Grey Flight and save the apprentices at Lake Landing*, she signalled – and Xanth could tell by the look on her face that it was useless to argue.

1135

And you? he signalled back.

We have the honour of the Great Library to uphold! Varis's hand touched her forehead and then her heart. She turned to the others. *Are you with me, librarian knights?*

In Centre Flight and Green Flight, all seventy heads nodded as one.

Then follow me!

Varis Lodd fed out a length of rope in a graceful arc, and her spidersilk loft-sail billowed out like an unfurling woodapple blossom. Around her seventy librarian knights did the same and, with a soft sigh, they sped away over the still waters of the Great Lake like silent stormhornets.

Xanth felt a hand on his forearm. It was Magda, tears streaming down her face. 'Make them come back!' she sobbed. 'Xanth, please! Hasn't there been enough useless sacrifice?'

Xanth turned back to her, the old haunted look in his face that she hadn't seen since the Reckoning.

'Stob Lummus and three hundred apprentices who have never flown before need our help to get to New Undertown. Varis and the squadron have laid down their lives so that we might succeed.' He gazed into Magda's eyes. 'A sacrifice, yes, Magda,' he said softly as the squadron approached the burning library in the distance. 'But not a useless one!'

·CHAPTER TWENTY·

THE THREE BATTLES

i

The Battle of the Great Library

The following morning, seemingly out of nowhere, an incoming leadwood log smashed into the side of the New Bloodoak Tavern with a great *crash!*, setting its foundations trembling and opening up a crack that ran from the bottom to the top of the eastern wall. Cleeve Hakenbolt shuddered, the paraphernalia at the front of his heavy sky pirate coat jangling, and gripped his pikestaff with white-knuckled ferocity.

'That was close,' said Rickett, the wiry ghost at his side. He peered up anxiously at the wall of the tavern. 'Another direct hit like that and the whole lot's gonna come crashing down on top of us.'

Cleeve nodded, the expression on his face drawn and sombre. 'What are they waiting for?' he snarled, poking his head up over the barricade of hastily constructed drinking troughs and tavern tables.

'They've got us surrounded. Why don't they attack?'

On the outskirts of New Undertown, the glade-eaters crouched like monstrous fire-bugs, gleaming in the dawn light. Their furnaces sparked and rumbled; their chimneys smoked. Behind them stood a vast mass of symbite goblins – gyle goblins, web-foot, tree and gnokgoblins, together with low-bellies and their lop-eared cousins. They shuffled from foot to foot miserably, and the air was filled with the sounds of their coughing and spluttering.

'They're softening us up,' said Rickett, his face appearing next to Cleeve's at the barricade. 'Using those infernal machines to batter Undertown to pieces, and then ... *Get down!*' he bellowed, as a huge boulder whistled overhead and crashed into a section of the barricades to their left.

Dusting himself down, Rickett saw a couple of sky pirates emerge from the rubble and begin repairing the shattered section of barricade with matter-of-fact efficiency. He turned to Cleeve.

'It'll take more than a few leadwood logs and boulders to soften you lot up. Tough as old Mire ravens, so you are!'

'Well said, Rickett, lad,' the sky pirate smiled. 'And as for you ghosts, this must seem like a home away from home, what with all this rubble!'

They laughed heartily as they peered over the barricade once more. Just then, there was a soft, whistling hiss from above, followed by a muffled thud. Rickett and Cleeve spun round to see a young ghost in a muglumpskin jacket and bone-armour standing before them. He coiled up the rope he'd just slid down on and tossed it over his shoulder.

'Care to share the joke, lads?' he said.

Rickett grinned. 'Just keeping our spirits up, Felix,' he said. His face grew more serious. 'Though Cleeve here was wondering why they haven't attacked yet . . .'

'They're firing up their furnaces with fresh lufwood,' came a voice behind them, and the three of them turned to see Deadbolt Vulpoon striding towards them, with the Professors of Light and Darkness in tow. 'When they're good and hot, they'll attack all right. And when they do . . .'

Felix clapped his friend on the back. 'We'll be ready for them, won't we, Deadbolt!' he said cheerfully.

'The sooner the better!' the sky pirate captain roared, waving a fist in the direction of the goblin army. 'If they think they can bash the best tavern in Undertown to bits and get away with it, they've got another think coming!'

Felix laughed – but when he saw the expressions on

the two professors' faces, he stopped. 'Forgive me, Professors,' he said gravely. 'I see from your faces that the librarian knights have had a difficult night . . .'

The Professor of Darkness bowed his head to Felix. 'My squadron covered the retreat from the slaughterer and woodtroll villages. I lost a hundred of my best knights.'

'And we fought in the northern fringe until we could fight no more,' added the Professor of Light simply. His white tunic was ragged and stained with blood. 'I lost more than half my squadron.'

Felix nodded. 'The population of the Free Glades is safe in the cloddertrog caves, thanks to the heroism of you and your knights,' he said quietly. 'Now we must make our stand together – ghosts, sky pirates and librarian knights alike – here in New Undertown!'

At that moment, a flurry of missiles flew overhead and smashed into the surrounding buildings, sending the group ducking for cover.

'We're all in this together, all right!' said Deadbolt darkly, spitting dust from his mouth and clambering to his feet. 'Like oozefish trapped in a barrel . . .'

A loud whistle cut him short. Felix looked up to see one of his ghosts standing on the upper gantry of the Lufwood Tower, pointing into the distance.

'Felix! Felix!' he called down. 'Over there!'

Felix unhitched his rope and hurled it high above his head, and in an instant, swung up onto the rooftops.

'That lad,' said Deadbolt, peering up after him, 'never stays still for an instant!' He put his telescope to his right eye.

The professors climbed to their feet and set off for the Lufwood Tower at a run.

'The third squadron!' said Deadbolt, focusing the telescope. 'I wonder what kept them? Hey, Professors!' He snapped the telescope shut and gave chase. 'Wait for me!'

At the Lufwood Tower, Felix landed on the gantry with a soft thud and scanned the horizon for himself. Far ahead and low in the sky, was a smudge of tiny specks, dark against the lightening backdrop. As they got closer, he could see that they did indeed form a squadron of skycraft, flying like woodgeese in their familiar V-shaped formation.

'There you are, sister,' he murmured. 'I was beginning to get worried . . .' He frowned. Something wasn't quite right. 'They're all over the place,' he said.

'That's just what I was thinking,' said the Professor of Darkness breathlessly as he climbed up the steps to join Felix, the Professor of Light close on his heels.

There was definitely something wrong with the squadron. Although there was a skycraft clearly leading at the front, followed by ten more in full sail and steady formation, and a sky-marshal darting back and forth bringing up the rear, the vast majority of the skycraft – almost three hundred of them – were wavering about uncertainly, their sails loose and flapping and their hanging flight-weights dragging them off course.

'Good old Varis. Looks like a full squadron,' muttered the Professor of Light. 'No casualties!' He shook his head. 'But what *is* wrong with them?'

'They're flying like apprentices,' said the Professor of Darkness. 'No sail discipline. And look at that flight-marshal. He's having to fly in circles just to keep them together!'

'Come on, come on!' Felix urged through clenched teeth.

As the fluttering skycraft came closer, the goblin army gathered round the glade-eaters noticed them. All at once a tremendous volley of flaming arrows and missiles flew up from its ranks towards the skycraft passing overhead. Almost immediately, the sounds of distant screams reached the onlookers in the Lufwood Tower as the goblin missiles found their mark.

Skycraft after skycraft was hit, their sails collapsing and their riders spiralling down to earth.

'Tack and dive!' urged the Professor of Light desperately. 'Pull in the nether-sails for Sky's sake! You're making yourselves easy targets!'

The squadron formation now showed ragged holes as it approached the outskirts of New Undertown and more skycraft were falling with every passing second.

'Come on, come on,' Felix muttered grimly. 'You can make it!'

Below them, the defenders of New Undertown had noticed the incoming flight, and cheers and cries and shouts of encouragement echoed through the air. At the front of the squadron, Felix saw the flight-leader and a tight formation of ten skycraft expertly adjust their sails and prepare to land. They came down silently in the square below the Lufwood Tower to the wild cheering of

ghosts and sky pirates –
which they ignored.
Instead, leaping from
their own skycraft, they
began signalling urgently to
the skycraft straggling behind.

One by one, they came in to
land, unsteadily and so lacking in control that most of
them slammed down and
their riders were
thrown from their
saddles and tossed
ignominiously to the
ground. The square was
soon thronging with
librarian knights, sky
pirates and ghosts, all

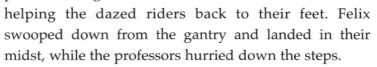

helping the dazed riders back to their feet. Felix
swooped down from the gantry and landed in their
midst, while the professors hurried down the steps.

'Varis!' he cried, rushing towards the flight-leader.
'Varis! What kept you?'

The flight-leader turned and removed her helmet and
goggles. Felix started back, a look of bewilderment on
his face.

'M . . . Magda?' he stuttered. 'Magda Burlix . . . But
where's my sister?'

The Professors of Light and Darkness jostled their way
through the crowd in the square to join Felix.

'But these are apprentices!' exclaimed the Professor of Light.

'From Lake Landing,' interrupted the Professor of Darkness. 'Sky be praised – we thought we'd lost you!'

'But where is Varis Lodd's squadron?'

Exhausted, Magda bowed her head, her face ashen white. A tear fell and splashed on her green flight-suit as she struggled to speak.

Stob Lummus, Assistant Master of Lake Landing, climbed from his skycraft and stumbled over. He gestured behind him.

'Xanth Filatine can tell you best,' he said. 'It is thanks to Magda and him, and their brave knights, that we made it this far.'

Felix turned. The last skycraft – that of the flight-marshal – was fluttering in to land. It had stayed airborne until the others had all landed. The carved ratbird prow was studded with goblin arrows; the sails ragged and scorched. Its rider climbed from the saddle and approached. There was blood on his flight-suit.

Xanth bowed solemnly. All round him, the ghosts and sky pirates were barking orders to clear the square and the librarian knights were helping the dazed apprentices to find shelter. Felix stood, completely oblivious to the missiles falling and the shouts to 'take cover!'. His eyes bore into Xanth's with a savage intensity.

'Tell me,' he said.

'We came down low across the Great Lake, what was left of us after the fight in the southern meadowlands,' Xanth began, his voice low but steady. 'That's when we saw it . . . The Great Library in flames, surrounded by goblin hordes and glade-eaters. It was plain that Lake Landing would be next. So Varis sent Grey Flight – the twelve of us – to save the apprentices, while she . . .' His voice faltered.

Felix's eyes never left his. 'What did she do?'

'I saw it all,' said Xanth, 'from the saddle of the *Ratbird* as I circled Lake Landing. It was a magnificent battle . . .'

'Magnificent?' said Felix fiercely.

'Yes,' said Xanth, his voice now grimly determined. 'Magnificent. In close formation, skimming the Great Lake, with Varis in front, the squadron charged the Great Library. They hit the shoreline with a murderous volley, the last they had, and then swarmed round the flaming building, ripping burning timbers from it with their flight-ropes, and raining them down on the goblins below. They fought till their sails were aflame and their skycraft were on fire . . . And then I saw them sail over the dark treetops followed by the enraged goblin hordes.'

Xanth's eyes were blazing now and his voice had risen.

'They followed them, like woodmoths to a flame, into the Deepwoods and away from Lake Landing until, one by one, I saw the flames go out. Then the goblin army streamed back, past the Great Library and towards Lake Landing. But by that time we'd got the apprentices airborne and were making for New Undertown.'

'So, my sister is . . .' Felix's voice choked.

'She sacrificed herself and her squadron for the

apprentices. Without the Battle of the Great Library, we would never have made it.'

Felix placed a hand on Xanth's shoulder. 'Varis would have been proud of you, Xanth Filatine,' he said simply.

The square was almost empty now, the skycraft tethered to mooring-poles beside the Lufwood Tower, and the defenders of New Undertown huddled behind the barricades. Overhead, the missiles continued to fall.

Felix was turning to go when Deadbolt arrived, Fenbrus Lodd at his side. The High Librarian was gesticulating wildly and booming in the sky pirate's ear. Behind them came a motley crowd of under-librarians armed with a mishmash of assorted weapons. Fenbrus stopped in front of Felix and glared round, red-faced with indignation.

'This sky pirate friend of yours thinks we librarian academics can't fight, Felix! The goblins burnt down our magnificent library, didn't they? Of course we're going to fight! You try and stop us. Tell him, Felix. Go on, tell him!'

Deadbolt rolled his eyes and shrugged.

'I'm ... I'm so sorry, my dear Fenbrus,' said the Professor of Light, turning away.

'Such a terrible loss,' murmured the Professor of Darkness.

'The Great Library?' said Fenbrus Lodd. 'Yes, yes. Time to think about that later. Now we must fight!'

Felix stepped forward. 'It's Varis, father,' he said softly.

'Is she back?' Fenbrus began.

Felix swallowed. He shook his head. 'She's not coming back.'

'You mean . . .' said Fenbrus again, his voice little more than a croaking whisper.

'Yes, father,' said Felix. 'Varis is dead.'

Fenbrus let out a small wheezing groan, the sound of a punctured trockbladder-ball losing its air. His beard drooped, the colour drained from his cheeks and it was as if his entire body – the bluster and bombast spent – shrank a little. Felix stepped forward, wrapped his arms round his father and hugged him protectively.

'She died bravely,' he said, 'sacrificing herself for the sake of others . . .'

Felix could feel his father's body trembling. 'Gone,' he heard him sobbing. 'Everything has gone.' The next moment, Fenbrus pulled away.

But Felix wouldn't let him go. He took him by the shoulders and stared deep into his eyes.

'Oh, Felix,' Fenbrus murmured, 'the books, the treatises, the barkscrolls. I can take their loss . . . Fresh young librarian schol-ars can be sent out to the four corners of the Edgelands. They can gather knowledge and write new books, new treatises, new barkscrolls. And the Great Library . . .' He shook his head. 'So magnificent . . . I can even stand *its* loss . . .'

He sighed. Felix held him tightly.

'But Varis. My beautiful, brave daughter . . .' Tears streamed down his pallid, puffy cheeks. 'Gone for ever . . . I don't think I can stand it.' He tried again to break away, but Felix maintained his grip. 'How can I go on without her?' Fenbrus wailed.

Felix looked down, his voice cracked and quavering. 'You . . . You've got me, father.'

Fenbrus looked into his son's eyes. 'You mean . . ?'

'Yes,' said Felix. 'I shall become a librarian. Together we shall rebuild the Great Library and replace the barkscrolls . . .'

For a moment, Fenbrus fell still. The next, Felix felt himself being pulled towards his father and wrapped up in his warm, strong embrace.

'Oh, son,' he whispered into Felix's ear. 'My dear, dear boy.' He pulled his head away and looked deep into Felix's eyes. 'Do you really think we could do all that?'

Felix nodded. 'Together,' he said simply. 'Together, father, we can do anything.'

At that moment, there came a series of whistles and cries from the top of the Lufwood Tower, and a booming voice filled the air.

'Freeglade Lancers, due south!'

Fenbrus and Felix pulled away from one another. The Professors of Light and Darkness both put their telescopes to their eyes and looked.

'Rook!' gasped Magda, grinning at Xanth through her tears. 'It's Rook!'

Xanth raised his hand and shielded his eyes from the low sun, just rising up above the horizon. Far ahead of

him, coming closer with every giant leap, was a band of Freeglade Lancers on prowlgrinback. Most of the mounts were heavy, stolid creatures in shades of orange and woodnut brown. But one – close to the centre at the front – was of a slighter, more sinewy build, and white with dark brown patches.

'You're right,' said Xanth. 'It *is* Rook.'

Bounding in from the north-west, emerging from the treeline and leaping through the colonies of hive-huts, the lancers were skirting round the fringes of the goblin army. Before the goblins had even registered that they were in their midst, the lancers had moved on.

As Magda and Xanth watched, the prowlgrins bounded through the air, leaping higher than the rooftops and dodging the arrows and spears of the goblins. A moment later, the lancers were flying over the barricades and tugging on the reins of their snorting mounts. Rook jumped from Chinquix's saddle and hugged his friends.

'You took your time getting here!' he panted.

His face was bruised, his arms grazed; his surcoat was torn and stained. Yet he was alive and, judging by the grin on his face, well.

'Rook, I'm so glad to see you,' said Magda, her eyes glistening with tears. 'Oh, Rook, where is it all going to end? This fighting. All this killing . . .'

Xanth patted her arm and drew Rook aside. 'She's been through a lot,' he said. 'We all have.'

Rook nodded. 'I know, Xanth, I know,' he said. 'And it isn't over yet. Look after her, Xanth, I must make my report.'

He turned and headed over to where Felix and his father stood, together with the two professors and Deadbolt Vulpoon.

'The glade-eaters,' said Rook. 'They're coming!'

Deadbolt Vulpoon nodded. 'The lad's right,' he said, and pointed to the wreaths of spark-filled black smoke coiling up from the distant machines as a thumping, roaring, screeching sound filled the air. The Professors of Light and Darkness exchanged glances.

'So, this is it, then, Ulbus,' said one. 'First the villages, then the library, now New Undertown itself . . .'

'Indeed, Tallus,' said the other. 'This is where we must make our stand.'

Rook frowned. 'The Great Library, destroyed?'

'Ay, Rook,' said Felix. 'And Varis, dead. My father has taken it very hard. He has lost everything.'

Rook reached inside his jacket, pulled something out and handed it to Fenbrus. 'Not quite everything,' he said. 'You still have Felix, and . . . this.'

Fenbrus found himself holding a familiar barkscroll, the words *On the Husbandry of Prowlgrins* emblazoned across the top.

'The beginning of the *new* new Great Library,' said Rook.

Fenbrus looked up, tears welling in his eyes. All round them now, the sound of the roaring, screeching glade-eaters echoed malevolently. Gripping the barkscroll, Fenbrus Lodd strode towards the barricades, his eyes blazing.

'This is not how it ends!' he bellowed. 'The accursed goblins may well have won the Battle of the Great Library, but they have not won the war!'

ii
The Battle of New Undertown

With an ear-splitting screech and a gut-wrenching roar, the mighty glade-eaters lurched forwards. They sliced through the barricades like an axe through matchwood, and onto the streets of New Undertown in a tumultuous frenzy of destruction. Towers were razed to the ground, street-lamps crushed and crumpled, cobblestones churned up and sent flying off in all directions.

With their battering-rams, their wrecking-balls, their spikes, scythes, chains and flails, the glade-eaters decimated everything which stood in their path. Building after building came crashing to the ground in a

rush of rubble, splintered wood and billowing clouds of dust.

Behind the monstrous machines came the symbites – gyle goblins, gnokgoblins, web-foot and tree-goblins – in a great stampede, viciously driven along by the whips of the flat-heads following close on their heels. In the distance, spread out across the eastern farmlands, stood the massed ranks of the hammerheads and long-haired goblins, looking on. At their centre, the clan chiefs clustered beneath an ornate canopy.

Grossmother Nectarsweet's huge cheeks were wet with tears. 'My poor darlings!' she blubbered.

'Calm yourself,' said Hemtuft Battleaxe. 'Hemuel Spume's glade-eaters will do the hard work. Your sym-bites will simply "mop up" any remaining resistance.'

'It's not the goblin way!' spat Lytugg the hammerhead disgustedly. 'My warriors need to bathe their blades in Freeglade blood!'

'Don't worry,' said Hemtuft. 'There'll be plenty of Freeglade blood for your warriors when we get to the cloddertrog caves!'

Beside him, Meegmewl the Grey and Rootrott Underbiter exploded into cackles of evil laughter.

In the distance, a cloud of dust and furnace-fumes rose up from New Undertown as the glade-eaters ploughed on. From his position on the steering-platform of the leading machine, Hemuel Spume wiped the dust from his spectacles and cleared his throat. Beside him, the Furnace Master pushed the gear lever forward, and the glade-eater roared as the power was unleashed through the drive chains. The machine smashed through the wall of a half-wrecked tavern and rumbled on towards the Lufwood Tower ahead.

As each building collapsed, the defenders of New Undertown seemed to melt away, while high above, the tiny specks of skycraft hovered like woodgnats, out of reach of the goblin missiles. Hemuel Spume permitted himself a thin smile of triumph. It seemed that his glade-eaters had knocked the fight out of this Freeglader scum. New Undertown would be his! He tapped the Furnace Master on the shoulder and pointed to the tower.

'TO ... THE ... TOWER!' he screamed in his ear above the roar of the furnace. Out of the corner of his eye, he noticed a sudden blur of green as something flashed past ...

With a gurgle and a splutter, the Furnace Master beside him slumped forward. The glade-eater swerved to one side, ramming into a tall statue and lurching on.

'I ... SAID, TO ... THE ... TOWER!!' screamed Hemuel, pulling the Furnace Master back – then stopping when he saw that his own long thin fingers were covered in blood.

There, sticking out from the base of the Furnace Master's neck, was a heavy leadwood bolt.

Now, all around, green skycraft flashed past, spitting deadly leadwood bolts down at the glade-eaters. Hemuel threw himself to the floor with a terrified squeal and curled up into a ball as the great machine trundled on, out of control. Around him, the other glade-eaters were also in trouble as their Furnace Masters fell, in turn, to the crossbow bolts of the librarian knights.

Soon the monstrous machines were beginning to collide with one another. Behind them, the goblins stumbled and slipped, jostling each other in their attempts to stay on their feet.

'Stay steady up there!' the flat-heads roared, whipping the symbites all the harder in their frustration and rage.

Above them, peering down from the rooftops, the pale figures of ghosts appeared. Securing their grappling-hooks, they swooped down on their ropes and landed on the steering-platforms of the glade-eaters. Hastily, they rammed the gears into full throttle, wedging the levers forward with chunks of broken wood, before leaping back to the rooftops on their ropes.

With a deafening roar, the glade-eaters accelerated, the hapless symbites struggling to keep up as their flat-head tormentors flailed at them with their whips. Through bartering-halls and merchant-towers, galleries, taverns, hostels and shops; market-stands, stables and stalls, the mighty glade-eaters smashed an unstoppable path. Ahead, North Lake spread out like a great, glittering circle of burnished silver.

Behind them, from alleyways and rubble-strewn passages, sky pirates appeared with cutlasses and pikestaffs, a sky pirate captain at their head. 'Take out the flat-head overseers!' he roared.

The symbite goblins turned and stampeded back the way they'd come as the sky pirates fell upon the snarling flat-heads. In front of them, at Lakeside, the glade-eaters roared on towards the water's edge, with the goblins on the furnace- and weapons-platforms throwing themselves from them with yelps of terror.

Twenty flat-heads lay at Deadbolt Vulpoon's feet as, around him, the sky pirates bellowed at the backs of their fleeing flat-head comrades. 'Come back and fight!'

'Not so brave now, without your machines, are you?'

'Freeglader!'

'Freeglader! Freeglader! Freeglader!'

All at once, an enormous explosion sounded from Lakeside as the first mighty glade-eater plunged into the lake, its furnace rupturing as it hit the cold water and spewing burning and hissing lufwood logs high in the air. A moment later there was another explosion, then another, and another, as glade-eater after glade-eater dropped down into North Lake and blew up.

Soon a thick steamy fog mingled with the dust in the rubble-strewn streets of New Undertown, and as each explosion sounded, it was greeted by a roar of approval from the ghosts, librarian knights and sky pirates clustered at the lake's shore.

In the eastern farmlands, the goblin army had been waiting. Beneath the ornate canopy, Hemtuft struggled to focus the captured sky pirate telescope on the hazy outlines of ruined buildings.

Then the explosions started.

Meegmewl the Grey spat noisily. 'I don't like the sound of that,' he said grimly.

Rootrott Underbiter nodded. 'Not good, not good,' he growled.

Just then, out of the thickening cloud of dust, burst the symbite goblins in a disorganized stampede, with the Freeglade Lancers snapping at their heels. As the terrified symbites ran towards them, the lancers fell back in a defensive line. Mother Nectarsweet gave a high-pitched scream.

'Look!' she screeched. 'Look what they've done to my darlings!'

As the last glade-eater plunged into the waters of the North Lake and exploded, a huge column of water burst forth into the air like a mighty geyser. Higher and higher it climbed before falling abruptly away. And there, where it had been just moments before, floating head-down on the surface of the water, was the body of the former Foundry Master, Hemuel Spume, his boiled skin looking pinker in death than ever it had in life.

The waters stilled, and the haunting sound of chanting voices echoed out across the surface of the lake from Lullabee Island at its centre.

'Ooh-maah, oomalaah. Ooh-maah, oomalaah. Ooh-maah, oomalaah . . .'

iii
The Battle of the Barley Fields

Lob hitched up his belly-sling and pushed back his straw bonnet. 'It's a sad business all round, and no mistake, brother,' he said.

'It is that, brother,' said Lummel, shaking his head. 'It is that.'

They were standing at the back of a great phalanx of low-belly spear carriers. Around them, the grey goblin archers, pink-eyed sling throwers and barb-spitters of the lop-eared clan clustered in an untidy rabble. Amongst them, standing out like ironwood pines, were huge tusked goblins, their massive clubs resting on their shoulders. Unlike the elite long-haired and hammerhead goblins, this was the untrained bulk of the goblin armies.

'Them poor symbites didn't stand a chance,' said Lob.

'And it'll be our turn next, brother,' said Lummel. 'To pay for the clan chiefs' glory with *our* blood.'

Next to them, a pink-eyed barb-spitter nodded, and a massive tusked goblin gave a low growl of approval. Lummel glanced at them sideways.

'Friends of the harvest?' he asked in a low whisper.

Ahead of them, spread out along the top of the ridge, their weapons, helmets and breast-plates glinting in the bright yellow sunlight, stood phalanx after bristling phalanx of the elite of the goblin army, many rows deep. There were flat-heads to the left, with curved scimitars and studded cudgels, and long-hairs to the right, vicious double-edged battleaxes resting over their shoulders.

At the centre – a head
taller than all the
rest and dominat-
ing the skyline
with their heavy
armour, their
crescent-moon
shields and fear-
some serrated
swords – were
the hammer-
heads.

In front of
them stood the
clan chiefs
beneath the
ornate
canopy, held
aloft by five
huge, tusked goblins.

Mother Nectarsweet of the symbites was sobbing uncontrollably – causing Meegmewl the Grey of the
lop-eared clan and Rootrott Underbiter of the tusked
clan to scowl at her with contempt. Hemtuft Battleaxe
picked at his shryke feathercloak distractedly, while
Lytugg of the hammerhead clan stepped forward and
addressed her warriors.

'The so-called invincible glade-eaters are no more,' she
bellowed, and a wicked smile spread out across her thin
lips. 'Now we shall fight the goblin way!'

*

Out of the ruins of New Undertown came the Freegladers.

On the right were the Freeglade Lancers, still proud and upright on their prowlgrins despite their tattered tunics and blood-stained armour. Rook and Chinquix were at their head, with Grist – the only one of his original comrades to survive – beside him. The lancers were down to eighty now and their prowlgrins looked thin and exhausted.

On the left, the sky pirates marched behind the braziers of their captains, with Deadbolt Vulpoon at their head. They'd polished their breast-plates, compass brass and telescopes, which now gleamed and glittered in the sunlight, and looked impressive despite their ragged greatcoats.

At the centre, led by Felix and his father, Fenbrus Lodd, came the Ghosts of New Undertown and a motley selection of ageing librarians from the Great Library, armed with clubs, scythes, sling-shots and catapults. The ghosts had fought hard but they knew that, numbering less than two hundred, their task against the thousands of goblins facing them was hopeless.

Behind them, leading their skycraft on the ends of tether-ropes and ready to take to the air at a moment's notice, came the librarian knights. Between the Professors of Light and Darkness walked Xanth, his dark eyes betraying both fear and pride. Of the nine hundred librarian knights, fewer than three hundred remained. Their ranks now included the callow apprentices from Lake Landing, led by Stob Lummus – a worried, haunted-looking Magda Burlix at his side.

Behind them all, the ruins of New Undertown smouldered, and beyond that, the white cliffs of the cloddertrog caves glimmered in the afternoon haze. There, holed up and waiting for news, was the defenceless population of the Free Glades, huddled together. All that was standing between them and the bloodthirsty goblin hordes was this rag-tag army.

Tramping through the fields of blue barley – the Waif Glen on one side and the dark fringe of the Deepwoods on the other – the Freegladers approached the huge goblin army, which rippled with anticipation. Felix stepped out and raised his hand.

'We shall stand and fight, here in the barley fields!' his voice rang out. 'And die if we must as Freegladers!'

'Freegladers! Freegladers! Freegladers!' came the response.

Ahead of them, the ranks of the flat-heads, long-hairs and hammerheads lurched forwards as if in answer to their challenge.

'Earth and Sky be with us all,' Fenbrus murmured by his son's side.

As the goblins bore down upon them, every Freeglader felt his heart race and his stomach churn. The ground itself trembled beneath the marching feet of the massed ranks of the goblins, and as they drew closer, the sun dazzlingly bright behind them, they started chanting – a single word, over and over . . .

'Blood! Blood! Blood! Blood! Blood . . .'

A hundred strides apart . . . Ninety . . . Eighty . . . The Freegladers could smell the foul odour of their enemies' unwashed bodies.

Seventy . . . sixty . . . fifty strides. They could see the tattoos emblazoned on their skins, and hear the sinister jangle of their barbaric battle-rings above the continuing *thud-thud-thud . . .*

Closer and closer. The goblins' chants had turned now into a frenzied, guttural howl mixed with a different noise . . .

Felix gasped. The noise wasn't coming from the ranks of the goblins. It was coming from the fringes of the forest to the east – a loud, yodelling cry that sliced through the still afternoon air.

The goblins seemed oblivious to it. Lost in their blood-lust, they thundered on, closing the gap . . .

Thirty strides . . . Twenty . . .

Now, he could see the reds of their bloodshot eyes. This was it. The Freegladers' last stand . . .

Fifteen . . . Ten . . .

All at once, the yodelling reached fever-pitch and out of the dark-green edges of the Deepwood forest came a great, seething brown mass which tore into the flat-heads on the goblin army's left-hand flank. Mighty goblin warriors were picked up and flung screaming through the air, as the ferocious beasts – all whirring claws and flashing tusks – tore through the goblin ranks like a blade through butterwood.

Rook leaned forward in his saddle as Chinquix snorted and skittered about uneasily. 'Banderbears,' he breathed. 'A convocation of banderbears!'

In front of the Freegladers, the elite of the goblin army was disintegrating. A flat-head swung his studded cudgel, only to have it knocked from his hands like a young'un's rattle – and his head crushed a moment later by a banderbear's tusked bite. A pair of long-hairs, their battleaxes swinging above their heads, were felled as one, as a huge, dark-brown banderbear struck out with one mighty claw.

First one, then two, then three hammerhead goblins were skewered on their own serrated swords, then tossed to the ground and trampled by roaring bander-bears, their fur red with blood.

Those not slaughtered threw down their weapons and fled back towards the mass of lop-ear and tusked gob-lins to the rear, who were looking on in dumbstruck amazement. The banderbears – now as red with goblin blood as the emblem on Rook's tunic – threw back their great heads and bellowed in triumph.

'WUH-WUH!!'

Chinquix gave out a shrill snort of alarm as, out of the mass of celebrating banderbears, three huge, blood-spattered figures approached. Despite their gory disguises, Rook recognized them instantly.

'Weeg! Wuralo! Wumeru!'

'Wuh-weela-wuh, Uralowa,' they yodelled in unison. *We have returned, he who took the poison-stick.*

Rook was about to leap from his saddle and embrace them when Grist clasped his arm.

'Rook!' he hissed urgently. 'Look!'

Rook followed his comrade's gaze. There, on the crest of the hill, coming through the blue barley towards them was the rest of the goblin army, their burnished metal weapons and armour glinting ominously in the evening sunlight.

Rook's heart sank. There were quite simply too many of the goblins to deal with. Countless thousands of them, appearing row after row after row at the crest of the hill and sweeping forward towards them. Not even the banderbears would be sufficient to repel this massive army.

There were tusked goblins, including snag-toothed and saw-toothed individuals, and ferocious underbiters. Tramping down the hills, they looked an impregnable force with their tooled leather armour rattling with battle-rings, their heavy visors and war-fists, and heavier war-clubs, reputedly embedded with the teeth of their opponents.

Marching between them were battalions of other goblins – lighter, more agile, yet no less deadly. Pink-eyed lop-ears, with their back-quivers bristling with poison-tipped arrows; tufted goblins of the long-haired clan, ruthlessly disciplined and skilled both in flailwork and swordplay; black-eared goblins with their characteristic long-pikes, clustered together in

their tightly-packed 'stickleback' formations.

There were furrow-browed and thick-necked goblins; tufted, crested and mossy-backed goblins; pink-eyed, scaly and septic goblins. And grey-goblins – thousands of them – fierce and fearless, and armed with their long swords and short spears, all keeping close together in their 'swarms' and waiting for the order to launch a mass attack on their enemy.

As Rook stared at them in horror, he knew that that order would not be long in coming. He braced himself. There in the midst of the goblin army he could just see the heads of the clan chiefs. Rootrott Underbiter, Meegmewl the Grey, Mother Nectarsweet, Lytugg the hammerhead, and there at their centre, Hemtuft Battleaxe, a hideous grimace of triumph on his long-haired face. They bobbed up and down in the midst of their goblins, as if trying to get a better view of their impending victory.

To his right, Rook saw Felix step forwards and stride towards the approaching goblins, sword in hand, his eyes flashing with defiance.

'Very well, then!' he shouted at the taunting faces of the clan chiefs. 'Let us end it now!'

Suddenly, Rook saw his friend drop his sword and sink to his knees, a look of horrified amazement on his face. The goblin army came to a shuddering halt, and five huge tusked goblins shouldered their way through to the front, poles clasped in their massive fists.

Rook looked up. On the end of each pole, instead of an ornate canopy, was a bloodied, severed head. Hemtuft's

hideous grimace greeted the astonished Felix and the
Freegladers. Beside him were the heads of the other clan
chiefs. Then a chant – soft at first, but growing stronger
by the minute – rose up above the clatter of weapons
being dropped to the ground.

'*Friends of the harvest! Friends of the harvest! Friends of
the harvest!*'

EPILOGUE

The Most High Academe and head of the Freeglades Council, Cowlquape Pentephraxis, stood on the upper gantry of the Lufwood Tower and let the warm sun soak into his tired old bones.

What a very long way he'd come, he thought with a smile. And not only him, but all of them in the Free Glades.

He gazed down at New Undertown. Already, the streets were clear of rubble, and the buildings were being repaired. Why, the New Bloodoak Tavern was almost its old self again. You could go down there any evening and hear Deadbolt Vulpoon telling stories of the Battle of New Undertown and the War of the Free Glades . . . War! It already seemed like a distant memory.

Waif Glen was full of goblins now, seeking the peace and tranquillity that Cancaresse offered, and the Goblin Nations were flourishing alongside the Free Glades. There would be no more war, Cowlquape thought, and smiled contentedly.

Over in the distance, the timber wagons of the woodtrolls trundled towards the Great Lake. The work both on the Academy at Lake Landing and on the new Great Library was already underway. He'd never seen Felix Lodd, or Fenbrus, so happy.

Looking towards the Ironwood Stands, Cowlquape saw two skycraft circling. Probably his old friend Xanth, he thought, and Magda – off to take a spot of tea with Tweezel the spindlebug. Yes, things really were getting back to normal . . .

A polite cough brought the Most High Academe out of his reverie, and he turned to see two low-belly goblins in splendid new straw bonnets standing before him.

'Lob! Lummel!' Cowlquape greeted the two newest members of the Freeglade Council. 'Welcome, Freegladers!'

*

The Foundry Glades were silent. The furnaces were all extinguished, and the dense pall of smoke that had hovered in the air above them for so long had thinned and disappeared. The goblin guards were gone and the workshops and forges empty. The slave workers had packed everything they could carry and left for the Free Glades and Goblin Nations.

In a small, upper chamber at the top of the Palace of Furnace Masters, a single occupant remained. He was seated inside the soak-vat, but the water was cold, the bubbles had stopped and the attendant gabtrolls who had oiled him, anointed him and rubbed him vigorously down were nowhere to be found.

'Hello?' he called out weakly. 'Hello? Is there anybody there? Where are my gabtrolls? I'm cold and I'm shivery and I can't get out on my own . . . Please, somebody . . . *any*body! Help me!'

Just then, to his right, he heard a *click* and the door opened. He turned.

'Flambusia!' he squeaked. 'It's you! Thank goodness!'

'So you remember your old nursie,' said the huge, lumbering creature, her bright eyes darting round the room jerkily as she hurried towards him. 'I thought you'd forgotten all about me.' She smiled, her teeth glinting.

'Forgotten?' Amberfuce laughed uneasily. 'Of course I hadn't forgotten . . .'

'All those times I tried to see you,' said Flambusia. 'Standing at that door, calling your name – only to be

1171

turned away . . . Beaten . . . Made to wash floors . . . And me, a nurse!'

'How awful,' wheedled Amberfuce. 'I had no idea.'

'Really?' she said, her eyes narrowing. 'You didn't hear my cries? My pleading?'

'No, no, nothing, Flambusia,' he said. 'I really had no idea.'

Flambusia's teeth flashed again. 'Tut-tut, Amby, dear,' she said, crouching down. 'And you a waif. Shame on you. But perhaps Flambusia can take care of you now, then?'

'Yes,' said Amberfuce weakly. 'Yes, that would be nice . . .'

The cloddertrog began pressing buttons, turning dials, switching levers, while Amberfuce looked on helplessly. The water inside the burnished metal vat began churning violently and suddenly began to steam.

'Ouch,' Amberfuce yelped. 'That's a bit *too* warm, Flambusia, my dear,' he said.

'Sorry, Amby, dear, I didn't quite hear you,' said Flambusia. 'What did you say?'

'Too hot!' squealed Amberfuce. 'Scorching, Flambusia!'

'I still can't hear you, Amby,' she said sweetly, giving the dial another violent turn. 'You'll have to speak up.'

'No . . . no . . . no . . . No, please, Flambusia! *Noooo!*'

*

The skewbald prowlgrin tethered to the sallowdrop tree snorted contentedly in the warm evening air. Its rider, a dark-haired youth in the uniform of a Freeglade Lancer, a sword at his side, stood on the small jetty gazing out over the still waters of North Lake to Lullabee Island. From the distant treeline came the far-off sound of a banderbear yodel.

The youth smiled, lost in thought. Then, as if sensing he was being watched, he turned – to find himself staring into the pale eyes of an old sky pirate.

'Lullabee Island,' said the pirate, his voice gravelly with lack of use. 'A place of dreams, they say.'

The youth nodded. 'I've been there,' he said, 'and dreamed the strangest of dreams . . . I was thinking about them just now.'

'I guessed as much by the way you were gazing at the place,' said the Mire Pirate, his sad eyes searching the youth's face. He cleared his throat and came to stand beside the youth on the jetty, his own gaze turning to the distant island. 'There was once a great sky pirate captain,' he said. 'I served under him a long, long time ago. He came from a large family. Lived in old Undertown in a grand house, with a beautiful room, a fabulous mural on its wall . . .'

The youth turned to look at the old pirate.

'It burned down,' he said. 'Tragically. He lost his mother, and his brothers.'

The youth's eyes opened wide. 'I dreamed that!' he said.

The sky pirate went on. 'He grew up to be a sky pirate

like his father. Took his wife with him . . . They had a baby . . .'

'But something happened,' the youth interrupted. 'I dreamed that, too. They had to leave their child . . . in the Deepwoods.'

The Mire Pirate nodded. 'But the captain found his child again, years later. I was there when he did. And that child grew to be as fine a sky pirate as his father, and his father before him. And I know, because I served under him, too – until . . .'

'Until?' asked the youth, hardly daring to breathe.

'Until we were wrecked in the Twilight Woods and I was lost . . . lost for such a long time . . . I don't know for how long . . . Shrykes found me. Sold me in their slave market. I escaped and came to the Free Glades, where I found my brother's son, Shem.' He paused. 'Shem Barkwater!'

The youth gasped. 'Barkwater? You said, Barkwater?'

The Mire Pirate nodded. 'Shem took me in, and gave me a home after all my wanderings. I was so happy. *So* happy . . . And then he met Keris, and imagine my surprise and joy when I discovered . . .'

'Discovered what?' urged the youth, half remembering his dreams.

'That Keris was the daughter of my sky pirate captain, Twig.'

'Twig!' exclaimed the youth. 'Captain Twig!'

'The very same. He'd married a slaughterer by the name of Sinew. It broke his heart when she died shortly after giving birth, but he did his best to bring his daughter, Keris, up, and he did a good job of it, too. When she grew up and left home, Captain Twig returned to his wanderings in the Deepwoods . . .'

'And that's where *I* met him!' said the youth. 'Living with banderbears!'

The Mire Pirate smiled. 'Yes, I heard tell of that . . . Well, his daughter married my nephew Shem, and the three of us lived so happily here in the Free Glades until . . .'

'Go on,' said the youth.

'They had a child. A beautiful little boy. Dark, curly hair. He was about four years old when they decided to take him to see his slaughterer relatives in their village. I pleaded with them not to. I *begged* them! But they laughed and set off just the same . . .'

'They wouldn't listen,' said the youth, staring out at Lullabee Island, his dreams coming back to him. 'They rode away into the sunset, and you stared after them, tears streaming down your face . . .'

The Mire Pirate nodded, his eyes glistening. 'When they didn't return,' he said, 'I went after them. I discovered their upturned cart, their scattered belongings and . . .'

Tears flooded down the old pirate's cheeks. 'Their poor, dead bodies. Killed by slavers, they were. But I found no trace of my grand-nephew, Captain Twig's grandson . . .'

'He was found by banderbears, looked after – and then discovered by Varis Lodd, who brought him to old Undertown, where he grew up in the sewers . . . He was . . . is . . .' the youth said hesitantly.

'You,' said the old Mire Pirate. 'Rook Barkwater!'

'And you, you are my great-uncle Tem!' said Rook, amazed. 'I dreamed it. I dreamed it all in the caterbird cocoon!'

The Mire Pirate nodded, his eyes full of sorrow and love, joy and loss. 'But there's one thing you won't have dreamed, I'll be bound,' he said.

'And what's that?' asked Rook.

'This,' said Tem Barkwater, fishing in his pocket and handing Rook a small, round object. 'I took it from your mother's dead hand,' he said, his eyes misting over, 'and I've kept it all these years. It was given to her by her father, who was given it by *his* father. It's yours now.'

Rook looked at the object in his hand. It was a small disc of ancient lufwood, decorated with a miniature painting of a youth staring back at him with a gaze that seemed eerily familiar. He frowned. It was the face he'd seen in the mural on the wall of the Sunken Palace of old Undertown; the face he'd seen in the caterbird cocoon dream.

A young knight academic in old-fashioned armour, with deep indigo eyes and a smile on his face. Behind him was the painted skyline of old Sanctaphrax, the lost floating city, worn, but still recognizable, with the Loftus Observatory at one of his shoulders and the twin towers of the School of Mist at the other.

Tem Barkwater smiled. 'It's your great-grandfather, Rook, lad,' he said, and placed a hand on his grand-nephew's shoulder.

Rook gazed at the portrait of the youth staring back at him.

'Your great-grandfather,' he repeated quietly. 'Cloud Wolf.'

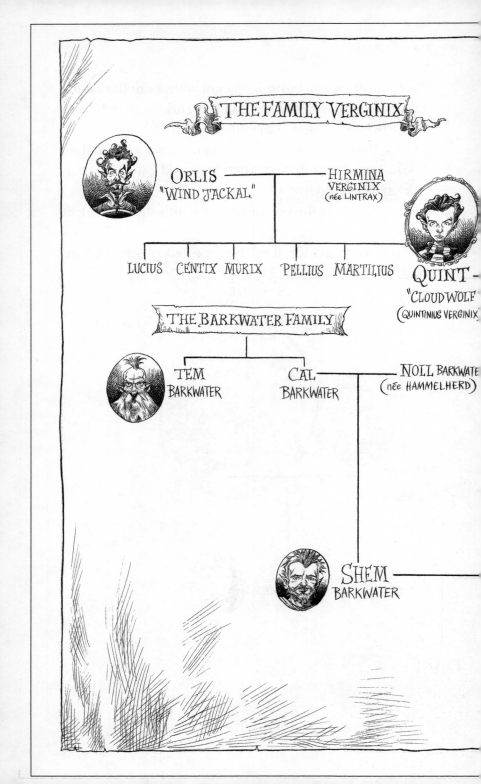

THE FAMILY VERGINIX

ORLIS "WIND JACKAL" ——— HIRMINA VERGINIX (née LINTRAX)

LUCIUS   CENTIX   MURIX   PELLIUS   MARTILIUS   QUINT "CLOUD WOLF" (QUINTINIUS VERGINIX)

THE BARKWATER FAMILY

TEM BARKWATER   CAL BARKWATER   NOLL BARKWATE (née HAMMELHERD)

SHEM BARKWATER

LINIUS
PALLITAX
(MOST HIGH ACADEME
OF SANCTAPHRAX)

YENA PALLITAX
(née VESPIUS)

MARIS
VERGINIX
(née PALLITAX)

TWIG
(ARBORINUS VERGINIX)

SINEW
VERGINIX
(née TATUM)

KERIS
BARKWATER
(née VERGINIX)

ROOK
BARKWATER

ABOUT THE AUTHORS

PAUL STEWART is a highly regarded author of books for young readers – everything from picture books to football stories, fantasy and horror. Together with Chris Riddell, he is co-creator of the *Far-Flung Adventures* series which includes *Fergus Crane*, Gold Smarties Prize Winner, and *Corby Flood*, Silver Nestle Prize Winner. They are of course also co-creators of the bestselling *Edge Chronicles* series which has sold over a million books and is now available in over thirty languages.

CHRIS RIDDELL is an accomplished graphic artist who has illustrated many acclaimed books for children, including *Pirate Diary* by Richard Platt, and *Gulliver*, which both won the Kate Greenaway Medal. *Something Else* by Kathryn Cave was shortlisted and *Castle Diary* by Richard Platt was Highly Commended for the Kate Greenaway Medal.

THE
EDGE CHRONICLES
FAN CLUB

Join the **FREE** Edge Chronicles Fanclub online!

Read Paul and Chris's diary and find out how they work together. Check out the awesome character gallery. Wonder at the interactive map. Play fantastic Edge games. Download wallpaper and much more.

Loads more to see and do!

www.edgechronicles.co.uk

Barnaby Grimes

Barnaby Grimes is a tick-tock lad – he'll deliver any message anywhere any time. As fast as possible. Tick-tock – time is money! But strange things are afoot . . .

Read all the adventures of Barnaby Grimes:

CURSE OF THE NIGHT WOLF
Join Barnaby as he battles an evil scientist and a terrifying werewolf!

RETURN OF THE EMERALD SKULL
Wonder as Barnaby fights to save those trapped in a school under a terrible curse!

LEGION OF THE DEAD
Gasp in horror as a legion of undead zombie warriors attack Barnaby – can he survive?

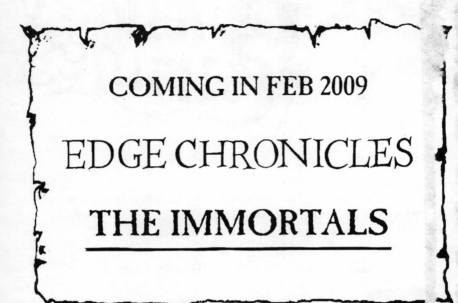

COMING IN FEB 2009

EDGE CHRONICLES

THE IMMORTALS